They were a special breed of men and women . . . as brazen, beautiful and hot as the desert skies

MEADE SLAUGHTER

Some said he loved too easily; some suspected he hated too hard, but everyone knew he got what he wanted . . . and he wanted it all.

TONY GIULIANO

A ruthless boss of bosses in control of all the ways men like to sin. He called Nevada his . . . and intended to keep it his private kingdom—no matter who he had to kill.

GARI

She was a tall, milk and honey show girl, as sexy and sizzling as the hot promises of the Vegas Strip. No man could resist her, not Meade Slaughter. Or his son.

DAVID SLAUGHTER

He inherited his father's passions but not his strengths, and Nevada offered all the seven deadly sins . . . illegal, illicit and irresistible.

A TALE THAT DAZZLES—AS FASCINAT-ING AND UNFORGETTABLE AS THE NIGHT LIFE, THE HIGH TIMES AND THE EXCITEMENT OF

NEVADA

NEVADA

Clint McCullough

NEVADA

This is a work of fiction. Although some well-known names and locales are included, the characters and the events described are products of the author's imagination.

NEVADA

Copyright © 1986 by Clindale, Ltd.

Published by arrangement with Lyle Stuart, Inc.

Library of Congress Catalog Card Number: 86-5720

ISBN: 0-312-90260-3   Can. ISBN: 0-312-90261-1

Printed in the United States of America

First St. Martin's Press mass market edition/June 1987

10 9 8 7 6 5 4 3 2 1

To the first lady in my life,
who gave me life,
my mother, Ruby McCullough

NEVADA

Prologue

The tall white-haired man watched the endless line of cars that moved, three-abreast, up and down the Strip. Like the sands of the desert that surrounded them, they seemed without number.

He opened the sliding glass door and stepped out onto the terrace. Rising from thirty-one stories below, the steady hum of traffic reminded him of swarming bees. The heat was stifling; 9:30 A.M., and the temperature had already reached 100.

The man left the terrace and shut the glass door. Bending over his desk, he stuffed some papers into the inside coat pocket of his dark western-styled suit. "I'm doing the tour," he told his secretary as he passed through the outer office.

Doors hissed shut and the elevator dropped swiftly into the bowels of the huge building, stopping several times to take on passengers. The white-haired man stood quietly in a corner, blue eyes intent on the flickering lights that marked their descent.

The quiet of the long ground-floor hall was disturbed by a distant murmur, a sound that grew in intensity as the man walked down the corridor.

An avalanche of noise rolled over him as he entered the

immense room. "Eight, the number's eight!" cried the stickman at a nearby craps table. "Now, eight the hard way!"

Chips fell softly on the green felt. The dice hit the end of
the table, then bounced high in the air. One twirling cube flew
over the head of a cigar-smoking man. "Off the wood, point's
no good," called the stickman.

The cigar smoker picked up the errant die and handed it
to a dealer who passed it to the slotman. Turning the die
around in his fingers, the slotman checked each side. Satisfied, he tossed it back on the table.

Gathering several sets of dice, the stickman pushed them
toward the shooter. The man chose two. "Damn!" burst out
a fat man near the center of the table. He laid two five-dollar
chips on Any 7. The dice bounced and rolled. "Seven!"
shouted the stickman. Money was dragged off the front line.
The fat man picked up the forty dollars won on the 7. Having
lost on the pass line, his win of the forty dollars brought him
almost even.

"Happens every time," the player on the shooter's right
said to no one in particular. "Throw 'em overboard, seven
out."

"New shooter! New shooter coming out!" cried the stickman.

The white-haired man moved on, pushing his way through
the milling crowd. The noise enveloped him. "Eee-leven!"
yelled a voice from a craps table down the line; shouts of joy
erupted in the wake of the call. People drifted toward the
table.

The man paused at a twenty-one table. The players bent
over their cards with silent determination. A lean man in a
short-sleeved shirt tapped a card in a downward motion. The
dealer slid a card from the shoe; it skidded to a halt in front
of the man. He lifted a corner and frowned, then signaled for
another hit. The next card was a ten. The man flipped his
cards face up. Twenty-six. The dealer swept the man's chips
into the tray.

The next player stood pat, sticking his cards under his
chips. And so on around the table. The dealer flipped his

cards face up, drew to 19. The player who had stood pat won; he had 20. The others lost.

Twenty yards away, in an elegant enclosure, a different game of cards was played. The ladderman nodded as the white-haired man approached, then returned his attention to the play. The white-haired man stood outside the enclosure and watched the action around the oval table. It was fast, and some players were betting the limit of four thousand dollars each hand. The tuxedo-clad croupier quietly gave instructions and announced winners.

Turning away from the baccarat game, the white-haired man entered the banks of machines that surrounded the pit, lined the walls and filled every available corner and niche of the casino.

"I got it! I got it!" a pants-suited woman with bleached hair cried, standing on tiptoe and looking across a row of black machines at her companion, pointing excitedly at a row of black bars that read, "JACKPOT, JACKPOT, JACKPOT." The white-haired man smiled. All that yelling for a nickel win of $5.00.

Coins crashed into metal trays, bells rang and electronic sound effects heralded wins and beat a space-age cadence to the pulling of handles and spinning of reels.

The big man looked down the rows of poker, twenty-one and keno video machines, not surprised to find them drawing more play than the slots. All sixteen progressive poker machines—linked together by computer—were in use, a giant overhead display flashing new higher winning amounts with each play.

A "Big Bertha" quarter slot machine dwarfed even the tall white-haired man. A young couple was playing it, the man inserting nine quarters each pull, the girl tugging at the long handle with both hands, mesmerized by the whirling banks of reels, hoping for the miracle of nine cherries in a row and a million-quarters win. The white-haired man silently wished them luck as he walked on. Big payoffs attracted more players.

As he passed through the rows of video machines, the man

felt suddenly out-dated, out of touch with this new breed of gamblers. The days when table games dominated Nevada casinos were past, green felt giving way to the steel and plastic of a new technology.

Surrounded by ringing bells, electronic bleeps, flashing lights, triumphant shouts and disappointed groans, the white-haired man was reminded of the old carnival days. In a nostalgic mood, he neared the main casino entrance.

A clickity, clickity, clickity sound—like a boy running a stick along a picket fence—made the man turn. A giant wheel of fortune spun while the dealer droned, " 'Round and 'round she goes, where she stops, nobody knows."

Two women watched the wheel intently. It clicked slower and slower. Their breath caught; they each had a five-dollar bill on number 20. Click . . . click . . . click. It stopped on 0. The dealer picked up the bills. The women laid down two more.

Again the wheel spun, blindingly at first. Clickity, clickity, clickity. " 'Round and 'round she goes . . ." the dealer said in a flat monotone.

The white-haired man stared at the spinning wheel. The scene faded. The dealer's voice drifted away. "Where she stops . . ." The crowd was gone, along with the hotels and the endless lines of traffic on the Strip. Blowing sand drifted across the desert wastes. It was another time and another place. . . .

BOOK ONE

1920-1937

1

"Step right up, folks!" cried the boy standing by the wheel. "For five cents, you can win a fortune!"

The small crowd of men, mostly farmers, stood in the hot California sun and looked up at the boy. Unruly hair, black as a raven's wing, sprouted from under the flat straw hat. Had he been a horse, the farmers would have judged the boy big and rangy with the promise of great strength, too tall and lean for the plow but a sure bet on the track. Good teeth, too —shining whitely in the dark-tanned face. But no horse ever had eyes like that! Pale blue orbs that peered out over the crowd with a mischievous glint.

A red garter encircled the boy's white-sleeved arm just above the elbow. He pointed his cane toward the big wheel. "A nickel, gentlemen. A nickel can bring you five dollars!" he urged, voice shifting keys as a sixteen-year-old boy's will.

"Aw, what the heck," said a sunburnt man, reaching inside his coverall's pocket. He laid a five-cent piece on the number 100. Two more men followed suit. Another put his money on the 10. The boy spun the wheel.

Clickity, clickity, clickity. The wheel stopped on 1. The boy picked up the nickels. A pause. The men put down more money. One doubled his bet. The wheel spun again.

The noise of the carnival surrounded them. The men didn't hear. Their eyes were glued to the wheel.

A man approached. He was of medium height, wearing a faded open-necked brown shirt and a wide-brim Stetson hat. An average-looking, thin-featured man who might have passed unnoticed if it weren't for the luxurious salt-and-pepper mustache that curled to sharp points on each side of his upper lip.

Stopping behind the crowd, he tipped back his hat and grinned up at the boy. The boy brushed a lock of hair out of his eyes and waved.

The man jerked a thumb toward a small fat man heading their way. The boy acknowledged him with a grin.

A lizard slithered through the dust, hesitated, eyes blinking rapidly. The lean man barely missed it with a stream of brown tobacco juice. The lizard disappeared under a wagon.

"Yahoo!" A man pushed his way up to the boy and held out a hand. The boy dropped in five nickels. More bets were laid.

The fat man climbed up on the platform. The boy yelled, "Gotta take a break. Go easy on Ben, here. He's the unluckiest man I know!"

The onlookers laughed. More money was wagered.

The boy fell in beside the mustachioed man. "Pretty good day, Charlie," the boy said.

"Not bad for a hick town," Charlie grunted. A gob of tobacco juice plastered a fly to a post.

"That must have been a ten-foot shot," admired the boy. The fly crawled out of the sticky mess, wings drooping.

Charlie squinted up at the boy from under his soiled cowboy hat. "Think I can do it again?"

"Forget it!" laughed the boy. "I'm not buying your lunch."

They continued walking through the crowded midway.

A strident voice made them turn. "If I can drive this nail into this piece of wood with just two strokes of the hammer, you should be able to do it with *three* strokes and WIN A PRIZE!"

Charlie and the boy stopped to watch a little man waving

a hammer aloft. Dripping wet, he couldn't have weighed 135. He shoved the hammer toward a husky young man in bib overalls.

The big man grinned. "All right, little feller," he said, "let's see you do it." The girl on his arm tittered.

The little man lifted the block of wood for all to see. A twelve-penny nail was embedded slightly in the wood. The crowd edged closer. He laid the block down and raised the hammer. *Wham! Wham!* The nail was driven in tight.

"Gimme," said the big man. He laid down 10 cents and reached for the hammer. *Wham! Wham! Wham!* The nail had half an inch to go. The girl giggled.

Her boyfriend stared at the nail, then at the little man. He tossed another dime on the counter. "Gimme another block," he growled.

"Come on," said Charlie, turning away.

The boy said, "I bet Jack used up a couple hundred blocks learning that trick."

A loud curse came from behind them. "Gimme another block!"

A tent shaded a group of people gathered around a table. In the center was a glass bowl tipped upside down. A frantic little mouse dashed back and forth, tiny feet scratching the sides. The rim of the table was covered with numbered holes.

"And there she goes!" shouted the operator. He lifted the bowl. The mouse made a beeline for number 1. The crowd groaned. The man retrieved the mouse and put it back under the bowl. "Bets down, folks!" he called. One finger caressed the number 2 hole.

Charlie chuckled. "Steb hunted all night for a male mouse. A cat cleaned him out yesterday." He nodded toward the table. "How much would you bet on the 2-hole in the corner?" he asked in a low voice.

"The works." The boy drew a straw from a pile of hay and stuck it in his mouth.

The glass bowl was raised. The mouse froze for a moment, nose twitching. It zipped into the corner 2-hole.

The mouse was under the bowl again. "Lay your bets,

folks!" cried the man. Underneath the table, he dipped a finger into a cup of vinegar, then rested it lightly over a number 1 hole. "Come on, folks!" he shouted. "Who's going to try for the big number 20?"

Charlie and the boy wandered over to the hot dog stand. "Three more days," said Charlie, "then we're on our way."

"Three more days of this heat is all I can take," said the boy.

"What's the matter, Meade? Can't you take it anymore? Isn't that sweat I see on your shirt? Or did you piss on your back?"

"Okay, smartass. You don't look so good yourself."

Meade looked toward the east, where brown foothills shimmered through the heat waves. "Even Iowa's going to look good after this," he said.

"Yeah."

"Catch a goldfish and win a prize!" shouted a barker. "One thin dime can win you a set of dishes!"

2

The train billowed black smoke as it started the ascent into the Sierra Nevada mountains.

Meade gazed out the window. The lush forest was a welcome sight after the dryness of the San Joaquin Valley. He turned his head and looked at Charlie who was sitting across the aisle. Charlie was slumped down in the seat, knees propped against the seat ahead, hat down over his face, arms folded across his chest.

The boy smiled affectionately at the sleeping man. Charlie was his mother and father, all rolled into one.

It had all begun two years ago, down in Texas . . .

* * *

Absently shuffling papers, the sheriff looked across the
desk at Charlie Brent. The boy sat in a chair, eyes fixed on
his feet. Charlie tilted his hat back and dragged on a cigarette. "Any reason why the boy can't come with me?" he
asked.

"You say you're the only kin," the sheriff said. "I can't find
anything that says different. We'd have to send him over to
Houston where they got a home—no way for a boy to live."

The sheriff tossed the papers in a pile. He looked at the
boy, then at Charlie. "The train leaves in half an hour.
They'll probably give me hell, but won't be the first time."

Charlie rose and stretched. "Did she leave anything?" he
asked.

The sheriff pulled out a drawer and removed a cigar box.
He handed it to Charlie. "That's it. The county took the few
bucks that was there for the buryin'."

Charlie lifted the lid and poked around. Some trinkets, a
few faded pictures, the boy's birth certificate. Thirty-four
years. A half-empty cigar box.

"The guy who did it," said Charlie, "where's he?"

"In Houston. He'll be dead by Christmas."

"That's less than six months. You Texans don't fool
around."

"We don't like murderers—'specially women killers."

The men glanced at the boy. He was still staring at his feet.

Charlie headed toward the door. "Gotta run," he said.
"I've got some things to pick up at the hotel." He paused on
the threshold. "Come on, boy."

"My name's Meade." Blue eyes stared defiantly at Charlie.

Charlie grinned. "Come on, Meade. We've got a train to
catch."

They had a lot of trains to catch. Charlie was a carney
man. He dealt in wishful thinking—the amusement parks,
the fairs, the traveling shows. *Step right up, folks! Laugh
a little! Take a chance! Win something!* Kids in bug-eyed
wonder, ladies hiding worn hands under lacey shawls, men
bent from too much labor and too little rest. *That's what*

it's all about, folks. For a few hours, a day, forget your worries. Pack up your troubles in the old kit bag! HAVE FUN!

As the train rolled out of the dusty Texas town, Meade left his mother behind, buried in a pine box under a crude wooden marker.

Maybe some of the girls from the house wept for her; Meade didn't know. None were there when his mother was lowered into the grave. No tears stained Meade's face. He hadn't experienced their salty taste since he was eight. That was when one of his mother's lovers had beaten him up. He had hated himself because he wasn't big enough to fight back. How he had wanted to pound the man's head into the floor! All he could do was stumble weeping out into the night, crying because of the humiliation rather than the pain. Knowing his mother wouldn't follow because she would get the same if she did.

Meade's mother had married a Kansas dirt farmer when she was sixteen. She was pretty and bright, with great hopes for the future.

The cruel Kansas winds quickly dried up her youthful enthusiasm. When opportunity came in the form of a dashing young drummer, she fled with her three-year-old son to Cleveland. Disappointment followed disappointment until the weary mother found it easier to accept "favors" from suitors rather than pennies for back-breaking labor cleaning homes and washing clothes.

Favors became cash payments and money soothed the reality that she had become a whore. Mother and son traveled from town to town, and the years took their toll. The worn face and tired body no longer brought a good price. Brothels in bleak western mining towns became a way of life. It was downhill all the way, right down to the little town in Texas where a drunken cowboy murdered her in a moment of uncontrollable rage.

The sheriff had found a recent letter from her brother, Charlie Brent, and sent him a wire. Charlie arrived two days later.

Now, as the train pulled into the Reno station, Meade

thought of the miles he had traveled the last two years. A lot of miles and a lot of towns like this. He gazed disinterestedly at the cluttered buildings that faced the tracks, brick exteriors dull with coal dust. Several saloons were in evidence, doors open in defiance of the Volstead Act, enacted last October to enforce the Eighteenth Amendment.

"Not much of a place, is it?" said Meade.

"A railroad town," said Charlie, reaching up to drag down an old metal suitcase.

After checking into a hotel, they walked south on Virginia Street, crossing at 2nd where Meade was nearly brained by two men loading a length of steel track on a truck. Charlie looked down the street at the trolley tracks that followed the bend at the bridge and disappeared into the residential district beyond. "Coming or going?" he asked one of the men.

"Goin'," the man said. "By the end of July, there won't be any trolley lines in Reno, except over to the Southern Pacific shops in Sparks."

"Looks like your town's going backwards," commented Meade.

"Shit no," snapped the man, suddenly aggressive. "Reno's gettin' bigger every day. It's just that people would rather drive cars than ride the trolley."

Meade grinned. "No offense meant."

The man nodded, still bristling, and went back to work.

"Stuck your foot in your mouth, didn't you?" chuckled Charlie as they reached the other side of the street. "People in these western towns are pretty touchy, and no one is touchier than a Nevadan. Most independent damn state in the Union."

Charlie paused under the shade of a big canvas awning and watched the traffic, evaluating the town through the eyes of a man whose living depended on accurately reading the crowd. He didn't miss the speakeasies tucked in between cleaners, hat shops, grocery and drugstores. For a population of ten or twelve thousand, the downtown area was bigger than normal, probably served an area fifty or more miles in every direction. He noted what looked like gambling halls just a half-block from the big Reno National Bank on the corner across the street. A jumpin' burg but still a burg.

Meade had a soda at Wilson's Drug while Charlie made a phone call. Charlie slid into the booth. "Drink up, boy," he grinned. "We're going for a walk."

Crossing the Truckee River bridge, they turned right, passing the Riverside Hotel, round brick turrets looming castle-like high above. Large homes appeared, surrounded by green lawns. Meade was impressed. This was a far cry from the dingy sight that had welcomed them at the train.

They climbed a hill and stood on a bluff that overlooked the river. "Wow!" exclaimed Meade, gazing in wonder at the huge mansions that sprawled in quiet splendor on the hilltop.

Charlie stopped in front of a brick gateway that had the name, TERHUNE, emblazoned on the metal arch that crowned the entrance to the most beautiful home Meade had ever seen. The two-story brick and stone mansion sat far back on what looked like acres of lawn, with tall trees lining the broad circular driveway.

Spitting his chaw of tobacco into a bush, Charlie started up the sweeping drive. "Holy cats," Meade said, hurrying to catch up, "are you sure you know where you're going, Charlie?"

Charlie peered at Meade from under his big cowboy hat. "What's the matter, boy? Don't you think I've got class?"

"Charlie, you might pass in a fancy saloon—but here?"

Charlie shot him a wry look. "Just tag along, son, and watch your old uncle in action."

The door was opened by a slender young woman with ash-blond hair and laughing brown eyes. "You've got to be Charlie," she exclaimed, thrusting out her hand. "Oh, hell," she said, pushing his hand aside and giving him a big hug. "I've heard so much about you that I feel we're sorta kin." She leaned back in Charlie's arms and added, "I'm Janice."

"Let go of my wife!" boomed a voice from the hall. "I always knew you couldn't be trusted with a pretty woman."

Meade looked past the grinning couple at a tall, broad-shouldered man who grasped Janice with one arm and threw the other around Charlie.

"Charlie, damnit," he rasped, "it's been six, seven years. And you don't look a bit different. Must have stopped aging at twenty-one."

"You don't look so bad yourself," Charlie replied. "If I got my figures right, you're two years younger than me, and I'm thirty-three. Damnit, you don't look a day over nineteen!"

Janice rolled her eyes up at Meade. "Sounds like a mutual admiration society."

"Hey," Charlie cried, tearing himself away, "meet my nephew, Meade. Him and me are partners."

The introductions over, which included the presentation of Grace, age three, and Tom, age five months, Bob Terhune and his guests retired to the library while Janice made for the kitchen. "At least I can fix you a good meal," she said, tossing her pretty head angrily at Charlie. "Imagine staying at that sleazy Elk Hotel when you could have stayed with us!"

Charlie and Bob nursed bourbons while Meade sipped on a beer. Scratching the back of his neck, Charlie looked around. "You've done all right, Bob," he said.

Terhune laughed, running his fingers through his wavy light brown hair. He surveyed the shelves of leather-bound books and dug the heels of his shiny boots into the thick carpet. "Janice keeps reminding me that I married money," he said, steel-blue eyes softening with affection. It was obvious that Terhune would have married Janice had she been penniless and not the only child of one of Nevada's wealthiest ranchers.

Charlie said, "What's doing, Bob? Your last letter said you're in politics."

Resting his drink on the chair arm, Terhune leaned back. "After the war, I won a seat on the city council. Janice's father has been a big supporter. I'm meeting a lot of people around the state. There's talk about bigger and better things. Who knows?"

Charlie looked at Meade. "I know you're wondering how Bob and I met." He grinned at Terhune, then turned back to Meade. "We met seventeen years ago—back in '03. I was working animals in the circus. When we stopped in Elko, this kid came up to me and asked if he could help shovel the elephant shit. Boy, what a deal! I got plumb wore out teaching him."

Terhune chuckled softly. "I'll never forget what an old cowboy said when I was walking home one night. He leaned over and took a big sniff, then jumped back. 'Boy,' he said, 'I've smelled horse shit and cow shit and chicken shit—but what kind of shit is *that?*' "

"The circus stayed in Elko for two weeks," continued Charlie, "and Bob came out every day. When we left for Salt Lake, he ran off with us. It was a month before his folks tracked him down. We got to know each other pretty good —been keeping up with each other ever since."

"What happened when your parents found you?" Meade asked Terhune.

Terhune shook his head, a shadow crossing his face. "My dad was going to beat the holy shit out of me, but my mother got between and said she would leave him if he did. My mother's a tough one. Dad backed down and walked out. He never had much to do with me after that."

Terhune was lost in thought for a moment, then he looked at Charlie. "When are you leaving?"

"Tomorrow morning. We're headed for Des Moines. Ever been to Riverview?"

"Hell yes! Stopped there on the way back from the war."

Terhune leaned forward and looked earnestly at Charlie. "You ought to stay in Nevada, Charlie," he said, raising a hand to block Charlie's protest. "I'm serious. This state's got a big future. We've got lots of plans. I'm looking right now at the state elections, maybe later Washington. Nevada will grow. You watch!"

"I believe you, Bob," Charlie said, "but I'm a carney man —not a rancher. There's only so many towns in this state, most of 'em no bigger than a pissant."

"Wait and see," Terhune said with a knowing smile. "Wait and see."

It was nearly midnight when Charlie and Meade returned to their hotel, a four-story structure facing the railroad tracks on Commercial Row. Before entering, Charlie peered down the street toward Center. "Let's mosey around a bit," he said, heading off in the direction of the Palace Club on the corner.

By the time the clubs closed at two A.M., they had visited a half-dozen. "Joints," Charlie muttered as he and Meade stood in a thick haze of cigar smoke and watched the action in a poorly lighted club. In one corner, a wizened, white-haired old man wearing a green eyeshade was dealing poker to four men while a group of onlookers crowded around.

Meade ran his fingers through his thick black hair. He felt conspicuous, not just because of his age but because he was the only one in the room not wearing a hat.

Poker and lo-ball were the most popular games, with whist, pan and 500 drawing a smattering of play. Gambling had been closed down in Nevada in 1910 but had slowly been allowed back into Reno over the last ten years, poker, lo-ball and slot machines returning to grace via the 1915 legislature, provided "the play was for drinks, cigars or other prizes whose value did not exceed $2."

The clubs were semi-private, and no women were allowed; however, illegal games like 21, craps and roulette were. Even if women had been welcome, no self-respecting lady would have wanted to descend into the dirty, unsavory basements that housed the Reno gambling clubs in the Twenties.

"I'd go nuts in a place like this," Meade said the next morning as they entered the train station. "Reminds me of the hick towns Mom and I lived in."

Charlie grunted and tossed the suitcase onto a baggage cart.

3

Even though they had been to the Riverview Amusement Park before, Meade and Charlie acted like two kids playing hooky—laughing, pointing, waving at friends.

Riverview opened in Des Moines in 1905. It was the home of the Scrambler, a giant whirling wheel with four cars on each arm, two riders to a car. There was the famous House of Mirth and a giant roller coaster with one and a half miles of track and eight heart-stopping dips that dropped all the way to the ground.

"Hey, let's have lunch and then ride the Scrambler," said Meade gleefully.

"How about let's ride the Scrambler and *then* eat lunch?" replied Charlie. He stuck his hands in his back pockets and looked up at the swinging monster, the screams of its passengers filling the air.

"Charlie baby!" cried a big-boned woman in overalls. She threw her arms around the hapless man and lifted him off the ground.

"Mandy," laughed Charlie, kissing her hard on the lips, "put me down before you break my bones."

Charlie stuffed his rumpled shirt back in his jeans. "Mandy," he said, "meet my nephew, Meade Slaughter."

Mandy grabbed Meade's hand and almost yanked his arm out of its socket. "Glad to meet you, boy!" she roared. "I'm Mandy Clark. Charlie and me—we go back a long ways."

Charlie grinned and said, "Still working them girls, Mandy?"

Mandy looked at him with rounded eyes. "Why, Charlie,"

she murmured, "you know all I do is operate a nice little bottle game—and it barely keeps me alive."

"Yeah," Charlie said with a leer. "I know how you 'barely' keep alive. You're the richest woman on the circuit, gal. And them nonexistent girls aren't making you no poorer."

"Come on, you mangy goat," said Mandy. "You, too, Meade. If I'm so rich, I guess I can buy you both lunch."

A lot of people dropped by while they ate. "Why don't you settle down here, Charlie?" asked a thin little man. Like the small man back at the fair in California, he operated the nail game. "With two strokes of the hammer . . ."

"Settle down?" exclaimed Charlie. "Hell, man, I like traveling. Besides, Meade needs a well-rounded education. He's not going to get that sitting still."

Mandy gazed skyward in silent supplication. "The poor lad," she intoned. "He's destined to be a graduate of the Charlie Brent Carney College." She threw her huge arms around Meade. "Stay with me, Meade," she pleaded. "I'll raise you proper."

"Har, har!" mocked Charlie. "Are you thinking of that *other* game you run?"

Later, as Meade and Charlie toured the grounds, Meade asked, "Does Mandy really run girls here?"

"Yep. Nice clean girls. Mandy never cheats a customer. She takes good care of the girls, too. Got a heart of gold. But she can be tough as nails when she has to."

Meade knew all about Mandy's other game. After all, he was his mother's son. A lively young whore had made a man of him just a few months before his mother was killed. At sixteen, Meade was already attracting a lot of attention from the opposite sex. He had reached his full height of six feet two inches and was filling out fast.

He wasn't handsome; his features were too blunt and rugged for that. The broken nose didn't help; he'd gotten that falling down a flight of stairs when he was ten.

But the girls took a second look when he passed. They noticed the unusual combination of dark hair and blue eyes, the aggressive walk, the smiling devil-may-care attitude that gave him the look of an oversized leprechaun. Older women speculated on the kind of man he would become and were saddened that it couldn't be sooner.

The summer and fall months passed quickly. Meade ran the Wheel of Fortune while Charlie operated the Fascination Game, a form of electronic bingo where the player shot balls into numbered holes.

As winter approached, they moved on to Miami. Other parks followed: Playland at Rockaway Beach, Atlantic City, Hershey Park, Lagoon Park. The months stretched into years. When Meade reached the age of twenty-two, they were running three concessions at the new Belmont Amusement Park on Mission Bay in San Diego.

4

She was tall, and her blond hair bounced with each springy step. She grabbed her escort's arm and pulled. "Look, a dart game. Bet I can beat you!"

"You're on!" The slim well-dressed man followed her to the booth.

It wasn't the Fourth of July or any other special day, but it became a special day on Meade's calendar—May 5, 1926.

Meade was turning from replacing some punctured balloons when he saw her. Their eyes met. Meade hoped she won everything in the booth. He hoped it took all day, a week, a month, a year!

Her companion threw down a dime, picked up two darts and handed one to the girl. "Okay," he said in a superior masculine voice, "let's see how good you are!"

The girl drew back her arm, the thin fabric of her dress stretching to reveal firm well-rounded breasts. A frown of concentration creased her brow; gray eyes narrowed. The dart missed one of the balloons on the top row by an inch. Meade almost cried with pain.

"Aha!" shouted the boyfriend. "Watch this!" His dart lodged third row down. A clean miss.

Meade silently cursed the darts. He cursed the balloons. He felt like grabbing a Panda bear and thrusting it at the girl, insisting that anyone who even *hit* the top row won a prize.

The boyfriend saved the day. "Once more!" he cried. Two nickels hit the counter. "Me first!" he yelled. Bottom row. *Thud.* Nothing.

The girl glanced at Meade, then drew back her arm. Again that tantalizing glimpse of a taut, full body. *Bam!* Second row down, middle. Glory be! She *had* won a Panda bear!

Instead of grabbing just any bear as was the custom, Meade leaned across the counter and wallowed in those deep gray eyes. "Which bear do you want, Miss—Miss—."

"*Shirley,*" she said brightly. "And I want *that* one."

Meade followed her pointing finger. "That one" was black and white with a red bow tie. He picked it up and handed it to the girl. Their hands touched, and again their eyes met. She was almost buried behind the three-foot bear.

Meade had an inspiration. He said, "You'll get tired of packing him around. Why not leave him here? You can pick him up when you leave."

Her eyes twinkled. "Sure, why not?" She looked at her escort. "Okay?"

"Why not?" he said, not sure he liked what was going on.

Meade almost went cross-eyed glancing around in anticipation of the girl's return. He invented ways of getting rid of the boyfriend. Just a few minutes alone! He could say a mad, red-haired man had leaped over the counter and seized the bear, then ran screaming toward the beach, clutching the bear and crying. Would the boyfriend rush off to the rescue? Fat chance!

He couldn't believe his eyes when he saw her approaching the booth alone. A customer had just left. Meade prayed for a sudden lack of consumer interest.

"Hi!" she said, flashing that big happy smile. "Got my bear?"

Meade searched the crowd. "Oh, *him,*" she said, voice bubbling with laughter. "We met some friends, and they wanted to ride the roller coaster. I said my stomach wasn't up to it. So here I am!"

Meade lifted the bear to the counter. Around its neck was a pink ribbon with a card reading, "Shirley."

"I would have put your last name and address on the card," Meade said bravely or desperately, he didn't know which, "but I just knew your first name."

"Shirley Reed," she said quickly. "Four fifty-two Ocean Street."

Meade didn't hesitate. "Phone number?"

"Plaza 6178."

Meade scratched the information on the card, then removed it from the bear's neck. "I better keep this," he said in a businesslike tone. "Kinda like a guarantee card."

She nodded her head. "You should," she said solemnly. "His stuffing or something might come out. You *do* fix those things, don't you?"

Meade patted the bear's head. "Ma'am, if one hair, just *one* hair falls out, I personally guarantee that the hair—or the bear—will be replaced." He picked up a card and wrote, "Meade Slaughter, Franklin 3319."

"That's the number of the hotel where I stay," he explained. "It's a community phone. You'll get me or I'll get the message. 'Course, most of the time, I'm here."

She picked up the bear and the card, then turned to leave. Mischievously, she looked back over her shoulder. "I'll count the hairs tonight," she said, smiling brilliantly. "I'll want to know if any fall out."

Meade was in a daze the rest of the day. Once, he dropped a dart on his foot. Dumbly, he stared down at the tiny missile as it quivered in his shoe. Cupid's arrow. Stuck in his foot instead of his heart!

Days passed. No phone call. No Shirley walking up with a smile. The card with her address and phone number was crumpled from overuse. It didn't matter; he had it memorized.

Charlie leaned against the hot dog stand. Squinting up at Meade, he said, "What the hell's wrong with you? I keep saying things, and you don't hear. You sick or something?"

"Do I look sick?"

"Don't know. You look like a guy who ate ten pounds of dried peaches, then didn't take a shit for a week."

"Ugh!" Meade looked disgustedly down at Charlie.

"It's a girl!" chortled Charlie. "I've seen you like this before—a dozen times. Right?"

Meade had to talk to someone about Shirley. He couldn't keep it to himself any longer. "Yeah," he said.

Charlie peered up into his face. "When did this happen? I haven't seen no action going in and out of your room lately."

"Charlie, she's not that kind of girl."

Charlie snorted. "What do you mean—not that kind of girl. *All* girls are *that* kind of girl."

Charlie was on his second marriage. After a year and a half, it was going sour. Charlie had never felt as Meade did. For that matter, had anyone ever been so desperately in love? Meade doubted it.

"Charlie," Meade said patiently, "she's not *that* kind of girl. She's the most beautiful thing you've ever seen. She can blind you with her smile."

"When you been seeing this gal? In the middle of the night? I haven't seen you with anyone who smiles and blinds people. I've seen you with Carl over there. He's sixty, ugly and missing one eye. What he's got sure isn't going to blind anyone."

"Charlie," Meade blurted out, "I haven't even gone out with her. I've only seen her once!"

Charlie choked on his hot dog and went into a coughing fit. Wiping the tears from his eyes, he croaked incredulously, "You've only seen her once? *Once?* And you're staggering around like a lost puppy? You—the scourge of the park circuit? You've left a trail of broken hearts from here to New

York. Times I've wondered if you've even got a heart, leaving all them pretty girls scattered in your wake. Men would stand in line for your rejects! By God, I can't believe it!"

Meade smiled weakly. "It's true. Oh Lord, it's true."

"Well, trot her out. Let your old uncle have a look!"

Pulling out the crumpled card, Meade stared helplessly at it. "I don't know if I've got the guts to call her," he said in a strangled voice.

Charlie slapped his palm to his forehead and groaned loudly.

Meade never made the call. She got to him first.

The phone almost fell from his trembling hand. "My bear is missing two hairs," she said sweetly.

"Two!" cried Meade. "Oh God, two! Never has anything like this happened. One maybe, but two—never!"

"What am I going to do?" she wailed.

"We have to meet right away! Tomorrow may be too late!"

"Horton Plaza by the fountain? In an hour?"

"Great! See you then." Meade started to hang up, then shouted, "Don't forget the bear!"

Strollers in the plaza smiled at the pretty blond girl and the tall dark young man sitting on a bench, heads bent over a giant Panda bear that sat between them.

"See," she said triumphantly. "Two hairs missing!"

"I'll have to take your word for it," said Meade. "I left my hair count card back at the booth."

"You didn't call," she said reproachfully.

Meade examined the bear's ears. "I was getting around to it. Scared, I guess."

"You were pretty brave at the booth."

"I was—I am!" Meade looked up and shrugged his shoulders. "It's just that I wasn't sure if you would see me. You know—like maybe it was just a joke."

Eyes round with innocence, she sighed deeply and said, "Well, we can certainly be thankful for the missing bear hair."

Jumping up, Meade grabbed the bear, then Shirley's hand. "Come on," he said, grinning broadly. "Let's put this critter in the car and go get a soda."

The setting sun outlined their silhouettes as they walked hand in hand past the arching waters of the fountain, the bear looking like some misshapened growth under the man's arm.

5

They were married on a bright Saturday afternoon in a little Methodist church on the outskirts of San Diego. It wasn't a big wedding. Shirley's father gave her away while her mother tried to look pleased; neither parent was happy about their daughter marrying a "carney man."

Shirley's older sister sat beside her mother with her husband and two children, her own displeasure barely concealed. Their brother, a senior at USC, viewed the whole proceedings with amusement and a secret pride in Shirley's defiance of their domineering mother.

An aunt came down from Los Angeles. Friends from the bank where Shirley worked filled two rows of seats. Well-wishers from the park gathered on Meade's side of the church. Charlie stood proudly at Meade's side as best man, looking somewhat stiff in the suit he had bought for the occasion.

That evening, Meade parked his Ford sedan in front of a motel in Oceanside, a sleepy town halfway between San Diego and Los Angeles. Laughing, he carried Shirley across the threshold.

There was no embarrassment. There hadn't been that first time, either, three months after they met. . . .

* * *

It was a lazy Sunday afternoon in August, and they were driving north along the coast. Shirley was crushed up against Meade, long legs straddling the gear shift.

Not long after passing through La Jolla, Meade pulled the car into a secluded grove of Torrey pines that nestled on a bluff high above the ocean. The only sound was the crashing of surf sixty feet below and the singing of birds.

Meade drew Shirley into his arms, and she nuzzled her face into his neck. Their lips met, tongues lightly touching. As Meade probed deeper, Shirley moaned softly. She shivered against the hand that wandered down her shoulder and closed over her breast.

Meade pulled back and touched her nose. "Know something?" he said in a husky voice. "This can get us into trouble."

Her eyes were at half-mast. "Worried?"

"No. You?"

"Try me."

Meade grabbed the blanket and picnic basket out of the backseat, and they walked in silence to a stand of young trees that formed a natural arbor. The ground was soft with pine needles and leaves, and their hips sank comfortably into the deep cushion as they rolled into each other's arms.

"You taste good," Meade said, nibbling on Shirley's lower lip.

"Mmmm," she murmured, pressing closer.

"Feel good, too," Meade said, gripping a taut buttock through the thin fabric of her shorts.

"You, too," Shirley said, slipping a hand under his shirt and running her fingers through the thick hair on his chest.

Meade pushed Shirley's bra up over her full breasts and licked the upright nipples. Her hips began to rotate as Meade's hand dropped down over her belly.

With one swift motion, Shirley slipped off her shorts and panties, kicking them with her sandals to one side. Rising on an elbow, Meade viewed her total nakedness for the first time. Shirley stretched luxuriously, basking in the admiration that filled her lover's eyes.

"My God," Meade whispered reverently.

"Not fair," Shirley said, reaching for the buttons on Meade's shirt.

Then it was Shirley's turn. Rising and sitting back on her heels, she studied his muscular body, the wide shoulders and lean hips, the engorged member that rose quivering from its nest of black curly hair.

They came together in an explosion of need and urgency, totally oblivious of their surroundings, intent only on satisfying the pent-up desires that had brought them to this moment.

Cries of release filled the air. Overhead, the birds fell silent, anxious eyes darting down at the two bodies that broke apart, then held each other as if they would never let go.

It had been like that from the beginning. Good. More than good—great.

"Mrs. Slaughter," Meade said as he broke open the bottle of champagne supplied by the gang at the park, "do you plan on taking advantage of me after we drink this?"

"No, Mr. Slaughter," she said in a deep-throated voice. "Before."

The champagne fizzled and lost its bubbles. It passed unnoticed.

6

"Do you want to get out and walk a little?" asked Shirley, stretching to look out the train window at the little town.

Meade sank deeper in the seat. "Okay if we stay here?"

"Sure, honey." Her finger traced its way down the side of his face. "You look tired."

Offering a lazy smile, Meade said, "I always get this way riding trains."

"Not me. I love it."

"Maybe I felt that way on my first trip. Don't remember."

Shirley playfully poked him in the ribs. "Meade Slaughter, world traveler!"

The train lurched and started to move slowly out of the station. As it neared the outskirts of town, a small graveyard came into view. They rounded the curve, and the town dropped out of sight.

Blinking his eyes, Meade dashed away that last glimpse of the sun-baked knoll where his mother's grave lay unattended.

A boy of fourteen had left this town nine years ago. A man was passing through.

Meade said nothing to Shirley about the little town or the little graveyard or the unattended grave.

Underneath the outward appearance of a showman, there was a deep, secretive side to Meade. Basically, he was an introvert. His early years had further nurtured the natural tendency to stay within himself. Dragged from town to town, he had played alone. As soon as he learned to read, he buried himself in books. The classics, *Tom Sawyer, Ben Hur* and *Uncle Tom's Cabin* became familiar companions. Reading would always be a passion with Meade. His actual schooling had been sparse, but he would go through life far better read than most college graduates.

Charlie, extrovert that he was, showed little finesse in introducing Meade to the mad, noisy life of the carnival. At first, the boy almost hated him. Charlie would put Meade on a box and wave at the passing crowd. "Yell, boy," he would say. "Yell until you get their attention. They've come to be entertained. Entertain 'em!"

Experience brought confidence. The boy on the box learned what Charlie meant about entertainment. People came to the parks, the fairs, the carnivals to have fun—hopefully to win something. They came with pockets full of change. The lucky ones left with dishes, candy, dolls and Panda bears. Most left with lighter pockets, but all left with lighter hearts. For a short time, they had let themselves go.

By the time Charlie and Meade settled down at San

Diego's Belmont Park, Meade was a seasoned carney man. They did well at Belmont, sometimes clearing over five hundred a week. They were partners, and Charlie shrewdly saw to it that a certain amount of money was salted away.

Two months ago, Charlie had led Meade out of the park and down to the beach. The sun was shining brightly, and sea gulls cried overhead. Removing his hat, Charlie searched the sky. Meade noticed the gray streaks in Charlie's thick hair. Charlie wasn't that old. Thirty-nine? Forty?

Spitting a stream of tobacco off to one side, Charlie wiped his chin on his sleeve and snorted, "Shit."

Meade knew that Charlie hadn't brought him to the beach to watch sea gulls. He stuck his hands in his back pockets and waited patiently.

"Know how much money we got in the bank?" asked Charlie.

"Nope. You keep the books."

"Just a little short of eleven thousand."

Meade whistled. "Not bad."

"Bad," muttered Charlie.

"Bad?" echoed Meade.

"Yeah. You see, Sarah and me are busting up—"

"So what else is new?"

Charlie ignored Meade's remark. "She'll go quietly if I pay her enough. She wants half of the bank account."

"So?"

"So she wants fifty-five hundred dollars. Where does that leave us? Up shit creek without a paddle!"

"Charlie, what's mine is yours. You would do the same for me."

Charlie hooked his thumbs in his belt and looked at Meade. "You're married now, boy. You've got responsibilities."

Meade said quietly, "You could have left me with that sheriff in Texas."

"Shit." Charlie's vocabulary was limited that day.

Gazing skyward at a screaming sea gull, Meade said thoughtfully, "I've got an idea. I'll get a honeymoon. You'll get rid of Sarah, and we'll make that money back by fall."

"What are we gonna do—all go to Niagara Falls and kick Sarah off, then sue the state for damages?"

Meade dropped on the sand and propped himself up on his elbows. He lit a cigarette amid chuckles. "That's an alternative," he said. "We'll keep it in mind." He waved the cigarette in the air. "I'm thinking about Playland in New York. They've got two hundred acres with people flooding the place. It's big enough that Mandy moved her stuff from Riverview. You read her letter."

"I'm listening."

"You stay here, and we'll go to Playland. We'll make money at both ends of the country. Shirley will be nuts about the idea."

The following day, a decision was reached. Charlie paid off Sarah. Meade wrote Mandy, and she made arrangements for them to open two concessions at Playland.

Shirley couldn't wait to leave. She was nineteen and had never been out of California. Her parents didn't share her enthusiasm; they had never accepted the marriage, certainly not this trip across the country. Their daughter was becoming a gypsy.

7

"Nevada is the only free state in the Union!" The words cracked out over the Denver audience. Men stirred uncomfortably in their seats. Fred D. Balzar, Governor of Nevada, was concluding a speech at the Colorado River Conference, a speech in which he had strongly defended his state's liberal divorce laws and tolerant attitude toward gambling.

It was late August, 1927. Prohibition was virtually ignored in Nevada, as were all laws that tended to curb one's freedom. Over thirty years later, another governor of Nevada, Grant Sawyer, would put it even clearer. "Our attitude toward life, save under the most urgent provocation, is relaxed, tolerant and mindful that if others are allowed to go their way unmolested, a man stands a chance of getting through the world himself with a minimum of irritation."

On the platform, Bob Terhune crossed his arms and let his eyes drift around the room. He knew what they were thinking, and like a true Nevadan he didn't give a damn.

Last year, Terhune had been re-elected to his second term as a Nevada state senator. He was one of the most popular men to ever achieve Nevada state office. He could stay as long as he chose.

Everything was coming up roses, but it hadn't always been that way.

Bob Terhune was born in a tiny hotel room in Elko, Nevada, March 16, 1890. He spent his first night in a dresser drawer.

His father was a tall, lean, brooding man who had been well educated back east where he had met Alicia Bennedict. She was two years his senior and had had a good deal to do with the decision to get married.

They wandered west in search of fortune and landed in Elko, in possession of two hundred dollars and a baby half-baked in the oven. Henry Terhune took a temporary job as the assistant manager of an Elko hotel; it would do until the child was born, then they would move on to San Francisco.

The child was born, but they never moved on. Henry's ambition never reached further than the managership of the hotel, and he got that a year after Bob arrived.

Realizing she would never attain her goals through her husband, Alicia decided to do so through her son. A former teacher, she took up her profession again. Bob played in the classroom while his mother taught. At three, he could write his name. At five, he was reading ahead of children twice his age. Alicia knew where he was going—to the University of Nevada. Opening in Elko in 1874, the university had moved to Reno in 1886.

Relegated to third place in the home, Henry Terhune took to frequenting the hotel bar more and more as time passed.

When Bob was fourteen and had returned from his escapade with Charlie and the circus, Henry took one last stab at his fatherly duties. When Alicia defied him in front of the boy, Henry slipped out the door and went downtown to the hotel bar. Soon afterward, he took to sleeping at the hotel and dropping by the home like a stranger sneaking in for a peek at family life.

Bob entered the University of Nevada at fifteen. He went home twice that first year, once at Christmas and once for his father's funeral. Henry Terhune had died under the wheels of a heavy wagon. Witnesses said he was so drunk he didn't know what hit him.

Alicia packed her things and followed her son to Reno. She taught school near the university and provided a home for Bob.

Bob was big and a natural athlete, a standout quarterback on the football team and a star baseball pitcher. That, coupled with good looks, made him highly popular with the girls.

At twenty-one, he received his law degree and went to work for a Reno attorney.

During his college years, Bob had worked part-time and summers for a local rancher. He kept up the habit even after going into law practice. His mother frowned at the idea, swearing he would be crushed under the hoofs of his horse or a thundering herd of cattle.

It was on the ranch that he met Sam Crowder, said to be the biggest cattle rancher in northern Nevada. They hit it off right away. Crowder liked what he saw. After sizing things up, he threw a little law business Terhune's way. They became good friends.

Their friendship took a new turn when Terhune met Crowder's only child, Janice. The apple of her father's eye, Janice had been raised by her father, her mother having died when she was three.

Janice couldn't keep her eyes off the tall, handsome young

man. At seventeen, with her father's wealth and power behind her, she was destined for the best. She decided Bob Terhune was just that. He didn't have a chance. Crowder was delighted.

They were married in 1915. It was one of the biggest weddings ever held in Reno. Everyone from the governor down was there. Crowder dragged his new son-in-law around until he had met every important person there. Crowder had big plans for Janice's husband.

Their first child, Grace, was born in 1917. That was the year that Terhune went off to war.

He returned in 1918 the conquering hero. He had been wounded in the Argonne forest while leading a charge that cleaned out a machine-gun nest. Captain Terhune's chest bristled with medals from his own and two foreign governments. He was welcomed back with a brass band and the works. Crowder was more delighted than ever.

Crowder presented Terhune and his budding family with his mansion in Reno. "Don't need it," he said, "I feel a lot more comfortable at the ranch."

Moving into the big house on the bluff above the Truckee River, the Terhunes quickly got re-acquainted. In 1920, Tom Terhune was born, instantly becoming the idol of his doting grandfather.

Grandfather and grandmother visited at different times; they didn't see eye to eye. For that matter, no one saw eye to eye with Alicia, not even her son. He avoided her as much as possible.

With the backing of his father-in-law, Terhune was easily elected a state senator on the Democratic ticket. He was soon a potent force at the bi-annual legislative sessions held in Carson City.

Rolling through the green farmlands of Utah on the San Francisco Overland, Governor Balzar said to Bob Terhune, "It's up to men like you to get our laws changed, Bob."

They were sitting in the wood-paneled first-class lounge car, cooled by the crushed-ice air-conditioning system. Leaning forward, Terhune refilled their glasses from his hip flask.

Balzar continued: "What in hell got into the legislature in '09 to outlaw gambling is more than I'll ever know. No one pays attention to it, but it's cramping our style and costing us tourist dollars. God, did you see what David of the auto association said last year—that Reno's picking up on the tourist trade, getting twenty cars going through daily? That's supposed to be big business?"

Terhune grinned. "Maybe with the Victory and Lincoln highways completed, we'll step up to *thirty* cars a day."

Balzar took a pull on his drink, then laughed. "That's about the pace a lot of our tail-dragging citizens would like to move at. I can see the slogan now, 'Fifty cars a day by 1930!' "

Tossing down the rest of his drink, Balzar looked earnestly at Terhune. "Getting the six-month divorce residency requirement cut down to three months this year will help. For my part, they could have cut it to one month. If a married couple can't get along, let them split up without a lot of trouble.

"It makes me sick when I think how we came within one vote of getting gambling legalized last March. One vote! It's sure as hell not your fault, Bob. You worked your ass off trying to get it through. We're just going to have to do our homework better next time. Damnit, Nevada's economy doesn't need a boost—it needs a kick in the ass!"

Terhune had heard this kind of talk a thousand times. The nation was enjoying a wave of prosperity, but little had trickled down into Nevada.

This year, the population of Nevada had reached 80,000. Reno and Elko had a fourth of it, with little towns like Tonopah, Winnemucca, Las Vegas and Ely getting a few thousand each. The rest were scattered over a state twice as big as England.

Balzar knew it would take men like Terhune to get Nevada moving. So did other powerful men around the state. They were determined to keep Terhune in state government until the right laws were written on the books. Then they had bigger things in mind for the popular state senator from Reno.

8

Meade locked the booth and walked along the darkened boardwalk. Sixty feet wide and four miles long, it was the pride of Atlantic City.

Shirley greeted him at the door with a finger to her lips. "He just went to sleep," she whispered.

Meade tiptoed into the little room and looked down on his son, David Slaughter, just four months old, a chubby thumb stuck securely in his mouth.

The child had added another dimension to Meade's life. He had felt a closeness with Charlie, something he had never experienced with his mother. With Shirley, it was a bursting of passions, a youthful flowering of love. Now, he felt pride. Nothing would be too good for his son.

Shirley set a glass of milk and a plate of cookies on the table. Sitting down, she wrapped the robe closer around her lush body. Meade grinned. "Baby, you look like you've never had a kid. I think I'd rather munch on you than these cookies."

Shirley glowed. More than anything else, she wanted to be attractive to Meade. She was an affectionate girl with lots of love to give. In turn, she needed to be loved completely and to be constantly reminded of that love. Meade more than fulfilled her wishes. A romantic at heart, he delighted in expressing his love by word and deed. He was always bringing her gifts that reflected the care he had paid to their choice.

Shirley was used to attention—she had been the baby of the family—and she had always been noticed by the opposite sex.

At first she was a pal to the boys, ready to attempt anything. When her tall lean frame began to fill out in her teens, "Skinny" Shirley suddenly began to attract boys in another way. She quickly learned to adjust; it was an exciting new adventure. She loved every minute of it.

She could have had lots of men, but all she wanted was Meade. She loved the big rugged man sitting across the table. Not once had she regretted her marriage.

Meade laid the cash box on the table. It was filled with bills and change. He shook his head as he counted the money. "I just can't believe it," he said. "We're rolling in dough. The whole damn country's getting richer every day. Remember Billy—the kid who unloaded the trucks down at the walk?"

"Little guy? Talks a mile a minute?"

"Yeah. Know what he did? He worked for four years and saved every nickel he made. Six months ago, he started putting it in stocks. He just kept on buying and selling. Last week, he quit his job. Harvey says he's worth over seventy-five thousand. Seventy-five thousand! Charlie and I have been working like dogs for ten years. Know what we've got? Maybe twenty thousand."

"Think we should buy some stock?"

Meade grinned sheepishly. "I already did."

A worried look creased Shirley's brow. "How much?"

"Five thousand. It's our money. I won't touch Charlie's."

Shirley squinted her eyes and looked him over. "I don't know if you'd fit on Wall Street," she said slowly. "You *are* getting a little class. You dress good. You talk good." She licked her lips suggestively. "You taste good."

Meade shoved the money box in a drawer, then pulled Shirley up into his arms. "To hell with Wall Street," he said gruffly. "Let's go to bed."

Three thousand miles away, the sun was just setting in San Diego, turning the sky a deep red and the crashing waves a foamy pink as they washed ashore at Belmont Park. As the last customers drifted out of the park, many paused to watch the fading rays disappear over Mission Beach, starkly outlining the giant roller coaster that dominated the skyline.

Hitching up his jeans, Charlie removed his cowboy hat and wiped the sweat from his forehead with a red bandanna. Another day, another dollar.

Like the rest of the nation, the West Coast was bathed in prosperity. With hired help, Charlie was operating five concessions.

Charlie had learned his lessons well, and Meade had learned from Charlie. The years in the parks and fairs had sharpened their instincts and prepared them for the years ahead.

9

The summer of 1929 found Meade and Shirley in Riverview Park. They had reached Des Moines via Panama City Park in Miami and Cedar Point in Ohio.

The strain of moving was beginning to show, but they were young and in love—and rich.

In June, Meade figured they had over $200,000 in stock. They kept ploughing all their earnings back into the market. The whole nation was living high on the hog.

From the beginning of 1928 to June, 1929, stocks had rocketed. General Electric rose from $128 a share to $396. RCA from $94 to $505, Montgomery Ward from $132 to $466. In three years, the average for twenty-five industrials rose from $186.03 to $469.49.

Meade tried to get Charlie to join him in the market, but Charlie was stubborn when it came to money. He bought a little stock, but most of his money went into a safe-deposit box in a San Diego bank.

As the summer wore on, hints of possible disaster came down from Wall Street. Few listened. The year before, Herbert Hoover had been elected as the "candidate of prosperity." He would bring to Americans a "chicken in every pot, a car in every garage."

On the Coast, Charlie tore the front page from the August 8th issue of the Hollywood *Citizen News.* The headline read, "STOCKS IN WORLD WIDE COLLAPSE." He mailed it to Meade with a warning to get out of the market.

Meade was already trying. Stocks that would have brought thousands now only brought hundreds, if that.

Instead of emptying Riverview Park, the cloud of doom that was settling over the nation seemed to attract even more people through the gates. They crowded into the park to seek temporary shelter from the disturbing pressures of the outside world. Through all the confusion and doubts, Meade observed this phenomenon, unconsciously filing it away for future reference.

There were periods of silence in the Slaughter household, as if Meade and Shirley were afraid words would lead to anger. They had never had a real fight. Their marriage was untested by financial stress; the great American dream had been theirs in bushels.

Shirley heard the news on the radio. A half-hour later, the door opened to admit her gray-faced husband. Swearing, he threw a big folder on the table. "Worthless!" he shouted. "The whole damn thing's worthless!"

They had used all their money, and the concessions, to try and save the stock they had. Only yesterday, they had siphoned off their last thousand dollars to the broker.

The date was October 29, 1929.

Later that day, Meade picked up a copy of *The New York Times.* The headline announced, "STOCKS COLLAPSE IN $16,410,030 DAY." Pointing at the copy below the headline, Meade said disgustedly, "Who the hell do they think they're kidding?" His finger stabbed at the words, "BUT RALLY AT CLOSE CHEERS BROKERS: BANKERS OPTIMISTIC."

America had been skidding toward a depression for some time. Europe, particularly Germany, had been in financial trouble through most of the Twenties. The stock market crash alone didn't drive America into the deepest depression in its history. As with all recessions, pessimism replaced optimism. Despair begat despair. People just gave up. They threw up their hands and said, "What good is it to try?"

Little David Slaughter gurgled in a corner while his parents sat hunched over the table, a pile of stock certificates lying between them. With a sudden sweep of his arm, Meade sent them flying across the room.

Shirley's eyes widened with shock. She had never seen him like this. He had always been so sure of himself. She stared at her husband as he jumped up and began to stalk back and forth.

The phone rang, and Meade made a dive for it. "Meade," Charlie said cheerfully, "I just got the note that you called. What's up?"

"Where have you been, Charlie? Haven't you heard about the stock market?"

"Oh that! Yeah, we got radios and newspapers here—cars and airplanes, too. We're getting downright civilized."

"Charlie, I'm serious. We're in trouble."

Charlie's voice tightened. "Whose 'we,' son?"

"Me and Shirley. You and me!"

"Hey, don't get so excited. Calm down and give it to me straight."

Meade did. Charlie had no idea how deep Meade had gone into the market. When Meade finished, Charlie asked, "That's it—nothin' more?"

"I owe the bank, some creditors around town."

"How much would it take you to get out of town clean?"

Meade hadn't told Shirley about the notes he had signed in the recent mad plunge to save his dwindling stocks. He wished he had called Charlie from somewhere else. Charlie's voice cracked over the phone, "Meade, are you there?"

"Yeah, I'm here," whispered Meade. Wiping his mouth, he blurted out, "I'm in pretty deep, Charlie. Twenty-five, maybe thirty thousand."

A gasp came from the table. Meade didn't dare look around.

The line sang, then Charlie chuckled softly. "By golly," he said, "when you do it big, you do it big, don't you?"

Meade gripped the receiver like it was a lifeline.

"Tell you what, son," Charlie said quietly. "Figure out just what you need, and let me know. I'll send you the money by Western Union. When things are cleaned up, come on out. I can use your help."

It wasn't until they arrived in San Diego that Meade learned Charlie had used almost every penny he had. Their combined bankroll stood at just under $700 when they entered Belmont Park to open their concessions the following morning.

10

Stepping off the train, Bob Terhune walked quickly into the San Diego train station. Dressed in a dark brown, western-style suit and carrying a matching overcoat, he was followed by a porter with his luggage.

"Bob. Hey, Bob!" Terhune looked around. Charlie was pushing his way through the crowd.

They shook hands. Terhune said, "Charlie, it's been ten, eleven years!"

"Remember this guy?" asked Charlie, pushing Meade forward, grinning like a proud parent.

Gripping Meade's hand, Terhune exclaimed, "Man, you've grown! With those shoulders, you would make a hell of a fullback. What do you weigh? Two-ten?"

"About two hundred," smiled Meade. "Enough."

In Terhune's hotel room, they raised their glasses. "To the death of the Eighteenth Amendment!" said Terhune.

"Amen," intoned Charlie.

Draping a leg over the chair arm, Terhune said, "Well, men, we did it. We're through standing still."

"Damned if you do, damned if you don't," said Charlie.

"Damned by just about every state in the union," Terhune replied dryly.

On March 19, 1931, Governor Balzar rose from his sickbed to sign a wide-open gambling bill for the state of Nevada. The act brought down a torrent of abuse from newspapers across the country. "Cancel Nevada's statehood," cried the *Chicago Tribune*. The *Dallas News* and the *Los Angeles Times* called Nevada a "vicious Babylon." An eastern paper cracked, "If you can't do it at home, go to Nevada."

It was Resurrection Day, Nevada style. From the dark basements and alleys the clubs' owners came, blinking and shading their eyes in the bright sunlight, welcome once more on the main streets of Reno, Elko, Winnemucca, Ely, Ruth, Kimberly and Las Vegas.

Hastily, they repaired old equipment and ordered new, throwing open their doors while construction crews pounded out a coarse symphony to the raucous cries at the gaming tables.

March 20th saw the press dashing about taking pictures of the great historical moment. Speaking with typical Nevada frankness, the *Nevada State Journal* observed: "Photographs of gambling games in operation were snapped to be sent to the outside world, the value of the photographs not at all impaired by the fact that they might have been taken anytime in the past few years."

In Reno, two men who had sharpened their skills in the silver and gold mining camps of Tonopah and Goldfield descended from their illegal gambling room on the second floor of the Palace Building and opened the Bank Club downstairs. The acknowledged gambling kingpins of Reno, Bill Graham and Jim McKay, were soon directing a myriad of operations from the "Big Store."

On the same afternoon that he signed the gambling act, Governor Balzar signed into law another controversial bill.

As of May 1st, the waiting period for non-residents seeking a divorce would be six weeks. Nevada's hold on the lucrative divorce trade had been broken a year ago when Arkansas and Idaho had reduced their residency requirements to match Nevada's three months. In the face of this, and the threat by other states to do the same, the 1931 legislature quickly put through a six-week divorce bill.

Last year, a decisive boost had been given to Las Vegas's economy. On September 17, 1930, over ten thousand gathered to watch Dr. Ray Lyman Wilbur, Secretary of the Interior, drive the first spike in the Union Pacific branch line that would reach twenty-two miles to the site of Hoover Dam, scheduled to be completed in 1936.

Las Vegans had done everything but put their prostitutes to work as school teachers in order to persuade the government to house the dam workers in their town. The giant cleanup campaign failed to impress Wilbur. He returned to Washington and recommended the construction of a town at the dam site.

With the state's new gambling laws, a nice chunk of the dam's huge payroll found its way into Las Vegas. As the dam became a tourist attraction, so did Vegas.

Terhune eyed the two men. "How's it going for you?" he asked.

Charlie shrugged. "We're getting by. People have to let go. Some are hiding their heads under pillows, but a lot are coming to the park. We're not rich, but we eat."

Refilling their glasses, Terhune planted his feet firmly in the carpet and looked down at the two men. "Charlie, Meade —you should look into moving up to Reno. Nevada's offering something you can't get anywhere else . . . freedom to gamble, freedom to get rid of your old lady without a lot of fuss and bother and freedom to get your ashes hauled by a nice clean girl who can make a living on her back and still walk the streets with her head up. In my state, a whorehouse is just another business."

Pointing at his guests, Terhune continued: "We've got a lot of new people moving in. Some are old-time gamblers who

know their way around. Some are assholes who don't know
shit from Shinola. They open a club one day, go broke the
next. Crossroaders are coming out of the woodwork. And
bust-out artists." Terhune shook his head in disgust. "Stupid
bastards! They won't last long in Nevada." His eyes were
suddenly cold. "Not as long as I've got anything to say about
it."

Hunching forward, Terhune looked hard at Meade and
Charlie. "We need men like you in Nevada. I want you in
Reno."

Sitting down, he threw his leg back over the chair arm, the
light glancing off his hundred-dollar boots.

Charlie whistled. "Bob," he said, "I darned near drowned
in all them words. And to think it all started with shoveling
elephant shit."

Meade's pale blue eyes were shrewd and calculating. "Mr.
Terhune—"

"Bob," Terhune interjected.

"Bob, why us? We run games of chance, but we're not
gamblers, not with cards and dice."

"Come and visit Reno," Terhune replied. "Look around.
See how many real gamblers you can count. With your background, you two are 'way ahead of the losers we've got up
there. Cards and dice? You'll learn. Come up and grow with
us!"

Meade and Charlie could almost feel the magnetic pull.
Terhune was the best kind of salesman; he really believed in
his product.

Charlie broke the spell. "Something like that takes a lot of
thought, Bob. We've been settled here a lot of years. Meade's
got a wife and son. It takes money to get started, and we don't
have much of that."

Terhune smiled. "Hell, we've got clubs starting up on
bankrolls that wouldn't choke a canary."

Charlie grinned back. "That's about the size of ours."

Leaning toward the two men, Terhune said earnestly, "At
least come up and look around. Make it a little vacation. I'll
show you the town."

Charlie looked at Meade. "Anything wrong with looking?"

"Okay with me."

11

Shirley gazed out the train window, eyes unseeing, ears closed to the sound of Meade and David laughing and playing on the seat beside her. Her thoughts weren't on the trip to Reno; they were turned inward, searching vainly for the happiness that had been eluding her the last two years.

Her marriage was a broken Humpty Dumpty, and she didn't know how to put it together again.

Her parents had told her she was a fool to marry Meade. They said he wouldn't amount to much, that he would never settle down. Shirley had fought back, defying her parents for the first time in her life. She loved Meade; there was no doubt in her mind that he would make his place in the world.

Then the stock market crash and the humiliating flight from Des Moines with barely enough money to buy their train fare and meals.

Now Meade worked seven days a week at the park, leaving at daybreak and returning late at night—exhausted, too tired to ask how the day had been for her, often falling asleep the minute his head hit the pillow.

Their sex life suffered badly, and sex was important to Shirley. She needed and wanted it. It was the most direct way in which Meade could show his attention and love.

Shirley wanted to believe that Meade still loved her. She *had* to. He continued to tell her so. But it wasn't the same.

The playful affection was gone. So were the little surprise gifts; there was no money for that. Shirley understood. It was just that the gifts had brought her so much joy; they were a constant reminder that he was thinking of her. Sometimes, Meade would bring prizes from the booth, but it wasn't the same.

A girl who had received attention all her life, Shirley had developed an insatiable craving for it. During the early years of her marriage, she had been the central figure. Not so now. There was the work. Always the work. And David. Sometimes, it seemed Meade paid more attention to his son then to his wife. Shirley was besieged with doubts. She was feeling unloved . . . and alone.

When she stepped down from the train in Reno, Shirley's mouth dropped with dismay. After the sunny cleanliness of San Diego, the dirty unsightly buildings that housed Commercial Row's gambling clubs and saloons were a shocking sight. Blond hair flying, she whirled to glare at Meade, angry words stifled by the appearance of Bob Terhune, smiling and welcoming them to the "Biggest Little City in the World."

"See, it says so right there," Terhune said as he drove under the steel arch that spanned Virginia Street, erected in October, 1926, to advertise the exposition that would celebrate the linking of the transcontinental highways the following June.

"Who thought that up?" Charlie asked, inspecting the arch with a slightly jaundiced eye. "The committee to save Reno from the rattlesnakes?"

The sight of the sparkling Truckee River and the beautiful Terhune mansion removed some of the sting from Shirley's disappointing introduction to Reno. Soon won over by Janice Terhune's cheery smile and forthright manner, she was shown through the house and presented to Grace 14, Tom 11 and Jim 2. Three-year-old David was quickly adopted by Grace and taken for a tour of the grounds.

The following day, they went out to the Crowder ranch. The rustic house set against a backdrop of rugged mountains and green meadows dotted with grazing cattle provided again another side to Reno. Shirley's first impressions were being dulled.

That night, snuggled up against Shirley in bed, Meade whispered, "What do you think, honey? Could you like it up here?"

"Maybe," she breathed into his neck, giggling softly as his hand crept down to her belly. "That tickles!"

His hand moved down further. "Does that?"

Her voice was husky. "Do you think this will make me want to move up here?"

"No, but I think it will make you want me to move up here," Meade said as he rose above her.

12

Not much of a club, considered Meade. A dozen players, half of them probably shills. A faro game, one 21 table, a roulette wheel that had seen better days. A far cry from last night.

With the Terhunes, they had visited the Willows and the Country Club where there were orchestras and entertainment to go along with the gambling. It had given Shirley a chance to dress up, and she had enjoyed herself, basking in the many admiring glances that had been cast her way. She and Janice had played roulette for a while, pooling their money and coming away $11 winners.

Meade was glad Shirley hadn't come along this morning. Commercial Row and Center Street were a part of Reno she could do without.

This was the fifth place he and Charlie had visited. The only real action they had seen was at the Bank Club, a real casino operation with several faro, craps, and 21 games, plus roulette, Chuck-a-Luck and a huge Pari-Mutuel wheel. The players were mostly in shirt sleeves and ill-fitting suits, a working crowd, a far cry from the formal dress of last evening.

That night Charlie told Bob Terhune that he couldn't see making the move to Reno right now, easing the refusal by implying that he might reconsider. Meade knew better. After what he had seen today, Charlie couldn't wait to get back to San Diego.

They returned to Belmont Park and said no more about Reno. It was a dead issue as far as Charlie was concerned. Shirley mentioned the trip a few times, but it was clear that she had no desire to live in Reno.

As 1931 drew to a close, Meade began to notice disturbing changes in his wife. She tended to snap at him over little things. When questioned, she would become angry and defensive, especially about where she had been during the long hours he was gone. If he had been a little older, a little wiser, a little less engrossed in his work, he might have caught on. But he was none of those.

Nineteen thirty-two arrived with little to celebrate. The nation was reaching up to touch bottom.

Yet the movie industry did a booming business during the Depression. The silver screen promised a momentary escape from reality. The enormous salaries of the big Hollywood stars stirred hope rather than resentment. The discouraged masses thronged to the theaters hoping that they, too, could go from rags to riches. They dreamed. For a while, they forgot.

The Ringling Brothers, Barnum and Bailey circus reached the pinnacle of its success during the 1930's, dazzling children and adults alike under the "Big Top" that seated ten thousand.

Belmont Park survived because it, too, offered an avenue of escape. It kept Meade and Charlie out of the breadlines.

13

They sat in the kitchen, the clock ticking past midnight. Shirley had been asleep when they arrived an hour ago.

"Not too many people today," Charlie said, refilling their glasses from a bottle of bootleg whiskey.

"Could have shot a cannon ball down the midway and not hit a soul," Meade replied.

Charlie stared down in his glass for a moment, then shook his head, looking up with his old familiar grin. "We'll just keep hanging in there, Meade," he said. "Plugging away isn't fun, but it gets the job done. Giving up is too easy these days."

Meade spoke the thought that had been running through his mind for days. "You could run our booths with some cheap help, Charlie. What about me going back to Chicago and taking over those concessions of Jim's? It'll give us a chance to pick up some extra money."

"That's crazy, Meade!" Charlie exclaimed. "They're starving back there."

"I thought just until winter sets in."

Charlie grumbled and protested, but Meade knew that the logic of the proposal would win him over.

"Honey," Meade said the following morning at breakfast, "got something we need to talk about."

Handing David a slice of toast, Shirley turned questioningly toward Meade.

"It's, uh, something Charlie and I decided last night," Meade said lamely, suddenly realizing that this wasn't going to be easy.

Shirley's silence didn't help matters. Leaning forward on her elbows, she waited attentively.

"Well, you see," Meade said, trying to pick his words carefully, "we need to make more money, but we can't get any more concessions at the park. I thought we could get Jack's, but he got a better price from an outsider and blew town without telling me."

"So what can you do?"

"I heard the other day about two concessions I can get, not at Belmont, though."

"Where?" Shirley asked suspiciously, lips compressing into a thin line.

"Uh, kinda far away," Meade said, grinning sheepishly and pushing a lock of hair out of his eyes. "At Riverview—in Chicago."

Shirley's mouth opened and closed silently, fishlike, a look of disbelief crossing her face. "You said Chicago?" she whispered.

Grinning cheerfully in spite of the storm that was darkening over Shirley's brow, Meade nodded and said, "Only for a few months. Until December."

"Only until December," repeated Shirley. Her voice became taunt, barely under control. "What about David and me?"

"You'll come with me, of course."

"Just like that! How nice! Do I jump up and start packing right now, or can I finish my breakfast?"

"Aw, come on, honey—"

"Don't 'honey' me!" snapped Shirley. "That's what you think, isn't it?" she yelled, eyes blazing with fury. "All you have to do is make a decision and your good little wife will smile and come trotting along! Maybe I would have a few years ago but not anymore. I'm sick of your decisions. They got us into this dump. If you hadn't thrown away all our money on the stock market, we'd be living and eating right instead of getting up every morning wondering whether we'll have enough food for dinner!"

Meade stared at Shirley in stunned silence, his mind refusing to accept what he had heard. A whimper made him look at the small figure on his left. David was hunched down in his chair, eyes large with fear. Meade smiled and patted his head.

"Asshole!" screamed Shirley. "Do you think it's funny?"

Meade's head snapped up. Who *was* this woman sitting across the table? This wasn't his wife! Not Shirley. Not the laughing girl who cuddled Panda bears and made love on the beach. He looked at her and saw a stranger.

Like the bursting of a dam, the words came tumbling and crashing down on Meade's head. He just continued to stare while Shirley vomited up the anger and resentment that had been souring inside her for years.

"It's all your fault!" she cried. "You sneaked behind my back and lost all our money trying to get rich. If it hadn't been for Charlie we'd be in jail! All you do is work. We never go anywhere. Sometimes I think you don't even know I exist! Mom and Daddy think I'm crazy for putting up with this. Now, you want to go back to Chicago!" Shirley spat the name out as if it might contaminate her mouth. "You want to go to Chicago? Then go—but without us!"

Standing beside his father, David tugged at his sleeve. "Daddy," he said, frightened, "why is Mommy yelling?"

Meade reached for the boy, but Shirley got there first, kneeling on the floor and drawing David close, looking at Meade like an angry lioness protecting her young. When she opened her mouth, Meade almost expected her to roar. "Go, if you want," she said in a tortured half-whisper, "but go without us."

Sinking to the floor, Meade put his hands on her shoulders. "I'm sorry, honey," he said quietly. "I didn't know you felt like this. I wish you had told me before."

The anger was gone now, leaving only emptiness. Tears flowing, Shirley rested her head on Meade's shoulder. They rocked back and forth in their misery. As he stroked Shirley's golden head, Meade pondered her words and silently wept for what once had been.

They were very close during the two weeks that followed,

with Shirley happy and relieved now that she had released the bitterness that had been bottled-up inside so long. Meade took time off from work for quiet walks along the beach. They held hands and talked and came together in the night with a passion renewed through understanding.

One such night, Shirley whispered softly, "Darling, I know you don't think now that it's a good idea for me to go with you, but I want to. I don't want to be left here alone." There was a note of fear in her voice that Meade couldn't identify.

They discussed the matter, and Shirley reluctantly agreed that a trip halfway across the troubled country wouldn't be good, perhaps even dangerous, for her and David.

As Meade's train rolled toward Chicago that first day in July, the Democratic Convention there was winding down. The promises and optimism expressed by the politicians made little impression on the jobless. Chicago was one of the hardest hit cities in the nation.

At Riverview Park, Meade struggled and often worked sixteen-hour shifts, returning to his grubby hotel room so tired that he sometimes slept in his clothes. When he packed for the return trip in November, he had made less than $900 profit.

As Meade stood in line at the Chicago station, he looked up above the ticket counter and studied the schedules. "Reno" caught his attention. A tingling feeling ran up and down his spine. Meade smiled and shook his head, but the feeling persisted.

When he purchased his ticket, he asked to be routed through Reno rather than to Los Angeles via Santa Fe. His step was lighter when he boarded the train.

Reno hadn't changed much. There were a few new clubs on Center Street, and the Western Club on Commercial Row had doubled in size. Near Douglas Alley, Meade noticed a clothing store where a small club had been last year.

Taking an upstairs room in a hotel that nurtured a bingo parlor in its bosom, Meade stayed overnight, drifting in and out of the downtown clubs, giving them a little play while he quietly observed the action. It wasn't encouraging.

As the train pulled out of Reno, Meade stood on the platform between two cars and watched the town until it disappeared from view. His business sense told him there was nothing there, but the tingling feeling wouldn't go away.

While in Reno, Meade had avoided the Terhunes. He wanted to think without interference. For that and other reasons, he said nothing about his visit to Shirley and Charlie.

14

The changes were subtle, but Meade noticed. Things were different when he returned to San Diego.

Shirley's laughter came a little too quick, and he caught her throwing him odd glances when she didn't think he was looking. More friends than usual were dropping by; Shirley didn't seem to be comfortable with him alone.

Charlie wasn't his normal cheerful self. Meade had always considered him an incurable optimist. He found Charlie's attitude puzzling.

Something was eating Charlie, and Meade wished he would talk about it. They had always respected each other's privacy; it would be unthinkable to come right out and ask him. Meade would have to wait until Charlie decided to open up.

It was Meade's misfortune to find out for himself.

He had become violently sick with food poisoning one day and had driven home. It was the middle of the afternoon.

At first Meade thought no one was home, then he looked in David's room and saw him sleeping. The sound of running water came from behind the bathroom door. He smiled to himself. Shirley was the cleanest woman in San Diego. She barely escaped being a prune, she took so many baths.

He headed straight for the bedroom. His stomach had settled down, but he felt weak as a kitten.

The bedroom was in disarray. That was strange. Shirley was a meticulous housekeeper. Stumbling over her clothing, he pulled the covers back. The odor was unmistakable. He had smelled it too many times before.

The sweat-dampened sheets were smudged with lipstick and crusting semen. If he had been here a half-hour earlier! Shock turned to rage, and Meade found himself standing outside the bathroom door, reaching for the knob.

Something stayed his hand as he stood there listening to the splashing sounds from the tub. Like a sleepwalker, he turned away and walked silently outside and got into his car.

Charlie took one look at him when he arrived at the park and closed the booths. They went out to Charlie's place and got roaring drunk.

Before they had crawled too deep down into the bottle, Meade slammed the table with his fist and pointed an accusing finger at Charlie. "You knew!" he shouted. "You *knew!*"

Nodding sadly, Charlie refilled Meade's glass.

"Why didn't you tell me, damnit?"

"There are some things a man has to find out for himself," Charlie said. His eyes softened. "You're the only son I got. I was dying for you, but what could I do? I thought about talking to Shirley, but I couldn't do it. It's something you have to work out for yourselves."

"How long has it been going on?" Meade asked hoarsely.

Charlie didn't pull any punches. "A year. Maybe more."

Meade didn't cry or curse or throw his drink against the wall. Charlie might have felt better if he had. He just drew his head down into his powerful shoulders and gripped the whiskey glass with whitened knuckles. Nearly a minute passed, then Meade said in a flat emotionless voice, pale blue eyes reflecting terrible pain and anger, "Who is he?"

Charlie had been dreading the question, even more the answer. He hesitated for a moment, then blurted out, "Damnit, I don't know!" His voice trailed off. "I don't know."

"You mean she's been going with this guy for a year and you don't know? I can't believe that!"

Leaping up, Charlie kicked the chair back and leaned over the table, staring down at Meade, eyes pleading for understanding. "Meade—son," he said with effort, "I can't tell you who because—because there's been too many. Try to understand. She needs a heap of love, lots more than you and me, more than most women. She needs attention, and she's been getting the wrong kind. She's confused, thinks it's love. Admit it; you haven't been giving her much time lately." Charlie swore and sat down hard.

Meade stirred his glass around and around in the moisture on the table. Charlie watched him apprehensively.

Meade looked up and his face was a tortured mask. "What happens now, Charlie? What would you do?"

"Damnit, boy, don't ask me what I'd do. You and me, we're two different people. You've got your way of doing things and I've got mine. What do *you* want to do?"

Meade continued swirling the glass in circles. "I'm not sure," he said slowly. "I *am* sure of one thing. I have to share the blame. I haven't paid much attention to Shirley for a long time." He looked sharply at Charlie. "I did spend a lot of time with her before I left for Chicago, and we hashed out a lot of things. Did you know that?"

Charlie nodded his head. "I knew something good was happening. Made me damn happy." He didn't mention his bitter disappointment when Shirley began to seek out new lovers not long after Meade's departure.

Meade said: "All I've been thinking about the last few years is getting the business back on its feet. It's been burning me up, this damn need to succeed. It's been hell going home and seeing my wife and kid doing without. Because of me! Because I threw away all our money back in Des Moines." Meade took another pull on his drink. "I thought the best way to show I cared was to make money. I saw things that made me wonder, but I've been too wrapped up in my own problems to try and find out."

Leaning back in his chair, Charlie said quietly, "If you feel that way, get in there and do something!" Meade shook his head and tried to clear his eyes. He poured another drink.

"Don't worry," Charlie said softly. "There's lots more where that came from."

15

Meade lifted David down from the train, then reached up for Shirley's hand. They stood close together as the blustery March winds flipped Meade's coat collar up against the back of his neck.

Bob Terhune hurried toward them, smiling and reaching out to grip Meade's hand. He greeted Shirley and tousled David's hair. "Let's get to the house," he said. "I'll have a man pick up your things."

It was good to be surrounded by the warmth and happiness of the Terhune home. Meade sank deep in a leather wing chair and watched the leaping flames in the huge rock fireplace. Shirley and Janice were upstairs. Bob Terhune had been called away on pressing state business.

Sipping on his bourbon, Meade reflected on the past few weeks. It had been a time of anguish and soul-searching such as he had never known. . . .

The morning after that long night of drinking with Charlie Meade wandered around the kitchen making coffee and toast, his thoughts on the bedroom where his wife slept on that soiled bed.

David appeared, and his father hugged him tightly. Dancing rays of sunlight brightened the room as Meade and David ate their breakfast. Love for his son washed away the last remnants of bitterness from Meade's heart. Only sadness remained.

Shirley entered the kitchen wearing a light blue frock, her

long blond hair freshly combed and shining. She looked so beautiful and clean. He had somehow expected her to look different.

Having already told Charlie he would skip work today, Meade headed for bed but not before surprising Shirley—and himself—by suggesting they go on a picnic that afternoon. Thus the day that had started so badly ended on a note of happiness. At least for Shirley. It had taken all of Meade's willpower to smile and act as if nothing had happened.

Weeks passed, and Meade spent more time with his family. Charlie watched closely as Meade went through the daily torture of wondering what Shirley might be doing behind his back, showing unusual strength for so young a man as he fought to keep his marriage together.

Shirley couldn't believe the happiness that had returned to her life. All she had ever asked was for Meade to love her; nothing else mattered. It had been so long since he had been attentive and caring. She could face anything as long as he loved her.

As long as he loved her. *Oh God,* moaned Shirley one morning. *What if he finds out?* She had just talked to her latest lover on the telephone, halting their relationship as firmly as she had done with the others before him. Only this time it was different. She wasn't getting rid of this one to seek another. She didn't need a new lover. Meade was all she needed, all she had ever needed.

It would have never happened that first time last November if Meade had shown that he loved her. She had been so lonely and confused, trapped between the constant nagging of her mother and Meade's indifference.

It was at this low point that she met Allen, a lifeguard at Ocean Beach. It had started innocently enough, a question about the tides, a wave of greeting a few days later, a little whale watching through Allen's binoculars. All discreet— hardly a love tryst with David running around between their legs.

Then one day Shirley arrived at the beach without David and with a lunch that was too much for her to eat. It was only natural to invite Allen to help her eat the extra food. Four hours later she was in his bed, her long legs locked around his waist, crying out with her third climax of the afternoon.

She returned home feeling loved and needed . . . and with a deep sense of guilt. During the month that first affair lasted the guilt lessened, largely due to her rationalization that it was all Meade's fault.

Allen was followed by Carl, then Walt. No affair lasted long; Shirley quickly became discontented and had to seek emotional renewal through new relationships.

No longer feeling unloved and unwanted, she tried to convince herself that she didn't care if her marriage came to an end. The last year had certainly proved that she was still a desirable woman; two of her lovers had begged her to leave Meade and marry them.

That was all past now. Once more, she felt cherished by the man she loved. Her happiness, however, was overshadowed by guilt and fear, most of all fear. San Diego was a small town; Meade might learn of her infidelities anytime. *Oh Meade, Meade,* she cried softly to herself. *I was so wrong. I know now that I never stopped loving you, not for a moment.*

Meade, too, had gone through his own kind of hell. At first, he had found it nearly impossible to make love to his wife, then as time dulled his imagination and his love endeavored to understand, he found comfort once more in their bed.

As time passed and the haunting look faded from Shirley's face, Meade felt that the battle was being won. All it had taken was a little love and attention. If he had needed proof of the effects of his neglect, he had it now. Meade's spirits rose as a new year arrived and the nation waited with hope for the inauguration of Franklin Roosevelt.

One day in February, Meade arrived home early to find Shirley and a young man in the kitchen, bags of groceries on the counter and a pot of coffee perking on the stove. Obviously uncomfortable, the man quickly excused himself and left.

"He was going by and helped me with the groceries," Shirley said, avoiding Meade's eyes while taking things out of the bags. Meade's heart sank at the defensive sound in her voice. Could this have been one of her lovers?

Turning, Shirley saw the look on Meade's face. She was pleading now, tears springing into her eyes. "I thought the least I could do was offer him a cup of coffee."

Meade believed her then; she wasn't that good an actress. "Sure, honey," he said, adding by way of an apology, "Sorry I had to bust in; guess I scared the poor guy away."

He would have let it go at that, but Shirley still needed reassuring. She said, "I thought it was the right thing to do. You do understand, don't you?"

Sitting on a chair, Meade drew her down onto his lap. "I do understand," he said quietly. "More than you'll ever know."

Shirley lifted her head from his shoulder and sat up straight, her large gray eyes filled with a strange mixture of curiosity and fright. "Do you really understand me, Meade?" she asked. "Really?"

"I really do, honey," he said, trying to pull her head back down on his shoulder.

Shirley had gone too far to stop now. Pushing against his chest, she said, "What do you know about me, Meade?"

He shrugged, uncomfortable about the direction this was leading. "Most everything, I guess."

"Everything?" she replied, lips trembling.

He sighed and nodded. "Everything," he said softly, adding a smile and lightly touching her cheek.

Shirley pressed his hand with icy fingers. The tone of his voice and the look in his eyes furnished absolute proof of his knowledge. "How long have you known?" she whispered.

"I got sick a couple of months back and came home in the afternoon. You were taking a bath, but the bedroom wasn't cleaned up." Meade paused, voice choking. "I—I had to get out. Charlie and I stayed up most the night drinking. He'd known about it for a long time. He's on your side, honey. He told me you need lots of love, that I've been neglecting you. I vomited my guts up, but I was sure of one thing. I loved you; I still do."

Laying her other hand over his, Shirley shook her head back and forth. "How can you still want me?" she cried softly.

"Because I love you; because it's my fault, too."

Shirley buried her face in his neck and cried until Meade thought her heart would break. He patted her back and stroked her hair. The deep sobs turned to sniffles. She found her voice and pleaded, "Take me away from here, Meade. Let's go somewhere new and start all over again."

That night Meade called Bob Terhune. He and Shirley would arrive in Reno in early March. Shirley didn't oppose the move. She would have followed Meade to the North Pole.

Charlie remained in San Diego; he still didn't believe in Reno. Besides, he knew it would be struggle enough for Meade and his family to survive the new venture.

Franklin D. Roosevelt was inaugurated as the thirty-second President of the United States on March 4, 1933. Two days later, the Slaughters arrived in Reno.

As Meade sat before the fireplace in the Terhune home, he wondered how far $2,500 would go. The only money he had taken from Charlie was for his share of the business. This was his venture and his alone.

16

Meade rented a building a stone's throw from the railroad tracks, a narrow cubbyhole fronted by Virginia Street with Douglas Alley on the left side. The former occupant had fled town a jump ahead of his creditors. After Meade settled with the men who had furniture and equipment in the building, he had $1,200 left.

The building was poorly lighted, the only outside light coming through a dirty plate glass window at the front entrance. The other entrance was in the rear, a small wooden door opening out the side into Douglas Alley. Meade studied the contents of the thirty-foot-wide room and shuddered.

The previous owner of the Tiger Club—the name was still painted on the window—had installed one craps table, two 21 tables and a Chuck-a-Luck game. The tables were in disrepair, walls and floor filthy, a dismal scene to a man who had spent much of his life in amusement parks and fairs where the atmosphere was bright and colorful.

"The first thing we've got to do," Meade said to Shirley the night after renting the building, "is clean the place up and get the equipment repaired. It needs light; it's darker than hell. A little color on the walls won't hurt."

They were sitting at the kitchen table in the small house they had rented on Stewart Street. Meade had been drawing on pieces of paper, showing Shirley ideas he had for the club layout. It was an exciting experience for Shirley; this was a new endeavor, and she was a part of it.

A dozen names for the club had been suggested and discarded. Then Shirley clapped her hands and cried, "I've got it. It's perfect! The wheel, you know, the one you said you ran at Belmont when you were a kid—the Plush Wheel!"

Meade leaped up and hugged and kissed her. "That's it. Beautiful! The Plush Wheel."

The name was painted in gold on the front window—elegant letters in the center of a large ornamental wheel. Passersby tried to peek in, but Meade had papered the inside of the glass. The interior work would take some time; he didn't want an audience.

They scrubbed and hammered and painted for three long weeks. As the time neared for the opening, Shirley's happiness waned. She wouldn't be helping Meade in the club; he considered it no place for a woman.

On April 23, 1933, the Plush Wheel opened for business. It wasn't much as openings go. No waving searchlights, no fireworks. At 5:00 P.M., Meade opened the door and stepped out on the sidewalk. The wind was brisk, and there was a chill in the air. Meade wore a bright red vest over a long-sleeved white shirt, black pants and boots. In the high-heeled boots he stood a head taller than most of the small crowd waiting outside, jet black hair stirring slightly in the breeze. There was an easy smile of welcome on his lips and a sparkle of good humor in his clear blue eyes.

Bob Terhune grabbed his hand. "Meade, you're a sight for sore eyes! By God, this town needs livening up!"

Meade stood at the door and greeted the welcoming Renoites. The residents were friendly and sincerely wanted him to succeed; business would be good for tonight. Starting tomorrow, he would be on his own. He would have to prove himself. That was another western tradition.

Meade hired three men, one for the craps table and one for each of the 21 games. He couldn't afford to switch to the new craps tables that were being introduced at the time, enlarging the layout from the field, come-line, six and eight to include hard ways, don't pass and the taking of odds. Actually, he didn't understand their mysteries any better than the majority of his customers. Besides, it took three men to operate the new tables, and he couldn't afford that. He contented himself with running the Chuck-a-Luck game and watching the house.

The patrons seemed a little dazzled by the bright colors and the circus posters that hung on the wall. Some openly scoffed. The competition wandered in and smiled. They quietly bet that Meade would lose his bankroll in a week.

It almost happened.

Meade was determined to run an honest game. Secretly, without Shirley's or Charlie's knowledge, he had been studying the gambling situation for over a year. It hadn't taken much research to learn that the house had the edge. He could run a clean game and still have the odds on his side.

Like many of the small operators in those days, the previous owner had operated a "flat store"—a crooked gambling house. The idea boomeranged. While the help was busting the customers they were busting the house, too.

Meade had done his best to hire honest dealers. It was not until later that he learned that the competition had guided every cheat in town his way. That first night, one of the 21 dealers and a partner took the house for nearly $200. It was a severe financial blow to Meade, but it helped bring about the most lasting friendship of his life.

About ten o'clock, a man entered the club. He was small with faded blue eyes and skin tanned a dark leathery shade. His jeans and coat were worn, cowboy boots scuffed. In even worse shape was the big hat he wore pulled down over his forehead. Meade watched him drift around the room, giving each table a little play. Evidently he was well known, as he was frequently greeted and spoken to.

There was no particular closing time for Reno gambling clubs. They just shut down when the place emptied. The Plush Wheel was down to two customers at midnight. A half-hour later they left, and Meade sent his help home.

He was beat. Already aware of the big loss at 21, Meade was afraid to check the cash box under the craps table. If he lost there, too, he was in big trouble first night out. He looked up and saw that the little cowboy had wandered back in.

"Well," the man said, watching him intently, "you made it through the first day."

Meade's smile was brief. He wished the man would go away, so he could finish making his count.

The man must have sensed Meade's mood. He stuck out his hand. "I'll be seein' you," he said in an unmistakable western drawl. "By the way, my name's Frank Smith. Most folks call me Smitty."

Meade hid his surprise as he shook Smith's hand. He had heard about "Smitty" Smith. He wasn't an old man—about forty-five—but he was already a legend in northern Nevada.

As a young boy, Smith and his prospector father had discovered a rich deposit of copper near Ely, Nevada. The younger Smith had taken his earnings and invested them in various mining ventures and land. His wealth was unknown, but it was said to be considerable.

Smitty grinned. "Bob Terhune says you're okay. That makes you okay with me."

"Thanks," said Meade, warming to the tough little man

with the shrewd eyes. "I've got to close up," he said. "Can
you hang around? I'll buy you a drink."

"You've got yourself a boy," Smitty said. Lighting a cigarette, he sat on a stool at a 21 table and smoked silently while
Meade counted his cash.

Chewing on the end of the pencil, Meade totaled the two
columns, then breathed a sigh of relief. He tapped the paper
and said to Smitty, "Guess it could have been worse. I lost
big at the table where you're sitting but made a little at craps
and the other games. All in all, it comes to a $110 loss."

Over whiskey at the Golden Hotel—prohibition was
openly ignored in Reno—Smitty introduced Meade to the
Montana Trim.

"There's a lot of ways of doin' it," explained Smitty. "The
way you got skinned was the most common. The dealer takes
the cards and cuts the corners real light with a razor—low
cards right top or bottom left, middle cards left top or bottom
right. He can use them to bust the player or the house. In
your case, it was the house."

Meade saw it all too clearly. "So, he and a friend took me."

"Right. They weren't too greedy tonight. They figure
there's plenty of time."

Meade studied Smitty. "Why are you telling me this? You
could just sit back and let me fall on my face."

Smitty paused and lit a cigarette. "I think you're the kind
of man we need in Reno," he said. "You're young, ambitious
and willin' to work hard. Most important, I think you're
honest. I kinda pride myself at bein' a good judge of character. It's helped me get where I am.

"This is my state. I was born here; I'll die here. I think it
was right when we legalized gambling, but I want to see it
treated right. That's goin' to take men like you. If you fall on
your face, I feel we'll be losin' a good man."

Meade flushed under the man's frank scrutiny. Impulsively, he held out his hand. "I'll do my best to attain that
standard," he said.

Smitty raised an eyebrow. "That's a pretty fancy word,
'attain.' Don't hear it around here much."

This time Meade did blush. "Sorry, guess I read too much."

"Don't be sorry," Smitty protested, holding up a hand. "We can use some class. God knows!"

Dawn was breaking when Meade arrived home. It had been a full night, one of thousands he would experience under Nevada skies.

He was aware only of the sheer joy of being alive. After he had looked in on his sleeping son, he tiptoed into the bedroom. Stripped, he fitted himself into the curve of Shirley's back. She awoke and ran a hand along his leg. "Morning, lover," she murmured as she turned into his arms.

17

The man flew out the door and crashed, arms flailing, into a parked car. The big white-shirted man in the red vest grabbed the dazed man by the coat collar and dragged him to his feet. Shaking the man until his teeth rattled, the big man growled, "You goddamned crossroader, you ever show up in my place again, I'll break your neck." With a snort of disgust, he threw the man into the gutter.

Heads popped out of nearby clubs, and men pushed to look at the bleeding man on his hands and knees in the gutter. Meade's message was savagely clear. Cheats had no place in his club—behind or in front of the tables.

Re-entering the Plush Wheel, Meade took the erstwhile craps dealer's place. "Sorry for the interruption," he said to the players. "I run an honest game; I don't want you to get busted out." He smiled. "I don't want to get busted out, either."

The men laid down their bets, a nervous laugh erupting from the pudgy man at one end of the table. Picking up the stick, Meade hooked the dice toward the pudgy man. "I believe you were rolling," Meade said. The man picked up the dice and prepared to throw.

Meade looked around the club. Things had quieted down. He breathed a sigh of relief.

He had spotted the "eight-ball" shortly after the man entered the club. By lucky chance, Smitty had pointed the man out just a week ago. Recognition and sharp vigilance caught the exchange of dice. The game quickly turned in the player's favor as the shaved cubes bounced his way. Seeing that the player and dealer were working as a team, Meade moved swiftly toward the table.

The dealer hissed a warning to his partner. When the player headed toward the exit, Meade made his choice and went for the dealer. As the "mechanic" crashed out into Douglas Alley, Meade was throwing the dealer out the front door and onto Virginia Street.

During the seven months since the Plush Wheel had been open, Meade's easygoing nature had been tested many times. Some men looked at his smile and failed to notice the big rugged frame and eyes that could turn to steel. It took a tough man to run a gambling club in Reno, and Meade quickly adapted.

At one point, Meade's bankroll had dwindled to less than $500. He had never been so frightened in his life. One big winner could wipe him out—or one cheat.

Without Smitty's advice and guidance, Meade wouldn't have survived those first few months. Countless hours had been spent in Smitty's room in the walkup hotel above the bingo parlor next door while Smitty educated him in the ways of gambling. Smitty was an ideal teacher, having learned the trade in rough mining towns like Goldfield and Tonopah, where Bill Graham and Jim McKay got their start before coming to Reno.

On the practical side, Meade furthered his education at the Plush Wheel. A slow turnabout had occurred four months ago; his bankroll now stood at $6,000.

David would be entering school after the first of the year,

and Shirley was talking about taking courses at the university.

Meade was acutely aware of Shirley's loneliness. In San Diego, she had had her parents and friends, most of whom she had grown up with. In Reno, she visited with Janice Terhune but had made no other friends.

Worst of all, Meade was spending even more time at the Plush Wheel than he had at Belmont Park. Shirley was showing signs of withdrawing again that worried him, but there wasn't much he could do about it except express his love at every opportunity.

Meade celebrated the end of Prohibition on December 5th by opening a small bar in the Plush Wheel, a happily accepted addition to the club that was becoming one of the most popular in town.

18

The bright August sunlight flickered off the giant wheels as the train screeched to a halt. Charlie had hardly stepped off the train before he was smothered in a bear hug. Stumbling back and straightening his rumpled shirt, he grinned up at Meade. "You're looking good, little feller," he said.

"You don't look so bad yourself," Meade replied, slapping his uncle affectionately on the shoulder, noting that the thick hair and mustache were flecked with silver.

They picked up Charlie's luggage and trudged down to Virginia Street.

Charlie paused in front of the Plush Wheel. It was closed; few clubs opened before noon. Shading his eyes, Charlie peered in the window. "So that's it," he said. Meade was pleased; he had looked heavenward when Charlie stopped, praying that he wouldn't hear, "shit."

By the summer of 1934, the Plush Wheel's business had doubled. For nearly a year, Meade had been pleading with Charlie to come to Reno. At first, Charlie had flatly refused, leaving no room for argument, but with the advent of the new year and a steady upswing in Meade's fortune, his protests had become less adamant.

Two weeks ago, Charlie had sold his Belmont Park concessions and wrapped up his business in San Diego. His bridges were cut, commitment total. He would make it with Meade or bust.

The future was looking great for the Plush Wheel.

It hadn't been that way in February. . . .

"Too damn quiet," Smitty said one night as he and Meade sat in the darkened club. "I think Giuliano is gettin' ready for the big push."

Meade nodded. It was going to come—as sure as God made little green apples.

Carlo Giuliano owned the Western Club, the big gambling house that dominated Commercial Row. He had started it as a basement club underneath the present location in 1915, staying within legal limits the first two years, then enlarging the club and adding illegal games such as craps and 21. Throughout the Twenties, the Western Club flourished while keeping a low profile below the first floor of the Maxton Building, payoffs to the proper authorities guaranteeing Giuliano protection.

When gambling was legalized, Giuliano moved his club upstairs, providing Commercial Row with a store nearly as big as Graham and McKay's Bank Club two blocks south and around the corner on Center Street.

With the legalization of gambling and the resultant publicity, Nevada was brought to the attention of every gambler and would-be gambler in the country. The majority came to gamble, but some came to reap the unending stream of money they imagined flowing into the coffers of the clubs. Gambling houses opened and closed practically overnight, or after a week, a month.

Some operators were completely inept; they depended on

luck alone. But Lady Luck could be a fickle bitch. Without warning, she could turn on an owner and strip him of his bankroll as swiftly as she could empty a customer's pockets into the club's cash drawer.

Others were cheated out of their bankrolls. Giuliano was only too happy to provide the crossroaders to do the job. It was a painless way to eliminate the competition, not that he wouldn't take harsher measures if necessary.

A few skilled operators survived in Reno. As long as they remained small, Giuliano left them alone. They were bothersome, like little dogs snapping at his heels, but he knew and understood that competition was the American way of life. After all, had he not gotten his start in this country by meeting the challenges of other business interests?

Arriving in 1901 in San Francisco from the coastal village of Scopello on Sicily's Gulf of Castellammare, Carlo Giuliano had quickly entered the exciting world of free enterprise. A squat, powerful man with a violent background in smuggling on Italy's coast, Giuliano set up a protection racket on San Francisco's docks.

Fourteen years later, when he saw the law closing in, he moved to Reno. It was the logical place to go; Reno had a solid Italian population, including some of his Sicilian cousins. By buying up several pieces of real estate, including the Maxton Building, and opening the Western Club, Giuliano let it be known that he planned to stay.

Carlo Giuliano brought with him to Reno his wife, five daughters and one son, Tony. When Tony was born nine years ago after four girls in five years, Giuliano thought he might be on a winning streak and went after boy number two. When his next roll in bed came up a girl, he cashed in his chips and started sleeping in another bedroom.

When Meade came to Reno, Giuliano sent Tony, now twenty-seven, to check out the Plush Wheel. Tony brushed Meade off as a "carney man, a punk who won't last a week."

Weeks passed, and Meade was still in business. Not only that, it looked like he had the potential to become serious competition. Giuliano tried to steal Meade's bankroll by infiltrating his club with cheaters, but it wasn't long before Meade's fierce reprisals made it impossible to find crossroaders to work the Plush Wheel.

Sitting in the darkened club and gazing out at the snow-covered street, Smitty said to Meade, "The word is that the old boy's bringin' in some outside muscle."

Meade fingered the gun tucked under his belt. "So I've heard."

Smitty's eyes traveled to the slight bulge under Meade's red vest. "You practicin' with that thing?"

Meade grunted, "Used up a couple boxes of shell shooting at rocks and trees—some jackrabbits."

"Hit any?"

"Trees and rocks? Sure. I've yet to hit my first jackrabbit."

"Trees and rocks stand still; jackrabbits don't. Neither do men."

Meade looked steadily at Smitty. "Men are a lot bigger . . . and slower."

"You know how I feel," said Smitty. "If they come in to wreck your club, shoot the sons of bitches."

"It's my place," Meade said in a barely audible voice. Smitty strained to catch his words. "Nobody takes what's mine without a fight."

19

The front door crashed open, and three men strode in, jostling players and equipment. Dealers and patrons backed away from the tables and drifted toward the rear door.

Moving out from behind the 21 table, Meade faced the men. "Get out of my club," he ordered. "I don't need your kind in here."

The man in front loosened his coat and hooked his thumbs

in his belt. "It's the other way around, bub," he growled. "We don't like *your* kind. *You* get out!"

Meade's hand slipped inside his vest. "Make one more move, and I'll put daylight through your leg."

The men hesitated. They had been told that the job would be a pushover, that they would have the "carnival man" chased out the back door and his club wrecked in minutes.

They looked warily at the big man in the red vest. With that hard face and frosty blue eyes, he looked like anything but a pushover.

Silently, one of the men slipped on a pair of spiked brass knuckles. The club was empty except for the four men.

Pulling out his gun, Meade aimed it at the leader's left leg. "You have ten seconds to get out," he said, voice flat and brittle.

The men shifted uneasily as Meade started to count, "One, two, three . . ."

Outside, several faces were pressed to the window. One of the onlookers later told the story in the bar at the Bank Club.

"There they was, them three guys standin' there with Slaughter holdin' a gun. Don't know what he was sayin', but he looked mean!

"Man, it happened so fast I almost missed it! One of them goons yanked out a gun. Bam! Slaughter's gun goes off and the guy's brains are splattered all over the wall. He hasn't even hit the floor and Slaughter jumps like a big cat and bashes another guy across the face with his gun.

"About that time, this other guy hits Slaughter low in the back with a pair of dusters. I thought that was it. Slaughter goes down on his hands and knees." The storyteller added a dash of bravado. "I was just about ready to go in and help."

The man continued: "The guy Slaughter hit is still floppin' on the floor. The guy with the dusters is like a wild man. He kicks Slaughter in the stomach and pulls a knife. About then, Slaughter picks up his gun and gut-shoots the bastard. I don't think the whole thing lasted a minute!"

Swallowing half his drink, the storyteller concluded, eyes sweeping his attentive audience, "Slaughter gets up. Boy, is he hurtin'! He grabs the guy he pistol-whipped and smashes him against the wall. He's yellin', but I can't hear what he's sayin'. Then he drags the guy—blood drippin' all over the place—out the front door and tosses him in the street. He may still be layin' there for all I know."

One man dead, another fated to die from stomach wounds two days later, a third with a smashed jaw and half his front teeth missing.

Reno buzzed with the news. Within days, the story had made the rounds in communities all over the state. Meade Slaughter was a modern-day folk hero; he had fought for what was his and won.

A message was sent to Carlo Giuliano by a man with a broken face, the words whispered with difficulty through crushed and bleeding lips. "That's what he told me," the lone survivor said to Giuliano's man who had bailed him out of jail and was hurrying him to a waiting boxcar. "He said to tell the boss to leave him alone or he'll blow his head off."

Shirley was asleep when Meade arrived home just before dawn, and he was sleeping soundly when she took David to school. One of the mothers told her about the fight.

Meade was rudely awakened when Shirley yanked the pillow off his head. He blinked up at his wife as she stood above the bed, fists on hips, tears streaming down her face, yelling and crying at the same time. Meade started to smile, then thought better of it. That might send her through the roof.

Meade didn't need to ask what was wrong. Key words were emerging from Shirley's nearly incoherent screaming. ". . . killers . . . fighting . . . guns . . . damn club . . . damn Reno . . . damn Nevada . . . home . . . want to go home . . . bastard!"

Meade reached up. "Honey—"

Shirley jumped back as if stung. "Don't start that!" she cried. "You're not going to soft-soap me out of this. I want to go back to San Diego. I hate this place!"

Painfully, Meade sat up and pulled on his pants. The sight of the livid bruises suddenly melted Shirley's anger. Tears

flowing, she dropped to the bed and hugged him. "Meade—
Meade," she pleaded. "Look at you; you'll get killed if you
stay here. Don't you know how much you mean to me, how
much I need you? Please, for both our sakes, let's leave."

Pulling Shirley close and stroking her hair, Meade said
quietly, "Honey, we can't go." Shirley stiffened, and he hurried on, "We're just getting on our feet. There won't be any
more trouble. Believe me! No one will bother the club now.
We'll never have another chance like this!"

Pushing herself away, Shirley looked up into his face, tears
blinding her eyes. "Meade, please, darling," she wept, taking
his face in her hands, "let's go back. I can handle it now.
Please—do this for me."

Meade stared down at his wife. It hurt him terribly to see
her like this. Her gaiety had been so infectious the day they
met and during those first years of their marriage. He would
do anything to see her happy like that again.

Or would he? Would he—could he—give up the club and
return to San Diego? He didn't believe in the supernatural,
but for years he had been unable to escape the feeling that
his fate was linked to Nevada. A feeling! How the hell do you
explain a feeling?

Shirley felt that if they returned to San Diego, she would
be happy. But what about Meade? She had never seen him
so excited and alive as he had been since coming to Nevada.
He thrived on competition and challenging the odds. Would
he be happy leaving all this? The answer pierced her mind
with pain. Lips slowly parting, she said dully, "All right
. . . all right. Let's not talk about it anymore. Okay?"

Meade showered while Shirley made breakfast. They ate
mostly in silence.

In contrast to the tense unhappiness at home, Meade found
the atmosphere at the Plush Wheel that night to be a festive
one, with many new faces around the tables and at the bar.
There were a lot of back-slappings and handshakes for the
hero of the hour, and Meade felt accepted as a Renoite at last,
a very high compliment indeed.

Three blocks away, a furious Carlo Giuliano sat in his

dimly lit office. He didn't notice that only a single bulb was burning nor did he hear the faint sounds of the Western Club drifting up through the floor. All his senses were zeroed in on the young upstart who had dared to threaten him. While he brooded and planned, his blunt fingers crushed and wadded a piece of paper into a tight little ball.

Three months after the fight at the Plush Wheel, Meade arrived home in the dead of night with a sudden craving for pancakes. While searching for the syrup in a top shelf, he found a half-empty bottle of whiskey. It looked too new to have been left by a former occupant.

With a deep sense of foreboding, Meade returned the bottle to the shelf. If it was Shirley's, how long had she been drinking? Not one to hold her liquor, Shirley had always stayed away from hard booze, drinking only cocktails moderately.

The pancakes forgotten, Meade sat down at the table and sipped a cup of coffee, considering his wife who slept down the hall.

Shirley had changed a lot during the last few months, no doubt about that. He had tried to coax her out of her increasing depression but to no avail. It was like San Diego all over again. Or was it? In San Diego, Shirley had put up a good front, maintaining a degree of sparkle and paying the usual careful attention to her appearance. Now, her moods were undisciplined, mercurial, presenting Meade with a different Shirley each day. Especially alarming was the way she had let herself go, many times neglecting to bathe and wearing her robe around the house all day, not washing the dishes or making the beds.

They had to talk. For Shirley's sake. For their son's. For their marriage which was sinking as fast as the level of that bottle. Meade looked at the clock. Three-fifteen A.M. He would get up at ten. David would be in school.

"You're up early," Shirley said when Meade came into the kitchen. She was sitting at the table smoking a cigarette, another habit she had picked up recently. A smoker since he was fifteen, Meade could hardly criticize, but this morning the ashtray full of butts, the coffee-stained oilcloth, dirty sink and slovenly appearance of his wife added up to a thoroughly disgusting picture.

Seeing the look on his face, Shirley clutched the neck of her robe. "There's coffee on the stove," she said, stubbing out her cigarette and starting to rise. "I'm going to take a bath."

"No!" Meade's voice was sharper than he intended. Shirley's eyes widened, and she stood slightly off balance, hands gripping the table's edge. Slowly sinking down into the chair, she inspected Meade's back as he poured his coffee. Her hands trembled slightly as she lit another cigarette.

Meade didn't beat around the bush, but he tried to soften the approach. "Honey," he said, sitting down and fingering his coffee cup with both hands, "please try to understand that I want to help. I'm worried about you." He pointed up at the top cabinet. "I'm worried about that."

"Spying on me! Is that what you've been doing?"

Waving his hands, Meade said, "I'm not spying on you. I'm just concerned. I was looking for something else when I found the bottle."

"I bet," Shirley said sarcastically.

"Honey, why—why do you have to drink the stuff?" Meade asked, reaching out for her hand.

"Because I like it!" she cried, slapping his arm away and jumping up. "It helps me pass the time. How else could I survive in this dump?"

Shirley reached up and grabbed the bottle of whiskey and headed out of the kitchen. "I don't care what *you* do!" she cried. "I'm going back to bed." She whirled around in the doorway. "And from now on, it's *my* bed. You stay out of it and stay out of my life!" Meade winced as the bedroom door slammed.

When Meade returned home from work that night, the bedroom door was locked. He slept on the couch.

Weeks passed, and the sleeping pattern remained the same. Except for the location of Meade's sleeping quarters. In order to rest undisturbed, he moved a cot into a small storeroom off the back porch.

Lovers once, now strangers. Communication was limited

to broken sentences, mumbled words and scribbled notes left on the kitchen table.

The whiskey was now easily accessible underneath the sink, and Shirley drank openly, sullen eyes daring Meade to interfere.

David became an innocent victim, especially when summer vacation arrived. There was little room in Shirley's inward thoughts for her six-year-old son. Each day he rushed outside to escape the dark gloom that had settled over the house like an undertaker's shroud. Meade tried to spend time with him, but the demands of the club made it nearly impossible.

It was this sad state of affairs that finally persuaded Charlie to come to Reno. Meade waited until mid-July before revealing his problems with Shirley. He needed Charlie's help so he could spend more time at home. If his marriage couldn't be salvaged, he could at least help his son.

Let's hope it works, thought Meade as he left Charlie at the hotel on that hot August night and headed toward the Plush Wheel. It's *got* to work! Tomorrow. Tomorrow he and Charlie would be together again, running the Plush Wheel as a team.

Two hours later, Meade looked up from the 21 table to see Charlie peering over the player's heads. "Couldn't wait," Charlie explained in answer to Meade's unspoken question. "Might as well get started today, don't you think?"

20

Lips touching, hands caressing, warm bodies on the beach. Dreams shared. Panda bears.

The marriage of Meade and Shirley Slaughter came to an abrupt end at 1:11 A.M., November 8, 1934. It had begun with tenderness and compassion; it ended in a moment of ugliness.

After Charlie's arrival, Meade and David enjoyed a brief happy time together. The summer sun was hot, and they spent a lot of time outdoors. Shirley never joined them. She clearly resented Meade's increased attention toward their son and shunned him even more, often staying in the bedroom while he was in the house.

Meade turned all his love toward David. He was a handsome boy, big for his age, with blond hair and gray eyes like his mother's.

They went fishing and rode horseback at Crowder's ranch. There were abandoned mines to be explored, mountains to be climbed, lakes to swim. By the summer's end, Meade knew he had accomplished half the battle; he had won back his son.

But he was losing his wife. Except for her physical presence, he had lost her already. She was leaving the house frequently now, timing her arrivals to coincide with his and David's. He never questioned where she had been, not that she would have answered if he had.

Meade decided to do nothing and hope for the best.

Soon after Charlie's arrival, Meade had tried to give him half his ownership in the club; he felt it only fair after the way Charlie had bailed him out in '29. Charlie flatly refused. He would accept only twenty-five percent, and he would pay for that. The battle raged for a week. They compromised. Charlie wanted to pay $5,000 for his percentage; Meade got him down to $2,500.

By October, the Plush Wheel had a bankroll of $25,000 and was doing a solid business. When the bingo parlor next door folded, they knocked out the dividing wall and expanded, doubling the size of the club.

When they held an expansion party, one of the first to congratulate them was Bob Terhune. He had arrived early with a large group of friends.

The club was packed, and Meade and Charlie were kept busy watching the action. Two club owners could never have contrasted more. Meade was wearing his white shirt, red

vest, black pants and boots. Charlie had exchanged his ill-
fitting slacks and shirts for tailored suits, flashy ties and
meticulously shined shoes. The chewing tobacco was gone;
he now smoked big cigars. Charlie clearly thrived on the
exciting fast-paced atmosphere of the Plush Wheel.

"Well, fellows," said Terhune, "it looks like I'm on my
way to Washington." Meade, Charlie and Bob Terhune were
sitting at the Plush Wheel bar. The big night was over, and
the club was closed.

"From what I hear," Meade said, "you've left your competition in the dust."

"About that," smiled Terhune. He was running for the
U.S. Senate on the Democratic ticket. His victory was assured.

"Going to close up your house here?" asked Charlie.

"Hell, no. Janice and the kids will stay in Reno. I'll be
coming back often. If I'm going to represent the state, I'll
have to keep in touch." He grinned and scratched his head.
"Besides, Janice would never fit into that Washington crowd.
She'd turn a tea party into a riot. She can't stand hypocrites,
and Washington's full of them."

Meade went home to an empty house. David was staying
at the Terhunes overnight, and there was no telling where
Shirley might be. He had stopped going out and looking for
her long ago. He picked up dirty clothes and washed the
dishes, then went to sleep on his cot in the back room.

Then it was November. The club opened at ten on a cold
wintry morning. The action was slow when the police chief
arrived at the side door. Catching Meade's eye, he motioned
for him to come outside. Meade joined him in Douglas Alley.

The chief's face was grim as he dug his hands down into
his heavy coat. "Meade," he said gruffly, "I came myself
because I felt I should be the one to tell you." He paused and
licked his lips. "It's your wife."

The cold was forgotten. A different kind of chill crawled
up Meade's back. "What about my wife?" he asked. There
was no telling what kind of trouble she might be in.

"Meade, how else can I say it? She's dead."

"Dead," Meade repeated in a disbelieving voice. The word echoed in his mind. Dead, dead, *dead!*

"How?" he whispered.

"A maid found her in a room at the Tourister Hotel. There were three empty bottles by the bed. The doctor who examined her in the room says it looks like alcoholic poisoning." An apologetic look. "They'll have to do an autopsy to be sure." Meade stared, unable to speak. The chief spread his arms in a helpless gesture. "I'm sorry, Meade. Sorry as hell."

Meade said, "Thanks, John. I appreciate your coming. Where is she?"

"Still at the hospital."

Meade nodded slowly. "I'll go tell Charlie. I'd better get over there."

"Sure."

As Meade rode the train to San Diego with Shirley's body in the baggage compartment and David sleeping in his arms, he let his mind drift back over the years. Shirley that first day at the booth, so happy and desirable, sparkling gray eyes regarding him boldly over the head of the giant Panda. The leap of his heart whenever they met, the thrilling touch of her hand, the quiet moments in the night, whispered words of love.

The tears began to flow. Bowing his head, he looked down on David's tousled head—hair the color of Shirley's, long lashes closed over eyes the same shade as hers. *Shirley, oh Shirley,* he moaned silently. *What have I done?*

Shirley's parents didn't speak to him at the funeral. Their hate was almost tangible. Even David was coldly received— as if Meade's blood had made him unacceptable.

Their hate stayed with Meade as he traveled back to Reno. They blamed him for Shirley's death. Perhaps, he thought, they were right.

21

"Meade, you're lookin' kinda peaked around the edges. Don't you think so, Charlie?"

"My thoughts exactly," Charlie said, nodding sagely at Smitty who sat next to him at the round table.

Meade set his bourbon glass down. "What's with you two?" he said. "You got nothing better to do than criticize my looks?" They were sitting in the Plush Wheel bar. It was early April, five months after Shirley's death.

Smitty squinted at Meade from under his old cowboy hat. "We're not criticizin'. Bein' your friends, we just think you need perkin' up." Smitty snapped his fingers. "I got a great idea. A little trip—that's what you need!" He looked to Charlie for support.

"By golly," Charlie cried admiringly, "you hit the nail right on the head!" He poked his cigar at Meade. "A trip—that'll do it."

Meade shot a sour look at the two grinning men. "I suppose you even know where I should go, too."

Charlie said, "Well . . ."

"South," Smitty said.

"How far south?" Meade asked.

"Oh, 'bout four hundred fifty miles or so," Smitty said.

Meade did some quick calculations. "Nothing down there but desert."

"Vegas," Smitty said.

"*Vegas?* Are you nuts? What would I do in a hick town like—" Meade stared at Smitty. "Are you talking about that wild-west thing?"

"For your information, it's called Helldorado," Smitty said. "It sounds like fun."

Meade burst out, "You can drop the whole town in one corner of Reno! That's a hell of a long ways to go for something that probably won't draw five hundred people."

"Meade," Smitty admonished, "you've been in Reno two years, and you're already soundin' like a northerner. You want to get ahead, you gotta set your sights high. Don't be so narrow minded."

"That's telling him, Smitty," Charlie said. "Go on down, Meade. It won't hurt you. Smitty will tag along."

Meade looked at Smitty. "You going?"

"I'd like to, but I ain't goin' alone."

"How come?" Meade asked suspiciously. Smitty couldn't care less about social affairs.

"I got friends down there," Smitty said, "Johnny Cahlan for one. He was born and raised in Reno. He's a reporter for the *Review-Journal* there now, been in Vegas since twenty-nine.

"The Elks is puttin' on this wing-ding, and Johnny's helpin' with it—most of the town is. You need to meet some of them people, Meade. Might come in handy sometime. Besides, I got investments down there; I can check 'em out while we're havin' fun."

Meade said, "Why didn't you say that in the first place? Going to count your profits is the only thing that makes sense."

Smitty looked wounded. "You don't think I'd go just to have fun?"

"Not likely."

"When you guys leaving?" Charlie said.

"Never said I was going," Meade said.

"Sure you will," Smitty said. "And there's goin' to be more than five hundred there—thousands, from what I hear. Death Valley Scotty's goin' to lead the parade. Clyde Zerby's puttin' the show on. Do you think he'd be involved with somethin' puny? They're buildin' a whole village for the thing. It's goin' to have bands, dancin', girlee shows, fire-works, you name it."

"Helldorado, huh?" Meade said.

"Yep. Sounds like a rip-snorter."

"Go with him, Meade," Charlie urged. "It's deader than hell here this time of year. It'll do you good."

Meade looked at the two men. He knew what was behind this. He wondered if it was just Charlie and Smitty or if Janice Terhune was in on this, too. Probably behind the whole thing; she was on a one-woman crusade to save what was left of the Slaughter family.

"Well?" Charlie said.

"When is it?" said Meade.

"Starts on Thursday, the twenty-fifth," Smitty said. "I got a buddy who will put us up at his house. The hotels are already booked; locals are rentin' out rooms. Does that sound like a two-bit party?"

"Hell, I don't know," Meade said, weakening.

"They're even sendin' a Pony Express rider with an invitation to Carson City," Smitty threw in.

"All right," Meade surrendered. "When do we leave?"

The two men grinned with triumph. Smitty said, "We got to go on Wednesday to make it for the openin' on Thursday night."

Meade groaned. Almost thirty-one hours by train, going via Salt Lake City. There was another route through Los Angeles, but most took the Salt Lake route. Only the hardy attempted the rugged two-day drive with an overnight stop in Tonopah.

Meade threw up his hands. "That gives me about ten days to get used to the idea," he said. "I hope to hell you know what you're doing, Smitty."

"Trust me, boy. Trust me."

"That's what I was afraid you'd say."

22

At high noon, Meade and Smitty stepped down from the train at the Union Pacific depot. They weren't alone; many of the passengers were getting off at Las Vegas.

"Hey, look at that!" Smitty exclaimed, pointing at the crowds and a big banner that spanned Fremont Street, welcoming visitors to Las Vegas, "The Gateway to Boulder Dam."

Carrying their suitcases, they walked along the tree-lined first block, a neat little park on each side. It was as if they had stepped back into the last century—women in bonnets and long crinoline dresses, bewhiskered men in western costumes and chaps. Hundreds milling about on the sidewalks and criss-crossing Fremont, the women's dresses trailing dust.

Smitty pointed his chin at Fremont between First and Second. "See that thing? It looks like a—" He stopped abruptly as a hand was laid on his shoulder.

"Like a jail, Smitty?" a grinning man said.

"Johnny!" Smitty cried, holding out his hand to John Cahlan. "I didn't recognize you under that mustache. You, neither, Jim," he added, shaking hands with a goateed man in a black hat and long-tailed coat. Smitty shook hands with several others, introducing them to Meade.

"This a welcoming committee?" Smitty said.

"Not quite," Jim Cashman said, stroking his goatee. "We're might sorry about this, Smitty—Meade—but you're both under arrest."

"Arrest!" Smitty yelled indignantly. "What the hell for?"

"No whiskers," Bob Russell said solemnly. "As Chief of

the Helldorado police, I'm empowered to slap you gents into the hoosegow." Russell pointed at the flatbed trailer parked in the middle of the street.

"Cripes!" Smitty exclaimed. "This is a damn kangaroo court!"

"Better believe it," Ernie Ward said.

Bob Russell signaled Kell Houssels and Pat Gallagher. "Haul 'em off, deputies."

A half-hour later, the dozen prisoners were led out to face the Helldorado judge who sat behind a bench on one end of the flatbed trailer. Judge Art Ham looked sternly at the men. "Got anything to say for yourselves?" he asked, a grinning bunch of bewhiskered men standing behind the defendants to prevent escape.

"We been railroaded!" growled one man.

"Damn unfair!" shouted another.

Judge Ham pointed at the first speaker. "Two bucks or spend an hour in jail."

The man howled but paid the fine. As did the others. Caught up in the spirit of Helldorado, they smiled as they bailed themselves out. The money was going to charity.

After Meade and Smitty had paid their two-dollar fines, they were led by a group of back-slapping deputies to the Apache Club. During the next hours, Meade was introduced to a steady stream of Las Vegans. Meade's confrontation with Carlo Giuliano's men fourteen months ago had made him a popular man all over Nevada.

At five, Meade and Smitty carried their suitcases to South Seventh. C.R. "Luke" Brandridge, Smitty's friend from the old Goldfield days, welcomed the two men. Luke's wife, Maudie, was at the Helldorado Village helping ready the booths.

At 6:45, the three men left the house and walked to Fremont Street, where the village spanned the south side of the block between sixth and seventh.

23

"Show me them hoochie-kootchie dancers!" Smitty said to Luke. They were standing with Meade in the middle of Pay Streak Trail, Fort Helldorado's main street. Fireworks were going off overhead, and bands were playing. With thousands of others, they had been swept inside after Lt. Governor Fred Alward cut the ribbon at the entrance.

"Save it," Meade said, heading toward the Last Chance Saloon, a weatherbeaten frame shack. The majority of the "buildings" were tents. All the furnishings were made out of rough planks, the timber having been brought down from Mt. Charleston.

Smitty got to see the Girlie-Girlie show and was properly impressed. They spent a while in the Pot-of-Gold gambling hall and saw the fat girl and the wild man. At the Wild West Show, they got separated, and Meade wandered along Pay Streak Trail. It was a happy crowd, made up of locals, dam workers and visitors from several states.

Meade ended up at the Helldorado dance hall. He leaned against the wall, a tall man in a black western suit, white shirt and dark string tie, his normal dress since the Plush Wheel was renovated two months ago.

With raven hair curling over his ears and collar and the long slim cigars he smoked, Meade was the image of a riverboat gambler. He fitted perfectly into the costumed Helldorado scene.

He didn't notice the girl at first. She was being swung around the dance floor so fast that all he saw was a mass of dark red hair and a long green dress. But the hair was worth watching—thick and hanging nearly to her waist with a tangled look that must have put the sturdiest comb to the test.

As they swept by, the girl glanced over her partner's shoulder and looked directly at Meade. Their eyes held, and Meade drowned in hers. They were light green, the color of ocean foam. She smiled, and Meade dipped his head, smiling in return.

It became a game, waiting for her return, Meade's heart beating faster each time she neared. Three more rounds and the dance ended. Taller than most, Meade looked over the heads of the dancers and watched another man claim the girl for the next dance. His heart sank. He'd never get near her at this rate.

A Virginia reel, the fiddlers sent the dancers off at a fast pace. The girl whirled past but not before she caught Meade's eye and smiled. Again and again. The next time, Meade pointed at himself, then at her. She flashed a big smile and held up two fingers. Grinning, Meade made a circle with a thumb and forefinger.

They went through the smiling routine while she danced with the next man, then Meade was making his way toward her as the number ended. A man approached the girl, but she shook her head, waving a hand toward Meade. The man bowed and backed off.

"I hope you told that guy that you're taken for the rest of the night," Meade said.

Her big eyes rounded. "But I don't even know you, sir!" She was laughing as Meade drew her onto the crowded dance floor.

"Meade Slaughter," he said, noting that she was about five feet two with a slender but well-endowed frame. Her plump breasts, pushed up by the high bodice, were liberally sprinkled with freckles.

"I'm Sandra," she said. "Sandra Farley. Where are you from, Mr. Slaughter?" She hung back in the circle of his arms, smiling up into his face.

Meade suddenly realized that they were standing in the midst of swirling dancers. He turned slowly, but neither showed any desire to join the frenetic procession. "First of all," Meade said, "I'm not Mr. Slaughter. I'm Meade—like the lake behind Boulder Dam, only with an 'e' on the end. Secondly, I'm from Reno. Your turn. Where are you from?"

She rolled her eyes. "I'm from all over. My pop's working on the dam. This is his third with Frank Crowe. For the last four years, I've been living with my aunt in Boulder, Colorado. I'm graduating from the university there this June."

They became aware of dancers bumping into them. Meade pulled her closer, and they moved along. The dance was coming to an end, and Meade said quickly, "Are you with anyone special?"

"I came with the family, but lost them in the crowd 'bout an hour ago. What do you have in mind?" A smile was twitching the corner of her mouth.

Meade felt like suggesting a trip to the moon. "Oh, I thought we might walk around for a while, check out the booths. Anything, as long as I can keep you to myself."

"You're on!" Sandra said gaily. "I'll get my purse." They walked hand in hand to a chair where she picked up an old-fashioned handbag. "My grandmother's," she explained, taking Meade's arm. They went out into the warm night.

As they strolled around the village, Sandra told how she had been born in Boise, Idaho, where her father had been working on the nearby Arrowrock Dam.

Joe Farley had served overseas during the war, then returned to bossing concrete crews on Gurnsey Dam in Wyoming, Deadwood in Idaho and Van Giesen in California. When the family moved to Boulder City in 1931, it was Sandra's fifth dam, the fourth for her younger brother and sister. Sandra, who would be twenty-two in October, hadn't stayed in Nevada long, leaving that September to attend the University of Colorado.

Sandra learned about Meade's early days with the carnivals and amusement parks. It was past midnight, and they were sitting outside the mining display, when Meade finally got around to telling about Shirley and David. Even in this short time, Sandra's opinion had become important, and he was afraid the revelation might send her away. He needn't have worried.

Sandra took his hand in both of hers, big green eyes sparkling. "I'm sorry, Meade," she said softly. "It must have been terrible for you and your little boy. How is he doing?"

Meade wanted to hug her. He told her about Janice and all she had done for David. While he talked, a burden lifted from his heart, and for the first time in years he felt the stir of long-suppressed feelings.

24

The next morning, Meade found Jim Cashman eating a late breakfast at the Sal Sagev hotel. They dickered while Meade had coffee and a short stack. A half-hour later, Meade drove a rented two-year-old Oldsmobile out of Cashman's auto dealership on North Main.

Unlike most of the streets outside a seven-square-block area of Las Vegas, the road to Boulder City was paved, having been completed in stages since the dam went under construction four years ago.

Shortly after noon, Meade drove through the guarded entrance into Boulder City, the government reservation of 800 homes that had been built to house married construction workers. Young trees lined the streets, and many homes displayed neatly trimmed lawns. Meade parked in front of one of these.

Sandra must have been watching because she opened the door after the first knock. She was wearing a long white dress, trimmed in a light green lace that matched the unusual color of her eyes. Meade looked the dress over and the small body it contained so nicely. "Your grandmother's?" he asked, smiling down at her upturned face.

"Yep," Sandra said, proudly dangling a drawstring purse from one finger. "I made this." She lifted a matching poke bonnet that was dangling down her back. "This, too."

"Nice," Meade said. "You're a lady of many talents."

"I can cook, too. Learned that from Mom." Sandra's mother was one of the head cooks at the giant Six Companies mess hall.

"Nobody home?" Meade said.

"Rich and Julie are off somewhere. Mom and Pops were gone when I woke up." An elfin grin. " 'Course, I didn't wake up until ten."

They stopped a few miles out of Boulder City and had lunch at the Railroad Pass casino. The time seemed to fly, and they barely made it to Las Vegas for the special matinee showing of *Star of Midnight* at the Palace Theatre.

Meade couldn't believe what was happening. He was thirty-one with a seven-year-old son, widowed only five months, and here he was sitting in a dark theater holding hands with a vibrant girl who had entered his life just last night. And thrilling to the pressure of their interlaced fingers just like a kid!

Over a decade had passed since those glorious first two years of marriage, when his whole life had revolved around Shirley. Could he ever feel that way again?

He glanced down at the mass of dark red hair that brushed his shoulder. Sandra squeezed his hand hard as Ginger Rogers and William Powell reached a tense moment in the romantic mystery. Meade's eyes returned to the screen. Maybe they were just caught up in the excitement of Helldorado. Then, maybe not. Time would tell.

Outside, Meade spotted Smitty talking to Pros Goumond, one of the owners of the Boulder Club. Waving, Smitty headed their way. He hadn't seen Sandra. A foot shorter than Meade, she was standing on tiptoe to catch a glimpse of the floats.

Coming to an abrupt halt, Smitty looked Sandra over and grinned. "So you're the gal who's takin' up all Meade's time," he said. "I'm Smitty." He touched the brim of his cowboy hat.

Sandra smiled and stuck out her hand. "I'm Sandra."

Smitty wiped his hand on his pantleg. He wasn't comfortable around strange women, but there was a twinkle in his eye when he shook her hand. He liked Sandra's western directness.

"Let's move down a block or so," Meade said. "The parade will be all bunched up here." They would have to find a curbside spot. Smitty wasn't much taller than Sandra.

They found a place in front of Ronzone's Dress Shop on Second, Sandra standing in front of Meade, Smitty to her right. As the parade started, Meade's arms crept around Sandra's waist, and she leaned back against his chest, hands covering his. Smitty didn't miss the movement, and a look of satisfaction crossed his face.

The parade route was short, seven blocks from Main to Helldorado Village, but over 12,000 enthusiastic watchers cheered the horse-drawn floats and Death Valley Scotty as he passed in his famous stagecoach. Jim Cashman was one of the parade leaders, joined by the likes of Rex Bell and his wife, Clara Bow, boxer Maxie Rosenbloom and Clyde Zerby.

The evening passed quickly—too quickly for the young couple suddenly caught up in each other's lives. They tried to take everything in—the Golden Wedding renewal between the Peter Pauffs with the Ed Von Tobels in attendance, the old-time fiddlers contest, the Apache band from Needles, dancing on the open-air platform to a jazz band.

Meade wasn't a good dancer, but with Sandra feather-light in his arms, he outdid himself. It was an unusual sight, women in pantalettes and hoops, men in cowboy garb and ten-gallon hats, whirling to the beat of modern music.

Boulder City bound, Sandra rested in the curve of Meade's arm, her glossy head comfortable on his shoulder. They didn't talk much; they didn't have to.

A mile outside the entrance to the little government town,

Meade pulled off the road and parked. They hadn't really kissed yet, just little playful pecks. Meade's lips sought Sandra's, and she eagerly threw her arms around his neck.

Minutes ticked by. Lips touching, Meade said, "I don't want this to end next week."

Sandra's eyes were shining. "Me neither. I've never felt this way—not with anyone!"

Meade wanted to say the same thing, but it was too early to compare his original feelings for Shirley with anything else. He smiled and sealed Sandra's lips with his. They clung to each other, and he was amazed at the strength in her small frame.

An hour later, Meade drove away from Boulder City, the car radio picking up Ray Noble and "The Very Thought of You" from a Los Angeles station. Las Vegas had no station of its own, and outside programs couldn't reach the little desert town in the daytime. Vegans had to wait for night and the more receptive airwaves.

25

Saturday was Boulder City Day at Helldorado Village, and Las Vegas was gearing up for the biggest crowd of the celebration.

The town was waking up later each day, the long nights taking their toll. Meade wouldn't be seeing Sandra until five. She was coming in with her family, and Meade was taking them to dinner.

Sandra and her family arrived, and Meade led them through the Las Vegas Club casino to the Smokehouse Restaurant. Seated around the big table, Meade looked at Sandra who was on his left. She was wearing yellow today, and a wide-brimmed white hat circled with a green ribbon. She caught his glance and smiled.

After dinner, Meade and Joe "Mud" Farley stood outside on the sidewalk while Sandra and her mother went to the restroom, Rich and Julie having disappeared into the crowd. Mud looked at Meade. "You and Sandra seem to get along pretty good," he said. It was both a statement and a question.

Meade stirred uncomfortably. He hoped this wasn't the preliminary to an interrogation. He was too old for that. "I like her a lot," Meade admitted. "I want to keep in touch after this is over."

Mud nodded, a slow smile crossing his face. "She's said the same thing about you. Sandra's not good at hiding her feelings. If she likes you, you know it, but if she doesn't, look out! We're close, me and her. She was our first and only child for years. Used to call her the best little gal by a dam site." Mud chuckled, and Meade joined in.

Mud looked Meade up and down. "I like you," he said. "Sandra tells me you're a widower and you got a young son. You treat my girl right, we've got no problems."

"I'll treat her right," Meade said, eyes locked with Mud's. "Count on it."

In the early hours of Sunday morning, Meade drove Sandra toward home, her head on his shoulder, hand in his. One more night, and Helldorado would be over.

They parked at the same spot as on the previous night, kissing and talking, not wanting to waste a minute of the little time left. Originally planning on returning to Reno on Monday, Meade was now leaving on Tuesday, giving them one more evening together.

26

On Monday morning, Las Vegas was trying to get back to normal. Elks Club members were tearing down Helldorado Village, and barber shops were doing a land-office business. A few men were emerging still wearing their mustaches, having decided to keep them as souvenirs.

Meade and Sandra had dinner at the Rainbow Club, then went for a drive. Meade had never been south of town, so he drove a few miles out on the Los Angeles highway, a graveled road full of potholes.

They passed the Pair-O-Dice Club, three miles from town. The wind was blowing, and dust swirled around the closed building, a lonely structure on a bleak stretch of desert.

A mile further, they found the Red Rooster open. Going inside, they had a couple of drinks and danced.

It was after ten when they returned to Las Vegas. At Sandra's urging, Meade drove a block north of Fremont to a row of clubs fronted by a common porch. Sandra hugged Meade's arm and eagerly looked out the window as they moved slowly along Ogden Street, a parade of club names showing up under the roof of the lighted porch—the Double O, Arcade, Star, Jazz, Pasttime, Arizona and Honolulu Inn. "Pops would shoot me if he knew I'd talked you into this," Sandra said, jumping slightly at the sight of a woman in silk pajamas sitting inside an open doorway.

"One more time?" Meade asked as they entered Second Street, enjoying Sandra's reaction to Las Vegas' famous "Block Sixteen," home of legal prostitution.

"Yes!" Sandra cried, rolling her big eyes. Meade turned right, and they circled to Ogden, passing the town constable riding his horse, a big ring of keys jangling from his belt. This time they saw a girl in a negligee, making Sandra whoop with wicked mirth.

As they started out of town on the Boulder Dam highway, Meade paused in front of the Meadows Club, operated by the Cornero brothers, Frank, Louis and Tony. Meade had been told that men with 30-30 rifles sat behind the parapets to guard against trouble. The casino did a good business, and the dining room was popular with locals, but Meade didn't want to take Sandra there. The Corneros were a tough bunch to deal with.

Approaching Boulder City, they parked at their customary spot. Their kisses were more urgent now; Meade would be leaving in the morning. Sandra was going back to the university. "Promise to write?" Meade said, smoothing Sandra's dark red hair.

"At least one letter before I leave next week," she promised. "And you'd better answer quick," she added, poking Meade in the ribs.

"Maybe I'll come to your graduation," Meade said.

"That would be super!" Sandra exclaimed. "June seventh. You won't forget?"

"I'm sure you'll remind me."

"I'll be going up with Mom and Pops to Washington in June," she said. "I'll try and talk them into going through Reno." A woeful look. "But the roads are so much better through California."

"How about visiting with me on the way back?" Meade said, expressing an idea he had been considering for days. "Janice Terhune will be glad to put you up."

Sandra's eyes sparkled. "Wouldn't that be keen?"

"You'll like Janice. She's family."

They talked until after one. The parting was hard, but June seventh was barely six weeks away. Meade had already made up his mind to attend her graduation. Sandra's family would be driving up from Las Vegas; Meade could take the train to Provo and ride with the Farleys to Boulder.

At 10:20 the next morning, Meade and Smitty got on the

Union Pacific for the trip through Salt Lake City to Reno. As the trains' arrivals and departures were special events in the little desert town, many of the residents were in attendance.

As the train pulled away, Meade and Smitty stood between two cars, returning waves. They went quickly inside to avoid the blowing dust from a brisk northwest wind.

27

"Sit down, Meade," Janice Terhune said, waving toward the kitchen table. "Try these little confections I baked. Good for what's ailing you." She placed a plate of doughnuts between the steaming cups of coffee.

"Nothing's ailing me," Meade grinned.

"Well, you have perked up some. Vegas must have agreed with you."

"You've been talking to Smitty."

"And Charlie. You know how he loves to gossip."

"Sounds like the pot calling the kettle black."

Janice combed her fingers through her gray-flecked hair. "Now, that's not nice, Meade. I'm a woman; we're naturally curious." She leaned forward, chin on fist. "Tell me about her."

Meade threw up his hands. "My third day back. Can't a man have any privacy?"

"Not with me. I'm your confessor, remember?"

"No, I don't. Since when?"

"Since right now," Janice said, nudging the doughnuts nearer. "Come on, I want a first-hand account. Is she as pretty as I hear?"

"Oh, hell," Meade mumbled through a mouthful of

doughnut, trying to look persuaded. He wanted to talk about Sandra; that was his main reason for dropping by.

"Well?" Janice persisted.

"She's pretty," Meade said. "With that red hair and those green eyes she stands out in a crowd. Got cute little freckles on her nose. Other places, too."

"*What* other places?" Janice demanded.

"Her shoulders. My God, Janice, we only went out a few times!"

Meade busied himself lighting a cigar. He puffed it to life. "She's going to be a school teacher," he said. "Graduating from the University of Colorado this June. She's smart, maybe too smart for me."

"Don't be a cow plop," Janice said. "You might fool some people, but humble you ain't."

Meade grinned. "Okay, but she *is* smart. Likes kids, too."

"Well!" Janice said, pretending wide-eyed wonder. "What's *that* supposed to mean?"

"Not a damn thing," Meade retorted. "Just thought you'd be interested."

"I am—" Janice's words were cut off as Jim Terhune raced into the kitchen, David close behind. It had rained yesterday, and the boys' clothes were splattered with mud. Two dirty hands reached for the doughnuts.

"Wash up first!" Janice ordered, lifting the plate high over their heads. Laughing, the boys raced out of the kitchen.

"And no running in the house!" Janice yelled, turning to grin at Meade as the bathroom door slammed open down the hall. "I should shoot 'em both, but I don't know what I'd do without all that noise." She couldn't have loved David more had he been her real son. With Grace, 18, in her first year at Vassar and Tom, 15, involved with high school and girls, Janice devoted most of her time to the boys.

The boys charged back in, holding out clean hands for inspection. "Two each, that's all," Janice said. "Milk's in the fridge." Sixty seconds later, the back door crashed shut behind the heavily laden youngsters.

A long silence, then Janice began to ask questions. That night, Meade wrote Sandra:

> . . . and Janice beat me to the punch. You're invited
> to stay at her place as long as you want. I know
> you'll be visiting your family, but I hope you'll
> spend part of the summer here.

Sandra's answer arrived the following week. She would go to Washington with her parents after graduation and arrive in Reno around mid-July. If Meade could stand her, she would stay until the end of August.

28

It was one of the hottest Julys on record. The doors to the Plush Wheel stood open. Inside, the overhead fans were going full blast. There were few players; everyone was waiting for the evening and the accompanying cool breezes.

"Here's mud in your eye," Smitty said, raising his glass toward Meade. They sat at a table near the bar, a big four-bladed fan chopping the air above.

"Forget the mud. Right now, I'd welcome a bucket of water on my head," Meade said as he watched two women come hesitantly into the club. Divorcées-in-waiting. He had seen them around town the past few weeks, drifting farther and farther from their "home" at the Riverside Hotel. A familiar routine. Tears and withdrawal at first, then increasing boldness with the passing of time.

The swank Fortune Club on Second Street drew most of these women. With its reproductions of Dutch masters and a beautifully appointed bar and restaurant, it contrasted sharply with the rowdy atmosphere of places like the Bank Club and the Palace on Center Street.

This was one of the reasons Meade had created a more conservative atmosphere at the Plush Wheel. Divorce was big business in Nevada. Hotels and a dozen dude ranches around Reno catered to the women who arrived almost daily to put a quick end to their marriages. It was even quicker for Nevadans, who didn't have to wait out the six-week residency requirement. A couple could fight at breakfast and be divorced by dinner time.

Smitty rose to leave, and Meade followed him outside. Giving Meade the thumbs-up sign, the little man pulled his hat down against the sun's glare, climbed into his battered pickup and drove off toward his ranch.

Meade looked at his watch. Four-twenty P.M. In a couple of hours, he would be relieved by Charlie. On June first, they had started opening the Plush Wheel at seven each morning. The days were never as good as the nights, but they helped pay the rent. The club usually closed around two A.M. A few times, it had stayed open all night.

Tourism was sparse. It was a long trip over the Sierras from the San Francisco Bay area. Some came by car and rail. There were a half-dozen daily flights at the United Airlines airport, and many stopped off as they traveled through Reno on Pacific-Greyhound. And there was the east-west traffic on the Lincoln Highway.

Clubs were still opening and closing. Many were nothing but clip joints, seamy holes that lived up to the preacher's concept of a gambling den. A few were well established—the Bank Club, the Palace, Giuliano's Western Club, the Plush Wheel—but the majority operated on shaky bankrolls.

A little place had opened last February on Virginia Street a few doors south of the Plush Wheel. With a background like Meade's and Charlie's in amusement parks and fairs, Harold Smith and his father, Raymond, had come to Reno to try their hands at running a gambling club. Their greatest success so far had been to provide a lot of laughs around town. They had no dice or card games, featuring only elec-

tronic bingo, played with nickels and dimes. They called their
place Harolds Club.

At night, there were few neon signs advertising the clubs.
Names were painted on windows, some on wooden signs.
Things were pretty quiet in Reno. Hardly a sleeping giant.
More like a child still sucking its thumb.

29

"It ain't fair!" yelled David, standing solidly in the doorway,
bristling with indignation. "I want to go, too!"

Sandra ran back to the porch of the Terhune home and
knelt in front of the seven-year-old boy. "We'll only be gone
for a few hours," she said quickly. "Didn't I take you on a
picnic the other day? And stop saying 'ain't,' little man, or
there won't be any more picnics!"

David grinned. "Okay, for you I won't say 'ain't' no
more."

Sandra looked at Meade and moaned, "This boy really
needs work on his English."

"Not today," Meade laughed. "Right now, it's you and me
and the lake."

As Meade headed his new Packard out of Reno toward
Lake Tahoe, Sandra hugged his arm and rested her head on
his shoulder. He smiled down at the tangle of dark red hair
that swirled in the breeze and gently grazed his cheek. As if
she sensed his look, she held his arm tighter.

Sandra had arrived in Reno two weeks ago, receiving Janice's instant approval and friendship. Charlie was captivated
by her, and Smitty acted as if he had been solely responsible
for bringing her and Meade together. Sandra was a giving
person and delighted in making new friends. It was a happy
time for all, including David, who looked on her as a com-

panion and a fellow conspirator in circumventing his father's wishes.

For Meade, it was a time of discovery. Sandra's sparkling unselfish personality brought a joy into his life he had thought no longer possible. It was almost frightening. He couldn't bear the thought of losing her.

Not that there was any danger of that. They grew closer each day, and it seemed they had known each other for years, rather than three short months.

"Penny for your thoughts," Sandra said, bringing him back to the present.

"Not worth that much," Meade said, hugging her close. They were climbing into the Sierras, the road narrow and twisting as it threaded its way through a corridor of tall pines.

Passing Mt. Rose, they reached the 8,900 foot summit and started down, catching glimpses of Lake Tahoe, then a sweeping view. Sandra stared at the great expanse of blue-green water. "It's gorgeous," she whispered, sitting on the edge of the seat and making little sounds of pleasure as they neared Crystal Bay.

"Oh, look, Meade!" she cried, pointing at a curve of white sandy beach. "Let's go there."

Gathering their things, they followed a path that led through the dense stand of pines that bordered the beach.

Sandra's feet sank in the sand, and she pulled off her shoes. "Last one in's a scaredy cat!" she yelled, kicking up sheets of sand as she raced for the water.

"Water's pretty cold," Meade called.

"Says you!" Sandra shouted back, wading into a small wave. A moment of stillness, then a tiny "Eek!" Sandra's green eyes were enormous as she turned to look at Meade. "I feel like I'm standing in an ice box," she bleated, lifting a foot to see if it was still attached.

Meade stuck his big toe in the water. "Not bad," he said, wading out to join her. "You get used to it. Tahoe's over six thousand feet up. We're standing in melted snow."

Sandra wiggled her toes experimentally. "I think the feeling's coming back," she said, pulling her dress away from her damp legs and fanning it in the warm air. She looked out over the lake. "I've never seen anything so big!" she exclaimed, gazing at the distant shoreline. "It's like an ocean stuck up in the mountains."

The temperature reached the mid-eighties, and they went swimming, their bodies quickly adapting to the cold water. As the afternoon shadows lengthened, they swam out to a round gray rock a hundred feet from the shore. Sandra hugged her legs to her breasts, watching the waves lap the sand. "It's so beautiful here," she said. "Wouldn't it be great to have a place like this to come to every summer?"

Meade looked up from his prone position. "With you, it would be."

Sandra smiled. "I wasn't thinking of anyone else but you."

"Better not," Meade said, pulling her down so her head was on his chest.

They didn't speak for a long time. Sandra sat up. "The sun's setting," she said. "It's going to be cold going back."

"Good thought," Meade said. He stuck his foot in the water. "There's only one way to do it, kid. Jump in and swim like crazy!" With a shout, he hit the water and ploughed toward shore. Sandra, a much better swimmer, beat him by ten yards.

Wrapped in towels, they sat on the blanket. "Nice and warm here," Meade said, watching Sandra as she wrung her thick mane of hair out on the sand.

"Perfect," she said, standing and shaking herself like a wet puppy. "Be back in a sec. I'm going to the ladies' room and change." She disappeared into the nearby trees. Meade followed suit, taking a deer path that led to a small glade.

Sandra was combing her hair when he returned. "Want to go somewhere and eat?" Meade asked.

"I'm not hungry. Can we stay here a while?"

"Sure." Meade sat down. "I don't have to be back at the club until morning. Plenty of time."

They talked, and the shadows became one, closing them in darkness. Sandra was in Meade's arms, their hands and tongues exploring. They had progressed to touching and feeling during the past two weeks, but only through their clothes. Sandra surprised Meade by opening her blouse and placing his hand over her naked breast. Her nipple was hard and surprisingly large.

"Honey—"

Sandra silenced Meade with her lips, moving closer so her breast flattened in his palm. Meade fingered the nipple and she moaned.

The blouse came off, and Meade ran his tongue over the taut little breasts, the moon barely illuminating the scene. Sandra's fingers tugged at the buttons on Meade's shirt.

Meade looked into Sandra's face. "Have you ever—" The words died in his throat.

Sandra touched his face. "No," she said, "I've been thinking about it a lot lately. I want it to be with you."

"But I haven't, we haven't—"

"Do you always talk so much at times like this?" Sandra chided, yanking at his shirt.

Meade glanced around. "Not here," he said gruffly. "There's a good clearing in the trees." They walked to the glade Meade had discovered earlier, Meade carrying the blanket, Sandra her blouse, breasts jutting in the moonlight.

Clothing was discarded. Sandra displayed herself to Meade's questing eyes and hands, unashamed, trusting. She buried her face in his neck. "I'm ready," she whispered.

"I don't want to hurt you," Meade said, rising carefully above her.

"Don't be a goose," she said, grasping his engorged member and guiding it to the darkness below her belly.

The tip was inserted, and Meade moved slowly, conscious of Sandra's small body, made even smaller by his bulk.

Grasping Meade's buttocks, Sandra pulled, raising her pelvis to meet his cautious thrusts. A moment of resistance, then Meade was fully inside, enclosed in a tight moistness that undulated and contracted with Sandra's quickening movements. "Wonderful!" she gasped. "Oh, Meade, it's wonderful!"

Then she came, a shriek of pure joy, legs trying to reach

around Meade's waist and failing, dropping so her feet hooked behind his ankles.

Meade's loins burned in the incredible warmth of Sandra's body. He felt like he was going to explode, all his energy focusing on the shaft locked so securely in its soft, unyielding prison. He burst inside her belly, crying aloud, mind reeling as Sandra frantically matched his movements.

They lay quietly side by side. Sandra smiled and touched his lips. "To think I've been waiting almost twenty-two years for this. If I'd only known." She snuggled close and went instantly to sleep.

The cold night air woke them an hour later. They dressed, laughing and stumbling in the darkness. Sandra insisted on rinsing the blanket out in the lake. "It's Janice's," she said as she scrubbed the dark stains away. "One look and she'd know." A soft laugh. "At least she'd know I was a virgin." Sandra leaned against Meade, hugging the wet blanket to her stomach. "I'm so glad it was you."

30

As Sandra laughingly put it, they were now playing house in earnest.

Meade had been living in a hotel since Shirley's death; David's brief stay at the Terhunes had become permanent, Janice insisting that Meade was in no position to properly care for the boy.

Three days after returning from Lake Tahoe, Meade rented a small brick house on North Sierra, a short walk from the university. It became the young couple's hideaway, a place to talk and make love all hours of the day and night. They didn't flaunt their new relationship, nor did they conceal it. Their friends took it for granted that they planned to marry.

They touched on the subject many times during the weeks that remained before Sandra had to return to Boulder and her teaching job. At first in a teasing way, as so often happens with lovers. The talk became more serious as Sandra prepared to leave, but neither was ready to commit. Meade was cautious after his failed marriage, and Sandra recognized this. She was a practical girl, with a common sense seldom found in one so young. So, they parted with much left unsaid.

They wrote often, and their letters were filled with expressions of love. Sandra was torn between her responsibilities as a new teacher and her desire to be with Meade. Meade became restless as his loyalties were split between the Plush Wheel and Sandra. Guiltily, he recalled how Shirley had suffered when he devoted most of his time to the club. He tried to tell himself that the Plush Wheel was established now, and the newness had worn off. But down deep he knew gaming was in his blood and the real growth was still ahead. He had plans and ambitions yet to be fulfilled.

They were disappointed when Sandra caught a bad cold right before Thanksgiving and was unable to travel to Reno. It hurt her to do it, but Sandra had to disappoint her parents and miss visiting them during Christmas vacation so she could see Meade. Joe and Ellen Farley understood. Sandra had always been honest about her feelings, and Meade's name had been appearing in her letters with increasing regularity.

A few days before Christmas, Meade drove Sandra to Lake Tahoe. Little snow had fallen in the basin, so they were able to reach Crystal Bay via Truckee.

Bundled up in heavy coats, they walked through the trees to the sandy beach. They had returned here several times last summer, and Meade laid the blanket on what they had come to call "their spot." A Thermos of coffee warmed them as Sandra leaned against Meade's chest, gazing at the beauty of the snow-covered mountain peaks that ringed the lake.

Meade lifted the stocking cap from Sandra's ear, his breath

steaming the heavy strands of hair that tumbled down. "Close your eyes," he said. "I want to show you something." Sandra squinched her eyes shut and wiggled into the warmth of his body.

She opened her eyes to see a full carat diamond ring gleaming under the dull winter sky. "I was going to save it for Christmas," Meade said, "but I wanted to give it to you here." His voice trailed off. The diamond sparkled in its blue velvet box, a delicate object in Meade's big hand.

With an audible gasp, Sandra reached out and touched the diamond with a gloved finger. Meade had said nothing about marriage since her arrival a week ago. It had been upsetting and she had been angry at herself for being so foolish. Just because she had made up her mind didn't mean he had to, too! Now, before her was the proof that he felt as she did. She recalled the hesitant tone in his voice. Did he think she would say no? She tore the glove off her left hand. "Put it on quick before it disappears!" she cried.

Turning, she knelt on the blanket while Meade slipped on the ring. She waved it in the air, delighting in its brilliance, then threw her arms around Meade's neck. "Does this mean what I think it does?" she growled, nibbling at his neck.

Much later, Sandra sat once more with her back pressed against Meade's chest. They talked about the wedding. "I'll have to finish this first year at school," Sandra said. "A June wedding would be wonderful but not practical. There's so much to do. Will August be too late?"

Meade said August would be fine.

Janice was delighted with the news, and Bob was told to mark off on his calendar the days before and after Saturday, August 29th, the day chosen for the wedding.

Christmas passed, then Easter. Sandra couldn't get away, so Meade visited her in Boulder. In June, Sandra went to Washington to be with her family. Arriving in Reno in late July, she was immediately caught up in a whirl of activities. The wedding was barely a month away.

31

Other plans were being made on Commercial Row. "Slaughter's got to be taken care of," Carlo Giuliano said to the big man slouched in a chair across the desk. They were in Giuliano's cluttered office above the Western Club.

The big man threw a leg over the chair arm. "I'm with you, boss," he said, discarding a cigarette butt and lighting another. "He's gettin' a lot of customers with all that honesty shit he keeps pluggin' in the paper. The bastard can't name you in the *Journal,* but he sure don't pull no punches with his mouth. He's never forgot that little ruckus a couple of years back."

"Me neither," growled Giuliano. "I couldn't believe it when he threatened me. *Me!* Killin' those two men has made it rough gettin' local talent. Graham says I should have taken care of Slaughter a long time ago."

"Don't know that Graham's got such hot advice," grunted the big man. "He's still got plenty of muscle in town, but I'll bet my ass that him and McKay go to the can for that horse race swindle. They've been livin' too high on the hog. They go, you can really take over."

Giuliano made a waving motion. "Graham's case will be in court for years. Now's what I'm thinkin' about, and I want Slaughter taken care of *now!*"

The big man sat back and rubbed his hands together, small eyes glinting in his scarred face. "I want in on this, boss. That bastard knocked me off the sidewalk the other day like I was shit—just stood there and dared me to make a move. I wanted to, but he's got good connections in town." He rubbed his knuckles, swollen and deformed from the boxing ring. "I'll take care of him good."

Giuliano regarded his bodyguard through thick cigar smoke, then nodded slowly. "Okay, Doug, but no killing. Just break him up good. I want him out of commission for months. Charlie Brent can't keep the club together without him. We'll bust Slaughter out or buy him out. Either way, we get him out of town."

Giuliano pointed a stubby finger. "Get a couple of boys from Rozini in Frisco. We're not takin' any chances on this one." Giuliano noted the quick flash of relief in Doug's eyes. The man was tough but not stupid.

"When do you want this to happen, boss?" Doug asked as he rose heavily from the chair.

"Soon as possible. Do the job in a quiet place. If you make it public, we've all got problems." Giuliano stabbed the cigar at Doug. "Especially you."

Without a word, Doug left. Good man, thought Giuliano. No questions; just gets the job done. Hard to find muscle and brains in the same body. Doug would get a nice bonus when this was done.

32

It was a happy time with David racing around telling everyone—including strangers on the street—that he was getting a sister. She was going to marry his dad and they were all going to live together. He couldn't get it through his head that Sandra was going to be his new mother. How could Janice be his mother and Sandra too? Janice was the only real mother he'd known; Shirley was just a dim memory.

Late Sunday night, Meade called and told Janice that he was going to close the club at one. No, he would drop by and see Sandra in the morning. "Tell her I'm hurt that she thinks taking a bath is more important than talking to me," Meade said, hanging up with a laugh.

When Sandra heard about the call, it was after midnight. "May I borrow your car?" she asked Janice, who was seated at the kitchen table going over a list of invitations to the wedding. "I'd like to surprise Meade. We can have breakfast at the Golden."

"Can't stay away from him for a minute, can you?" Janice smiled, pointing at the keys hanging on a hook. "Go ahead, make a fool of yourself, chasing a man around in the middle of the night."

It was warm outside, and Sandra tossed her sweater into the passenger seat of Janice's Cadillac. As she crossed the Truckee River, she noted that it was ten minutes to one. She passed the Plush Wheel on Virginia Street and turned right on Commercial Row. Meade's Packard was parked beside the railroad tracks. Using her key, Sandra opened the Packard's door and scooted down in the seat.

A movement caught her eye. It was Meade! No, three men headed her way. Darn! Don't spoil my surprise! She sank down further.

When she looked again, the men were gone. Then she saw Meade coming out of Douglas Alley. A sight that never ceased to thrill her. A big dark-haired man moving confidently, surprisingly light on his feet for his size. She started to duck down.

She wasn't sure what it was at first. Then it was horribly clear. Three running figures descended on Meade, clubs whirling in the air. Meade went down as a scream rose in Sandra's throat. "Meade! Meade!" Her voice was magnified in the close confines of the car.

The clubs rose and fell. Unthinking, uncaring, Sandra hit the ground running, running to help her man. Ninety-eight pounds of girl leaping into the fray. Bare hands against baseball bats. Furious. A little wildcat leaping on the back of a man, scratching, biting.

Meade was in a bad way. One arm broken, ribs cracked,

blood running from a deep cut on his forehead. Even at that, he nearly throttled one man before he was beaten off and knocked once more to the ground.

He saw Sandra. "No!" he shouted, trying to rise, arm hanging bent, useless. A roar of pain escaped his lips as a bat came down on his leg, breaking it with a brittle snap, white bone ripping through his pants, glistening in the muted light.

Yanking Sandra from his back, the man grabbed her by the hair and threw her to one side, but not before she had torn the bandanna from his face. Through a bloody haze, Meade recognized Doug Clausen, Carlo Giuliano's bodyguard.

As Meade crawled toward Sandra, a bat slammed into his lower back, knifelike pain blurring his sight. He tried to move, but his good leg wouldn't work.

Clausen raised his bat, eyes intent on Meade's unbroken leg. As the bat came whistling down, Sandra leaped in the way to protect Meade. The bat smashed into her head with a sickening crunch. Without a sound, she fell across Meade, dark blood swiftly matting her hair.

The attackers froze, then fled into the night. A girl! Maybe dead. She'd been hit hard enough.

The imported thugs were out of town in minutes, driving fast toward the California border.

Carlo Giuliano was enraged.

"You fuckin' idiot!" he screamed at Doug Clausen. "If that girl dies, all hell's going to break loose. I can't buy protection for a deal like that!" Giuliano crushed his cigar out and stomped around the office. He pointed an accusing finger at Clausen. "Did anybody see you?"

Clausen stirred uncomfortably in the chair and shook his head. "Nobody." He wasn't going to mention the loss of his mask; he'd tackle that problem when and if it came up. He felt the back of his neck, his hand coming away bloody. "That broad came out of nowhere!" he rasped, reaching back again to touch the scratches Sandra had made on his neck. "Damn little bitch!"

"You better hope nobody saw you," Giuliano snapped. "You better damn well hope so!"

33

Tumbled dark red hair, the pulse in the slender neck beating, beating, faltering . . . still.

Gentle fingers pushed the heavy strands of hair aside. Pain-filled eyes, welling with tears, vainly sought for life.

Meade cradled Sandra's head on his chest, knowing that had help arrived immediately it would have been too late.

Meade's heartbreak was beyond imagination, transcending the terrible pain that wracked his body. But only above the waist. He felt no pain from the fractured right leg. No response from the left leg. Except for his right arm, his limbs were useless.

Numbing spasms seized Meade. He fought desperately, refusing to relinquish these last few moments with Sandra, devouring every feature of her silent face. Eyesight fading, he stroked her hair and traced a finger down her left arm, touching the diamond ring. Tears blurred his vision, then a darkness fell that was blacker than the huge steam locomotive that loomed silently on a nearby siding.

They were found by a blackjack dealer whose car was parked beside Meade's. Thinking both dead, the dealer ran across the street and phoned the police from the Elk Hotel. A small crowd followed him back. Meade was recognized. "Jesus Christ!" shouted a man. Meade was moaning softly.

It was past two when Janice was awakened by the heavy tone of the door chimes. The news left her sagging against the doorjamb, face ghostly white. She willed herself to speak. "Meade? How bad is he?"

The police officer said, "Quite a few broken bones. Hard

to say what's happened inside. They're working on him now."

"Charlie Brent should be notified."

"Jack Lomas is over there now."

Janice hugged her arms and moved back into the hall. She shook her head, and tears trickled down her cheek. "Damnit, Harvey," she said, "there was going to be a party here Friday night. For Meade and that poor dead girl. Pretty soon, I've got to pick up the phone and tell her parents there won't be a wedding. Just a funeral! Goddamn! Listen to me and listen to me good, Harvey Cox!" she cried. "I want you and that bunch you work with to turn this town upside down and find the bastards that did this. I've got a pretty good idea who did it, and so do you." She glared at him for a moment, then stalked out of the room.

34

"Compound fracture of the leg, fractured arm, broken ribs, forty stitches on his forehead, concussion, ruptured spleen—all that will heal in time," the doctor said to Charlie and Smitty.

But there was more, stunning words that erased the relieved looks on the faces of the two men. "One of the blows smashed a vertebra in the lower back. There's a strong possibility that the nerves are destroyed. If so, he'll never walk again. I've called in a specialist from San Francisco; he'll be here tomorrow."

Smitty rocked on his heels, hands stuck in the back pockets of his jeans. "You sure, Stan?" he said.

"Hell, no. That's why I called in the specialist. But I'm going to be surprised if I'm wrong."

"Does Meade know?" Charlie asked, trying to absorb this additional tragedy.

"No, and he's not going to—not until we're sure, and he's strong enough. He's got all he can handle now."

"When can we see him?" Charlie asked the doctor.

"Maybe in two-three hours," the doctor said. "The police have first crack. He's the only lead they've got."

The following Monday morning, the doctor sat on the edge of the bed, tapping a clipboard on his knee. Meade said, "So that's it; my legs are gone."

The doctor nodded. "We can operate to relieve the pain, but it's not going to make your legs work."

Meade shook his head. "No operation. I'll live with the pain." The doctor left.

I'll live with the pain. I wish it would hurt so much that I could forget! At times during the past week, Meade had feared he was losing his mind, the anguish almost too much to bear. One powerful emotion had sustained him—a consuming thirst for revenge. Could half a man avenge Sandra's death? He refused to accept defeat.

Swathed in bandages, one leg in traction, Meade recalled the last few days. Janice had become the catalyst in his life.

She was the first at his bedside. The police had to wait. It wasn't easy to say no to Janice Terhune.

Kissing Meade, she pulled up a chair and gripped his hand. Revealing that Sandra's parents were on the way, she wept unashamedly, dabbing the tears from Meade's eyes with her handkerchief. "We'll do it together, Meade," she said. "Don't worry about David. I'm explaining the best I can. He'll be here this evening. It's going to be tough because he'll ask questions. It'll be tougher when the Farleys get here."

Meade tried to speak, but the words wouldn't come. He closed his eyes, and tears ran down his cheeks. Janice sat beside him for a while, then slipped from the room.

Meade gave little information to the police. He had been attacked by three men wearing masks and had no idea who they were.

The police had no clues and expected the investigation to

reveal nothing. It was a relief. Beatings—and killings—had been engineered in the past by the likes of Giuliano and Graham, but they had been carried out quietly, with no willing witnesses. The death of the girl made this one especially bad. The last thing Reno needed was for a club owner to be found the guilty party. Let it appear like a grudge beating, a loser lashing out.

Only Charlie and Smitty knew the truth. "I recognized Doug Clausen," Meade said that first day. "He's the one who killed Sandra."

"But you didn't tell the police," Smitty said curiously.

"And I'm not going to. They'll botch it, and Giuliano will go free."

Smitty tilted his hat back and squinted at Meade. "You're not goin' to let them get away with it." A statement rather than a question.

Meade spoke slowly, voice slurred by medication. "It's going to take me a while before I can get around. I'm going to take care of this personally. It's something I've *got* to do."

Charlie and Smitty glanced at each other. If Meade's revenge depended on the use of his legs, it might take forever.

The meeting with Joe and Ellen Farley was more difficult than Meade had imagined. Desperately tired from the long drive, faces drawn with grief, they looked ten years older than when Meade had seen them in Las Vegas.

Meade's secret fear that he would be blamed for Sandra's death was quickly dispelled when Ellen rushed to the bedside and kissed his cheek. Joe couldn't speak. He rested a gnarled hand on Meade's shoulder.

The funeral was held in Reno, and Sandra was buried in a cemetery a few blocks from the brick house where she and Meade had loved. A construction child, Sandra had no hometown. Reno was perhaps the nearest thing.

Meade was unable to attend the funeral. The Farleys left the following Monday. They talked about seeing each other again, but Meade wondered if it would ever happen. The memories would be painful.

Within a few days of the doctor's telling Meade he would

never walk again, the word was all over town. "Guess what," Charlie said. "A guy's been nosing around wanting to buy the club. Says he's from Kansas City. Maybe he is, but I'll bet the money's from Commercial Row."

"Has he named a price?" Meade asked.

"Nope. Just wants to know if we'll sell. Are we interested?"

Meade looked at the far wall, then at Charlie. "I've been thinking. I might be. You with me?"

Charlie's smile warmed the room. "You bet, son. Just say the word."

Three weeks later, the Plush Wheel was sold for $100,000. The following day, an ambulance rolled into the Reno station and backed up to a Pullman car. Meade was carried on a stretcher to a double-bedroom suite, Charlie and Smitty keeping a watchful eye on the proceedings.

At 1:11 P.M., Tuesday, October 6, 1936, the powerful diesel engine rumbled along Commercial Row past Giuliano's Western Club and out of Reno, swiftly picking up speed as it streaked toward the destination for which it was named, the city of San Francisco.

Never seen again, the world was allowed to rot." Guess what?"
he managed. "You're leaning up against something to beat the
clock. Save us a trip to Kansas City. Maybe I'll stay but I'll be
the hammer's from Centerville Row."

"He ad-libbed Vendor," Mindy asked.

"Listen, I just want to know if . . . if I can't . . . we do into a
prayer?"

Mindy looked at the far wall, then at Charlie. "I've been
thinking," I might be . . . you with me?"

Charlie's smile went to the room. "Vendor, you just say
the word."

Three weeks later, the Wurtch Whey worked and he arrived
in the morning after an ambulance rolled over, the hope of home
and backed up to a Pontiac . . . Mindy was carried off a
stretcher to a double ball room smile, Charlie said, settling
leaning a very long pardon the proceedings.

At 11:40 A.M., Doc Jay Dempsey, Esq., the hospital free
lot square grabbed at an Commercial Row East Columbia
Western Club and 60 ... ? . . . Times, while it's up to size. As
it attended . . . good the celebration, or which it was formed
the one pot Santa France...

BOOK TWO

1937-1949

1

"Know any carpenters?" Meade was propped up in a special hospital bed, a whiskey glass clutched in his hand. He and Charlie were having their regular evening drink.

"Tom Bailey's pretty good," Charlie said. "He used to build houses, but with the way things are he's doing odds and ends at the park."

"See if you can send him around tomorrow."

"Okay." Charlie puffed on his cigar. "Ready to get at it, huh?"

"Good a time as any."

They had moved into this house four months ago. It faced the Great Highway and the Pacific Ocean. A mile north was Golden Gate Park and just beyond Chutes-at-the-Beach, where Charlie operated three booths on the midway.

Charlie no longer dressed elegantly, but he hadn't returned to chewing tobacco. He had learned to love cigars.

When they first arrived in San Francisco, nurses had attended Meade around the clock, then only during the day. A month ago, Charlie had returned home to be met by a red-faced nurse. "I will not put up with that man for another day," she snapped at a bemused Charlie. "He curses and does the opposite of everything I tell him. If I let him

117

smoke a little, he smokes twice as much. Today was the last straw. When I took his cigars away, he threw the bedpan at me!"

"It was empty!" Meade roared from the bedroom.

The nurse was paid. Charlie carried the whiskey bottle and glasses into the bedroom. Meade glared. "I ain't saying nothing," Charlie grinned.

"No more nurses," Meade said, reaching for his glass. "Leave things on the nightstand where I can reach them. I can work the bedpan and empty it in a bucket."

"Aw, shit," Charlie moaned.

"I'll save that until you get home."

After a few days, Charlie stopped worrying. Meade was doing a lot of reading and was much more content.

Sipping his bourbon, Charlie studied Meade. He had dropped forty pounds, prominent bones in his face producing a skeletal effect. His once dark skin was pale and unhealthy looking, hair dull and listless. His mind was as sharp as ever, and he had been smiling of late. A good sign.

Not one doctor had offered hope, and several had been consulted since arriving in San Francisco. In time, Meade's legs would wither away until they were lifeless twisted appendages to an otherwise healthy body.

Meade refused to accept the bleak predictions, and Charlie struggled to share his disbelief. But it was hard to ignore the reports. And Meade's condition. He had no feeling below the waist.

Meade never talked about that August night. Sandra's name was never mentioned. Meade hurt deeply, but he also hated. His hate gave him a powerful reason to walk again.

2

"Planning on hanging yourself?" Charlie asked, peering up at the pulleys and ropes that dangled from the ceiling.

Meade shot Charlie an indulgent look. Biting down on his cigar, Meade seized the rings that hung above his head. "Watch this," he said. Straining, veins popping out on his forehead, the long scar there turning red, Meade pulled until his shoulders lifted several inches from the bed. He eased himself down. The cigar fell on his chest, and he batted the hot tip away. "Better leave that out next time," he panted.

"Not bad," Charlie said, getting out the bourbon. He looked down at Meade's sweat-stained face. "You'll get some real workouts on that."

Meade reached for a new cigar. "Hell, this is only the beginning!"

A few weeks later Charlie returned to find Meade displaying a curious device that took up half the bed—a long padded board, hinged in two places. Ropes led from the board up to pulleys, then down to rings.

"Gonna need help," Meade grunted. "Have to get on this thing."

Charlie helped him on the board, lifting Meade's useless legs over the ropes that were attached to the lower section.

Meade scooted down so one hinged section was at his lower back, the other at his knees. He reached up and pulled one set of rings. His hips and legs rose slightly off the bed. Gritting his teeth, Meade slowly lowered the board back on the bed.

He grabbed the other set of rings. This time, the section at his knees was raised. Meade took two pulls, flexing his legs. Breathing hard, he looked up at Charlie for approval.

Charlie didn't have to fake his enthusiasm. Meade's mental and physical condition had improved since he had started exercising with the rings. This new device couldn't hurt, and it offered hope. If everything failed, at least Meade would be better able to accept defeat.

Tom Bailey, the carpenter who had built the "contraption" (Charlie's name for it), took to dropping by when things were slow at the park. Soon, it was an everyday occurrence. He helped Meade on and off the hinged board, adjusted ropes and gave encouragement. When the visits became regular, Meade insisted on paying Bailey. He knew Bailey had a wife and children and was barely getting by. When Bailey protested, Meade swore and slammed the flat of his hand down on the bed. "Damnit, Tom, do you know what those worthless nurses cost me? A hell of a lot more than I'm going to pay you! Now take the money or get your ass out." Tom spent half the day at the park, the other half with Meade.

Meade sweated and cursed and sometimes cried out with pain as he hauled on the ropes that must lift him from his private hell. Charlie shook his head at Meade's accomplishments. By summer, Meade could raise his body up and down on the hinged board for half an hour without raising a sweat. His shoulders, chest and arms hardened into great slabs of muscle. Gradually, his legs regained flesh and tone. Then the miracle happened.

It was mid-July. Charlie arrived to find Tom Bailey standing at the foot of Meade's bed. They were both grinning like idiots. "Show him, Tom," Meade said. "I don't think the miserable carney really thought it would work."

Tom lifted the covers, exposing Meade's toes. "The left one," Meade said. "Watch the left one."

Charlie's jaw dropped. Meade's big toe was moving. It was *moving!*

"My Gawd!" whispered Charlie. "MY GAWD! You did it, boy. You did it!" Charlie carefully grabbed Meade's foot.

"Let me be the first to shake your toe." He looked at Meade affectionately. "You stubborn son of a bitch. You couldn't take no for an answer."

By fall, Meade was moving both feet. The house rang with the sounds of sawing and hammering as Meade prepared for his next offense.

Tom Bailey built a set of rails from the bedroom into the living room. Three feet apart, they allowed Meade to brace himself as he tried to walk. It was tough going, and Meade took many a fall before he could move a few feet from the bed.

Christmas was just a week away when Meade took three tottering steps without the aid of the rails. "Tom," Meade said, sweat pouring down into his eyes, "we'll be walking on the beach by spring."

From the beginning, Meade had laid down an order. No one was to know about his progress. When Janice brought David and Jim to visit every few months, the men played their roles well. Equipment was removed and Meade stayed in bed.

Meade hated deceiving Janice. He trusted her completely, but Janice had to remain innocent and thus protected.

David was nine now, a tall handsome boy with the blond good looks of his mother. Although he enjoyed being with his father, he didn't seem saddened to leave. Meade wondered if he was losing his son.

3

Meade's shout from the kitchen greeted Charlie when he entered the house. "Hey, Charlie! We've got a visitor!"

Smitty sat across the table from Meade. "You old bastard," Charlie said, his face lighting with pleasure. "Meade didn't say anything about you coming."

"Didn't know it myself," Smitty said, brushing his cowboy hat off the table, making a place for Charlie. "Just decided yesterday to hop a train and come down."

Charlie gestured toward Meade, who sat in a large padded chair. "What do you think of our boy?" he said proudly.

"Had to see it for myself," Smitty grinned. "Fuckin' doctors, what do they know?"

This was Smitty's first visit in three months, and Meade's condition had improved dramatically during that time. It was no longer a question of whether Meade would recover, just a question of when.

"I want it to be August," Meade said. "August tenth, to be exact."

"Now, Meade," Smitty reasoned, "you can't set up a thing like this with a certain date in mind. Not this far ahead, at least."

"I know," Meade said heavily. "I just said I'd *like* it to be the tenth." A pause. "I looked it up. It's a Wednesday."

"A slow day," Smitty said. "That's a point in its favor."

Charlie didn't comment, a silent observer. Violence was foreign to his nature. Meade had tried to keep him out of this. Two years ago, Charlie would have asked to be left out. Before Sandra's death. Before Giuliano had nearly destroyed this man he loved like a son.

"I want them both," Meade was saying.

"Should be no problem," Smitty said. "I've been checkin' on and off. Clausen's almost always with him. They always leave about the same time, usin' that little alley."

They discussed the details, going over a map Meade had drawn on a piece of butcher paper. Smitty would get the guns and line up a car.

When Smitty left, he was carrying $5,000 in cash. It didn't seriously dent Meade and Charlie's bankroll. They still had over $70,000 in the bank.

Meade exercised even harder, pulling himself between the rails until he dropped with exhaustion. He graduated to

crutches in February, a cane in April. Later that month, as
they stood on the beach, cold water swirling around their
ankles, Meade looked down at Tom Bailey and said, "The
cane goes next month."

And it did. By July, Meade was walking miles each day in
the sand. He had never felt so healthy, so strong.

One evening, Meade and Charlie were sitting on a sand
dune, waves licking at its base. Charlie broke off a blade of
grass and chewed on it thoughtfully. "I keep worrying," he
said. "Have we left anything out?"

"Not that I know of," Meade said. "We're giving ourselves
plenty of time. I'm aiming for the tenth, but if it's not right,
I'll wait." Meade looked at Charlie. "Wish me luck?"

"All the luck in the world. Sure you don't want your old
uncle to go along for the ride?"

Meade smiled. "Not this trip. We'll be back together again
soon."

The following week, Charlie stood on the sidewalk and
watched Meade and Smitty drive off. He didn't go inside until
the lights of Smitty's pickup disappeared in the fog.

4

Smitty's ranch was fifteen miles north of Reno, at the end of
a narrow dirt road. It suited Smitty, who preferred a solitary
life.

The morning after they arrived, Smitty took Meade down
to the basement. He layed a double-barreled shotgun and an
army Colt .45 on the workbench.

Meade hefted the shotgun. It was a twelve-gauge, big
enough to blow a hole through an elephant.

While Smitty went into town, Meade sawed off the shotgun
barrels, shortening them to twelve inches. Putting the shot-

gun, pistol and shells into a burlap sack, Meade left the basement and went upstairs.

Darkness was falling as Smitty drove into the low hills, the burlap sack resting on the seat between him and Meade. Parking in a small canyon, Smitty gathered wood and started a fire that lighted a fifty-foot area.

Meade slipped two shells into the shotgun. Legs braced, he aimed at a brush cedar and pulled the trigger. A three-inch limb fell to the ground.

Meade rubbed his hand on his pants. "It's going to take practice," he said. "Damn thing almost broke my arm."

Meade worked with the shotgun and the pistol. The last few times, he hung the shotgun over his shoulder by a leather strap and wore a long overcoat.

The next two weeks, Meade read during the day and practiced with the guns at night. Every few days, Smitty went into town for groceries. Then August tenth was just two days away.

The night of the ninth, Meade and Smitty headed into Reno. Adjusting the shotgun strap, Meade checked the shells in the left overcoat pocket, the pistol in the right. Pulling on a pair of tight woolen gloves, he settled a wide-brimmed hat on his head. He picked up a half-empty bottle of wine and waited for Smitty to stop.

Wandering along the railroad tracks like an aimless hobo, Meade crossed to the other side of Commercial Row three blocks east of the Western Club. Several times, he had to step over sleeping drunks that lay across the sidewalk. He sat against a wall at the mouth of an alley, facedown, hugging his knees.

A Ford sedan rattled past, Smitty at the wheel. He parked half a block away.

A freight train thundered by, shaking the ground. Meade shook off a hobo who tried to strike up a conversation. He stole a look at the door at the back of the alley. It had been August tenth for over an hour.

Light splashed on the rough brick surface. A big man stepped out of the doorway and walked toward Meade. A foot crashed into Meade's side. "Move it, bum!" snarled Doug Clausen. Meade scrabbled out of the alley and hunched down on the sidewalk, feet in the gutter. Clausen gave him a passing kick as he walked toward the big LaSalle.

Parking the car in front of the alley, Clausen got out and held the back door open. A squat powerful man emerged from the alley and prepared to get in.

Meade staggered toward the two men, clutching his side as if in pain. "Cocksucker," Clausen lashed out, bunching his fists and advancing on Meade. "I'm gonna bust your ass."

Snapping upright, Meade whipped out the shotgun. He gazed dispassionately at the man he had last seen standing over Sandra's lifeless body.

Clausen's mouth dropped. With a gasp, he reached for his gun. As it came free, the right-hand barrel of the shotgun erupted, tearing a great hole in Clausen's stomach just above the groin, lifting him off his feet and spinning him brokenly into the car.

Wheeling, Meade aimed the gun at the dark man standing petrified by the door, eyes rounded and staring. A child seeing a ghost. "You!" he croaked, eyes dropping to Meade's legs. "But you can't walk!"

"I can walk, Giuliano," Meade said in a calm, almost gentle voice. "I got my legs back, but I'll never get back the girl this scum killed. You have to pay, Giuliano. You understand, don't you?"

The shotgun roared, buckshot expending its full force into Carlo Giuliano's face. Brains, bone and facial tissue splattered redly over the car and into the street.

It was August 10, 1938, exactly two years from the date Sandra was killed.

5

Meade lay low at the ranch while Smitty kept up his normal routine, dropping into town every few days. They had slipped out of Reno quickly, everything going according to plan.

Meade had leaped over Giuliano's body and hopped into the Ford sedan as Smitty braked alongside the LaSalle. As the Ford crossed the tracks, Meade tore off his coat and hat, throwing them in the backseat along with the shotgun. He stuffed the gloves in his pocket.

Parking on 5th Street, they walked to North Arlington and got into the pickup. Smitty lit a cigarette as the lights of Reno faded behind them. "You got 'em both," he said matter-of-factly. "Now you can stop lookin' back."

Meade didn't take offense. Smitty was right. He should look forward now. He laid his head back and closed his eyes.

The Ford sedan was found that night. Like the guns, it was untraceable. "Town's in an uproar," Smitty said when he arrived back at the ranch the day after the killing. "Tony Giuliano has turned the bulls loose on the street. They're comin' down on everybody they think might know somethin'. Tony's put up a ten thousand dollar reward for whoever finds his old man's killer."

"I heard," Meade said, pointing at the radio.

"They've brought in the FBI. The police think the hit was professional, imported talent."

Meade raised an eyebrow. "That I didn't hear."

"Got it from the chief. Lou and me had coffee just before I left."

The investigation came to a dead end. After two weeks, Meade and Smitty figured it was safe to leave.

They drove to Sacramento where they caught a train headed south. Two days later, they arrived in Las Vegas.

6

"Sure we ain't in hell?" Smitty said, standing in the shade of the Apache Hotel and squinting at the heat waves rising from the pavement.

Meade shrugged. "Feels good after the fog in San Francisco." He was dressed once more as he had been at the Plush Wheel—dark western suit, white shirt and black string tie, black boots. The coat was tossed over his shoulder.

Las Vegas had changed little since their visit three years ago. If anything, business had slowed. With the completion of Boulder Dam, thousands of workers had left the area.

Last night, Meade and Smitty had made the rounds, renewing acquaintances and meeting new arrivals to the gambling community. There were surprised looks over Meade's recovery but no direct questions. Meade's injury had been well publicized in the state.

Meade started down the street, a big broad-shouldered man with a massive chest and heavily muscled arms. From under the thick wavy black hair that fell over his forehead and partially covered the jagged scar, pale blue eyes mirrored the pain of experiences unsuited to his years. There was a hardness to his face, but it was softened by a hint of humor on his lips. A good face, reflecting a balance of strength and compassion.

They stopped in front of a shuttered single-story building, standing between an office equipment company and a barber shop. Smitty unlocked the door.

Eyes adjusting to the darkness, Meade scanned the cloth-covered tables and the bar in a far corner. Walking slowly around the room, he looked under sheets, pulled on slot machine handles and ran his fingers through the dust on the bar. He looked at Smitty, who stood in the doorway. "Better than I expected," Meade said.

Smitty flicked his cigarette into the street. "Needs fixin' up. A good operator can make it pay. Nothin' wrong with the location or layout. The guy was workin' on too short a bank-roll."

Meade took a last look around. "Let's see the lot," he said. Smitty handed him the key. Meade locked the door and followed Smitty to a corner lot two blocks away.

Meade walked to the center of the lot, boots kicking up puffs of dust. Hands on hips, he looked up and down Fremont. People were drifting in and out of the stores and clubs. Not many women. Las Vegas was a man's town in the summer, many of the women going to the California beaches to get away from the heat.

Meade walked to the sidewalk and stamped the dust from his boots. "Maybe I should have stayed in bed and let you do the work," he said to Smitty. "You did pretty good without me."

In February, Smitty had purchased the lot for Meade. The club had been picked up by paying the past-due rent, satisfying creditors and giving the former owner $1,000 in cash. All negotiations had been done through a lawyer; Smitty and Meade hadn't been involved.

At the lawyer's office, Meade signed the papers that put the lot in his name. The club's lease and equipment also. Back outside, Meade looked down at Smitty. "Thanks. I owe you."

"Hell," Smitty said, "I'm just goin' along for the ride. Might be interestin'. Come on, want to show you somethin'."

Smitty drove south on the Los Angeles highway, still unpaved and a mess of potholes. Dust and sand swirled across the road and obscured their vision. There was little to see—

rocks, creosote bushes, dried weeds. Three miles from the city limits, they passed the Ambassador Club, once the Pair-O-Dice. As usual, it was closed for the summer.

Smitty slowed and pulled off to the right. "Got seventy-five acres here," he said, pointing. "Got it dirt cheap."

Meade peered through the blowing dust. "Dirt seems to be the right word."

Smitty shot him a pained look. "If you're smart, you'll buy the hundred acres next to mine—won't make a dent in your bankroll."

A long freight train rolled by a half-mile to the west, trailing smoke. Meade shifted his gaze to the bare stretch of land. A car passed, headed toward California, a tumbleweed stuck under the front bumper.

Meade considered Smitty's words. He didn't know what the little man was worth, but it must be considerable. His advice shouldn't be taken lightly.

Wrapping his arms around the steering wheel, Smitty stared down the lonely highway. "Los Angeles is growin' like a weed," he said. "Someday, it'll be twice as big as the San Francisco Bay area, maybe bigger. When the L.A. people want to gamble, they'll come to Vegas. It's a hell of a lot closer than Reno.

"When the war comes—I don't give a damn what Roosevelt says, it'll come—this country will come out of the Depression like a scalded cat. Someday, there'll be forty, fifty thousand people livin' here." Smitty nodded at Meade's incredulous look. "Don't laugh; it'll happen." He waved at his land. "I bought this 'cause people will come through here before they get to Vegas. A club out here will catch a lot of business that will otherwise end up downtown."

Meade threw up his hands. "You've sold me. Let's go buy some real estate."

As they headed back into town, Meade twisted around for a last look. A small dust-devil was dancing its way across the barren landscape. He would have to trust Smitty's judgment. Right now, it didn't look like much of a buy.

One of the first things Meade did was send for Tom Bailey. Bailey was glad to make the move; he was finding little work in San Francisco. He would arrive with his wife and two children next week.

One night, Smitty brought two men to the hotel room. Bob Thompson was five feet ten inches, balding and built like a beer keg. He looked in his late thirties.

Six feet tall and slender, with light brown hair and steel gray eyes, Don Milton was five, six years younger than his companion. He radiated danger, like a coiled rattlesnake.

Quietly, concisely, Meade outlined his needs. Twenty minutes later, the two men shook hands with Meade and Smitty and left.

Meade walked to the window and looked down on Fremont Street. "This isn't going to be easy," he said. "Traipsing around with two bodyguards!" A quick look at Smitty. "You sure this is necessary?"

"Meade," Smitty said sharply, "sometimes you're as stubborn as a Missouri mule. Do you need to get run over by a truck to learn your lesson?" The flashing hotel sign cast a bluish tint on their faces.

Smitty said quietly: "Meade, you're not the kinda guy who's gonna sit still. You're a competitor. Most operators will be content with their little clubs and won't think of branchin' out. Not you. You'll work like hell buildin' this club; then when it's done you'll be bored stiff. So you'll build somethin' bigger. That's the way you are. You'll always be lookin' for new mountains to climb."

Smitty waved a hand. "There are a few operators in

Nevada who'll get wild hairs, like Carlo Giuliano's son, Tony. They'll want to grow, and if you don't fight back, they'll grow right over you. Maybe you don't like the idea of havin' bodyguards now, but I think in time you'll be damn glad you've got 'em."

Meade set his whiskey glass on the sill. "I guess you're right, Smitty," he said heavily, turning away from the window. "It's just that I'm used to taking care of things myself."

"Not anymore. You're gettin' too big for that."

The following three months were busy ones for Meade. While Tom Bailey and a crew remodeled the club, Meade acquired licenses, interviewed prospective employees and performed the myriad duties necessary to the opening of the club.

Choosing the name for the club was easy. For some reason —perhaps as a final insult—Meade's Reno club had been renamed Club Golden. The records showed that the Plush Wheel name and symbol were available. Meade registered both, assuring him of their exclusive use. With deep emotion, he watched workers attach the sign to the front of the building. Once more, the familiar elegant letters surrounded the large ornamental wheel. The gold leaf words, PLUSH WHEEL, brought back a rush of memories. Silently, he vowed to never let the name leave his control again.

The word of Meade's return swept through Nevada like wildfire. It was more than news to one man; it was a revelation. Tony Giuliano's fist crashed down on the desk. "Slaughter!" he shouted. "He's the bastard that did it!"

If Meade hadn't been bedridden, he would have been the prime suspect in the killing of Tony's father. Until now, Tony Giuliano had written Meade off as a defeated man who had left Reno happy to escape with his life.

Tony knew Meade had the motive, but the clincher was the date. August tenth. The same date Slaughter's fiancée had been killed. It was too much of a coincidence—his father being killed on the tenth and Meade reappearing in Nevada shortly after.

"I saw Slaughter with my own eyes, boss," said the man

standing in front of Tony Giuliano's desk. "He's walkin' as good as you and me—bigger and meaner than ever. I ducked out real quick and drove all night to get here."

Giuliano snapped, "Get Dave Follin and take care of the bastard. The ten grand reward will be yours."

"Not me, boss. Slaughter's got Bob Thompson and Don Milton. They don't leave him for a minute." He twisted his hat in his hands. "Between them three, they could stand off an army."

Giuliano studied his fingernails. "Thompson and Milton," he mused. He looked up at the nervous man. "The bastard means business."

The man continued to twist his hat.

Giuliano pulled out a wad of bills, peeling off two large ones and tossing them on the desk. "That's for the information," he said. "Now beat it and let me think."

"Thanks, boss," the man said, snatching up the bills. He hurried downstairs to the casino.

Tony Giuliano leaned back and stared blankly at the wall, dark eyes burning with the same intensity his father's had. At thirty-two, Tony was a stamped-out version of his father— dark, squat, powerful. He had taken up the reins of his father's empire with a confidence born of strength rather than inheritance. He had the complete allegiance of the small army of men that worked in the Western Club and other business enterprises, such as the Cribs down by the Truckee River where two dozen prostitutes toiled and sweated to make him rich.

Tony Giuliano considered the problem of Meade Slaughter. "Patience is somethin' you gotta learn," Carlo Giuliano had once told his hot-tempered son. "If you got a job to do, do it. If it can be done right away, good. If it takes a little longer, that's okay, too. The important thing is to do it right. Do it right, and you don't have to do it over again."

"Well, Papa," Tony Giuliano said to the empty office, "we didn't do it right the first time. Next time, it'll be done right —if it takes me the rest of my life."

8

The Las Vegas Plush Wheel opened on November 8th. "Just like old times," Charlie said, puffing on a big cigar and watching the crowd.

"You look pretty good in that suit," Meade said. "Glad to be back?"

"Didn't know I missed it so much."

Smitty weaved his way across the room, followed by Jim Cashman. "Real nice, Meade," Cashman said. "Keep this up and you'll have to buy a new car to fit the image."

"Well, I'll know who to go to for one, won't I?" Meade grinned.

"How's Reno?" Charlie asked Smitty. Meade knew Charlie missed the town.

"Movin' along," Smitty said. "They come and they go. Got a guy named Bill Harrah who ain't doin' bad. He opened a bingo parlor on Center Street last year—went bust after two months. Came back this July and started up on Commercial Row. Bought the Tango Club on Virginia last week. Looks like he'll do okay. He's a long drink of water, thin as a rail." He looked at Charlie. "Thought you might know him."

"Me? How come?"

"He used to run a bingo game for his dad in Venice, near L.A. Thought you might have bumped into him in your travels."

"Nope."

Smitty glanced at Cashman. "He was smart to come to the big city instead of this little ol' town."

"Ha!" snorted Cashman. "We've got eight thousand peo-

133

ple here. You may have us beat in size but not in ambition. Give us time, we'll choke you in our dust!"

Smitty peered at Cashman, faded blue eyes twinkling. "One thing you'll never be, and that's spelled s-o-p-h-i-s-t-i-c-a-t-e-d."

"Surprised he knows how to spell it," muttered Cashman, determined to get in the last word.

During the Christmas vacation, the Terhunes brought David down for a visit. Meade had spoken many times with Janice and Bob on the phone and they had known of his recovery for months, but it was still like a miracle to see him walking again.

Leaning back in Meade's arms, Janice looked up at him through happy tears. "You big lug," she said affectionately, "you wouldn't listen to anyone, would you? Just went out and showed 'em!"

Meade had a mild shock of his own. David had gained three inches in height since he had last seen him. Next April, David would be eleven, and the top of his head already reached Meade's shoulder. It was a cautious meeting; father and son had seen little of each other during the last two years. Meade wished he could have the easy relationship with David that existed between his son and Janice. He silently vowed to spend a lot of time with David when he came to live in Vegas after school was out next June.

Meade and Bob Terhune discussed politics and the strong possibility of war in Europe. Nothing was said about Carlo Giuliano's death; if Terhune suspected anything, he wasn't talking about it.

Las Vegas received a boost of sorts in 1939 when Clark Gable's wife, Rhea, came there for a divorce. The Chamber of Commerce wasted no time taking advantage of the event. Five hundred dollars were allocated for the biggest publicity campaign in the chamber's history. Pictures were taken of Mrs. Gable riding horseback and playing golf, swimming in Lake Mead and climbing Mt. Charleston. The pictures, along with quotes from Rhea Gable about what a wonderful place Las Vegas was, were sent to one hundred of the country's

leading newspapers. Las Vegas was letting the country know
that Reno, the divorce capital of the world, had an aggressive
and worthy competitor.

In October, 1940, Meade started construction on the corner lot down the street. Tom Bailey was the prime contractor.

Fremont Street was becoming a beehive of activity, and the
gambling clubs might have stretched on there forever if the
powers of booze and friendly persuasion hadn't been used on
Thomas E. Hull by two zealous town boosters.

9

When Jim Cashman and Robert B. Griffith, Secretary of the
Las Vegas Chamber of Commerce, heard that Tom Hull, a
hotel man out of Palm Springs, was in an inebriated state in
Bakersfield, California, they rushed over to that little farming
community and whisked Hull across the border and into the
Apache Hotel.

Sometime during that long night, Griffith went home,
but Cashman continued to match Hull drink for drink, determined to at last persuade the hotel man to build in Las
Vegas, something Hull had been considering for two years.
Lightning flashed over Mt. Charleston in the distance as
the two men sat in easy chairs on the Fremont Street sidewalk, talking, arguing, regularly refilling their glasses from
the bottle resting between them on the pavement. At 4
A.M., they rose unsteadily to their feet and shook hands.
Hull had agreed to build a hotel on Highway 91 just south
of the city limits. He would pattern it after his El Rancho
hotels in Fresno and Sacramento; it would be called the El
Rancho Vegas.

Hull purchased thirty-five partially wooded acres for
$5,000 and arranged a loan through the First National Bank

of Las Vegas. His motor hotel and casino would be elaborate and expensive; $300,000 was a lot of money in 1940.

On February 21, 1941, Meade opened the new Plush Wheel on Fremont Street. Bob Terhune officially launched the club by spinning the huge roulette wheel that stood near the entrance; it had been designed as an exact replica of the early Reno Plush Wheel sign.

Slot machines ringed the room with table games in the center. A long bar ran along the back wall—dark mahogany with stools covered in rich brown leather.

Upstairs, a bingo parlor—seating one hundred—took up three-quarters of the space, offices the rest.

Less than two months later, on April 3rd, the El Rancho Vegas opened to a huge splash of publicity.

A special preview opening was held on April 1st, with 590 invited guests attending, many from towns along Highway 91 —from Barstow, California, to St. George, Utah. Hull arrived in western clothing at the height of the party to welcome the crowd, and the evening wound up with a community sing.

The El Rancho was a sprawling complex with stone and stucco exteriors and cedar shake roofs. From the main lobby and casino, sixty-three bungalows branched off to the back and sides. A windmill rose above the administration building; when everything was completed in six weeks to two months, the windmill would have whirling neon-lighted blades.

Seven acres of trees and shrubs were still in the process of being planted, and a large swimming pool sparkled in the sun. Luckily, the El Rancho sat atop a huge underground artesian lake; it consumed 10,000,000 gallons of water a month.

"Come as you are," was Hull's advertising theme, and the people came, dropping cash on the El Rancho's tables that would have otherwise ended up downtown.

Not all the visitors to Las Vegas that summer were welcome. "Boss," said Bob Thompson, "Sedway's downstairs. He wants to see you."

Meade leaned back in the chair and rolled the long cigar

around in his fingers. "Okay," he said to Don Milton. "Bring him up."

The news of Moe Sedway's arrival in Las Vegas last week had spread fast. Sedway was an outsider, a representative of the eastern mob.

Sedway was in Vegas to set up the Trans-America Wire Service. Trans-America was challenging the Continental Press Service, which handled virtually all the bookmakers west of Chicago, including Las Vegas. Meade had not yet set up a bookmaking operation, but it was under consideration.

Sedway, a small man, followed Thompson into the office. Thin black hair met in a widow's peak over a sloping forehead, batlike ears and a thick nose looking as if they had been intended for a much larger man. He had quick movements and watery dark brown eyes.

Ignoring the outstretched hand, Meade waved Sedway to a seat in front of the desk. Sedway lit a cigar and perched on the edge of the chair.

"What can I do for you?" asked Meade.

Sedway laughed and said in a high nasal voice, "I think you got it backwards. I'm here to do somethin' for you! I been sent out here to arrange a wire hookup with Trans-America. You could do real nice with us."

"But I don't have a racebook," Meade said mildly.

"You will. You will! It's perfect for an operation like this." Sedway leaned closer, chewing on his cigar. "There's waits between races. What are your customers goin' to do? They're goin' to play the tables and slots. You get business both ways!"

Meade said, "The town's already got a wire service. It's worked good enough so far."

"Them bums!" cried Sedway. "They don't know nothin'. They're a bunch of assholes." Pulling the cigar from his mouth, he jabbed it at Meade. "We got a goin' operation in Arizona, and we're moving into California. We'll be so big Continental will fold. You need to get in on the winnin' side now!"

Meade lit another cigar and studied Sedway. "What will your service cost me?" he said softly.

Sedway said eagerly, "I want just a little piece of the action."

Meade's look was deceptive. "You mean we pay you for the service—then give you a little extra as a bonus."

"Yeah," Sedway said brightly. "That's it!"

"And why should we do that, Mr. Sedway?" Meade said with an inquiring look on his face. "Why should we give you a bonus?"

Sedway's eyes were almost crossed with concentration. Meade's reaction had him confused. He had heard that this big man sitting behind the desk was tough as nails. Hell, he was a pussy cat!

"You give me a bonus," replied Sedway, "because I give you protection."

"Protection from what?"

"Why—hell, from jerks like that Continental bunch. They ain't goin' to like it when we move in."

Meade rose, startling Sedway, who leaped to his feet. Meade said, "I'll have to think about this. I may not even put in a racebook."

Sedway bounced up and down on his toes. "But you'll go with us if you do—right?"

"No," said Meade. "I didn't say that."

"You better," Sedway rasped out.

"Are you threatening me?" Meade asked.

Sedway was tired of playing around. "Call it what you want," he snapped.

"I'll tell you what you can do," said Meade, voice suddenly cold, "you can get out of my club and don't ever come back!"

Sedway was apoplectic, spittle flying all over the desk. "You don't talk to me like that!" he screamed.

In a flash, Meade was around the desk. Grabbing the lapels of Sedway's coat, he lifted the spluttering little man high against the wall. Sedway dangled in Meade's grip like a bug-eyed monkey on a clothes hook.

Meade's voice was sharp and clear, like the sound of a

hammer striking an anvil. "Get out of my sight, little man,"
he said, casually tossing Sedway toward the open door.
Thompson handed him his hat as he went out.

"Got a nice touch, boss," Milton said admiringly.

"So has Sedway's boss," said Meade.

Milton nodded. "Siegel's been in California about four
years. He's big there—gambling, narcotics, broads. He wants
to get bigger. They say he likes Vegas."

Sitting down, Meade put his feet on the desk. His words
were calm, measured, uncompromising. "I'm running a
clean, honest store. That's the way it is. That's the way it
stays. You men are here to help me protect what's mine. That
means you're siding with me against Bugsy Siegel. If you
want out, now's the time to do it."

"We'll stick," Milton said. "Bob 'n' me talked this thing
over when Sedway hit town. We're with you."

Meade grinned. "I'd have been surprised as hell if you had
backed out."

Sedway continued to push Trans-America in Las Vegas,
but he never came near the Plush Wheel again.

Most Vegans thought R. E. Griffith, a Texas theater
owner, was out of his mind when he purchased thirty-five
acres for a hotel a little over two miles south of the El Rancho
on Highway 91. In most Vegans' minds, one hotel was all the
traffic could bear.

Club 91, once the Pair-O-Dice, then the Ambassador Club,
was on the site Griffith bought. Guy McAfee had come up
from Los Angeles in 1939 and tried to make a go of the place
as Club 91. Like others before him, he had failed. Griffith
planned to incorporate Club 91 into the design of his new
hotel.

Griffith had been planning a hotel in Deming, New Mexico, when he stopped off in Las Vegas on his way to California to buy materials. After he and his architect nephew, Bill
Moore, took a look around, Deming was forgotten.

On the morning of December 7th, Bill Moore was driving
toward Las Vegas with the plans for the Last Frontier Hotel
when he heard on the car radio that the Japanese had bombed

Pearl Harbor. He didn't know it then, but he was also hearing about the biggest boost to the Las Vegas economy yet.

Even without World War II, Las Vegas was slowly coming awake. More than 800,000 tourists visited the area in 1941. After seeing Boulder Dam and Lake Mead most gave the gambling clubs some play.

Reno boomed in 1941. It seemed that Californians had suddenly become aware of the "Biggest Little City in the World." They streamed over the Sierras to try their luck.

The really lucky ones were the club owners. Tony Giuliano doubled the size of the Western Club. Harolds expanded in every direction. Bill Harrah added the Reno Club to his growing business.

It was the beginning of a new era.

10

It was a bright cold January morning, a little over a month after Pearl Harbor. Bob Thompson parked the car in front of the Plush Wheel; Milton and Meade got out and stood on the sidewalk. Digging fists into the small of his back, Meade looked up and down Fremont Street; it was already lined with cars.

When the war broke out, Vegans feared that business would slump as the result of gas rationing. That worry was quickly set aside.

Meade followed Milton into the club, Thompson close behind. Charlie waved from behind the bar; playing bartender was his favorite pastime.

Meade sat on a stool while Charlie poured two cups of coffee. "How're things at the ranch?" Charlie asked.

"Just like home on the range," Meade grinned. Last summer, Meade had bought a ten thousand acre ranch fifte miles west of town. The prime reason for the purchase was David.

David hadn't come to live with Meade in the summer of 1939 as planned. Because Meade's work had been so demanding, it had been decided to wait another year. That, too, was postponed. It was not until the spring of 1941 that Meade began to plan seriously for David's arrival. He knew it could be put off no longer; he and his son were becoming strangers.

The problem of housing was the first consideration. Meade was living in a hotel; that certainly wouldn't do.

"Why don't you buy a little ranch?" Janice suggested over the phone.

"A *ranch?*" Meade yelped. "Janice, have you been drinking?"

"No, Meade darling," she said sweetly. "I've heard about some good buys down there; you can't lose buying good range land. But most important, you'll be providing a home for David. I don't have to tell you how tough this transition will be for all of us."

"I know; I think about it all the time. Hate to admit it, but I'm scared. Know what I mean?"

"I sure do," Janice replied in an assured, understanding voice. "That's where a nice place in the country will help. David's nuts about horses. Frankly, he's a better rider than any of my kids. It's going to be pretty rough if you put him in one of those dusty little houses downtown."

Meade groaned. "Do I have to become a rancher?"

Janice laughed. "You don't have to do anything, Meade. It would just be kinda nice if you did. Tell you what, how about me coming down and looking around for you? I'm an old hand at property buying."

In less than six weeks, Meade was a cattleman. Janice found an excellent working ranch, complete with three hundred head of cattle. A crew of four moved the beef, tended fences and performed the chores.

Janice brought David and her youngest son Jim down in June and stayed in the ranch house two weeks, smoothing the way for father and son. Even with her help, it was a difficult time. When Janice left, Meade felt like he was a stranger, tearing a thirteen-year-old boy from his mother's arms.

As time passed, things got a little easier. But Meade knew that life must be dull for David; he was used to the hustle and bustle of the Terhune home and Reno. Having his own horse helped, and David spent most of his time with the ranch hands. The Mexican housekeeper wasn't much company; besides, she spoke little English. When school started in the fall, David made new friends, but the remoteness of the ranch wasn't conducive to frequent visits. Meade tried to spend time with David but found it difficult to get away from the club. Not the best of arrangements, but Janice agreed with Meade that a son needed a father.

While Meade and Charlie talked at the bar, the sound of hammering and sawing drifted down through the ceiling. The club was being tripled in size. Tom Bailey was adding three stories, the top two to be a hotel. They were also expanding out over the parking lot. A lounge and entertainment stage were being built on the third floor.

Gambling clubs never closed for remodeling; they stayed open as if nothing were amiss. It was a way of life in Nevada.

Slot machines whirred and roulette wheels spun to the rhythm of jackhammers. Players ignored crumbling ceilings and showering dust. Walls came and went. Rows of slot machines disappeared only to reappear across the room. Later, they would be replaced by a poker parlor. It was like a mad game of musical chairs. If you were away from the bar too long, you might return to find a craps table in its place.

Meade leaned on the bar and said quietly to Charlie, "Got a call from Smitty last night. The Chase Building is out. Harolds is taking part of it; they've got an option on the rest."

Charlie couldn't keep the disappointment from his voice. "So that's it," he said gloomily. Charlie was going to run the new Reno club, but first they had to find a location.

"Nope," smiled Meade. "Best thing that ever happened."

"Tell me," Charlie said impatiently.

"The Harding Building is available. It's bigger and can be

fixed up easier. The Chase is better for Harolds because it's right next door; otherwise, I think they'd have taken the Harding."

"When did it go on the market?" asked Charlie. "I thought the Harding family didn't want to sell."

"It's not on the market yet. Bob Harding told Smitty yesterday. He and his wife are breaking up, and he needs settlement money. His brothers said they'd go along with the sale."

"How much?"

"Two hundred thousand. Cash. What we don't have and can't borrow from the bank, Smitty will loan. That cagey old prospector's got more money out than a fucking bank."

Their Reno attorney handled the paperwork. Nevada Investments, Inc., a corporation totally owned by Meade and Charlie, purchased the building for $185,000. Remodeling would begin as soon as Tom Bailey could get away from the expansion work on Fremont Street.

During that early part of 1942, Moe Sedway made the big move. Access to the wire service—available to any club that paid the fee—was cut off completely. Anyone who wanted to make book, and it was impossible to do so without a wire service, had to give Sedway a piece of the action. The clubs fell in line. Sedway was off and running.

11

"Bugsy's at the Apache," Milton said. "Marty saw him go in about an hour ago."

"Wonder if he'll come here," said Charlie.

"No way," said Milton. "I knew Siegel back east. He's a tough son of a bitch—I'll give him that—but when he moves, he wants the odds in his favor. When he looks at us, the numbers don't come up right."

"It's all this growth that's attracting bastards like Siegel," said Meade. "They say Carson City's going to set up a commission to supervise gambling. As far as I'm concerned, the sooner the better."

The 1931 legislature had legalized gambling in Nevada and established county fees based on the number of games operated in each club. The revenues were allocated to the state, counties and towns. Though legal, licensed and taxed, the gambling industry was not regulated by enforcement at the state level.

Charlie said to Milton, "I'm curious. What's Siegel like?"

Milton scratched his chin. "He's no dummy. A real snappy dresser. Good looking, too. The way he laughs, you'd think he's the sweetest guy alive. Don't believe it. He's got a real short fuse—a temper that goes off like a bomb."

"He didn't get where he is selling Bibles," commented Meade.

"He ran with Lucky Luciano," said Milton. "Had connections with Dutch Schultz and Capone. He's been around."

That Saturday night, Meade, along with Milton and Thompson, was making his habitual rounds of the clubs to check the action. As he entered the El Rancho lounge, Milton nudged him toward the left. "Don't look now, boss," he said quietly, "but Siegel's here."

After they had ordered drinks, Meade lit a cigar and looked around. In a far corner sat a group of men. Meade recognized Sedway and a downtown club owner. Sedway was talking excitedly to a strikingly handsome man. Smiling and waving away Sedway's obvious objections, the man stood and walked toward Meade's table.

Siegel was slim with dark hair and moved with the effortless grace of a natural athlete. He was wearing an expensively tailored pin-striped gabardine suit and alligator shoes.

Siegel looked down at Meade. "Mr. Slaughter," he said politely, "can we talk a few minutes?" He glanced at the two bodyguards. "Alone?"

Meade nodded at Thompson and Milton. They picked up their drinks and moved to a table out of earshot.

Sitting down, Siegel thrust a hand across the table. "My name's Benjamin Siegel, Mr. Slaughter. My friends call me Ben."

Meade shook his hand. "Meade Slaughter," he said.

Siegel lit a cigarette. "Nice little town you've got here. I like it. Might live here someday." His voice was soft, but there was a challenge in his eyes.

A cocktail waitress approached the table. "Buy you a drink, Mr. Siegel?" Meade said.

"Ben," Siegel corrected. He looked up at the girl. "Honey, bring my glass from the table over there." As she hurried off, he smiled at Meade. "I'm still workin' on a full one, but I'll let you buy me a drink the next round."

Meade picked up the thread of the earlier conversation. "Vegas is a nice little town," he said. "I've made it my home. I'd hate to see it messed up."

Siegel surprised Meade with his candor. "By someone like me?" he said, smiling widely.

Meade couldn't help but laugh. "Maybe, Mr. Siegel."

"Ben," Siegel said. "Look, I'll call you Meade; you call me Ben. Okay?"

"Can't do any harm."

Siegel leaned forward on the table. "I won't deny it," he said earnestly. "There's been talk around town about you and me knockin' heads. I say bullshit! We're both businessmen. You've got your way of operating; I've got mine. We both want the same thing—to make dough. Right?"

Without waiting for Meade's reply, Siegel continued: "This town's big enough for both of us. Know why? 'Cause it's goin' to get bigger!" Eyes widening with excitement, Siegel rapped his knuckles on the table. "I've been around. I've got a nose for money, and this place makes my nose twitch like a rabbit's. The war's makin' this country boom. Lots of yokels movin' to L.A. to work ain't never goin' to go back home. The whole L.A. area's goin' to bust its seams. A lot of those people are goin' to come to Vegas to try their luck. Millions of suckers will be leavin' their dough here!" When Siegel said, "millions," his eyes grew big as saucers. All they lacked were dollar signs flashing on and off.

Finishing his drink, Meade signaled for the waitress. After he ordered, he turned back to Siegel. "Vegas will grow," Meade said. "Nevada will grow. If I didn't believe that, I wouldn't be here. I'm not afraid of competition; the Constitution gives us the right to compete." Meade bounced ice around in his glass with a finger. "Matter of fact, I like competition. Adds spice to life. Gives you a chance to win and beat on your chest. Like a gorilla that beats its opponent and drags the female off into the jungle."

Siegel chuckled. "You're talkin' my kind of language, Meade." A boyish grin brightened his face. "Know somethin'? I like you!"

Meade felt the power of that winning smile; he wondered how many had been so charmed just before they were shot full of holes.

Meade chose his words carefully. "If I'm honest with myself, I have to admit I'm a selfish man; most of my thoughts are centered on my business, my future.

"I'm not really interested in what the other guy does, as long as it doesn't affect me." Meade leaned back in his chair and looked directly into Siegel's eyes. "If you want to open a club next to mine, that's *your* business. I believe in the survival of the fittest. Keep it clean, so will I. You do good, I'll benefit. That works both ways."

Laughing loudly, Siegel exclaimed, "Meade, we're gonna get along fine!" People stared, especially the men at Sedway's table across the room. "Son of a bitch!" Siegel slapped the table with a loud crack of his open palm. "Let's join up. We can own this whole damn state!"

Meade smiled and shook his head. "Thanks, but no thanks. I'm a loner. I like doing things my way."

Siegel said, eyes twinkling, "Yeah, I know."

Meade looked at his watch. "I've got to get back to my club."

Siegel rose and held out his hand. "Let's shake, Meade. Hell, we got better things to do than fight."

They shook hands and went their separate ways.

12

"Welcome back," Smitty said with a broad grin. They stood under the arching sign that spanned Virginia Street, proclaiming, RENO, THE BIGGEST LITTLE CITY IN THE WORLD.

"Wonder if everyone's as friendly as you are," Meade said drily, stretching tired muscles that had cramped during the long train ride from Las Vegas.

"Friendly town, friendly people," said Smitty. " 'Course, like any town, we've got a few ornery folk."

"I bet," said Meade, glancing down Commercial Row where the huge Western Club faced the railroad tracks.

"Speakin' of ornery folks, we kinda miss Graham and McKay. They may be a little mean, but they did things in style."

"Nine years and an eleven thousand dollar fine each. It could have been a lot worse. They've got three years out of the way now; bet they don't do the whole nine."

"No bet," grunted Smitty.

Meade and Smitty crossed Virginia Street to a building fronted by a wooden safety tunnel that covered the sidewalk. Tom Bailey met them as they entered through a rough plank door. "A little noisy in here," he shouted above the pounding of hammers and the roar of power equipment. "Haven't had a quiet day in weeks. We're working twenty-four hours a day."

For the next hour, they toured the four floors of the Harding Building. The opening of the Reno Plush Wheel was set for three months from now—hopefully, for New Year's Eve.

That night, Meade was sitting in a bar off Douglas Alley when Eddie Sahati came in. Sahati and his brother, Nick, owned the Normandie Club near the airport and the Stateline Country Club on the south shore of Lake Tahoe.

Eddie Sahati was a powerful man, six feet tall and over two hundred pounds with jet black hair. A Syrian and—according to Harold Smith—the absolute, ultimate gambler, Sahati had come to Reno by way of San Francisco where he had been a bookie. Like Meade, he never went anywhere without two bodyguards. When Sahati joined Meade, his men sat with Thompson and Milton. The four men kept close watch at a nearby table.

Meade and Sahati had just completed their first round of drinks when Tony Giuliano walked in with three men. Chairs scraped; Thompson and Milton straightened, eyes glued on Giuliano.

Tony Giuliano was halfway into the room before he spotted Meade. He turned to leave.

Jumping up, Sahati hurried to Giuliano's side. While Meade watched, the two men argued quietly. Leaving Giuliano, Sahati walked quickly over to Meade.

"Meade," he said in his surprisingly soft voice, "I've been telling Tony that you two ought to get together. You ought to patch up whatever is between you." Tapping his thick chest, Sahati added, "I said I would sit in. You know you can trust me. What do you say?"

Meade glanced at Giuliano, who was glaring at him from across the room. Meade ground out his cigar and looked up at Sahati. "Oh, what the hell, Eddie," he said resignedly, "tell him it's okay."

While Sahati was talking to Giuliano, Meade got up and told his men what was going on. He arrived back at the table at the same time as Sahati and Tony Giuliano.

The two sworn enemies sat down without a word. Sahati ordered drinks. When they arrived, the men drank silently.

Sahati cleared his throat. The two men looked at him expectantly. "I stuck my neck out tonight," began Sahati, "because it's a bad thing that's going on between you two."

He swiftly raised a hand. "I don't know what it is, and I don't want to know. Pretty soon, you're going to both have clubs in Reno. I don't expect you to become friends, but I think you can learn to live in peace. We owners don't want action that's bad for the image."

Meade and Giuliano stared at Sahati, glanced warily at each other, then looked down at their drinks. Meade shook his head and said to Sahati, "Shit, Eddie, this isn't going to work."

Sahati's face suddenly turned red with anger. "Why the hell not?" he snapped. "Are you going to give each other some kind of disease?" Sahati's voice rose an octave. "Maybe you're both fuckin' afraid!"

"I'm not afraid," muttered Tony Giuliano. "I'm not sure I want to talk."

Swirling his drink around in the glass, Meade said quietly to Giuliano, "I think all Eddie wants to hear is that we'll both forget the past. I've got no quarrel with you. It's all right with me."

Hands flat on the table, Tony Giuliano stared open-mouthed at Meade, lips trembling as he fought a losing battle for control. With a scream of rage, he bounded to his feet, kicking the chair away. The bodyguards leaped up, guns drawn while patrons hit the floor. "You goddamn bastard," yelled Giuliano, shaking his fist at Meade. "Sure it's all right with you. It's *my* father who's dead!" Giuliano slowly backed away from the table.

Sahati sat quietly, both hands on the table. Rising, Meade slipped a hand under his coat. Milton's voice floated across the room. "Don't do it, boss. We've got things under control."

Meade stared coldly at Tony Giuliano. *Sure your father's dead,* Meade thought. *But so is Sandra.* Giuliano clinched and unclinched his fists, shaking with silent fury. Bunching around him, his friends hustled him out the door.

Returning their guns to their holsters, the bodyguards sat down. Overturned chairs were uprighted, and excited voices filled the room. Several men made a fast exit; in an hour the whole town would know.

Meade sat down. "Hell, Eddie," he said, "I'm sorry."

"Bad for business; bad for business," intoned Sahati.

Sticking to Meade like glue, Thompson and Milton moved him swiftly to his hotel room. Meade smoked a cigar and read the paper, then went to sleep.

Don Milton stuck his head in the door the next morning. "Somebody to see you," he said. "Senator Terhune." He stepped aside, and Bob Terhune walked in, face tight with anger.

"Bad news gets around fast," Meade commented drily.

Terhune didn't bother shaking hands. "Damn right," he said sharply. "It's just lucky that I happened to be in town. This thing could have been out of control by tonight."

Meade adjusted his tie and watched Terhune intently.

Bob Terhune looked every bit the powerful U.S. Senator he was. His voice cracked with authority as he pointed a long bony finger at Meade. "I've been your friend for over twenty years, Meade," he said, "but that doesn't mean shit right now. I've got a lot of interests, but the biggest one is this state. I'm fighting in Washington so we can keep our gambling while you're doing your damnedest to put us back in the horse and buggy days!"

It was Meade's turn to get angry. "Look here—"

"I'm not through yet," interrupted Terhune, fists on hips, jaw outthrust. "Not by a long shot!" He shook his big frame. "Have you any idea how many people would like to shut us down? One hell of a lot! If enough get together, they can do it. All they need is an Old West shootout in a Reno saloon between two owners. That's all they need."

"Aw shit," Meade said disgustedly, sitting down on the bed.

Pulling up a chair, Terhune sat down in front of Meade. "I've talked to Eddie Sahati," he said in a calmer tone, leaning forward, hands clasped. "He told me what happened. So Giuliano made the first move. That wouldn't make any difference in the headlines. The goddamn preachers would be pounding the pulpits from California to Maine."

Terhune rubbed his big knuckles. "For your information, I've already been to see Tony Giuliano. I told him the same thing I'm going to tell you." Terhune sat up straight, eyes suddenly cold. "You cause trouble in my state, and I'll run your ass out so fast you won't know what hit you. Friendship won't mean a fucking thing."

Terhune sighed and made a despairing gesture. "Meade," he said quietly, "when you pulled off that miracle in San Francisco and came back to Nevada, it didn't take me long to put two and two together. What happened to you and Sandra was nasty business—terrible! After Carlo Giuliano got killed, I asked myself what I would have done had I been in your place." He paused and took a deep breath. "I might have done the same thing. You did it nice and clean, and it's all in the past. All I ask is that you back off and leave Tony Giuliano alone. He told me he'd go along. What about you?"

Meade nodded and smiled at his friend. "Sure, Bob. That's what I told Giuliano at the club. You can count on me."

Terhune stood and slapped Meade on the back. "Come on, you son of a bitch," he said heartily. "You can buy me breakfast. You owe me something for all this trouble."

A few blocks away, Tony Giuliano paced back and forth in his office, the man sitting in the high wing-back chair following his movements like a spectator at a tennis match. Stopping behind the desk, Giuliano hunched his powerful shoulders, giving the appearance of an angry buffalo. "I'm going after Slaughter," he said slowly, enunciating each word carefully, his voice a low growl. "I'm going after him in a nice, legal, businesslike way—American style. When I get through, he's going to be past history in Nevada."

The seated man rested his chin on steepled fingers, silver hair glinting in the light of the desk lamp. He knew Tony Giuliano was a determined man, just like his father. If Tony decided something, he'd do it or break his back trying. At 36, two years younger than Meade Slaughter, Tony Giuliano had a lot of years with which to accomplish his goal. As Carlo

Giuliano's lawyer, Henry Lawton had wisely guided his client through many pitfalls, legal and illegal. He was serving the son in the same manner.

Tony Giuliano said: "I want you to look into Vegas, Tahoe, any place in Nevada that looks good for business. We'll expand here. I've got more dough than that carnival barker will ever see. I'll grind him," spit out Giuliano. "I'll grind him, and someday I'll own him."

13

Bill Moore greeted Meade and Smitty at the door. "Come to see the big new failure on Ninety-One?" he grinned.

"Yep," said Smitty, easing his way through the crowd that filled the lobby of the Last Frontier Hotel. It was the night of October 30, 1942. Highway 91's second resort hotel had thrown open its doors to the public for the first time just a few hours ago.

"Well, we did it," Moore said, obviously pleased with himself, waving an arm around the huge lobby with its open-beam ceiling, sandstone fireplaces, wagon-wheel lights with Pony Express lanterns and buffalo heads mounted on the walls.

" 'The Old West in Modern Splendor,' " mused Meade, referring to the theme Griffith and Moore had chosen for the Last Frontier. "You sure as hell accomplished that," he said to Moore. "Don't let Hull know I said it, but when it comes to splendor, you've got him beat."

Moore said: "The ones I want to beat are all those locals who told us we were nuts to build out here. Damnit, they can't see beyond Fifth and Charleston! Everybody backed Hull to the hilt. When we announced our plans, they told us that the El Rancho could handle all the traffic on 91, said it

would be years before another hotel could make a go of it.
Didn't give us the chance of a snowball in hell! Know where
I got encouragement? From Siegel, no less! He's heavy in the
Hollywood crowd—runs around with George Raft, Cary
Grant, Barbara Hutton. Hell, Jean Harlow is godmother to
one of his daughters! Anyway, Siegel says that Vegas is going
to become a big Hollywood playground. He says he's going
to build here; I believe him." Moore glanced at the crowd.
"We'll show that downtown bunch; they'll be eating their
words by Christmas!"

"No argument from me," said Meade, cupping his hands
to light a cigar. "Far as I'm concerned, a lot of the downtown
boys have their heads in the sand—and there's a lot of it
between here and Charleston."

Moore said, still obviously upset by the lack of support
from the local merchants and town leaders, "War restrictions
and the static from town made it rough getting supplies.
Thank God we had connections in Texas, but it was a hell
of a long way to truck materials."

Meade smiled and patted Moore on the shoulder. "All's
well that ends well," he said.

Moore nodded and tipped back his big cowboy hat.
"Damnit, I like this town. There's lots of room to grow here,
and I intend to be a part of it. We're after tourists, sure;
without them we're out of business. The whole damn town
is. But first, last and always we're going to cater to the locals.
We're not going to cut off our noses to spite our faces."

"Here, here," said Smitty.

Moore grinned. "Come on, let's do the tour."

They entered the Gay 90's Bar, complete with Texas long-
horns and saddle bar stools, stirrups and all. Smitty ran a
hand along the huge mahogany bar, a gnarled finger tracing
a deep cut. "Looks like the real thing," he said slyly.

"You're not going to bring that up again?" said Griffith,
who had joined them. Meade and Bill Moore smiled at each
other behind Griffith's back; the story about the bar had
reached legendary proportions.

Not long after the railroad auctioned off 1,200 lots on May

15, 1905, and Las Vegas became a town, the old solid mahogany bar had been hauled from San Francisco's Barbary Coast over the Sierras and down to the Arizona Club on Block 16. When Griffith saw the bar, he immediately made an offer. It was scarred with bullet holes and knife cuts and was shiny from nearly a century of elbow rubbing—the perfect piece to add to the collection of collectors' items Griffith and Moore were scrounging up from all over the west. It was agreed that the bar would be delivered when the Last Frontier was nearing completion.

When it arrived, Griffith almost screwed himself into the desert with rage. The bar had been completely refinished. Gone were the bullet holes and knife cuts; it looked like it had just been built.

The bar was left outside and sandblasted, then attacked with knives, followed by bullets fired from pistols and rifles. As the lead flew, so did the story. The bar was given a suitable place in Nevada history.

Moore took Meade and Smitty through the casino. The ceiling was covered with the hides of paint ponies, and paintings of nude women hung on the walls. It was an eye-filling sight, but most of the patrons were too intent on the action at the tables to look.

"We're going western all the way through," said Moore. "The El Rancho thinks they've got something with their riding stable. We're going to have that, too, but wait until you see our stagecoaches. They'll be collecting guests from the Union Pacific and the airport. They want the west—by God, we'll give it to 'em!"

Moore took special pride in the Ramona Room where Gus Martell and his Fifth Avenue Orchestra were playing. "Vegas will be a big entertainment spot someday," he exclaimed. "We're going to be booking a lot of top shows."

Meade was listening, but his mind was on the one hundred acres he owned a half-mile south of the Last Frontier.

14

One month. Had it only been one month? David leaned forward eagerly as the bend of the track revealed the lights of the tiny hamlet of Verdi in the distance. He wondered if Janice was already waiting at the Reno station. No, too early.

Turning from the window, David looked at his father. Meade was stretched out in a lower berth of the private compartment, a file folder on his chest, intently studying several typewritten sheets, flipping the pages back and forth. Unable to contain himself, David blurted out, "We're going to be there pretty soon, Dad!"

Meade sat up and looked at his watch. "Another twenty minutes," he said, smiling at David's eagerness. He kneaded his shoulder muscles; it had been a long ride up from Las Vegas.

They had left at 2:28 A.M. the preceding day on the City of Los Angeles, changing in that city to the Southern Pacific Owl and arriving in Oakland at 8:10 this morning. The Pacific Limited was scheduled to get them into Reno at 9:05 tonight.

David gazed at the darkened window; it yielded nothing but his reflection, but he knew that deep snow covered the Sierras. "The skiing's going to be great!" he exclaimed. "Wish you could come up with Mom and us this weekend." The "Mom" came easy. David had been calling Janice Terhune that for over eight years, ever since Shirley's death.

Meade said, "I wish I could, too, but I'm going to be pretty busy." Busy indeed. After a six-year absence from Reno, the

Plush Wheel was returning, not on the New Year's Eve date originally planned but in the third week of 1943—Saturday, January 23rd.

As general manager of the new club, Charlie had moved to Reno three months ago; he had never liked Las Vegas and was happy to return to the town he had come to think of as home. Mike Doltz, an old-time gambling man from Kansas City now managed the Vegas Plush Wheel.

David wished his dad could spend more time with him. He knew it was impossible this weekend, but there had been other occasions when he hadn't been *that* busy. David had learned to hide his disappointment. How often he had longed for times like that one at Lake Tahoe three summers ago when he was twelve; he had never felt so close to his father . . .

The moon was full—glinting off the white sandy beach near Crystal Bay, upstaging the stars that sprinkled the sky.

"Dad," said David, "when did you buy this place?"

"About four years ago."

"When I was a little kid, huh?"

Meade's teeth flashed whitely in the darkness. "Yeah, when you were a little kid."

"It sure would be nice to have a cabin here," David said wistfully, peering around at the giant pines that framed the beach. "Lots of kids I know stay at the lake all summer."

"Maybe I'll do that someday," Meade said.

David counted on his fingers. "Seven years ago; I was eight." Clutching his fingers, he said, "That was when San—" He looked up, startled. "I didn't mean—"

A moment of total silence, then Meade reached out and ruffled David's white-blond hair. "It's okay," Meade said softly, surrendering to the lure of this special place. "It's okay to talk about her. We probably should have a long time ago. It was just too hard for me at first. I thought maybe you had forgotten her."

"Forget *Sandra?*" David cried. "She was my best friend! We had lots of fun together. I was real happy that she was going to live with us." A small careful smile. "I thought she was going to be my big sister."

Meade's voice was quiet, understanding. "I guess nobody can replace Janice as your mom."

David kicked some bark off the log they were sitting on. "No, I guess not," he said slowly, making circles in the sand with his foot. "But Sandra sure came close."

"This was for her, you know."

"What?"

"This land," Meade said, his waving arm encompassing the five-acre lot. "I bought it as a surprise. I was going to give it to her after the wedding. I asked her to marry me here."

David looked around with renewed interest. "You really liked her a lot, didn't you?"

"A lot. You'll never know how much."

"That was what Mom told me after Sandra di—died. We talked a whole bunch. She thought Sandra was swell, too."

Impulsively, Meade put his arm around David's shoulders. "That's right, David," he said, voice low with emotion. "She was really swell. She loved you a lot."

"I know," said David, nestling closer to his father. "I bet you miss her a lot."

Meade gazed out over the lake, eyes picking out the rock he and Sandra had sat on that warm summer day. "Every day," Meade said quietly. He held his son in his embrace for several long moments, too moved to speak.

They talked until late that night—about a lot of things they had never discussed before. David was ecstatic. His disappointment was almost tangible when he awoke the next morning to find Meade gone, already two hours on his way back to an emergency meeting in Las Vegas. . . .

As the train rolled past Verdi heading toward Reno, David cast a furtive glance at Meade, who was once more engrossed in his papers. David's attitude toward his father was one of near worship. Meade was a godlike figure—bigger than life. David knew that others viewed Meade the same way. Once he had overheard some men talking about the time his father

had killed two men in his Reno club. They had described the
event in awed tones, lesser men according rightful tribute.

Once David had dreamed about following in his father's
footsteps; by the time he reached his mid-teens he knew that
could never be. He'd never measure up. Never.

David had a lot going for him. Already six feet tall, he had
inherited the blond good looks of his mother. That, coupled
with the drowsy gray eyes, left many a teenage girl weak-
kneed and cow-eyed in his presence. He would never have the
massive build of his father, but his lean hard body had earned
him quite a reputation as a hard-driving halfback slicing
through the opposing lines on the football field. David had
the brains and ability to be a good quarterback, but he lacked
the most important ingredient; he didn't like to lead.

David was a follower. It was very important that he be
accepted by his peers, and only in that was he aggressive. He
had seen frowns of disapproval from his father over his eagerness to please his friends. Meade had absolutely no understanding of such behavior. Meade never said anything. Just
those frowns of disapproval. David returned his gaze to the
window and thought about Janice waiting at the station.

On the evening of January 23rd a light snow was falling,
but it didn't dampen the spirit of the crowd that thronged
into the Reno Plush Wheel.

The four floors of the remodeled Harding Building contained three craps tables, eight 21 tables, a poker and bingo
parlor, two hundred slot machines, keno and several smaller
games such as Chuck-a-Luck and roulette. Also housed in
the building were three bars and two restaurants. The giant
roulette Plush Wheel dominated the entrance.

The din was enormous, the unique sound of the Nevada
casino, a mixture of jangling slots, croupier's calls and
player's cries—all overridden by the constant blaring of the
PA system.

Most of the top help at the club had been imported from
outside Nevada. The casino manager, Israel "Izzie" Silver,
was from Cincinnati, as were three of the pit bosses. A shift
boss and two pit bosses were from Cleveland, others were

from Chicago, Louisville and Miami. This was a pro's game; Meade wanted the best.

Meade had other men lined up. This fall, he was going to begin his most ambitious project yet—a hotel-casino on his land south of the Last Frontier.

Highway 91 had also become Bugsy Siegel's lodestone. Having received the go-ahead from Lucky Luciano to build a gambling palace in Las Vegas, Siegel had recently purchased forty acres a mile south and across the highway from Meade's property. Siegel had been promoting the project to his underworld friends for over a year. With Luciano in prison at Great Meadow in New York, Meyer Lansky, the man who held the purse strings for the mob, had released the money for the land purchase.

Siegel's acreage was still barren wasteland when the newest Plush Wheel opened the following May. Money had been rolling into Las Vegas at an amazing rate; Meade had already paid off the loans on the Fremont Street Plush Wheel. New loans had been negotiated to complete the Highway 91 complex, but the future promised their quick repayment.

The newest Plush Wheel was built on the same pattern as the El Rancho Vegas. One hundred twenty guest cottages surrounded the central building which contained the casino, lounge, restaurants and theater-restaurant. The exterior was a combination of stucco and stone—the stucco white, the stone native.

The interior of the main building featured clean modern lines; Meade didn't pursue the western theme so popular in the area. The lobby was small, a forerunner of the minuscule lobbies that would grace future gambling hotels. All available space was to be used for the casino—the heart and soul of the complex.

Wine-colored carpet covered the casino floor. Six craps tables and twelve 21 tables stood in the center of the big room. There were two roulette wheels and a poker parlor. Slot machines lined the walls and crowded every available space. At the entrance stood the now-famous Plush Wheel.

The opening of the newest Plush Wheel was a gala affair.

Most of the owners dropped in to view the latest addition to the southern outskirts of the city of Las Vegas. Wilbur Clark, who with S. P. Barbash had purchased the El Rancho in March, talked excitedly about the future of Highway 91. He confided that he had plans for a lavish place across the road.

As the war appeared to be winding down, local leaders worried about the losses that might come about with the closing and cutbacks at Basic Magnesium and the Army Air Force base; the population of the town had grown from 8,000 in 1940 to 20,000 in 1944.

Maxwell Kelch, who had come to Las Vegas in 1939 and started radio station KENO the following year, was chosen to head the Chamber of Commerce. He immediately instituted an advertising campaign, using New York's J. Walter Thompson Company to promote Las Vegas. So successful were the newspaper, billboard and magazine promotions that Las Vegas had to maintain a housing office, directing tourists to private homes willing to rent rooms; the local hotels and motor courts couldn't handle the business on peak weekends.

Bugsy Siegel gained another foothold in Las Vegas when his cohorts David Berman, Moe Sedway and Gus Greenbaum purchased the El Cortez Hotel from Marion B. Hicks and Johnny Grayson on March 28th. Hicks and Grayson had opened the 91-room downtown hotel in early November, 1941, to a big splash of publicity.

In November, Franklin Roosevelt was re-elected president for an unprecedented fourth term. The Allies were battling in Europe. In December, General Douglas MacArthur kept his word and returned to the Philippines.

History was also being made by a thin pale-looking crooner who had risen from modest beginnings in Hoboken, New Jersey, to become one of the highest paid performers in the country. Francis Albert Sinatra was destined to become one of the greatest draws for big-time gamblers Nevada would ever know.

15

Bob Terhune leaned on the corral fence and watched David Slaughter cinch down the saddle on a nervous wall-eyed cowpony. David's back muscles rippled under his thin shirt as he put his boot into the stirrup and prepared to mount.

"That kid's grown," said Terhune, looking down at Meade, who was resting on one knee and peering through the rails.

"Hard to believe," said Meade. He glanced up at Terhune. "When I was seventeen, I had already been three years on the road with Charlie."

An eruption of noise and dust drew their attention back to the corral. David was seated on the back of a whirling, twisting, screaming animal that was determined to dispense with its rider. Sand and rocks flew as steel-shod hoofs pounded and kicked. Suddenly, David flew across the corral like a shot from a cannon. Ploughing into the fence, he quickly rolled under the rail to the outside and safety. The riderless horse continued to buck its way around the corral.

A leathery bow-legged cowboy snaked a rope around the animal's neck and twirled the other end around a snubbing post. Quieting down, the horse stood spread-legged, sides heaving.

"Welcome—again," chuckled Terhune, grinning down at David who was stretched out on the ground, elbows in the dust and shoulders propped up, a disgusted look on his face.

Meade lit a cigar and eyed his son. "Ready to give up?"

"Hell no," grunted David. "I'll ride that bastard if it kills me."

"Might just do that," Meade said drily, secretly proud—glad whenever David showed determination and drive.

This was the third time David had been thrown this morning. The horse had been broken once, but that had been years ago. It had been brought off the range last week.

Meade and Bob Terhune headed toward the ranch house while David climbed back into the corral. Meade stopped and watched David pick up his hat and slap it against his leg, raising a small cloud of dust. The old cowboy held the horse's head while David climbed on.

"Stubborn cuss, isn't he?" grinned Meade.

"Wonder where he got it."

They sat on the porch and opened cold bottles of beer. Drinking deeply, Meade observed his friend. Bob Terhune's hair had turned iron-gray, enhancing his already distinguished looks. Last year, he had been re-elected to his second term as U.S. Senator from Nevada. He was a power in both his home state and Washington.

Terhune said, "The state's growing too fast, Meade." Grinding the cigarette stub under his boot heel and resting his feet on the porch rail, he continued: "I'm damn glad the legislature is finally going to set up more state controls. It's more of a money thing than anything else, but it's a step in the right direction.

"Vegas is worried about gangsters moving in. They've got good reason with Siegel and Greenbaum; their backgrounds leave a lot to be desired."

"We need outside talent," said Meade. "None of my top men came from Nevada. The more outsiders we bring in, the more careful we'll have to be. We need an unbiased investigating team. State controlled. Too much chance for graft on the local level."

"The state will get involved," said Terhune. "It'll benefit. More controls call for more revenues. The state should get more from gambling. Their twenty-five percent share of county license fees averages thirty thousand a year. Chickenfeed!

"I'm from the north, but I'm the first to admit that Vegas

can't be controlled by a few men four hundred fifty miles away." The seven tax commissioners—the governor, the chairman of the state Public Service Commission and representatives of mining, agriculture, banking, livestock and business—all lived in the Reno-Carson area. They served without pay, met twice a month and had only two investigators for the whole state.

On May 6, 1945, Governor Vail Pittman signed into law the bill that empowered the Nevada Tax Commission to make rules and regulations governing the conduct of gambling in the state. A one percent tax on gross gambling revenue was levied; it brought in $500,000 the first year.

It was not until 1948 that two metal quonset huts were obtained from the highway department and erected side by side on the grounds of the State Capitol in Carson City, proclaiming the new state headquarters of the Tax Commission. The southern Nevada headquarters was the investigator's bedroom.

The new supervisor and his investigators had a lot to learn, but they learned fast. On one of his first days on the job, Supervisor Bill Gallegher was approached by a newsman complaining about a man running a flat store down the street. Gallegher nodded knowingly, then went to a nearby club and asked a 21 dealer what "flat store" meant. He returned to the quonset hut and wrote, "Crooked gambling joint," in his fast-growing dictionary of gambling terms.

Three days before the atomic bomb was dropped on Hiroshima, Guy McAfee announced plans to build a one million dollar gambling palace on Fremont Street. It would be called the Golden Nugget.

The war over, the lights came back on with a vengeance. The *Las Vegas Age* referred to Vegas as the "Battleground for neon lighting." The popular downtown clubs—the Boulder, Las Vegas Club, Pioneer, Biltmore, Plush Wheel, Frontier, El Cortez, Club Savoy and Monte Carlo—lit up the night, while on the Gay White Hi-Way, as Highway 91 had come to be known, the El Rancho, Last Frontier and Plush Wheel flashed their neon messages to the incoming tourists, competing with smaller clubs like the Grace Hayes Lodge (once the Red Rooster), the Casa Vegas, Val Sneeds, Bon Aire and the Players'.

A smiling piano player with strange mannerisms was entertaining in the Last Frontier lounge. He was paid $400 a week. He called himself Liberace.

Across the highway and a mile south of the Last Frontier, Bugsy Siegel broke ground for his new hotel. He called it the Flamingo.

16

"Hold it a minute," said Meade, leaning forward, looking out the window from the backseat of the car.

Pulling off the highway, Thompson parked on the shoulder. Heavy rain, driven by a violent wind that rocked the car, obscured their vision.

"Nothing much going on," said Milton.

Meade watched as men worked on the concrete forms. "You sure as hell couldn't get me to work in that."

Thompson said, "Siegel's paying fifty bucks a day. Thinking about it keeps those guys warm."

The national wage had nearly doubled during the war, from $24.20 to $44.39 for a forty-eight hour week, but $50.00 a day was unheard of, even for skilled labor. Carpenters, electricians, plumbers and masons fought for jobs on Bugsy Siegel's hotel.

April, 1946, was experiencing the impact of runaway inflation in the United States. From Pearl Harbor to the end of the war, over $100 billion had been saved by the American public. They were now ready to spend it, and goods were hard to find. The black market flourished, despite frantic efforts by Washington to curb it. Nylon stockings sold for five

dollars a pair and recapped tires for twenty. Beef went for a
dollar a pound on the hoof. Cars were purchased with hundreds of dollars in bonuses passed illegally to dealers. Inflation doubled, then doubled again. Nineteen forty-six saw the
cost of living rise seventy-five percent.

Bugsy Siegel started the Flamingo—or the Fabulous Flamingo as he preferred to call it—in the midst of all this
soaring inflation. His original building estimate to Lucky
Luciano and Meyer Lansky in 1943 was one million dollars;
at the present rate it would exceed five times that.

Siegel's backers didn't fall into the category of a normal
lending institution; they had unhealthy ways of voicing their
disapproval.

By the time construction began on the Flamingo, materials
were almost impossible to find. Nearly everything had to be
purchased through the black market. Happily, Lucky
Luciano had influence with the Teamsters Union, so Siegel
was able to receive his supplies.

Rumors spread about truck drivers delivering materials in
the morning, stealing them back at night, then redelivering
them the next day. A risky business, considering Siegel's
reputation. It was said that some rested quietly in the cement
foundations of the Fabulous Flamingo.

Gamblers are a restless breed, and they proved that in
April of 1946. On Highway 91, Sanford Adler took over the
El Rancho, Milo Stoney the Kit Carson Club, Flash Warner
the Bon Aire, Duke Wiley and Eddie Elias the Casa Vegas.
Downtown, Kell Houssels bought the El Cortez from Moe
Sedway and partners.

It was also in April that the Las Vegas city commissioners
considered annexing the southern strip of Highway 91 into
the city. When the owners protested, the plan was dropped
for fear it would discourage further development.

The building on Highway 91 didn't discourage downtown
growth. On August 29th, Guy McAfee's Golden Nugget
opened, proclaiming itself the most lavish gambling palace in
the world. Two days later, Sedway and friends held the grand

opening of the El Dorado Club, located in the Apache Hotel building where Tony Cornero's S.S. Rex had been.

By the fall of 1946, the Gay White Hi-Way was being referred to as "The Strip." Local boosters said that someday it would be more famous than Hollywood's Sunset Strip.

The Hollywood crowd had been flocking to Las Vegas since the El Rancho was built in 1941; now it was the Los Angelenos' turn. So many came to Vegas that one man said, "Las Vegas is the greatest little California town in Nevada."

Sitting in the car, Meade glanced back toward town. A myriad of colored lights blinked on and off. If the messages could have been decoded, they would have undoubtedly spelled, "Money. Money. Money."

17

Meade and Bugsy Siegel sat in the corner of the Plush Wheel lounge. Tinsel and bright bulbs decorated the walls, and a Christmas tree stood on the counter behind the bar.

Siegel was excited. "Goddamn, Meade. Just a few more days!"

Meade chuckled. "I'll be glad when you get that glorified whorehouse open," he said. "Then maybe we can drink in peace."

Siegel grinned. If anyone else had called the Flamingo a glorified whorehouse, they might have been looking down the barrel of a gun. Not Meade. Over the months, he and Siegel had formed a companionship of sorts. Last summer, Siegel had taken to dropping by the Plush Wheel for an evening drink. At times, Meade would join him. Soon, it was a daily ritual.

The two had a little in common. They were about the same age; Meade was forty-three, Siegel forty. In their respective professions, they were successful. There, the comparisons ended. Siegel was a man who lived to control others. Meade controlled himself. Siegel felt that strength in Meade and looked forward to their meetings, like a ship seeking a haven in a storm.

"It's goin' to be grand, Meade, grand!" enthused Siegel. The Fabulous Flamingo was having its opening the day after Christmas, 1946, four days away. Meade and Siegel had argued fiercely about that. Meade had said it was suicide to have an opening between Christmas and New Year, but Siegel wouldn't listen. He *had* to get the Flamingo open, even if it was still uncompleted; he needed money coming in, not out.

Siegel waved his arms expansively. "George Jessel, master of ceremonies! You can't beat that bastard for handlin' a crowd. I talked to George Raft last night. He can't wait to come over and help his old buddy. You're goin' to be one of the first to shake his hand, Meade. Right up front!"

Siegel was certainly going all out for the first night. Joining Raft as official greeter was Jimmy Durante. Xavier Cugat's band would entertain in the big showroom, along with Rosemarie, Tommy Wonder and the Tune Toppers.

Siegel was still waving his arms. "Planes full of the best Hollywood's got! Can't you see it?"

Meade felt that if he closed his eyes he would see hundreds of surplus B-29s circling the Vegas airport, waiting to land and disgorge their celebrity passengers.

The opening of the Flamingo held the undivided attention of everyone in Vegas, especially the club owners. Siegel's hotel could have considerable impact on Las Vegas's future.

The opening was also receiving the attention of another interested group; they were holding a convention thirty-five hundred miles away on the island of Cuba. The meeting was taking place at the Hotel Nacional in Havana.

That fall, the call had gone out to underworld leaders throughout the country that Lucky Luciano would arrive in Havana from exile in Italy in December to preside over a congress of the Unione Siciliana. Delegates began arriving after mid-December, and the convention began on December 22nd. The upper floors of the hotel were set aside exclusively for the delegates' use.

One of the first orders of business at the convention was to recap Siegel's activities in Las Vegas. Meyer Lansky, a boyhood friend of Siegel's, broke the alarming news that outside investors were talking about becoming active in the hotel's management. This was the main reason for Siegel's rush to open the hotel before it was completed.

Lansky also dropped the bombshell that Siegel's girlfriend, Virginia Hill, had made several trips to Zurich. More than three hundred thousand dollars had been deposited in a numbered account. Considering this and the fact that Hill had leased an apartment in Switzerland, it appeared that Siegel had provided himself with a bolt-hole in case of failure in Las Vegas. Lansky believed his old friend was skimming mob money.

The delegates voted unanimously to put out a contract on Siegel. It was decided, however, to wait and see what happened at the Flamingo's opening. If it went well, they might reconsider Siegel's fate.

18

On Christmas Day, the Flamingo stood like an olive-green castle in the midst of a barren desert.

The following morning, the Fabulous Flamingo was surrounded by acres of lush green grass. Flower gardens bloomed, and shrubs dotted the landscape. Fully grown date trees and rare cork trees from Spain were scattered throughout the grounds. It seemed that Siegel was more than a prophet; he was a miracle worker, too.

Meade and Smitty leaned against the car. "Shit fire and

save matches!" exclaimed Smitty. "If I hadn't been here last night, I think the shock would have killed me."

Last night, they had watched the crews hurrying about the hotel grounds. Working under a battery of lights, a small army of men had spread truckloads of rich top soil, shaped and terraced the dirt, then covered it with acres of mature lawn, plants, shrubs and trees.

Meade said, "Got the old tux brushed off?"

Smitty grimaced. "What's this country comin' to? A man has to put on a tuxedo to get into a gamblin' store!"

"Siegel's ad says come as you are," said Meade in a bantering tone. "Go ahead. Look like something that crawled out from under a rock. I'm going to show those Hollywood types that Nevadans have class, too."

Smitty hooked a thumb toward the Flamingo. "Some class your buddy Siegel has! Most of the money for that joint came from ex-bootleggers who went straight, and they got their loot from Murder, Incorporated, of which Mr. Siegel was a top dog."

Meade shook his head. "Smitty, you are the nosiest character I know. You'd be hell on wheels at an old wives' sewing bee."

"Knowin' and yakkin' are two different things, son. I use my knowin' to make money, not to spread nasty stories— 'specially about fine upstanding citizens like Bugsy Siegel." Smitty peered up at Meade. "Anyway, if you insist, I'll wear a tux to the big party. Frankly, I'd rather stay at the ranch and talk to the cows."

That night, Thompson drove up to the Flamingo entrance. A parking attendant waited while the two bodyguards opened the doors for Meade and Smitty. Looking elegant but somewhat uncomfortable in their tuxedos, the four men gazed up at the weaving searchlights that strove unsuccessfully to pierce the heavy clouds. They hurried inside to get out of the blowing rain.

They were overwhelmed by the odor of flowers. They were everywhere, filling the lobby and the casino.

"Meade, over here!" Siegel was standing in front of a huge

spray of flowers. He was handsome as a movie star in his expensive tuxedo, a pink carnation stuck in the lapel.

Meade immediately recognized George Raft. "George," said Siegel, "I want you to meet my good friend, Meade Slaughter."

"Glad to meet you, Meade," said Raft, looking more like a gangster than Siegel. It was said that Raft had connections with the underworld. Maybe it was true or maybe Raft had played too many gangster parts. Siegel was certainly a connection; he and Raft had been close for years.

Jimmy Durante seized Meade's hand. "Pleased to meetcha," he said in his gravelly voice.

Meade looked at the flowers that surrounded Durante. "Nice flowers."

"Yeah," cracked Durante. "Reminds me of a cemetery wit' crap tables."

Siegel laughed. "You gotta learn to show respect, Jimmy."

Durante's big nose signaled a left turn toward Siegel. "I tell you what I respects," he growled. "I respects the money this joint represents."

Meade and Smitty admired the casino. The effect was that of a posh country club, with crystal chandeliers sparkling overhead and thick carpet underfoot. It was a marvel. Nothing like it had ever been seen in Nevada.

Meade scanned the action. Good, but not what one would expect for an opening night. There were lots of diamonds and furs, and he recognized several Hollywood stars.

The two men surveyed the room. "Little slow, wouldn't you say?" said Meade.

Smitty nodded. "Weather hasn't helped."

Meade said, "Freezing rain, lousy conditions at the airport, big Christmas letdown, no reasons to keep people away." He spied some owners at the bar. "Let's join that bunch and cry together in our beer."

"Make mine whiskey," said Smitty, leading the way.

In Havana, the delegates of the Unione Siciliana gathered in a conference room to await the news from Las Vegas. The report arrived in the early morning hours. The crowd hadn't been up to expectations, and a remarkable thing had happened in the casino. It had lost money.

It was decided that nothing would be done about Siegel until the hotel's financial structure was reorganized. Immediate steps would be taken to throw the Nevada Projects Corporation into bankruptcy. A new corporation would be formed with original investors receiving pennies on the dollar.

On February 6th, 1947, the Flamingo closed its doors.

19

It was through Bugsy Siegel that Meade met Cindy Guest.

One night, Siegel entered the Plush Wheel lounge, Virginia Hill on one arm, Cindy on the other. Virginia was an attractive woman, but Cindy literally lit up the room. Meade sat up straighter in his chair. Milton whispered from the next table, "Lord give me strength."

"You're fired," breathed Meade. "Go to your room."

"Can't, boss. I gotta stay here and protect you."

Meade rose and looked down on the shiny platinum blond head. "Meade," said Siegel, "meet my friend, Cindy."

China blue eyes twinkled as she looked up at Meade through long lashes. Wrinkling her nose, she flashed a quick elfin smile. "Hi, Meade," she said throatily, holding out a slender hand. Cool fingers laced around Meade's.

"Hello, Cindy," said Meade, experiencing an acute loss when she withdrew her hand.

They sat down and drinks were served. "Cindy's been waiting out her six weeks," Virginia explained in her marked Southern accent. "I knew her in Hollywood. She's an actress."

"A *struggling* actress," corrected Cindy, her deep throaty

voice sending chills of excitement up Meade's spine. "I just do bit parts."

While Siegel talked exuberantly about the Flamingo's reopening next Saturday night, Meade watched Cindy. She had a graceful way of running her fingers through her long silver hair, little frown lines appearing and disappearing as she followed the conversation.

Cindy looked directly at Meade. "Ben says this is your place," she said, blue eyes wide and attentive.

Meade grinned and replied in a drawling voice, "Just a little ol' country boy tryin' to make a livin'."

Siegel brayed with laughter. "Don't let him fool you, Cindy. This little ol' country boy owns three joints in this state."

The conversation returned to the reopening of the Flamingo. Nearly a month ago, a large ad had announced the "official" opening of the Hotel Flamingo. The same ad had mentioned that tomorrow, February 6th, the hotel would be closed so completion work could be done. At the "official" opening on March 1, the Andrews Sisters would entertain. It didn't mention that a new corporation would reopen the hotel.

A few more days and Siegel would be facing his moment of truth. It was beginning to tell. A small tic jumped at the corner of Siegel's mouth as he drummed the tabletop with restless fingers. The drumming stopped, and he pulled a wad of bills from his pocket. "Gotta get back to work," he said, jumping up and dropping a twenty on the table.

"Keep it," said Meade, waving the money away.

"Yeah," grinned Siegel. "What am I tryin' to make you rich for?" He gestured toward a leggy girl who was serving drinks across the room. "Let her have it. The kid needs all the tips she can get." Meade smiled. A top cocktail waitress in Vegas made ten times her salary on tips.

Picking up her purse, Cindy prepared to rise. Meade said hastily, "Do you have to leave? I thought we might have dinner."

"Sure you don't have to get home to your wife?" Cindy asked.

"Nope."

"Fancy that. Two lonely people."

Siegel helped Virginia Hill into her fur coat. "I think I've heard somethin' like this in the movies," he laughed. His final words were tossed over his shoulder as he turned to leave. "Don't do nothin' I wouldn't do." He was still chuckling and throwing Meade knowing glances as he went out the door.

The headwaiter led Cindy and Meade to Meade's private booth where their conversation warmed over a bottle of Dom Perignon. With skillful maneuvering, Meade was soon listening while Cindy talked.

She was twenty-seven, born and raised in Los Angeles. "A native Californian. There aren't many of us around!" she said.

The winner of several beauty contests, she had earned a screen test. Surprisingly, it had gotten her a contract with Warner Brothers. She had never reached stardom, but earned a steady living.

Three years ago, Cindy had married an actor. The marriage had been bad from the start; they had been separated for a year. Ronald Guest was living with his current girl friend in Cuernavaca, Mexico.

"That's it," concluded Cindy. "End of scene. Cut, print. Now, let's hear about you."

Meade offered a lazy grin. "My life's an open book."

"I'll bet," Cindy said, resting her chin on a small fist. Suddenly, she wanted to know all about this big rugged man sitting across the table. He was so different from the matinee idols she knew in Hollywood. Blue eyes clear as the desert air; the scar on his forehead looking like it had been scratched there by a tiger. She tried to imagine a ring in one ear and a red scarf tied over his thick black hair. Give him a cutless and a knife in those strong white teeth, and he'd make Errol Flynn look like a pansy. She glanced at his big hands as they toyed with the champagne glass. What would they feel like touching her? Somehow she knew they would be gentle, sensitive. She shivered involuntarily.

The waiter bent over the table and poured the last of the champagne. "Another bottle?" Meade asked Cindy.

"Okay," she replied, "but you may have to pour me in bed." She clapped her hand over her mouth. "I didn't mean that the way it sounded," she gasped.

Meade laughed, waving away the grinning waiter. Looking directly at Cindy, he said, "For that privilege, I'd buy two more bottles."

Cindy dropped her eyes and blushed prettily, then succumbed to soft laughter. Looking up, she said impulsively, "Meade, I like you! There I go again—speaking my mind. Cindy, I keep telling myself, you've got to keep your big mouth shut. Never works. Never works." The laughter was deeper now, inviting Meade to join in, making it impossible for him not to.

Later, riding in the back seat of Meade's Cadillac, Cindy whispered in Meade's ear, nodding toward the bodyguards in the front seat, "Are they *always* with you?"

Drawing her close, Meade whispered back, "One sleeps at the foot of my bed."

"How *exciting!*" giggled Cindy.

Meade kissed Cindy goodnight at her motel room door; they had already made a date to see a show that night. "I'm not getting up until noon," Cindy said, running light fingers down Meade's face.

In the car, Milton and Thompson exchanged glances. "I think the boss is in love," said Thompson.

"Yeah," said Milton. He stared out at Cindy and heaved a deep sigh. "Me, too."

20

The scene at the Flamingo was frantic. Workers were everywhere—adding a touch of paint, moving furniture into the ninety-seven guest rooms, hanging pictures, cleaning, polishing. In the midst of it all, appearing and disappearing like a whirling dervish, was Bugsy Siegel. He was a driven man, motivated by the knowledge that his very existence was linked to the success of the hotel.

Meade and Cindy attended the reopening on Saturday night. It was cold and windy, but the casino was crowded. Siegel's face was wreathed in smiles; his hotel was now a success.

The smiles disappeared in a fit of screaming anger the following morning. Raving back and forth in the counting room, clutching the tally sheets and waving his arms—creating small breezes that stirred the stacks of bills—Siegel bellowed, "How can we lose in the casino and hotel *both?*"

The counters stared at their machines and prudently kept silent.

The loss wasn't just a one-night occurrence; it lasted for over a month. In May the Flamingo finally went into the black, and Siegel breathed a sigh of relief.

Also in May, another hotel was started on the Strip, a mile north of the Flamingo. Wilbur Clark, two brothers and several investors had raised $300,000 to begin the hotel's construction. It would be called the Desert Inn.

After a few months, funds ran out. The stark bones of the framing skeleton rose above the creosote bush, a ghostly monument to dashed hopes.

21

Benjamin Siegel died on the night of June 20, 1947. He was hit by five slugs from a 30-30 carbine—one in the head and four in the body. Three other bullets missed. The shots were fired from outside the living room window at 810 North Linden Drive in Beverly Hills. It was 10:30 P.M. The killer was never found.

Siegel's death sentence was carried out almost six months to the day after it had been handed down at the Havana conference. The January reprieve gave Siegel a brief moment of glory in May when the Flamingo finally showed a profit. The morning of his murder, he was smiling and talking with unbridled enthusiasm about the future of the Flamingo Hotel and Las Vegas.

The prophet died but the dream lived on. The desert would blossom far beyond Siegel's wildest expectations, and giant hotels would rise as glittering memorials to his prophesy. The Bible says that a prophet is not without honor except in his own country. Siegel received no honor from his underworld friends—only death.

Al Smiley, a friend of Siegel's who had been visiting with him that night, slowly picked himself up from the floor where he had dived at the first sound of gunfire. Upstairs, Virginia Hill's brother, Chick, huddled in a bedroom with his girl friend and Hill's secretary, Jeri Mason.

Later, the three gathered in the living room to view the carnage. Virginia Hill had found it convenient to be in Europe at the time.

Another gathering would soon be taking place at the Flamingo Hotel. It would also be comprised of a group of three.

They were Gus Greenbaum, Morris Rosen, a longtime gambling figure out of Miami and Havana, and Moe Sedway, a childhood friend of Siegel's. Greenbaum and Rosen would manage the hotel and casino and Sedway would be in charge of public relations.

Virginia Hill barely escaped Siegel's fate. She was allowed to live providing she kept quiet and returned most of the money she and Siegel had salted away in Switzerland.

Nevada was still rocking from the repercussions of Siegel's death when Harry Sherwood, owner of the Cal-Neva Lodge at Lake Tahoe, was shot and killed. The two murders made national headlines. Front-page stories proclaimed that Sherwood had once been in partnership with some notorious West Coast gambling figures. The man who shot Sherwood was believed to be Louis Strauss, better known as "Russian Louie," a hit man for the eastern mob.

Carson City was shocked. Gangsters, it was said, were threatening to take over the state.

Undaunted, the Strip continued to grow. In July of 1947, not long after the Players' Club had been taken over by Wilbur Clark, Milton Prell and friends opened the $500,000 Club Bingo on the southeast corner of the Strip and San Francisco Street, directly across from the El Rancho. The Club Bingo advertised the world's biggest and most expensive parlor.

In October, a new hotel was begun north of Wilbur Clark's uncompleted Desert Inn. It was called the Thunderbird, and the builder and part-owner was Marion Hicks.

Years later, the Thunderbird would squat like a massive toad amidst a shining array of elegant hotels, an ugly sister in a glamorous family. A writer would describe the Thunderbird as, "Warehouse modern with Navajo decals, some beginning to peel."

22

"Give me a nickel or I'll never speak to you again!" Cindy demanded, extending an imperious hand, palm upward, holding her striking five foot six inch frame in a regal pose that would have put Greta Garbo to shame.

"Nuts to you," grinned Meade, looking past Cindy at the Plush Wheel-emblazoned slot machine that was waiting to gulp down the requested nickel. Poking a finger at the tip of her nose, he growled, "You crazy little noodle-head, you've already dumped a whole dollar in that thing. Much more and we'll have to wash dishes for our dinner!"

"Oh, Meade," she said, touching his arm and blinking rapidly. "I'm sorry. I would never have asked if I'd known you were down to your last nickel." She plunged a slender hand into her purse. "Here," she said, holding out a dollar bill, batting her long eyelashes. "I hope you'll accept this small token of my affection." She patted his arm. "And you don't ever have to return it." Turning and sadly regarding the silent machine, she uttered a loud sniff. "And it was going to pay off. I just *know* it was!

Whirling, she cried, "Feed me, Meade," pulling him along through the long rows of slot machines. "It's past two, and if I don't eat, I'm going to die!"

My heart's skipping just like my feet, thought Cindy as she seized Meade's arm and accompanied him through the casino of the Strip Plush Wheel. She had never known anything like this in her life, had never felt so damn *good* all over.

The last three weeks had passed like a speeded-up film, a montage of colorful scenes lovingly spliced together, creating patterns of happiness, excitement, tenderness and passion.

When she first arrived in Las Vegas, Cindy had dreaded the six-week residency wait for her divorce; she expected to be bored to death. She had started marking a calendar, counting down the days to when she could return to Hollywood. Now she didn't care if she ever went back.

What was happening to her? She had asked herself that last night, curled up in the delicious warmth of Meade's embrace, their bodies still heated from making love, Meade asleep, holding her spoon-fashion in his arms.

Cindy wriggled her bottom closer, causing Meade's limp penis to slide into the dampness between her buttocks. Slowly rotating her hips, she felt the warmth of arousal in her loins. Stop it, Cindy, she silently ordered, giving herself a mental slap on the offending posterior. If you wake him up, the poor man won't get four hours sleep. You can sleep all day!

Is this really Cindy Clark? (She always thought of herself by her film name, not by her married name which she was dropping with her marriage two weeks from now.) This can't be the Cindy who's always in charge, the girl who never really cares when it comes time to say goodbye, controlling men, controlling but never loving. Including her husband. That was sure a dumb move, Cindy girl. Two crazy people on a weekend fling in Mexico suddenly deciding to go through a ceremony that took less time than the border crossing. Two topsy-turvy years together, then a year of separation. Whoopie! Over soon. You're dumb, Cindy. Just plain *dumb!*

Admit it, you're not really dumb. You always got top marks in school, and you've got a mind quicker than a hummingbird. That's what Jack told you. Good old Jack. What a lovable sweet guy. How does nice lovable Jack stack up against Meade? How does any man? Oh, damn, thought Cindy, wriggling closer to Meade, my whole world's flopped upside down.

I've always wanted a strong man, and now I've got one. Boy, have I! Cindy played with Meade's little finger. He's got me twisted all around that thing, she silently conceded, both thrilled and appalled at the knowledge.

She rubbed the offending finger over the dark areola of her breast, feeling the nipple responding, hardening, reminding her of that first time.

Their third date. Pretty quick but it was a miracle it took so long. Just touching set off more sparks than a welding machine.

They had been dining at the Flamingo as guests of Bugsy Siegel, who had dropped by earlier to chat. That was an hour previously. Two bottles of Dom Perignon previously.

Cindy lifted her glass. "A toast," she said merrily.

Meade touched his glass to hers. "Let's see," he said, scratching his head and grinning, "this must be about number fifteen. Right?"

"Be serious, you dunce; this is a serious occasion," Cindy said, stifling a delicate burp. Clearing her throat, she stared at the ceiling. "Now look what you've done," she cried, setting her glass down on the table. "You've made me forget what I was going to say!" She gazed down into the glass as if the amber bubbles held the answer. "Aha!" she announced triumphantly, snapping her fingers and raising her glass. "It's a very original toast; that's why it was so hard to remember. To us!"

"Original, my foot!" protested Meade. "That was toast number three, and *I* made it! Think of another one quick or I'll pour this stuff on the floor."

"Okay," Cindy fired back. "How about to our first—uh, kiss?"

"Did that days ago."

"Our first hug?" Eyes brightly hopeful.

"Done it hundreds of times."

"Our first, our first . . ." Cindy's forehead wrinkled with concentration. "Oh darn," she exclaimed, shoulders drooping in defeat. "What's left?"

"Maybe we could look it up in a medical book," suggested Meade.

"I don't have one," Cindy said despairingly.

"I do."

"Where?"

"My office. Take us five minutes to get there."

They stared at each other for a long silent moment, not trying to hide the hunger in their eyes. An unspoken agreement; as clear as if it had been shouted from the rooftops. Rising, Meade held out his hand. Fingers interlocked, they walked wordlessly out to the waiting car.

"Wait in the bar," Meade said to the bodyguards after they had arrived across the highway at the Plush Wheel. "I'll be in the office."

Cindy felt that her knees were turning to jelly as Meade led her by the hand into the dimly lit office. A ghostly statue in a white clinging gown, Cindy waited while he opened the door that led into his private quarters. Meade turned, smiling, and Cindy moved silently into his arms. They kissed in the doorway, two dark figures becoming one, casting a long shadow on the bed beyond.

Reaching up, Cindy cupped Meade's face in her hands. "Give me five minutes," she whispered, briefly pressing her lips to his and then disappearing into the bathroom.

Feeling as giddy as a virgin bride, Cindy worked the gown down over her hips, heavy breasts swinging free as she bent forward to step out of the silken garment. With quick urgent movements, she stripped off her nylon stockings, garter belt and lace panties, scooping everything up and throwing it in a haphazard pile on the vanity.

Standing naked before the floor-length mirror on the door, Cindy arched her body and bounced lightly on her toes, smiling with satisfaction at the way her breasts jiggled firmly above her deep rib cage. Her eyes dropped to where the fine golden hair revealed the pink lips of her swollen sex. Sucking in her breath with a hiss of anticipation, Cindy turned away and used the toilet, then washed herself, carefully applying powder and perfume. Wrapping herself in a big towel, she turned off the light and entered the darkened bedroom.

She sat on the edge of the bed and kissed Meade, thrilling to the feel of his hands as they removed the towel and pulled her under the covers.

Cindy snuggled up against Meade's naked body, nuzzling

his neck while he caressed her hair and ran light fingers over her back. Meade kissed her eyelids, behind her ears and along the jawline to her mouth, gently parting her lips with his tongue. Moaning with pleasure, Cindy opened her mouth, intertwining her tongue with Meade's.

Magic. Perfectly tuned to one another. Marveling that they had found each other. Startled, a little frightened at the depth of their passion. Kissing, holding, touching, feeling, prolonging with delicious agony the moment when they would come together in a rite as ancient as Eden.

Neither taking the lead, moving in faultless harmony as if they had loved in another life. Positioning for the final union, praying that the end would only be the beginning.

Legs spread wide, hands gripping Meade's buttocks, Cindy gasped as the full length of Meade's thick penis penetrated deep into her body. "Don't move, darling," she begged, lifting her long legs and wrapping them around Meade's hips, locking her ankles and drawing him in even deeper. Suddenly, her eyes were blinded with tears, tiny droplets sparkling in the soft light cast down from the window.

Deeply moved, Meade kissed Cindy's wet cheeks, tenderly brushing the silver-blond hair from her forehead. A smile broke across Cindy's face, and she reached up to touch Meade's lips. "You feel it, too," she whispered.

Meade nodded, knowing in that instant that they were one in mind as well as body.

Mouths joined in a deep kiss, their bodies began to move in unison, Meade's strokes slow and even, the thrust of Cindy's hips in perfect concert.

The tempo increased until the bed shook with the violence of their lovemaking. Their movements became erratic, naked hips rolling and driving, wet flesh making uneven slapping sounds.

Cindy tore her mouth away from Meade's and bit hard into the rumpled sheet, body taut, face reddening. Muffled screams filled the room as she reached a shattering climax, muscles contracting in uncontrollable spasms, clamping down on Meade's penis, squeezing warm semen into her belly in fitful spurts. Meade's cries joined Cindy's as they continued to thrust and buck, refusing to stop until the last tiny remnant of orgasm had been achieved. The moment came; gradually their undulations slowed, then halted, passion giving way to deep contented exhaustion.

Cindy's china blue eyes were as big as saucers. She looked up at Meade, still locked in her embrace, and breathed, "Oh, wow. Oh, wow. Oh, wow, wow, wow." A dimple appeared, and she laughed softly. "That was a first, and I mean a *first!*"

Grinning, Meade tried to free himself. "Oh, no, you don't!" cried Cindy, scissoring her legs even tighter around Meade's hips. "I want you to stick around."

"Stick around is right," Meade said. "That stuff is like glue. We'll be attached forever."

"Yummy!" giggled Cindy. "Let's try it."

Laughing and tossing about, they finally came apart. Rolling away, Cindy crawled to the foot of the bed and peered over the side, glistening rump high in the air. "What are you doing?" Meade asked, eyes devouring the exposed vagina, puffed lips white with semen.

Cindy looked back, long silver hair framing her upside-down face, staring at Meade between her spread legs. "I'm looking for that bodyguard that sleeps here," she said, fighting back a giggle, losing the battle and collapsing on her back in a paroxysm of deep belly laughs.

Meade couldn't resist Cindy's laughter. It seemed to well up from the very depths of her soul, a contagious merry disease. Laughing, he hauled her back. With a lot of squirming and wiggling, they got their bodies facing in the right direction, adjusted the pillows and blankets and promptly fell asleep.

Meade's last thoughts were of Milton and Thompson waiting in the bar; he made a mental note to wake up in an hour. He did and so did Cindy. The bodyguards had to wait another two hours. Well satisfied with the results of their second session, Meade and Cindy appeared in the bar at 4 A.M., their faces incapable of fooling even the tipsiest customer. Silently, Milton handed a five dollar bill under the table to

Thompson. He had bet they wouldn't make it out before daylight.

Three days later, Meade moved Cindy into a rented house a few blocks south of Fremont Street. The word was passed around town. Cindy Clark was Meade Slaughter's girl. Hands off.

23

An early spring, greening the fields and low foothills, a thick luxurious carpet sweeping up toward towering Mt. Charleston twenty miles away. Cindy's eyes gazed up at the snow-capped peak outlined in blue. So beautiful; an ice cream cone feeding the sky.

She leaned forward, gloved hands resting on the horn of the big western saddle. Sadie—Cindy's name for the old mare Meade had felt it safe for her to ride—bent her head down and cropped off a clump of grass. Cindy smiled and slackened the reins so Sadie could continue her hungry quest, recalling the words of the old wrangler who had taught her to ride. "You're goin' to spoil that old horse, Miss Cindy. Yank her head up when she tries to grab a bite. Show her who's boss or she'll be takin' you places where you don't want to go. Look at her—fat as a pig, feedin' her all that candy and stuff." Toby shot Cindy a disgusted look, but it didn't come off. "Aw shi—shoot, Miss Cindy, you're goin' to do what you're goin' to do, so get at it."

Cindy reached down from the saddle and pulled Toby's hat down over his eyes, then whipped Sadie into a semblance of a gallop. She looked back as Toby waved his hat in the air, grinning and shaking his head. It was well known around the ranch that he worshipped "Miss Cindy." No one blamed him; the whole crew was in love with her.

It was just over a year since she had met Meade, a wonderful year filled with loving, laughter and happiness. She had returned to Hollywood once for a small part in a film, but the strain of separation had been too much for both her and Meade. Her agent had continued to pester her with job offers, but so far she had refused. He had called yesterday with an offer that seemed too good to be true, a leading part in a big budget movie starring Cary Grant. Meade's face had lit up when he heard the news. "Imagine silly Cindy and cuddly Cary!" She loved the nicknames he had given her. Silly Cindy indeed! If only she didn't laugh so much. Phooey! Life is supposed to be fun. Long faces are for churches and funerals!

There had been only one dark spot during the past year—David. Cindy hadn't met him until she and Meade had been going together for several weeks.

"Cindy, this is my son, David," Meade had said. They were standing in the living room of the big ranch house; David had been slouched on the couch, reading a *Popular Mechanics* magazine when they entered. Awkwardly, he rose to his feet, unsure what to do with the magazine, finally dropping it on the couch.

He dipped his head. "Hello, Cindy."

"Hi. I've heard a lot about you," Cindy said, looking up at the tall nineteen-year-old boy. *He doesn't look like Meade at all,* she thought. She studied the fine features, the deep gray eyes, the slightly curled blond hair. *How beautiful his mother must have been!*

"All good, I hope," said David, glancing from Cindy to Meade, a smile flickering across his face, shuffling feet wrinkling the big hooked rug.

Taking Cindy by the arm, Meade led her to a big overstuffed chair. "Sit down. I'll get some coffee brought out." He stuck his head in the kitchen. "Maria! How about some coffee?"

A voice answered from the back of the house. Meade drew up a chair and sat down beside Cindy. David was on the couch, crossing and uncrossing his legs.

"I hear you work for Tom Bailey," Cindy said to David.

She had met Bailey last week; he was now one of the biggest contractors in Nevada, building homes and commercial buildings.

"Yeah," said David, looking quickly away from Cindy.

Meade tried to keep the conversation going. "Cindy's an actress, you know."

"Yeah, you told me." David idly thumbed through the magazine at his side.

Looking quickly at Meade, Cindy saw the anger crossing his face. She lightly touched his arm, then said to David, "Meade says you do a lot of riding. I've never been on a horse in my life. Is it okay if I meet your horse? He won't bite me, will he?"

David's face brightened for the first time since they had entered the room. "Thunder? Naw, he's a little frisky, but he won't bite. Not unless you feed him sugar the wrong way."

"How do you do that?" Cindy asked, leaning eagerly forward, eyes brightly interested.

"You've gotta hold your hand out palm up and flat," David said. "Like this. That way he picks up the sugar without biting your fingers."

"Show me. Please!" Cindy had leaped to her feet, a look of happy anticipation on her lovely face.

"Sure," said David, getting up. He looked at Meade, who stood beside Cindy. "You coming, too, Dad?" There was a note of anticipation in his voice, as if he hadn't expected his father to be interested.

" 'Course," smiled Meade. "I haven't seen old Thunder for quite a while."

"Come on, Dad," protested David. "Thunder's not old; he turned four in June."

Meade looked down at Cindy. "David's had Thunder since he was a six-month-old colt; raised him on this ranch."

"His father was a champion Quarter Horse," David said proudly. "Won a lot of races in Arizona and California."

"Well, let's go, you two," Cindy said, already standing at the door. "Who's got the sugar?"

David grinned. "Keep a box in the tackroom."

"Hold the coffee, Maria," Meade said to the fat Mexican woman standing in the kitchen doorway, holding a coffee pot and cups. "We'll be back in a little bit."

It went well that first morning. Cindy was a beautiful grown-up child, loving the big black horse, rubbing his velvet soft muzzle, crying with delight as he delicately picked the sugar cube from her open palm.

The happy times might have continued had Meade and Cindy not been so enamored of each other, eyes and bodies speaking their own private language, creating a small world David found impossible to penetrate.

As the afternoon wore on, David grew quieter and quieter, finally excusing himself, saying he had to meet a friend in town.

A sensitive, discerning woman, Cindy had been painfully aware of the tension between father and son. For the first time, she had seen Meade uncomfortable—unsure how to act around David. From previous conversations, she had gathered bits and pieces about Shirley and Janice, how David had lived in Reno with his foster mother, coming to live with his father after five years absence.

"Meade," she said that night, carefully choosing her words, "do you and David spend much time together?"

Meade looked at her sharply; they were sitting on the living room couch at her home. "Some," he said slowly, knitting his brows as if he had never faced the question before. "I'm not much of a horseman and about the worst skier in Nevada; that's where most of David's interests lie. We've gone fishing a few times, but I don't think David enjoyed it much. Seems like we don't have much in common." He smiled at Cindy, a strange, sad smile. "Why, honey? Does it show?"

Cindy's eyes were loving, frankly honest. "It shows, darling," she said simply. "I hope I didn't make it any worse; I don't think David was very happy to see me."

Meade's jaw tightened. "He could use a lesson in manners."

"Please, darling, he's confused. He needs understanding, not a lecture."

Meade drew her close. "Think so, huh?" She nodded. "Okay, honey, we'll give it a try."

As winter approached, Cindy became a part of a hopeless triangle. She didn't tell Meade about the way David had gradually cut her off until he spoke only a few barely polite words whenever she came out to ride Sadie, purchased by Meade with the unspoken hope that David would teach her to ride. When Toby started teaching her, Cindy said it was because David's work kept him away much of the time. Meade had silently accepted her explanation, a tightening of his lips the only indication of his disbelief.

When Meade was with Cindy, David minded his manners; he even posed with her for a picture on his twentieth birthday on April 26th, a month ago.

Sadie's loud whinny jerked Cindy out of her reverie; she looked around to see David approaching on Thunder. He was wheeling his horse away when Cindy waved and kicked Sadie in the ribs. Reining in, David waited under a big tree; it was obvious by his expression that he would rather ride on over the hill.

"Hi," said Cindy. "Nice day, isn't it?"

"Yeah," said David, cruelly yanking Thunder's head away from Sadie's.

Cindy didn't get angry often, but when she did it was impossible to hide. She reached out and patted Thunder's nose. "That wasn't nice," she said, shooting a disapproving look at David.

"My horse," he retorted. "I'll treat him any way I want." Pulling on the reins, he turned to leave.

Cindy seized Thunder's bridle. "David," she pleaded, "can't we be friends?"

"Why do we have to?" David snapped. "You've got Dad; isn't that enough?"

Cindy's eyes widened, and her jaw dropped. "I don't *have* your dad," she exclaimed. "We're friends, good friends. I've always wanted you to be a part of our friendship; Meade wants it, too."

"I'll bet!" sneered David. "We'd look great—all three of us in bed!"

"David!" cried Cindy, really angry now. "What a terrible thing to say! I'm ashamed of you; you're old enough to know better."

"A hell of a lot closer in age to you than Dad is! What do you see in him? His money?"

"That's enough, David! I don't have to put up with this!"

"No, you don't. Why don't you leave, then maybe I'll have a chance to know my dad!"

Backing Sadie up a few paces, Cindy stared at David. "Oh, David," she said softly, tears springing into her eyes, "you shouldn't feel that way. Your father loves you; he'd be with you more if you'd let him."

"Bullshit!" shouted David. "I saw little enough of him before you came. All he could think about was making money. Now that you're here, I never see him. I wish you'd go back where you came from!"

Cindy was crying openly now. "Oh, David, you're so wrong, so wrong. I don't want to drive a wedge between you and your father. I want to make things better, not worse!"

David answered with youthful cruelty. "By marrying him, I suppose. Then you can go around saying you're my mother. Do you think that will make any difference? Do you think you can replace my mother? How about Sandra? Can you replace her? Will Dad ever love you as much? You're out of luck! Nobody can replace Sandra. Dad's never been the same since she died!"

Cindy's face turned deathly white, frozen with shock. Who was Sandra? Meade had never mentioned her.

David laughed, a harsh shrill sound. "You didn't know about Sandra, did you? She and Dad were going to get married, a long time ago when I was eight. She was killed when some guys beat Dad up. He's never looked at another woman since. You're the first, and I'm surprised it's lasted this long."

The tears were flowing now. "No, I didn't know, David,"

Cindy said brokenly. "But it doesn't make me love your father less; it makes me love him more—because it shows what a kind and loving man he is. You should be very proud of him." Cindy rode closer and gave Thunder's bridle a little shake. "Please, David, can't we be friends?"

"Get out of our lives," hissed David, yanking Thunder's head away. "Get out of our lives and then maybe Dad and I can get along."

Cindy sat unmoving on Sadie for a long time after David disappeared over the ridge. One side of her wanted to get a whip and beat David black and blue; the other wanted to cry with him over the childhood experiences that had left such scars on his mind and heart.

24

"Meade," Cindy said a few days after her fight with David, "would you be angry with me if I took that part Lee called about?"

"I'm sleeping, woman, don't bother me," Meade said, lying contentedly on his back in the big bed, Cindy's naked body sprawled haphazardly over his, long strands of her silver hair on his chest.

Cindy pinched his nipple, making him flinch. "I'm serious, Ding Dong," she said. "You seemed to like the idea; besides, I think you want to get rid of me."

"You're right," Meade said, looking solemn. "You've got to go. You crawl all over me at night and keep me awake. Everytime you turn over you hit me in the face with your boobs."

Cindy's eyes opened wide, and her mouth formed a big O. "Meade Slaughter, that's the most horrible thing ever said to me!" She sat up and cupped her breasts, then bounced them up and down on her hands. Experimentally, she touched her nipples, smiling as they sprang to rigid attention. "Boy," she said, head bowed as she gazed intently down at her chest, "do you know how many men would give ten years of their lives to get slapped in the face with these?"

Meade groaned. "You're hopeless, you little jerk!" Grasping Cindy's chin between thumb and forefinger, he tipped her head up. "Now what's this about leaving me?"

"Dunce! Not leaving you. Just going away for a while."

"How long's a while?"

A little timid now. "A couple of months, maybe three."

"A while? That's an eternity! We tried it once before. Didn't work worth a damn."

"We can see each other at least once a week. I can fly here or you can fly there."

"Not the same."

"But you said you want me off your back—or is it your chest?"

"Chest, face, legs, everywhere. Shit, come here, woman."

"Not until we decide."

"Decide what?"

"Don't be a dummy. Whether I go to Hollywood or not." Meade blinked. "You're serious? Really serious?"

"Yes, I'm serious, dunce! Why else would I bring it up?"

"I'll be damned."

"Well?"

"Really want to go, huh?"

"Darling, I've thought a lot about it. You say I'm not a kept woman, but you won't let me spend a nickel of my own money. I've got a few dollars, you know." Cindy grinned at Meade's perplexed look. "I'm the original independent woman when it comes to money. Been saving ever since I started on my own, got a nice savings account and some stocks, AT&T, General Motors, stuff like that."

Cindy took a deep breath, disturbing Meade's concentration. "I like to earn my own way." She poked Meade in the ribs. "Of all people, you should understand."

Meade nodded reluctantly.

"Now what do you say, Mr. Slaughter?"

"What can I say, Miss Clark? Go with my blessing, but I'd better see you at least once a week. Any less and I'll have to find another lady to occupy this house."

Their lovemaking was more urgent that night, lasting into the small hours of the morning. After Meade fell asleep, Cindy lay quietly beside him, pressing her breasts against his chest. Her face-slappers! She started to smile, then burst into silent tears. *Oh, Meade, Meade, do you know how much I love you?* Thank God she had willpower—just enough to get her through.

The first week in June, Cindy got into her red Buick convertible, a Christmas gift from Meade, and drove off toward Hollywood, waving gaily at Meade as he stood on the sidewalk. The Strip passed in a blur of tears as she headed south out of town.

25

"What the hell got into that kid?" demanded Meade. He and Tom Bailey were sitting in the downtown Plush Wheel coffee shop; Bailey had called Meade earlier and asked for the meeting.

"He's only twenty, Meade," Bailey said in a mildly disapproving voice. "When he's with other guys, he doesn't know how to say no."

"You mean he can't stand on his own feet," growled Meade.

Shaking his head, Bailey raised a hand. "I didn't say that."

Meade cursed and slammed down his coffee cup. "I ought to beat the shit out of that kid! There's no reason for what he did. I give him all he needs."

Bailey paused, then said quietly, "Meade, we've been

friends for a long time. I hope you'll let me get this said." He paused again. "You said you've given David all he needs. That's partly right. You've given him everything but yourself." Bailey pointed a stubby finger at Meade. "How much time have you spent with that boy?"

Meade bristled angrily, then calmed under Bailey's cool, steady gaze. Tom Bailey was a good family man with a loving wife and two happy well-adjusted children. When it came to relationships, Bailey was the authority, not he.

He had tried; damnit, he had tried! But had he tried hard enough? It seemed like every time he and David got together, they fought. Had they *ever* got along? Yes, when he had taken up the role of father and mother before and after Shirley's death. And there were the good times with Sandra. Meade winced. Would he ever be able to forget her? He might as well try and stop breathing.

If only he and David could have been together during those crucial formative years! It would have been impossible in San Francisco, but he *could* have sent for David sooner after he got to Vegas.

When David did arrive, he was a homesick boy of thirteen, wandering around the ranch with no companions but the cowboys and Maria. He missed Janice terribly—and Jim Terhune, his younger "brother." David finished grade school and went through high school meeting Meade coming and going. Now this.

A few weeks ago, materials started disappearing from Bailey's job sites. It got so bad that Bailey hired two men to patrol the locations. Last night, they had caught a group of boys red-handed. One of them was David. To protect David, Bailey recorded the boys' names and let them go. Each parent had been notified. Meade was the last.

Meade sighed. "You're right, Tom. No matter how much time I've spent with David, it hasn't been enough." He looked at his watch. "Where is he?"

"Should be at the ranch. You didn't stay there last night?"

"No. I worked late at the office and slept there."

Meade stood and tossed a silver dollar on the table. He

clasped Bailey's hand. "Thanks, Tom. You did the right thing."

Meade saw David's Ford coupe in front of the ranch house. David was in the kitchen. He looked up, then quickly back down at his plate.

Pouring a cup of coffee, Meade sat across from his son. David glanced at Meade, a sullen expression on his face. "I guess Tom told you."

Meade nodded. "Why?"

David shrugged his shoulders. "I don't know—somethin' to do."

"Something to do?" snapped Meade. "What are you going to do when you really get bored—rob a bank?"

David pushed aside his plate. "I've got to get going."

"You're not going anywhere until we get this talked out!"

David gripped the table until his knuckles went white. "What's there to talk about?" he burst out. "I stole some stuff. I'm not going to do it anymore. Satisfied?"

Meade bit the words off one by one. "I'm not going to be satisfied until you treat me with respect. I'm your father, damnit!"

David mumbled, "Sometimes I wonder."

"What did you mean by that crack?" Meade demanded.

David studied the tablecloth. "Nothing."

Meade slammed his fist down on the table. "Answer me, boy!"

David's head whipped up, eyes burning with sudden anger. "The only time we sit down to talk in years and you yell and call me 'boy.' That's it, isn't it? 'Boy, do this. Boy, do that. Boy, stop bothering me. Shut up, boy.' Why shouldn't I wonder if you're my father? You sure as hell don't act like one!"

Meade fought to control his anger. "Okay," he said, "I'm not doing this right. Let's start over."

"Can't we wait until tomorrow?" David said listlessly. "I've got some guys to meet."

"Goddamnit!" shouted Meade, "is that more important than our talking?"

"You call this talking?" David shouted back. Jumping up, he turned to leave.

Meade was on his feet. "You don't leave this room until I say so!"

David whirled around, fists clenched. "Or what? Are you going to put out a contract on me? Maybe blow me away like you did Giuliano?" David's face turned white, sudden fear leaping into his eyes as he backed slowly away. The words had just slipped out.

Grabbing David's arms, Meade shook him until his teeth rattled. David was big, only an inch shorter than his father's six feet two inches, but he was helpless in his father's grasp. Pulling David forward until their faces almost touched, Meade demanded, "Where did you pick up that shit?"

David struggled in his father's iron grip. "Around," he murmured. He averted his eyes. "Around town."

Meade gave David another shake. "Is this what you and your worthless buddies do, sit around and talk about the hits your father's made?"

David shook his head and pushed on Meade's chest. "Let me go, Dad. I'm not a kid anymore. Quit pushing me around."

Releasing David, Meade looked at him contemptuously. "What are you going to do? Fight back?" He raised a hand as if to hit David.

David had been in a lot of fights and reacted without thinking. He took a swing at Meade.

Moving with blinding speed, Meade swept David's arm aside and smashed a big fist into the boy's stomach. David crashed into the wall, then slipped down into a sitting position, clutching his stomach and groaning.

Meade sank to his knees, reaching out a trembling hand to touch David's knee. "I'm sorry, David," he said in a stricken voice. "Jesus, I'm sorry."

"Leave me alone," David said through clenched teeth. "Just leave me alone."

Rising, Meade looked down at David. "I'll come home early, and we'll talk. Okay?"

David stared at the floor and nodded.

When Meade got home that night, David was gone. His closet and chest of drawers were empty. He had even taken his saddle from the barn.

There was nothing left to remind Meade that he had a son.

26

"I'm wondering who's the biggest ass—him or me."

Cindy brushed a stray lock of hair from Meade's forehead. "I hope you're not expecting me to answer *that*," she said, crinkling up her nose and trying to tease him into a smile.

Patting her leg, Meade rested his head against the cushion. "I'm not very good company, am I?"

Cindy smiled. "Another question? I'm not answering that one either."

Meade pulled her roughly into his arms. "I've missed you," he said, burying his face in her hair and rubbing her back.

"I've missed you, too. It's been a whole six days—seems like a month."

"You'd better get back pretty soon or I'll start looking around. Lots of pretty girls in Vegas."

Cindy held up a small fist. "Try it, buster, and I'll rearrange your face."

"Who said that—Cagney?"

"No. Clark. It's in a movie about a tall, dark, handsome man in Vegas who can't keep his hands off a gorgeous, sexy blonde. They spend a lot of time in bed."

Meade growled and began to munch on Cindy's shoulder. Moving his lips downward, he slipped off the straps of her gown and began to suck greedily on her nipples. "I said bed, not couch," moaned Cindy as Meade stripped off her panties.

"Do you really care?" asked Meade, playing lightly over her clitoris with his finger.

"No. Oh God, no!" gasped Cindy, spreading her nylon-encased legs, fumbling frantically with the buttons on Meade's shirt.

Rising quickly, Meade threw off his clothes. "Let me," Cindy said, reaching up to pull at his shorts. Breathing deeply, Meade looked down at Cindy's blond pubic hair, shining moistly below the black garter belt.

Meade sucked in his breath as Cindy gripped his throbbing penis. Slowly, she worked it up and down, intently watching the loose skin as it covered and uncovered the blood-engorged head. Moving her left hand down between her legs, Cindy rubbed herself in unison with her right hand strokes. Faster and faster, until she suddenly pulled her knees up to her breasts, opening herself wide to accept Meade's swollen member. Cindy was driven deep into the cushions as Meade entered her body, a violent encounter that lasted only a few moments, ending with an explosion of pent-up passions that left the participants too exhausted to move.

"Meade," Cindy said from the depths of the cushions, "I'm not sure being apart is a good idea. It's awfully frustrating. People die of heart attacks getting excited like this, you know."

"Who's excited? They could drop an atomic bomb in the middle of the room, and it wouldn't even faze me."

"I don't mean *now,* dunce; I mean *before.*"

"Got a point there. Any suggestions?"

"I'll be back in a month." A deep sigh. "If we last that long."

It was several hours before the subject of David came up again. "Don't worry," Cindy said, cuddling closer to Meade in bed. "He'll turn up. He's not out looking for trouble. Bet he's scared to death, wishing he'd never left home."

"Hope you're right, honey. I've been a damn fool, and I intend to make it up to him." He shook his head. "If he'll let me."

"You'll call as soon as you hear something?"

Meade hugged Cindy tight. "Sure, honey."

Three nights later, Meade got a call. "David's here," Janice Terhune said. "He spent a week in San Francisco, then made a beeline for our house. Poor boy," she chuckled softly, "he's all tuckered out."

Meade suppressed his feelings of relief. "Ran home to Mom, huh?"

Janice's laughter tinkled in his ear. "Know something, Meade?" she said gaily. "You *are* a cow plop."

Meade ground out his cigar. "Okay, Mom, where does this leave David? Does he live with you happily ever after?"

"How about for a while? He can get a job, then attend university this fall. It's only a mile or so from the house. Jim's going there."

"Will he do it?"

"Sure. We've already talked it over."

Meade laughed. "Why are you asking me? You've got everything decided."

"Daddy's still got the last word. Is it okay?"

"You know it is." Meade's voice turned serious. "Think it will be okay with David and me again?"

Janice's voice was hesitant. "Give it time, Meade. Don't push it. Okay?"

"Okay. Tell him . . . tell him I'm really sorry. I'm sorry as hell about what happened. I'll send up some money. You'll need it; the kid eats like a horse. Tell David to let me know if he needs anything. He's still my kid. Don't let him forget that."

"Gotcha. Meade, you're kinda sweet, even if you are a cow plop."

A soft *click.* Meade dropped the receiver in its cradle and lit a cigar.

27

Five stories high, Vegas Vic waved his arms and repeated over and over again, "Howdy Podner."

" 'Peers to me like 'Howdy Sucker' might be more appropriate," Smitty observed.

Meade laughed. "Guy McAfee might agree with you. Told me yesterday that the Golden Nugget cleared one hundred fifty percent of its original investment in the first year."

Smitty emitted a low whistle. "Now *that's* a profit. How come McAfee didn't invite me into that little project?"

"You're not from Los Angeles."

"Figured somethin' like that. Pretty soon us native Nevadans are goin' to get scarce around here." Smitty peered up at Vegas Vic, towering above the Pioneer Club. "Still say 'Howdy Sucker' would sound more appropriate."

A block away, the monotonous amplified voice began to fade; it was replaced by the blast of a public address system. "Don't those damn things ever stop?"

Meade looked up into the neon-lighted night sky. "Maybe around four or five in the morning when things are dead."

Smitty scanned the crowds gathered in the street to play blackout bingo. "Never seen anything like it," he grunted. Hundreds were on the sidewalks and in the alleys marking cards. Some knelt in graveled parking lots while others squatted on the pavement; they even filled out cards on each other's backs. Loudspeakers blared out the numbers. On big days, thousands played bingo in the streets, games often reaching astounding payoffs of $7,000.

An elbow jostled Meade. Angrily, he brushed cigarette ash

from his coat. "Now you see why I don't come downtown much. I'll take the Strip anytime."

"Glitter Gulch," said Smitty. "The name fits."

"Everybody thought so when it was the winner in that contest a couple of years ago. Now the Chamber wants to call it Casino Center. They can try, but I'll bet Glitter Gulch sticks."

They sat in a booth at the El Cortez coffee shop. "Reno's like a boom town," Smitty was saying. "Talked to Charlie yesterday. Ten thousand people a day through the club!"

"I know. He says Harolds is doing even better."

Smitty leaned on the table. "I didn't come down here to talk about Smith and Harrah."

"Figured as much."

Smitty lowered his voice. "Giuliano has his sights 'way past Reno. He's doublin' the size of the Western Club—that's no news." Smitty crushed out his cigarette. "He's goin' to build a club at Tahoe. 'Bout a half-mile from Stateline."

Meade nodded. "I've heard rumors."

"Rumors no more. Fact."

Meade absently stirred his coffee. "I've been thinking about Tahoe."

"Come on, Meade," Smitty chided, "you can't start playin' catch-up with Giuliano."

Meade said angrily, "Damnit, Smitty, you know better than that!"

Smitty's face hardened. "Do I?"

Meade tossed the spoon on the table, shaking his head and grinning ruefully. "Hell, Smitty, you've got the right to think that. Damnit, maybe I *am* playing catch-up, but I really think Tahoe has a future."

"Me, too. I've been buyin' up lots around the lake for years. Where would you build a club?"

"The north end, by the Cal-Neva."

Smitty shook his head violently. "Don't do it, Meade. The South Shore is where the action'll be."

Meade raised an eyebrow; he respected Smitty's judgment. "Think so?"

"Damn right. It's a lot closer to California traffic, easier to get to, and the weather ain't goin' to close the road. Stateline's on a cross-country highway; they'll keep it clear. The Cal-Neva shuts down every winter!"

Smitty leaned closer. "Stateline may not have much goin' in the winter, but at least they stay open. Tahoe's goin' to grow. Someday, there'll be thousands livin' there all year around. Tahoe's like a rollin' snowball—it'll get bigger and bigger."

"South Shore," mused Meade. "I'll look into it."

Smitty tapped the table. "Now I've got some big news; you ain't goin' to like it."

"Shoot."

"Giuliano's got fifty acres on the Strip south of the Flamingo, same side of the road. He's had it for years. Kept it under another name. He's goin' to start buildin' next year."

Meade's eyes narrowed. "Fact?"

"Fact. I saw the papers. Got a friend in high places—been payin' him for information for a long time. He gets rich; I get richer."

Meade nodded. Smitty looked like a cowboy down on his luck, but he had to be one of the richest men in the state. Meade said quietly, "Giuliano on the Strip."

"Gonna put you two roosters in the same barnyard."

Meade stared at Smitty through the cigar smoke. "Never knew two roosters to get along unless one was boss."

"Can't have feathers flyin' on the Strip," Smitty said. "The owners won't put up with it, the state either. I thought gettin' the news early will give you time to get used to the idea."

"Maybe I can handle it, but what about Giuliano? He's the one who blew up in Reno."

"He must be figurin' he's got himself under control or he wouldn't be comin' down here."

"Speaking of catch-up, sounds like that's what he's doing."

"It's occurred to me."

"We've got some tough bastards down here. Greenbaum could eat him alive."

"Maybe. Maybe not. Don't sell Giuliano short. He may be homegrown, but he's tougher than shit."

Meade switched the subject. "What do you think about Greenbaum taking over the Flamingo?"

"Can't knock it. Greenbaum's colder than a son of a bitch, but he's a sharp operator. Besides, anybody who gives Sanford Adler a black eye is okay with me. Gettin' Adler out of the Flamingo is the best move so far. I knew Adler when he used to run the Cal-Neva. He's nothin' but a cheatin' bootleg operator. Word ain't worth shit. Obnoxious as hell. Always screamin' his head off over somethin'.

"But Greenbaum has a bad habit, I hear. They say he can't stay away from the tables."

"It's hell when an owner bellies up. Stay with the house; that's the way I see it."

"The word is that the money he owes the mob is going on the tables. When it comes to gambling, Gus is a born loser."

"Speakin' of the Flamingo," Smitty said, "my little bird told me that they're addin' a hundred rooms, the Thunderbird, too. You goin' to join the race for rooms?"

"I don't know," said Meade. "Think I'll wait for a while. This trend toward fancy hotels has got me puzzled. Maybe it's the way to go. If it is, I'm outdated."

The two men walked back toward the Plush Wheel; they passed a bar, the aroma of booze drifting out into the street. Smitty chuckled. "Sorta like Smith's whiskey waterfall."

Meade laughed. "A carnival gag all the way. Might have worked if it was Coke."

Last week, Harolds Club had installed a tumbling rock waterfall behind the bar in the Covered Wagon room on the second floor. The rock was rock. The water was whiskey—Old Forrester.

Thousands rode the first escalators in Nevada to view the spectacular sight. The waterfall drew oohs and aahs; it made an impression that affected more than sight.

The following day, a UP story said: "It wasn't long before gamblers, many of whom hadn't had a nip since breakfast, were leaving the joint in droves, listing first to starboard, then to port. Worse, the patrons soon found themselves wearing fume hangovers."

Old Forrester was replaced with tea.

As Meade and Smitty strolled through Glitter Gulch, winners screamed while losers hurried away with long faces, fleeing the demons that had driven them to this final madness. Loudspeakers brayed. Lights flashed on and off. Slot machines clanked and groaned with the weight of their contents, spewing forth small amounts to keep the customers happy, who pulled the handles with silent determination, coin wrappers littering the tiled floors at their feet.

Smitty grinned up at Meade. "Your little town's growin', Meade. Might be bigger than Reno someday."

28

It was a beautiful late-summer day; the temperature was in the mid-seventies at Lake Tahoe, a vast relief after the stifling heat in Reno.

The big dark man touched Tony Giuliano's arm. "Thought you might be interested," he said, pointing toward where a construction crew was working on the skeleton of Giuliano's new casino. "See that blond kid up on top—the one holding onto that beam?"

"Yeah."

"That's Meade Slaughter's kid." The big man grinned at Giuliano's startled reaction. "I thought that would get to you."

Giuliano shot him a puzzled look. "What's he doin' up there?"

"Working. Like the rest of those poor slobs."

"How come? He could get a lot better deal with his father."

The big man shook his head. "Not anymore. His dad kicked him out."

Tony Giuliano's eyes widened. "Where did you get that?"

"Mario."

"Mario," repeated Giuliano. "Whatta you know."

The big man was Sam Rozini. Years ago, he had been in the rackets in San Francisco with Tony's father. Now he was big in the dockworkers' union. Rozini had driven up from San Francisco to visit with Tony and Mario Gatori, his grandson.

Gatori was a black sheep, an outcast in the family. He had been raised in New York City, where he had become a street-wise, hard-fisted tough, fighting and stealing, nearly driving his mother out of her mind. At twenty-two, he had almost gone to prison. Only the influence of his grandfather had kept his record clean. Rozini had told Mario he would help him on one condition—that he leave New York.

Rozini had called Tony Giuliano, telling him about Mario Gatori's troubles. "I think he'll be all right if he gets in the right place," Rozini said. "I don't expect you to put him to work in your club right away. Let him work up to it. Put him on the construction crew and see how he does. If he gets out of line, dump him down a mine shaft."

Very few knew that Giuliano owned a construction company; it was to his advantage to keep his name out of it. Contracts might have been studied closer if it were known that Tony Giuliano was involved.

Mario Gatori arrived in Reno excited about the prospects of getting into the gambling scene. His grandfather had spelled it out for him; he would have to earn his way into the casino. Mario showed the proper respect for Giuliano and worked hard. He had one attribute that Tony Giuliano prized; he knew how to keep his mouth shut.

That night, Giuliano had Mario Gatori meet him at the Stateline Country Club bar. They sat at a small table in a far corner.

"How's it goin', Mario?" Tony Giuliano asked, smiling pleasantly.

"Great, Mr. Giuliano. Great! Never thought I'd like workin' like this, but I do."

Giuliano laughed. "Maybe you'll like it so much you won't want to work in my club."

Gatori shook his head and grinned. "Not that much. That's my dream—workin' in a casino!"

Giuliano sat back and laced his fingers together. "I like what you're doin'. Keep it up, and your dream will come true."

Mario Gatori beamed with pleasure.

Giuliano took a long pull from his drink, then set the glass down. "There's somethin' you can do for me."

"Anything. Name it," Gatori said eagerly.

"There's a guy workin' with you—name's David Slaughter. Know him?"

"Tall guy, blond hair."

"That's him. Know who his father is?"

Gatori nodded, eyes guarded. There was bad blood between Tony Giuliano and Meade Slaughter; their clash in Reno had reached legendary proportions.

Giuliano said, "Does the Slaughter boy know you have any connection with me?"

Gatori didn't blink. "I don't talk. You tell me to keep quiet, I keep quiet."

Giuliano relaxed and smiled. "Good!" He threw a hundred dollar bill on the table.

Mario Gatori stared at the bill, then looked questioningly at Giuliano.

"I want you to make friends with the Slaughter boy," Giuliano said, pushing the bill toward Gatori. "Use the money for what you like, maybe take a little and entertain Slaughter. I want him to love you like a brother."

Gatori cleared his throat. "Should I know why?"

Laughing loudly, Tony Giuliano sat back in the chair. "How can I tell you when I don't know?" he said. He sat up straight, and his cold voice sent shivers up and down Gatori's spine. "I may not know now but someday I will. When I do,

I want a nice direct pipeline." Giuliano pointed a blunt finger at Gatori. "That's you."

In the Polo Lounge of the Beverly Hills Hotel, Meade Slaughter was also the main topic of conversation, although in this case he had a very lovely champion. For the past hour, she had been the center of attention in a room that had hosted some of the most beautiful women in the world.

"Cindy, I can't see you doing this; it's . . . it's just not natural!"

"What *is* natural?"

The slender man tinkered with his martini glass. "Got me there, Cindy," he said morosely. "Why did I ever get mixed up with the original independent woman?"

"Couldn't help it. I drew you like a moth to the flame."

"And burned my wings off. Cindy, do you realize what you've done to me?"

"No. What?"

"You've grounded me. Cut me off at the knees. Left me a babbling idiot, incapable of entering into a new relationship. Everytime I think I've found a new girl I compare her with you. It's sad. Sad! Ever seen a flower wilt right before your eyes?"

"Maybe you go with blooming idiots?" Cindy offered helpfully.

Laughing, Jack raised his hands. "Okay, I give up. But tell me why you're determined to bury yourself on the desert."

"We've been through that before," Cindy said patiently. "His name is Meade Slaughter, and he's six foot two with black wavy hair and the bluest eyes you've ever seen. He's got shoulders as wide as a barn door, and he looks like he eats nails for breakfast. Besides," she said, resting her chin on a small fist, "I happen to love him."

Jack groaned. "There you go, hitting below the belt again."

"You asked," Cindy said sweetly.

"All right, I'm a glutton for punishment. Cindy, you've made my life miserable for three years. You'd think I'd learn, but I keep coming back for more. At least I've seen you once in a while since you've gone native, but now you're talking about getting out of pictures completely. Be honest with me —how can you do that? I've been around the acting game for a long time. It gets in your blood. You get addicted to it; if you don't get a fix, you wither and die."

Cindy's eyes were no longer laughing. "I've thought about that, Jack. Really, I have. I've thought about a lot of things. I'm not a giddy little schoolgirl building castles in the air. Things go wrong. That's life. You're right about one thing— I'm independent as hell. If I'd been around forty years ago, I'd have been whacking men with women's suffrage placards."

Cindy's eyes softened. "I know what love is now. Real love, the kind that gets inside and fills up your whole body until you feel like you're going to burst. Nothing can take that away from me. Nothing."

Her last words pierced Jack's heart. Before he met Cindy, he was a happy-go-lucky fledgling director, intent only on being among the best in his profession and the leading man in an endless array of ladies' lives. Tall and slim with thick rust-colored hair and sleepy brown eyes, he had had his pick of beautiful women.

Cindy changed all that. Vows of bachelorhood forgotten, he pursued her with the same dedication he applied to his work. It was a brief affair, lasting only a few months, ending with Cindy's trip to Las Vegas to gain the freedom that Jack secretly hoped would clear the way for their marriage. His world came to an end when she called to tell him about Meade. She wasn't one to play games. He hadn't made it any easier by continuing to see her; it was pure masochism.

Cindy touched Jack's arm. "You're sweet, Jack," she said gently. "I do love you; you're the best friend I have."

"Friends," Jack repeated, offering a lopsided smile. He squeezed her hand and kissed her on the cheek. "That's better than nothing."

They met next at the studio. Cindy was glowing. "I'm on my way," she said gaily.

Jack watched her walk across the set, happily waving
goodbye to friends. Tucking the heavy script under his arm,
he turned and walked slowly toward the back lot.

29

"How long before I start knitting little things?"

"You're nearly three months along. You'd better have
everything done by September 26th."

Thank you, Santa Claus, for this belated gift! Cindy left the
doctor's office in a daze, unmindful of the March wind that
whipped her long hair around her face. "Wow, oh wow, oh
wow," she repeated softly, sitting in her car and slapping her
gloved hands together. "Do something, Cindy. Don't just sit
here!"

As if it had a mind of its own, the car headed north out
of town. Ahead, Mt. Charleston filled the sky with snowy
whiteness. Cindy parked the car on the side of the road and
looked up at the twelve-thousand-foot peak. That's where it
happened. Right up there! "Are you satisfied?" she shouted,
glaring at the mountain as if it were a living thing.

Five months ago, she had driven back to Las Vegas, a
crescendo of joy building in her heart as the miles fell away.
Because of the pressures in completing the film, she hadn't
seen Meade for three weeks. If only the car could fly! It was
dark as she drove past the lights on the Strip, her heart
pounding as she neared her house.

She couldn't believe it when she turned the corner. No
black Cadillac parked out front; no lights on inside the house.
A mixup? No, she had talked to Meade last night, and he
knew how punctual she was. Something important must have
happened at the club. What could be more important than

her return? Hurt and fighting back tears, Cindy slipped her key in the lock.

The lights blazed on, and Cindy froze in the doorway. The living room was filled with flowers, and a three-tiered cake rose majestically on the coffee table, a tiny blond doll in a blue gown standing daintily in the white frosting. Beside the cake was a silver ice bucket holding a magnum of champagne. Gaily wrapped gift boxes were on the mantel, in her favorite chair, one even dangling by a string from the ceiling light. A huge banner spanned the wall over the fireplace, displaying, "WELCOME HOME, CINDY," in bright red. Meade was standing by the light switch, grinning from ear to ear. He opened his arms wide.

"Meade. Oh, Meade!" cried Cindy, flying into his arms, laughing and crying at the same time, nuzzling her face into his broad chest while he stroked her hair. "You dunce," she murmured. "You great big beautiful dunce!"

They kissed long and hard, and their bodies responded accordingly. "The cake! The champagne! The gifts!" yelled Cindy, kicking and squirming as Meade carried her into the bedroom.

"Shut up, woman," Meade growled. "You've got to pay for them first."

Somehow they managed to throw off their clothes without ripping seams or tearing off buttons, falling onto the bed in a tangle of arms and legs.

Later, Cindy knelt on the living room floor in her new silk robe; paper, boxes and gifts scattered all around, the top of the cake demolished and the champagne bottle upended in the bucket. She grinned up at Meade, who sat contentedly smoking a cigar on the couch. "I don't think I've done enough to earn all this," she said mischievously. "It may be a long time before I can pay it off."

Meade smiled and rubbed his chin. "You've got good credit with me; I'll accept it on the installment plan."

The weeks slipped by, and it was Christmas. Meade surprised Cindy by renting a cabin on Mt. Charleston. What astounded her most was that he was willing to leave the clubs in other hands for three days. A Christmas miracle in itself.

On Christmas Eve, they pulled a sled through the snow and chopped down their very own tree, then spent the evening decorating it with ornaments, candy, homemade wreaths, pinecones and—Meade considered it a stroke of genius—colorful pairs of Cindy's panties.

Their days were filled with laughter, sledding, hiking and snowfights, the nights with making love in the big oak bed and on the thick rug in front of the fireplace.

Cindy was showered with gifts on Christmas Day, including a full-length black mink coat. Among Meade's gifts was a pair of platinum cuff links with the letters MS set in diamonds. Cindy's eyes shone with anticipation when he opened the red velvet box. She had planned this for so long, wanting to express her love in some special way. She was rewarded by an expression of tenderness she had never before seen on Meade's face. Afterward, they made love amidst the scattered papers and string, the flickering firelight dancing over their glistening naked bodies.

Those three days had been heaven, thought Cindy as she gazed up at Mt. Charleston. Now this little bundle from the same place!

Now what, Cindy girl? There was a logical solution; this kind of thing happened a lot in Hollywood. She could ask around and find the name of a doctor who would professionally and discreetly take care of the problem. Problem? Is that what the baby is? Hey, don't get sentimental!

Since when have you liked kids? Not much future in it if they have to grow up the way you did. Thank God, you had a grandmother who took you in when you were seven, after your dad took off and your mother turned to booze and drove her car off the cliff at Pacific Palisades.

"Well," Cindy said aloud as she started the car. "That settles that." Driving home, she made her plans. She would tell Meade she had to go to Hollywood to settle some matters with her agent. He would believe her; he had no reason not to.

It was not until that night that her thoughts turned to other things, things she might have put off for another six months or a year. Damn! Why couldn't life be simple?

Despite what she had told Jack, she missed the creative fulfillment she received from acting. Without Meade, she would have been driven to despair in Las Vegas. Isolated from her previous world and the world around her, she spent most of her time keeping herself and her little jewel-box of a house in readiness for Meade's appearances.

She had to face what had been bothering her more and more of late. She had no *roots*. She had a past and a present but no future. No goals, no challenges. She was drifting aimlessly—toward what?

Now we get down to the nitty-gritty, Cindy thought as she lay in the dark quietness of her bed. Just what is it you want? Wouldn't it be great to have it all? Meade, marriage, acting, a child. There. You've said it. Marriage. That child part just slipped in. Pretty natural, considering what you've got growing inside your tummy.

Marriage. They had never discussed it. It hadn't seemed important in the beginning, but it had been on her mind a lot of late. Marriage would give her a sense of *being*. Then she could kiss Hollywood goodbye forever. She would pitch in and help Meade. There would be outlets for her creativity. She could help in the design and decorating of his clubs, fix up the old ranch house, even help form a little theater group. She would have *purpose*.

What about Meade? Ah, that was the $64,000 question. He would have unhappy memories about his first marriage, but that hadn't kept him from planning to marry Sandra. Sandra! David had said nobody could replace her. Was that just the raving of an angry boy or was it true? Meade had never mentioned her; that wasn't good.

Speaking of David, what about him? She had seen him when visiting Reno with Meade. David still wasn't friendly toward her, and his relationship with his father was strained at best. Even if David did disapprove of her, he would never live with his father again, so that wouldn't be a daily conflict in their lives.

Now the biggest question of all. If Meade should bounce in that door tonight and ask her to marry him, everything would be fine. She would say yes and suggest that they get married as soon as possible; otherwise, things might get embarrassing six months from now. Bad enough explaining a three-month premature baby. Especially if it weighs ten pounds!

Well, there's not much chance of Meade asking, so what should she do? See that doctor and go on as if nothing had happened? No, I'm not sure I want that, Cindy concluded. Oh God, what am I talking about?

Cindy lay awake long into the night.

30

"Meade?"

"Hmmm?"

"You aren't really asleep, are you?"

"As a matter of fact, I am. Who are you—the tooth fairy?"

"Snow White. She gets bigger billing."

"I'm Grumpy. Leave me alone."

Reaching down from her sitting position against the headboard, Cindy lifted one corner of the pillow. "Your eyes are open. You're faking."

Meade pulled the pillow back over his head. "Go away," he said in a muffled voice.

Cindy dropped her magazine on the floor beside the bed. "I'm lonely. Talk to me."

"Can't. I'm asleep."

"Meade Slaughter, it's past noon. You've had your eight hours and then some. Awake; the world awaits!"

Meade groaned and tossed the pillow aside. "Why do you have to look so pretty and clean in the morning?" Meade said. "Makes me feel like something that crawled out from under a rock."

"Tell you what, Grumpy. Why don't you shower while I throw a little breakfast together?"

"Good idea. When you see me next, I'll look like Prince What's-his-name."

"Charming."

"Right."

It's now or never, Cindy thought as they sat on the living room couch having their after-breakfast coffee. "I finished that script Lee sent me," she said. "It's a good part. He's going to be pretty angry if I don't take it."

Meade looked sharply at Cindy. "I thought you were through with that stuff. You said you were reading the script to make your agent happy."

"I was. At first. But it's made me think, Meade, I can't sit here and wilt away."

Meade put his arms around her shoulders. "You don't look like you're wilting, honey. You look great to me."

"Be serious. How would you like it if you were doing nothing with your life?"

"Hey," Meade said, tilting Cindy's head up. "What's this?"

There was no turning back now. "Darling, I'm not the kind to do nothing with my life. You know I'd rather be with you than anything else in the world, but I'm still an artist of sorts. Someone once said that there's no one unhappier than a person with creative talent who's not using it."

Meade said, "That's the way you feel? Like you're burying yourself?"

"No, darling, not burying myself. I've never been so happy as I've been the last two years." Cindy reached up and touched his cheek. "I love you. In many ways, you're my whole life. But I'm still an *individual.* I need to express myself. Acting has been the most satisfying way for me."

Meade looked puzzled. "Is that what you're saying? You'll be happy if you can keep on acting?"

Cindy shook her head. "There's more to it than that." She struck a small fist into her palm. "Oh damn, whatever I say, it comes out wrong!"

Meade took her hand. "Take your time, honey. I've got lots of time."

Cindy rested her head on Meade's shoulder, her heart pleading with her to stop. Oh God, how she wished she could! "It's just . . . just that I don't know where I'm going," Cindy said, lacing her cold fingers through Meade's. "Not just where *I'm* going—where *we're* going." *There, I've said it!*

Meade's arm stiffened around her shoulders, and his hand closed tighter over her hand. "Things have been good the last two years," he said gently.

"Oh, darling, wonderful! I couldn't ask for more."

"But you are," protested Meade.

Cindy bowed her head and nodded. "I guess you're right. Please try to understand!"

"I'm trying, honey. Let's get this straight. You want us to stay together, but you also want to act. Is that it?"

"Yes . . . sort of." Cindy bit her lip, then burst out, "Are we going to go on like this forever?"

Meade slowly expelled his breath. "That's it, isn't it? It's us that's bothering you most."

Cindy nodded. "Mostly." She looked up quickly. "I'm a person, Meade. A *person!* You've been my whole life for two years. You still are—so much it scares me. I would like to go on, but not on this basis. I don't want to be a bystander in your life; I want to be a part of it. It would give my life meaning. I need acting now because that's all I've got. I can turn my back on it if there's something better to replace it."

"Marriage," Meade said quietly. "That's what it all comes down to, isn't it?"

Cindy began crying silently. She tried to speak but couldn't. Slowly, she nodded her head. "Yes," she whispered.

Several moments passed. Meade hugged Cindy and said,

"Don't cry, honey. You're always so happy. It kills me to see you like this."

Cindy sniffed and rubbed her nose. "I feel like a fool."

"Maybe we're both fools," Meade said musingly. He squeezed her hand. "Okay if I don't say yes or no right now? This takes getting used to."

"Of course," Cindy said, moving closer into his embrace. "I've only been thinking about it seriously for a few days."

"It's been a long time since I've thought about marriage," Meade said in a low reflective voice.

"Sandra, wasn't it?" Cindy said softly.

Meade pulled away from Cindy, an astounded look on his face. "Where did you hear about her?" he asked in a barely audible tone.

"David."

"David? I didn't know you were that friendly."

"We aren't. It wasn't the best of days. He was angry with me and said I could never replace Sandra in your life."

"Oh." Meade looked like he had received a blow to the heart. "When was that?"

"A year and a half ago."

"A year and a half ago," Meade repeated. He looked at Cindy with anguished eyes. "Yes, I loved Sandra very much. When she was killed, something in me died with her." He paused and rubbed his big hands together. "I haven't had much luck with love. Maybe I'm a jinx." He reached out as if to touch Cindy, then withdrew his hand. "I don't want to mess up your life."

Cindy seized his hands. "I don't expect you to love me like you did Sandra, but I need your love. I want to spend the rest of my life with you but not if you don't feel the same way."

Meade's eyes were pleading. "Give me time to think, honey. A few days. Please!"

They talked for another hour, then Meade went off to work. There was a quiet desperation about their next two nights together; by mutual consent, neither brought up the subject of marriage.

On the third day, Meade dropped by in the afternoon to

say he had to go up to Reno for three days. "I'll have the answer when I get back," he said, smiling wanly. "Funny, I'm usually quick when it comes to making decisions." He ran his fingers through Cindy's hair. "This is a big one, maybe the biggest one I'll ever make in my life. I want it to be right." He drew her into his arms. "I'll call tomorrow night."

Cindy clung to Meade for a long time, seeing him only as a blur as he walked out the door to his car.

31

Las Vegas dropped out of sight as the Bonanza Airlines C-47 climbed into the evening sky. Banking slowly, the aircraft set a course for Reno.

Meade sat by the window, a heavy briefcase in his lap. Across the aisle, Don Milton and Bob Thompson were playing cards. Meade started to unzip his briefcase, then turned to gaze out the window. The briefcase was forgotten as his mind drifted back to the little house on Ninth Street. Cindy would probably be fixing dinner. She had been trying out a lot of gourmet dishes lately, products of a fancy cookbook Meade had given her for Christmas.

A wonderful two years, Cindy had said. A gross understatement. Cindy had brought so much joy into his life. Closing his eyes, he saw her mischievous grin and heard her bubbling laughter. He smiled at the happy picture.

Another picture replaced Cindy's—out of focus, blurred by time, worn and crumpled from overuse by the fingers of his mind. Sandra. So much promise! Their marriage would have been the best. If only he could be sure it would be the same with Cindy.

His reflection mocked him in the darkened window. What

makes you so sure things would have been perfect with Sandra? How much time did you *really* spend with her? What new things would you have learned about each other over the years? Could it be that you've put Sandra on a pedestal and measured all other women by that unfair yardstick? You've been with Cindy for two years—four times as long as with Sandra. Have you discovered qualities in her you can't accept? Come on, name them!

Is it true? thought Meade. Have I been unfairly comparing Cindy with Sandra? Did Sandra's death and the ensuing years combine to create a flawless person, an unattainable image that no woman could match? Have I closed my heart to love because my love lies buried in that cemetery in Reno? Would Sandra wish this for me? She would be the last to want that.

Admit it, Meade, there are so many things you love about Cindy—her unquenchable spirit, her smile, her touch, the beauty within matched only by the loveliness without.

Meade's eyes opened wide, and he stared at his face in the mirrored glass. You love her! You thick-headed bastard, you love her! What a fool you've been, letting the past dictate to your heart! Sandra would have to be laid to rest in a sacred part of your memory; it was time for the living.

His mind made up, Meade wondered why it had taken him so long. He was seized by a sudden feeling of loneliness, a feeling that increased as the plane took him further from the one he loved. He would call Cindy as soon as the plane landed. No, better yet, he'd wrap up his work tomorrow and fly back that night. They could get married the next day.

Meade barely slept during the next twenty-four hours, rushing about trying to complete in one day what had been scheduled for three. Even Charlie couldn't pry from him why he was pushing himself so. Meade would just grin and look mysterious.

Shortly before midnight, the Cadillac pulled up in front of Cindy's house. Meade dismissed the bodyguards and walked quickly to the front door. Stepping into the entrance, he turned on the light and called out, not wanting to frighten Cindy.

No answer. Strange. Cindy was a light sleeper, usually waking up when he opened the front door. Hurrying down the hall, Meade flipped on the bedroom light. He stood in the doorway, mouth agape.

The bed was empty, unused. All of Cindy's things were gone from the dresser, the top newly dusted. Heart sinking, Meade threw open the closet doors. Nothing. The rods were bare.

Then he saw it, propped against the headboard of the bed. With shaking hands, he tore the envelope open, revealing two sheets of light blue stationary.

Dearest Meade,

My heart is breaking as I write this. It's late at night, and I must hurry. There are so many things I have to do.

My darling, I love you more than I can ever say. You have given me enough happiness to last a lifetime, and it will have to last that long because I'm going away.

Why? you ask. Because, darling, for things to work, we would have to love equally. I could have waited for your answer, but I saw it in your eyes. One has to be very sure about these things, and I know you aren't. You understand, don't you?

You are wondering why I didn't wait. I barely have the strength to do this. I might have lost my resolve if I talked to you. That would have made things worse.

When you told me you would call tomorrow night (tonight now), I knew I had to leave immediately. So, I will be gone when you call. I hope I don't worry you too much, darling.

Please, Meade, don't try to find me. Let's think about the good times and get on with our lives. Remember that you are loved—always.

Cindy

Shocked beyond belief, Meade searched the house, finding nothing of Cindy's left. Her car keys were on the kitchen table, the signed pink slip alongside. The car was in the garage, a bright red memorial to its former owner.

Meade called the airport and contacted an agent he knew, asking him to check the flight records. The man called back in ten minutes; a Cindy Clark had flown to Los Angeles at 1:05 that afternoon.

Hanging up, Meade wandered through the silent house, lost in a whirlpool of despair. If only he had called last night! He looked at his watch. 12:33 A.M. There was nothing he could do until morning. Where should he start? Cindy's agent. Lee, a last name that was decidedly English. Entwistle! He would call him first. Maybe it would be better to take an early plane and see him at his office.

Meade stopped in the middle of the living room and shook his head, shoulders slumping in defeat. He wasn't thinking straight; he had to get some rest. He walked to the empty bedroom and sat on Cindy's bed, wearily slipping off his coat and loosening his tie. Undressing, he got into bed, falling asleep with his arm reaching out where Cindy should have been.

He was up early and talking to the agent at nine. "Cindy? No, I haven't heard a thing. I was getting ready to call her. If she doesn't sign that new picture contract this week, Universal is withdrawing the offer. What's the matter with that girl? It took years to get her where she is; now she's throwing it all away!"

Meade said, "Will you tell her I called? I've got to hear from her—right away."

"Glad to, old chap, if I hear from her. Damnit, what's got into her?" There was a tone of accusation in his voice; no doubt he blamed Meade for Cindy's odd behavior.

Giving Entwistle his number, Meade hung up and paced his office, furiously trying to recall names of friends Cindy might have mentioned. He drew a blank, only first names, casually dropped now and then. Cindy had told him once that she didn't want to bring her Hollywood life into theirs.

She had no family that he knew of, her grandmother having died several years ago.

He called Warner Brothers where Cindy had worked when she first came to Hollywood. He was informed that Cindy Clark was not among their current actresses and coldly refused any information as to her whereabouts. A dead end.

Meade went about his work the next few days in a state of utter frustration, creating such an upheaval in the clubs that Charlie called him, demanding to know what was going on. "Damnit, Meade, you left Janie in tears today, and she's the best goddamn secretary in Nevada. Izzie said you bit his head off when he called about last week's count. What's got into you?"

"Nothing," Meade said, unwilling to discuss the matter. "Something I've got to work out. Sorry I shook Janie up. Tell her I'll take her to lunch next time I come up. Okay?"

"Sure," Charlie said, softening a bit. "Anything your old uncle can do to help?"

Meade's voice was low. "Wish you could, Charlie, but this one's my problem—all the way."

"I understand," Charlie said quietly, seeing it all too clearly now. Something was wrong between Meade and Cindy. He recalled Meade's rush to return to Las Vegas, a look of happy anticipation on his face. What had happened? He'd find out eventually. Nothing he could do but wait. "Okay, son," Charlie said. "In the meantime do your uncle a favor and take it easy on the help."

Entwistle's call came later in the week. "I'm holding the damnedest letter you've ever seen," he said in his clipped English accent. "Came in this morning. Cindy says she is through with acting and I'm to take her off my list. She thanks me politely for all I've done and wishes me luck. That's it, nothing more."

Meade's heart sank. "What's her return address?"

"That's even curiouser. There isn't any. The letter was mailed in Santa Monica."

Hanging up, Meade sat a long time at his desk, staring at the silent telephone. How could Cindy drop out of acting like that? It had been her whole life until she met him. Would she go that far to avoid him? If she was out of acting, he had no lead from which to start searching.

That afternoon, he flew to Los Angeles and hired a private detective agency, instructing them to spare no expense finding Cindy Clark.

The weeks slipped by and became months. Meade gave up the lease on the little house on Ninth Street and sold the red Buick convertible. Outwardly, he showed nothing of the pain and loneliness he experienced every waking hour. Only Charlie knew. Not because Meade had said anything—he hadn't mentioned Cindy since she left. Charlie knew because he loved Meade like a son and felt his hurt as if it were his own.

Gradually, Meade got back into the swing of things, but his heart continued to lurch every time he saw a girl with long blond hair. He was paying a heavy penalty for a misplaced loyalty to the past.

The word got around town that he had broken up with Cindy, but no one dared to bring up the matter in his presence. Cindy became a memory; many beautiful women had come and gone in Las Vegas and many more would follow.

Meade paid the detective agency off and cancelled the search. Like Alice down the rabbit hole, Cindy had dropped completely out of sight.

BOOK THREE

1950-1956

1

"Wilbur Clark was wearing so many diamonds, he looked like a lighthouse," Meade said. "Searchlights, flowers, beautiful women, the press brought in from all over the country —the works. Governor Pittman was there and what looked like half of Hollywood. We thought the Flamingo opening was something. This made it look like peanuts."

Charlie leaned over the table in the Reno Plush Wheel restaurant and studied the pictures in the Las Vegas *Review-Journal.* "The ad says, 'Come as you are,' but I don't see any jeans or cowboy shirts. Lots of furs. Too bad this isn't in color. A pink tree in the lobby?"

"Wilbur likes pink," Meade said, recalling the opening of the Desert Inn two nights ago, April 24, 1950. "The Inn's painted pink, and he had that pink Joshua tree inside for opening night. It was loaded with pink carnations; every woman who came in got one. I think Nevada's got some of the best showmen in the world."

"Good shows, too," Charlie said, reading the ad. "Edgar Bergen, Vivian Blaine, Ray Noble and His Orchestra."

Meade pushed his coffee cup aside and rested his elbows on the table. "The Strip offers something you can't find anywhere—the chance to act like a millionaire even if you're a working stiff."

"We had lots of working stiffs in the parks," said Charlie, rolling his cigar from one side of his mouth to the other. "Ever miss those days?"

"Sometimes. I guess everybody looks back now and then and misses the good old days. You?"

"Not much. In some ways, this isn't much different, only the stakes are higher. I kinda like staying in one place. Getting old, I guess."

"Hell, you're looking better every day."

Charlie grinned. "Sixty-two and a lot of white hair, but still built like a boy where it counts. Ask any of the fortunate women in my life."

Meade laughed. "At least you're not marrying them."

Charlie shot Meade a sour look. "I'm getting older, not weaker in the head."

David walked into the restaurant and sat down in a booth near the entrance. He was accompanied by a slim, dark-haired young man. Meade lifted a hand in greeting. David acknowledged with a wave, then turned back to his companion, who sat with his back to Meade.

"Who's the guy with David?" asked Meade.

Charlie glanced over the back of the booth. "Mario Gatori," he said. "They pal around a lot."

"Gatori," mused Meade. "Don't recall ever seeing him before."

"You're not around here much, you know. Besides," Charlie added, watching Meade closely, "you don't visit the Western Club often. That's where Gatori works—deals twenty-one."

Meade stiffened. "The hell you say."

"Nothing to worry about. He just works there. Seems to be a pretty good friend to David."

Meade was silent for a few moments, lost in thought as he watched his son and Gatori carry on an animated conversation. How long had it been since he and David had been so free and easy with each other? Had they ever?

Charlie said: "Bill Harrah asked me to bring you by. We were on the phone this morning. He wants to buy you a drink."

Meade stood up. "Let's go," he said.

Meade stopped by David's booth. "How are you, David?" he asked, big hands resting on his hips.

"Okay," David replied, looking up at his father, then glancing quickly away. "Meet Mario Gatori; he's a friend of mine."

"Mario," Meade said, extending his hand.

The young man's hand was slender, but his grip was strong. "Glad to meet you, Mr. Slaughter," he said in a surprisingly mellow voice. Jet-black hair fit his finely featured face like a short curly mop. That, combined with long silky eyelashes, gave him an innocent, almost angelic look. Until you looked at his eyes. They had the dark shiny look of a newly split lump of coal, and they were old beyond their years. Twenty-five going on sixty, thought Meade as he released Gatori's hand.

After Meade and Charlie left, Gatori said admiringly, "Never saw your dad up so close. Damn, he looks bigger than a house!"

David watched Meade's broad back disappear out the door, then turned back to Gatori. "Just think how he looked when I was a kid. Talk about big! More like a building than a house." The pride was still there, along with the hate, and the resentment and the feeling of inadequacy.

Inadequacy. David had thought about that last night lying in his bed at the Terhunes'. He seemed to go through an emotional upheaval every time he thought of his father. It angered him. He didn't give a damn what his father thought, so why should he get so bothered?

2

"I'm not waiting to get drafted," said Jim Terhune. "I'm enlisting—in the Marines."

David sat on the edge of the chair and stared at his friend. "When did you decide that?" he asked in an astounded voice.

"I've been thinking about it for a couple of weeks, and made up my mind this morning. You're the first to know."

Nearly eight weeks had passed since Sunday, June 25, 1950, when North Korea opened fire on a forty-mile front, raining death across the 38th Parallel on South Korea.

The two Koreas were wards of the United Nations, thus the North Korean attack was an act of war against the United Nations, of which America was a leading member.

Americans were shocked to learn that their great military might had dwindled to a fourth of Russia's. U.S. troops in Japan, according to General William F. Dean, had deteriorated to a force that was accustomed to "Japanese girl friends, plenty of beer and gooks to shine their shoes."

Within six weeks, units of the National Guard were called up, and the draft quota was set at 600,000.

"Why the Marines?" David asked Jim Terhune.

"Why not?" replied Jim. He was a year younger than David, having had his twenty-first birthday in late May, ten days before he graduated from the University of Nevada. He didn't have the size and height of his father. Of the three children, Jim looked the most like Janice—the same slender build, ash-blond hair, light brown eyes. He was four inches shorter than David's six feet one.

David studied his friend. "You're really going to do it, aren't you?"

"I said I was, didn't I? Look, Dave, if I don't join, I'm
going to get drafted. At least the odds say I will. I don't want
to be some infantry slob. The Marines are a professional unit.
If I'm going to fight, I want a guy next to me who knows what
he's doing."

David stood up, jaw set. "Let's go before I change my
mind," he said, heading for the door of his room.

Jim grinned and slapped his friend on the back. "Now
you're talking. I knew you'd do it."

Janice accepted the news with her usual calm. Meade's
reaction was one of surprise, mixed with pride. "I'll be
damned," he said to Janice, who had called him with the
news.

"At least they'll be together," Janice said. "That makes me
feel better."

"Me, too. When do they go?"

"Two, three weeks. They'll know for sure on Tuesday."

"I'll be up next week. We'll throw them a farewell party."

"Like I've always said, Meade—you're a champ."

Three weeks later, David and Jim arrived at Camp Pendle-
ton, near San Diego.

As the war raged in Korea, another battle loomed on the
Las Vegas horizon. The soldiers were from Washington; the
war was against crime.

On May 26, 1950, the Special Committee to Investigate
Crime in Interstate Commerce, soon to be known as the
Kefauver Committee, held its first hearing in Miami. Before
it was disbanded in May, 1951, the committee traveled
32,380 miles in the United States, held hearings in fourteen
cities and gathered millions of words in testimony from eight
hundred witnesses.

The audience for such hearings would not normally have
been large. But the advent of television changed all that.
There was little daytime television in 1950, so local stations
filled their dead time with the Kefauver hearings. Millions
were given a thorough indoctrination in the influence of
crime in the United States.

Estes Kefauver, a six foot three inch Democrat senator

from Tennessee, became a familiar image, one of the most identifiable men in America. It helped launch him on an unsuccessful bid for the presidency in 1952, a loss which undoubtedly caused Nevada to heave a great sigh of relief.

On November 15, 1950, fresh from stinging sessions in Detroit and Philadelphia, the panel hit Las Vegas.

For all the hoopla, it wasn't much. The closed-door hearing lasted one day—nine hours interrupted by a sight-seeing trip to Boulder Dam. Kefauver expressed his personal conclusion in one sentence. "As a case history of legalized gambling, Nevada speaks eloquently in the negative."

Bill Moore, a member of the Nevada Tax Commission representing "Business"—the business being his part ownership in the Last Frontier—was a special irritant to Kefauver. Moore's referring to everyone on the committee as "Fella," including, in Kefauver's words, "even the dignified Senator Tobey from New Hampshire," grated on the committee's nerves.

When the Tax Commission was formed in 1948, licenses were automatically granted to established casino owners, some of whom had felonies on their records. When asked about this, Moore replied, "Are you going to throw out a man with a three-and-a-half-million-dollar investment?"

Counsel Halley mentioned a Detroit gambler who had been granted a license in Nevada, a man who had a long record of illegal operations in other states. "Sure," Moore said in his easy Texas drawl, "but that is no sign that he shouldn't have a license in a state where it is legal."

Halley stared at Moore. "It makes no difference to you whether he gambles in a state where it is not legal?"

"No," answered Moore firmly. "How else is he going to learn about the business?"

A bit of fun was poked at the committee when pranksters had messages blared simultaneously from hotel loudspeakers that echoed over the Strip. "Paging Mr. Frank Costello; Mr. Bugs Lansky wanted on the telephone; Mr. Joe Adonis, please; paging Mr. Tony Accardo."

Wilbur Clark was blasted by the "dignified" Senator

Tobey for his choice of partners in the Desert Inn. "Before you got in bed with crooks to finish this proposition," sputtered Tobey, "didn't you look into these birds at all?"

Clark smiled and said, "Not too much. No, sir." When Vegans heard about this, they chuckled silently. After looking at the framework of the Desert Inn drying in the desert air for twenty months, Clark would have gone into league with the devil to bring his dream to fruition.

Tobey, whose caustic tongue spared no one during the hearing, barked at Clark. "You have the most nebulous idea of your business I ever saw. You have a smile on your face, but I don't know how the devil you do it."

Wilbur Clark bestowed a brilliant smile on the glowering senator. "I've done it all my life," he said, his smile widening even more.

In later hearings, when the committee interviewed one of the "birds" Clark had gone into partnership with, Moe Dalitz uttered a one-liner that raised him to revered status in Vegas.

Regarding Dalitz's investments, Senator Kefauver asked, "Now, to get your investments started off you did get yourself a pretty good nest-egg out of rum running, didn't you?"

Dalitz leaned forward and spoke clearly into the microphone, "Well, I didn't inherit my money, Senator."

At the Las Vegas hearing, little Moe Sedway, no longer under Bugsy Siegel's shadow and shining on his own as a small percentage owner in the Flamingo, thoroughly confounded the Kefauver Committee, fielding their questions with double-talk. The committee wasn't able to draw from him the names of the real owners of the Flamingo.

In his book about the hearings, published in 1951, Kefauver coined two new words, "Siegelized" and "Binionized." He said when a state or a community—in this case Nevada and Las Vegas—had been "Siegelized" or "Binionized," his opposition to legalized gambling was firm.

He referred to Bugsy Siegel, dead four years, as the former "gambling boss" of Las Vegas.

Lester (Benny) "Cowboy" Binion was very much alive and doing well in Las Vegas.

After his initial partnership with J. K. Houssels in the Las Vegas Club, Binion had opened the Westerner Club on Fremont Street. He had lost his license briefly when one of his bodyguards, Cliff Helms, shot and killed an ex-convict in the boiler room of the Las Vegas Club.

Kefauver's main attack on Binion was for his running feud with Herbert Noble, a former competitor in Dallas. Kefauver's book referred to two of Noble's nicknames—"The Cat" and "The Clay Pigeon."

Lieutenant George Butler of the Dallas Police Department, who assisted the Kefauver Committee as a special investigator, testified that at the time (1950), Binion had made nine attempts on Noble's life. Noble had been shot in the head and the leg, even shot at while recuperating in the hospital from another murder attempt. Bombs had been placed in his home and airplane. One bomb accidentally killed Noble's wife when he decided to drive another vehicle. This feud, which had begun in the late thirties, continued, according to Butler, even after Binion moved to Las Vegas.

On one occasion, Butler caught Noble fitting one of his airplanes with bombs, so he could fly to Las Vegas and bomb Binion's home.

The matter was ended on August 7, 1951, when Noble was blown apart by a bomb planted under a cattle guard next to his mailbox. It was never proved that Binion was involved.

When the committee held its final hearing in New York in March, 1951, Virginia Hill testified that she hadn't gone out much in Las Vegas because she was allergic to cactus. It brought a good laugh in Vegas. Cactus was rare but creosote plentiful on the Strip.

The committee's summation of the Las Vegas hearing was not unexpected. Reno was also castigated, with Bill Graham and Jim McKay referred to as having "controlled Reno politically and financially."

The summation concluded: "It seems clear to the committee that too many of the men running gambling operations in Nevada are either members of existing out-of-state gambling syndicates or have had histories of close association with the underworld characters who operate those syndicates.

"The licensing system which is in effect in this state has not resulted in excluding the undesirables from the state but has merely served to give their activities a seeming cloak of respectability."

The committee concluded that no proposal for legalized gambling carried any guarantees of success. In Kefauver's words, "Every plan (proposal) that was suggested, when subjected to impartial analysis, seemed to play right into the hands of the Siegels, Costellos, Sedways, Binions and others, large and small, of their ilk."

Nevadans couldn't have agreed with him less.

3

David threshed about the hospital bed, moaning feverishly. Hands gently pressed against his chest, holding him still, calming him. The dream was returning . . .

The icy wind howled across the bleak Korean mountaintop. Jim Terhune was bundled up beside him a few yards from a deep chasm. They had been talking about Janice. "Ever think about your real mom?" Jim asked.

"Some," David said. He couldn't really remember her. Pictures were all he had.

"What about your father?" Jim said softly, his voice almost lost in the wind.

Even in his dreams, David could feel the anger. But Jim's reasoning had won out. And the new maturity Korea had so swiftly bestowed. . . .

* * *

David's body relaxed on the hospital bed as the words from his letter to Meade flashed in and out of his delirium. "I love you, Dad. . . . You see things different out here. . . . I was wrong when we got in that fight. . . . I hope we see a lot of each other when I get back." The signature at the bottom, "Your son, David." He had sent it—days, weeks ago? . . .

He was sitting against a rock with Jim, wolfing down a Thanksgiving dinner piled high on a tin plate. The food was turning cold faster than they could eat it. Never mind, the war would be over and they would be home by Christmas.

Shots and the blaring of bugles. A soldier's face disappearing in a splash of red. The attackers were Chinese. The 1st Marine Division's retreat from the Chosin Reservoir, fighting overwhelming odds, carrying their wounded, leaving their dead, struggling to reach the port of Hungnam, forty miles away. . . .

David cried out, awakening the sleeper in the chair by his bed. "No! No!" David shouted. He could still see Jim Terhune reaching out, a surprised look on his face, blood spurting from a great hole in his neck. "Jim!" David whispered. The scene faded, replaced by a long mound of dirt—Jim and eighty-three others buried in an icy grave, tears making dirty rivulets down David's bearded face as he trudged away.

Twelve days, and they still hadn't reached Hungnam. Another ambush. David spun like a broken doll, left arm smashed and bleeding. The pain, the terrible pain! Hungnam. Doctors. A long plane flight. How much was real and how much a dream?

A dark figure loomed over the bed. "Water," David gasped.

His head was raised, a glass held to his lips. "Thanks," David murmured. He drifted off to quiet sleep.

It was still dark when he awoke again. The pain was steady, throbbing, insistent. David tried to move and cried out sharply.

A glass was lifted to his parched lips. The sheet was straightened over his trembling body, and a hand felt his brow. The room ceased spinning, then began to spin again. He was drawn down into a bottomless pit.

Rays of sunlight slanted through the venetian blinds and produced a soft glow. David looked up at the ceiling. It no longer rippled like a white sheet in the wind. His body was bathed in sweat, making him shiver slightly under the light covers.

The pain made him wince. A full minute passed before he got up the nerve to reach across and touch his left shoulder. Trembling fingers traced the bandages, splints and straps that enclosed his arm. David almost sobbed with relief. During the retreat, in Hungnam, on the plane across the Pacific, every lucid moment had been filled with the fear that he would lose his arm.

A heavy-set nurse strode into the room. She looked at David's quizzical expression and smiled. "So you're back in the land of the living!" she said jovially, feeling his pulse. She studied her watch and nodded approvingly. Pulling out a thermometer, she gave it a snap with her wrist. "Think you can keep this in your mouth without biting it in two?" she asked, popping it in before David could answer.

When she removed the thermometer, she said, "Good, very good!" She looked down at David and smiled. "This is the first time in a week that your temperature's been normal. Looks like you're going to make it after all."

Quickly and with surprising gentleness, she stripped the bed and changed the sheets, then David's gown. "There," she said, wiping David's face off with a damp cloth. "That's better. We couldn't have you looking like a drowned puppy when the doctor comes." She cocked her head to one side. "You've been getting a lot of special treatment here. That's some father you've got."

David's eyes widened. "Father?" His voice was a croak.

"Yep. He's been here ever since you arrived. Poor man, he hasn't had much sleep. He's spent most of his time with you."

David digested the shocking news. "Where am I?" he asked.

"San Francisco Memorial. You were brought here straight from Fairfield-Suisan Air Force Base. Your father saw to it that you got the best of everything—doctors, private room, the works."

"Where is he?"

"Resting in the doctors' lounge. He was dead on his feet —and getting in the way." She grinned. "Actually, he's pretty popular around here, bringing us flowers, candy and stuff. It's a con job, but we love it."

David was dazed. It was too much all at once. "My arm," he said, "how—"

The nurse held up her hand. "Doctor Hansen will be by in a few minutes. He'll tell you everything."

When the doctor arrived, he read the chart, then sat on the edge of the bed. "Well, David," he said, peering down through thick horn-rimmed glasses, "you're a lucky young man. When you arrived, we thought you were going to lose your arm. When we got past that crisis, we thought we were going to lose *you*. You developed a bad infection and a temperature to go with it. Things started to look better two days ago when your temperature started dropping. You'll be okay now, but you're going to have to take it easy for a long time."

He fiddled with a gold pen, turning it around and around in his hands. "You'll never have full use of your left arm. We've done what we could, but it's a makeshift job at best. With the proper therapy, you'll be able to lift small things, put your clothes on, drive a car, normal things. But you'll have to be careful and exercise regularly. Your arm may give you pain for the rest of your life. Chances are, it will."

David asked in a low hoarse voice, "Am I okay otherwise?"

"Nothing to worry about. You have a couple of other wounds, one in the leg, another under the arm. They'll heal up before long." The doctor smiled. "You seem to favor the left side; that's where all the damage is."

David looked around. "When will I see my father?"

The doctor stood up. "This afternoon. You're pretty washed out." He stuck the pen in an outside pocket. "Don't worry. You'll have lots of time to talk."

David slept right through the afternoon. When he opened his eyes, the window was dark, but the hospital corridor was filled with bustling sounds. A lamp glowed on the right side of the bed. Meade was slumped down in a chair reading a newspaper.

David's voice was just above a whisper. "Dad?"

Meade's head snapped up. He was on his feet in one swift motion, the newspaper falling to the floor unnoticed. They stared at each other for several long moments, too filled with emotion to speak. David was amazed to see tears in his father's eyes. He felt his own eyes filling and tried unsuccessfully to raise his head.

Meade moved to the side of the bed and grasped David's hand. "How are you, son?" His voice was deep, comforting.

"Okay, I guess. You?"

Meade's grip tightened. "Right now, I feel like a million dollars. It's been hell the last week. You've been pretty sick."

"You've been here all week?" David attempted a smile. "Who's been minding the store?"

Meade sat on the bed. "To hell with the store! I'm with my son. That's more important than anything."

David thought his heart would leap out of his chest. "You really mean that?" he blurted out, tears sliding down over his cheeks.

Meade took a deep breath before answering, fighting to keep from choking up. "More than you'll ever know, David. I've got a lot of making up to do. I hope you'll let me be a real father to you from now on."

Neither said anything for a time. David asked, "You got my letter?"

"I got it. I can't tell you what it meant to me. I mailed a letter to you the same day, but that was right before Thanksgiving, so I guess you didn't get it."

David shook his head, staring up in wonder at the face that he had silently worshipped—and feared—for so long.

The broken nose, the jagged scar on the broad forehead, the rugged features that seemed to have taken on a gentle look just for him, the piercing blue eyes that were now filled with tears.

Meade's voice was husky, barely under control. He smiled crookedly. "You were right about one thing. It's easier to say things in a letter than face to face." Meade yanked some tissues from a box and blew his nose. "Anyway, I wrote that I loved you and wanted us to make a new start at life when you got back. I still feel that way—more than ever."

Then Meade did something David could never recall him doing before. He bent down and kissed David on the cheek. David dug his fingers into his father's thick hair and held his face next to his. Healing moments that bridged a gap of seventeen years. Not since Shirley's death—not even then— had they experienced such closeness.

Meade sat up and wiped his eyes. He said, "The doctors say you can be released in a week to ten days." He paused and a look of apprehension crossed his face. "I hope you'll come back to the ranch. I can arrange for a full-time nurse to help until you can get around." He looked at David, eyes silently pleading. "Is that all right with you?"

David smiled. "Sure, Dad. I wouldn't want anything else."

Meade brightened, and they talked for a while about the move, about Christmas only six days away. Meade filled David in on the war news, which didn't look too good.

David was visibly tiring, and Meade hurriedly switched the subject. "There's something else we've got to talk about, son," he said, studying David's face carefully. "If you're not up to it, we'll put it off for a while."

David bit his lip and shook his head. "No, let's get it over with. It's about Jim, isn't it?"

Meade nodded. "It's been tough, especially on Janice. Bob's been home the last week." Meade stared at the wall above David's head. "They had Jim's funeral three days ago. The military doesn't know if they'll ever be able to retrieve the body. A small box of Jim's things came back on the plane with you." Meade looked at David. "Bob and I agree that as soon as possible, he should bring Janice down to see you. We think it will be good for both of you."

David recalled that windswept plateau and Jim's shining eyes as he talked about his mother. It was replaced by another picture—an ugly mounded scar in a frozen gully. David looked up at his father. "I want to see her, Dad," a mixture of anticipation and misery in his eyes. "Tell her that, will you?"

4

"The one in red—who's she?"

The small dark man grinned at David in the candlelight. "That is none other than Penny Ann Carter, better known in our fair city as Gary West—'cause she's tall like Gary Cooper and has boobs like Mae West."

David stared at the statuesque dark-haired girl on center stage, flanked by two beauties on each side, the five girls' arms lifted high, touching hands and smiling over the footlights, the audience showing its appreciation with claps and cheers.

The other showgirls, two blondes, a redhead and a brunette—in costumes of yellow, green, pink and orange—were knockouts, but David only had eyes for the tall centerpiece whose thick dark brown hair tumbled down in luxurious abandon on her naked shoulders.

She was nearly six feet tall, even taller in her red spike heels, scarlet feathers towering four feet above her head. Satin gloves reached to just above her elbows; a flimsy sequined corsetlike costume was her only clothing. All in brilliant scarlet, sequins and feathers blinking and waving under the powerful lights.

Her breasts were spectacular. Large, firm, heavy. Out of proportion to the slenderness of her body. She gazed out over the crowd with a look of unapproachable disdain. A haughty queen favoring her subjects with her presence.

"We haven't got anything like this in Reno," David said, eyes glued to the stage.

His companion laughed. "If you want sawdust up to the ankles, go to Reno. You want to see broads, come to Vegas."

When the show ended, David kept staring at the empty stage. The room was swiftly emptying, and a crew was clearing the tables, stacking the chairs.

"Want to meet Gary?" the man asked.

David looked around eagerly. "God yes!" he exclaimed. A puzzled look crossed his brow. "Gary? You really call her that?"

"Sure. It was a joke at first, but the name stuck. She's been using it for years—spells it G-a-r-i."

The man reached for the phone behind the booth. Al Spaatz was one of the pit bosses at the El Rancho. He had known Meade since the mid-forties and had offered to have David as his guest for the show. This was David's first real night out since returning to Las Vegas from the San Francisco hospital two months ago. He was painfully thin, left arm resting in a cloth sling.

Spaatz's voice was quietly persuasive. "No, honey, this ain't some high roller gone all mushy over those great boobs. He's a nice clean-cut young guy who's father is a friend of mine—Meade Slaughter. Yeah, Slaughter as in the Plush Wheel. Okay, we'll wait."

Spaatz hung up and put the phone back. "She'll be out pretty soon," he said.

David said, "Sounded like she wasn't anxious to come."

Spaatz drummed his fingers on the table. "This is one broad with a mind of her own. She doesn't like to be set up on short notice."

David nodded. If a big spender liked a showgirl and she

was available for action, it was usually the pit boss who negotiated the meet.

"Gari's got funny ideas," said Spaatz. "Like we don't tell her, she tells us. Sometimes, I feel like sockin' her."

They rose as the girl approached. Her dark hair was tied in a pony tail that hung halfway down her back. A loose navy-blue sweater minimized her breasts. She wore jeans and canvas sneakers. A huge purse hung from her right shoulder, bumping her hip as she strode purposefully toward them. There was a no-nonsense way about her walk, and her eyes were cool as she looked from Spaatz to David and back to Spaatz.

"Gari," said Spaatz, "this is David Slaughter. David, meet Gari."

"David," she said in a low husky voice, standing hipshot, tawny eyes appraising him quietly, an eyebrow lifting slightly at the sight of his arm in a sling. She glanced at Spaatz as if to say, *Well, I've met him. Can I go now?*

David was tongue-tied. He felt like a sixteen-year-old on his first date. He tried to think of something to say, and the words came tumbling out, "You don't mind being called Gari?" Oh God, was that the best he could do?

"Not really," she said, a hint of amusement in her voice. "I'm from South Haven, Indiana. Gary isn't too far away. It's a familiar name."

Spaatz laughed. "Gari must like you, David. She's already told you more than she's told me."

Gari shot Spaatz a wry look, shifting the strap of her heavy purse to a more comfortable position. Spaatz snapped his fingers and said, "Hey, Gari, why don't you and David grab a bite to eat? I know you kids are starved after the show. You can eat right here. I'll send out some prime rib. Okay?"

Gari shook her head. "Not tonight, Al. I—"

"Aw, come on, Gari. David doesn't want to eat alone."

David broke in, "It's all right, Al. Maybe Gari and I can get together some other time."

Gari glanced at David and saw the embarrassed, hurt look on his face. Her eyes softened, and she said to Spaatz, "Oh hell, Al, now that you mention it, I am hungry." She smiled at David, easing the severity of her classic features, making her less handsome and more beautiful. No longer untouchable. Mortal.

David's face lighted up, adding color to the unnatural pallor of his face, revealing for a flashing moment the carefree young man who had gone off to war nine months ago. It made Gari glad she had changed her mind.

A bottle of Piper-Heidsieck arrived a few minutes after Spaatz left. David said, "Looks like Al wants us to enjoy our dinner." Their conversation hadn't amounted to much yet, trivial subjects—what shows were in town, a brief description of Reno, a town Gari had never visited.

Gari eyed the tall tulip glasses and their sparkling contents. "I'm not exactly wearing the proper clothes for champagne," she said, plucking at the coarse material of her sweater.

"Who cares?" David smiled, lifting his glass. "To Gary, Indiana!" he offered, suddenly confident, feeling more alive than he had in months.

When the food arrived, David pointed at Gari's rapidly diminishing plate. "I like a girl who enjoys eating," he said. "Tells a lot about her character."

Gari looked at David suspiciously, looking for some underlying meaning. God knows she had heard enough since arriving in Las Vegas seven years ago! Satisfied it was only a teasing remark, she said, "I was raised on a farm. We put in hours of work before we ate. Used to get up while the moon was out. By the time meals came around, we were starved. We ate big heavy meals, lots of meat, potatoes and gravy. We worked it off before it had a chance to settle in."

"Hey!" David exclaimed. "I was raised on a ranch, too."

"In Nevada?"

"Right. Fifteen miles out of Vegas."

"Not the same. Bet it has thousands of acres."

"Ten thousand."

Gari's laugh was short. "We had less than a hundred."

David stared. That would hardly feed one beef in southern Nevada.

Gari sat up straight and pulled the pony tail over her shoulder. She began to plait the dark strands into a thick braid. "Enough talk about me," she said firmly. She pointed at David's injured arm. "Tell me about that. An accident?"

"Guess you could call it that," David said. "A pretty big one. Korea."

"Ah." A soft explosion of breath. "Up to talking about it?"

The words came slowly at first, then faster and faster as David poured out his story. Gari's tawny eyes never left his face during the long recital, her hands busy braiding and unbraiding her hair. David's voice was filled with pain as he told about Jim Terhune's death, the mass burial, the final days of retreat through that snowbound hell.

A look of pride and unspoken feeling lighted his face as he described his father's vigil at the hospital. His eyes were shining as he talked about Janice, their emotional meeting, her determination to come with him to the ranch and care for him during the first critical weeks.

"No impersonal nurse is going to take care of my boy," she had snapped at Meade and Bob, turning back to David, not seeing the smiles and relieved looks that passed between the two men. Janice had been shaken and deeply depressed by Jim's death and David's injury, an unnerving experience for Bob who had come to rely heavily on her strength and unquenchable spirit over thirty-six years of marriage.

Janice didn't ask for David to be brought to Reno. She had noticed immediately the change in Meade and David's relationship. This was not the time for them to be separated.

"She stayed at the ranch until three weeks ago," David concluded. "I may eventually go back to Reno. I like it there. For now, I'm staying here. Dad and I have a lot of catching up to do." Another story. Not ready yet to be told.

David's face was pale, the strain of the long night having taken its toll. Gari glanced at her watch. "It's past four," she said. "Time to break up this little session. Frankly, you look like death warmed over." She smiled, letting him know she had appreciated his company. "Thank you for putting up with me. I haven't been in a very good mood tonight."

David asked quickly, the youthful eagerness back in his voice, "Can we do this again—soon?"

Gari was going to say no, then she recalled that look of hurt embarrassment that had made her change her mind earlier. "Let's think about it, David," she said, standing up abruptly, pulling the purse strap over her shoulder. "I won't say no, and I won't say yes. How about a maybe?"

David grinned. "Good enough for me," he said, dropping a large tip on the table. As he walked beside Gari toward the exit, his pace quickened. Rather than being discouraged, he felt strangely elated. This was one challenge he was going to meet head on.

5

Meade glanced at the kitchen clock. One-thirty-two P.M. Pushing the plate and silverware aside, he lit up a cigar. While he went through a pile of correspondence, Maria, the Mexican housekeeper, removed the dishes and refilled his coffee mug. Meade stared glumly at the steaming liquid. His fifth cup since getting up. Much more and he would be floating—and dancing—his way to the bathroom.

His eyes shifted toward the hall and David's bedroom. Smiling, he recalled his frantic call to the El Rancho this morning at five. He was sure something terrible had happened to the boy on his way home, driving as he was with the aid of only one arm.

Meade was surprised to find himself talking with a chuckling Beldon Katleman. "What the hell are you doing up so early?" Meade demanded, relaxing, sure now that everything was all right.

"I'm not up early; I'm up late," Katleman replied. "Haven't been to bed yet. I understand you're worried about your boy, afraid he's lost or something." Katleman laughed softly. "He left here about twenty minutes ago. In a manner of speaking, he *is* lost. He had a late dinner with Gari West."

"I'll be fucked!" Meade blurted out. "Gari West? You're sure?"

"Swear it. Scout's honor."

"My poor defenseless son!" Meade moaned, not sure whether to laugh or cry.

"Hey, Meade, Gari's not a barracuda. She's all right. A little prickly at times but aren't we all?"

"Not me. I'm always sweet and lovable."

"I think I'm going to be sick."

A long pause. "Gari and David, huh?" Meade murmured dolefully.

"Yep. Had dinner in the Opera House, then David waltzed the lady out to her Cadillac. She took off in a cloud of dust, and your son headed for home. Should be there anytime."

"Tell me something, Bel. Is there anything that goes on there that you *don't* know about?"

"I haven't bugged the rooms yet," Katleman said cheerfully.

"I'm going to bed," groaned Meade, dropping the receiver into the cradle. He went to his room and shut the door. All David needed was to arrive home and find his father waiting up.

Meade was lighting another cigar when David entered the kitchen and dropped wearily into a chair. "Have a good night?" asked Meade, smiling at David's haggard face.

David's eyes came to life. "Yeah," he said, grinning from ear to ear.

"How's the arm?" Meade said, reluctant to explore the reason for David's suddenly animated face.

"Not bad," David said, flexing the fingers of his left hand.

"The exercises are helping. I can tell the difference already. The doc gave me some new ones yesterday."

"Did he say how long it will be before you can get rid of that sling?"

"He thinks I should stop using it as soon as possible. Doesn't want me to get dependent on it. I'm going to start leaving it off a few hours every day."

"Still hurts?"

"Some. I'm getting used to it. Got those pain pills if it gets too much."

Meade's curiosity got the best of him. "Have a good time last night?"

The big smile was back. "Had dinner with Gari West. She's a showgirl at the Rancho Vegas. Know her?"

"I've seen her on stage, haven't met her." Meade leaned forward, elbows on the table. "What's she like?" He had his own ideas on the subject but wasn't about to make them known. The fabric of their new relationship was too loosely woven for that. The important thing now was to show interest, to encourage David to share. Meade wanted desperately to be a part of his son's life.

"She's nice," David said. "She grew up on a farm. Used to milk cows. How about that?"

Meade grinned. "Maybe that's where she got that corn-fed look. She's got to be at least six feet tall."

" 'Bout that," agreed David. "She was wearing tennis shoes last night, and I didn't top her by much."

Meade watched as David deftly lit a cigarette. He was getting good at doing things one-handed. Meade asked the question he wasn't too anxious to have answered. "Going to be seeing her again?"

David's response was immediate. "You bet!" He smiled and ran his hand through his rumpled hair. "It's going to take a little persuasion, but she'll come around."

Meade's eyebrows lifted. David usually got his way with women; it was his greatest success to date. And Meade had expected Gari to pounce with or without David's encouragement. David's position would be very attractive to a girl on the make.

David noted Meade's surprised look. "She didn't say no," he explained. "She left things up in the air."

"Playing hard to get?" Meade suggested, keeping his tone light.

David frowned. "I don't think so. She doesn't seem the type to play games. She's no shrinking violet," he added.

"Tough, huh?"

"No. Oh hell, I guess so. She's pretty direct. Reminds me of a couple of teachers I had. You know, the kind that used a ruler a lot."

Meade chuckled. "Sounds like someone to run from, not to."

"True," David admitted. "It's kind of a challenge." He leaned back as Maria set a plate of bacon and eggs on the table. Picking up a piece of bacon, David waved it at Meade. "No one that beautiful can be that mean." He shuddered. "Not like Miss Shields. Remember her? The one with arms like Joe Louis and a mustache?"

"Hell yes. She scared me, and I wasn't a little kid!"

"Well, Gari's not like that."

"No mustache, huh?"

David looked pained. "You're a bundle of laughs this morning, Dad."

Later, David was studying a full-page ad in the *Review-Journal* when something made him glance up. Meade was staring at the newspaper with a look that sent a chill up David's spine. It all came back in a rush—the long-standing feud between his father and Tony Giuliano.

Another memory. A hot July day three years ago when he had taunted his father with the killing of Carlo Giuliano, Tony's father. A whispered story. Blurted out in a fit of rage. In this same kitchen. Crashing to the floor under the fury of his father's attack.

"David?" David's head snapped up. Meade's eyes were concerned, questioning.

David shook his head. "I must have been daydreaming,"

he said, realizing that his face had betrayed his thoughts.

"It's that, isn't it?" Meade said, stabbing a finger at the advertisement. David nodded—a minute jerk of the head, afraid to speak, suddenly unsure of himself.

As if by unspoken agreement, their eyes dropped to the open newspaper. Tomorrow night, Giuliano's four-million-dollar Fantasia Hotel was opening on the Strip a half-mile south of the Flamingo. Entertainment would be provided by Harry James and a lavish Hollywood revue. The press was being flown in from all over the country. Thousands of invitations had been sent out. Leading politicians from Nevada and neighboring states were expected to attend, along with a large number of motion picture personalities. It threatened to eclipse the two days of festivities that opened the Desert Inn a year ago.

Meade crushed out his cigar and nodded slowly, as if answering a question in his mind. He looked at David. "Someday, you're going to take my place in the business. It's only right that you know what you're up against. To be forewarned is to be forearmed." Meade sighed heavily and leaned back in the chair. "What do you know about this thing between me and Giuliano?"

David was speechless, stunned by this invitation into forbidden territory, but thrilled by the confidence Meade was showing in him and his future. Still, he was unwilling to take the lead. His words were hesitant, accompanied by a shrug of the shoulders. "Not much. A few stories, rumors mostly. You know."

Meade rested his chin on a big fist. He hadn't shaved, and the stubble of his dark beard scratched his knuckles. How much should he tell David. What did he *need* to know? Meade thought of the ways in which he had closed Shirley out of his life. And Cindy. He sat up straighter. Not anymore. It was time to show trust as well as love.

"It all began back in thirty-three," Meade began, gathering his thoughts as he went. "You turned five three days after we opened in Reno. Don't suppose you remember that." Meade smiled, and David grinned back, shaking his head.

"Anyway," Meade continued, "the Plush Wheel opened on the twenty-third of April, and I figure that old Carlo Giuliano had someone snooping around that night. Next to Graham and McKay, he was the biggest operator in town. He didn't like competition anymore than they did. When the Plush Wheel started to grow, Giuliano began to push, siccing crossroaders on us. When that didn't work, he got rough."

The kitchen clock ticked loudly as Meade described the encounter in February, 1934, that left two men dead. David's eyes widened with sudden understanding when Meade told how he had recognized Giuliano's bodyguard the night Sandra had been killed and he had been left beaten and paralyzed.

Meade plunged ahead, sparing no details as he recalled the almost two years during which he had fought to regain his health, climaxing with the shotgun slaying of Carlo Giuliano and his bodyguard. David sat frozen in his chair, his face a study in contrasting emotions, fingers playing nervously with a napkin.

"Tony Giuliano figured out I killed his father," Meade concluded. "It wasn't hard. I showed up in Vegas right after that, walking, healthy again. The motive was there. Smitty advised me to take on fulltime bodyguards. I thought he was wrong at the time, but I don't now." A pause. "Tony Giuliano's never forgotten, much less forgiven. I found that out when he blew up at me in Reno. Remember?" David nodded. He had been fourteen at the time, visiting with the Terhunes. The news had been all over town.

"I didn't want you to know this," Meade said quietly. "But I couldn't see any way to avoid it. As long as Giuliano's alive, we've got to be on our guard. I don't know about his son; let's hope he's more coolheaded. You're about the same age. Same with me and his father." Meade smiled tightly. "If we lived in Italy, it would be a perfect set-up for an old-fashioned vendetta." Meade waved a hand in dismissal. "I may be blowing smoke. Hope to hell I am."

After a long silence, David looked at his father, eyes shining with understanding and compassion. "I'm glad you told me, Dad," he said. "For what it's worth, I'm with you."

They smiled at each other across the table. Sharing the moment as equals.

6

"Some bash," said Smitty.

Meade grunted something unintelligible. Chewing on his cigar, he stared out the window of the parked car at the lines of vehicles that waited to enter the grounds of the Fantasia Hotel. Powerful searchlights criss-crossed each other in the clear night air.

Meade gazed at the huge hotel that sprawled over forty acres. He smiled at the memory of Bugsy Siegel's words when they first met. "Millions of suckers will be leavin' their dough here," he had cried, arms waving, eyes wide with excitement. Meade had considered Siegel a fanatical visionary that night nine years ago. Not anymore. It was beginning to happen.

In a strange way, Meade missed Bugsy Siegel. Like many owners, he felt that Siegel's enthusiasm and drive had awakened them to the real potential of this once lonely stretch of highway. Without Siegel's determined, certainly destructive, passion to make his dream a reality, nights like this might still be years away.

Watching the crowds that spilled out into the parking lot, Meade thought of his Strip hotel, suddenly so small and plain, a motel compared to the rich luxury of the Fantasia. Giuliano had the jump on him. For now.

The silence was broken by the scratching of a match as Smitty lit a cigarette. He had arrived on a Bonanza flight that afternoon. "Wanta see what all this commotion is about," he

NEVADA   251

had said when Meade picked him up at the airport, grinning slyly from under his old cowboy hat.

"Didn't miss a trick, did he?" Smitty commented, leaning forward in the back seat of the Cadillac to get a better view of the action across the highway.

Meade shot his friend a pained look, then said to Milton, "Let's check out the other clubs. Start with the El Rancho."

It was past midnight when they ended up at the Flamingo. Gus Greenbaum greeted them as they entered the casino. "Meade, Smitty," he said in his wheezing, gravelly voice. "I thought you would be down the road." He waved an arm at the subdued room. "Seems like everyone else is."

Smitty said, "Giuliano gets his night. I wouldn't want to pay out what this is costin' him."

Greenbaum thrust out a heavy jaw. "That kind of cost a man can handle. I'll fly in a thousand live ones any day. That's a condition I like." He spit out his next words. "What I don't like is losin' money to some chickenshit crossroader."

Meade raised an eyebrow. "Troubles?"

"Troubles past," growled Greenbaum. "Caught a twenty-one dealer workin' with a friend. Don't know how long it's been goin' on. Must have taken us for twenty grand."

"Troubles past," Meade said. "You've taken care of the problem?"

"Damn right," snapped Greenbaum, eyes cold as tombstones. "I was handlin' problems like this when those bastards were in diapers." A hard grin crossed his face. "We had a nice little talk. They won't be botherin' us anymore." Greenbaum didn't elaborate, leaving it up to their imagination as to how far his "persuasion" had gone.

Meade said, "The word will get out. It'll save us all money." When they were ready to leave, Meade turned to Greenbaum and said with a sly smile, "Whenever you feel lucky, come over to my place."

Greenbaum growled, "You're funny, Slaughter. Real funny."

"Just a friendly gesture," Meade said pleasantly. The last time Greenbaum gambled at the Plush Wheel, he had left behind more than $10,000 in markers. Regardless of how well he knew the percentages, Greenbaum couldn't stay away from the tables.

Before returning to the Plush Wheel, Meade had Milton make one more pass by the Fantasia. It was three A.M., and the parking lot was still jammed. Meade stared at the glittering lights that adorned Giuliano's huge new hotel.

Smitty's voice barely reached Meade's ears. "Your tail feathers are stickin' straight up, boy. Feel a little crowded in the old barnyard?"

7

"David, you're crazy. Absolutely crazy!" Gari stood in the middle of her living room, bare toes digging into the deep carpet, fists planted defiantly on her slim hips. She shook her head, and the thick pony tail whipped across her back. "What the hell are you?" she shouted, tawny eyes ablaze. "Some kind of masochist?"

Lifting his arms in a helpless gesture, David stared with dismay at this bewildering creature. Glaring back, Gari crossed her arms over her chest and stuck her jaw out pugnaciously. All that was needed to complete the picture was a pair of boxing gloves to go with her gray sweatshirt and jeans.

David said, "All I said was—"

"I know what you said, David. For God's sake, don't repeat it!"

"Gari," David pleaded, his voice faltering as Gari poked him in the chest with a long finger.

"Look, David," Gari said, poking him repeatedly for emphasis. "We're seeing each other at least twice a week, and half that time's spent in the sack. Can't you be satisfied with that?"

David backed away from the stabbing finger. "Damnit, Gari," he argued, frustration creeping into his voice, "I want you all the time—not just once in a while. I—"

He was backed up against the wall. The finger was a fist now, making solid thumps on his chest. "Nobody owns me, David," Gari snapped. "So don't give me that shit about having me all the time! Do you think a piece of paper will give you that right?" Turning away abruptly, Gari dropped down on the couch, long legs stuck out straight, arms folded across her chest. She studied her scarlet-painted toenails angrily.

"Gari," David said hurriedly, anxious to get the words out before Gari could stop him, "what have you got against marriage? Don't you believe in it?"

Gari looked up at David. He looked so woeful that she almost reached out to pat his hand. She suppressed the feeling, gripping her arms tighter, as if they might betray her and touch this unhappy boy.

To her, he was no more than that. A boy. Gari was two years older than David, but she felt positively ancient in comparison. Seven years in Las Vegas had helped bring about that miracle.

Gari had arrived in Las Vegas a vastly different girl from the one who had run away from home the year before. During that year, her rebellion had been complete. The owner of the restaurant where she worked initiated her into the act of sex, but she soon outgrew him, seeking new adventures by giving herself to a variety of men with a fervor that was almost religious. One was a photographer, and he got her into the beauty contest that eventually brought her to Las Vegas.

Gari wasn't in Las Vegas long before an older showgirl sat her down and taught her a valuable lesson. "Look, honey," the tall blonde said, shaking her finger in Gari's face and wagging her head with the wisdom of four years' seniority, "you don't give it away. Not unless you're so damn ugly that free is the only way you'll get it. I've been watching you— letting guys lay you for the price of a meal and a bottle of champagne. Cheap stuff at that!"

Gari (she was still known as Penny then) opened her

mouth to protest, but the blonde raised a hand. "Don't get me wrong. You don't need to sell yourself like a whore. Not for cash on the dresser and, whoopee, into bed. You can get it in other ways. Like chips while you lean on the guy's shoulder at the crap table. Lead 'em on right, and they'll load you with gifts. I've got a dozen furs and enough diamonds to start my own store. And I didn't get my car on time payments. Chips and gifts can be turned into cash." Her lips curled, and she said drily, "The Johns get a bigger charge that way. They think you're doing it for love."

Why not? Gari reasoned. She might be headstrong and rebellious, but she was also practical. Forced responsibility at an early age had seen to that. At eighteen, she was mature far beyond her years.

Gari knew she wouldn't remain young and desirable forever. The working life of a Las Vegas showgirl was short, usually terminating in her early twenties. The competition was brutal. A constant flow of gorgeous young girls poured into Las Vegas. Fresh, eager faces, girls who had been fawned over and singled out by admiring males from the time they were in their early teens.

Gari "registered" with various pits on the Strip, making it known that she was available. Before long, she learned to accept cash along with the gifts, the money often paid by the hotel on behalf of the customer.

The glamour soon faded, and it became a demanding job, adding longer hours to her already long nights. As the years passed, and armed with the knowledge that she had become one of the most popular showgirls on the Strip, Gari became more selective, limiting her "dates" to one or two a week, if that.

When she reached twenty-five, Gari knew she was one of the lucky ones. Her face and body were holding up well, and she could probably continue for several years on the Strip. More important, she had built up a sizable nest-egg. She could throw over the Vegas scene whenever she wanted.

Then David bounced into her life like an unwanted puppy, a puppy that turned into a stubborn bulldog when she tried to shut him out. After two weeks of calls, flowers and cards, she gave in. It hadn't been unpleasant. David was young and good-looking, a fun companion. A far cry from the majority of her escorts.

David's voice, insistent, demanding, jerked her out of her reverie. "Well?" he said. A bulldog again.

"Well, what?" Gari said grumpily, peering up at him from under thick eyelashes. Her arms were still folded across her chest, long legs extending between David's as he stood spread-legged above her.

"You know," David replied, tousled blond hair falling down over his high forehead, face drooping with the woeful charm that had attracted Gari the first time they met.

"O Lord," Gari said resignedly, straightening up on the couch. "Sit down, David," she said, patting the cushion by her side.

David dropped onto the couch and tried to put his arms around her. "None of that," Gari admonished, pushing him away, moving to the other end of the couch and hugging her knees up under her chin. She squinted at David through half-lidded eyes.

David grinned. "You're cute when you look like that."

Gari's eyes opened wide. "I am *not* a cute person, David," she snapped. "Not now. Not ever! Now shut up and listen."

Gari raised a big toe as if signaling for attention. "How many reasons should I give why it won't work?" she said. "Ten, twenty? I can come up with that many if you want. Not to mention the fact that I have absolutely no desire to get married."

"What's wrong with marriage?" David pressed.

"What's *right* with marriage?" Gari retorted.

"Well, uh, it's kinda nice. Gives two people a chance to do things together. Have kids."

"Oh boy," Gari said. "Do you realize how *dumb* that sounds?"

David shrugged and grinned. "It was sort of off the top of my head. Give me a minute or two and I'll do better."

"Spare me, please!" A pause. "Do things together. Like we

were doing in the bedroom a while ago? You don't need marriage for that."

"I'm talking about always. Not just once in a while."

Gari sighed. "Morning, noon and night, I suppose."

"Right!" David said brightly.

"Wrong," Gari said, a heavy tone entering her voice. "Everyone needs a rest." She lifted her chin off her knees and stared directly at David. "Is that your concept of marriage? Fucking day and night?"

"Gari," David said, a distressed look crossing his face, "you're too nice to talk like that."

"Oh GAWD, David," Gari cried. "Now we come to one of the *big* reasons. You call me nice? What do you think I've been doing in Las Vegas the last six, seven years? Living a life of celibacy?"

"Aw, Gari, let's not get into that."

"Why not? It's got a hell of a lot to do with this conversation."

"What's past is past. I'm talking about now—the future."

"Past? Come on, David. Do you think I've been living only for you the last few weeks?"

Gari winced at the hurt look on David's face. Damnit, did she have to be so rough? "David," she said quietly, eyes softening, "I'm sorry, but you must have known." She dropped her chin back on her knees. "You did, didn't you?"

Nodding, David dropped his eyes. "I guess I did," he admitted. His head snapped up, and his gray eyes locked with Gari's. "But that doesn't mean you're not a nice girl!" He tapped the left side of his chest. "*I* think you're nice, and that's what matters."

Gari was shocked at the tears that welled behind her eyes. She looked quickly to one side, and got her emotions under control. When she glanced back, David was reaching out a hand, eyes pleading. "Oh, David," Gari said, batting his hand away gently, "let's not get emotional. But I do thank you for the vote of confidence."

"Don't you understand?" David burst out. "I love you. Isn't that a good reason for getting married? Love?"

"It's a good reason," Gari nodded. "If both parties feel the same way." She jumped to her feet. "The problem is that I don't feel that way." She looked down at David, suddenly sad. "I'm not sure I'm capable of love."

Rising to his feet, David took her hands in his. "I'm not going to give up," he said determinedly. He squeezed hard. "If you don't like me, tell me now. That's the best way to get rid of me."

Gari gave him a swift kiss on the lips, then turned around, long pony tail flying. "I can't say that, David. I *do* like you. But that's all." She waved a hand in a shooing motion. "Now go away. I need to be alone for a while."

Gari crossed her arms and stared at the wall. She didn't move until the door closed softly behind her.

8

Meade sat in a secluded corner of the El Cortez coffee shop. It was 11 A.M. Fremont Street was beginning to wake up.

A few more days and the big Memorial Day weekend would kick off the summer season. May had been exceptionally hot; it would be 102 today.

The gloomy news on the front page of the *Las Vegas Sun* was in sharp contrast to the bright sunlight outside. Chinese troops had torn a gaping hole in the U.N. lines in eastern Korea. MacArthur had recently been fired by Truman, and General Van Fleet was gathering American forces for what seemed an impossible push toward the north. Allied planes had flown over one thousand sorties yesterday while United Nations troops continued to withdraw before the enemy.

The headlines reminded Meade of those anxious months last fall—scanning the papers daily, wondering where David was and how he was faring. Well, he knew where David was now. As to how he was faring, that was a matter of opinion.

They had talked last night, a certain showgirl the main subject. Nothing new, only this time Meade was struck with the seriousness of the situation.

Two and a half months ago, Meade had considered it a passing thing. All he had to do was be patient and keep his opinions to himself. It would blow over.

But it hadn't. Wishful thinking. Meade had struggled to understand. When he was David's age, he had been madly, helplessly in love with Shirley. What if someone had suggested that he was only infatuated, that it would "blow over"? He would have responded with a swift fist to the jaw! No one—not even Charlie—would have dared interfere.

Meade was no longer the young man who had knelt in the surf and cried his heart out over Shirley's infidelities. Nor was he the hopeful lover who had briefly dropped his defenses to lose Sandra in a sudden act of violence. Certainly not the man who had let his misguided feelings pervent him from enjoying happiness with Cindy. Six months ago, Meade had reached a new plateau of emotional maturity when he had wept in his office over David's letter from Korea. It was a sign of this maturity that Meade was willing to lower his defenses, risking again the pain of involvement, something he had avoided with increasing purpose over the years. A realist, Meade knew this had been a selfish act. But practical. No involvement; no hurt.

Like David was hurting last night when he stuck his head into Meade's office a little after seven. "Doing anything important?" David asked.

"Are you kidding?" grinned Meade. "If I dropped dead, nobody would miss me for a month. Maybe I should hire less competent people, then I'd be more appreciated." Meade waved at a chair. "Sit down. Eaten yet?"

Dropping in the chair, David fumbled for a cigarette. He said, "No, but I'm not hungry."

Meade's eyes narrowed. David had a lot of nervous energy and seemed to always be eating. Not that it showed on his lean, lanky frame. Meade noted the jerky way David lit his cigarette, the drawn look on his face. "Arm bothering you?" Meade asked cautiously.

"No more than usual," David said. He dragged on the cigarette and stared at the floor.

Meade sat back and rocked his chair slowly. He unwrapped a cigar, the paper making a sharp, crackling sound in the silent room.

David looked up and said tentatively, "You know I've been seeing Gari."

Meade nodded, forcing himself to smile.

"I like her a lot," David continued. He hesitated. "I asked her to marry me."

Meade's heart sank. The goldbricking bitch! He had been afraid of this from the beginning. He fought to keep his face impassive. "And?" he said, watching David closely.

"She said no," David said flatly.

Meade brought his chair down hard and stared at his son. "When did this happen?" he asked.

"A month ago the first time. Lots of times since. This afternoon."

"She give a reason?"

"None that made any sense. She just keeps saying no. Until today," he added morosely.

"Today?" Meade prompted.

"Yeah. She told me to never ask her again. If I do, she won't see me anymore."

Meade experienced unreasonable anger. Who was she to refuse his son? Did she think she was some goddess on a pedestal? He mentally shook himself. Damnit, be glad for unexpected gifts! He asked David, "What are you going to do?"

"I don't know," David said in a low voice.

Meade was seized by a feeling of déjà vu. He had lived this moment before. Then looking at David's anguished face he understood. Briefly, he had seen the mother, not the son. Meade shuddered. Was David destined to follow in his mother's footsteps?

"There are lots of other girls," Meade said softly, guard-edly.

David's head snapped up. His voice was tense, challenging. "Not like Gari."

Meade retreated swiftly. "Can you go on seeing her knowing how she feels?"

David sat up, confidence returning. "That's just it," he said, "she doesn't know *how* she feels. Her parents had a lousy marriage, so she thinks all marriages are lousy." He looked at Meade defiantly. "Ours could be good. All she's got to do is give it a chance."

"But you say she isn't going to do that," Meade said, knowing that David was reasoning with his heart, not his head. He rocked quietly back and forth in the chair. The ball was in David's court now.

"I'm going to keep seeing her," David said stubbornly. "If I keep my mouth shut about marriage, everything will be okay."

For a while, maybe, thought Meade, recalling his own hurt of long ago. But you'll be dying bit by bit, wondering how many others are enjoying her body, receiving the affection you want so badly for yourself. It had taken all his strength to survive the crisis with Shirley. Would David survive his? Meade glanced at his son's despondent face. The risk was too great. Whatever it took, he must see that it was avoided.

Meade did his best to cheer David up over dinner and drinks. When they parted at midnight, David was smiling and more relaxed but just as determined to continue his pursuit of Gari.

That was last night. Meade pushed the newspaper aside and signaled for another cup of coffee. He considered again the idea that had been forming in his mind all morning. Risky, but the more he thought about it the more it made sense. She sounded reasonable. She hadn't leaped at David's proposal. He had to give her that.

9

With a snort of disgust, Gari threw the needle and thread down on the kitchen table. Muttering to herself, she tramped barefooted into the bedroom and dug her eyeglass case out of the nightstand drawer.

Settling back in the dinette chair, she placed the glasses firmly on her nose and threaded the needle on first attempt. Sighing contentedly, she began to mend a rose-colored bra. A fluffy pile of panties awaited her ministrations. The air-conditioner hummed quietly. Gari glanced at the clock. Five hours before she had to leave for the first show of the night.

The doorbell rang, making Gari jump. She looked around angrily. Just when she was getting started on an oft-postponed project! She frowned. It couldn't be David; he had called earlier to say he was flying to Reno for the day to do some things for his father. Resignedly, Gari tossed the glasses on the panties, smoothed the white T-shirt down over her jeans and padded to the apartment door.

The man was tall with shoulders that seemed to fill the doorway. He had thick black wavy hair, rugged features and eyes the color of clear morning sky. He wore a dark western suit with a string tie to match. Beads of sweat ran down over a jagged scar that gleamed whitely on his darkly tanned forehead. It was fiercely hot outside.

Hiding her surprise, Gari squinted into the bright sunlight. "May I help you?" she asked.

"I'm Meade Slaughter," the man said. His voice was deep, resonant, used to command.

Gari nodded, a tall slender figure firmly rooted in the doorway, face impassive.

"I, well, I thought we could talk," Meade said, shuffling his feet like a kid caught playing doctor. He looked past Gari into the darkened interior of the apartment, a questioning look on his face.

"Sure," Gari said, stepping aside, motioning Meade in. She shut the door and looked up at her unexpected guest, feeling suddenly uncomfortable. In high heels, she looked down on most men. Beside this one, she felt almost tiny. She hurried past Meade and dropped into a chair, waving him toward the couch. Meade seemed as relieved as she to sit down. Settling into a cushion, he withdrew a cigar from an inside coat pocket.

Gari wrinkled her nose. "If you don't mind," she said, "I'd appreciate it if you wouldn't smoke."

Meade blinked. "Sorry." He shoved the cigar back inside his coat, then looked at Gari curiously. "David smokes."

"Not here. I have to put up with it outside my home. Here, I don't. And David smokes cigarettes." Again that wrinkling of the nose. "Not cigars."

Meade couldn't help smiling. "I've heard you aren't afraid to speak your mind."

Gari was instantly alert. "Who told you that?"

"David, Beldon, others. You've got quite a reputation around town."

Gari went rigid, and her tawny eyes blazed. "Just what does that mean?" she snapped.

"Hey," Meade said, holding up his hands, palms outward. "No need to take offense. I didn't mean anything."

"Didn't you?" Gari said, leaning forward, jaw outthrust, hands gripping her knees. She thought of the sewing left undone. Damnit, why couldn't she be left alone? She looked at Meade who was stirring uncomfortably on the couch. "Just why are you here, Mr. Slaughter?" she asked, as if she didn't know. It was a demand more than a question.

Meade stared at Gari. This wasn't working out at all. What the hell did David see in this bitch? She was about as attractive as a cornered wildcat! Curbing his rising temper, Meade said, "I came to talk about David. He's pretty messed up. I thought we could discuss how to help him."

Gari relaxed in the chair, and concern replaced the anger in her eyes. "Messed up?" she said.

Encouraged, Meade asked, "Do you know about the emotional problems David's been through?"

Gari touched the side of her face with a long finger. "Some. I know his mother died when he was young. He had a rough experience in Korea."

Meade cleared his throat. "Has he said anything about his relationship with me?"

Gari shook her head. "Not much. He doesn't have to. It's just—there." She hesitated, and her eyebrows lifted. "You mean a lot to him."

Meade was pleased. "Yes," he said softly. "And I care for him." Meade cracked his knuckles, making Gari wince. "It wasn't always that way, you know."

"Oh?" Gari tucked her long legs under her body and rested her chin on a fist, her anger and sewing forgotten, curiosity aroused.

With a sincerity that impressed Gari, Meade told of the years he and David had been apart while the boy lived with Janice Terhune and the difficulties they had experienced when David came to Las Vegas to live. He didn't spare himself as he described the fight that had caused David to leave home and return to Reno. "Things have been fine since David came back from Korea," Meade concluded. He was relaxed now, idly watching Gari's slender fingers plaiting her hair into a thick braid. Her movements were quick, sure, unconsciously sensual. He glanced at her face. She seemed to be totally unaware of her task.

Meade reached for a cigar, then dropped his hand abruptly. The window air-conditioner hummed in the silence. Gari released the heavy braid. "You said he's messed up. How?"

Meade stared at Gari for a long moment, then took a deep resigned breath. He had set the direction of this conversation; he couldn't stop now. He said, "David's mother was pretty emotional. Things got her down a lot." He paused, knowing how one-sided this could sound, especially to a woman. "For a year before she died, she was so depressed that I couldn't reach her—no one could."

"How did she die, Mr. Slaughter? David never told me."

Meade shook his head. "I'm not ready to get into that." He saw her expression and shook his head angrily. "She didn't commit suicide, if that's what you think."

Gari shrugged.

Meade continued, "When David talked to me about you the other night, he was really depressed; it scared the hell out of me. It was his mother all over again." He looked pleadingly at Gari. "I don't want to lose my boy."

Gari tapped the chair arm. "What do you want me to do? You must have something in mind."

Meade spread his hands, palms up. "Can you let him down easy—cut it off?"

Gari cocked her head to one side and eyed him thoughtfully. "Maybe you can explain that, Mr. Slaughter."

Meade sat back and rubbed his hands together. "David told me about this—this marriage thing." There was a note of contempt in his voice.

Gari colored at the thinly veiled insinuation. "Yes," she said, a gleam of anger appearing in her eyes. "And I told him no. I assume he told you that?"

Meade nodded. "He did. I appreciate your honesty."

"So how do I 'cut him off'?" Gari said with a touch of sarcasm.

Meade's eyes flickered and hardened. "I don't know," he said. "I thought you might have some suggestions."

"Look," Gari said, feet dropping to the floor. "What else *can* I do? I've told him I won't marry him." She shot Meade a heavy look. "That's what you want, isn't it?"

Meade nodded. "Yes," he said in a quiet voice. "That's what I want."

Gari hadn't expected it to hurt, but it did. She was clearly nothing but dirt under his feet. She took a deep breath. "You don't think much of me, do you?"

Meade's voice was suddenly cold. "No, I don't. Vegas is a small town. The word gets around."

Gari's face was burning now. She leaped to her feet. "You'd better leave," she said in a barely audible voice.

Meade didn't move. He looked up at her, no trace of remorse on his face. "We still haven't decided about David."

Gari bunched her hands into fists. "What in hell is there to decide? I said I won't marry him. What else can I do? Hit him over the head with a baseball bat?"

Meade rose and towered over Gari. "Nothing like that," he said, chewing on his lip. A pause. "Maybe . . . maybe if you left town. Then he'd know it was over for good."

Gari was speechless. Her mouth opened and closed. She seemed to have difficulty breathing. Her long arms stiffened, hands knotting into fists. She stood on tiptoe and glared into Meade's eyes. "Leave town?" she choked.

Meade glared back. "Why not? It's a reasonable alternative. Of course I'll make it worth your while. I'm not a poor man, and any reasonable figure you come up with I'll see that you get it in cash, on the barrelhead."

Gari's breasts rose and heaved under the thin T-shirt. "Reasonable?" she whispered. "You call that reasonable?" Her voice began to rise. "That's what you've wanted all along, isn't it?"

Meade lifted his shoulders. "Maybe," he conceded.

Gari's face turned red, and she looked like she was going to explode. "I've got a short answer to that!" she yelled. "Fuck you!" She shook a fist in Meade's face, beyond reason now. "You're a bastard, a real bastard! Your poor wife. No wonder she was depressed. No wonder David ran away!"

Meade almost hit her. It was that close. His rage came from deep within, and he seemed to grow in size. "You fucking whore!" he shouted. "You're nothing but a slut. You aren't fit to wipe my son's feet, leastwise marry him. You leave or I'll run you out of town. You're not going to ruin David's life!"

Gari was so angry she was crying. And frightened. It added fuel to her anger. To be afraid of such a bastard! She picked up a heavy metal figurine. "Get out!" she screamed. "Get out before I kill you!"

Meade looked at her silently, hands on hips. His anger subsided as he stared into her tear-streaked face. "All right," he said, voice reduced to a low rumble. "I'll go." He backed up until his hand was on the doorknob. He glanced at the heavy figurine in Gari's right hand, then looked into her tawny eyes. "I guess I popped off," he said quietly, embarrassed over his loss of control, fearful of the consequences. "I'm sorry." Then as Gari relaxed her hold on the figurine, he blew it. "Think about what I said. I can make it financially worth your while."

Gari's mouth dropped open, and she turned deathly white. Drawing back her arm, she advanced on Meade with long-legged strides, face ugly with rage. "You lousy bastard!" she screamed.

With one swift motion, Meade stepped outside and shut the door. He heard the lock click behind him. From the second floor landing, he saw his two bodyguards standing beside the car, anxiously looking up. Meade started down the steps.

Inside, Gari leaned against the door, head thrown back, tears and sweat pouring down her body. She walked to the coffee table and replaced the figurine with trembling hands. Wandering about the living room with a dazed look on her face, she started to kick a chair, then remembered her bare feet.

She went into the bathroom and washed, pausing to look at her face in the mirror. With a shake of her head, she turned out the light and went into the dinette. Sitting down and slipping on her glasses, she picked up the bra. The needle was stuck halfway in the fabric. Carefully, she pushed it through, drew the thread tight, then repeated the motion the opposite way.

Silently, she began to weep. Her glasses clouded, and she shook her head, splashing the lenses and making it impossible to see. Tearing off the glasses, she wiped her eyes with a forearm. A deep sob tore through her chest, and she dropped her head onto her arms. The tears flowed, and she abandoned herself to her misery.

Minutes passed. Raising her head, Gari grabbed a pair of panties and wiped her eyes and face. Hiccuping and snuffling, she gazed into the living room. It was the same as an hour ago. Nothing had changed. But it had.

Fucking whore! Slut! You're not fit to wipe my son's feet!

Gari pushed a spool of thread around and around in slow circles. Something had been brought to a head this afternoon. Something that had been much on her mind of late. David had started her thinking. David. She smiled. He was really sweet. The smile turned to a grimace. To have such a father! God, she had never hated a man so much!

David's marriage proposal had not touched her lightly. It had made her take a closer look at herself, her future. Much of what she saw, she didn't like.

How many years as a showgirl did she have left in Vegas? Three? Five? Then what? She couldn't live here. Not that she didn't like the town. She had come to love the sunny climate and easy western friendliness.

What could she do if she stayed. Be a cocktail waitress? Good money, but hectic, no real future.

If necessary, she could live for some time without working. She had built up a sizable nest-egg, allowing herself only one real luxury, her white Cadillac convertible. She pampered it like a baby, taking it to Cashman Cadillac every few weeks for a check-up. Jim Cashman teased her unmercifully, but she doggedly refused to stick to the more widespread factory schedule.

There was her "other life" to think about. It would be almost impossible to live it down in Vegas. Only recently, she had overheard some men talking about a promiscuous showgirl. "If she had as many sticking *out* of her as she's had stuck *in* her," joked one man, "she'd look like a porcupine." The men had laughed loudly. It was real funny.

For Gari, that life was about over. Perhaps David had had something to do with that. He had shown her the first real love she had ever known. He accepted her for what she was. And loved her. Of that, she had no doubt.

David didn't know it, but he had made inroads with his unrelenting proposals. The more she had felt herself weakening, the more she had resisted him. She didn't love David, not in the romantic sense. But she cared.

Gari dropped the spool on the table. Why not? She could be a good wife. Faithful. God knows she had had enough men for two lifetimes! They could live in Reno; David had always said he wanted to live there.

What would his father do if they married? Cut David off? No, not much chance of that.

If David was forced to make a choice, Gari knew she would win. But as much as she hated the father, she didn't want that. It could destroy David. And it would be cheap of her to get at the father through the son. She couldn't be that petty.

Gari looked at the clock. Two hours to go. She picked up the bra and began to hum as she resumed her sewing. David would be back tomorrow. They would talk.

10

"I have a Miss Penny Carter on the line."

Meade shot a puzzled look at the intercom, then stiffened with shock. Penny Carter was Gari West's real name. David had told him often enough.

Meade had been in a turmoil ever since the disastrous meeting yesterday. He had even considered flying to Reno last night and talking to David. What could he say? "Look David, I went to see your girl today and tried to get her to leave town. Lost my temper and called her a whore." Shit! He was caught in a trap of his own making. With no way out.

"Mr. Slaughter, are you there?"

"Yes," Meade said to his secretary. "Put her on."

"Mr. Slaughter?" No mistaking that voice. Low, with a husky quality that under other circumstances he might have called sexy.

"Yes, Miss Carter," Meade said. "What can I do for you?"

Gari's voice was firm, uncompromising. "I wouldn't be calling if it weren't for David." A pause. "I want the best for him as much as you. Will you accept that?"

"Yes," Meade said, willing to agree to anything to keep peace. He added quickly, "I'm sorry about—"

"Please, I've got some things to say and not much time. I sent David out for some things; he'll be back before long."

Meade swore softly to himself. David had gone straight to her place from the airport! He drew a hand across his eyes. "All right, Miss Carter. I'm listening."

Her voice was hurried now. "David doesn't know what really happened yesterday. He knows we talked and had some differences. That's all."

Meade's heart leaped. "Thank you, I—"

"Don't thank me yet. There's more."

Meade almost groaned out loud. He felt like he was riding a roller coaster.

"I told him you came to see me because you were worried about him, and we didn't get along. I had to say that because there's going to be no way we can hide our feelings in the future." Meade sat up straighter. Now what the hell did *that* mean?

Gari continued, "I don't like you, Mr. Slaughter—any more than you like me. But I don't want to drive a wedge between you and David. It's important that you believe that."

It was impossible to doubt the sincerity in her voice. "I believe you," Meade said.

"David and I had a long talk this afternoon," Gari said. "I want you to hear this from me, so you won't fly off the handle at David. Okay?"

The phone was slippery in Meade's hand. "Okay," he said.

Gari dropped the bomb. "David and I are getting married."

Meade slumped down in the big leather chair. He wasn't angry. He didn't want to fight anymore. His son's welfare was at stake. "That happened pretty quick," he said.

"Yes," Gari agreed. "But David has been asking me for months, you know."

Meade searched for the right words. She was doing this for David. They had a common cause. "Do you love him?" he asked.

"I care for him. I enjoy being with him. I'm not sure I know what love is. Do *you*, Mr. Slaughter?"

"There were times I thought I did. Now, I'm not so sure. It involves a lot of sacrifice. I didn't do too well in that department."

The line hummed for a long moment. "Then I think we understand each other," Gari said.

"Have you made plans?" Meade asked.

"That's one reason I called. David wants to move to Reno and work in your club there. Will you let him?" There was an anxious tone in her voice.

Meade took a deep breath. "I told you I don't want to lose my son. I'll go along with it."

"Thank you," Gari said, obviously relieved.

Meade didn't want to beg. "Will I be included in your wedding plans?"

Gari didn't answer right away. "It's not going to be much. We're going to be married by a J.P. In Reno. We don't want any publicity."

"David won't understand if I'm not there," Meade said.

"I know," Gari replied. "He knows I don't like you; I can't hide that." She hesitated. "I told him the feeling's mutual. He's torn up about it. We shouldn't make it any harder."

"Then I'm invited?"

"Yes." Gari's voice hardened. "But don't take that as a blanket invitation to be a regular house guest. We know what we think about each other."

Meade felt desperate. "We can change, can't we?"

"Let's not fool ourselves," Gari said sharply. "Maybe you can forget things easily. I can't. Answer me truthfully. Have you changed your mind about me?"

"I think you're an honest person," Meade said. He grinned in spite of himself. "I admire your spunk."

"Come on," Gari said heavily. "You haven't answered my question. Do you still think I'm a whore who doesn't deserve your son?"

"Shit!" Meade cried. "Don't you ever give up?"

"Well?"

"Okay, damnit. But I can change, can't I?"

"Maybe. Time will tell. I'm sure David will be seeing you tonight. He won't know about this talk." A pause. "I'm going to do my best to be a good wife." Another pause. "See you at the wedding."

Meade was listening to a dead connection.

11

"Meade, sometimes you haven't got the brains of a pissant!"

"Aw, shit, Charlie, do you have to jump on me, too? I'm beginning to feel like a football."

"Serves you right," Charlie chortled gleefully from behind his desk. "I can't believe it—done in by a woman!"

Meade shot his uncle a sour look. Unwrapping a cigar, he waved it in the air. "You smoke one of these things around her, and you're going to get done in, too. She'll hand you your head."

Charlie grinned. "Sounds like she's got spirit. I like her already."

Meade groaned. "The whole world's against me!"

"I feel for you, boy."

Meade looked affectionately at his uncle, resplendent in a

light blue vested suit, alligator shoes propped unceremoni-
ously on the desk. Charlie had aged well. At 64, he looked
in his fifties. With his shock of white hair, the mustache and
the ever-present cigar, he looked a lot like Mark Twain.
Meade smiled. A long way from the old tobacco-chewing
days.

Charlie's face turned serious. "Glad to hear everything's
okay with you and David."

Meade said, "I was worried about how it would turn out.
We were both on pins and needles." His mind went back over
the scene he had described earlier to Charlie.

It was early morning. Meade was standing at the edge of
the pit area in the Strip casino. Across the room, he saw
David enter and raise a hand. He was smiling. A hopeful
sign. Meade pointed toward the coffee shop, and they met at
the entrance.

"Let's grab a bite to eat," Meade said.

"Okay, but no booze for me." David grinned and made a
slashing motion across his throat. "I've got champagne up to
here."

"Celebrating?" Meade asked casually. The champagne
was probably what David had gone out for when Gari called.

David's eyes turned wary. "Yeah," he said. "I came over
to talk about it."

"You don't mind if I drink?" Meade said, smiling, trying
to ease David's mind.

"Drink away!" David answered quickly. He shot his father
a sidelong glance. "I might wait for you to have a couple
before I tell you the news."

"Sounds ominous," Meade said, resting a hand on David's
shoulder.

David smiled mysteriously.

After they had ordered dinner and Meade was nursing a
bourbon, David looked at his father, apprehension on his
face. He cleared his throat. "Is it okay if I don't wait for that
second drink?"

"Shoot."

David nervously stubbed out his cigarette. "It's about me

and Gari," he said, the wariness back in his eyes. "She told me you saw her." No accusation, just a questioning look.

"I hope you won't hold that against me," Meade said. "I was worried. You're my son, and I care for you. You were pretty unhappy, and I thought I could help. It's important that you believe that."

"Sure, Dad," David said. If he felt otherwise, he was covering it well. He frowned. "Guess things didn't work out too good."

"We had a few words," Meade admitted. He ran a finger around the rim of his glass. "We're both a little hard-headed."

David's head jerked up. "You can say that again!" he grinned.

Meade proceeded carefully. "She's got spunk," he said truthfully. "I told her so." He didn't add that he had told Gari that just a few hours ago.

David's face lighted up. He hadn't expected any kind of compliment. Taking a deep breath, he plunged right in. "Gari and I are getting married."

Thanks to advance warning, Meade displayed a calm exterior. "I figured that was it," he said, tapping cigar ash into a tray. "When's it going to be?"

David stared, mouth hanging comically open. Meade's casual acceptance was the last thing he had expected. "Just like that, Dad?" he blurted. "No arguments?"

Meade's face could have won a poker tournament. "What for?" he said, smiling easily. "You're over twenty-one." Meade stuck his hand across the table. "Congratulations, son."

"Hey, Dad, thanks!" David cried, seizing Meade's hand, a big smile splitting his face. "I'll be damned," he added happily. He looked around and signaled the waitress. "I think I'll have that drink after all."

They got down to practical matters. "Where are you going to live?" Meade asked. As if he didn't know.

"We, uh, thought maybe Reno. Can I work up there, Dad? We'd like to get away from Vegas." A tortured look crossed

David's face. Meade was relieved. David wasn't totally naïve about his bride-to-be. Strangely, Meade was pleased with the mature way David had accepted the bitter facts. His son was growing up.

"Then you'll want to work in the Reno club," Meade said encouragingly.

"Will that be okay?" David said eagerly. "It won't take me long to get back in the groove."

"No problem. I'll call Charlie later and set it up."

"Great!" David looked like he could walk on air. No longer inhibited by worry, his happiness was complete. He glanced at his watch. "Gari's second show will be over soon; she'll want to know how things went." He looked at Meade, the troubled look again in his eyes. "Will things be okay between you and Gari?"

Meade recalled Gari's unfriendly words on the phone. "It may take a while," he acknowledged. "I'll give it my best." Adding hopefully, "I'm sure she will, too." Meade stared at the glowing tip of his cigar, then looked at David questioningly. "Back to my original question, got the date picked out?"

"Not exactly." The smiling bridegroom now. "Next month sometime."

"Am I invited?"

"You bet!" David thrust out his jaw aggressively. "If you're not there, I won't be!" Meade smiled. Well, it had taken something to wear Gari down.

The tortured look returned briefly to David's face. "Something else, Dad. Gari—we, well we want to keep this just between us. Okay?"

"Sure." Meade was glad they were moving to Reno. It was tough living down a reputation in Vegas. He hoped it wouldn't follow them. Not much chance. Las Vegas and Reno had little use for each other. Their north-south rivalry was like that of San Francisco versus Los Angeles, only worse.

David stood up. "Okay if I run? If I don't tell Gari, I'm going to bust."

Meade smiled up at his son. "Soon as you get all the particulars down, let me know. Need anything, just yell." He paused. "Of course, there are some things I can't help you with. Not even God!"

David laughed and swiftly exited the coffee shop.

Charlie's voice brought Meade back to the present. "I'm going to this shindig, you know."

Meade's head jerked. "Shit, man, don't tell *me!* Tell that wildcat that calls herself a woman." Meade had held nothing back. Charlie knew all about the disastrous visit with Gari and her phone call. Meade had also voiced his reasons for objecting to the marriage. "Give her a chance," Charlie said. "You haven't exactly lived an angelic life. Me neither." He picked up a pen. "Got her phone number?"

"Are you crazy? At least go through David. You make that call and you'll be a ruined man. If nothing else, think of me. I need that flea-bitten mind of yours intact."

Charlie muttered, "Leave it to me, boy. I might teach you a few things."

A long moment of silence. "I've been thinking," Meade said. "Maybe I should buy the kids a house, give them some cash to furnish it."

Charlie squinted through the cigar smoke. "Peace offer, huh?"

"Damnit, Charlie," Meade yelled. "Can't I just be a nice guy?"

Charlie nodded his head solemnly. "Difficult, but possible." His face brightened. "I like the idea! Do it. Got any places in mind?"

"Hell, I just thought about it."

"Tell Janice. She's got her finger on that kind of stuff. Smart head for values, too."

"Good idea." Meade's face dropped. "She'll want to be at the wedding."

"Naturally. Did you think David would leave her out?"

"Guess not. What about Gari?"

Charlie mumbled under his breath, "Better give Janice her phone number, too."

"What did you say?"

"Nothing," Charlie said, looking up innocently. "Just talking to myself. Comes with old age."

"I bet." Meade had gotten the gist of it. It was Charlie's neck. He was old enough to know better.

Two days later, Gari got a phone call. "Miss Carter?" The man's voice had an easy midwestern drawl.

"Yes." Gari was sitting on the couch. She lifted the phone off the floor and put it in her lap.

"My name's Charlie Brent. I'm David's great-uncle. I wanted to call and offer my congratulations." The warmth in his voice made Gari smile.

"Thank you," Gari said. "David's talked a lot about you." She searched for something else to say. "It's all happened so quick."

A soft chuckle. "No point in drawing things out. Surprises are more fun."

"I hope you're right," Gari said lightly.

"I *know* I'm right. Trust your old uncle. You *will* be my honorary niece, won't you?"

"If you want," Gari said, liking him. A pause. "You might change your mind when you see me."

"Got horns or something?"

"No," Gari laughed, suddenly feeling good all over, sensing that something special was happening.

"When's the wedding? I gotta start cleaning my fingernails."

Gari didn't give it a thought. "We'll know definitely in a week or so. David will let you know."

"Good. I'll be there with bells on." The soft chuckle again. "I'm looking forward to meeting you, honey. I think we're going to be friends."

Gari's eyes were sparkling. "I think so, too." A wishful tone. "I've never had an uncle."

"You've got one now. You and David get up here. I need company."

Gari hung the phone up in a daze. A whole new world was opening up. Marriage. A new town. She smiled. A new uncle.

So much more than she had hoped for. The doubts were fading, and her affection for David was deepening. Because of him, she was getting a chance at this new life. She set the phone back on the floor.

Gari was halfway across the room when the phone rang. Afterwards, she strongly suspected a conspiracy. Two plotters sharing the same phone. "Is this Penny Carter?" A woman's voice now.

"Yes."

"I'm Janice Terhune. I don't know if you've heard about me from David."

"Oh, yes! He told me all about you the first time we met."

"Bless that boy! I heard a rumor that you two are getting married. Any truth to it?"

"I think so. If I don't chicken out."

The laughter was rich, contagious. "I'll hold your hand if you want."

Gari smiled into the phone. "I may need it."

"Well." The voice was businesslike now. "How about you and David hotfooting it up here? I'm dying to meet you, and maybe I can help. Looking for a place, things like that."

Gari felt bowled over by the fast-moving events. "I guess we can," she said hesitantly. "I'm quitting my job Friday night. Maybe next week?"

"Fine. You and David can stay at my place. My husband's back in Washington, but he's not going to miss the wedding." Gari sighed. So much for the quiet ceremony.

Time passed swiftly, with events merging into each other like a whirling kaleidoscope. When Gari and David arrived at the Reno airport, Janice and Charlie were waiting. It seemed the most natural thing in the world for Gari to move into Charlie's arms and give him a big kiss. Love at first sight. "Hey," said Charlie, whose chin came to just above her breasts, "no horns!"

The deep love between Janice and David was clearly evident. With one arm still around David, Janice reached out for Gari. A petite figure with graying hair, she smiled up at the tall girl. "You're beautiful!" she exclaimed with western frankness. A mischievous grin. "I've heard about you Indiana corn-fed girls. And you used to milk cows! We're going to get along fine."

Gari had never known such warmth and friendliness. She had always been a loner, avoiding close friendships, uncomfortable around strangers. She surprised herself by joining in the friendly chatter as they drove into town, taking frequent glances out the window at the passing scene. Reno was so different from Las Vegas. The streets were well-ordered, lined with trees that had reached maturity many years ago. It all seemed so *settled*.

The Terhune mansion left her open-mouthed and staring. She had never seen anything so beautiful. From the high bluff, she gazed down at the fast-moving, clear waters of the Truckee River. Definitely not Las Vegas, where it rained less than four inches a year. She hugged herself and looked out over Reno. A new life. Could she forget the past? She'd damn well better!

The next morning, Janice took Gari and David across the river to Riverside Avenue. A few blocks west of Virginia Street, she parked in front of a big two-story colonial home, shining with a new coat of white paint. Huge oaks surrounded the corner lot, and the riverbank was just across the narrow street. With puzzled looks, the young couple followed Janice past the "For Sale" sign to the front door. "Like it?" Janice asked as she dug the keys out of her purse.

"It's beautiful," Gari said softly, looking up at the spreading tendrils of vines that reached all the way to the roof. She glanced at David. "We can't afford this!" Her eyes went to the sign, then to Janice. "That says 'For Sale,' not 'For Rent.'"

Janice smiled brightly. "Let's take a look anyway."

They wandered through the huge living room, the airy country kitchen, dining room and four bedrooms. "Three baths!" exclaimed Gari. Standing in the middle of the high-ceilinged hall, she lifted her arms helplessly. "This must cost a fortune." She shot David a mournful look. "I'd have to go back to work."

"But do you like it?" Janice persisted.

"I love it!" Gari said. She looked at David. "Don't you?"

"Yeah, sure . . . but . . ." He lifted his arms, mimicking Gari's helpless gesture.

"Good!" Janice said, heading for the stairs. "Follow me, children." Mystified, Gari and David stayed close behind. Marching out the front door, Janice took a strip of paper from her purse, peeled off the backing and slapped the paper firmly across the sign. "There," she said in a satisfied voice.

Gari and David stared at the big red SOLD that blotted the sign. "Huh?" David said dumbly.

"A little something from Meade," Janice said with a big smile on her face. She was enjoying herself enormously. "Oh, yes," she added as if it were an afterthought, "you've got an account set up at Home Furniture downtown." Janice grinned at the bewildered couple. "Well, don't just stand there!"

Gari's tawny eyes returned to the sign. "No, no," she whispered, long dark hair swirling as she shook her head back and forth. The words echoed in her mind. *Whore! Slut!*

"Gari," Janice said sharply, "I'm going to be straight with you. I know there have been some problems between you and Meade. I've known him since he was sixteen, and I'll grant you he's not perfect. But he can be sweet at times. This is his way of saying he's sorry. It carries no obligation." A pause. "If you won't do it for yourself, do it for David," she added gently.

Gari looked at David. His eyes were pleading. She glanced at the sign, at Janice, back at the sign. With a small gesture of defeat, she murmured, "All right. You've got a persuasive way about you, you know."

Laughing, Janice touched her arm. "All us cowgirls do; you ought to know that."

Smiling down at Janice, Gari said, "You were pretty sure about this, weren't you?"

"Hell, yes," Janice chuckled. "You may be in love, but you're not crazy!" She waved an arm at the big house. "That's one of the best pieces of real estate in Reno. Look at

that garage. Big enough for three cars." She grinned at
David. "Not that you'll need them. You can walk to work
and downtown from here."

Janice looked across the river at the huge mansion that
dominated the bluff. "We're going to be neighbors," she said,
turning back to Gari. She dropped the keys into Gari's hand.
"I'm going to leave you two lovebirds alone. Home Furniture
is three blocks that-a-way. Everything's set. Order to your
heart's content. Bye!" Gari and David stood rooted beside
the sign until Janice's car disappeared around the corner.
Then they hurried toward the front door to take a closer look
at their new home.

With so much to be done, the wedding date was changed
from June to July. Toward the end of June, Gari and David
drove north in Gari's white Cadillac, and Gari took up temporary residence with Janice. It was convenient. Gari could
walk to their house and downtown.

Finally, the day arrived. A brilliant, warm Saturday afternoon. It was a civil ceremony; Gari had held firm on that. In
the crowded living room—with guests spilling into the dining
room and hall—Charlie gave the lovely bride away. And she
was indeed lovely, standing over six feet tall in her white satin
heels, dark hair falling softly on bare shoulders, tawny eyes
glowing behind the gauzy veil.

Meade stood beside David. As promised, Janice was there
to hold Gari's hand if necessary.

After the wedding, the guests moved out on the lawn for
a reception that lasted into the evening. Actually, it went on
past midnight, several hours after the young couple left to
spend the first night in their first home. Tomorrow, they
would fly to San Diego for two weeks on the beach.

David carried Gari across the threshold, wedding dress
and all; it had seemed unnecessary for her to change for a trip
of less than half a mile across the river. Stumbling, red-faced,
David squeezed through the doorway with his burden and
staggered into the hall. Filled with champagne and the happiness of the moment, they were laughing uncontrollably.
"You're going to break something!" Gari screamed as David

whirled her around, a high-heeled foot barely missing a vase filled with roses.

David stood Gari on her feet. "We made it," he grinned. She wasn't sure if he meant the marriage or the simultaneous entrance; they weren't exactly normal-size people.

Hand in hand, they ascended the broad staircase and entered the huge master bedroom. The canopied bed, never used, beckoned silently. "It's been too long," David said, taking Gari into his arms and kissing her hard.

"Hmmm," Gari murmured, closing her eyes, glad that they had not had sex since her arrival in Reno to prepare for the wedding. It had been a small victory, perhaps silly considering her past, but it had seemed suddenly important to her. Whether he understood or not, David had gone along. It hadn't been easy for him; Gari could feel his hardness now.

She pressed against him, experiencing a responsive stirring in her loins. A physical girl, Gari had enjoyed sex from her first introduction to it as a teenager. That was all it was to her. Sex. She had orgasms, but there was no mental or emotional involvement. As if she were bestowing a gift on a body that wasn't hers.

In Vegas, where her sex was usually with paying strangers, Gari's orgasms had been few and far between. Because he cared and sincerely tried to please, David had brought her to orgasm on most occasions. Nothing mind-blowing, but physically satisfying. Gari had no illusions about finding a man who could satisfy her completely.

But she wanted to try with David. He had helped bring about so many changes in her life. Gari opened her mouth, and their tongues touched, probed, intertwined. David ran his hands down her back, seizing her buttocks and pulling her against his erection. "Oh God," he gasped. "You feel so good I could eat you up."

"Why don't you?" Gari whispered into his ear.

"Too many clothes," David muttered, feeling around the back of her dress. "How do you get this thing off?"

Laughing, Gari turned around and pointed over her shoulder. "Little fasteners," she said. "See?"

"Gotcha," David said. His hands were clumsy as he worked with the tiny buttons and clasps.

In moments, Gari was out of the wedding dress and sitting on the bed, peeling off her nylons while David threw his tuxedo in an untidy heap on a chair. "Sure you know how to use that?" Gari teased as David dropped his shorts and turned around, his swollen penis swaying back and forth like an elephant's trunk.

"I think I can remember," he grinned as he approached the bed. Gari had just removed her bra, and her breasts thrust out proudly, impossibly large for her slender frame, nipples centering the dark areolas like dull copper pennies. David's penis came fully erect as Gari layed back and hooked her thumbs over the tops of her white panties, pushing them down over her hips, drawing up one leg and revealing the pink lips of her vulva as she slipped the panties off one foot, then the other.

"Don't move," he said hoarsely, spreading her legs apart, licking the inside of her knees, moving up slowly toward the thick mat of hair that was sparkling with sweat droplets.

"The bedspread!" Gari cried, trying to twist away. "It'll be ruined!"

"To hell with the bedspread," growled David, grabbing her legs. He wasn't about to stop now.

"David!" With a powerful kick, Gari pushed him away and rolled to the top of the bed, tearing back the covers and throwing them to the floor with one quick motion. "There," she said in a satisfied voice, falling on her back and spreading her legs. "Now where were we?" Gari looked up at David who was standing by the bed, an angry look on his face, penis drooping in defeat. "Oh, come on, David," she smiled. "It only took a second. Just think of the cleaning bill we saved!" Spreading her legs wider, she held out her arms.

David just stood there, sulking. "Please, David," Gari said softly, "not on our wedding night." Sitting up, she took his hand, then laid back, drawing his head down on her breast and guiding the nipple to his mouth. It turned instantly rigid as he licked the tip. Soon, he was sucking hungrily, his hardened penis stabbing at Gari's leg. "Am I forgiven?" she asked as he rolled on top of her.

David was smiling now, that boyish grin that never failed to strike a responsive chord in her heart. "Yeah," he said, lifting himself so she could grasp his penis and guide it into the moistness between her legs. He began to move, driving deeper and deeper. Thrusting upward, Gari tried to match the rhythm of David's frantic movements as he swiftly neared climax.

Too soon for her. Much too soon. Maybe she should have let the bedspread go. Pushing the thought from her mind, Gari increased her efforts, pulling David hard against her belly. Seconds later, David cried out, and Gari felt the pulsing of his penis as it released the pent-up semen.

Gari woke in the middle of the night. David was asleep on his back, snoring softly. She stretched, and a hand touched her soft mound. No orgasm on her wedding night. A bad omen? No, just one of those things. There would be lots of other nights. She smiled. And days. She'd get even during the next two weeks in San Diego. Still smiling, she drifted off to sleep.

Across the river, Janice Terhune glanced at the clock as she turned off the kitchen light and headed toward the bedroom where Bob was already asleep. Two-sixteen A.M. Yawning widely, she passed the guest room where Meade was staying.

Meade and Gari—what a pair! They had prowled around each other yesterday like two big jungle cats, eyes wary, putting on outward appearances that fooled everyone but those in the know. Janice shook her head and hoped for the best.

12

Gari walked along the Truckee River, long tanned legs flashing under the light summer dress, a bulging paper bag swinging in her right hand. She stopped and leaned over the rock wall. The ducks spotted her instantly and headed quacking for the bank. Calling softly, Gari reached into the bag and withdrew a handful of bread crumbs. With a wild beating of wings, the birds leaped and dived for the crumbs that descended on their heads.

Turning away, Gari continued walking along the river, the ducks in hot pursuit. Gari waved gaily to a woman watering her lawn, then stopped to throw more crumbs.

Has it only been a year? Gari mused as she leaned on the wall and watched the ducks quarrel over the food. She looked back at her home, the green-shuttered windows almost hidden by the trees and the bend of the river. Las Vegas seemed a million miles away.

So much had happened, so many changes. Gari patted her slightly rounded stomach. December would bring the biggest change of all. Six months from now. About the fifteenth. Gari had never dreamed she would welcome a baby. Or marriage, for that matter. Or close friends.

The ducks clamored for more food. Gari reached into the bag and created a snowstorm of bread crumbs. Some settled on feathered backs and were quickly pecked off. Do ducks fantasize? Gari wondered. She hoped so. It would make their lives easier.

Clutching the near-empty bag, Gari walked slowly along the river. She had never wished on a star, but one had fallen at her feet. She touched her stomach. This little one would learn to dream.

Gari glanced over her shoulder, and a smile of delight lighted her face. She dumped the rest of the crumbs over the wall and hurried toward the distant figure with long-legged strides. Waving, Charlie quickened his pace. They met under a big spreading oak. Grabbing the wadded bag from her hand, Charlie stuffed it in a pocket, then hugged Gari close. "How are you, honey?" he asked, standing back, holding her arms and running his eyes up and down her slender frame. Grinning, he gently poked Gari's stomach. "How's little Ann?"

Laughing, Gari took his hand. "Charlie, why are you so sure it's going to be a girl? Doesn't David have anything to say about it? Or me?"

"Nope," Charlie said confidently, taking Gari's arm and aiming her toward home. "And she's going to be just like you." He looked up at her, and held his arms out in a cradling position. "I want a little Gari to hold." He nudged her with an elbow. "You're too big."

Gari gave him a playful push. "You really know how to hurt a girl, don't you?"

"Hey, young lady, I had a special reason for coming by. How about having lunch with me at the Mapes?"

"You're on. But I've got to change. It'll only take a few minutes."

"You look good enough to me," Charlie said.

"In this dress? I don't have nylons on!"

Charlie leered. "So I noticed."

"Dirty old man."

Charlie settled into a living room chair while Gari ran up the stairs. "Careful, girl!" he yelled. "That's little Ann you're bouncing around!"

Gari stopped on the landing and stuck her tongue out. At the end of the hall, she entered the huge master bedroom that took up the whole end of the upstairs floor, the big bed looking like a tiny island in an ocean of light blue carpet.

Tossing off her dress and putting on a garter belt, Gari sat on the edge of the bed and pulled a nylon up over one leg. She hummed softly as she adjusted the strap, thoughts straying to the man downstairs. Charlie had become the loving father she never had. Their love for each other was unaffected, equally shared. At times, it made Gari feel guilty. She wished she could care as deeply for David. She had come to love him, but it wasn't a total commitment. Not the way she felt in her own special way about Charlie. She hoped in time that she would feel the same for David. He had certainly given their marriage his best.

From the start, David had been loving and attentive. Marriage had matured him; he was more settled, taking a serious interest in the club and his future. Charlie planned to advance him as rapidly as possible. Not too fast. David was only twenty-five. He would have to learn how to handle authority. As the owner's son, it would be harder to earn respect.

Charlie stood up as Gari appeared at the head of the stairs. She had changed into a white dress with spaghetti straps and a full skirt that swayed lightly with the movement of her hips. In deference to her escort, she wore low-heeled open-toed shoes, gold to match the ribbon in her hair and the big cat eyes that sparkled as she descended the stairs.

"Holy Moses!" Charlie exclaimed, gazing up with frank admiration. "I've died and gone to heaven." He took her hand as she reached his side. "Maybe we better drive. You'll cause an accident crossing the street."

"We walk," laughed Gari, reveling in his praise. "Junior needs lots of exercise."

"Ann."

Gari sighed. "Come on. Let's feed her."

After lunch, they rode the elevator to the Skyroom. Overlooking the Truckee and catty-corner across the river from the Riverside Hotel, the twelve-story Mapes Hotel had opened five years ago. It was the tallest hotel in Nevada.

As the cocktail waitress walked away, Gari turned to Charlie. "After that big lunch, one gimlet will probably put me to sleep." She noticed his fingers nervously fidgeting with a napkin. "Charlie," she said sharply, "will you please light up a cigar? You're about to have a fit."

"Does it show?" he said, eyes twinkling.

"It shows," Gari said. She plucked a cigar from Charlie's coat pocket and stuck it in his hand. "Don't expect me to light it for you."

Charlie pushed his chair back and lit up. "You're an angel," he said, puffing contentedly.

"That's stretching it a bit," Gari said drily. Her eyes softened. "You know I'd do almost anything for you."

Charlie looked out the window at the tree-lined streets and the distant mountains. "Meade's coming up tomorrow," he said softly.

"I said *almost* anything, Charlie."

"Hey, don't go jumpin' the gun. I just thought we could have lunch—you, David, me and Meade."

"Oh."

"Think you can handle that?"

"My God, Charlie, it's not like I never see him. He's been over for dinner several times. We've gone out with him a few times, too."

Charlie raised his glass in salute. "Hoo—ray!"

Gari waved a fist in the air. "Sometimes I could poke you."

"For what?" Charlie cried, wide-eyed and innocent. "For trying to set up a friendly lunch?"

"It's more than that, and you know it. You're as bad as my ducks. You keep pecking away. I've told you, I can't be a hypocrite. I just don't like that man!"

Charlie tapped the table. "It proves what I've known all along. You and him are too much alike. A couple of blockheaded stubborn Missouri mules!"

"Ha!" Gari snorted. "Don't you dare compare me with that man!"

"That man," Charlie said meaningfully, "happens to be your father-in-law."

"Do you have to remind me?"

Charlie threw up his hands. "I think I need another drink," he said, turning around and looking for the waitress.

"Me, too," Gari said quickly. "There's something about this conversation . . ."

Charlie made a twirling motion with his finger, then pointed at their drinks. The waitress smiled and turned toward the bar. Charlie looked at Gari, who was gazing pensively out the window. He loved this girl. And Meade had been like a son to him for over thirty years. He wished he knew of a way to get them together.

Meade's attitude toward Gari was changing. Not long ago, he had grudgingly admitted that things were working out better than expected. The news of Gari's pregnancy—David had called Meade the moment they were sure—had elicited a phone call from Meade.

"How do you like that?" Charlie said. "Me a great-great-uncle and you a grandfather."

"Really great," moaned Meade. "Can't you see me sneaking in to see my own grandkid?"

"Aw, come on, Meade. Gari's not like that!"

"How do you know? You've got blinders on when it comes to that woman!"

"Look, that gal's done wonders for David. He's turning out as steady as a rock. He's going to be a fine executive in the company someday."

A reluctant tone. "I have to give Gari credit for not poisoning David against me. There's a strain because of the way things are between me and her, but it's not critical. I have to thank her for that."

"Ever thought of telling her?"

"Hell, yes, but she'd probably bite my head off! I'm going to be a chicken and let matters take their own course. Maybe the baby will help break the ice."

Charlie laughed. "I always knew you were a coward when it comes to women."

"*Anybody* would be a coward when it comes to this one!"

When Meade called yesterday to say he was coming up, Charlie had suggested that they all get together for lunch.

Meade agreed, but he was only going to compromise so far. Gari had to give some, too. Stubborn mules! This could go on forever.

13

On October 7, 1952, the corner of San Francisco Street and Highway 91, the location of the Club Bingo since 1947, was the scene of another big opening on the Strip. Milton Prell, from Los Angeles via Butte, Montana, with a group of investors that included Al Winter, Bobby Gordon and Johnny Hughes, proudly welcomed the public to Las Vegas' newest marvel, the Sahara Hotel.

Built by Del E. Webb, who received twenty percent of the hotel as part of his fee, the Sahara boasted the biggest casino, the biggest swimming pool, the biggest theater-restaurant and the biggest stage in town. Ray Bolger and Lisa Kirk headlined in the Congo Room for a two-week run. The $5,000,000 Sahara was a solid winner from the beginning.

Smitty peered up at the two lifelike Watusi warriors that guarded the entrance to the Congo Room. "Sure they won't jab us with them spears?" he said. "They look real enough."

Meade grunted a reply that was lost in the noise of the crowd. Hands jammed in his rear pockets, he gazed through the doorway at the staff preparing the Congo Room for the first show of the night. Chewing on his cigar, eyes thoughtful, he noted the specially woven carpet with its arrows and shields, the tropical plants, the murals depicting the caravan life of Sahara desert nomads.

Smitty looked at Meade questioningly. "You seem a mite testy," he said. "Got a dill pickle up your ass?"

Meade shot his friend a sour look, then started to move through the packed casino. "Let's get some coffee," he said.

They passed the Casbah Lounge, where the Legion-Aires were entertaining. Music from alternating groups had been crashing into the casino continuously since the Sahara threw open its doors for the first time that evening.

The African theme was everywhere, starting with the lobby that resembled a Moroccan garden court. Tropical plants and native murals were strategically placed throughout the hotel. Milton Prell called the Sahara the "Jewel of the Desert." Many were inclined to agree, although there were some friendly hoots and hollers from owners down the road. With typical Las Vegas warmth and hospitality, competitors downtown and on the Strip had welcomed the Sahara with large display ads; it was a Las Vegas tradition of long standing.

Settling into a booth in the Caravan Room restaurant, Smitty looked around. "If the food's as good here as it was at the Club Bingo, they'll do all right."

"They'll do all right," Meade said. "Like the Flamingo, the D.I. and Thunderbird are doing all right." A pause. "And the Fantasia." A reluctant admission that Tony Giuliano's hotel was flourishing.

Meade tore the wrapper from a cigar. "Jake Friedman will have the Sands open in December. That's going to put six hotels on the Strip that will make the El Rancho, Frontier and the Plush Wheel look like glorified motels." Meade puffed the cigar into life. "We squeeze a couple of hundred into our showrooms and think we're doing great." He waved an arm. "These places are doing double that and more. Not to mention everything else they've got that's bigger and better."

"So?"

"So we're outdated." Meade waved his arm again. "*This* is the future, and I'm going to be part of it."

Smitty's faded blue eyes narrowed. "What you got in mind?"

Meade leaned his elbows on the table, excitement entering his voice. "I want to go big, Smitty. Real big. The Sahara's got two hundred forty rooms; I want five hundred. To start.

I like the Sahara's shopping area. Vacationers buy a lot of things. Why not right at the hotel? Throw in a barber shop and a beauty salon. A health club. Tennis courts." Meade's eyes gleamed. "A golf course."

Smitty was smiling. "I'm listenin'."

Meade said: "Benny Binion told me that when Moe Dalitz said the D.I. was going to build a golf course, he thought it was the dumbest thing he'd ever seen a gambler do. Benny wasn't alone in his opinion. A lot of owners thought Moe and Wilbur were going off the deep end. Now, they're thinking different. The D.I.'s having that golf tournament next year. It's going to draw a lot of attention to Vegas. Something big besides gambling." Meade tapped his cigar on the ashtray. "Those building lots around the golf course are going to bring good money. That's what I want. Maximum use of the land. A complete package—hotel, casino, shopping, recreation, golf course, lots."

"What about the government building restrictions?"

"I'll do the same thing Prell and Friedman did. They beat the new construction ban by remodeling. Prell remodeled the Club Bingo, Friedman La Rue's restaurant." Meade grinned. "I'll remodel my place, too. Just like they did. From the ground up."

Meade had Smitty's total attention. All his adult life, Smitty had devoted himself to one thing—making the most from the dollar. He had never married; it would have diverted his attention, diluted his control. He planned his investments carefully, not hesitating to pay money under the table for inside information and special favors. Known for his ruthlessness in business dealings, he had made few close friends. He was liked, in a wary, distant sort of way. If he wanted, he could turn on the charm, but that didn't happen often. His business competitors feared and hated him.

Smitty was a throwback to the old west. Had he been born fifty years before, he would have packed a gun and shot it out over the water rights to the land he wanted. With over forty years of shrewd investments behind him, Smitty was worth millions.

He was a loner—trusting no one. Until he met Meade. Meade had won his trust almost from the beginning. Older by years, Smitty had latched onto Meade that night in the tiny Virginia Street Plush Wheel because he had a gut feeling that Meade's ambition was backed by an aggressiveness and strength few men possessed. Smitty was seldom wrong in his judgment of men; this inborn perception was one of his greatest assets. In Meade's case, he had been proved wrong in only one area; he had underestimated the strength and resolve that continued to drive Meade toward greater heights.

Smitty prompted, "Let's hear what you've got in mind."

Meade let his breath out in an explosive burst. "I'm going to build a whole new Plush Wheel on the Strip. New layout, design, everything."

Smitty nodded, eyes slitted. "You're goin' up in Reno and downtown. No other way *to* go. On the Strip, you can go up, down and sideways. A hundred acres is a lot of land. Five times what the Sahara's got."

"A hundred isn't enough," Meade said, shaking his head. "I want a golf course, building lots, the works. I need more land."

Drawing his lips back over tobacco-stained teeth, Smitty said wolfishly, "Fancy that. I just happen to have seventy-five acres next to yours."

"Hell of a coincidence, isn't it?" Meade said, grinning back.

"Watch your shirt, boy," Smitty said. "I may be wearin' it."

They haggled price back and forth the rest of the evening and all the next day, finally settling with a handshake. Their lawyers were given the task of working out the details. Thanks to the booming prosperity of the last ten years in Las Vegas and Reno, Meade had entered the negotiations nearly debt-free. He emerged obligated to a sizable mortgage and low on cash. "Like the old days," chuckled Smitty. "Keeps you on your toes, workin' with a short bankroll."

"Thanks a lot," Meade said drily. They were seated in the lounge of the Strip Plush Wheel. Meade continued, "Smitty,

you'd think with all your money that you'd buy a new hat.
I'll swear that relic is the same one you were wearing the day
I met you."

Smitty picked up the battered, sweat-stained cowboy hat.
"It's a little tarnished, that's all," he observed. He punched
out a couple of dents. "I'm used to it. Look at that," he said,
kneading the pliable crown. "Soft as a baby's ass. Fits my
head like a glove."

"Shut up and buy me a drink."

As the cocktail waitress walked off, Smitty watched
Meade's eyes follow her swaying bottom. "I see you still
notice the ladies," he said.

"Smitty," Meade said patiently, "I'm not dead yet."

"Speakin' of ladies, when's Gari due?"

"The doc says December twelfth."

Smitty wasn't afraid to tread on dangerous ground. "Some
showgirls make damn good wives. They get all them silly
ideas out of their heads before they hitch up. They can settle
down without spendin' half their time wonderin' what they
missed."

Meade nodded, refusing to be baited. Next to making
money, Smitty liked a good argument best. Meade said,
"David seems to be doing well—at home and at the club."

"How about that arm? When I last saw him, he was favor-
in' it a lot."

Frown lines wrinkled the livid scar on Meade's forehead.
"That bothers me. He's been sticking to the exercises, but
there's no improvement. If he uses it too much, the nerves go
haywire. Lots of pain. Charlie's in the process of pulling him
off the tables and putting him into administrative."

"Can't the doctors do anything?"

Meade shrugged. "They've talked about an exploratory
operation. No guarantee. David says no. Can't blame him.
All that pain and trouble—maybe for nothing. He gets by
with pain pills."

The phone rang at the back of the booth. Meade picked it
up. "Hi, Charlie, how's—" Meade's face turned white, and
his jaw tightened, muscles forming knotted cords. "When did

it happen?" Meade said, jabbing his cigar out in the tray. He wiped a big hand across his forehead. The phone crackled, and Meade asked, "How's David taking it?" Meade nodded, face anguished. "I'll charter a plane. Be there as soon as possible."

Meade hung up. Smitty was stunned to see tears in the big man's eyes. "It's the shits," Meade said. "Janice Terhune was killed an hour ago in an auto accident."

"Aw, hell," Smitty said, voice stricken, eyes blinking as he absorbed the shocking news. "I loved that gal. Didn't have a hateful bone in her body." He shook his head sadly. "Poor Bob. Jim gone two years ago, now this. He worshiped that woman." Smitty stared at Meade. "Bob got the word?"

Meade nodded. "He's on the way." Meade dialed the number of Vegas Air. He put a hand over the mouthpiece. "You coming?"

"Are you kiddin'?"

An hour later, they were winging their way toward Reno.

14

It was a beautiful, crisp fall day. The sun was shining brightly down through the trees on the mourners, a huge crowd saying farewell to the daughter and only child of Sam Crowder, one of Reno's pioneers. Janice Terhune was being laid to rest beside her father. Two plots over was the simple headstone that marked Jim Terhune's empty grave; his body had never been returned from the mass burial site in North Korea.

As one of the pallbearers, Meade stood under the awning at the graveside, silently urging the minister to complete the sad proceedings. Meade considered these traditional rituals to be unnecessary torture. He wanted to remember Janice as he had known her when she was alive. And how alive she had been! His mood lightened as he recalled the times she would become exasperated with him and call him a "cow plop."

Meade looked across the flower-covered casket at Bob Terhune. Two nights ago, Meade and Charlie had met Bob at the airport. Meade had been shocked at the sight of the senator's sagging figure as he descended the ramp, accompanied by his aide, Max Verdon. As unobtrusively as possible, Verdon was supporting Terhune by one arm. Three inches taller and forty pounds heavier, Terhune looked like he would collapse without Verdon's help.

Tom Terhune left Meade's side and seized his father in a tight embrace. Tom looked much like Bob in his younger day —tall, broad-shouldered with light brown hair and blue eyes. Bob's hair was still thick and wavy, but it was nearly white now. The last few hours had aged him; he looked ten years older than his years.

Tears were bright in Bob's eyes as he took Meade's hand. "Meade," he said brokenly. Meade could only cover his hand and nod. They had both loved Janice.

While Bob talked with Charlie and Tom, Meade's eyes met Max Verdon's. The lean leathery man shrugged helplessly. In his late thirties, Verdon had worked for Bob ever since receiving his law degree in 1938. A graduate of the University of Nevada, Verdon was born on a ranch thirty miles north of Reno. His native shrewdness had seen him through many political wars, and he had become Bob's indispensable right arm. Looking more like a cowboy than a political sharpshooter, Verdon walked over and held out his hand. Meade said, "Sorry we have to meet under these circumstances, Max."

"It's rough," Verdon said in a Washington-cultured western accent. He rolled his eyes toward Bob. "He's taking this harder than I would have thought. Bob must have depended on Janice a lot more than we knew."

"We all did," Meade said. "I feel like someone's kicked a prop out from under me."

Verdon nodded, shoulders hunched, hands shoved in the back pockets of his suit pants. In many ways, Verdon reminded Meade of Smitty. A polished version. Verdon said, "How's David?"

"At home, looking like he's been pole-axed. Janice had a protective way about her. She was like a mother hen. First sign of trouble, you dived under her wings." He smiled sadly. "She could make room for everyone and still take in a few strays."

"That's Janice. You said it in a nutshell."

Soon it would all be over. Meade lifted his eyes from the mound of freshly dug earth and glanced at Bob, standing woodenly between Tom and his daughter Grace, eyes glued to the casket, a beseeching look on his face—as if he could will some comfort from the body within.

Meade looked at Smitty on his right; the little man was gently slapping his hat against his leg—a new hat, Meade had noticed earlier. Charlie was next to Smitty, white hair contrasting sharply with his dark suit. On Meade's left, Gari was leaning slightly against David, holding his arm. Her bulging stomach had thrown her off balance, making it difficult for her to stand straight. She dabbed her eyes with a handkerchief. A few nights ago, she and Janice had been sewing a cover for the crib.

David's eyes were hollow and red-rimmed; he had slept little for days. Jim's death in Korea had been a terrible shock, but losing Janice had been the most traumatic experience of his life. Meade shook himself and returned his attention to the service.

When it ended, the gravesite was crowded as friends approached the family to offer condolences.

Gari was visibly drooping. "You look tired," Meade said softly.

Gari's eyes widened. She hadn't expected sympathy from Meade, not even at a time like this. She smiled wanly. "It's been a long day."

Meade looked at David. "Any reason to stay?"

David glanced at the milling figures under the awning. "We're not doing much good here," he said, throwing a final look at the casket. He took Gari's arm. "Let's go," he mur-

mured brusquely, heading toward Charlie's powder-blue
Cadillac. Charlie joined them as they walked along the graveled path.

Meade waved goodbye to Smitty who was deep in conversation with a local banker. No harm. Smitty had paid his
respects. Time to go on living.

Charlie made coffee while David took some rolls out of the
breadbox. Touching one, he said, "Janice and Gari baked
these the other night when they were sewing baby things."
Hands on the counter, he stared down at the plate, eyes
blinking.

Charlie glanced over his shoulder at David's back, eyes
momentarily meeting Meade's. Meade shrugged and continued laying out the dishes.

Gari stuck her head in the doorway. "Sure you don't need
help?"

"We're doing fine, honey," Charlie said affectionately.
"Go sit down. We'll be right behind you."

Several hours later, Meade and David were alone in the
living room. Charlie had gone to the club, and Gari was
upstairs asleep. The afternoon shadows were lengthening,
plunging the house into semi-darkness. Neither man bothered to turn on a light.

David put his drink on the end table and stared out the big
bay window, absently rubbing his bad arm. He dropped his
hand and turned to his father. "Dad," he said quickly, "what
was she like?"

"Janice?" Meade said, a surprised look on his face. David
knew her as well as anyone. Better than he did.

"Not Janice," David said. "Mom."

Meade almost dropped his drink. He sat up, shadows criss-
crossing his face as he leaned forward. "Why now?" he said
curiously. "You haven't brought her up in fifteen years."

David stared back unblinkingly. "I started thinking about
her today. I've always thought of Janice as my mother, but
that's not right, is it? I never missed my real mother. I guess
I was too young, and Janice was always there." David held
out his hand. "Tell me about her, Dad. Please."

Meade gripped his whiskey glass with both hands. Looking into David's gray eyes—so like his mother's—Meade nodded slowly. "You're right," he said. "You should know about your mother. I shouldn't have waited for you to ask." Meade had a sudden attack of remorse. He had closed the door on Shirley's memory, not just for himself but for David as well. He had no right to do that.

"I was only six when she died," David said. A moment of pregnant silence. They weren't ready to discuss that yet. "I have some pictures," David continued. "Janice put them in a little book." Meade's head snapped up. He felt ashamed. He had never thought of saving pictures for David. But Janice had. He could see her—sitting at the kitchen table, pasting Shirley's pictures in an album, preserving them for David. All these years and it had never been mentioned.

David's voice broke into Meade's thoughts. "She was pretty, wasn't she?"

Meade smiled, glad now that David had brought the subject up. They could escape the sadness of this day with remembrances of happier times. Meade recalled the first meeting with Shirley. "Your mother was more than pretty," Meade said. "When I saw her that first time I thought she was the most beautiful girl in the world. She knocked me off my pins."

David stood up. "Come on, Dad. Let's go for a walk." He grinned. "You can smoke. It'll help loosen your mind."

They crossed the narrow street to the river. Gari's ducks were alongside in an instant, clamoring for food. "Should have brought something," David said, watching their frantic efforts to get attention. "Gari's spoiled them silly." He lit a cigarette; Meade was already puffing contentedly on a long thin cigar.

As they walked along the riverbank, Meade told David about the dart game, the bear, the "missing hairs" and the romance that had resulted from that chance encounter.

They walked slowly along the river. Memories—like the rushing waters at their feet—flooded over Meade. How different things looked with the passage of time. If only he had been more mature, less selfish, more understanding. If, if, if. The story of his life.

David's voice was hesitant. "You really loved her?"

"A lot," Meade said, studying the glowing tip of his cigar. "A hell of a lot."

"Dad." Meade looked up. "I don't remember much about you and Mom together. But I remember Sandra." Hesitating. "And Cindy." David continued quickly, "I acted like a spoiled brat around her. I didn't know why then, but I do now. I was jealous." He shook his head ruefully.

Meade stopped, grinding the cigar out under the heel of his boot. "Nothing to explain," he said. "You had reason. I wasn't paying much attention to you." He began to walk along the river. David fell in beside him.

Hands in pockets, staring at the ground, David said, "You loved Mom, and you loved Sandra. You told me about Sandra at the lake. Remember?" Meade nodded. David shot a sidelong glance at Meade. "You loved Cindy, too. That's why I was jealous." David stopped and faced Meade. "Can you really love more than one woman? Is it the same each time, or do you love the most at first, then less as you go along?"

Meade looked at his son. It was dark now, making it difficult to distinguish David's features. "Now that's a mouthful," Meade said, smiling crookedly. Picking up a stone, he pegged it into the river.

Meade gazed at the homes on the opposite bank. "I was head over heels in love with your mother," he said quietly. "A lot of people don't believe in love at first sight, but I do. It happened to me.

"It was a gut-wrenching, one-of-a-kind experience. I guess it happens to everyone. The first time you go off the deep end. There's kind of an innocence about it. I even thought about writing poetry. Me! Suddenly, I believed in miracles because one was happening to me. Nothing was impossible. I felt like I could lick the world. Just touching Shirley's hand sent chills up my back. And when she said she loved me—God!"

Meade watched the bubbles of aerated water that gleamed

whitely on the river's dark surface. "I knew I'd die if I couldn't have her. I *knew*—I positively knew—that I couldn't go on if we broke up. Without her, life wouldn't have been worth beans. You know the feeling—optimistic one minute, scared spitless the next. Call it puppy love, but it was damn serious to me. I loved your mother, and she loved me. It was great at first. The best." A pause. "It wasn't too good toward the end, but you don't want to hear about that, do you?"

David shook his head. "Not after this morning. Maybe never. I just want to hear good things." He shuffled his feet in the thick coating of leaves that covered the ground. "There is one thing, though. I've never heard from Mom's parents; I don't even know if they're alive. It's never really bothered me—hard to miss someone you don't remember much. Just curious, I guess."

"For all I know, they're still alive," Meade said. "They never liked me. I was just a carnival man . . . footloose, worthless. They gave your mother a hard time, especially after we went broke in twenty-nine. They had a bunch of grandchildren, so I guess it was easy for them to forget you. I wish I could say some nice things about them, but I'd be a hypocrite if I did."

David shrugged. "Just wanted to know. Doesn't sound like I've missed much." He leaned against a thick tree trunk. "We had some good times with Sandra. It was sort of . . . comfortable. Know what I mean?"

Meade smiled and nodded. It was good, this special thing they were sharing. In the distance, he saw the living room lights come on; Gari would be wondering where they were. David stared at the lights, enjoying the warmth of his father's hand on his shoulder.

Meade broke the silence. "You want to know about Cindy?"

"Do you mind?"

"No. It's been three years. It hit me hard when we broke up. I guess you don't know much about that. Nobody does, not even Charlie." Dropping his hand, Meade started back toward the house. "I didn't even realize how much I loved her until it was too late." Meade shook himself as if throwing off an invisible burden. "I flew back from Reno to ask her to marry me. She was gone—left a note saying she loved me but I didn't care enough for us to stay together. I looked for her for almost a year, even hired a detective agency. She just disappeared."

David was deeply moved; he had never expected his father to open up like this.

Silently, they walked toward the glow of the porch light. The front door opened. Clutching the neck of her robe, Gari peered down at the two men. They looked guiltily at the frown that wrinkled her forehead. "I was starting to get worried," she said. "I even called Charlie." She smiled, letting them know all was forgiven. "He told me you were both big enough to take care of yourselves." She stepped back into the hall. "Come on in. I've got a fresh pot of coffee on."

15

On the morning of December ninth, the ducks waited at the riverbank with increasing impatience. By ten o'clock some were swimming out into the middle of the Truckee to get a better look at the door of Gari's home. Such neglect was unthinkable; they were usually fed before nine.

They would have a long wait; Gari had been taken to St. Mary's Hospital shortly before 3:00 A.M. With a definite show of independence, the baby had decided to arrive a week early.

After they arrived at the hospital, David was shooed out of the room by the nurses. He hurried to the nearest telephone. "Jumpin' H. Jehoshaphat!" yelled Charlie. "I'll be there before you hang up!" The phone went dead.

David looked at his watch. 3:36. Well, Meade had told him to call as soon as Gari went to the hospital. He would have called anyway. He wanted to shout it from the hospital roof.

Meade answered on the second ring. "I figured that was it," he said gruffly, sleep still heavy in his voice.

"I had to tell you, Dad," David pleaded, mistaking Meade's gruffness for irritation.

"Hey," Meade said quickly, "I'd have shot you if you hadn't."

"I'll let you get back to sleep," David said, suddenly anxious to check on Gari.

"Sleep, are you nuts? I'm coming up. I'll jog Hal out of bed and be there by nine." Meade had been using Hal Williams for charter flights a good deal of late. He had even been talking about buying a plane. Williams, a pilot for Vegas Air, was also a licensed mechanic. He and Meade got along well, and Williams would gladly come to work for the Plush Wheels fulltime. It made sense; there was a lot of company travel going back and forth between Las Vegas and Reno.

Hanging up, David looked around just as Charlie puffed his way past the nurses' station. "Well," Charlie demanded, "where is she?"

"Room 206," David said. "But you can't go in." He grinned. "I'm the only one allowed."

"The hell you say!" Charlie snapped. "No damn nurse is going to keep me away from my girls." He peered at David. "You're teasing your old uncle, aren't you."

David nodded, grinning even wider. "Just like you're teasing me about Junior being a girl."

"Teasing? You think I'm kidding about *that?*" Charlie exploded. A crafty look entered his eyes. "How much you betting?" After all, this was Nevada.

David threw caution to the winds. "Fifty bucks!" he cried joyfully.

"You got a bet," Charlie grinned, pulling out his wallet. "Shall we have Doc hold the money?"

David slapped his back pocket. "I left my wallet at home. I'm lucky I remembered to bring Gari along!"

"I'll trust you, son," Charlie said, returning the black secretarial wallet to his inside coat pocket. He couldn't resist getting in a final jab. "It's *me* that's going to have to do the trusting, 'cause *you're* going to do the paying."

At 8:37 A.M., December 9, 1952, Gari gave birth to a seven-pound ten-ounce girl. Ten minutes later, the doctor walked into the waiting room. "A girl!" he proclaimed as he emerged through the swinging doors. "Mother and daughter are in perfect shape."

"I'll be damned," David said, mimicking Meade's favorite expression. He dropped into a chair, a silly grin on his face.

The doctor had barely disappeared when Meade came out of the elevator. "Had a tail wind part of the way," he said. "Made it sooner than we expected." He stopped short and stared at the two grinning faces. "It's over?" he said incredulously.

"It's a girl!" David shouted, grabbing Meade's hand and pumping wildly. "They're both okay. We'll be seeing them in a few minutes."

"I'll be damned," Meade said. He shot a sour look at Charlie. "You're going to be big-headed for sure now."

Charlie's look only proved Meade right.

They followed the doctor down the corridor to where a plate-glass window covered the upper half of one wall. The doctor tapped on the glass, and the nurse picked up a tiny bundle. The baby was asleep, and all they could see was a wrinkled face and wisps of light-colored hair.

David's nose was pressed against the glass. All he could say was, "Wow."

Charlie was beaming as if he'd personally engineered the whole thing. "Ann," he said softly, touching the glass. The baby's eyes flew open. "Did you see that?" Charlie cried. "She knows her name!"

The doctor signaled the nurse to return Ann to her crib. "Let's go see Momma," he said, moving off at a quick pace.

"David," Gari said weakly, lifting a hand as they entered the room. David seized it in both hands, too filled with emotion to speak.

Kissing her cheek, Charlie pushed a strand of sweat-dampened hair off her forehead. "We're proud of you, honey," he said. "We've seen *Ann*"—he grinned, putting emphasis on the name. "She's going to be as pretty as you."

"You said it would be a girl," she whispered, smiling up at him.

" 'Course," he said cheerfully. "Maybe you'll pay more attention to me in the future."

Meade stood in the background, thoughts flashing back to a year and a half ago. He saw this girl who was receiving so much love as she had looked that afternoon in her apartment —shaking with anger, hurt, tears streaming down her face, screaming her defiance. Meade wished he could disappear. He had been so wrong, so goddamned wrong!

Gari turned her head and saw Meade. Suddenly, they were alone in the room, seeing only each other. Squinting woozily, Gari noted the softness of Meade's look, the steel-blue eyes that were no longer challenging. She smiled tentatively, and he moved quickly to her side. "How are you, Gari?" he said quietly.

"I'm okay," she said, looking up into his face, studying each feature as if she had never seen him before.

Meade covered her hand with his. "That's quite a little girl you've got," he said. "I'm going to stick around, and we'll have a party when you get home."

16

"Henry," Tony Giuliano spoke excitedly into the telephone, "did you see the *Journal* this morning?"

"Right here on my desk," replied the attorney. "I was getting ready to call you."

Giuliano said, "The funeral is tomorrow. Think we can move before?"

"I don't know," Henry Lawton said hesitantly. "Maybe we should let them bury him first."

Giuliano drummed his fingers impatiently on the desk. "I guess you're right," he said, hating the delay. "Make it first thing Friday then."

"I'll have my secretary clear my calendar for the whole day."

Replacing the receiver, Tony Giuliano leaned back smiling in his chair. He had waited fifteen years for this moment. In a few days, it would be his.

Old man Taggert had once owned thousands of acres in and around the Lake Tahoe basin. Twenty years ago, at the age of seventy-three, he sold off all but the choicest pieces and retired to the ranch headquarters outside Carson City. Despite the many generous offers over the years, he had steadfastly refused to sell the remaining Lake Tahoe acreage. Lean as a snake and whipcord tough, Taggert hung onto the land and his life, claiming he was saving the property for his son and daughter. No one believed him; he was saving it for himself. He wasn't going to give it up while he lived.

Like he was saving his money for his children. Bill Taggert was thirty-four when his father retired. Neither he nor his sister, Caroline, had seen any of the small fortune their father had socked away. Six years younger than her brother, Caroline married in her mid-twenties and moved to Reno. Bill and his family lived and worked at the ranch headquarters, a series of run-down buildings rapidly approaching self-destruction. He had seen little extra money from his tight-fisted father, and there were times he and his sister thought they might die before the old man did.

Tony Giuliano coveted only one piece of that Lake Tahoe property—thirty acres stretching between Highway 50 and the beach, less than a mile from the California border. It was there that he would build his crowning achievement, a complete hotel-casino resort complex.

Fourteen years ago, he had approached old man Taggert

and had been curtly brushed off. No room had been left for future negotiation.

Tony had sought out the son. Bill Taggert was more than willing to make a deal, but without the father's approval he was powerless.

Tony could only wait and watch the land double in value, then triple, then triple again. Fortunately, his own worth increased astronomically during Nevada's boom years of the forties and early fifties, so he was prepared to meet whatever the final price might be.

Now the old man was dead. The papers were already drawn up, only a few blank spaces had to be filled in.

Pulling a thick file out of a drawer, Tony thumbed through the drawings of his dream hotel. He lifted out a color photograph of the artist's rendering. The painting had been an extravagance, and it was one of Tony's best-kept secrets. He gloated over the picture of the highrise hotel with the lake and towering mountains in the background. It would take time to put it together, but he should break ground within two years. Tony put the file back in the drawer. Fifteen years. Two more days and it would be his.

Late Friday morning, Tony was talking with the casino boss at the rear of the Western Club when Henry Lawton appeared at the entrance. As Tony approached, Lawton walked quickly toward the stairs that led to the second-floor office. Tony followed.

Closing the door, Tony looked with anticipation at Lawton's bulging briefcase. "Let's see it," he said eagerly, rubbing his hands and smiling.

Lawton didn't move. For the first time, Tony took a good look at the lawyer's face. It was pale, strained. Lawton said uncomfortably, "Better sit down, Tony."

"What da hell for?" snapped Tony. "You got it, don't you?" When he became excited, Tony's English got sloppy. And he was easily excited. Like his father, Carlo, he had a short fuse.

Dropping the briefcase, Lawton sat down heavily. "I don't," he said quietly, looking up at Tony with tired eyes.

"You don't?" yelled Tony. "How come you don't?"

"Because it's already been sold," Lawton said wearily.

"Sold! What the fuck do you mean sold?" Tony screamed. Lawton glanced at the closed door, then looked back up at the raging man. Even if the sound drifted down into the casino, the employees wouldn't pay any attention. They were used to Tony's outbursts.

"When did it happen?" Tony demanded, his dark face ugly with a boiling anger that made his body shake.

"The papers were filed the morning after the old man died."

Tony Giuliano's fists were clenched, his squat powerful frame as taut as a violin string. "How could it happen so quick?" he shouted. "I've been talking to Bill Taggert for years. How come he didn't see me first?"

Steepling his manicured fingers together, Henry Lawton stared calmly at Tony. Lawton had been counselor to the Giulianos for over thirty years and was used to such scenes. Carlo's temper—which was best described as rabid—had been passed on to his son. Lawton was well paid for his services, but there were times he felt it wasn't enough. Like now. Clearing his throat, he said, "It's taken me all day to search this out. Money was paid in advance with the deal to be closed immediately upon the old man's death."

"I offered that to Bill Taggert a dozen times!" Tony cried.

"It wasn't paid to Bill; it was paid to his sister."

"His sister! What the hell's she got to do with it?"

"As much as her brother, maybe more; she was made the executor of his will. The old man must have trusted her more than the son." Lawton paused. "The front money was paid out over two years ago. I don't think Bill even knew about it until the day before yesterday. Evidently, the daughter wasn't so trustworthy as the old man thought. Probably didn't take Bill long to get over his mad; he's been broke most of his life." Lawton slumped down in his chair. "No matter; it's done."

"The hell it is!" shouted Giuliano. "Find out who the buyer is. I'll give him the fastest profit he's ever seen. Everyone's got a price." Tony stood over Lawton, square-fingered hands planted firmly on thick hips. "Get me his name. I want that land!"

"Forget it, Tony," Lawton said, looking up and shaking his head. "I know who the buyer is. He won't sell."

"Like hell he won't," snapped Tony. "Give me his name. I'll close the deal by tomorrow."

Lawton sighed and prepared for the explosion. "Slaughter," he said flatly. "Meade Slaughter."

For a moment, Tony Giuliano was too stunned to speak. Then he seemed to swell as the hot blood rushed to his face. Enraged, he whirled and raked his arm across the desk, knocking papers, pencils and a bottle of ink to the floor. "Slaughter!" he bellowed, leaning across the desk, howling like a wounded animal. He spun around and faced the lawyer. Lawton was aware that Carlo had killed more than once in his rise to power; he knew now that Tony was just as capable of murder as his father. Had Slaughter been in the room, he'd be a dead man. Tony's trembling fingers were brushing the lapel of his coat, inches from the gun that rested in a shoulder holster.

"Slaughter!" Tony repeated, literally spitting out the hated name, saliva dripping off his chin. "He killed my father, now he's tryin' to wreck me. So help me God, I'm gonna kill the bastard!"

"Tony," Lawton said mildly, trying to break through the man's irrational behavior, "there's never been any proof that Slaughter killed Carlo."

"Proof!" Tony screamed, shoving his face inches from Lawton's, "who the fuck needs proof? You know damn well Slaughter did it. You want to fight me on that, then get the hell out and stay out!"

Lawton stirred uncomfortably under Tony Giuliano's wild glare. Not even with Carlo had he faced anything like this. He tried to remain calm. No use arguing. Besides, he had always secretly believed Slaughter was guilty of Carlo's death. He had also known the reason for Slaughter's action. Frontier justice. Not the way Tony saw it. All Tony knew was that his father had been murdered. To hell with the reasons. Tony hungered for revenge—pure and simple. Lawton held up his hands in surrender. "All right, Tony," he said. "Let's say Slaughter did kill your father. What does it have to do about this land deal? Do you really think he did that to get back at you? There hasn't been a stir for ten years."

Tony stepped back, a look of paranoia on his face. "Slaughter never gave up," he said. "If he could get away with it, he'd have killed me, too. But he knows that kind of shit don't go in Nevada. I keep myself protected, knowin' how crazy he is." Tony waved his arms wildly, and the spittle flew. "He'd do anything to hurt me. He's fuckin' crazy—*crazy!*"

Lawton let out a deep sigh. Trying to reason would be futile, likely disastrous. Best to leave and hope Tony would cool down. He picked up the briefcase and stood up. "I'd better go, Tony," he said, hoping he could leave without being subjected to another outburst. "I'll call Monday," he added lamely.

Tony gazed at him malevolently. "You do that," he said. Lawton left quickly, closing the door quietly behind him.

Tony kicked the empty ink bottle against the wall, then gathered up the pencils and papers, tossing them into a drawer. He went behind the desk and sat down in the ancient wooden swivel chair.

Tony knew that he stood alone in this fight. He had only one son working with him in the clubs. The other, Mike, worked in Tony's construction firm. Only twenty, Mike was a big powerful boy with his father's temperament, but he wasn't suited for the gambling business. Reluctantly, Tony had to acknowledge that Mike was too slow and methodical, a kind way of saying he wasn't too bright.

Louis was another matter. Nearly six feet tall, slender and darkly handsome, Louis would be twenty-three in a few months. He had more brains than the rest of the family put together. Not that Tony's wife Sophia and his eighteen-year-old daughter Carla had much to add to Mike's. Lately,

Sophia and Carla had been living in San Francisco more than in Reno, carried away as they were with the cosmopolitan life of the city. It suited Tony. He had tired of his wife years ago, and Carla seemed like a stranger.

Louis was a dutiful son. He had defied his father only once. That was when he insisted on attending the University of Nevada, something he was able to do when a burst eardrum had kept him out of Korea. "What the fuck do you want to get more school for?" Tony had demanded. "How's a college education goin' help you in the club?"

Louis had quietly resisted, and Tony had given in. If Louis had screamed and ranted as Mike would have done, there would have been a battle royal. But that wasn't Louis' way.

Tony was proud of Louis. He was a good boy, and there was no question of his loyalty. Now that he had graduated with honors from the University, Tony bragged about his son's achievement, making it sound as if it had been his idea all along.

Tony ran a powerful hand over the scarred surface of the old oak desk. It had been his father's. He wished the old man was here now. They could plan together, and they would be of one mind, one purpose. Louis was going to be his able right arm one day, but he wasn't really suited for this kind of work.

Tony considered his options. Killing an owner in Nevada was suicide. The unwritten law had been laid down when a heavy influx of outsiders started coming to the state in the forties. Disputes were to be kept out of the state. Don't kill the goose that lays the golden eggs. There hadn't been any known gambling-related killings in Nevada since Harry Sherwood had been shot at Lake Tahoe in 1947. Lincoln Fitzgerald's shooting in Reno two years later had always been considered the work of an amateur. And Fitzgerald had lived.

Meade Slaughter was heavily protected. His original two bodyguards were now security chiefs in the Las Vegas Plush Wheels, Bob Thompson downtown and Don Milton on the

Strip; however, Slaughter still kept two men with him whenever he left the Strip hotel's premises, which was his headquarters.

Tony hit the desk with frustration. He couldn't go after
Meade Slaughter. It was too damn risky. There was something else to think about, something he didn't want to admit.
Slaughter was an extremely dangerous man. He had killed
four men that Tony knew of, one his father.

But he *had* to even the score with Slaughter for this latest
insult. As for his father's murder, he had vowed vengeance
for that long ago. He was in no hurry. Just thinking about
it gave him pleasure.

This land grab was an attack on him personally; his pride
was involved. Tony looked up suddenly, black eyes glinting,
a smile breaking across his face. He would go after Slaughter
the same way. Personally. Tony picked up the phone and
called downstairs to the pit boss. "Is Gatori on the table
now?" Tony asked. The pit boss's voice crackled over the
phone. "Have Pete take his place," Tony said. "I want to see
Gatori right away—in my office."

A few minutes later, Mario Gatori entered the office. He
still had an angelic look, enhanced by his short black curls
and long eyelashes, but Tony knew Gatori was everything
but an angel. He had come here to escape troubles with the
law in New York City. He hadn't changed his ways, only the
methods. He was more subtle now. Tony was sure that only
he and his informants knew of Gatori's illegal activities in
Reno.

"Sit down," Tony said, waving at a chair. He saw Gatori's
eyes flick to the fresh ink stain on the floor, the bare desk.
No surprise, no questioning look. Tony liked that. Mario
Gatori knew how to mind his own business, and he was
street-wise far beyond his twenty-seven years.

Tony had his anger in check now. He asked Gatori, "You
still seeing the Slaughter kid?" He already knew the answer;
little happened in Reno that he didn't know about.

"Yeah, sure," Gatori said, picking his way cautiously.

"We get together for lunch, breakfast, a drink—things like that."

"How's he doing?"

Gatori shrugged. "Okay, I guess. Had a kid a couple of months ago."

"Happily married?"

"Hell yes!" Gatori burst out. "With a wife like that, who wouldn't be?"

Tony sat back and put his hands behind his head. "Tell me about him. Everything you know."

Mario Gatori talked, with Tony asking a question now and then, probing, prompting, searching.

Gatori stopped and stared at his lighted cigarette for a long moment. "That's about it," he said. He looked at Tony. "That what you wanted to know?"

Tony nodded, elbows resting on the desk, fingers laced together, rubbing his thumbs against each other. Neither spoke as Tony lighted a cigar, then sat back, the old swivel chair creaking in the silence. Several minutes passed.

Tony sat up straight, feet thumping on the floor. He pointed the cigar at Gatori. "The kid's arm—it bothers him a lot?"

Gatori nodded. "All the time. They took him off the tables because of it. It acts up, hurts like hell."

Tony's eyes narrowed. "He takes pain pills?"

There was a glint in Gatori's agate eyes; he was catching on. "Yeah," he said softly. "Eats 'em like popcorn."

Tony leaned on the desk. "Okay, Mario," he said, biting off each word decisively, "here's what you do." Gatori sat impassively while Tony spelled out what he wanted. Gatori didn't show it, but he was stunned at the knowledge that Tony had of his outside activities. Tony didn't condemn, nor did he threaten exposure, but Gatori knew what would happen if he didn't carry out Tony's orders. He would have anyway, even without the large sum Tony said he would pay. Mario Gatori knew on which side his bread was buttered.

By the time Gatori left the office, Tony was in a much

better mood. Taking the papers out of the drawer, he put
them back on top of the desk. The empty ink bottle, he tossed
in the wastebasket. He looked down at the stain on the carpet. He'd get that taken care of tomorrow.

17

Plans were spread out on the big table in the conference room
next to Meade's Strip office. Along the walls were a score of
full-color renderings and murals. Charlie grinned, chewing
on his cigar, as happy as a kid in a candy shop. "Son of a
bitch!" he chortled. "It's like old home week."

Meade peered over Charlie's shoulder at the mural of San
Diego's Mission Bay beach with Belmont Amusement Park
in the background. "We'll have at least thirty pictures like
this scattered through the casino and lounges," Meade said.
"All the best parks in the country—Coney Island, Playland,
Cedar Point, Queen's, Palisades, you name 'em."

Meade picked up a rendering of the exterior of the new
Strip Plush Wheel Casino and pointed to the wheel of fortune
that stood in the entrance. "A new Plush Wheel design," he
said. "None of that fancy gold filigree on our wheels now.
More modern. That goes for the sign too." Meade indicated
the Plush Wheel on the roof of the casino. A thirty-foot copy
of the wheel inside, it would turn slowly, pause on a number,
move to another, pause, move. At night, it would be il-
luminated by a brilliant array of neon lights. In conjunction
with the opening of the new Strip Plush Wheel next year, the
wheels—inside and out—would go up at all three clubs.

"Nordstrom's good," Charlie said, studying the casino
drawing: table games in the center pit, slot machines crammed in every available space, murals of the parks and rides
hanging on the walls. "He's tied everything together real

nice. It'll be great when we get all the clubs looking the same."

"As far as I'm concerned," Meade said, "Nordstrom's the best. He can't be over thirty-five, but he's everything Bartlett said he was. Did you know he's a fourth-generation architect? He probably bleeds drawing ink."

Meade had retained Gunther Nordstrom last November. These plans and drawings were the result of nearly six months of research, endless conferences and experimental designs.

"See anything you don't like?" Meade asked as Charlie wandered from picture to picture.

Charlie nodded, jabbing his cigar at the big drawing that dwarfed most of the others. "That damn golf course," he said. "Bunch of idiots running around after a little ball. Izzy puts in all his spare time on the course. Only thing wrong with him; otherwise he's the best damn casino manager in the business."

"I've got a couple of managers down here who might disagree with you," Meade said drily. He admired the layout of the golf course. Designed by Robert Trent Jones, it would be a thing of beauty, sprawling over one hundred acres and covered with lush grass and trees, leaving ample room for one hundred fifty choice lots.

Meade said, "When I see this, I don't think about the game. All I see are dollar signs."

Meade reached for a tall canvas that was turned face against the wall. "I've saved the best for last," he said, standing it on a table. "Like it?" he asked, stepping back and examining the color painting, so real it looked like a photograph. "It's a ways down the road," Meade added. "A couple of years, at least. We'll duplicate it at Tahoe."

The building towered over the casino, rising fourteen stories above the desert floor. To date, all the Strip hotels were one- and two-story complexes that rambled over acres of land. This was a new concept and not without critics. Some even said that the porous sandy soil couldn't support such weight. But land prices were soaring, and going up seemed the only way to meet future demands.

Meade said, "There's talk about a Miami group building a highrise near the Thunderbird. They may beat us to the punch. We've got a lot to do before we get to this."

"Who else's seen this?" Charlie asked, waving an arm around the room.

"You, me, Nordstrom and his staff. We'll spring some of it to the public when we break ground next month." Meade pointed at the painting of the highrise. "That stays on ice for a while."

Charlie nodded approvingly. "What about Zed and Archie?" he said. Zed Atkins managed the downtown Las Vegas Plush Wheel and Archie Greenburg the Strip hotel.

"They'll get a look," Meade said. "All the top people will. Same with your bunch in Reno. I'll bring everything up next week."

"Let's not go too far down the management line," Charlie said. "You know how people change jobs in this business. Worse than women trying on hats."

"It's a fact," Meade agreed, taking down the picture of the new hotel and facing it against the wall.

18

"David, look out!" Gari screamed.

"What? Hey—" David looked around just as the boom hit the seat of his bathing trunks, propelling him into a brief flurry of motion before he hit the water. "Aaaugh!" he spluttered as he surfaced, spitting out a mouthful of water.

Scrambling on all fours over the deck of the little sailboat, Gari chased the whipping line, ducking under the wildly swinging boom, finally securing the flopping canvas in a burst of effort that left her sprawled on her stomach, panting as she wrapped the rope around a cleat.

Gari looked for David. He was swimming toward the boat. "Oh God," he cried, "it's cold!"

Leaning forward on her knees, Gari waited for David to come alongside. She giggled, bit her lip, let out a loud laugh, bit her lip again. Losing the battle, Gari hugged her sides and surrendered to convulsions of laughter.

Finally she reached down and yanked David on board, slithering and flopping about like a beached whale. "What a lovely shade of blue!" Gari exclaimed, grabbing a towel and rubbing David's dripping back and legs. Rolling him over, she toweled off his front.

"I think I'll live," groaned David. He looked up into Gari's laughing face. "Think it's funny, huh?"

"I'm sorry, David," Gari said, losing control again, "but you should have seen yourself. Kicked in the ass by a sail!"

Whooping, David knocked Gari on her back, then sat on her stomach, tickling her sides. He stopped suddenly, leered, then jerked the top of Gari's bathing suit down over her breasts.

"*David!*" Gari yelped as he bent down and grabbed a swollen nipple between his teeth. Tasting the colorless liquid that squirted into his mouth, David murmured, "Yum, yum. Plenty here. Enough for me and Ann."

Gari stopped wiggling and grabbed David's hair. "You know that turns me on," she gasped. "Why did you have to start it here—when we can't finish?"

David glanced around; there were no other boats nearby. "Who says we can't?" he grinned. "From the shore, they'll think we're wrestling."

"Uh, uh," Gari said, shaking her head. "You can munch a little bit, but that's all. I'm not going on public display, no matter how horny I am." Gari moaned and scratched David's back. "That's good." She shifted his head to her other breast. "Bite it." David nipped the tip, ran his tongue over the areola, around the nipple, then seized it with his teeth. He slipped his hand down over her mound. "Yes, yes!" Gari urged, spreading her legs and rotating her hips. She let out a little cry. "I can't believe it; I think I'm going to come!"

Gari bucked and rolled as David's fingers blurred with movement. It was over in moments, Gari's cries muffled by the hand she clapped over her mouth. Silence. Rolling on her side, Gari sighed. "Do you realize it's been two weeks?" she said.

"I do now," David said, taking her hand and closing it over his throbbing penis.

"Well, hello there," Gari said, rising to her knees, naked breasts swaying. She pulled David's trunks down and gripped him with strong fingers. Bending down and running her tongue inside David's ear, she began to work her hand up and down, slowly at first, then faster and faster. David's climax was almost as fast as hers. Gari kept pumping until semen coated his stomach and her hand. "Feel better?" she teased, slippery fingers caressing his shrinking member.

"Yeah," David whispered, suddenly tired. "Know something?" he said, raising his head and grinning. "I'm not cold anymore!"

"Wonder why?" Gari said, releasing his penis and cleaning her hand on a towel. Wiping David off, she pulled up his pants. "We'd better watch out," she said, looking furtively over her shoulder. "People get arrested for things like this."

"I can see the headlines," David grinned. "Mr. and Mrs. Slaughter caught masturbating on Donner Lake."

Gari made a face and pulled the bathing suit up over her breasts. "Sounds awful when you put it like that."

"Didn't seem awful to me," David yawned. He looked Gari up and down. "Hey, you're looking good for a momma of five months."

Gari ran her hands over her flat stomach and trim hips. "Not bad if I say so myself," she agreed. She frowned at her breasts. "The upstairs department needs a little work."

"You're the one who insisted on breast-feeding the baby," David reminded her.

While David attempted to get the boat underway, Gari stretched out on the little deck. Two hours ago, they had christened the *Lady Ann* with a glass of champagne poured over the bow. The rest of the bottle they had consumed as they drifted out into the lake, Gari reading from the instruction book while David worked the confusing array of ropes and pulleys. Gari glanced up. The single sail was filling with wind. "Not bad!" David called, sitting down and working the tiller as the boat began to move.

Gari and David had visited Donner Lake several times last summer; it was a short drive from Reno, just across the border in California. The sparkling little lake inspired them to buy a sailboat. They had picked up the *Lady Ann,* a 4-meter Sunfish, yesterday.

Closing her eyes, Gari let her body sway with the gentle movements of the boat. It had been nearly three weeks since they had sex. David had always been the aggressor when it came to sex. Until three months ago. It had happened gradually. Several nights missed with no expression of desire. Once, a week passed. Then two. This latest stretch was the longest.

At times—increasingly of late—David seemed to drift about in a cloud of euphoria. Gari had teased him about it. In the beginning. Then she became alarmed. Frightened when Charlie brought it up a week ago.

David had been letting things go at work. He was forgetting important matters, often showing up late for work with no excuse and an uncharacteristic lack of concern. Punctuality had been one of his attributes, something he had learned from his father.

Since last December, David had been working in the credit department at the Plush Wheel. The problems with his arm had forced him to stop working as a dealer, and his new job was the first step in a carefully planned administrative training program.

Hoping there might be some explanation for David's strange behavior, Sam Devon, the credit manager, discussed the matter with Charlie. As puzzled as Devon, Charlie suggested that they watch David closely for a while. If it became necessary, Charlie would talk to his grand-nephew.

Weeks passed, and Charlie knew he could no longer avoid the issue. He took a round-about approach, luring Gari out to lunch and bringing the subject up over cocktails. Admittedly he was passing the buck, but Charlie, too, was seeking a reasonable explanation.

There was none. Gari's fears were added to Charlie's. "Think it's his arm?" Charlie asked.

Gari shrugged helplessly. "I don't think so. If anything, it seems to be better. Did you know the doctor advised another operation?"

"Morley?"

Gari shook her head. "Doctor Morley had a specialist look at David last November." Her eyes darkened. "He said that if a reconstructive operation didn't work, amputation might be the only way to end the pain."

"Shit!" Charlie blurted. "Sorry," he added, shaking his head, "but that's a helluva shock. How come nobody told me?"

"David doesn't want anyone to know. He made me promise." Gari hugged her arms across her chest. "He won't even consider an amputation." She shuddered. "I don't blame him."

"Me neither," Charlie said, a note of horror entering his voice.

"There's something else," Gari said.

Charlie blinked. "Shoot," he said.

"David hasn't seen Doctor Morley for nearly two months. I found out at the Johnsons' party last week. When the doctor brought it up, I just acted dumb."

"Did you ask David?"

"Yes. He said his arm is better. I believed him because he's cut down on his pain pills. I'm thankful for that. He was taking too many."

Charlie shook his head in defeat. "So where's that leave us?"

"Nowhere," Gari said tiredly. She looked around as if seeking help, then turned back to Charlie. "I think I should be the one to talk with David."

There was no argument; Charlie didn't like confrontations. "Does Meade know anything?" he asked.

Gari frowned. "I'm not sure. When he showed us the plans of the new hotel, David was going through one of his 'dazed' spells. Know what I mean?"

"Kinda half here and half not?"

Gari nodded. "Meade was talking about the plans, and David was staring out the window, off in another world." The scene was still vivid in her mind.

Meade had smiled at the figure slumped in the leather chair. "Are you with us, David?" he said.

David's head snapped up. He grinned sheepishly at Meade, who was standing by the rendering of the highrise. "Sure, Dad," he said, sitting up and running his fingers through his thick blond hair. "Daydreaming, I guess."

"You're forgiven," Meade said, dropping in a chair near where Gari sat nursing Ann. Waving his arm, Meade looked at his audience. "What do you think?" he asked.

"Pretty nice," David said, glancing at the pictures scattered around the living room. He looked at Gari. "What do you think, honey?"

"I think it's wonderful," she said.

"Now the real work begins," Meade said, pleased with her reaction. He grinned and pointed at the blanket that covered Ann's head. "Want to sell the kid and work on the project?"

"He's mean," Gari said, looking down and touching Ann's fat little cheek. Gari looked up at Meade, tawny eyes flashing. "I'd take you up in a minute if Ann weren't around." Her eyes softened, and she looked down again. "But she is."

Meade cleared his throat. "If that critter's full, let me hold her."

Gari poked Ann's cheek, and the tiny mouth made a half-hearted nibble. "Not only full, she's asleep," Gari said. She lifted Ann and laid her over her shoulder.

Gari handed Ann to Meade, amazed as always at the gentleness with which he handled his granddaughter. She noted the tender look on his face as he laid Ann in his lap. Four months ago, she wouldn't have believed it possible.

After a half-hour of small talk, David rose abruptly. "Have to get to work," he said.

Gari looked at the mantel clock. "You've got an hour yet."

"I know. I promised to meet Mario for coffee."

"Oh." A flash of disapproval appeared in Gari's eyes. David didn't notice; he was already leaving the room.

Meade's voice broke the heavy silence. "Does David see Mario much?" One eyebrow was raised. *He* hadn't missed Gari's look.

"Some," Gari said. A pause. "Quite a bit, really." Shaking her head, Gari looked away, angry with herself for letting her feelings show.

Meade shot Gari a penetrating look, then switched his attention to the sleeping baby. He busied himself adjusting the blanket around Ann. He glanced up at Gari, chewed his lip, then continued fiddling with Ann's blanket.

Gari was impressed. Meade knew something was wrong, but he wasn't going to pry.

While Gari put Ann to bed, Meade packed the pictures away. They talked about the designs over coffee and while they loaded the cases in the car. Nothing of a serious nature was said about David, not then or during their two meetings since.

Gari rolled on her stomach as David guided the *Lady Ann* across Donner Lake. She peeked at her husband through the long strands of hair that covered her face. Why the sudden shifts in mood—happy one day, down the next? The bursts of confidence followed by defeated silence? Days, weeks of sexual indifference, then unexpected passion like today?

A week had passed since she had told Charlie she would talk to David. She sighed and laid her head down on her arm. It couldn't be put off much longer. She wasn't afraid to face David. It was just so damn *confusing!*

What about Mario Gatori? Gari's eyes narrowed. She had formed an instant dislike for the man. Knowing David regarded Mario as a close friend, she had tried to be cordial. It wasn't easy. Gatori was too sure of himself, handsome in a dark sinister way that undoubtedly attracted many women. Gari had met men like him in Vegas—survivalists relying on animal instincts, egos exceeded only by their contempt for women.

David and Gatori spent a lot of time together, too much as far as Gari was concerned. She had considered and quickly dismissed the thought that she might be jealous. From the beginning, her relationship with David had been a case of David needing her, not her needing him. It bothered her, however, to see him become dependent on a man like Gatori.

Gari's breasts pressed painfully against her bathing suit. "We'd better get home," she called to David. Sitting up, she hefted the top of her suit. "If Ann doesn't lower the level, these things are going to pop."

David laughed and began a long sweeping turn. "Let me try," Gari said, crawling toward the stern. Moving over, David handed her the tiller. "Hey," Gari cried, "this is fun!"

They skimmed across the lake. Their course was erratic, and once the sail lost the wind. It would be a while before they could tackle a big lake like Tahoe.

19

It was early morning, and the hot August sun beat down on the two men. "All we need is a wind," Smitty grumbled as a giant landmover rolled by, making them jump back to avoid the trailing cloud of dust.

"Progress, Smitty, think of it as progress," Meade grinned, clamping his white teeth firmly over the long thin cigar.

"I call it dirt," Smitty muttered, slapping his hat against his leg, sneezing violently as dust drifted up into his nose.

Meade watched the dozen vehicles that moved back and forth over the one hundred acres that lay behind the Strip Plush Wheel. The golf course was taking shape. The archi-

tect, Robert Trent Jones, expected to start planting trees and
grass in October. The five lakes would be filled at the same
time.

Of the one hundred fifty lots around the course, Meade had
reserved several of the best for himself. Twenty-eight had
already been sold. He figured the balance would be sold
within six months of the golf course's completion.

"Things have changed since thirty-eight," Smitty said as
the Cadillac rolled over the unpaved construction road behind the Plush Wheel.

Leaning back in the deep cushions of the rear seat, Meade
looked beyond the skeleton of his new casino at the Sands
Hotel that stood between the Flamingo and Desert Inn. "Almost too fast," Meade mused. "We've been making so much
money it scares me. Sometimes, I long for that little two-bit
club in Reno."

"Like shit!" Smitty snorted, shooting Meade a cynical
look. "Bet you think like that once in a blue moon. And I
ain't never seen one."

Meade shrugged and grinned. "Well, I do get sentimental
at times. I miss the days when everybody knew everybody.
Not that Vegas is that big, but we're not the friendly little
town we used to be."

"True," Smitty said, lighting a cigarette. Pale blue eyes
took in the restaurants, motels and service stations that dotted the Strip. "You blow a bubble long enough, it's goin' to
bust," Smitty continued, dragging on his cigarette, eyes shifting upwards as the shadow of the casino frame darkened the
car.

Meade said, "The Sahara's added two hundred forty
rooms, D.I. two hundred, Thunderbird one sixty." He
pointed at the new building. "I'll be adding to this over the
years, but I'm not going to tear it down in order to grow.
We've got to look ahead when we design a new hotel. Costs
are going up; investors can't plan on a hundred percent return on their money in two-three years anymore."

Smitty nodded, shivering slightly as the air-conditioning
chilled the sweat on his shirt.

"Been meanin' to talk to you about somethin'," Smitty said to Meade as they walked around the construction site. Smitty stopped and peered up at Meade. "About last night."

Meade sighed. "I think I know, but go ahead."

"The man's changed!" exploded Smitty. "I can't believe how he's changed!"

Meade kicked a piece of wood. "He drinks a lot."

"A lot, hell!" Smitty exclaimed. "He was drunk. I've known Bob for fifty years, and I've never seen him drunk. Until last night."

They moved into the shade of the building, Meade hunching down on his heels and chewing his cigar. Smitty sat on a pile of lumber and lit a cigarette. "The man looks like hell," Smitty said. "It's like somebody jerked his cord, and the lights went out."

"Janice," Meade said.

"Hell, yes—Janice," said Smitty. "I always took Bob for a big strong man who could hold his own anywhere. Not anymore. He must have depended on Janice a lot more than we knew."

Meade stared at the ground and saw Bob Terhune the way he was last night at dinner, the first time he and Smitty had seen him since the funeral. The easy assurance was gone, a defeated look in his eyes. Bob Terhune's hair was snow white, his frame bent, walk shuffling. He did too much back-slapping, talked too loud and tended to laugh at peculiar times. He grabbed at the cocktail waitress when she brought their drinks, fingers exploring her body under the skimpy costume. The stories must be true, thought Meade. Less than ten months since Janice's death, and the rumors had been rampant about Terhune's sexual exploits in Nevada and Washington.

Meade looked up at Smitty. "You think you know a man, then you don't. I hope he slows down before he ruins his career."

Smitty shrugged. "He's sixty-three. About retirement time."

NEVADA   325

Meade grinned. "You're sixty-five. Are you going to lay down and die?"

Smitty's head jerked up. "Shit no! I'm just gettin' started."

"Maybe that's the way Bob feels," Meade said, standing up.

"I'm still motivatin' good," grunted Smitty. "Bob's like a walkin' corpse. If he keeps this up, he won't have any choice."

Meade nodded. Nothing more to add. Circumstances change; people change. He was certainly in no position to judge.

Smitty rose and looked at the men working three stories above. "Looks hotter than hell up there," he muttered. "I'm goin' back to the ranch before I melt down." With a wave of his hand, he headed toward his old pickup that was parked by the construction shack. Meade returned to the Cadillac.

Smitty lived on the ranch with Meade now. Although his business interests were scattered all over Nevada, Smitty was investing more and more in the Las Vegas area. He visited Reno once a month, but most of the time he sat on the porch of his remodeled bunkhouse "clippin' coupons," as he put it.

Meade watched as a girder was lifted to the top of the giant structure that would house his new casino and showroom.

20

Charlie leaned across the desk and refilled Meade's glass. "Good bourbon's like medicine," Charlie said as he topped off his drink. "Protects the body against all kinds of disease."

Meade's eyes were hooded, thoughtful. "Know something, Charlie?" he said. "I've been in Reno two hours, and I've learned all kinds of interesting things. Like the club's making money hand over fist, the broads never looked better, and bourbon makes good medicine. But I've got this funny feeling that this isn't why you called me up here so urgent like. What's up—you getting married?"

Charlie's drink went down the wrong way. "God no!" he coughed. His face dropped, and he shook his head. "Even that wouldn't seem so bad, considering."

Meade sat up, intent. "I'm listening," he said.

With a swift jab, Charlie stubbed out his cigar. "It's David," he said quickly. "I should have said something a long time ago, but I kept hoping it would blow over."

Meade stared at the wall calendar. "It's been two months since I was here last—been up to my neck with things on the Strip, the golf course opening last month, construction headaches coming out of my ears. Too damn busy making money, I guess." He looked across the desk. "I'm not blind, Charlie. I've noticed things. Figured it was none of my business. Thought maybe there were problems between David and Gari."

"Not that," Charlie said emphatically. "I've talked to Gari. She's at her wit's end." Charlie slapped the desk with the palm of his hand. "David's going downhill, and there's no damn reason for it!"

Pushing his drink to one side, Meade leaned forward. "Tell me," he said wearily.

Charlie said, "He doesn't seem to be with it, wanders around like he's not here. Makes mistakes, forgets things. Damnit!" Charlie burst out, angry, frustrated. "He's not responsible worth shit! Never know when he's going to turn up for work or when he's going to leave. If you point anything out, he just grins. Words roll off him like water off a duck's back!"

"You've talked this over with Gari?"

"Dozens of times. The last time yesterday. That's why I called you. We need your help."

"We?"

"We," Charlie snapped. "Me and Gari."

"She wants _my_ help?"

"David's your son, damnit. Gari wouldn't ask for your personal help in a million years. We've got to pull together. For David's sake." Charlie yanked a cigar from an inside pocket. "What we need is Janice. She left a big hole in all our lives." They had talked earlier about Bob Terhune's problems.

"Have you talked to his doctor?" Meade asked.

"What for? David hasn't seen him in six months."

Meade got up and walked around the room. "Guess I've really been out of touch," he said, stopping at the window to look down on Virginia Street.

"You can't be everywhere," Charlie said.

"You said it," Meade murmured. "But, he's my son. I should have cared enough to check things out." Meade whirled, and Charlie was taken aback at the pain in the big man's eyes. "Do you know what David's actions remind me of?" Meade said. "Do I have to spell it out?"

Charlie laid his cigar in the tray. "Don't read something into this that isn't there," he said softly. "Lots of things are different this time."

Meade turned back to the window. His voice was barely audible. "Shirley used to go off into her own world. If things bothered her, she would just close everything out. Including me." He looked at Charlie. "Is David doing the same thing to Gari?"

Charlie sighed. "Some. They're not communicating." He looked up at Meade, defiant. "That gal's hanging in there. Sometimes, I think she's got more guts than you and me put together. She isn't running; you can believe that."

Meade nodded slowly. "You don't have to sell me on her. She may not believe it, but I can change my mind."

"Good," Charlie said, chewing his cigar with satisfaction. "That'll make it easier."

"What easier?" Meade said suspiciously.

"You and her talking. It's all set up."

"Just like that," Meade said, leaning over the desk. "Do I have any say?"

"Nope," Charlie replied, grinning sardonically. "You're

pretty good at manipulating people. Thought I would turn the tables a bit. Got any objection to meeting with her?"

Meade sat down heavily. "No, of course not." He raised an eyebrow. "Aren't you sitting in?"

"Got work to do," Charlie said, waving at a stack of papers. "Besides, I've talked about this until I'm blue in the face. Maybe you and Gari can come up with a new angle."

"Being as you've got everything else planned, when's this meeting coming off?" Meade said.

Charlie looked at his watch. " 'Bout an hour. David's supposed to be on the job at six." He looked at the now darkened window, the neon lights flickering a myriad of colors against the pane. "At least he's supposed to be here." Charlie turned back to Meade. "That's another part of the mystery. If he's late, I can never catch him at home. Gari's says he's gone for long stretches, didn't make it home one night."

Meade slumped in the chair. "That's serious."

"That it is," Charlie agreed.

"Another woman?"

"Gari says no."

"What about David's friends?" Meade asked.

"He hangs out a lot with Mario Gatori," Charlie said. He shook his head at Meade's look. "Now don't go off on a tangent. You've had a thing about Gatori for years—just because he works for Giuliano. Gatori's not my kind of guy, and Gari doesn't think much of him, but I can't see any harm in him going around with David. There's no proof about anything, anyway. I'd step careful there if I was you. Him and David are pretty close."

Meade grunted something unintelligible. He got up and stood looking out the window. He was silent for a long time. "Do you know it was nineteen years ago this month when Shirley died?" he said quietly. "Whenever November rolls around, I think about it." The flashing lights etched his face eerily. "I should have done more for her, Charlie. I was too damn selfish." Meade turned. "I still am, but I'm going to do my damnedest to help David."

"I know you will, boy," Charlie said softly. For a moment, they were thrown back in time, Meade opening his heart, Charlie understanding, offering consolation.

The porch light was on when Meade walked up the steps. When Gari opened the door, Meade immediately noticed the dark circles under her eyes. She had lost weight, but her eyes were clear, strong, like the set of her chin.

"Come on in, Meade," she said, stepping aside, closing the door and following him into the living room.

"Where is she?" Meade said, looking around.

Gari smiled. Her old self again. "Upstairs, asleep, I hope." She saw the longing in Meade's eyes. "I'll take you up, but you've got to promise not to wake her. I had to do everything but tie her down tonight."

Meade grinned. "Scout's honor," he said, raising a hand.

Ann was sleeping on her stomach, rear end up in the air, a chubby fist clenched tightly in front of her nose. Fine blond hair covered her eyes and part of her cheek. Meade reached down in the darkness and tenderly moved the silken strands behind her ear.

Meade moved silently away from the crib. He grinned at Gari as they stepped into the hall. "If you hadn't been looking, I'd have tickled her awake." He stopped and looked back into the room. "God, she's a little beauty!"

Gari's eyes softened. She touched Meade's arm. "Let's go down to the kitchen; I've got a fresh pot on."

Meade set his cup down and looked at Gari across the table. "One month from now. I can't believe it's been a year."

"Tell me about it," Gari said, glancing down at her slender waist. On December 9th, Ann would have her first birthday. Meade and Charlie were competing to see who could shower her with the most gifts.

Gari tilted her head toward the upstairs room. "You're spoiling her, you know."

"It's the prerogative of a grandfather," he said loftily.

"Hummpf," Gari retorted. She got up and refilled their cups.

The big kitchen clock ticked loudly. Meade cleared his throat. "Guess we've got to talk," he said lamely.

Gari's eyes met his. "How much has Charlie told you?"

"Not much. He said David's in a fog a lot." A pause. "He said he stays away from home . . . didn't even come home one night. When I started to ask questions, he told me to wait until I saw you."

Gari ran her fingers through her thick dark hair. "I feel like we're plotting behind David's back."

"Don't think that. He needs help, and we're all he's got."

Gari acknowledged this with a jerk of her head. "It happened slowly," she said, gathering her thoughts. "I first noticed it about March. I would say things, and he wouldn't hear, seemed to be drifting away." She looked at Meade, tawny eyes questioning. "That's the way he was the day you showed us the plans. You noticed, didn't you?"

Meade nodded. "I didn't think too much about it. I wasn't seeing him every day like you."

"Nothing since?"

Meade stirred uncomfortably. "Looking back, I can think of other times. I didn't know what was going on, so it didn't bother me." A shrug. "How many times have I been up since April—four, five times?"

Gari just stared down into her cup.

"I've been busier than hell down south," Meade continued, a defensive tone in his voice. Impulsively, he reached out and took Gari's hand. "I'm sorry, Gari," he said as she lifted her head and looked into his face. "I should have paid more attention." He dropped her hand and played with the handle of his cup.

Gari got up quickly and went to the stove, her back to Meade. "You don't have to be sorry," she said quietly, blinking her eyes. "You had no way of knowing." She lit the burner, still reluctant to turn around.

"I wanted to come up lots of times," Meade said. An embarrassed chuckle. "I guess you know I'm nuts about Ann." His cup rattled in the saucer. "You guys are the only family I've got. We've got to pull together."

Tears threatened to well in Gari's eyes. She lifted the lid and peeked inside the coffee pot. Once more in control, she turned with the steaming pot. "I'm glad you feel that way. I never had much of a family either."

Meade looked up, interested. "I didn't know." He grinned, seeking to break the emotional spell. "We'll have to delve into that sometime."

"How about thirty years from now, when I'm old and gray?"

"*You* old?" Meade exclaimed. "What about *me*? My hearing will be gone by then!"

They laughed together. A moment of silence. Meade said, "Do you have any ideas why David's acting this way?"

Gari bit her lip. "At first I thought it might be something to do with his arm. But it seems to be better. He's not using near as many pain pills. And he's stopped seeing the doctor. Did you know that?"

"Charlie told me." Meade hesitated. "What's he like around the house—when he's around the house," he added grimly.

Gari waved a hand helplessly. "It's like Charlie told you. He's just not with it. He doesn't seem to *care*. He's moody. One day he's happy, the next down in the dumps. It's like" —she struggled for words—"he's not *there.*"

"You talked to him?"

"Several times. At first I teased him about his daydreaming. Then it wasn't funny any more. After Charlie brought it up, I had a serious talk with David. That was in July. He waved it off. Didn't get mad, just laughed and told me I was worried about nothing. It was like talking to a pillow. The last time I talked to him was a week ago." She pulled her hair over one shoulder and combed the dark tresses with her fingers. "It wasn't very pleasant. He's getting moodier." Her fingers began to unconsciously plait her hair into a thick braid. "He was closed up like a clam and stomped out. I could have handled it easier if he'd waved his arms and yelled. I didn't see him until the next day."

"That was the time he was gone all night?"

"He was like a spoiled little boy. I could have popped him one!"

Meade smiled approvingly. "It's going to take a lot to get you down," he said. "I'm glad to see that."

"Having Ann makes it easier," Gari said, glancing toward the stairs. She looked at Meade. "Do you have any idea what it could be?"

"You don't think it's his arm?"

Gari shook her head.

Meade popped his knuckles, making Gari wince. "Sorry," he said, "bad habit of mine." A pause. "This business of being away from home a lot. Not another woman?"

Gari shook her head emphatically. "No, I'm sure of that."

Meade raised one eyebrow.

"I'm sure," Gari said firmly.

Meade opened his mouth, then clamped it shut.

"All right," Gari said. "You want to know why I know, don't you?"

"You don't have to tell me," Meade said, but the questioning look was still there.

"Several things," Gari said, dropping her braid and ticking off the points on her fingers. "One, this is a small town. Things get around. You know that. Two, a woman can sense these things. Three—" She closed her fingers into a fist. "This gets personal," she said, adding, "but with my past, why should I be embarrassed."

"Gari!" Meade said sharply, making her jump. His big finger was pointed rigidly at her nose. "Your past died when you married David. All you've got is a future." He pointed upstairs. "That's part of the future up there. In my book, you're A-Number-One. Okay?"

The tears were bright now, and Gari made no effort to hide them. "Thank you, Meade," she whispered.

Meade reached out and covered her hand with his. "Friends?" he said.

"Friends," she answered, laying her other hand over his. Several moments passed. Still holding Meade's hand, Gari began slowly, "David has no interest in sex anymore. In the beginning, he was perfectly normal—more than normal. Then he began to taper off this spring." She squeezed Meade's hand hard. "We haven't had sex in nearly two months!"

"I'll be damned," Meade said.

Gari withdrew her hands. "It's not another woman. He just hasn't any interest anymore." She blushed brightly. "He's even tried a couple of times and hasn't been able to."

"I'll be damned," Meade repeated.

Gari pounded a fist on the table. "Sometimes I could cuss a blue streak!"

Meade grinned, confident in their new relationship. "I seem to remember you doing that once."

Gari's eyes sparkled. "Thanks for reminding me; I'd almost forgotten."

"I'll bet," Meade said, still grinning.

They were silent for a time. "So where do we go from here?" Gari said.

Meade said, "You and Charlie have talked to David. Guess it's my turn." A pause. "What about David and Gatori? Charlie says they spend a lot of time together."

Gari made a face. "I don't like that man."

"Me neither. I've got my reasons. What are yours?"

Gari didn't hesitate. "He's too smooth, too sure of himself. He can't be over thirty, but he's been around. He's from New York; I guess people grow up fast there, in the city at least." Gari looked at Meade, eyes flashing. "He looks at me like I'm a piece of merchandise. He doesn't want to love women; he wants to own them."

Meade nodded. "I've seen some of that. What does David see in him?"

Gari waved a hand. "David's not a leader; I recognized that before I married him." A little laugh. "Probably just as well; I'm not much of a follower." She frowned, then continued, "David leans on Gatori. How much Gatori influences him, I don't know. Anything is too much."

"Do you think Gatori has something to do with this?"

Gari bit her lip, then shook her head. "I've thought a lot

about that." She hesitated. "I—I even considered that there might be something going on between them. You know. But that's out. Gatori's not the type."

Meade looked away. "The ball's in my court now," he said. "I'll talk to David tonight after he gets off."

"He shouldn't know we've talked," Gari warned.

"Don't worry. I'll approach it from the business angle. He's been talked to by his boss and Charlie. It's logical that I should be next."

They parted at the door, both apprehensive, wishing each other luck. Meade would return in the morning to see Ann. He promised to come up more often. Gari was to let him know immediately if things got worse. Meade would definitely be up next month for Ann's birthday.

When David's shift ended at two in the morning, Meade met with him in Charlie's office. Meade expected to see some dramatic changes, but David looked healthy, perhaps a little thinner, nervous, but that could be expected. David was amiable and seemed truly apologetic for his behavior on the job. Meade was hampered in his questioning because he couldn't reveal his conversation with Gari.

It was frustrating. Meade had to choose his words carefully, all too aware of how he had lost Shirley and had once driven David from his home.

The meeting ended in the Plush Wheel coffee shop, David promising to be more attentive on the job. Both were happy to switch the subject to Ann's birthday party. David was proud of his daughter, spending the final half-hour talking about her remarkable abilities, displaying pictures, several showing Ann walking about in a long housecoat at nine months.

Meade passed on the results to Gari when he went by the house to see Ann that morning. David was still asleep, so they were able to talk quietly in the living room, in between Ann's determined efforts to dominate the conversation.

Meade returned to Las Vegas, disturbed, a sinking feeling in the pit of his stomach. There was little he could do except wait.

21

It was Saturday night, and the Reno Plush Wheel was packed. Charlie was in the pit talking to Izzie Silver, the casino manager. As Charlie turned to leave, he clutched at his chest and gasped. Silver grabbed him by the shoulders. Charlie tried to speak. A tremendous spasm jolted his body. Eyes rolling up into his head, he sank to the floor, Silver easing him down. Loosening Charlie's tie and unbuttoning his coat and vest, Silver shouted over his shoulder, "Get an ambulance. Fast!"

No need to hurry. Charlie had died instantly when the second heart attack ripped his heart apart.

Within minutes, Silver was on the phone to Vegas. Meade received the news in stunned silence. The wire hummed. "You there, Meade?" Silver said.

"I'm here," Meade said in a tortured half-whisper, gripping the receiver until his knuckles cracked. "Hold everything until I get there. I'll leave right away."

Breaking the connection, Meade dialed Bob Watkins, owner of Vegas Air. It was past midnight, and Watkins was in bed. He would have the plane ready by one-thirty.

Meade started to replace the phone behind the private booth in the coffee shop. He stopped, then set the phone back on the table. His call was answered before the first ring was finished, as if the receiver was already being lifted. Meade could barely hear the answering voice.

"Gari?" he said.

"Yes." She was crying.

"You've heard," Meade said.

"About ten minutes ago," Gari said. "Just a minute."

335

Meade heard her blowing her nose. The receiver rattled as she picked it up again. Her words were choked, voice filled with anguish. "It's like a bad dream. I was asleep when David called me."

"He at work?"

"Yes. He should be here anytime."

"Gari, I—" Swallowing, Meade continued, "Charlie practically raised me. I know how you feel, believe me."

Gari blew her nose again. "He was always there whenever I needed him. Do you understand?"

"All too well. I guess I figured he'd be here forever."

"Me, too."

"I'm leaving in about an hour. I'll stop at the club, then come straight to the house." A pause. "How's David taking it?"

"All right." Grief filled her voice. "He wasn't as close to Charlie as I was." Meade heard the baby start to cry.

Dawn was breaking as Meade walked up the sidewalk toward the big vine-covered house. The door opened, and for the first time he held Gari in his arms. As they clung to each other tightly, Meade looked over Gari's shoulder at David, who stood in the doorway. His eyes were bloodshot from lack of sleep, but he wasn't feeling the pain that Gari was.

Gari stepped back and wiped her eyes. She lifted her head proudly, unashamed of her tears. "It's been a long night," she said, moving into the shadow of the hall. "Come on in, Meade."

They talked for an hour, then Meade went off to make arrangements at the funeral parlor. To make matters worse, it began to snow. By mid-afternoon, a fierce wind was howling down from the Sierras. The funeral was set for Wednesday, March 3rd, three days from now.

The snow was heavy on the ground the day of the funeral, but the sky was clear. Standing by the graveside, Meade stared down at the coffin that held the remains of the man who had guided him through so much of his life.

Why didn't you tell me? Meade silently asked. The doctor had told him that Charlie had had two mild heart attacks in the last year and a history of heart trouble for some time.

The attorney had delivered a letter to Meade on Sunday afternoon, the day after Charlie's death. It was hand-written in the big scrawl that Meade had first seen on letters to his mother forty years ago. It was dated June 12, 1952:

Meade, Old Partner,

When you get this, I won't be around to say anything, so I had better get it said now. You know how I hate to write letters, so this will be short.

My will lays it all out. The twenty-five percent I own in the corporation, I am leaving to you, also, all my assets left over from the cash and things I'm leaving David, Gari and Ann. You will know what to do with your part. I don't have to tell you to use it wisely. You will do that.

My first will left my interest in the corporation to David. I'm worried about him, Meade. That could send him off the deep end. I'm leaving David $25,000.

I'm leaving $100,000 in trust for little Ann, with you and Gari as trustees. David may not like this, but I want the money invested wisely. You and Gari will do that. I know you love Ann dearly and will approve of this.

Gari's a wonderful girl. No daughter could have given me more happiness. I'm leaving her $25,000. See that she spends a nice hunk of it on herself. Stick by her, Meade. Help her all you can. Help David. He's a good boy.

You and me, we went through a lot together. I've never been sorry about that little trip down to Texas when I picked you up. I hope you feel the same way.

Your uncle, Charlie

Meade reached up and felt his breast pocket. Charlie's letter crinkled under his questing fingers.

Smitty coughed lightly. Meade looked down at the bowed head of his friend. Holding his hat against his leg, Smitty gazed fixedly at the ground. A slight breeze stirred his thinning hair. He's getting old, thought Meade. All my friends are getting old.

Gari wept softly while the will was read the following day.
Meade had insisted that they bring Ann; the little girl was a
vital part of Charlie's legacy. When Ann reached up to pull
at a button on her mother's coat, Meade lifted the child onto
his lap. She immediately went to work dismembering his
black string tie.

David sat through the proceedings with little show of emotion, except for a nervous scratching, a habit he had picked
up of late. Meade had first noticed it on his last visit to Reno,
three weeks ago.

That afternoon, after David had gone to work, Meade and
Gari sat in the living room. Ann was taking a nap.

Charlie was still uppermost in their minds. Meade had
been reminiscing about his years with Charlie on the carnival
and amusement park circuit. They were good memories, full
of instances that made them laugh. "He was a man who was
always giving," Meade concluded. "He never asked a favor
of anyone."

Gari said, "I still can't believe what he did for Ann—and
me."

"That was Charlie's special way of saying how much he
cared. Ann will be a rich lady when she turns twenty-one."

Eventually, the subject got around to David. "It's not
good," Gari said. She was sitting on the opposite end of the
couch, long legs tucked under her body, facing Meade. "His
moods are getting wilder. When he's up, he's almost too
happy; everything seems like a big joke." She picked at the
nubby material on the back of the couch. "When he's down,
he's really down—and it's happening more often. He gets
sullen, irritable, really upset at times—even at Ann."

Meade looked at her sharply. "Ann? What does he do?"
Meade's eyes were hard; Gari thought carefully before she
spoke.

"He doesn't really yell at her," Gari said. "He just cuts her
off, walks out of the room. Now that she's walking, she's all
over the place, gets into everything that's not tied down or
locked up. She's learning to open drawers, the little snoop.

"The other day, she got into David's cuff link box and

scattered things all over the place. Ordinarily, he would have laughed. He grabbed the box from her and almost knocked her down. I got in on the act and told him to slow down. He threw the box down and walked out."

Meade said, "If he gets mad at Ann, he must get mad at you."

"Sometimes," she acknowledged. "But I'm not little like Ann. I can give as good as I take. More, if I'm pushed. It hasn't come to that yet."

"But you think it will." A statement rather than a question.

Gari traced a long finger around the edge of a cushion. Her tawny eyes met Meade's. "It looks that way. It hasn't been easy these last few months. I can't talk to him. He either laughs or gets mad, depending on the mood he's in." Gari looked around. "I love this house, and in the beginning I loved Reno. Then Janice died." She cocked her head to one side. "Janice was the first close woman friend I'd had in my life. Imagine! I never knew until I came here what a closed life I'd led."

Frowning, Gari continued, "Things were still good between me and David then." She smiled. "And I had Charlie. Then David began acting strange. But Charlie was always around when things got rough." She shivered and hugged herself. A wry grin. "Maybe it's the weather." She glanced at the frosted window. "What I'd give for just one warm sunny day!"

Meade smiled, but his eyes were concerned, troubled. "I'd send you and David on a vacation to Mexico tomorrow if I thought it would do any good."

"Funny you should mention that. A few weeks ago, I suggested we go to San Diego for a week. He wasn't even interested."

Meade got up and added another log to the fire. Turning he clasped his hands behind his back, the leaping, snapping flames outlining his big frame. "I have to talk to him straight this time," he said. "I don't see any other way. Do you?"

Gari bit her lip, then shook her head. "No. Things can't

get much worse." She ran her fingers through her hair. "You'll have to tell him we talked, won't you?"

Meade said quietly, "I'll be hamstrung if I don't."

"Then do it," Gari said, dropping her feet to the floor. "We have to get to the bottom of this before it ruins us all." She stood up and pulled the blue sweatshirt down over her jeans. "If it were just David and me, maybe we could let it go for a while, but Ann's involved, and I don't want her to get hurt." Gari's eyes flashed, a mother protecting her young. "Physically *or* mentally."

Meade moved away from the fire. "I might as well get it over with," he said. He stopped in front of Gari, searching for the right words. "David's my son," he began. "It seems only natural and right that I stand up for him first." He looked down at Gari, standing shoeless in heavy woolen socks. "You and I started off wrong. It was my fault, and I'm sorry for it." He raised a hand when Gari started to speak. "Let's forget all that." A sad smile. "Our family is dwindling fast; we've got to be together on this. I guess what I'm trying to say is that I understand what you're going through. I'll support you no matter what you decide." He hunched his shoulders, eyes pleading. "Ann means a lot to me." A smile. "And I think we can be good friends. Promise to talk to me before you do anything drastic?"

Gari nodded mutely, eyes glistening. The last few days had taken their toll of her emotions.

Meade slipped on his heavy overcoat. He was pulling on his gloves when Gari said, "Something else, Meade. I wasn't going to bring it up, but it may be part of this. David's spending a lot of money. I thought at first he was gambling, but I haven't heard anything about it. I'm sure I would if that was it."

"How much is a lot?" Meade asked.

"Five hundred, a thousand a month."

Meade pursed his lips. "That's a lot—on his salary."

"I know. We had some saved up. Not anymore."

"And now he's got twenty-five thousand," Meade mused. He looked at Gari. "Should I bring it up?"

Gari shook her head. "I think that would be too much at once. You've got enough to talk about as it is."

As before, Meade and David met in Charlie's office. The room looked the same, right down to the big picture of Gari and Ann on his desk. But this meeting was totally different from the one four months ago.

"You and Gari—talking about me?" David yelled. He and Meade were standing a few feet apart. David's hands were tightly clinched, face white with anger.

"David," Meade reasoned, "she's worried, so am I." He waved a hand around the office. "So was Charlie."

"Charlie?" David said incredulously. "How long has this been going on?"

"Charlie talked to me first last November," Meade said evenly.

"November," David repeated. "Did you talk to Gari then, too?"

No use denying it. "Yes," Meade said.

Backing away, David threw up his hands. "Can't I trust *anyone?*"

"Don't talk that way," Meade said, dismayed at the direction things were going. "We're with you. We want to help. You've got a problem; admit it."

"I'm not admitting anything!" David shouted, moving toward the door. "Especially not to you!" His face was twisted with sudden hate. "You've pushed me around all my life. Now you've got Gari on your side. You used to hate each other. What's going on? Are you fucking her?"

Two swift strides and Meade was between David and the door. He seemed to swell and tower over David, who was only an inch shorter than his father. "Don't ever say anything like that to me again," Meade said, voice flat, each word enunciated clearly in the quiet tenseness of the office.

David's anger went as quickly as it had come. He moved back, appalled at what he had said. "I'm sorry, Dad. God, I'm sorry," he said, sitting down in a chair, hands over his face.

Meade's anger also melted. "Let me help, son," he said, laying a hand on David's shoulder.

David looked up as Meade sat across from him. Tears ran down his face. "It's something I have to work out for myself, Dad," he said. "I've—I've been real nervous lately. Things bother me that shouldn't." He looked around desperately. "Sometimes, I think I'm going nuts."

"Why don't you go in for a complete medical checkup?" Meade said. "I'll get you the best there is."

David's face went white. "No, I don't need that," he said quickly—too quickly. His eyes were frightened, like an animal's. "There's nothing wrong with me. I feel fine." He rubbed his shoulder. "My arm hasn't bothered me in a long time."

"This is more than your arm," Meade said. "Look what it's doing to you." He pointed at David's shaking hands. "You can't go on like this; it's tearing you apart. Gari, too. She wants the best for you. Like I do."

David nodded, clasping his hands tightly together. "I believe you." A pained look. "You won't tell Gari what I said?"

"Of course not. I know you didn't mean it." A pause. "What about it? Will you let me set up a doctor's appointment?"

The fear was back. "Please, Dad. Give me a little time to work it out. I know I can!"

Meade was pressing now. "How long?"

"A month? If I'm not better then, I'll get that checkup." A crafty look crossed his face. He was buying time, Meade knew. For what?

Meade and Gari compared notes the week after he returned to Las Vegas. She and David had had a long talk, and David was trying hard. He was spending more time at home, and they were trying to work things out on a daily basis. Things were improving, and Gari was grateful.

22

"I don't give a damn who did it wrong," Meade snapped. "Tear it down and rebuild it."

"But Mr. Slaughter," argued the man, "it took a week to make it—and that was with overtime. We'll never have it ready on time!"

Meade glared down at the man. "Get it done, or I'll find someone who can." Spinning on his heel, he walked quickly away.

The foreman looked balefully at the huge oak case that was to grace the entrance of the new Strip Plush Wheel casino. "Okay, you guys!" he yelled at a group of men. "You, you and you," he pointed. "Get a dolly and take this thing back to the shop. Move!"

Meade paused to go over things with Tom Bailey. Bailey said, "At times like this, I wish we were back in your bedroom in San Francisco swapping lies."

Meade grinned. "It wasn't all talk; think of all the contraptions you built."

Bailey looked around the huge room. "Your contraptions are getting bigger, Meade. Who would have dreamed this then?"

Meade bared his teeth in a wolfish grin. "Me. Did you think I planned on lying on my back the rest of my life?"

They turned back to the plans Bailey had unrolled on a twenty-one table. The last-minute jobs were piling up, with the grand opening of Las Vegas's newest casino set for four days from now, Friday, April 23rd. It had been hectic for the last month, only now it was getting worse.

As Meade headed for the elevator, he watched as a man

wearing a carpenter's apron stopped to check the bottom of his shoe, leaning on a slot machine for support. Sparks flew, and the man yelped. Meade grinned. Las Vegas and static electricity were old friends. Carpeting was an excellent conductor.

Upstairs, Meade met with the hotel's press agent, Bob Lakely. Lakely had ad proofs and posters laid out on the big table, each featuring the Donn Arden revue.

"Things are coming along," said Lakely, making a note on a large yellow pad. "The press will start arriving day after tomorrow." Forty thousand dollars was being spent on travel costs and a big private party in the showroom on Friday afternoon.

A secretary stuck her head in the doorway. "Telephone, Mr. Slaughter." Pointing. "You can take it over there, extension three."

"Meade?" It was Gari. Her voice was strained, hoarse. Meade sat on the edge of the desk, stomach muscles tightening.

"I didn't want to bother you," Gari continued, "but I can't put it off any longer."

"David?" Meade said, glancing at Lakely who was bent over the conference table.

"Yes. He hasn't come home in two days. I thought he was at least showing up for work, then Izzie called a while ago wondering where he was. We—we had a fight, Meade. A bad one. I wasn't surprised when David didn't come home the first night. But I'm worried now. I wouldn't have called you otherwise."

Meade's voice was sharper than he intended. "I thought David was getting better."

"That was weeks ago," Gari replied. "I'm sorry," she added defensively. "Things have fallen apart so fast lately."

"Oh hell, Gari," Meade said, wiping his brow. "What I need is a swift kick in the ass. As if *I* had all the answers!" Meade checked his watch. "I'll be up there by seven."

"No, Meade. Please! I can handle this. You've got too

much to do there." Was it fear he heard in her voice? Meade shook his head. Not Gari!

Meade said, firmly but gently, "I know where I'm needed."

"Please, Meade." She was pleading now.

"Gari," Meade said, puzzled with Gari's strange behavior, "I *have* to help. This isn't just you and David. Think of Ann. We need to work together, not pull apart."

Silence. Gari sighed. "All right, Meade. I'll be waiting."

"I'll stop by the club, then come straight to the house."

Breaking the connection, Meade dialed the Reno Plush Wheel. Pressing his hand over the mouthpiece, he called to Lakely, "Have your girl call Vegas Air. I want their Cessna ready to leave in half an hour. I've got to make Reno tonight." Lakely hurried from the room.

"Get me Silver," Meade said into the phone. "This is Slaughter."

In moments, Silver was on. "I expected your call," he said gruffly.

Meade snapped, "Why the hell didn't you let me know? What kind of store are you running? Some kind of country club?"

Silver was tough; he didn't scare easy. "Maybe I should have told you, but I thought I was doing the best for all concerned."

"Enough," Meade said wearily. "Call Chief Logan. Tell him to keep this close to the vest; I don't want anything leaking out. Have him put out a quiet check on David. He's got to be around close."

"Right."

"I'll be up in a few hours." Meade hung up and hurried toward the exit.

"What about the rest of the layouts?" Lakely called.

"They're all yours," Meade shouted over his shoulder.

"The police have a big fat zero," Izzie Silver told Meade. He had met Meade at the Reno airport, and they were riding into town in the back seat of the Plush Wheel limousine. "They've run a check on the whole area—nothing."

"I don't understand it," Meade said. "David's been acting like he's been losing his senses. Any ideas?"

Silver shook his head, face expressionless. He had ideas, but he wasn't going to voice them. If he was correct, he didn't want to be around when Meade found out.

Meade got out at the house. "Call me if anything comes up," he said. "I'll be by in the morning."

When Gari opened the door, Meade knew instantly why she hadn't wanted him to come. Even in the darkness of the hall, he could see the dark bruise on her right cheek. The swelling was going down, but it would be days before her face would be back to normal.

Pulling herself up to her full height, Gari stood tall and slender in the narrow confines of the hall. "Now you know why I didn't want you to come," she said. She touched the high collar of her wine-colored robe. "Not pretty, is it?"

Meade was boiling with anger. That a man could hit a woman was beyond his comprehension. And that that man should be his son! Shame replaced anger, and misery filled his eyes. Their roles were reversed, and Gari touched his arm in sympathy. "Meade, it's all right. It will go away."

Meade clasped her by the shoulders. "Will it?" he asked, giving her a little shake. "Will it go away inside?"

"I don't know," Gari said honestly. "I'm not walking out. Not yet, anyway." She stepped out of his grasp. "This isn't like David. None of this is! He was always so kind. He's not a violent man. That's the only reason I'm not leaving!"

"Tell me what happened," Meade said, looking away from the bruise that marred her lovely face.

"Coffee first," Gari said, turning toward the kitchen. She filled their cups and sat down. "David seemed to be improving at first," she began. "He was really trying; it was like he was fighting a battle inside. His promise to go to a clinic if he didn't get better was on his mind a lot. That's what set him off—when he realized he was getting worse."

"How was he getting worse?" Meade asked.

"Physically, mostly. He must have lost ten pounds during the last two weeks. He was throwing up and had several bad cases of diarrhea. Saturday, after he had thrown up his lunch, I said I was going to call the doctor. He blew up." She snapped her fingers. "Just like that. Grabbed the phone out of my hand. I thought he was going to tear the whole thing out of the wall. Thank God, Ann was asleep! It was frightening; he was like a maniac, shouting and screaming. I got mad and told him to shut up and act his age. That did it. Wow! He hauled off and hit me. I banged into the sink and held on. Then I got *really* mad! I called him every name in the book and told him to get the hell out. That scared him. He backed out the door saying over and over again that he was sorry. I guess I should have called him back, but I was too damn mad and hurting too much to care." Gari's eyes narrowed, and she bit her lip. "I still get mad everytime I think about it."

Meade's voice was flat, brooking no argument. "When we find him, he's going to get professional help. He's gone too far this time."

Gari's response was a short, quick nod. "Where could he have gone?" she said.

"Who knows? Maybe we should check with Gatori."

"Not me. I think he'd get a kick out of that—me having to check with him."

"I'll find someone at the club who can do it casually."

"Meade," Gari said, "you can't waste any more time here. It must be a madhouse down there. I'll take care of things on this end."

"No, you won't," Meade said, making Gari sit up, not liking the tone of his voice. Meade smiled. "I'm not about to pick a fight with you!" He readied himself for the storm. "When I go back, you and Ann are going with me. I'm not leaving you here alone."

"What?" Gari's jaw dropped. "Go with you? What for?" She waved an arm. "This is my home!"

"I know, Gari," Meade reasoned, "but you've got to think of Ann—and me." He had an inspiration. "You can help me get ready for the opening! I can use some of those brains you've got tucked away."

She was tempted. Slowly, she shook her head. "No, Meade." She touched her face. "Besides, can you imagine the gossip this would cause?"

"No one will see you," Meade said. "You can work at the ranch."

"It's sweet of you to offer," Gari said, getting up and returning with the coffee pot, "but I can't do it."

"Why not?" Meade wasn't used to being defeated.

Gari sat down and rested her elbows on the table. "Can you imagine what it would do to David to come home and find us gone?"

Meade chewed on his lip. What could he say?

"I know you're afraid for Ann," Gari continued. "Don't be. I can take care of myself—and her."

"I'm sure of that, but—"

"But nothing, Meade," Gari said, sitting back and clasping her hands together. "You do your job; I'll do mine."

Meade spent an hour on the phone checking on things in Vegas, then talked briefly to the Reno police chief. After sleeping a few hours in the guest room he was on his way to the airport. The plane was over Walker Lake when the sun broke over the horizon.

Looking down at the small town of Hawthorne, Meade realized that Ann had slept the whole time he was in Reno; he hadn't even held her once. Glancing back as Hawthorne slipped out of view, he wished that he had been able to persuade Gari to leave with him.

23

Opening night, and David was still missing. Dressed in a black tuxedo, Meade stood at the door greeting the crowd. As in all Las Vegas openings, civic leaders and club owners were there to offer congratulations and encouragement. Many came to gamble. Meade hoped none would be as lucky as Beldon Katleman, Farmer Paige and several others when they almost won the Thunderbird away from Marion Hicks and Cliff Jones on opening night in 1948.

But even that was a small worry in comparison to Meade's concern about David. Meade had been in daily touch with Gari. On Wednesday, he had told the Reno police to put out discreet inquiries in neighboring states.

"Congratulations, Meade," Jake Friedman said, Carl Cohen standing quietly behind him. A small man in a gaudy cowboy hat, Friedman looked even smaller beside the tall, broad-shouldered Cohen.

Grinning up at Meade, Friedman said in his deep, thickly-accented voice, "Think all this flash and glamour will put the Sands out of business?" He pulled out a wad of $1,000 bills. "How much do you want to bet we beat your socks off?"

Cohen looked down on Friedman, a benevolent guardian angel. "Don't pay any attention to him, Meade," Cohen said. "He's just jealous."

"Jealous?" Friedman cried, whirling to face Cohen. "Who's side are you on, anyway?" Friedman spread his arms to encompass the huge room. "Why should I be jealous of this?" He grinned widely at the audience he was gathering; he loved to put on a show. "That's some lighting display outside, and that carousel bar is pretty nice, but real gamblers aren't looking for fancy stuff. Give 'em a blanket and a pillow, and they're ready to roll!"

"That's telling 'em, Jake!" a voice in the crowd shouted.

"Is that why you built such a junky place, Jakie?" Meade asked.

Pushing his cowboy hat back off his forehead, Friedman laid a hand over his heart. "You really know how to hurt a guy," he said, a pained look on his face.

The long night finally came to an end. "How was it?" Gari asked when Meade called the next morning.

"They're saying it's the biggest thing to hit Vegas," Meade said. "But they say that everytime a new hotel opens."

The calls continued, and the attempts at humor were less successful. Eighteen days after David's disappearance, Meade got a call at his office.

"Mr. Slaughter, my name's Martin. I'm with the San Francisco Police Department. We have your son. I talked with the Reno authorities. They said it would be best to call you direct."

Meade sank down in the big leather chair. "Is he all right?"

A moment of hesitation. "He's not injured."

"Give it to me straight," Meade ordered, refusing to be in the dark any longer.

"Your son is a full-blown heroin addict, Mr. Slaughter," Martin said in a rasping voice.

"Heroin," Meade whispered, shocked, disbelieving. "You're sure?"

"I'm sorry, Mr. Slaughter."

"Where did he get it? Nevada's got some of the toughest drug laws in the country. David was in Korea. Could he have started there?"

"Hard to say," Martin said in a tired voice. "The things I see make me sick. Drugs are becoming a big problem here; they're going to get bigger. We're picking them up off the streets every day. That's how we found your son."

"Where is he?"

"The county hospital. It's the best we can do," he added apologetically.

"Is there a good hospital up there I can get him in?"

"Several. They're expensive."

"Damn the cost!" Meade exploded. "I want the best for my son." He continued in a calmer tone, "I'll be there first thing in the morning. Can I see you then?"

Martin gave him directions and a phone number. They arranged to meet at nine.

Meade didn't go directly to San Francisco, and he didn't go alone. Of late, he had been moving about a good deal without bodyguards. But for this trip, he took two, especially picked out by Don Milton.

When the plane landed at the Reno airport at five P.M., the

Plush Wheel limousine was waiting. Meade had the driver let him out at the house; rooms had been reserved for the men at the Mapes. They would be leaving for San Francisco at four in the morning.

"David?" Gari asked, a fearful look on her face.

"Yes," Meade replied, taking her arm. "He's safe." He felt her muscles relax under his grip.

They sat on the couch, Ann gurgling on Meade's lap. "Where is he?" Gari asked.

"San Francisco. He's—he's, oh hell, how else can I say it?" In a few terse words, Meade recalled this morning's phone call.

Gari was horrified. "Heroin! How, Meade, how?"

"*That* I'm going to find out," Meade said grimly. "I feel like a damn fool. I've kicked around a lot, but when it comes to drugs I know about as much as Ann."

"What happens now?" Gari asked.

"I have a meeting with Martin at nine. Then I'm going to find a place where David can get straightened out."

"I'm going with you."

"No," Meade said. "Let me handle this."

"He's my husband," Gari said, flashing him a warning look.

"That's right, but you can't help him now. All I can do is sign papers and pass out money where it's needed. It's going to be ugly. Why go through it?"

Ann stood on the couch between them, trying to figure out who was the most susceptible to a good con job. She decided on Meade and gave him her best smile. He picked her up, and she shouted with glee.

Gari watched them for a moment. She said, "I'd fight you, Meade, but you're right. Will you stop on the way back?"

"Of course. I shouldn't be gone more than a day or two. I'll call as soon as I know something."

Lt. James Martin leaned forward on the desk and contemplated his visitor. Earlier, he had observed the two men who had accompanied Meade into the station. They moved with professional ease, missing nothing. Hard men—and their boss was tougher than both of them put together.

Martin said, "We found your son in an alley off Hyde Street. He was going into withdrawal."

"You can tell?"

"Usually. The first few days are the worst. Your son had all the signs—tears, runny nose, hot and cold flashes, nausea."

Meade's voice was hard. "Someone got him started. Any way of finding out?"

Martin shrugged. "We've got men on the street all the time. We're batting about ten percent."

The doctor at the county hospital met Meade in the hall. "You can't do better than Holton Sanitorium, Mr. Slaughter," he said. "They've got the best staff in the state; there's none better in the whole country."

"How quick can I get him out of here?"

"You'll need the necessary papers; my secretary can help you with that. The judge will have to okay the move. No problem. Your son can be at Holton tomorrow."

"May I see him?"

The doctor looked sharply at Meade. "Are you sure you want to? It's not a pleasant sight, believe me."

"I'm willing to take the risk," Meade said quietly.

The doctor led Meade to a special section of the hospital. The doors were made of heavy steel with tiny barred windows in the upper half. The doctor stepped to one of the windows and looked in. Moving to one side, he motioned to Meade.

Meade peered into a cell lighted by a single light bulb high in the ceiling. The walls were padded, the light protected by a metal screen.

Meade barely recognized the writhing figure on the single cot. David's arms were bound in a straitjacket, legs drawn up in a fetal position. Low moans issued from cracked lips. His face was running with sweat, cheeks twitching erratically, pupils contracted, body twisting and jerking.

Tearing his eyes away from the window, Meade said, "How long does this go on? Can't you let him down easier?"

The doctor shook his head. "Our policy is cold turkey. Your son is at the peak of withdrawal. He'll start tapering off tomorrow. Holton may have a different approach. My advice is to leave it up to them."

Meade accompanied the doctor to his office. Two hours later, he walked out into the sunlight. Another trip downtown and David could be moved to the Sonoma Valley.

That afternoon, Meade visited Lt. Martin. "Can you recommend a top detective agency in town?" Meade asked. "I want the best."

Martin returned Meade's cold look; they understood each other. Martin said, "One of our retired top men opened a place a few years back. He's good, and he keeps his mouth shut. If anyone can help you, Branch Thorton can." A pause. "Don't expect too much. Even the best can't work miracles."

The next afternoon, Meade returned to San Francisco from the Sonoma Valley where David had been admitted to Holton Sanitorium. They had informed him that it might be as late as Thanksgiving before David could be released.

Meade made one last stop before flying off to Reno. "I want answers," Meade said, handing Branch Thorton five $1,000 bills. "I want names, dates, places. I'll take care of the rest."

24

"Gari, we've got to talk."

"I know," Gari said, watching intently as the water ran down the drain. Meade was drying the last of the dishes; Gari had had dinner ready when he arrived from San Francisco.

Gari wiped her hands on a towel. "Let's go in the living

room," she said, turning and hanging up her apron. She was wearing a fashionable high-necked white blouse and light green skirt, long legs encased in nylons, open-toed white high-heeled shoes on her feet. "I'm tired of looking dowdy and dragging around like the world's coming to an end," she had said when she met Meade at the door. "We do have something to celebrate," she added, looking to Meade for understanding. "David's all right and being taken care of."

"That we do," Meade said, smiling his approval. The rich smell of cooking filled the hall, and Ann was yelling from the kitchen. It was like coming home.

Dinner past and Ann in bed, Meade sat across from Gari in the living room, silently preparing his arguments. The first hurdle would be the biggest. Booted feet resting on the leather footstool, Meade regarded his daughter-in-law, composed and waiting, legs drawn up under her on the couch, shoes discarded on the floor. "Gari," Meade began, "I have to know. How do you feel about all this? What do you want to do?"

Gari smiled crookedly. "You shouldn't have asked me that. Know what I want to do? I want to run away. I'd like to wake up in some strange place and find it's all been a bad dream. That's what I'd *like* to do." She made a helpless gesture with her hands.

"You don't have to explain," Meade said. "I'd be surprised if you felt differently." He asked what he needed most to know, "What about David; how do you feel about him?"

"Oh boy," Gari said, heaving a deep sigh. Her eyes met Meade's. "I told you a long time ago that I would try to be a good wife; maybe I should have tried harder." She shook her head as Meade opened his mouth to speak. "No, let me finish.

"I'm not going to play the martyr and blame myself for David's problem; how he got started on drugs is more than I know. Maybe he was on them when we met, but I don't think so; the big changes didn't come until last year. I think" —she stopped and bit her lip—"I think I would leave him if there was some other reason for his behavior. But drugs! I

know a little more about them than I did a few days ago."
She pointed at a pile of books on the coffee table. "I got these
from the university library." She leaned forward, the light
revealing only a slight discoloration where David had hit her.
"Heroin addiction can be cured, Meade, especially in the
early stages. David hasn't been hooked since he was a kid.
Even if it happened in Korea—and I don't think it was there
—he would have been on it for less than four years. He's got
a chance—a good one."

Gari sat back, hands clasped in her lap, jaw set. "I'll give
it a try with the man I married; that's the man I hope will
be coming home. I went into our marriage with my eyes
open. I wasn't deeply in love." A small smile. "We talked
about that once, remember? I'll probably never know what
real love is like," she added sadly. "Unless it was what I felt
for Charlie. Do you understand, Meade—*really* understand?"

"Gari—" Meade raised his hands, dropped them. "What
do you want me to say—that I feel what you feel? How can
I? I'm not you. I haven't lived through this like you have.
Love? God, leave that to the poets and song writers! Do I
understand what you're trying to say? I *think* so; I *want* to.
I'm with you whatever you decide. Is that what you want to
hear?"

"Oh Meade, anything helps. I seem to need a lot of assurance these days."

Meade decided it was now or never. "I've got a sugges-
tion," he said, trying to make it sound spontaneous.

"What?"

"David's going to be away for at least six months. You said
you would like a change of scenery. Why not stay at the
ranch for a while? Maria went back to Mexico six months
ago, and the house is a mess. I'm living on the Strip most of
the time, but I'd like to move back to the ranch house. But
not before it gets fixed up."

Meade continued quickly. "That'll be your job. I'll supply
the funds, no questions asked. Have the place air-conditioned
first; I don't want to suffer through another summer. You can

decorate and refurnish it to your heart's content." A grin. "Just remember it's a man's house, no pink curtains in the bedroom."

Meade tossed in his final argument. "It will be good for Ann. She can get outside more. You can introduce her to a few cows and horses." Meade waited apprehensively.

"Okay," Gari said.

"Huh?" Meade blurted, mouth open, a stupid look on his face.

"I said okay. Isn't that what you wanted to hear?"

"Well, I—" Meade sat up and grinned broadly. "I'll be damned," he murmured. "What changed your mind?"

"Who said I changed my mind? You just asked me."

"The other day you said—"

"That was before we knew what was happening. I'm for it now. Besides," she said, resting her chin on a fist, "that old house does need work. I wasn't there five minutes last summer, and I wanted to run screaming out the door."

"That bad, huh?"

"That bad. Better watch your pocketbook. It may cost more than it's worth."

"Have a go at it. I plan on living there the rest of my life."

So Gari returned to Las Vegas, this time with a baby, her white Cadillac convertible packed to capacity, and the little sailboat *Lady Ann* hitched behind. Meade hadn't liked the idea of her driving alone, but she had set her foot down. He couldn't wait a week to go with her, and it would take that long for her to get ready. Furthermore, she was perfectly capable of taking care of herself.

Gari arrived at the ranch in mid-May, and within a week the house looked like it had been in the path of Sherman's march to the sea. Throughout most of the summer, a constant stream of carpenters, plumbers, electricians and painters flowed through the sprawling old ranch house, transforming it into a handsome showplace, the new white-painted exterior gleaming brightly in the shadows of the huge surrounding oaks and cottonwoods.

And Gari made a friend—of sorts. Meade had been concerned about putting her and Smitty close together. In general, Smitty regarded women as a pain in the neck, and that attitude would go over like an iron cloud with Gari. If they ever locked horns, Meade hoped he was in another state.

Surprisingly they hit it off. Their relationship was nothing like the one Gari had had with Charlie. It was more like two predators meeting and deciding it was better to share the territory than to chance dying for it.

One night in August, Meade sat on the porch of Smitty's bunkhouse. Their chairs were tipped back, feet on the rail. Smitty was industriously whittling on a stick. A few feet away, the windmill creaked, and water surged and splashed into the big tank high above.

Smitty pointed up. "Somethin' soothin' about that old relic," he said. "It's like me—goes like hell when it ain't tied down."

Meade listened to the hum of the big blades. "We've got to use pumps for irrigation," he said, "but that old gal is going to keep on working as long as I'm around."

Smitty grunted and kept on whittling.

Meade looked off toward the lights of Vegas, fifteen miles away. "I talked to Thorton today," he said.

"Anything new?"

"No. He's convinced David's source wasn't in San Francisco. His undercover man's been in Reno for three weeks. I think Thorton knows what he's doing; I'm sticking with him."

"Gari know anything about it?"

"No. I'm going to handle this my own way. She can't be any part of it."

The windmill continued to whir and creak. Meade thought about the many decisions he had to make. One of them involved Gari; he had another project in mind for her. He didn't want David returning to Reno when he was released.

25

"Gari, you sure you know how to run this thing?"

"Shut up and enjoy yourself."

Meade looked back apprehensively as the *Lady Ann* moved away from the dock. The boat didn't seem big enough for one, much less two.

Her dark tan contrasting sharply with her white one-piece swimming suit, Gari expertly guided the sailboat around an anchored houseboat. "We're off!" she yelled gaily as the big sail filled with wind. The *Lady Ann* seemed to leap forward as she picked up speed and headed out into Lake Mead.

"How did I ever get talked into this?" Meade groaned, hitching up the new swimming trunks he had bought for the occasion.

"Because you're daring and anxious to try new things," Gari said, grinning as Meade squirmed to find a more comfortable position.

"Like getting a sunburn. Do you realize how many years it's been since I've worn a bathing suit?"

"It's good for you. You need some fun in your life."

"Drowning isn't fun."

"If you do, it'll be your fault."

"Tell that to my insurance company," Meade said, looking up at the billowing sail. "I hate to see your head get any bigger, but you're pretty good with this thing."

Gari shot him a satisfied look. "If that's a compliment, I'll accept it." A smug smile. "I've learned a lot this summer, if I must say so myself."

As the *Lady Ann* skimmed across the lake, Meade lay back and stared up at the clear blue sky. Despite his earlier misgivings, he was beginning to enjoy himself. Not bad, considering he had been practically shanghaied aboard. After a summer of practice, Gari had been ready to show off her skills, and Meade was the logical choice. Smitty mistrusted any body of water bigger than a bathtub.

Following lunch on a small beach in Boulder Canyon, they rested in the shade of the *Lady Ann*'s sail. Meade raised himself up on one elbow. "You awake?"

Gari rolled over on her back. "Barely," she said, fighting back a yawn. She squinted up at Meade. "Uh oh, vacation's over."

Meade grinned. "Just want to talk."

"Fire away."

"I don't want David going back to Reno, not for a while at least. I think you feel the same way. Right?"

Gari nodded. "I'm afraid, Meade. He must have had contacts there for that stuff. I want him to have a fresh start, with no one knowing what happened. Our story about a nervous breakdown seems to be holding up, but—" She waved a hand. "On my last visit, David was worried about going back. He didn't say anything; I just knew. I'm sticking to orders and not talking about what put him there. He didn't need to be told; he doesn't want to talk about it at all."

From the beginning, they had been under strict instructions not to discuss with David the reason for his hospitalization. The first meeting in June had been difficult, with Meade seeing David first and paving the way for Gari. They had flown back to Vegas with mixed feelings—shocked at David's wasted physical condition, encouraged by his positive attitude. Since then, he had improved markedly; he was back to normal weight, eyes clear, tanned, showing no signs of harm from his addiction. A new problem now. He was anxious to come home. The doctor had told Meade and Gari to expect this. It was a critical time. The patient might become rebellious, not understanding that an early release could cause a relapse. It was imperative he remain at Holton another seven weeks.

"Here's what I have in mind," Meade said. "Nothing permanent, one step at a time. You guys live at the ranch; you'll have more privacy there. David can work in public relations on the Strip, and you can help me in administration." Meade stabbed a stick into the dirt. "Take a few weeks when David gets out, go to New York, travel around, take it easy with no set schedule. All on the house, of course." He looked anxiously at Gari. "Sound okay?"

"I like the step-by-step idea. You *know* I want the job. The trip would be a good way to get reacquainted. Not going back to Reno right away makes me feel a lot better." A wistful smile. "I'll miss my home—and my ducks, poor things." She made a face. "David should get back on his feet without Gatori around. If that jerk doesn't already know what's going on, he'll know quick enough if we move back to Reno. I don't trust that bastard; the whole town would know in a week."

Meade stood up and dusted the seat of his trunks. Reaching down, he pulled Gari to her feet. Still holding her hand, he shook it up and down. "Congratulations," he grinned. "You are now Vice-president in charge of Special Projects."

"Vice-president!" squeaked Gari. "Isn't that going a bit too far?" Her look belied her words; she was obviously thrilled with the idea.

"Consider it a practical move," Meade said, releasing her hand. "It will expedite matters. Vice-presidents get faster service."

"*Presidents* get even better service," Gari shot back, grinning.

With his mission accomplished, Meade thoroughly enjoyed the return trip. Only one problem remained, and it was a big one. With David's homecoming less than two months away, there was no positive news from Branch Thorton. Meade had hoped for results by now; the undercover investigator had been in Reno for five weeks.

Meade got the word ten days later. "We have the information you want," Thorton said over the telephone.

"Everything?" Meade asked quickly.

"We're satisfied."

"I'll be up tomorrow. About noon?"

"I'll buy you lunch. We can talk business after."

While Meade's secretary made flight arrangements with
Vegas Air, Meade instructed Don Milton to have the same
two security guards ready for an early morning flight.

He hated to lie to Gari, but he had to keep his meeting with
Thorton quiet. He told her he was flying to Reno and would
return the day after tomorrow. It was a half-truth; he would
return via Reno; he hadn't seen Izzie Silver for over a month.

It was a beautiful, clear September day in San Francisco.
Returning from lunch at the St. Francis, Meade and Branch
Thorton sat down in the big paneled office. "It's all here,"
Thorton said, tapping a thick file. He pushed it across the
desk to Meade.

Thorton lit a cigarette and checked the mail while Meade
flipped through the pages of the report. From time to time,
Thorton would glance up at Meade. For all the reaction
Meade displayed, he might have been reading the morning
paper.

Meade closed the files. "No copies, right?" he said, looking
steadily at Thorton.

"That's it," Thorton said, pointing at the file. "My inves-
tigators only know bits and pieces, the one who worked in
Reno knows the most. I typed the report myself, no carbon.
We all have short memories."

Meade said, "You have the final bill?"

Thorton handed him an itemized sheet. Reaching inside
his coat, Meade took out a wallet. He handed several large
bills to Thorton. They shook hands. "It's been a pleasure,
Meade," Thorton said. Meade nodded; the feeling was mutual.

The night Meade returned to Vegas, he drove out to the
ranch. After dinner with Gari, he walked over to Smitty's
bunkhouse. Twenty minutes later, Smitty knew everything.

Meade shifted his feet on the porch rail. "I want it cleaned
up before David comes home," he said.

"That doesn't give you much time."

"Four weeks."

"You're goin' to need help," Smitty volunteered.

"Thought maybe you might know of a couple of good men."

"That I do. They're gettin' a little long in the tooth for this kind of work, but they're tough as nails and know how to keep their mouths shut."

"When can you see them?"

"They're workin' a claim of mine—'bout a hundred miles north of here. I'll drive out tomorrow."

"Want me to come along?"

"Better let me see 'em first. They've been out on the desert so long, I'm not sure they speak English. They trust me. Strangers make 'em edgy." A dry chuckle. "They might shoot your leg off." Smitty paused to light a cigarette. "You think Gatori was in this alone?"

"That's the way the report reads. I'll do a little investigation of my own." Meade looked sharply at Smitty. "These friends of yours squeamish?"

Smitty's laugh was short. "They're goin' to be askin' the same thing about *you*. These boys handled some nasty jobs for me when Tonopah and Goldfield was boomin'." Another laugh. "They might even teach you a thing or two."

Meade grunted his satisfaction.

"How far you goin' with this thing?" Smitty asked.

"Make any difference to you—or your friends?"

"Nope. Just askin'."

Meade's voice was flat. "Gatori can't live after what he's done."

"Figured that."

Meade stood up. "Tell your friends I'll make it well worth their while—in hard cash. This will never go any further than you, me and them. They can stay in the old cabin out by Mt. Charleston while we put it together."

26

Tuesday, October 19, 1954, was just one hour old when Tony Giuliano walked out of his Lake Tahoe club. With the summer season over, he was making only one inspection trip a week up from Reno now.

Until last year, he had shut the Tahoe club down every December 1st through April 15th, but South Shore was much busier in the winter now, largely due to the aggressive busing campaign by Bill Harrah. All the clubs along Highway 50 at the lake had benefited. Not so at North Shore. Even the road was closed there for the winter.

Tony Giuliano and his bodyguard walked toward the big gray Chrysler, footsteps echoing in the darkness, tall fir trees standing like majestic sentinels around the parking lot. The lot was deserted except for a dozen cars and two aging cowboys weaving and staggering toward the club entrance.

It happened so fast that neither Giuliano nor his man had time to react. The blackjack had no sooner smashed into the bodyguard's skull, then Tony was heaved into the passenger side of the Chrysler's front seat.

Tony Giuliano found himself sitting in the back seat with a gun jammed into his ribs. The pistol was huge, with a barrel that looked a foot long, and the hand that held it was lined with age, fingers scarred and gnarled from hard work. Giuliano looked into the face shadowed by the sweat-stained cowboy hat, and he felt the cold hand of fear. The eyes that stared back were faded and narrowed into a permanent squint from over a half-century of desert sun. They may have been blue once, but now they were washed out, empty, telling Tony Giuliano nothing.

The man reached inside Giuliano's coat and removed the gun from the leather shoulder holster. When Giuliano started to speak, the ancient revolver was jammed painfully into his side. "Shut up," the man said. The voice fitted the owner—dry, toneless, old.

As the Chrysler rolled east on Highway 50, Giuliano observed the driver. The two men were much alike, only the driver had a livid burn scar that covered the right side of his face. Whatever had caused that damage had destroyed most of the ear, leaving only a few shriveled remains. The man would stand out in a crowd anywhere.

A frightening thought. The driver wasn't concerned about being identified—had he been, he would have covered up that scar. Where were they taking him? Giuliano wondered. What for? If this was a kidnapping for ransom, it was no ordinary one; certainly these were no ordinary kidnappers!

The driver pulled off the highway onto a narrow dirt road that threaded its way through a dense forest. After several hundred yards, the big car jolted to a stop. The driver turned, and Giuliano gave a start. The man's right eyelid drooped hideously, half-covering an eyeball filmed with milky blindness. The other eye glinted in the darkness. "Open your mouth," the driver said in a flat emotionless voice.

Giuliano hesitated, and the big pistol was taken from his side and shoved up under his jaw. "Open," Giuliano's seat companion said, grinding the barrel painfully into the soft skin.

Giuliano opened his mouth, and the driver stuck a rag inside, tying a long strip of cloth around the captive's face to hold the gag in. The driver then held the gun on Giuliano while his partner tied Giuliano's hands behind his back.

Leading Giuliano to a dark blue Pontiac nearby, the men shoved him in the back seat and tied his legs. The door slammed, and he was left alone.

Wrenching his head around, he watched as his bodyguard was tightly bound and put in the back seat of the Chrysler. Were they taking them to separate places? No, the two old cowboys were headed his way. They got in the front seat, the

scarred man still driving. The car lights flickered over the
Chrysler for a moment, then they were heading back toward
Highway 50.

The highway began to drop toward Carson City, leaving
the big trees behind. The car slowed, turned off to the right,
tires crunching over rocks and twigs as they followed a crude
trail. Several times, the car barely moved as it crawled over
big rocks in the road. Once they went down a steep slope and
crossed what must have been a dry creek bed. Giuliano's
captors remained silent, smoking and keeping their attention
on the road.

Despite his fear, Tony Giuliano was angry. Kidnapping an
owner was unheard of in Nevada. This kind of foolishness
would bring down the wrath of every owner in the state. A
successful kidnapping would put them in danger of a similar
fate.

The car stopped. They were in a big open area, surrounded
by huge boulders. No buildings, no signs of life.

The men got out and went to the trunk. There was a clang
of metal as they pulled several things out and threw them to
the ground. Giuliano twisted around, but all he could see was
the raised trunk lid, reflecting the three-quarter moon above.

When the men returned, they were both wearing belted
holsters, and their pistols were identical. Giuliano recognized
the guns; there were several on display at Harolds Club. They
were Colt 45s, usually found only in museums and on western movie sets. These were no museum pieces, however. They
were oiled and well-cared for, and their owners wore them
comfortably.

The back door was yanked open, and a big bowie knife
appeared in the scarred man's hand. "Stick your legs out,"
he ordered. When Giuliano obeyed, the man bent and cut the
rope that bound Giuliano's ankles. The knife pointed away
from the car. "Walk."

Giuliano took several steps into the natural amphitheater.
The moon was bright, and the great boulders cast long for-
bidding shadows on the ground.

"That's enough," the scarred man said. The other man

walked around to face Giuliano, the .45 again in his hand, the long barrel pointed at Giuliano's stomach. "Stand nice and easy," he said. "Jack's goin' to cut you loose." Again, Tony Giuliano felt a chill. They weren't even afraid to reveal their names!

The rope fell from Giuliano's wrists, then the cloth was cut that secured the gag. "Take it out," the gun wielder said.

Gratefully, Tony Giuliano pulled out the saliva-soaked rag, throwing it to the ground. Free, able to speak, self-confidence returned and along with it his celebrated temper. "What the hell's going on?" he demanded.

"Now that's interestin'," Jack said, standing beside his partner and looking Giuliano up and down. "You sure you got this right, fella? You're standin' in front of the gun, not behind it. If I was you, I'd be a little more polite."

"Look," Giuliano said in a conciliatory tone, "let's sit down and work this out. I'll see you get enough cash to last you a long time."

"Money?" Jack exclaimed, letting out a harsh laugh. "You think we want *money* from you? Shit man, you're way off target!"

"What *do* you want?" Giuliano asked, puzzled, afraid.

"Don't think you're goin' to like it," the scarred man said, adding ominously, "You'll learn soon enough."

Tony Giuliano stared at the big revolver while Jack picked up two objects from behind the car. He moved past Giuliano carrying a pick and shovel. Tossing the shovel aside, he drew a big rectangle in the dirt with the pick. "How's that, Hank?" he said, standing back and admiring his work. Tony Giuliano almost jumped. He had both names now.

"Not bad," Hank said, slitted eyes moving quickly to the rough sketch, then back to Giuliano. "A little crooked but what the hell. Our friend here can straighten it out."

Jack looked at Giuliano, the dead eyeball moving in tandem with the good one. "C'mere, bub," he said, holding out the pick.

Giuliano didn't move. Hank waved the big pistol. "Better go," he said conversationally. "I won't shoot out any vital part, but this ol' gal takes out a pretty big chunk no matter where she hits."

Tony Giuliano edged away from the menacing barrel, one foot scuffing the wavy line in the dirt. "Careful!" snapped Jack. "You're ruinin' my artwork." Hank gave a short bark of laughter.

Jack carefully retraced the broken line with the pick while Hank sat on a nearby rock. Satisfied, Jack handed the pick to Giuliano. "Dig," the scarred man said, pointing at the drawing on the ground.

Tony Giuliano gripped the pick handle with both hands, glancing back and forth apprehensively at the two men.

"I said dig, asshole!" exploded Jack, all pretense at humor gone. "What the fuck do you think a pick's for, cleanin' your teeth?"

Giuliano began to swing the pick. He was a squat powerful man with bullish shoulders, but he hadn't done any manual labor for thirty years. After he had broken the soil inside the lines, he stopped and held up his hands. "I need gloves," he said, looking pleadingly at his captors who were now both seated on the rock.

"Ain't got none," Hank said. He looked at Jack. "What about them rags in the trunk?"

Standing up, Jack ground his cigarette out under a boot heel. He peered at Giuliano from under his big black Stetson. "They might work," he said speculatively. His next words froze Tony Giuliano into immobility. "Why the hell should we save his hands? He ain't goin' to need 'em much longer."

"Go get the rags, Jack," Hank said mildly. "Let's humor the poor son of a bitch."

Giuliano opened his mouth to speak. "No talkin'," Hank said, wagging the .45 like a big finger. "Save your breath for workin'."

Jack returned with two oil-soaked rags. "Wrap these around your hands," he said, tossing them on the ground by Giuliano. "Then git to work. We want to get to bed before daylight. We're gettin' too old for this kind of shit."

The pick rose and fell. From time to time, Tony Giuliano

would shovel out the loosened dirt. The sweat poured down his back, and his throat was dry. He didn't have to be told what he was doing; he already stood knee-deep in his own grave.

Tony Giuliano stopped and leaned heavily on the shovel handle, shoulders heaving, shirt soaked with sweat. He had abandoned his coat long ago. "Can't we talk about this?" he begged, words coming out in short gasps.

"Keep diggin'," Jack growled.

The moon's light was fading when Jack called a halt. "Come on out," he said to Giuliano, whose head and shoulders were all that remained above ground.

Slowly, painfully, Tony Giuliano pulled himself up over the edge of the hole. He lay on his side, taking ragged breaths, not caring about the dirt that seemed to fill every pore.

The two men walked over and looked down into the hole. "Pretty nice," Hank observed, kicking aside a lump of wet dirt that had stuck to his boot. "Seems a shame to fill it up again."

Cupping his hands, Jack lit a cigarette, the milky eye glowing grotesquely in the flame of the big kitchen match. "Let's get it over with," he grunted. "I'm pooped."

Three good eyes shifted to Tony Giuliano's prostrate form. Hank said, "Think he should be wearin' the coat, don't you? Don't seem right not to have him dressed up."

Jack nudged Giuliano's leg with the pointed toe of his cowboy boot. "Git your coat, pilgrim. You're wastin' time."

Half-bent over, Tony Giuliano moved to where his coat lay. He was struggling to button the front when he felt a warm fluid running down his leg. In his fright, he had pissed himself.

"C'mere," Jack said from beside the hole.

Tony Giuliano shuffled over to where Jack stood, too tired and defeated to protest.

"Get back in," the scarred man said, pointing down into the hole.

Giuliano looked from Jack to Hank, who had moved

closer, the .45 held at hip level, pointing directly at Giuliano's stomach. "Please—" Giuliano said, voice breaking.

"Do what he says," Hank said quietly, eyes as cold as the sweat on Giuliano's back.

"Now!" Hank ordered. Two long-barreled .45s were now aimed at Giuliano.

He would have backed away, but the hole was only two feet behind. Tony Giuliano shook his head, resigned to his fate. "What difference does it make?" he said in a tortured half-whisper.

"A lot," Jack said, a grin stretching the livid scar. "We don't have to move you afterward."

It was suddenly important to Giuliano. "Why are you doing this?" he asked, spreading his reddened hands. "Can't you at least tell me that?"

Jack shook his head. "Nope. Are you gettin' in that hole the easy way or do we have to do it for you?"

Tony Giuliano shook his head. He wasn't even sure if he could move if he wanted to. "I'm not going in there," he said hoarsely.

Jack heaved a deep sigh. Shoving the pistol in its holster, he seized the pick. Swinging it back and forth, he moved toward Giuliano. "This is goin' to be messy," he said in a resigned voice. "Goin' to hurt a lot more, too," he added as he swung the pick far back behind his shoulder.

Tony Giuliano threw up his arms. There was no questioning the intent in the man's one good eye. "I'll get in," Giuliano said dully. He dropped over the side and fell on his knees, eyes looking fearfully up into the darkness.

The two men appeared at the edge, both holding guns. A terrible smell filled the hole. "He shit himself," Hank said disgustedly, wrinkling his nose. "Stinks worse than a pig. Let's get this over with!"

Tony Giuliano dropped his head, hands grasping his knees. Long moments passed. He looked up. Only one man stood at the edge of the hole. He wasn't holding a gun.

Tony Giuliano peered up at the tall menacing form. This wasn't one of his captors! They weren't half his size. The man spoke, and Giuliano's heart leaped. "Know why you're here now, Giuliano?" the man said.

"Slaughter!" Giuliano cried. Shrinking down in his own filth, he looked up with horror at the giant apparition.

"That's right, Meade Slaughter. I have a son, David. I think you know him."

Giuliano shook his head wildly. "I've never met your son!"

"Funny," Meade said, continuing to speak quietly. "I thought you had a real interest in him. Wonder where I got that from?"

"I don't know! I don't know!" Tony Giuliano shouted in his terror.

"Maybe this will refresh your memory," Meade said, glancing over his shoulder and signaling. The two gunmen appeared carrying a heavy burden. They threw it into the hole. Tony Giuliano screamed as it crashed into his back and drove his face into the mud.

Giuliano scrambled out from under the clinging object, crabbing on all fours, pushing his back hard against the side of the hole, knees drawn up as he tried to make himself smaller. The object rolled over slowly, revealing the battered face of Mario Gatori. There was a blood-stained hole in his forehead. The back of his head was blown away.

Towering above Giuliano, Meade lit a cigar, then tossed the match into the hole. "You should be proud of your boy," Meade said. "He followed your orders to a T—did a nice job on David." Taking out the long cigar, Meade studied the glowing tip. He looked back down at the cowering Giuliano. "First a pill to ease the pain in David's arm, then a lot of pills. Pretty soon, pills weren't enough." Meade puffed on the cigar, the end coming redly to life. "Morphine's good for pain," Meade continued. "Of course, you know that. Interesting how morphine and heroin go together, isn't it?"

Tony Giuliano finally found his voice. "I don't know—"

"Shut up," Meade said tiredly. "Gatori didn't die right away. We got all the facts first. Have to say this for him: He didn't talk right away. Tough bastard. Too bad he had to die so young."

Meade threw the burning cigar into the hole beside Giuliano. He shoved his hands deep in his coat pockets and stared down at his old adversary. "I've been asking myself this question over and over again the last day or so—what am I going to do with Tony Giuliano? I considered staking you out on the desert and feeding you to the buzzards. My friends here learned how to do that one from the Indians. Not a bad idea, but messy and time consuming. Besides, the more I thought about it, the more I realized that killing you isn't the thing to do." Giuliano was so stunned he hardly heard Meade's next words.

"Killing an owner can raise a stink that might hurt the whole state. It'd be like cutting off my nose to spite my face. No, I think I'm going to let you live, Giuliano." Meade pointed a big finger down to where Tony Giuliano crouched. "If you ever get any smart ideas about getting even, remember yourself *now.* " Meade's voice was suddenly hard, stinging like a whip. "Remember it good, you son of a bitch!"

Shaking himself, Meade said in a quieter voice, "Why don't you use Gatori like a ladder and climb out? Maybe you should check his pants first. They may be cleaner than yours."

Tony Giuliano stared dumbly down at the corpse. "Forget it. The guy shit his pants when he died," Jack said, moving up beside Meade.

Meade nodded. "Come on up," he said to Giuliano. "We'll think of something."

With what seemed the last of his strength, Giuliano pulled himself out of the hole. Groaning, he lay helplessly on a pile of fresh dirt.

Making a face, Meade stepped back. "He can wear these," Hank said, tossing a pair of overalls on the ground beside Giuliano. A rag landed on Giuliano's back. "Wipe your ass with that," Hank added.

Meade sat on a rock while Giuliano cleaned himself up. "All right, Giuliano," Meade said as the shivering man pulled on the overalls, "grab a shovel and fill the hole. Throw your dirty stuff on Gatori. Let it rot with him."

Light was streaking the eastern sky when Giuliano stamped down the last shovelful of dirt. Meade waved him to a rock. "Sit down," he ordered. "We'll talk, then you can be on your way."

Sitting down, Tony Giuliano wiped the sweat from his eyes. His swollen split fingers were spread clawlike; if he closed them, the blisters would stick like glue.

"The boys will take you back to your car," Meade said. "Your bodyguard's not going to know much. He's your man; you can keep him quiet.

"You'll have to make up a story about your car going off the road and having to dig it out. Might be a good idea to bash it up a bit."

Meade paused and flicked some dust off his pants. "I don't have to tell you to keep the law out of this. Besides, we don't want to give the state a bad name, do we?" he added sarcastically.

Standing up, Meade regarded Tony Giuliano with open contempt. "I hope I've convinced you I mean business. I have everything covered if you try something stupid, so don't try anything," Meade said in a deadly voice. "Don't even think bad thoughts. Move against me, and you'll take a long time dying."

Turning away, Meade dismissed Giuliano with a wave of the hand. "Get out of my sight, Giuliano. You make me sick."

27

"You have to understand that David is a very nervous, frightened young man."

Meade and Gari glanced at each other, then back at the doctor.

The psychiatrist leaned back in the high-backed swivel chair. "David and I have spent a good deal of time together the last few months," he said, clasping his hands over his ample stomach. "He's a very sensitive man." He shot a speculative look at his attentive audience. "May I speak frankly?"

"Please do," Gari said quickly. Meade nodded his agreement.

The doctor turned his gaze on Meade. "Perhaps—perhaps, David is too sensitive for your line of work, Mr. Slaughter."

Meade's eyes narrowed. "Doctor Jacoby, are you saying that David shouldn't work in a casino?"

A shrug. "I don't think that's for me to say. There are some facts to consider. David's your only heir; it's logical that he will take over your business someday. Correct?"

"That's my intention," Meade said, wondering what this was leading up to.

"There's a lot of pressure in your work," Jacoby continued. "David's described it very well." A smile. "I've been to Reno once, never to Las Vegas. It can be exciting, but I don't have to tell you that.

"What you must understand is that some people aren't built to work under pressure—particularly the kind of pressure one finds in a gambling club. I'm not saying David won't adjust, but it's going to take time—and a lot of patience on your part. Whatever you do, don't rush David. Let him feel his way." The doctor studied Meade carefully. "There's a possibility that David won't want to stay in your business. Are you prepared for that? Can you handle it if he wants out?"

The question jolted Meade. How often had he asked himself the same thing? Years ago, he had faced the fact that David lacked the aggressiveness and desire necessary to make him a successful leader. He had hoped that time and experience would strengthen David and prepare him for his future as head of Nevada Investments, Inc. The question had always been there—would David shrink from responsibility? Would the Plush Wheels pass to new ownership on Meade's death? Meade glanced at his daughter-in-law, sitting calmly by his side. If only David had her strength and drive! He shook away the unsettling thought.

Jacoby was waiting, rocking gently in his chair. Meade finally responded. "I've always considered the possibility, Doctor. It won't be easy, but I'll do what's best for David. As you know, David will work in public relations when he and Gari get back from New York. I won't push him; he can work in any area he wants." A pause. "I don't have to tell you how important it is to me that he remains with the company. But if he wants to go, I won't stand in his way."

Jacoby smiled, and Gari shot Meade a grateful look. They knew, especially Gari, how difficult that speech had been.

Gari spoke up, "Doctor Jacoby, how does it look for David? Is he really off that stuff? Can he go back?"

"Mrs. Slaughter," Jacoby said heavily, "to be addicted to heroin is like being addicted to alcohol. You can't guarantee that a patient won't fall back into old habits. Of course, heroin is not as accessible as alcohol.

"The alcoholic and drug addict seek the same thing—only in different degrees. They are both seeking relief from anxiety, a temporary lift from depression, an artificial way to cope with life. They become dependent on drugs—and believe me, alcohol is a drug—to a point that their tolerance level becomes unbelievably high. The more they use, the more they need to achieve the euphoria they seek.

"What I'm trying to say, Mrs. Slaughter, is that a cured patient is cured only as long as he can learn to handle daily problems without artificial stimulants. If he can reach that level comfortably, then he is truly cured. Unfortunately, until they reach that point, they must fight daily to keep from taking the easy way out . . . falling back on the drugs that provided them with the escape they so sorely need. David developed a high level of tolerance for drugs. Going back into the outside world will be a traumatic experience. It won't be easy."

"How high a tolerance did David develop?" Meade asked.

"He had become tolerant to five thousand milligrams of

morphine a day. A clinically effective dosage of pain relief is
in the fifteen to twenty milligram range."

Meade and Gari stared at the doctor, shocked into silence.
Gari fumbled with the snap on her purse. "It's a wonder it
didn't kill him," she whispered.

Jacoby nodded. "Many die of overdose. Drugs have been
on the American scene for a long time, more so in the east.
Before long, it will become critical out here."

Meade searched the doctor's rounded face, the rimless
glasses magnifying the brown intelligent eyes. "How can we
be of the most help to David?" Meade asked.

"Understand. Show you care. Listen. Don't plan a year
ahead. Take it one day at a time.

"David respects you, Mr. Slaughter. Even fears you. He
wants to love you. He's not sure you want that love—even
less sure that you will return it." The doctor included Gari
in his glance. "I wish I could be of more help. I can only try
and point you in the right direction. If you sincerely want to,
it can be a rewarding experience."

Meade and Gari looked at each other. "We want to,"
Meade said, speaking directly to her. Gari smiled her agreement, not hiding the anxiety in her eyes. Meade understood;
she would be bearing the biggest responsibility.

David joined them in the private waiting room off Jacoby's
office. He was carrying a leather suitcase—part of a matched
set Meade had bought him and Gari for their trip—and
looked like a tourist returning from a satisfying vacation. His
gray suit, white shirt, black-striped tie and black shoes were
new, recently purchased by Meade and Gari in San Francisco. Dropping the suitcase, David took Gari into his arms.
"You feel great, honey," he said, controlling his voice with
difficulty.

Gari murmured something into his neck, then stood back,
grabbing his hand. "Let's get out of here," she said, voicing
their collective wish.

Sitting in the back seat of the rented limousine, the glass
partition closed between them and the two Plush Wheel
security guards up front, they discussed the trip. David, Gari

and Ann would be flying out of San Francisco International tomorrow for New York City.

"How's Ann?" David asked Gari, trying to look everywhere at once, taking in the sights as the Cadillac rolled through the beautiful Sonoma Valley.

"She's fine," Gari said. "Should have heard her scream when we left her with the baby sitter this morning. It's a wonder they didn't toss us out of the hotel! They're not used to Nevada ranch girls on Nob Hill."

"Can't wait to see her," David said. They were entering the little town of Sonoma. "Look at that!" David exclaimed, pointing at a gaily decorated storefront. "They've already got Christmas stuff up."

"Six weeks away," Meade said, adding drily, "Wouldn't be surprised if they start pushing Christmas in October before long. Anything for a buck."

The talk turned to Las Vegas. When told three weeks ago, David had raised no objection to Gari's new job. There had been concern that he might resent his wife working alongside him. He was definitely happy about not returning to Reno and thought that living on the ranch was a great idea.

Meade brought David up to date on the Strip Plush Wheel. "We'll start construction on the highrise in the fall," he said. "If we weren't in such a solid financial position, I'd hold off. Some of the owners are worried about all this building."

"On the Strip?" David said.

"The Strip, everywhere. You know about Bill Moore and the D.I. group opening the Showboat out on Boulder Highway last September. Looks like they're going to do well. They're catering to locals—the way the Last Frontier did under Moore. The Showboat has to; they're off the beaten track for California tourists . . . and they're eighty-five percent of our market."

Meade continued, "Walter Parman's California Club's been open downtown for almost a year and doing good, same with the Lucky Strike." Meade threw up his hands. "But the Strip, hell, who knows? The way we've been making money the last ten years, everybody wants in on the act. We've got investors from back east, California, Florida, even St. Louis, who think the Strip's located at the end of the rainbow. So there are several more places in the works. Smitty's predicting a bust. I'm listening. He's cagey as a fox, and he's wired into everything that goes on in the state—a cowboy version of Norman Biltz."

"What's Smitty worth, anyway?" David asked. "I've always wondered."

"You and a lot of other people," Meade laughed. "He could probably buy the whole Strip if he wanted to."

David whistled softly. "That much?"

"Just a guess. I'm not about to ask him."

"Me neither. I wouldn't put it past him to blow my leg off!"

"Oh, pooh," interjected Gari. "He's not so bad once you get to know him."

The noon sun cast a flickering row of shadows on the car as they passed over the Golden Gate Bridge. Meade relaxed and enjoyed the view of the bay and the glittering city. Tomorrow, David, Gari and Ann would be on their way to New York. He would return to Nevada, able once more to concentrate all his efforts on business.

28

Within a week, Tony Giuliano knew about David's release from Holton Sanitorium. Through an intricate spy system, he kept up on all the happenings in the state, especially anything to do with Meade Slaughter.

Meade Slaughter. In the beginning, he had sneered at him, considering him no threat, a carnival type who wouldn't last in Reno a month. That was in 1933, over twenty years ago. Later, when Meade became his father's enemy, he became Tony's also. They were close in age, Meade twenty-nine and

Tony twenty-seven at the time. Four years later, Meade killed Carlo Giuliano, and Tony's hatred became an obsession as he vowed to avenge his father's murder.

Tony Giuliano's hate intensified with the years. After Senator Bob Terhune's warning, Tony dropped consideration of physical violence, building the vast empire inherited from his father, watching Meade's activities, waiting for some sign of weakness, a chink in the armor through which he could thrust and destroy his enemy. He couldn't take Meade's life, but he could strip him of his power. For a man like Meade, that was another form of death.

When Meade purchased the Lake Tahoe property that he had wanted so badly, Tony Giuliano considered it an act of war. It was possible that Meade never knew of Giuliano's interest, but Tony wouldn't believe it for a minute.

In a fit of rage, Tony moved against Meade through his son. Perhaps, if he had taken time to consider the implications, if this latest insult hadn't been like the proverbial last straw, if he had had more control over his psychopathic temper, Tony Giuliano might have stayed his hand. Perhaps. For a brief time, he savored the sweet juices of revenge. They turned sour during the most terrifying night of his life.

Again and again, he would dream of the pick rising and falling and moist dirt piling up on the ground. He would look up and see the grotesque face of the aged gunman looking down, the dead milky eye following his movements, the big Colt .45 rock-steady in the gnarled hand.

The dreams were always the same. Backing away, the terribly scarred man would be replaced by a huge dark figure. It would grow and grow until it seemed to reach the very stars, and the laughter that boomed down sounded like thunder. Pointing a finger that blotted out the light of the moon, the fearsome shadow taunted him, calling him a coward and less than a man.

Dwarfed by the giant apparition, the scarred gunman reappeared, grinning evilly, pointing the pistol at Tony Giuliano's face. A great belch of flame. Darkness.

Tony would wake up screaming and drenched with sweat.

The shame was his alone. He and his wife were separated now; she lived in San Francisco with their daughter. Louis had married his college sweetheart, and they lived in Reno with their year-old son. Mike, three years younger than Louis and just turned twenty-one, was living and working on one of Tony's construction projects in Elko.

It was shame that Tony felt most of all. Repeatedly, he would relive the humiliation of kneeling in his own filth, meekly awaiting his fate, staring up from this servile position at his enemy, gratefully accepting his reprieve, scrambling over Mario Gatori's corpse and up to freedom.

When Sam Rozini had asked about his grandson, Tony had said that Gatori had quit and gone back to New York. Rozini stated that he would break Mario's neck if the ungrateful bastard gave his mother a bad time.

Tony Giuliano faced the two men seated across the desk. The topcoats hanging on the rack dripped water on the worn office rug. The first heavy snow of the season had fallen last night. In two weeks, it would be Christmas, a time that meant nothing to Tony except that it brought more customers into his clubs.

Tony looked at Louis. "You'll be responsible for Tahoe. Don't push Angie; work with him, and keep me informed. Do a good job, and you'll move on to Vegas. You'll need a few more years first. This ain't no kid's game."

Henry Lawton winced at Tony's brusque words. Couldn't he use a little diplomacy with his son? Small chance. Tony didn't know the meaning of the word. Lawton glanced at Louis, who was listening attentively to his father. Did Tony appreciate his son's intelligence and maturity? Possibly deep inside, but his stubbornness and ego would never allow him to admit it.

"You see anything wrong?" Tony asked Lawton.

The white-haired attorney rested his chin on steepled fingers. "No. Building at Tahoe can't miss, not with the growth up there. The old club's outdated, too small." He didn't mention that the new building site on the east side of Highway 50 was far inferior to the lakeside parcel Meade

Slaughter had purchased. That subject was taboo in this office.

Tony stubbed his cigar out in the tray. "Vegas?" he said, eyes still intent on Lawton.

"Downtown's booming; building on Fremont Street will pay off," Lawton said. "Those extra two hundred rooms at the Fantasia are filled every weekend, so that was a good move." Lawton scratched his ear. "You have the same reservations as I have about the Strip. Standing pat sounds like a good idea to me."

Tony's hooded eyes said nothing. "I put up with Vegas for the money," he said, "but it ain't Reno." He looked at the two men. "We go up six stories here with a hundred twenty-five rooms, build a new club and motel at Tahoe and do nothing for a while on the Strip. Agreed?"

The men nodded. Even if they had disagreed, objecting would have been a waste of breath. Holding total ownership of all his business activities, Tony Giuliano's control was absolute. Of all his employees and advisors, only Louis and Henry Lawton were allowed to freely express their opinions, Louis because he was Tony's son and heir apparent of the gambling corporation and Lawton because of his experience and long association with the Giuliano family.

After Louis and Lawton had left, Tony Giuliano sat unmoving behind the old oak desk, dark eyes roving the cramped office, seeing everything but seeing nothing. Less than a month had passed since that terrifying experience on the eastern slope of the Sierra Nevadas. Try as he might, the memories were with him every waking hour. He knew that in time they would relax their hold on his consciousness, but they would always be there—prodding, taunting, giving him no peace until he had triumphed over Meade Slaughter.

29

"See you sometime this morning?"

"Your place or mine?" Gari smiled into the phone; it had been painted white to match the feminine decor of her office.

Meade was learning to rely on Gari's judgment for many things. Her position in the company hadn't been accepted by all; there had been signs of resentment from some. Gambling had always been a man's game, and Las Vegas was a man's town. Women dealers had worked briefly downtown toward the end of the war but none had ever worked on the Strip. Harolds Club had hired one of the first women dealers in Nevada in 1938 (the first being the wives of Pappy and Harold Smith). That dealer, Doris Rose, was one of many in 1943 when Harolds announced they would hire no more men for the duration of the war. Women dealers were now a common sight in Reno.

Later that morning, seated in the private booth beside Meade, Gari gazed out the third-story window of the Lake Room. "Wonder what the wind's doing to our many construction projects?" she mused. Nothing was visible beyond the center of the Strip.

"Oh, they're working; you can bet on that," Meade said. "The Riviera and Royal Nevada have set their openings for late April. They'll have to go like hell to make it."

"The Royal Nevada's already got problems; they're getting way behind on salaries. That's going to cause trouble.

"Moe Dalitz doesn't give the Dunes a prayer. None of the owners have any gambling experience. I go along with Moe. Just because they've done well in the restaurant business in

Providence, Rhode Island, doesn't mean they'll make it here."

Meade chuckled. "Gambling experience isn't everything. Nobody has more than Tony Cornero. He and his brothers opened the Meadows on Boulder Highway back in thirty-one, and he's been running gambling ships on and off ever since. Not to mention his short term at the S.S. Rex downtown. Now, he's an instant businessman, selling stock out of his briefcase. The Stardust's almost half done, but as far as I know, Frank Fishman's the only one who's got all his money. Tony paid him six hundred-fifty thousand for that thirty-two acres next to the Royal Nevada."

Gari bit off a piece of celery. "I feel bad about the Last Frontier changing. It was such a friendly place." She made a face. "The 'New Frontier.' Silly name. What's wrong with the old ways? I don't even know if I'm going to the opening next month. Are you?"

"Got to. I'm an owner, remember?" Meade said, smiling at Gari's indignant remark. Old ways? Turned twenty-nine in January and she's talking about *old* ways?

The talk strayed to other things, but they were back to the original subject during dessert. It was hard to stay away from it. Everywhere one went—on the Strip, downtown, Boulder Highway, even Westside—there was building activity. Hotels going up, remodeling, neon signs bigger and more spectacular than their predecessors, all designed to outdraw the competition and grab off a portion of the endless flow of wealth. Or was it endless? The debates went on—in the casinos, at meetings of financial and civic leaders, on the sidewalks and in the bars. And nothing was more controversial than the Moulin Rouge.

"I don't know," Meade was saying. "It's a hell of a risk."

"It will give the Negroes a place to go. It'll be a captive clientele. That's bound to help."

"But how much money will they bring in? Two million for a hotel on Bonanza Road! Hell, half the streets are still unpaved in Westside!"

Gari set her coffee cup down with a bang. "How long can

this segregation go on?" she demanded. "It's crazy. Even the Negro entertainers can't stay in the hotels where they perform! Look at Sammy Davis. He'll headline at the New Frontier after it opens next month, but he won't be able to stay there. He'll stay where the rest of them do, at Ma Harrison's in Westside." Gari strangled her napkin with strong capable hands. "I think it's great that they'll have their own hotel. I hope they make it, and what's more I intend to visit the Moulin Rouge when it opens!"

Meade made a clapping motion. "Bravo!" he cheered softly, grinning at Gari, her face made even more lovely by the red flush of anger. "Keep things in perspective, lady. I understand that Joe Louis has been offered some points in the Moulin Rouge, but the owners are white, Jewish to be exact. Ever eat a Reubens' sandwich?"

"Don't get off the subject."

"I'm not. The Reubens are the principal owners."

"I know that. Do you think my head's buried in the sand?"

"No, but it looked like it when we came in from the outside."

Laughter. They had many arguments with neither coming out a clear winner. Two strong-minded individuals learning respect for each other.

Meade cleared his throat. "How about stopping by my office on the way back?"

Gari tilted her head to one side, forefinger touching her temple. "Ah, now we get down to the nitty-gritty," she said. "You've been leading up to this all morning, haven't you?"

A sheepish look. "Maybe. I'd like to put it off, but—" He lifted his hands.

Gari sighed. "Let's go," she said, rising and dropping the napkin on the table. The meal suddenly felt heavy on her stomach.

They sat in a corner of the big office, where several leather chairs circled a round coffee table. Gari kicked off her shoes and put her nyloned feet on the low table. "You talk first," she said, throwing her head back and closing her eyes.

"While you sleep?"

Gari's eyes popped open, and she glared at Meade. "I'm not sleeping, damnit!" she snapped.

"Gari—" Meade lifted his heavy shoulders. "This is hard for both of us. Let's not fight. Okay?"

"Sorry. Touchy subject, touchy woman."

"David's drifting away again," Meade said. "At least we know how he's escaping this time. He's been hitting the booze pretty hard."

Gari nodded wearily. "I know. He started drinking when we were back east. I thought it was a reaction to getting out, that he'd slow down. I couldn't say anything. We were both on pins and needles as it was."

"That bad?" Meade said.

"Worse, maybe," Gari replied, closing her eyes for a moment. She looked at Meade. "We had two bad fights, one in New York, another in Miami. The second time, he went out and got drunk. That's why we came home a week early."

"I wondered what happened. One day you're going to Bermuda, the next you're on the way home." Meade smacked a fist into his open palm. "Damn, I wanted it to work!" He saw the fire in Gari's eyes. "Sorry," he said, raising a hand. "We both wanted it to work." Softly. "It's been rough for you, hasn't it?"

"I've managed," Gari said simply. "The worst part has been the job. Not that I haven't loved it! If it weren't for the other problems, this would be the happiest time of my life."

Dropping her feet off the coffee table, she sat up. "I'm not a hypocrite, Meade, but I've had to be lately. I've had to come to work after a fight and smile and act like nothing's wrong. David and I are seen together here all the time, and we put on a good act. He's as anxious as I am to keep things quiet." An angry toss of the head. "At least we agree on *that!*"

"How bad is it, Gari?" Meade asked sympathetically. "We agreed not to talk about this after David got out. I broke that promise today because I've been at wit's end the last few weeks." A pause. "Bob Lakely didn't see the need to take

David along to Reno today, but I insisted. You've probably figured that out by now."

Gari tucked her feet up under her on the chair. "I was catching on," she said. "Took a while. I'm not too sharp these days." She combed her fingers through her hair. "How bad is it? Going downhill, with the drinking, temper tantrums and everything else." She made a slashing motion with her hand. "You sure you want to hear this?"

"I can't help if I don't know what's going on," Meade said. "You can't keep fighting this battle alone."

A defeated shrug. "All right. You know about the drinking—the *social* drinking that is. Is it getting around?"

"Lakely talked to me about it. Public relations people have a reputation for drinking their lunches, goes with the territory, I guess. Lakely and his crew can handle it; David can't. Last week, he made an ass out of himself at an advertising club meeting. Lakely tried to get him to slow down. David got mad and walked out."

Gari sighed. "Like he does at home. Meade, he's drinking so he won't have to face life, and if that isn't enough, he runs. Booze is just a substitute for drugs, and I'm afraid that's the next step. Drinking won't be enough unless he stays drunk all the time," she added bitterly.

"Is he taking off much? Where does he go?"

"Two-three times a week lately. Some bar, I suppose."

"Funny I haven't heard."

"No shortage of bars here. Besides, who'd notice? It wouldn't be anything unusual unless he caused a disturbance."

"Think that might happen?"

"I don't know. I suppose." A frown. "Maybe he just blows off steam at home. Better there than where everybody can see him. Except—" Gari bit her lip.

"Except what?" Meade said.

Gari's eyes flared, and she said angrily, "Yelling is one thing. Getting physical is another. I can take care of that. It's Ann I'm worried about."

"Ann?" It was almost a shout. Meade jerked upright, and his big fists were clinched. "Has he—?"

Gari broke in. "No, Meade. Please, nothing like that. I'm just afraid that it might happen."

"*Something* has happened," Meade insisted.

"He's shouted at her, made her cry. She doesn't scare easily, but she's only two."

"Does he hit her?" Meade pressed. He couldn't imagine anyone hitting Ann. He worshiped his tiny granddaughter.

"Oh, Meade," Gari said, an amused look on her face, "all children have to be punished now and then." She made circling motions with her finger on her skirt. "He spanks her at times. Nothing drastic. It's just, well, what if he loses control like before?"

Meade recalled Gari's swollen face, the livid bruise. "There can't be another time," he said harshly. "Not for Ann *or* you."

Silence. They stared at each other. "That sounds pretty final," Gari said softly.

"Oh, shit," Meade groaned, rubbing his chin with the back of his hand. "How final is it, Gari? With you and David? Is there any hope?"

"It's like a disease, isn't it?" Gari said, choosing not to answer directly. "That's what Doctor Jacoby called it, a disease like alcoholism." She sat up, feet planted firmly in the thick carpet. "I always thought of alcoholics as weaklings who couldn't control themselves. One of the girls I went to grade school with had a father like that. She despised him. The only time he acted strong was when he was drunk. He thought he could lick the world then. Only it was his wife and children who got licked.

"So when Doctor Jacoby talks about it being a sickness, I have a hard time understanding. Did you know I called him a few weeks ago?"

"No," Meade said, not surprised.

"Jacoby recommended re-admittance. He insisted on it, actually," Gari continued. "He said the next step is for David to go back on drugs. He brought up the sickness thing again."

She took a deep breath. "If I could think—*really* think—of David's problem as a disease or a sickness, whatever you want to call it, maybe I could handle it. But I can't. I've tried, Meade. I've tried!"

"Well, I asked," Meade said heavily. A forced smile. "I'm not shocked, you know. I had lots of hopes last November. The last month or so . . ." His voice trailed off.

"So did I, Meade," Gari said, a defensive tone creeping into her voice.

"I know you did," Meade said, running a hand across his brow. "You've got some tough decisions to make. I mean *we,*" he amended quickly.

Gari's look was steady, uncompromising. "Once it's over, I won't go back," she said. "We have to settle that right now."

"Nothing to settle," Meade snapped, feeling helpless, unreasonably angry. "That's between you and David."

"*Between* me and David?" Gari cried, stung by his abrupt words. "What do you think we're going to have—a nice friendly conversation? We're talking about divorce, Meade. D-i-v-o-r-c-e. I can't talk this over with David, not the way he is. I just have to go!" She finished on a shrill note. Her fists were clinched, long fingernails digging into her palms, face white as she struggled for control.

Meade felt awful. Damnit, how could he be so insensitive? He rose quickly and grasped Gari's upper arms, lifting her to her feet. "I'm sorry, baby," he said, drawing her close. Gari stood stiffly in his embrace, fists close together against his chest.

Gari whispered into Meade's shoulder, "What's going to happen to David? He'll feel betrayed. Maybe I *am* betraying him. Most of all, I'm worried about Ann. Don't you see?" She was almost pleading.

Meade rubbed her back. He felt clumsy, inept, with this big leggy girl in his arms. "David has to go back to Holton," he said, knowing it was the only solution. "I don't want you doing anything. I'll talk to David. After he's straightened out, you can break the news. It's the best way, Gari. You'll still be living at the ranch and working here." He held her at arm's length, smiling. "You didn't think you could get out of your job, did you?"

Gari blinked; her lashes were damp. Shaking her head, she tried to return Meade's smile. "It is the best way, isn't it?" she asked anxiously. "It would be such a relief to postpone things for a while. Am I being a coward?"

Releasing Gari, Meade stepped back. "No, Gari," he said. "You're not a coward. David can't be faced with this now. He has to be cured first. It may take a year or more. Can you wait that long?"

"Oh, Meade," Gari said chidingly, "do you think I'm so anxious to be a divorced woman? I have a beautiful daughter and a wonderful job." A smile. "And a pretty nice father-in-law. I can wait for as long as it takes."

30

Meade was talking into the phone, "So if you agree, we'll be flying out in about an hour."

"Oh, Meade, does it have to be this way? It seems so cold. I won't be able to say goodbye. He'll never understand."

"Jacoby says we should bring him up immediately. No matter what we do, David won't understand. Not now, anyway."

"He'll be under sedation the whole time? He'll wake up in that place?"

"It won't be that abrupt; they're going to keep him under medication the first week or so."

"But—"

"Gari, there's no easy way," Meade broke in. "I had hoped for something better than this, but it's gone too far to back off now."

A deep sigh. It was 1:36 A.M. Gari had been sleeping on the couch, waiting for Meade's call. "I know you're right," Gari said. "It's just such a difficult decision. Will Doctor Nelson be flying up with you?"

"Yes."

"Then do it, Meade. When will you be back?"

"Tomorrow night, the next morning at the latest. I'll call if that happens."

"I'll go crazy if I stay at home. Okay if I go to work?"

"Of course. I'll see you as soon as I get back." Meade hung up, knowing that Gari would get little sleep the remainder of this night.

Meade walked into the bedroom that adjoined his office; he had been staying at the Strip Plush Wheel for nearly a year now, ever since Gari moved to the ranch. "How is he?" Meade asked, gazing down at the sprawled figure on the bed.

The doctor rose from the chair and stood beside Meade. "He won't wake up for several hours," he said. "I gave him a pretty healthy dose."

"We'll be leaving in a few minutes. I want him under all the way."

The doctor nodded. Ted Nelson maintained an office at the Strip Hotel. Much of his practice was devoted to the care of Meade's employees and guests.

The two security men lifted David and carried him out the private exit to the waiting limousine. Meade and Nelson got into the back seat with the unconscious man. Meade held his son tightly as the heavy car rolled silently down the Strip, the bright lights casting ghostly shadows over the occupants.

As the plane took off with David strapped to a stretcher, Meade looked with disgust at the chafed knuckles on his right hand.

Gari had called him a few minutes after nine; he was eating dinner in the Plush Wheel coffee shop. "David's in pretty bad shape," Gari said. "We had a fight—over Ann. He was sitting in the kitchen, and she was chattering away. David yelled at her to shut up—screamed is a better word. Scared her half to death. While I was trying to calm her down, he left." A pause. "I know we agreed to give it a week or so, but maybe we shouldn't wait. What do you think? Meade, I can't take much more of this!"

Meade glanced around the crowded restaurant. The day after he and Gari had talked, he had flown to Reno. Returning this morning, he had gone directly to the downtown Plush Wheel to meet with Zed Atkins, the General Manager. Meade hadn't seen Gari in three days. He said into the phone, "Do you know where he went?"

"No, but I know he's been going to the Starlite Bar in North Las Vegas; at least he's been bringing home a lot of their matches."

"As good a place as any to start," Meade said. "I'll leave right away."

Meade took one precaution before he left; he informed the Strip Plush Wheel security chief, Don Milton, where he was going. Meade had been extra cautious since the confrontation with Tony Giuliano, taking security guards with him on trips and excursions outside of the hotel. Not tonight. He had to do this alone.

The Starlite Bar was on Lake Mead Boulevard just off the Salt Lake Highway, a single-story building sitting in the middle of a large paved lot. Flashing lights advertised pool, pinball machines, slots and poker. The lot was half filled with cars and pickups. The Starlite catered to locals.

Entering, Meade moved to one side until his eyes adjusted to the dim interior. He spotted David right away. He was seated at a large round table with a dozen men. They were laughing and talking loudly, showing the effects of the empty beer bottles shoved haphazardly together.

Stepping under a soft overhead light, Meade raised his hand, catching his son's attention. A look of consternation crossed David's face. Several of the men followed David's gaze to where Meade stood. Meade signaled for David to join him. Reluctantly, David obeyed.

"Can we go somewhere and talk?" Meade said.

"What about?" David asked, a mixture of worry and anger in his eyes.

"Things," Meade said. "We can have a drink at my place."
A wave and a smile to ease the tension. "It's quieter there."

"I don't know," David said, looking down at his feet.
Another glance over his shoulder. "Can't it wait until tomorrow?"

Meade's voice hardened. "Tonight," he said, no longer
smiling.

David straightened up, not liking Meade's words, a stubborn look crossing his face. "I'm not going," he said, a slight
slur slipping into his voice. He turned to leave.

"David—" Meade grabbed David's arm.

"Let me go!" David cried, shaking himself free. Three of
the men got up and headed their way.

Meade was angry, angry at letting himself get into this
situation, angry at David for acting so foolish. "You're going
now," Meade snapped, seizing David's arm and steering him
toward the door.

"What's going on, Davey?" the biggest of the three men
asked. He was holding a bottle of beer, looking Meade up and
down.

David glanced at the men, then at his father. He had seen
this look on his father's face before, and he was well aware
of the violence contained inside that big frame. The grinning
men had no idea who Meade was. If a barfight erupted, it
would make the front pages. The horrifying thought sobered
David. He held up his hands, frightened. "It's okay, guys,"
he said. Nodding at Meade, he added, "I'd forgot that I'd
told him to pick me up." David threw in the clincher.
"There's enough money on the table to buy drinks for the rest
of the night. Enjoy yourselves."

The big spokesman looked at Meade, then David. "You
sure, Davey?"

"Yeah, no problem," David said.

The big man grunted, shooting Meade an insolent look.
"Okay, Davey," he said. "Thanks for the drinks." His companions followed him back to the table.

Once outside, David whirled on Meade. "What the hell are

you trying to do?" he shouted, pointing at the closed door. "You made me look like an ass in there."

"Not here," Meade said, glancing at a couple standing by their car, watching. "I'll explain when we get to my office."

"Save it," David snarled, pulling out his car keys. "I'm going home."

Meade looked around. The couple had gone inside. The lot was deserted. "You're going with me, David," Meade said, yanking the keys out of David's hand and dropping them in his pocket.

"Bastard!" David screamed. For the second time in his life he took a swing at his father, and the results were the same, only this time Meade hit him on the jaw. The heavy blow seemed abnormally loud in the early morning quietness. Meade caught David before he hit the ground and half-carried, half-dragged him to the black Cadillac. Putting David in the front seat, he got quickly behind the wheel. Twenty minutes later, he pulled up outside his office. David was still unconscious, but he was rolling his head and moaning. Unlocking his private door, Meade got David inside and on the bed. Meade made two phone calls, one to Don Milton to tell him he was back, the other to Ted Nelson. Before leaving for the Starlite, he had asked the doctor to wait until he returned.

A knock on the door. Nelson slipped in and laid two pills on the nightstand. Bending over David, he checked his eyes and pulse, then went into the bathroom. He returned with a glass of water. "Will they work fast?" Meade asked as Nelson set the glass on the nightstand.

"Two-three minutes, maybe five," Nelson said. "I'll wait in the office." He hurried out; David was waking up.

Gripping his son's shoulder, Meade said softly, "David?" David began to moan. Meade repeated, "David?" Louder this time.

David's eyes opened. He tried to rise, but Meade held him down. "Take it easy, son," Meade said.

David felt his jaw. "Let me up," he muttered, pushing Meade's hand away. Meade sat back, ready, waiting.

David rested his back against the headboard. Yanking several tissues out of the box on the nightstand, he dabbed at his mouth. The tissues came away bloody. "Satisfied?" David asked, eyes filled with hatred.

"I'm sorry, David," Meade said. "I just wanted to talk."

"You have a funny way of going about it," David said, dabbing away more blood. He glared at Meade. "You wanted to talk, talk. When you're through, I've got some things to say." A glance at the clock. "I'd be home asleep if you hadn't butted in."

Meade spread his hands. "For one thing, I wanted to talk to you about your drinking. Why are you hanging around a place like the Starlite? It's a dump. You can get in all kinds of trouble there."

"That's my business," snapped David. "How did you know I was at the Starlite? Are you spying on me?"

Meade ignored the question. "Let me help you, David. I know it must be rough getting started again. Drinking's not the answer. It can lead to other things." The inference hung in the air like a heavy cloud.

"It's Gari, isn't it?" David demanded, refusing to be diverted. "She's been snooping and talking to you."

"David—"

"You two got to be great buddies while I was away. I could tell the difference right away. Even while we were back east, it was Meade this and Meade that. I got sick of hearing your name!" David's voice rose. "I know what you're trying to do. You want her for yourself!"

Meade's mouth dropped open. "Of all the—"

David was raving now. "You two have been ganging up on me for two years now. Why couldn't you leave me alone? I'd have been all right." Suddenly, he was crying, head bowed, chest heaving.

"David," Meade said softly, moving closer. He put his arms around his son. "We want the best for you. You've got to believe that."

"What *is* best for me?" David cried.

Meade wanted to tell him that he should return to Holton Sanitorium. He wanted to tell him many things, most of all that he loved him. It would be useless to say any of that now. He had to lie to his son. He put the two pills in David's hand and lifted the glass of water. "Take these, David," he said. "They'll make you feel better."

Leaning against Meade, David swallowed the tablets. Meade set the glass back on the nightstand. He held David, talking quietly, reassuring his son even as he deceived him. Within minutes, David was unconscious.

31

One August morning, Meade stuck his head in Gari's office. "Let's take a drive," he said. "Got something to show you."

Gari shivered in the front seat of the air-conditioned car. "Cold, hot, cold, hot," she muttered. "I feel like a walking case of malaria."

"Want me to turn the heater on?" Meade grinned.

Gari looked at the shimmering heat waves rising from the pavement. "Thanks, I'll suffer through this somehow." She hugged her bare shoulders. The thin summer dress covered the essential parts but little else.

Meade guided the car along the road that meandered through the lush green golf course. Many of the trees scattered throughout the hundred acres had been planted full-grown, others would reach maturity in a few years. Dotted with lakes, the golf course was a beautiful oasis. Several luxurious homes faced the course; a score more were under construction.

Meade stopped beside a huge lot that overlooked the fairway and a sparkling lake. "Like it?" he asked. New stakes with red ribbons marked the boundary lines. "Actually, it's two lots," Meade added.

Gari looked out her side of the window. "It's lovely," she said. "Like having the biggest lawn in the world for a front yard." She turned toward Meade, eyes shining brightly. "You're going to build a house!"

Meade grinned. "Right! Like the idea?"

"I think it's wonderful," Gari said. "You don't know how guilty I feel living at the ranch, with you in that dinky little office bedroom."

Meade was smiling broadly now. "You *should* feel ashamed. I'm ordering you to vacate the ranch by January first. I want my house back!"

"Wha—" Gari's face was a study in comic surprise.

Meade poked the tip of her nose. "It took a month, but I've persuaded Nordstrom to design your house." Meade looked at his watch. "He'll be arriving at McCarran Airport in an hour. He said he was too busy, but the idea of working with you tipped the scales. I think he likes your legs."

Gari stared at Meade, glanced out the window, looked back at Meade. "The heat's got to you," she said at last. "Meade Slaughter, what are you up to?"

"Nothing," Meade said innocently. "I think my special vice-president *and* hostess should have a home that reflects her lofty position. Sort of a showplace, if you will."

"What's this hostess bit?" Gari asked suspiciously, shooting Meade a sidelong glance, studying the lot with new eyes.

"You know, someone to grace special events—golf tournaments, meetings." A big grin. "Boat races. It's the latest thing."

Gari's eyes softened, and she twisted sideways, left arm thrown over the back of the seat. "Meade, why are you doing this?" she asked. "Truth now. No fibbing."

"Truth?"

"Truth."

Meade leaned back against the door, one foot depressing the gas pedal slightly to keep the engine from overheating. "For one thing," he began, "we *do* need a hostess, and you're the perfect choice." He gestured toward the lot. "A show-place home will be great for publicity; most of it can be a charge-off. The ranch is okay, but Ann will be in school before long. She needs more of a permanent home, to be closer to you during the day. I know it's hell to keep good help out there in the boonies. This way, you can get to work in a few minutes, not in the hour or so it takes now. We've never talked about it, but I'm hoping you're going to stick around. I'd like to think you'll make Vegas your home. The house will be yours, no matter what you do."

Gari's eyes had never left his. "That's it?" she said quietly.

Meade sighed and folded his arms. A guilty look. "I know what you're thinking—that I'm doing this to insure your staying. I won't stand in your way if you want to leave. You have several options, including the home in Reno. Whatever you decide, I'll see that you're financially secure. I don't want you to leave."

A whisper. "And David?"

Meade closed his eyes for a moment. "David. What happens when he gets out? If he stays with the company, he'll probably work in Reno; he always liked it better there. Jacoby's made it clear that it will never work with you two in Vegas, especially working in the same place. Maybe Jacoby's right, and David shouldn't even return to Nevada." A tortured look. "It scares hell out of me that he might be institutionalized the rest of his life. All I can promise is that I'll do everything I can for you and Ann. Is that enough for now?" An attempt to lighten the mood. "Will you accept the house and quit bitching?"

Gari's voice was husky. "All right, Meade," she said, knowing how important it was to him. "And you're not bribing me, either. I have no desire to leave Vegas."

Meade left Gari with Nordstrom and went to the coffee shop for lunch.

David was very much on Meade's mind as he walked through the casino to his office. He had seen his son five times since his return to Holton Sanitorium four and a half months ago. The first visit had been a disaster; David wouldn't even speak to him. Gari had received only a few mumbling words.

The second time hadn't been much better, with little improvement on the following visits. It had been difficult for Gari, having to hide the fact that their marriage was over. David hardly acknowledged his father, blaming his incarceration on Meade.

After the last visit, David had told Jacoby that he believed something was going on between his father and Gari. Jacoby had suggested that Gari come alone next time.

32

Through the combined efforts of architects, contractors and landscapers, all coordinated by Gari with the energy and drive of a field general, Gari's new home was completed a month early. Christmas, 1955, would be celebrated in style, but first there was to be a special dinner. That was set for Friday, December 16th. Gari had hoped to combine it with Ann's third birthday on the 9th, but even her remarkable abilities couldn't pull that one off.

The final furnishings for the 6,000 square foot ranch-style home had been delivered just a few hours ago, and Gari and Ann had taken Meade and Smitty on a grand tour immediately upon their arrival. It had been a difficult task, with Ann running ahead and stealing her mother's lines. At one point, Gari stopped, folded her arms and glared down at her tiny blond daughter. "Ann Slaughter," she said, tapping one high-heeled foot, "I was so glad when you started talking. Now I wish I could reverse the process."

"What's reverse?" Ann said brightly, violet eyes aglow.

Gari aimed her daughter the opposite way down the hall. "That way," she said, pointing.

"Oh," Ann said, slipping under Gari's arm and dashing back to the lead position. "Come see the 'antry!" she yelled. She hadn't got her p's right yet.

It was a beautiful home, and as much as Gari complained about its size and extravagance, Meade knew that she loved it. "Big house for a big girl," Meade had said on one occasion. She liked that, too.

Candlelight, chateaubriand, Dom Perignon, everything prepared by Gari. "Us farm girls know lots of things," she said, accepting the men's praise with a pleased smile.

Later, sitting in the huge living room, with Ann forcefully retired to her room, Gari made a shocking announcement. "Go ahead and smoke a cigar, Meade," she said. "You can smoke, too, Smitty. You're both going to be coming here a lot, so I'm changing the rules." A wry look at Meade. "I've learned to put up with it at work. Why not here?"

"Gari, you don't have—"

"Shut up, Meade. You might talk me out of it."

Meade watched Gari as she described to Smitty the landscaping of the grounds. She was talking animatedly, eyes sparkling, slender hands making descriptive designs in the air. The Plush Wheel was her life now. In addition to her other duties, she had taken to the hostess job like a duck to water. Next month, she would break a bottle of champagne fourteen stories above the desert floor at the topping-off ceremonies of the Strip Plush Wheel highrise.

Despite the hotel problems on the Strip, Meade had gone ahead with the original building plans. The highrise, with its 420 rooms, was scheduled to open in mid-May. Nineteen fifty-six promised to be an exciting year, with the groundbreaking for the Lake Tahoe Plush Wheel set for the week before the opening of the highrise.

But everything—the Christmas season, Gari's happiness with her job and new home, the challenging new year—all were overshadowed by the knowledge that David was incarcerated in Holton Sanitorium. Meade had spoken with Dr. Jacoby by telephone last week, and the report had been dis-

couraging. David's moods were mercurial. He would rise to
the heights of elation, then fall into the darkest despair, all
within hours. Gari had visited only twice since August,
Meade only once. Meade hadn't even seen David on that visit
a month ago.

"Give it time," Jacoby had said to Meade. They were in
the doctor's office, David having refused to see his father.

"Will he ever learn to make it out there?" Meade asked in
an anguished voice, waving in the direction of the gate that
was guarded twenty-four hours a day. "He can't stay locked
up the rest of his life!"

Jacoby said: "There's a good deal of medication on the
market, more coming out every day. With a knowledgeable
doctor and proper medication, he should find his place in
society again."

Meade's face twisted with distaste. "Pills! You're saying
he'll have to depend on pills the rest of his life?"

"It's not the end of the world, Mr. Slaughter," Jacoby
answered mildly. "Millions are surviving that way. Some are
very important people."

Meade smiled ruefully. "Sorry, Doctor. I guess I expect
too much."

"I know it's hard for you," Jacoby said. "God knows, I say
that to parents all the time. Take it a day at a time; that's the
best advice I can give."

Meade looked out the window that overlooked the manicured lawn enclosed by the walls of the sanitorium. "He's a
good-looking boy," Meade said in a low voice, eyes following
David as he walked across the green grass, closely followed
by an attendant. "He has the coloring and looks of his
mother." Meade turned toward Jacoby. "She was a beautiful
woman, you know."

Jacoby nodded. "David told me."

Meade looked back out the window. David and the attendant were walking up a small hill. Meade watched until
David's blond head disappeared over the rise.

Gari's voice brought Meade back to the present. "Well, I

think it's terrible," she was saying. "I think Meade and the other owners should do something about it!"

Smitty grinned at Meade. "She's got the bit in her teeth. Better duck."

"Did I miss something?" Meade asked, noting Gari's straight back and flushed face.

"Somethin' about the Moulin Rouge," Smitty replied. He enjoyed watching Gari in action, as long as he wasn't the target.

"Oh, no," Meade groaned.

"Oh, yes!" Gari retorted. "It's sad. They were doing great, Meade. That third show was a fantastic idea. All the entertainers from the Strip and downtown would show up and have impromptu jam sessions. I lost a lot of sleep going out there, but it was worth it. Then, boom! It's closed. They were making a profit! If it had been catering to whites, it would have made it."

"Like the Royal Nevada?" Meade shot back. "Come on, Gari, the Moulin Rouge failed because the prime lender backed out at the last minute. And don't say the other hotel owners were behind that," he added sharply. "It was some insurance company that reneged; I don't even know which one."

Five months after opening in Westside, the Moulin Rouge closed abruptly at 4:30 P.M., October 10th, having been served with a writ of attachment by two labor unions for back wages that it was unable to pay. There was talk about watered-down stock and an investigation by the Securities and Exchange Commission.

"Bob Bailey and the others worked hard to make a go of it," Gari continued, refusing to concede defeat. "Everybody went there—Frank Sinatra, Dean Martin, Tallulah Bankhead, Donald O'Conner, you name them." She pointed a rigid finger. "How often did you go, Meade Slaughter? I must have asked you a dozen times!"

"Whoopee!" Smitty crowed, grinning from ear to ear.

"I went several times, and you know it," Meade fired back.

"Ha! Listen to the man. Several times. Once, twice?"

"So what?" shouted Meade. "I didn't sink the place. Finances did, not color!"

Gari leaned forward, pounding a knee with her fist. "This segregation's got to stop!" she cried.

Meade threw up his hands. "How did we get on *that* subject? Are you using the Moulin Rouge to get on your soapbox?"

"Mommy, what are you and Grandpa yelling about?" Ann was standing in the hall entrance, clutching a teddy bear by one ear, the other hand hitching up her pajama bottom.

"Oh, honey," Gari said, "we're not yelling, just discussing things."

"Some discussion!" cackled Smitty.

Gari looked daggers at Smitty. "Stay out of this!"

"Now you're yelling at Uncle Smitty," Ann said, violet eyes round and interested.

"Help!" wailed Gari, holding out her arms for Ann, scooping the little girl into her lap. "Discussion's over," Gari said, smiling at the two men, rocking Ann to-and-fro.

"Nuts," Smitty said. "Just when it was gettin' good."

Meade stood up, laughing. "Come on, Smitty," he said. "Let's get out of here while we're still alive." He walked over and lifted Ann into his arms, giving her a big hug and kiss. "Hurry and grow up, sweetheart," he murmured into her silvery hair. "I need you to protect me from your mother."

33

The call came three nights later. "We don't know how he did it," Dr. Jacoby said in a deeply troubled voice, "but he was missing when we made the midnight bed check. We've searched the grounds. The authorities in town have been notified."

Sitting up in bed, Meade dropped his bare feet to the floor. He glanced at the luminous dial on the clock: 1:05 A.M.

"Do what you have to," Meade said gruffly. "I'll be there as quick as I can." A pause. "Damnit!" he snapped. "I thought you had good security there!"

Jacoby said, "I know apologies are not in order at the moment, Mr. Slaughter, but please accept my sincere regrets."

With a curt goodbye, Meade broke the connection, then dialed Hal Williams. Recently, Meade had purchased a twin-engine Cessna, hiring Williams away from Vegas Air. It was a feasible move; Meade was shuttling between Las Vegas and Reno on a weekly basis. Soon, Lake Tahoe would be added to the circuit.

Gari's eyes were frightened when she opened the door. "David?" she said hesitantly.

Meade stepped inside and closed the door. In a few terse sentences, he told her what had happened. "I'll call as soon as I know anything," he concluded.

Gari touched one of the large buttons on her robe. "Where can he go, Meade?" she said, eyes wide, voice anguished. "He must be so alone!" Guilt was there, too. Perhaps this wouldn't have happened if she hadn't abandoned him.

"I don't know," Meade replied, also feeling guilt. "How he got away is a mystery to me." He looked at his watch. "I'd better get going." He squeezed Gari's arm and hurried out to the car.

Jacoby steepled his fingers and looked across the desk at Meade. "A desperate man can be very clever, Mr. Slaughter," he said. "Somehow, your son fashioned a key. Very crude, but it worked. We found it outside the building.

"David hid in the car of one of our male nurses. Once outside, he knocked the man out with a tire iron and took his clothes. He tied the man up and put him in the trunk, drove to Sacramento and parked next to the state capital park. One of the state policemen heard the banging on the trunk lid." Jacoby glanced at the wall clock. "That was about an hour ago, nine-thirty. The car was only three blocks from the bus station, so the police are checking that. Considering the nurse left here at eleven, they must have reached Sacramento between two and three this morning. Buses have left in every direction since then. The nurse had only about eighteen dollars, so David can't go far."

"Which way?" Meade said in a barely audible voice. "Can he make it to Vegas on eighteen dollars? Reno? That's a lot closer, and maybe he's got friends there."

"I mentioned Reno when the police called. They'll check it out."

Meade looked at the clock. "Did they say how many buses have left Sacramento for Reno?"

"One at three-thirty, another at five. Three since then."

Meade did some quick calculating. "If he caught either one of those first two, he could be there now."

"If," Jacoby said, leaning heavily on the word. "Reno seems the logical choice, but he could be off in any direction."

Meade stood up. "I've got a good detective firm in San Francisco. We'll fly down there now. The owner's name is Branch Thorton. Give him all the help you can."

As Meade drove through the gate at Holton, David was entering the First National Bank of Nevada on the corner of Second and Virginia Street. He had stayed out of sight until the last minute; the Reno Plush Wheel was half a block away.

The teller greeted him warmly. He was David's age, and they had gone to grade school together. David requested his bank balance, then wrote out a counter check. The teller looked at the check. "Taking it all out, huh?"

"Might as well," David said. "I live in Vegas now, don't come up here much anymore."

The teller winked. "Aren't planning on hitting the tables, are you?"

"Maybe," David grinned, going along with the joke. He leaned forward and kept his face hidden while the teller counted out the cash.

"Twelve thousand eighty-eight dollars and thirty-one cents," the teller said. The stack was surprisingly small; David had asked for one hundred- and five hundred-dollar bills.

"Thanks," David said, stuffing the money into his pants' pocket.

"Next time you're up, let me know," the teller said. "I'll buy you a drink. Hey, and Merry Christmas!"

"Same to you," David said, lifting a hand as he turned and hurried toward the door. Stepping outside, he crossed Second Street and headed south on Virginia, away from the main casino area. His home was only a few blocks away, but he didn't dare go there.

An hour later, he checked into a small motel, a large package under his arm. He shaved and showered and put on the new suit he had purchased. The hat felt strange; he had never worn one before.

Discarding the old clothes in a waste basket, he walked a few blocks to the Greyhound Bus Depot and boarded a bus to Oakland.

34

Meade stood in the huge lobby of the Fairmont Hotel and looked up at the Christmas tree that nearly reached the twenty-five-foot-high ceiling. The tree was a Nob Hill tradition. Laden with 100 strands of tinsel and 2,000 ornaments, the Oregon white fir glittered amidst the ten golden Corinthian columns.

Branch Thorton said, "Takes your breath away, doesn't it?"

"It knocks me out every time I see it," Meade said. A group of carolers strolled by, singing "Silent Night." Meade turned away, feeling only sorrow. Had it only been sixteen hours since Jacoby's call?

In Meade's room, Thorton was completing his report. "The Reno police had checked the airlines, train stations and bus terminals by the time my men got there. They've been checking hotels and car dealers all afternoon. He emptied his account at the First National Bank on Virginia and Second —a little over $12,000. With that kind of money, your son has no end of options. Know where he got it?"

"His uncle died two years ago and left David twenty-five thousand. I talked to David's wife. She never knew what he did with it. Guess this is what's left."

The two men stood at the window, watching the lights below. "I'll have dinner sent up," Meade said. He looked around the room. "I had to pull strings, but I've reserved this room and the one next door through the first. With Christmas and New Year's coming up, it was the only way I could be guaranteed a place to stay. For all we know, David might be heading for New York, but I'm going to stay here until we know for sure. My secretary's on her way; she'll take the other room. I want one of your men with me whenever I leave the hotel. I could use some of my own security staff, but I've got to keep a lid on this thing. There are only two men I really trust, and they're both security chiefs. Can't break them away."

At that moment, the subject of their search was disembarking from a bus in Oakland and flagging down a cab for the Bay Bridge crossing to San Francisco.

He registered at an old hotel on Geary Street, a few blocks from San Francisco's Tenderloin district. Several square blocks of neglected hotels, apartments and assorted buildings, the Tenderloin offered every vice imaginable.

Hiding most of his money inside his shoes and in the lining of his jacket, David put two one hundred dollar bills inside his shirt and ten dollars in his pants' pocket. He carried no identification; his wallet was at Holton. Hands shaking with anticipation, he left the hotel and turned toward Polk Street. Within minutes, David was swallowed up in the darkness and squalor of the Tenderloin.

So passed the first night after David's escape from Holton Sanitorium, father and son less than two miles apart, one asleep on Nob Hill in the stately grandeur of the Fairmont Hotel, the other visiting sleazy bars until he finally made a buy in an alley off O'Farrell.

The next morning, Gari called Meade. "I've canceled my Christmas party," she said. "I can't have it now, not with you in San Francisco and David God knows where. My secretary's calling everyone now. Thankfully, it's not a big list. How long will you be there?"

"I don't know. At least another week. I'm going to stay until we get a lead. Thorton thinks David will come back here. He's familiar with the area, and—" Meade halted in mid-sentence, reluctant to go on.

"And what?" Gari demanded. "You don't have to coddle me, Meade. I'm a grownup girl."

A heavy sigh. "He can get anything he wants here; he probably knows where to go."

"At least that will narrow down the search, won't it?" Gari asked in a helpless voice.

"Yes," Meade answered quietly. "If this is where he's headed."

Silence. "Christmas is only four days away. Ann will miss you." A pause. "So will I."

For the first time in years, Meade felt the tug of loneliness. "Same here," he replied. "Maybe I can come down for the day."

"Oh, could you? I'll fix a nice dinner. Just us and Smitty."

The day passed with no news. Another day. Another. Then it was Saturday morning, the day before Christmas.

Meade called Gari. "Sorry, baby, but I can't come down. You'll have to do with Smitty."

Gari's voice was husky. "Will you call and talk to us tomorrow? Ann keeps asking about you. Poor thing, she doesn't understand."

"Frankly, I don't either. Lousy timing, isn't it?"

"The worst. They'll be concentrating on San Francisco now?"

"Yes. I told Thorton to offer double overtime. This is disrupting a lot of plans."

Christmas came and went. New Year's, 1956, was three days away. The city was quiet, girding up for the big New Year's Eve celebrations. Life in the Tenderloin continued with little change. Stolen articles were exchanged, pimps bargained with customers, fights broke out in bars and alleys and elderly couples, too poor to move out of their island of misery, huddled together in cold apartments, fearful of answering the door or going out at night.

David knew no fear as he walked along Turk Street, surrounded by flashing lights and raucous cries. He had never felt so good. These were his people and this was his home. He waved at a leggy blonde across the street. He had bought her services the second night here. It was the greatest fuck he'd ever had; they'd both been high on drugs. The next day, David had left the Geary Street hotel and rented a room in the Tenderloin. He wanted to be closer to the action.

He was wearing a moustache now, dyed brown like his hair. With the hat and dark glasses he wore all the time, he felt safe from discovery. His confidence had been momentarily shattered yesterday when a bartender told him his picture was being flashed around. By cops? Private detectives, the bartender said. He had recognized one.

David went right out and bought an overcoat and adopted a bent-over shuffling walk. This, coupled with the fix he gave himself, erased his panic. He was back on the street two hours later, feeling like a king.

David figured he had enough money to keep himself supplied for at least four months. By that time, he would have established enough contacts to insure his future. As long as he could buy what he needed, nothing else mattered. He had never really lived until now.

By the morning of January third, Meade was in a quandary. He had never been away from his hotels so long. The two rooms at the Fairmont were piled with papers, and his private secretary, Marcia Teller, had had to hire temporary secretarial help. Although she had gone home for Christmas, she was having a hard time. In nearly thirty years of marriage, she had never been separated from her husband for more than a day.

Meade decided to give it another week. He told Marcia she could go home on Saturday, four days from now. He would stay until Monday.

Even as he told Marcia his plans, the matter was being decided fifteen blocks away. "Hey, Davey, I got some great shit," Easy Harry said. "Just came off the boat."

"Let's see," David said. They were standing on the second-floor landing of an old hotel, safe from prying eyes.

Easy Harry dangled the small plastic bag in front of David's face. "Pure as the fallin' snow," Harry said, jumping the bag up and down. The white powder made a small cone as it settled back. "I'll sell you the whole batch—special price!"

"How much?" David asked, eyes following the bag as it swayed back and forth.

"One big one. You'll be in heaven for weeks."

David studied Easy Harry warily. No one knew how much money he had hidden inside his shoes. Men would kill here for a fraction of that amount. "Give me a day," David said. "Okay?" He had to make finding a thousand look difficult.

"That's cool," Harry said. "By noon tomorrow."

"Here?" David said.

Harry nodded. "Noon," he repeated. "Come late, this shit is gone." He held the bag up toward the single light bulb that hung from the ceiling.

"I'll be here," David said. He was sweating; it looked like great stuff.

The following afternoon, David moved two blocks away. The private detectives were still working the streets, and he had his precious stash of heroin to protect.

Checking the door to make sure it was locked, David put some of the powder in a smaller bag, and stuck the balance behind an old blanket on the top shelf of the closet. He'd find a better place tomorrow.

Taking off his jacket and shirt, he tossed them carelessly on a chair. He kicked off his shoes and padded to the suitcase on the chest of drawers. Unzipping a small shaving kit, he took out a spoon, eyedropper and hypodermic needle. He filled the eyedropper with water from the glass on the nightstand.

Sitting on the bed, David wrapped his belt tightly around his upper left arm, then pumped it at the elbow. The veins swelled. Satisfied, he put some powder in the spoon and added a drop of water. Striking a match, he held it under the spoon until the solution cooked. He held the spoon carefully while he sucked the white substance up into the hypodermic needle. Raising the needle, he extracted the air bubbles. He pumped his arm again, then inserted the needle into the distended vein. Droplets of blood tinted the solution pink. Slowly, David pressed the plunger down, sending the heroin rushing into his bloodstream. He unstrapped the belt and lay back.

It hit his heart with the impact of a jackhammer. His body lifted and jerked spasmodically. He rolled on his stomach as an orgastic warmth flooded his body, scrabbling hands clutching at the sheet.

Minutes passed. He opened his eyes. "Wow," he whispered. The faded wallpaper was ripping like it was full of worms. He closed his eyes and savored the greatest hit he'd ever had.

Late that afternoon, he took another hit, and again at midnight. He woke in the early morning hours and stared at the ceiling. Scratching his face, he experienced an odd sensual pleasure. In the eye of a hurricane, he knew a few lucid moments. He thought of Gari and Ann. Since arriving in San Francisco, he had blocked them out of his mind. They came back now with a rush of emotion that almost hurt. God, how he loved them! What would they be doing now? Asleep, of course. What he'd give to be with them right now. Would they want to see him? Ann would. Gari?

His father's face appeared on the ceiling. "Damn you!" David cried, his voice little more than a croak. Gari's face materialized and merged with Meade's. One image, shimmering, revealing first one face, then the other, mocking him. "Damn you both!" David shouted. He struggled to a sitting position and reached for the plastic bag. He increased the solution.

By mid-morning, he was floating on a warm cloud in a great wavy cave. He lost all track of time in his search for bigger and more powerful thrills. The fading sunlight was streaking the half-closed blinds as he filled the charred spoon to overflowing. His hands were shaking so hard that he had to rest the spoon on the nightstand while he filled the hypodermic. Pushing the plunger down, he fell back on the bed, the needle still sticking in his vein.

Branch Thorton called Meade Sunday evening; the police were sending a car to the Fairmont.

"Drug overdose," the medical examiner said, lifting the sheet for Meade's identification.

Meade stared down at David's unshaven face, the brown dye fading into uneven streaks. Nodding his recognition, he walked quickly away. An officer was waiting in the hall. "I'm sorry, Mr. Slaughter," he said, "but you will have to sign some papers. We'll need instructions for disposal of the body."

"Let's get it over with," Meade said brusquely, moving so fast that the officer had trouble keeping up. Branch Thorton was standing by the entrance. Thorton was a seasoned professional, but there was a look of genuine concern on his face. They shook hands silently.

After Meade signed the papers, Thorton joined him at the door. "My car's out front," Thorton said. "I'll drive you to the hotel."

At five the next morning, Hal Williams eased back on the controls, and the Cessna lifted off the runway at the San Carlos airport. Rising over the bay, Williams set a course for Las Vegas.

David's body was being shipped to Reno. Meade had called Gari last night. They would fly together to Reno for the funeral. David had left no will, but Meade knew he would want to be buried near Janice Terhune.

35

The three men stirred uneasily. The telephone conversation had been short. Tony Giuliano's face was ashen, and his hands were visibly shaking when he hung up.

"Beat it," Giuliano ordered, making a waving motion with his hand across the desk. The men slipped out of the office, mystified, glad to be returning to their jobs in the casino downstairs.

Tony Giuliano stared at the closed door. Fifteen months had passed since that fateful night on the eastern slope of the Sierras. The memory had been crouching in the dark recesses of his mind, gnawing at his consciousness, occasionally entering his dreams with quick, savage thrusts—until this phone call brought it snarling and ripping through his carefully laid defenses, leaving him exposed, vulnerable, petrified with fear.

One of the undertakers had called from Miller's Funeral Home. David Slaughter's body had arrived an hour ago from San Francisco. He had died of a drug overdose.

Giuliano's mouth silently formed the word, "Overdose." He had an irrational urge to run and hide. To where? Meade Slaughter would find him; the man wasn't human.

What *was* Slaughter going to do? Would he seek additional vengeance? An eye for an eye?

The more Giuliano thought about it, the less likely it seemed that Meade Slaughter would pursue the matter. Slaughter knew he would be prepared this time. If a shooting war resulted, the repercussions would be felt statewide . . . and in Washington.

No, thought Giuliano. Meade Slaughter won't do anything.

A knock on the door. "Yeah?" yelled Giuliano. He straightened up in the chair.

Louis stepped inside, tall, slender, immaculate in a pinstriped suit, holding a sheaf of papers.

Tony lighted a cigar while his son pulled a chair close to the desk. Puffing the cigar to life, he said casually, "Got a call from Willie at Miller's Funeral Home. Meade Slaughter's kid was brought in last night. Died of an overdose—drugs."

The papers hung above the desk in Louis' rigid hands. "So that was it," he said quietly. "I heard rumors. Drugs! Funny, he didn't seem the type. We were together in grade school for a while; he was a couple of years ahead of me. Got along with everybody. Good-looking guy." Black eyes narrowed in a fine-featured face. "I know how you feel about his father, but I wouldn't wish that on anybody. Drugs! Maybe he got started in Korea. He wouldn't be the only one. He couldn't have been over twenty-eight."

Tony shrugged. "Tough luck. What matters to me is how it'll effect Slaughter's setup. Shouldn't do anything. It's always been a one-man organization. Good managers, but Slaughter's the big honcho."

"Like what we have," Louis said, a smile on his dark face, ignoring the flash of irritation on his father's face. At 26, Louis had a whip-cord toughness that would suit him well in his chosen profession. Some of Tony's employees had been fooled by Louis's slender build and patrician good looks, thinking him an easy mark. They had quickly revised their opinions. "He'll bend, but he won't break," a pit boss had once said. An apt description.

Tony looked at his son through the dense cigar smoke. "You know how I feel about runnin' a business," he said. "Keep it in the family, and there's only one boss. No outside ownership, no banks gettin' their hooks into you." Tony sat back and hooked a thumb toward his chest. "That's why *I* own everything. Your mother got a nice settlement with the divorce, but she didn't get any of the business. You and Mike will get everything when I'm gone, but until then I'm the boss." A heavy look. "With you and Mike married, I've got to keep everything protected. I ain't goin' to be partners with somebody's wife.

"Women!" Tony spat out. "They're nothin' but trouble."

"Everybody to his own opinion," Louis said. He glanced down at the papers on the desk. "We've got more important things to talk about."

"Sure," Tony said. He nodded approvingly. The kid had guts.

For the next hour, they went over the figures on the new Lake Tahoe casino. The foundations had been poured last fall. Framing would begin when the snows melted in the spring. The casino would be a two-story structure with attached single-story motel units angling to the rear like wings.

The talk returned to David Slaughter's death and the Plush Wheels. Tony Giuliano said, "Slaughter's been movin' like hell; everything he does seems to come up roses. He's been lucky—so far."

Tony pointed at Louis. "There's one big difference between the way he and I operate. Know what that is?"

Louis shook his head.

"Money!" Tony exclaimed. "Hard cash. Slaughter has always worked on a short bankroll. He's stretched himself so damn thin his bank account would disappear if you turned it sideways. Luck's all that saved him. Lucky timing. He got into Vegas just before the town started to boom, then he moved out on the Strip when there was no way you could lose."

Tony's fingers drummed a swift tattoo on the desk. "Look at all the trouble on the Strip last year, the Riviera almost goin' under, the Dunes ready to go any time. That deal the other night at the Royal Nevada was crazy. New Year's Eve, the joint's jumpin' and the sheriff hits the cage with a writ. Like pushin' a panic button! Dealers grabbin' chips, bartenders emptyin' cash registers. Some of 'em left IOUs; guess they thought it was the only way they'd get paid.

"The Royal Nevada was bad timing. Just the opposite from Slaughter's. When he bought on the Strip, land was cheap. Could buy it for a song. Hardly any competition. Customers were linin' up before a new hotel was finished. Hell, even when we built the Fantasia in fifty-one, we had to start buildin' extra rooms the day we opened. Everybody did."

Tony stubbed his cigar out in the tray. "I've been lucky, too, but I haven't had to rely on luck. I've got plenty of money behind every move I make. I can roll with the punches. Somebody hits a lucky streak on the tables, I don't have to panic. If Slaughter gets pushed too hard, he's goin' down. Someday, he'll take one chance too many. Think of him like a big building on a little foundation. One big push, he goes over." Tony made a shoving motion. "When the time comes, I'm goin' to be the one to do it."

"Wilbur Clark went in too deep," Louis said. "And the outsiders ate him up."

"Exactly!" Tony replied, slapping the desk top with a big hand. "That's the way the smart boys work. At first, the pigeon wants their dough and ninety percent of the operation. They wait. Pretty soon, he'll take sixty percent. Then forty. The creditors start screamin', and he's goin' to lose everything. He ends up with five percent, and he's happy to get that." Tony Giuliano leaned forward and regarded his son through hooded eyes. "I'm a patient man," he said, voice hardening. "Someday, Slaughter's goin' to push his luck too far, and I'll be there to yank the rug right out from under his feet."

BOOK FOUR

1956-1977

1

Smitty tossed the old sheepskin coat in the booth and sat down across from Meade. Slapping his hat against his leg, he grunted, "Damn rain's runnin' down my neck."

"It's a wonder that old museum piece doesn't collapse down around your ears."

Smitty looked hurt. "There you go again—insultin' my greatest treasure."

Meade looked around the Desert Inn coffee shop. Most of the customers were employees. It was still too early in the morning. Early in Vegas was anytime before ten.

Meade picked up their earlier conversation. "Bill Harrah isn't going to stop with the Gateway. I know he's dickering with Nick Sahati for the Stateline."

"Some think Harrah's crazy," Smitty said. "I think he's crazy like a fox. With the Gateway Club and the Stateline Country Club and that busin' idea, he'll make Tahoe hum."

"Busing," Meade said, shaking his head with admiration. "That's one hell of an idea—a string of Greyhounds running up Highway 50 and dumping a captive audience at Harrah's door. A free ride with the cash and coupons they get back, but I'll bet very little goes back with them. Probably a lot of moaning and groaning on those buses when they roll back down the hill."

"Yep," agreed Smitty. "And before long, they're ready to go back and try again."

"The skeptics argue that most of the busers are retired with just a few bucks to spend, some too broke to do anything but go along for the ride. You can figure that every bus leaves a lot of change in the slot machines. Bill's smiling all the way to the bank."

Smitty looked at Meade slyly. "Bet it makes your ass itch when you think about your thirty acres at South Shore."

Meade grinned. "Funny you should mention that."

"Oh, shit," groaned Smitty. "Here we go."

Meade's smile widened. "Don't you think I ought to get in on a little of the action?"

"A little or a lot?"

"Hell, *all,* if I can get it!"

It was Smitty's turn to grin. "That's what I've always liked about you, Meade. You're so meek and willin' to share."

"Takes one to know one," Meade said pleasantly.

"What you got in mind?" Smitty asked.

"I want to start small, with plans for expansion. A casino with maybe ten table games, a couple of hundred slots. I can keep fifty rooms filled every night in the summer, two hundred probably, but I don't want a lot of empty ones in the off-season. Being right off Highway 50, we'll pick up some travelers, even in the winter."

"Sounds reasonable."

"It's going to take a chunk of money," Meade said, shooting Smitty a quick glance. "You wouldn't happen to know someone with some loose change he might want to loan, would you?"

Smitty studied his fingernails. "Got to pare these things down when I get home," he mused. He looked at Meade, and bared his teeth. "Bank's open anytime. Get your act together and amble over to my place."

David had been buried three months ago. January had been particularly rough on Meade and Gari. Publicly, announcements had to be made, covering up the real cause of David's death. Privately, feelings of guilt had to be acknowledged, reckoned with and laid to rest. Things were slowly returning to normal as March came to an end. To Ann, David was only a fading memory. The man in her life was Meade.

2

The morning after the May ground-breaking at Lake Tahoe, Meade and Gari traveled to the North Shore. They took the long way around, following Highway 89 past Emerald Bay, through Tahoe City and Kings Beach, sitting in the back seat of the Cadillac that had been brought up from Reno's Plush Wheel. Two plainclothes security guards were in the front seat, one driving, the other enjoying the scenery. Meade was taking no chances; he was in Tony Giuliano's territory.

Old habits die hard, Meade thought, his eyes pausing briefly on the two men up front. He glanced at the left side of his coat; it didn't have that barely perceptible bulge anymore. The shoulder holster had gone in the late forties. Like single-owner clubs, it was becoming a thing of the past.

They crossed into Nevada and Crystal Bay, where they bought coffee and doughnuts at a small bakery. A half-mile beyond, Meade had the driver pull off into a heavily wooded area. Through a break in the trees, a wide stretch of sandy beach glittered under the clear blue sky.

Picking up a blanket and one of the bakery sacks, Meade grinned at Gari. "Let's go exploring."

They walked slowly along a narrow path, Meade in his customary black suit, white shirt, string tie and dress boots, Gari in a light summer dress with low sandals on her feet. Rays of sunlight filtered down through the tall pines and created a cathedral-like atmosphere. They were silent until they stepped out on the wide expanse of white sand. "Oh, lovely!" Gari burst out, gazing eagerly at the twenty-mile length of blue-green water. She whirled and looked up at Meade. "Wouldn't it be fun to sail the *Lady Ann* up here?"

"Maybe for you," Meade said, adding with a grin, "You go down out there, you're not coming up. That thing's fifteen hundred feet deep."

"Oh, pooh," Gari retorted, refusing to be baited, folding her arms across her chest and looking back at the lake. Kicking off her shoes, she wriggled her bare feet in the sand. "Come on," she urged, grabbing the blanket and sack out of Meade's hands and setting them on the ground. "Let's go wading!"

"You're crazy!" Meade cried, pointing at the shoreline a hundred feet away. "That water will freeze your toes off. You'll be using crutches the rest of your life!"

Gari spread the blanket. She stood in front of Meade, long legs spread wide apart, a hand on one hip, the other pointing at the blanket. "Sit down and take your shoes off," she ordered. "Your coat, too. You'll look funny enough as it is, wandering around out there."

"Aw, come on, Gari," Meade pleaded.

Gari's eyes were dancing, but she continued to point. "You promised me a fun time on the beach. Are you going to be a spoilsport?"

Meade groaned and sat down. Pulling off his boots and socks, he rolled up the pants to his three hundred dollar suit. "The coat, too?" he asked, looking up at Gari who grinned and nodded. Sighing deeply, Meade stood up and dropped the coat on top of the boots. "Let's go, kid," he said resignedly, taking Gari's outstretched hand. "Don't blame me if we both end up in the hospital."

The water was cold, and they both made appropriate noises when the first wave lapped over their feet. It was soon forgotten, and they walked for nearly a mile in the wet sand. Turning, they headed back toward the blanket.

Meade made an encompassing gesture, indicating the

curve of beach ahead and the dense forest of trees that hid the highway beyond. "Pretty, isn't it?" he said. He pointed toward the trees. "Imagine a cabin up there, maybe a roaring fire, looking out a big plate-glass window at a full moon over the lake."

"Why, Meade!" Gari exclaimed, smiling up into his face. "You're a romantic!" She looked up at the trees wistfully. "Wouldn't it be nice?"

Meade spread his arms. "This is mine, you know."

Gari stopped abruptly, dark hair flying as she turned toward Meade. "Yours? How long have you had it?"

Meade thought a moment. "Twenty years."

"Twenty *years*? Gari's mouth dropped open as she looked up and down the beach. "How big is it?"

"Five acres."

Gari's eyes grew even larger. "Five acres? How could you keep it secret all this time?"

Taking Gari by the shoulders, Meade aimed her toward the distant blanket. "A man's entitled to keep a few things to himself," he said, moving away from the water and cutting across the warm sand. He paused a moment while Gari caught up. So David had never told her. No need to tell her that David knew. He didn't want to spoil her happiness with sad memories.

Gari was excited. "Five acres. From where to where?"

Meade pointed at a tall ponderosa pine. "Starts at that big tree and goes just past that big rock in the lake."

"You could have your own dock!" Gari cried.

"With a sailboat, I suppose," Meade grinned.

"Well . . ." Gari grinned back. "The thought did occur to me."

They reached the blanket and sat down. Gari poured coffee from the Thermos and laid two doughnuts on paper napkins. They were silent for a long time.

Gari was doing some quick calculating. David's mother had died when he was six, twenty-two years ago. Meade had bought the land after that. She was curious but didn't want to pry. She and Meade had always respected each other's privacy. She asked, "What were things like back then—when you bought this land?" She would take the indirect approach.

"Not much different," Meade replied. "Oh, there were less vacation homes, and it wasn't built up around the Cal-Neva like it is now.

"There are plans for development east of here, but it won't affect this place." He wrapped his arms around his knees and stared out over the lake. "Whatever I do here, I want it to fit. I'm not going to bring in bulldozers and make it fit into *my* plans." A long pause. "This holds a lot of memories for me."

"Good ones?" Gari said softly. She knew they were; it was evident in Meade's voice and the look on his face.

Meade looked at the big rock in the lake. Almost a minute passed, and Gari thought he wasn't going to answer. She nibbled on a doughnut, wishing she had minded her own business.

Meade's voice startled her; it had been so quiet. "Good ones," he said. His next words left her holding the half-eaten doughnut suspended in mid-air. "This was going to be a wedding present."

Gari looked at Meade and saw the deep sadness. "Oh, Meade, I'm sorry," she said. "I didn't mean—"

Meade smiled and touched her arm. "You're family. You have a right to know."

Gari swallowed and looked away. Family. Meade had comforted her so many times. Could she comfort him? Would he want her to? She moved a little closer.

"Her name was Sandra," Meade began. He looked at Gari. "Ever hear about her?"

Gari nodded. She had been trying to remember the name. A whisper. "David said she died."

Meade's voice turned suddenly harsh. "She was murdered —a few weeks before we were to be married."

Gari stared, unable to speak.

Meade's eyes softened, and he smiled. "We came up here that summer; I asked her to marry me maybe a few feet from where we're sitting. We swam out to that big rock. Sandra fell in love with this place. I traced the owner. He lived in Oakland and needed money. I didn't tell Sandra I had bought it, meant to surprise her with it on our wedding day."

In a low voice, Meade described that final night on Commercial Row, the car parked in the darkness by the tracks, the lonely wail of a freight leaving Reno, the attack by three men swinging clubs, the horrifying moment when Sandra appeared leaping on an assailant's back, throwing herself across Meade's body, falling soundlessly from the terrible blow to her head. "It was a long time before I looked at another woman," Meade concluded quietly. "For one thing, I spent a long time in San Francisco, learning to walk again." He made a waving motion. "I think it's time I did something with this."

Gari hugged his arm and rested her head against his shoulder. She was crying softly. "Do it," she said fiercely, grabbing a napkin and wiping her eyes. "Build a cabin and enjoy some good times here. That's what she would have wanted."

Meade slipped an arm around her shoulders. Several minutes passed. They watched a motorboat leave Crystal Bay and pick up speed as it headed out into the lake. "You're right," Meade finally said. "We'll get to work on it." He released Gari and pulled his socks and boots on. He stood up and looked around. "Ann will love it here. We'll make it a happy place." He helped Gari up, squeezed her hand, pointed. "A little dock will fit right in, with a sailboat, of course." He grinned at her. "Looks like you've got another project."

3

Nearly a year passed, and the Tahoe Plush Wheel was a month away from opening. Smitty sat in Meade's office at the Strip Plush Wheel and watched the art director and Bob Lakely going over the ad layouts with Meade. "Can you take it from here?" Meade asked. "I've got to run."

"Sure," Lakely said. Meade began throwing papers into a briefcase.

After the press agent and art director had left, Smitty said to Meade, "You're busier than a whorehouse on Saturday night. Does me good to see a man work."

Meade kept on stuffing papers. "Maybe you ought to get off that skinny butt and do a little work for a change," he grunted.

Feeling the back of his jeans, Smitty exclaimed, "By golly, it *is* skinny! Here I was thinkin' I was gainin' weight."

Meade snapped the case shut. "Know something, Smitty? What you need is a good wife—someone to take care of that tender body in its old age."

Smitty looked at Meade like he'd done something that smelled bad. "Meade," he said dourly, "sometimes you come up with the damnedest things! Why don't you just tell me to shoot myself. It's lots quicker and a hell of a lot less painful." Bending down, he picked his hat up off the floor. Clapping it on, he squinted at Meade. "And another thing, I'm not old; I'm not seventy yet."

"How can you get any closer?" Meade demanded. "You've got less than eight months to go."

"That makes me sixty-nine—a very *young* sixty-nine."

They parted at the side entrance. Meade got into the backseat of the Cadillac and rested his head against the cushion. "Let's go to the bank first," he said to the driver.

The third stop was at Tom Bailey's office. Bailey now had a statewide construction company, with several hundred employees. His headquarters was in a new building off Sahara Avenue. After spending a half-hour with Bailey, Meade returned to the car. "That's it," he said wearily. "Back to the shop." He closed his eyes as they pulled out onto Sahara.

"Holy shit!" the driver yelled. Meade's eyes snapped open. He looked out the side window just as a weaving car smashed into the limousine. A tremendous crash and Meade was thrown against the far door. A split second of pain, then darkness.

"Mr. Slaughter, my name is Doctor Jeferies. You've been in an accident. Do you understand?"

Meade blinked his eyes and peered up at the clouded image. He blinked again. The face bending over him took on definition. The doctor had gray hair and wore black horn-rimmed glasses. "I understand," Meade said slowly. "How bad am I?"

The doctor flashed a light into Meade's eyes. "Lucky," he said. "Your driver is down the hall with a broken hip. Looks like all you've got is a mild concussion."

"What about the guy that hit us?"

"Not guy—gal. Not a scratch! Know why she hit you?"

"She hit us on *purpose?*"

"Yep. She had just put her last nickel in a slot machine at the Sahara, had been playing for almost twenty-four hours. Started with dollars and worked her way down. When she lost that last nickel, she ran screaming out of the casino. Got in her car and aimed it at the first car she came to—yours."

"Where is she now?" Meade asked.

"Under observation at the county."

A nurse looked inside. "May I see you a minute, doctor?"

Jeferies called over his shoulder as he walked toward the door, "Be right back."

The door had hardly closed, when the doctor stuck his

head back in. "Do you know a beautiful lady—tall, dark hair, great legs?"

Meade grinned. "Sounds like my mother."

The doctor withdrew, and Gari walked in. She looked quietly down into Meade's smiling face. "Those bandages become you," she said huskily, sitting on the bed and taking his hand. "You big jerk, you scared me half to death. I was in the middle of a meeting when the hospital called. I just jumped up and ran for the door." She laughed softly. "Then I remembered that my shoes were under the desk." She pressed his hand. "Think I'll ever get civilized?"

"You do and you're fired," Meade said.

The doctor returned. "I see your mother found you," he said.

"Mother?" Gari said.

"Little joke between me and the doctor," Meade explained. He looked at Jeferies. "When can I get out of here?"

"If you'll follow my orders, today. Otherwise, about a week."

Meade's eyes narrowed. "What orders?"

"Stay in bed and rest for a week."

"And if I don't?"

"You might do irreparable damage to your brain."

"What brain?" Gari muttered under her breath.

Meade shot Gari a sour look, then said to the doctor, "Okay, I'll take it easy—but not here. Take a walk, girl, I'm getting up." He started to pull the sheet back.

"Hold it, Mr. Slaughter," the doctor ordered. "I said tonight; that's four hours from now. We've got some tests to make first. And you're not walking out. You go out on a stretcher and in an ambulance."

Meade burst out, "That's the dumbest thing I've—"

Jeferies held up a hand. "It's either that or you can stay right here." He appealed to Gari. "This man shouldn't move around for several days. Can you make him understand?"

Looking squarely into Meade's eyes, Gari said, "You bet your ass I can, doctor."

Jeferies smiled his approval. "If you ever decide to be a nurse, look me up," he said. "I like your style."

That night, Gari and Smitty followed the stretcher out to the ambulance. Gari got inside with the attendant. "Nice lookin' nurse you've got," Smitty said merrily.

"See you at the ranch," Meade said.

The heavy ambulance rolled quietly away from the hospital. Bright lights began to flicker. They passed a marquee with Jack Benny's name in huge black letters. "Hey!" yelled Meade. "This isn't the way to the ranch."

Gari smiled at the attendant. "Ignore him," she said. "He gets this way often."

The ambulance turned off the Strip. Blinking in rapid sequence, neon lights depicted a swooping roller coaster, a slowly turning ferris wheel and a whirling merry-go-round. Glaring at Gari, Meade opened his mouth to speak.

Leaning forward, Gari pressed her fingers over his lips. "You're going to my place," she said firmly. "We'll talk about it when we get there."

"Mummf!" Meade continued to glare.

The ambulance stopped, and the rear doors opened. "Welcome to the ranch!" Smitty chortled.

"Traitor," Meade mumbled.

"Grandpa!" cried Ann as they entered the door. "You look like the man on the Dunes!"

Meade laughed and felt the bandages on his head. Maybe he did look a little like the thirty-foot turbaned sultan that stood on the roof of the Dunes Hotel.

Smitty left a little after eight. Gari had to carry Ann to bed. "Can't I sleep with Grandpa?" she yelled as Gari packed her out.

Returning, Gari laid a cord with a buzzer by the bed. She said, "If you need me, push that button."

"Where did that come from?" Meade asked.

"I had a clever electrician hook it into the intercom system."

Meade grinned. "You're a very efficient lady."

"Thank you," Gari said, making a little bow. "Now I'm going to show how efficient I am." With a few swift movements, she straightened the covers, fluffed the pillows and turned out the light.

"Hey!" Meade protested. "I'm not ready to go to sleep."

Gari's voice came out of the darkness. "Oh, yes you are. Pills are on the nightstand. Take two—no more than two— every four hours. Water's in the glass."

"My God, you sound just like a nurse. Did I ever tell you about the one I threw a bedpan at?"

"No," Gari said. "It can wait until tomorrow. 'Night." The door shut softly.

Mumbling to himself, Meade swallowed the pills. Minutes later, he had fallen into a deep, dreamless sleep.

4

"They were for your protection more than anything else," said the doctor as he removed the turbanlike bandages. He cleaned and re-bandaged the deep cut on Meade's forehead. "You're going to have a nice scar there. Not as big as the one on the other side, but pretty impressive. I've got a friend who does great reconstructive work. He can fix your forehead as smooth as a baby's behind. He's in L.A. Want his number?"

Meade shook his head. "I can live with it," he said. "Hell, I'm not entering any beauty contests."

"It's your face," Jeferies said cheerfully, zipping up his black bag. "Take it easy for the rest of the week. You can go back to work on Monday." He glanced at the papers scattered over the bed. "Looks like you're working anyway."

Meade was on the phone when Gari came in. She shot him a disgusted look as she picked up some papers off the floor. When Meade hung up, she grabbed the phone and set it out of reach. "If you don't leave that phone alone," she snapped, "I'll have it disconnected."

"Why don't you go back to work?" Meade grumbled. "Your boss might fire you if you keep skipping out."

Throwing Meade a sour look, Gari muttered, "If he keeps on being such a bastard, I might quit. I've seen a whole new side of you since you moved in here. You—"

"Moved in here!" Meade shouted. "I was shanghaied, dragged by the heels, duped—"

"Shut up, I'm talking. You've been doing all kinds of sneaky things—smoking too many cigars, working when you shouldn't, phoning all over the state, not to mention the way you've subverted Ann." Gari pointed at the connecting door. "Imagine sending a five-year-old child into my room to look for a box of cigars! She was half under the bed when I caught her."

"Well," Meade grinned sheepishly, "she found them, didn't she?"

"Little imp," Gari said, bursting into laughter. "When I dragged her out, she was holding onto the box like her life depended on it." Still laughing, Gari added, "Meade, that was terrible. You're turning my daughter into a criminal!"

They talked for a while, then Gari went back to work. Meade proceeded to smoke five cigars while he wrote notes and made endless phone calls, keeping a sharp ear out for a surprise raid by Gari.

Late that night, Gari sat on the edge of Meade's bed. "That's it," she said, tossing a small notebook to one side. "Another exciting day at the Plush Wheel." She glanced at her watch. "Do you realize it's past eleven? You should have been asleep an hour ago." She started to rise.

Grabbing her wrist, Meade pulled her back down. "I've already had enough sleep for a month," he said. "How about fixing drinks? Bourbon and water for me."

Gari frowned. "I don't know. The doctor said—"

Meade glared menacingly. "Get those drinks, woman. If it kills me, at least I'll die smiling."

Gari's eyes widened. "Well!" she exclaimed, standing up quickly. She hurried out of the room.

Midnight came and went, and they were in a mellow mood, a third round of drinks nearly finished. Gari was quite proud of the way in which she had maneuvered Meade into talking about Sandra. She had avoided any mention of Shirley. There was an air of mystery about her death that she didn't want to probe.

"That was nineteen thirty-six," Gari said. "You mean you've never had a steady girlfriend since?" She was lying on top of the bedspread, propped up against the headboard beside Meade.

Meade stirred uncomfortably under the covers. Had she gone too far? David had told her about Cindy, but the details were sketchy.

"There was one," Meade said at last. "Her name was Cindy."

"Nice name," Gari said, keeping her voice neutral. "What was she like?"

Another long silence. Then, "Blonde, pretty—no, beautiful. She had the bluest eyes you've ever seen. She was an actress."

"When did you meet her?"

"Let's see. Forty-seven. The Flamingo was getting ready for its big grand opening on March first." He grinned. "As opposed to its small grand opening the day after Christmas."

Gari waited, long fingers impatiently tapping the glass balanced on her stomach. "And?" she said.

Meade was still grinning. "Guess who introduced us?"

"Meade," Gari fumed, "will you please get on with it?" She peered at him through a pleasant haze. "Who?"

"Benny Siegel, no less. Bugsy to most of the world."

"Wow!" Gari was properly impressed. "What was she doing with him?"

"She was a friend of Ginny Hill's—Siegel's girlfriend. Well, Benny brought Cindy and Ginny over to the Plush Wheel for a drink. Cindy and I hit it off real good. We went together for a couple of years."

Gari stared down into her glass. She had seen the look on Meade's face. Cindy had been special. Very special. There was a dullness in the pit of her stomach. Was he still carrying a torch? After eight years? What if he was? Why should it matter to her? With one quick motion, she swallowed the contents of the glass. "Didn't work out, huh?" she said, turning her head toward Meade.

The pain in Meade's voice was almost tangible. "She just went away one day and never came back."

"Do you know why?" Gari said in a small voice.

"She left a note, said I didn't love her enough. I knew then that I did, but it was too late." Meade's voice was barely audible.

"Did you try and find her?" Gari whispered back.

"Did everything. Hired a detective agency. She'd just disappeared. She even wrote her agent saying she was getting out of the business."

They lay side by side, taking a great interest in the far wall. A minute ticked by. Another. "I'd better get to bed," Gari said, glancing at her watch. "Almost two. I'll be half asleep on the job."

Meade yawned. "Talk to your boss. Maybe he'll let you come in late."

"Are you kidding? The man's an ogre—goes around beating defenseless women with a whip."

"Hmm." Meade looked up at Gari who was now standing beside the bed. "Goodnight, baby," he said. "Thanks for listening."

"I wasn't being fair," Gari said, looking down at her hands. "I had heard a little about Cindy. I wanted to know more."

Meade smiled. "Well, now you know. Go to bed, girl."

" 'Night." Gari turned out the light and opened the connecting door. "You must have loved her very much," she said.

"Yes," Meade's voice answered in the darkness. "She was quite a lady. That's all in the past now."

It was a long time before Gari went to sleep.

On Thursday, Meade graduated to the living room. That afternoon, Gari returned from the office to find Meade crawling around on the living room floor with Ann on his back. "Look, Mommy!" cried Ann. "Grandpa and me are horsing around!"

Arms folded across her chest, foot tapping the floor, Gari glared down at Meade. "You have absolutely no sense," she said, trying to look angry. "The doctor said a week. That's next Monday, Tuesday to be exact."

"Nothing wrong with my head," Meade said. "See?" He butted his head gently against Gari's legs. "Sound as a dollar."

"*Hard* as one, anyway," Gari replied, stepping back and dropping her hands to her hips. She sat down and kicked off her shoes. "Go ahead; mess up what few brains you have left."

Watching Meade and Ann play, Gari thought of how much he had changed over the years. It was hard to believe that she and Meade had hated each other once; they were such good friends now. Gari had had two brief affairs during the past year, but each time she had caught herself comparing the men to Meade. They had come up sadly lacking.

Lying on his back, Meade was holding Ann high above his head, laughing while she kicked and screamed with delight. Meade was so big, Ann so tiny, one with jet black hair shot with gray, the other with long tresses the color of harvested wheat. Had Ann been his daughter, Meade couldn't have loved her more.

On Friday night, Meade and Gari dined by candlelight. It was a late dinner, and Ann was in bed. The chef at the Lake Room had prepared a lavish meal. A bottle of Dom Perignon rested in the silver ice bucket.

Smiling, Gari raised her glass. "To the indestructible Meade Slaughter. May he go forth to conquer more worlds!"

"I'll drink to that," Meade said, touching his glass to Gari's. He took a long sip, then held the glass toward her again. "To the greatest nurse in the world. The only time in my life being sick was fun!" They laughed and clinked their glasses.

Much later, Meade rose from the living room couch and stretched. "Better get your beauty sleep," he said. "Just think, tomorrow you'll have the whole house to yourself."

Gazing up at Meade, Gari said ruefully, "It's been so crowded with you here. Six bedrooms, five baths, a living room as big as a football field, separate quarters for the housekeeper." She stood and straightened her dress. "I've even considered having Mrs. Hemshield move into the house. This house is built for a *family*, Meade, and a big one at that. Ann and I just rattle around."

Meade looked shocked. "You don't like it?"

Gari smiled and shook her head. "I love it! It's just that it's so awfully big."

Meade gave Gari's chin a squeeze. "You'll find a good man to share it with. Nothing will please me more. You're too much woman to live alone."

Gari regarded Meade for a long moment, a quizzical look on her face. "Think so, huh?" she said.

"Know so," Meade said, kissing her on the forehead and giving her a quick hug. He patted her cheek. " 'Night, baby."

Gari stood by the couch and watched him go down the hall, a big man moving with catlike grace, strong, confident, a solid force in her and Ann's lives. She picked up her shoes and tidied the couch.

In bed, Gari stared at the dark ceiling. Tomorrow, Meade would return to the ranch. Suddenly, she realized how happy she had been the last few days, knowing that Meade would be there when she got home, the long talks they'd had. It struck her like a physical blow. She cared for Meade—not like a daughter-in-law or friend—like a *woman!* It had been there for a long time, teasing her emotions, playing havoc with her mind. Oh God, Gari silently moaned, twisting her hands together, head rolling back and forth, stunned with the revelation, acknowledging that it was true.

She looked at the connecting door. What did Meade feel? She thought about the other night when he had talked about

Cindy. He had loved her; it had been so obvious in his look, the tone of his voice. Could he care again, perhaps even love? Gari hugged the pillow to her breasts. They had become so close over the last three years. Had he been as blind as she?

She considered the problem. There was the subtle approach, workable but not her style. The direct frontal attack could be disastrous, but it would quickly settle matters one way or the other. "Damn!" she burst out softly. Feeling both fright and delicious anticipation, she stared at the connecting door.

5

Meade's sleep had been restless, filled with disquieting dreams.

For the first time in years, he dreamed about Shirley. She was standing at the carnival booth in San Diego, smiling happily with a big panda bear in her arms. Sandra replaced Shirley. She was lying beside Meade on the beach at Lake Tahoe. Meade reached out to take her into his arms. She faded away, and Cindy was riding across a low mountain ridge on Sadie, platinum hair streaming in the sunlight, a sparkling smile on her face as she waved at Meade. He tried to wave back, but his arm wouldn't move. Cindy waved again and was gone.

Then a strange thing happened. Gari appeared and whispered his name. His arms encircled her naked body and drew her close. Her lips touched his. Their tongues entwined, and he seized her firm buttocks.

Meade's eyes flew open. This was no dream! Burrowing closer, Gari punished his mouth with hers. Meade gripped her arms and pushed her away. "Gari," he whispered, "what is this?"

"What do you think it is?" she hissed. "I'm raping you!"

"You're *what?*" Meade spluttered.

"Raping you," Gari repeated. "It would have been better to have talked it over, but you wouldn't have listened to reason."

"*Reason?*" Meade rose on one elbow and looked down at Gari. The covers fell away, exposing her breasts in the soft moonlight. Meade's eyes traveled from Gari's face to her breasts, then back to her face. "This has got to be the—"

"—dumbest thing I've ever heard." Gari finished for him. Looking off to one side, she muttered, "Boy, oh boy," heaving a deep sigh that caused Meade's eyes to drop to her breasts.

With an unsteady hand, Meade pulled the sheet up under Gari's chin. "Where's your robe?" he demanded. "You're going back to your room."

With one swift motion, Gari kicked the covers completely off the bed. "Make me," she dared, glaring up at Meade, arms folded across her breasts, legs pressed close together.

It was hard for Meade to keep his eyes on her face. He made a half-hearted attempt to reach for the covers. "Oh hell," he groaned, lying down and pulling Gari close. "Will you kindly explain yourself?" he murmured into her hair while he caressed her naked back.

Gari's face was buried in his shoulder. "I didn't know how much I wanted you until tonight," she said in a muffled voice. "I've been next door thinking about it for over an hour. I decided that nothing would happen if I waited for *you* to make a move. Boy, that would be like waiting for the Second Coming!" A soft chuckle. "We haven't even had the first coming yet."

Gari tugged lightly at the thick hair on Meade's chest. "I'm glad you sleep naked," she said. "That way, we can get right down to business."

"You awake?" Gari whispered.

"Uh, uh," Meade said, stroking her hair.

"Know something?" Gari said.

"What?"

"That was pretty good."

Meade smiled in the darkness. "That's putting it mildly."

Pushing Meade on his back, Gari looked down into his face. "Lie still," she said, raising her body over his, breasts swinging heavily over his chest. Slowly, she lowered herself down on his engorged penis. As she moved up and down, Meade grasped her breasts, thumbing her nipples to match the beat of her buttocks on his hips.

Drenched in sweat, they worked silently, prolonging the end as long as possible, reveling in the special thrill of this first time together. Gari began to moan and move faster, then Meade gasped as he lost control. With an explosion that reeled their senses, they climaxed together, Gari falling down into Meade's arms, too exhausted to move.

Minutes passed. "Am I too heavy for you?" Gari asked.

"You can stay there all night," Meade said contentedly.

"Mmm."

Later, Gari slipped down beside Meade and rested her head on his chest, throwing a long leg over his stomach. "Oops," she said, reaching down to feel herself. "I'm dripping all over you."

Meade laughed softly. "Drip away."

"Don't you think I should clean up?"

"Not for my sake," Meade said. "I like it—adds to the pleasure."

"Mmm." She gave him a quick hug. "You'd better get some sleep," she said. "I want you to be ready when we wake up in the morning. We've got a lot of making up to do."

"It *is* morning."

"Well, I mean later."

"What about Ann?"

"Tomorrow—I mean this—is Saturday. Mrs. Hemshield gets her up. It's my day to sleep in late." Gari nibbled at Meade's chest. "I locked my door and came in through the connecting one. Locked yours, too." She flicked her tongue over his nipple. "You were a dead duck the minute I came into this room. I was scared, but I was determined to go through with it."

"Know something?"

"What?"

"I'm glad you did."

Gari sighed and snuggled up closer.

6

It was early Monday morning. Meade had not returned to the ranch as planned. Gari's huge rambling home had become a refuge for two people discovering each other after years of acquaintance.

An hour ago, they had gone for a stroll along the golf course, Gari carrying a sack of bread crumbs. With a lake only fifty yards from the house, she had built up a whole new following of ducks. Some were wild, but others had been planted, most of them by Gari in the middle of the night so the neighbors couldn't see her. After all, there was a limit.

Returning to the house hand in hand, Gari rested her head briefly on Meade's shoulder as they approached the pool. That was when Smitty's voice broke the spell.

Smitty was sitting at one of the round metal tables, a cup of coffee in one hand. Leering, the sun glancing off his balding head, he cackled, "I'd volunteer to act as chaperone, but I believe I'm a mite late."

Picking up Smitty's old hat, Gari crammed it down over his ears. "Dirty old man!" she cried as she fled into the house.

Meade tried unsuccessfully to wipe the smile off his face. "Go ahead and say it," he said, sitting down and pulling out a cigar. "I'm a dirty old man, too."

"Don't know about dirty but sure dumb," Smitty said. He

shook his head. "When it came to Gari, I used to wonder if you had an IQ over twenty."

"Think you're pretty smart, don't you?" Meade said, puffing the cigar into life. "Coming here after the fact and acting like you knew all the time."

"Not just me," Smitty burst out, waving his arms expansively. "*Everybody* knew, you fool. Whenever you two got together, the sparks flew so that anybody within thirty feet was endangered. And them looks you gave each other! Enough to make a turtle dove blush. Guess it took a good knock on the head to wake you up."

Meade groaned and drew his hand across his brow. He looked sharply at Smitty. "If you know so much about women, how come you never got married?"

"That's *why* I never got married, sonny," Smitty chortled. He hooked a thumb toward Gari as she approached, carrying a tray. " 'Course, I never had a chance at one like that. Might have changed my mind."

"What's this?" Gari asked suspiciously, setting the tray down on the table.

"Nothing important," Meade said. "Smitty just likes to run off at the mouth."

Smitty lit a cigarette while Gari poured coffee. He grinned at her as she sat down beside Meade. "You're lookin' good, girl," he said, noting the bloom that a weekend of lovemaking had brought to her face. Gari flushed and smiled, the severe lines of her classic features giving way to a loveliness that Smitty had never seen before.

Smitty's eyes dropped to Gari's low-necked dress and the heavy breasts that pressed against the thin fabric. Pursing his lips, he whistled softly. "Say, why don't you go over to the Dunes and look up Major Riddle?" he said. "He did so well takin' them little stickum things off the girls' nipples in that Minsky's Follies last January, he's bringin' the show back in the fall. You join up, and them old geezers will be droolin' in their drinks."

Gari threw her napkin; it floated down limply over the toast.

Still puzzled, even a little frightened at the intensity of their new relationship, Meade and Gari went back to work. They saw each other only once during the day and thought they did well covering up their unsettled emotions. They didn't do well covering up their good spirits, however, and there was much speculation as to the cause.

That night, a high-level conference was held in the middle of Gari's big bed. It was quite informal, with Gari sitting naked, legs straddled over Meade's hips. She squirmed her bottom, still damp from lovemaking.

Meade's hands gripped her slim waist. "How can I be serious when you do that?" he groaned. He looked up past Gari's jutting breasts at her smiling face. "You *are* listening, aren't you?"

"Of course I am." She squirmed some more. "I'm just not sure we're on the same wave length." She looked down into Meade's anguished face. "Okay, I'll be good." She sat down hard, making a small squishing sound.

"Thank you. Thank you very much," Meade sighed. "Now, where were we?"

"In bed?" Gari offered helpfully.

"Woman, will you get serious?" Meade grinned and tweaked a nipple. "Maybe, you'd better get under the covers."

"Nope. I'm staying right here. Say your piece, Mr. Slaughter."

"All right. Let's start with my age. I'm fifty-three; you're thirty-one. That's—"

Gari's long hair cascaded down around Meade's face as she bent over him, eyes ablaze. "I don't ever want to hear that again," she snapped. "Never!" She glared down at Meade, strong hands squeezing his shoulders. "I'm perfectly aware of our age difference. I didn't know I was doing it, but I guess I've been thinking about it for a long time. For sure the last few days."

Gari sat down hard on him, still glaring. "I'm not going to worry about forty years from now. *Today* is what counts, and today I'd rather be with you for a year than spend forty years with a man who can't make me half as happy or give me half the satisfaction you do." Gari yanked at the thick black hair on Meade's chest, making him yelp. "Got that, mister?"

Meade raised a hand to protest. Grabbing it, Gari bit his forefinger. "Not a word," she warned.

Meade looked to see if his finger was still attached. Wiggling it experimentally, he grinned up at Gari. "I got the message," he said. He stroked her breasts. "Want to get married?" he blurted, shocking himself and Gari.

Gari's eyes widened. "Well!" she exclaimed. She shook her head. "I don't think either of us are ready for that—maybe never. Besides," she said, "I've already got your last name."

"So what do we do?" Meade asked.

"You told me what to do the other night—find a good man to share this house with." Cocking her head to one side, Gari smiled. "I'm not sure how good you are, but you're a man. I've learned that first hand."

"Live here?" Meade asked, trying to keep his mind off the clinching and unclinching of Gari's buttocks.

"Why not?"

"People will talk."

"Do you care?"

"I was thinking about you and Ann."

"Forget about me. Ann will think it's the greatest thing since riding her pony in the Helldorado parade. We can't explain it to her now; she's too young. We can do it later if we're still together." Gari eyed Meade thoughtfully. "I'm a one-man girl."

"You mean I have to give up my widow woman?" Meade cried.

"Who? Where?" Gari wasn't sure if he was joking.

"Name's Mabel. Lives in a shack about thirty miles out of town. I take her a sack of groceries once or twice a week. She calls me her stop-and-come market."

"Crumb!" Gari yelled, swatting Meade with a pillow. She settled back down over his hips. "Well?"

"Sounds good to me," Meade said. "When do we start?"

"Right now," Gari said, reaching down to fondle him.

7

"You beat me to the draw, Meade," Bill Harrah said as they walked through the bustling crowd at the opening of the Lake Tahoe Plush Wheel. "We'll both be real busy come Memorial Day." Next week, Bill Harrah's new club would open at Stateline, across Highway 50 and a half-mile south of the Plush Wheel.

"Meade!" cried a booming male voice. "This sure is a hell of a lot bigger than your first opening in thirty-three!"

Meade turned to face Bob Terhune. He recognized the brunette on Terhune's arm as a high-class hooker from Reno. "Bob," Meade said, shaking Terhune's hand. "Don't tell me you came all the way from Washington just for this."

"Sure, why not?" laughed Terhune. "Actually, I had other things to do—pushed dates around so they coincided with yours. Got to keep a perfect record; haven't missed one of your openings yet."

Bob Terhune turned and grabbed Harrah's hand. "Glad to see you, Bill."

"How are things in Washington, Bob?" Harrah said.

"Busy. Runs me ragged sometimes, but I'm still alive and kicking." Bob Terhune squeezed the brunette's arm and winked. "Ask Kathy." The girl's look was less than humorous.

They talked for a while, then Terhune dragged the girl off into the crowd. "It's enough to make a grown man cry," Meade said to Bill Harrah, watching the senator's back. "I've never seen a man go downhill so fast. It's been five years since Janice died. Bob's aged twenty." Meade slashed his hand in a downward chopping motion. "He doesn't just drink, he's a drunk! And the women. I've heard he's developed some strange habits. God, and to think he's representing us in Washington!"

Bill Harrah shook his lean frame. "He's represented Nevada for a long time, Meade."

"Maybe so, but I think we'd better start looking for another man. I just hope Bob keeps a tighter rein on himself back in Washington."

"He's on some big committees," Harrah said. "A lot of people in this state think he's God. It won't be easy to dislodge him."

A smile of genuine pleasure spread across Harrah's face. Following Harrah's gaze, Meade saw Gari approaching with long-legged strides. Wearing a clinging white gown, dark hair tumbling over her shoulders, she swept through the crowd like a ship under full sail.

"Gorgeous," said Harrah, a man who truly appreciated a beautiful woman. "You'd better watch out, Meade. I might hire her away from you. She would be a real asset to my organization."

"Hi, Bill," Gari said, pecking him on the cheek. Harrah smiled when he saw the way she looked at Meade. So much for any ideas about hiring her away from the Plush Wheel.

Gari left, and the two men ended up in Meade's office where they could talk in peace. An hour passed.

"There you are!" The men looked up, startled. "Meade, half the world's out there waiting to see you," Gari said. Stepping inside, she held the door open. "You, too, Bill. A construction type is standing at the bar drinking our champagne. He awaits your presence, something about a door that looks crooked." The curve of a smile. "If you wouldn't make yourselves so indispensable, people might leave you alone."

8

The Tahoe Plush Wheel was a big success, and the summer of 1957 saw it flourish beyond Meade's wildest dreams. Most of the owners at the lake profited, but none came close to the big three at Stateline—the Plush Wheel, Harrah's Club and Harvey Gross's Wagon Wheel. A mile and a half away, Tony Giuliano prepared to double the size of his casino.

Bill Harrah had plans of his own. Having purchased the Nevada Club between his club and the California border, he would remodel and build a $3,500,000 theater-restaurant next year.

Meade was already envisioning a highrise hotel at his lakeshore sight. Years away from reality, it was important to start planning now. Increased residential and commercial growth around the lake had resulted in the formation of the Lake Tahoe Area Council last April. Made up of Nevada and California residents and interested parties, the group would carry out anti-pollution studies and act as coordinators between government entities. It boded ill for the future of large hotels.

Meade strolled through the Vegas Riviera casino with Gus Greenbaum. Labor Day was right around the corner, bringing to an end the summer rush. The dinner crowd had just spilled out of the Clover Room, and the tables were crowded.

Greenbaum stopped to scribble his name on a pad held out by one of the pit bosses. As the pit boss walked away, Greenbaum shot a satisfied look at Meade. "Got a live one in from Texas," he said. "He's signed over a hundred grand in markers this trip. He's good for 'em, too. He gets home, we get paid within a week."

445

"A few premium customers can keep a place going," Meade said, watching the crowd. He grinned at Greenbaum. "I could use some of your contacts."

"Ha!" Greenbaum rapped out hoarsely. "I've seen some of your action. They can come over to my place anytime."

"Speaking of customers," Meade said, "did you see Irv Goldwin last night? That poor son of a bitch was walking around in his own blood, but he wouldn't quit. Left thirty thousand in markers at the PW."

Greenbaum's eyes narrowed. "Yeah, I saw him. He signed some paper here, too."

Meade paused, lighting a cigar. "We'll get our money," he said. "He won't pay as fast as your Texas man, but he'll pay."

Greenbaum passed a few words with a cocktail waitress who had just come out of the pit. Like most of the girls who worked the area around the tables, she was special.

Only the most attractive were given that position. It was not out of the ordinary for a girl to earn hundreds of dollars in tips during a single shift.

The cocktail waitress laughed at something Greenbaum said. He gave her a pat on the rump as she left.

Studying Greenbaum's gaunt frame, Meade wondered how he maintained the combined pace of gambling, booze and women. Greenbaum had had half his stomach removed before returning to run the ailing Riviera. In Las Vegas, his doctor advised a strong narcotic to ease the pain of the cancer that was slowly killing him. Agreeing, Greenbaum became a controlled addict.

Greenbaum glanced up at the long, narrow ceiling mirrors. "The boys will be busy tonight," he said. With sharp-eyed supervisors walking the catwalks and watching the action below the one-way mirrors, cheaters and dealers were kept honest.

They stood in the doorway of the theater-restaurant. Tables were being cleared for the late show. Hooking a thumb toward the stage, Meade said lightly, "What you need is a big name, Gus. Somebody like Mario Lanza."

An asthmatic laugh gurgled up from Greenbaum's chest.

"Sure," he said, measuring Meade with a jaundiced eye. "I'll do that; right after you run him for a couple of weeks."

Meade smiled at the memory of the fiasco at the premiere opening of the New Frontier three years ago. Advance publicity had pre-sold all four weeks of Mario Lanza's run. On opening night, eight hundred people, including over a hundred newsmen, sat in the sparkling new Venus Room and waited for Lanza's appearance. The eight o'clock curtain time arrived, passed; 8:15. 8:30. Every ten minutes, one of the owners would try and explain the delay. The explanations got weaker as time passed. At 9:30, it was announced that Lanza would appear in fifteen minutes. Just before ten, an owner announced, most regretfully, that Mario Lanza had a severe throat condition. He would not appear.

The severe "throat condition" was a bad case of booze and tranquilizers. Jimmy Durante filled in that night and the hotel arranged for stars like Ray Bolger and Gisele MacKenzie to complete the tenor's run. Lanza left Las Vegas the next day.

Meade turned away from the Clover Room. "I think I'll pass on Lanza," he said. "The revue we've got fills our place."

"Broads!" burst out Greenbaum. "That's what people want to see. Minsky's saved the Dunes last year; the show's still packin' 'em in. Bare boobs on ice at the T-Bird, naked Japs over at the New Frontier. The Stardust's only been open two months, and it's in solid. That Lido show 'bout knocked me out the first time I saw it. The French know how to do it right."

"The Trop's bringing in a French show," Meade said.

"They better do somethin'," Greenbaum said. "Imagine Houssels havin' to bring over a shoppin' bag full of money to bail out the cage. If he takes over, they might have a chance. But they'll need the broads, too."

Greenbaum observed the heavy action in the pit. One craps table was surrounded by players and a platoon of spectators. The stick man was pointing and calling off payoffs, the crowd noisily voicing its approval.

Smacking his fist into an open palm, Greenbaum wheezed, "It gets to you, Meade. I tried to stay away from it for a while down in Phoenix. Fought comin' back, but after I got here, it was like comin' home." His shoulders slumped. "It ain't been the same since Davie died last summer. Now, there was a man! With him around, I could stand up to anybody."

Greenbaum's next words were barely audible. "The boys want me out," he said bitterly. His wave encompassed the packed room. "When I came here, the joint was goin' belly up. Now look. We're makin' so much money, we're swimming in it!" Gus Greenbaum's hollow eyes surveyed the room. "I'm not goin'," he said in a low rasping voice. "This is my town, and I'm stayin' here."

Meade had occasion to remember those words three months later. It was the morning of Wednesday, December third. Meade had just arrived at the Riviera for an 11:30 appointment with Benny Goffstein. A strange look came over the secretary's face as Goffstein's voice crackled in her ear. "Go right in, Mr. Slaughter," she said. Her eyes followed Meade as he entered the office and shut the door.

Benny Goffstein was sitting behind the desk, burly frame hunched over, face white. He was staring at the phone. Looking up, he said, "Sit down, Meade." His speech was slow, halting.

Goffstein waved helplessly at the phone. "I called Gus' home in Phoenix a few minutes ago. A cop answered. All he said was, 'The Greenbaums have passed away.' Then he hung up."

Meade's answer was a slow explosion of breath. "Son of a bitch," he whispered.

The *Review-Journal* reported it that afternoon. Last night, Gus and Bess Greenbaum had been murdered, nearly decapitated by deep slashes to the throat. Some of Bess's hair had been yanked out by the roots. The weapon had been one of their own butcher knives.

9

In 1960, Ray Abbaticchio, a former FBI agent and newly appointed head of the Gaming Control Board, produced what was to become known as the "Black Book." The book surfaced to haunt Frank Sinatra in 1963.

The Black Book was nothing more than a loose-leaf binder, the kind seen on thousands of school yards and campuses. It contained eleven mimeographed sheets. Later, Governor Sawyer would add one more sheet, a controversial move that would cost him re-election.

When the Black Book came out in October, 1960, it contained the rap sheets of eleven "undesirable" characters. The joke went around that Abbaticchio stuck names on the wall and threw darts to determine the entries. Whatever the method, one hundred copies were delivered to Nevada casinos. None of the eleven were to be allowed in a casino, given a room or allowed to eat in a restaurant. Any owner who broke that rule would lose his license.

In mid-July, 1963, Sam Giancana, a Mafia leader out of Chicago and a nominee in the Black Book, paid a visit to Frank Sinatra's Cal-Neva Lodge on the North Shore of Lake Tahoe. Phyllis McGuire and her two sisters were entertaining at the Cal-Neva. Giancana moved in with Phyllis. Giancana avoided the casino, but he did receive a visit from his friend, "Frankie." Neither was aware that Phyllis McGuire's chalet was under surveillance by the Gaming Control Board, this as a result of a tip by the FBI.

"Sinatra's goin' to lose his ass," Smitty said. He and Meade were sitting on Smitty's porch, enjoying the cool September evening.

Meade nodded in the darkness. "With the complaint issued, they'll have a full Control Board hearing. If Sinatra shows up, it's going to be hell. That temper of his can blow the thing wide open."

"Life was a lot easier in the thirties," Smitty said, lifting his feet to the rail. "You paid your rent and fees, bought a little equipment—you were in business. If you didn't make it, you crawled out of town with your tail between your legs."

"It's not just the restrictions," Meade said. "It's the money. What we used to build a hotel for won't even pay for the foundation now."

"It's gettin' hard for one man to build a hotel," Smitty said. "If your backers drop out, you're done for. Look at the mess Frank Carroll's in with the Landmark. He shoulda stuck with those apartments and not tried to beat out the Mint with the tallest building in Nevada. It's an ugly son of a bitch sittin' out there half finished.

"You can say the same for the TallyHo. It won't last the year out. Them Loews are crazy, thinkin' they can build a big fancy hotel on the Strip without a casino."

"We can do without any more hotel failures," Meade said. "We're just recovering from that bunch six years ago."

"Hoffa wants to put twenty percent of the Teamsters' money in Nevada," Smitty said.

"We're going to need it. They've already made their presence known, backing that sixteen million for Harolds. Sixteen million! And the Smiths still control the operation."

"That'll seem like peanuts down the line," Smitty said, flipping his cigarette butt over the rail. "People like you and Bill Harrah will have to figure out other ways of raisin' money. Banks won't be able to handle it, and the Teamsters have only so much money to spread around." Smitty shot a speculative look at Meade. "There's a way, but you won't like it."

"Try me."

"Go public."

Yanking the cigar out of his mouth, Meade gaped at

Smitty. "Go *public?* Give up ownership after all these years I've fought to keep it? Are you nuts?"

"Said you wouldn't like it," Smitty chuckled. "It's goin' to take big organizations to handle things in the future. Like Del Webb, even bigger. I think it's a good thing, Webb buyin' the Sahara. That with the Lucky Strike and Mint is a bigger chunk than any one man can handle, not if you want to keep ahead of the competition. Prell and his group did all right, but they didn't have the financial muscle to get into the really big time."

Running a hand over his bald head, Smitty looked at Meade. "Nobody likes to give up part of his business. But if you've got to sell some to raise money, the best way is to go public. As long as you don't sell off control, you're still the boss. Use the new capital wisely, and your fifty-one percent is worth twice as much as your hundred percent used to be."

Meade knew better than to totally reject Smitty's advice. "I'll have to do some thinking about that," he said.

"Do that. The state's already lookin' into it."

"Oh?"

"Yep. It's bein' kicked around in Carson City. It'll be a while before anything's done. They've got to figure out how to bring in outside shareholders without makin' 'em all get licenses."

Meade grinned at his friend. "I ought to be onto you by now. You've always been a jump ahead of everybody else. It's a wonder you're ear isn't full of dirt, you've got it to the ground so much."

"It ain't makin' me any poorer," Smitty said modestly. He pointed a skinny finger at Meade. "Think about it. Think *hard* about it. You can't keep growin' like you are on your bankroll, not even *mine.*" A sly look. "Even if it is substantial. You're goin' to need lots of money to carry out those plans that are rollin' around in your head."

"You're sure bank money won't do it? They're loosening up in their attitude now."

"No way. We're talkin' millions. Not tens—hundreds."

"Come on, Smitty," Meade chided. "That's going a bit far."

"Wrong again, friend. The day's not far off when a hundred-million-dollar hotel will be commonplace. I may be past seventy, but my eyes can still read a column of figures, and my brain knows when two and two make four."

Meade looked out across the field where a herd of Black Angus grazed in the moonlight. He had plans for three of his locations. The Fremont Street club would continue with just routine improvements; it had produced a steady profit for twenty-five years.

He had visions of highrise hotels in Reno and at Lake Tahoe. For the Strip Plush Wheel, he wanted a twenty-, perhaps even a thirty-story hotel with a casino three times as large as the present one. Others were expressing similar dreams. Smitty was right. There would have to be new ways of finding money.

Crushing the cigar stub out under his heel, Meade said, "How long do you think it will take before the state okays casinos going public?"

"Somewhere between five, ten years," Smitty said. "It'll be a big legal hassle, but it'll get done. It's the only way to bring new blood into the state—the kind we want, anyway."

Meade stared out into the darkness.

Reaching down, Smitty poured bourbon into the two glasses beside his chair. Handing one to Meade, he said, "Tell that brat of yours to get out and visit her horse. He 'bout bit my arm off today, hasn't been out of his stall for a week."

Meade smiled at Smitty's reference to Ann as his child. It happened often. Even at home. "I'll give her a jab," he said, adding proudly, "That kid is into everything—plays, parties, even politics. She'll probably run for President someday."

"If looks alone will do it, she'll be a sure winner."

"She's going to be a beauty," Meade agreed. "Worries the shit out of me sometimes. Two more years and she'll be in her teens. The boys will be banging on our door."

Smitty said, "Gari will know how to handle it."

Meade laughed. "Can you imagine some poor kid getting

out of line and having to face Gari? Talk about a fate worse than death!"

"They don't make women like her any more," Smitty said. "She kinda reminds me of an Indian princess I met down in Phoenix once. She was supposed to be descended from the Aztecs." He cast a sidelong glance at Meade. "Ever tell you about her? No? Well, it was back about nineteen ten . . ."

10

Meade sat in the Strip Plush Wheel lounge booth across from the man he had known for almost forty-five years. Bob Terhune had been a strong, virile young man when they first met, burning with ambition, eager to meet life's challenges. Meade had looked up to the older man with a mixture of envy and awe.

There was nothing to envy now. Bob Terhune was 75, but more than age had ravaged his face and body. For fourteen years, he had been moving steadily down a one-way path, plunging headlong toward the oblivion that waited at the end. Strewn along that path were broken promises, misues of political power, sexual excesses and a capacity for drink that had become legendary.

Janice's death. It had started then, Meade thought as he observed his old friend. Bob had loved Janice deeply; it was still difficult for him to talk about her. And he had depended on her strength. The inherent weakness had always been there; Janice's death had merely brought it to the surface.

Local elections were only a few days away. Terhune was stumping for James Steadway, candidate for Clark County District Attorney. Steadway's opponent was leading; it would take Bob Terhune's influence to put him over the top.

Their discussion about the race had been short and angry.

Meade was a member of the opposition. He knew that Steadway had received money and support from undesirable sources. Favors would be returned if Steadway was elected.

"I miss old George Wingfield," Terhune was saying. "He must have gone through millions in his day." A chuckle. "The best stunt he ever pulled was mailing those bricks for the Goldfield Hotel through parcel post. Picked up an error in the rates and found that they were cheaper to mail than ship. George was a cagey one. Had guts, too. He was a credit to the state of Nevada."

"Not much left of Goldfield now," Meade said. "Tonopah either. Wingfield and his group ruled Nevada from Reno for a long time. Bet he never dreamed that Vegas would become the biggest city in the state."

"Me neither," Terhune admitted, lighting a cigarette with shaking hands. "Hell, even the city of Vegas couldn't project the growth. They could have annexed the Strip easy back in the early forties. By the time they woke up, it was too late." Finishing the drink, Terhune waved for another round.

Turning back to Meade, he said, "I dropped by the Fantasia yesterday. They're going to fifteen stories next year. Louis Giuliano and I had lunch together. That boy's done well since he took over. He's got a lot on the ball, not hot-headed at all like his father. They work okay together, but it's mostly long distance. Tony doesn't get down here once a month, if that. I'm sure that suits Louis. Tony'd be on his back every second if they were closer together."

Terhune waited until the girl had replaced their drinks and left. Leaning forward, he said in a low voice, "I'm glad I was able to step in between you and Tony. You've learned to live together. That's good. There's plenty of room for you both in the state."

Downing half his drink with one swallow, Terhune continued, "Remember when I came down to San Diego and asked you and Charlie to move to Reno? Hell, I told you guys to stay there in nineteen-twenty! Was I wrong?"

Meade smiled. "I don't know about the first time," he said,

"but you were right in thirty-one. We should have jumped right then."

Terhune stared down into his drink. "Charlie—God rest his soul—was a stubborn bastard, worse than a Missouri mule. But when he made up his mind, he went all the way."

Laughing, Meade said, "He took to Reno like a duck to water. He was out of those old cowboy duds like they were full of lice. The chewing tobacco went out the window right behind them." Meade shook his head. "I miss Charlie. He was the only father I ever had."

Sadness filmed Terhune's eyes. "We're burying all our friends, Meade. I'm afraid to look at the obituaries anymore."

They were silent for a long minute, lost in private memories. Meade lit a cigar, then asked, "How do we look back in Washington these days? That damn Black Book and Sinatra's troubles have made Nevada a ton of headlines."

Catching the cocktail waitress' attention, Terhune made a circling motion in the air. "One more, then I've got to run," he said. A lewd wink. "Got some ashes to be hauled."

Ten minutes later, Meade watched his friend weave out of the Plush Wheel lounge. Turning for one last wave, Bob Terhune disappeared into the crowded casino.

11

She was a stunning woman with an aristocratic bearing. Max Verdon wondered about her heritage. How in hell had she gotten in *this* business? A mental shrug. It took a classy dame to pull down her kind of money.

Dropping her mink stole on the bed, she turned toward Verdon, the low-cut dress revealing full breasts and a spectacular figure. Moving toward Verdon with catlike grace, she asked, "Will I do?" She arched an eyebrow and mocked him with a smile.

Eyes roaming the tall lovely girl from head to toe, Verdon nodded slowly, the hint of an answering smile on his face. "You'll do," he said in a dry western voice. He waved toward a chair. "Let's talk a few minutes. Your client will be here in about a half-hour."

Seated across from the girl, Verdon said, "You've come recommended as the best." She acknowledged the compliment with a slight dip of the head. "You're not only supposed to be the best in there," he continued, nodding toward the bed, "but you're supposed to be the best up here." He tapped the side of his head.

"Bryn Mawr, '61," she said pleasantly, adding, "Top of the class."

Verdon thought the world had run out of surprises. "How come this?" he asked, glancing around the room.

"Money," she said brightly, flashing even white teeth. "Money and the independence it buys. I like being my own boss. Two, three more years of this, I'm leaving a rich woman. Any decisions I make after that will be the result of deliberation, not desperation."

"I'll be damned," Verdon said admiringly. "Know something? I think you'll make it!"

"Thank you, Mr. V.," she said, dipping her head once more.

Verdon got down to business. "You'll probably recognize your client. He's Senator Terhune; they don't come any bigger politically in this state."

The girl nodded. "I read the papers." She combed her fingers through her long black hair.

"What I've got to say," Verdon said, "you won't read in the papers. I've been with Senator Terhune for twenty-five years, been his right-hand man for twenty. He's a great man." A pause. "But he's getting old. He drinks too much and has picked up a few bad habits. That's where you come in."

There was no expression in the girl's large dark eyes.

Verdon stirred uncomfortably under her frank gaze. He said, "Mary said you can handle any situation, so I'm trusting you. For all I know, the sex might not be much—maybe nothing. The senator's a shadow compared to what he used to be. Keep him happy. He's got a big job to do tomorrow. We need him in top shape."

"He doesn't go in for rough stuff, does he?" the girl asked quietly. "I won't be any part of that."

Verdon shook his head. "No S & M. That's the least of your worries. He'll be a pussy cat."

Verdon handed the girl his card. "My room number's on the back. Call me as soon as you leave. I'm just down the hall."

A short time after Verdon left, Bob Terhune arrived. "My God," he exclaimed, holding her at arm's length, "you're beautiful!"

"I'm glad," she said, smiling up into his face. "I want everything to be beautiful for you tonight." She took him by the hand and led him to the couch. Stepping behind the tiny bar, she said, "Bourbon all right?" Terhune smiled his acceptance as she knew he would; Max Verdon had supplied the bottle. Mixing a weak martini for herself, she carried the drinks to the couch and sat down beside Terhune.

Taking a long pull on his drink, Terhune stared at the girl. "I can't get over how beautiful you are," he said.

Running her hands over her tight-fitting black dress, she said softly, "I can get more beautiful whenever you want."

"Later," Terhune said, patting her hand. "I'm in no hurry. Are you?"

She pressed his hand. "I'm yours for the night. There's no rush at all."

Sinking down into the cushions, Terhune held out his glass. "How about a refill?"

Returning with the drink, she kicked off her shoes and knelt beside the senator. "You look uncomfortable in that coat and tie," she said. "Want to take them off?"

"Sure," Terhune said. She helped him with the coat, then

removed the tie. Terhune smiled and patted her head. "Good idea! I feel better already."

For the next hour, Terhune drank steadily while he talked. It was a confused, rambling soliloquy, words coming in short, disjointed bursts. As his head began to nod, the girl unfastened the buttons on his shirt and began to play with his nipple.

"You're very persuasive, my dear," Terhune said, reaching out to fondle her breast.

The girl moved closer, lifting out a breast and thrusting the nipple into Terhune's mouth. He sucked noisily while kneading the other breast through the thin fabric of her dress. Moaning, Terhune made himself more available. She stripped his pants and underwear down to his knees.

Terhune lifted his face from her breast. "Put on a show for me," he whispered hoarsely. "It'll work. I know it will," he added desperately, struggling to remove his pants. With her help, he was soon stripped, rubbing his crotch. "Bring that chair here," he said, pointing.

She placed the chair directly in front of him.

"Take off your dress," Terhune said. "Just the dress." He pointed at her three-inch spike heels. "Put those on."

Stepping into the shoes, she unzipped the clinging dress and dropped it over the back of a bar stool. Bob Terhune's greedy eyes took in the black lace panties and silk stockings held up by a frilly garter belt, the taunt breasts hanging free and inviting.

"Come here," he said gruffly. She faced him while he ran a hand over her soft pubic mound. Briefly, he explored the cleavage between her legs.

"Turn around," he panted. "Bend over the chair so I can touch you from behind."

Bending over, she thrust her buttocks in Terhune's face. Sweat broke out on his forehead as he ran his hand over her tight bottom. Spreading her legs, he felt around her crevices. His hands were shaking as he drew her panties down. She lifted her feet one at a time as he removed the panties from around her ankles.

Breathing hard, he spread her buttocks and examined her anus. He explored it with his finger. Drawing her closer, he ran his tongue around the inside of her thighs, then drove it deep inside her body. He flicked it around, then withdrew and licked her buttocks, finally her anus. Again and again, he teased it with his tongue.

Looking back between her legs, the girl saw that he was growing. She didn't have to simulate pleasure as she moved her body to the rhythm of his tongue. He was an expert at oral sex.

His face still buried in her buttocks, Terhune fumbled inside his coat, pulling out a large dildo which he slipped inside her vagina. He continued to lick her anus while he worked the dildo in and out, slowly at first, then faster and faster. She began to moan loudly. As her body began to move more violently, Terhune masturbated, increasing the tempo to match her movements.

Suddenly, the girl shuddered and cried out, gripping the chair and jerking her bottom eratically. Even as she climaxed, she continued to watch the frenetic movements of Terhune's hand. A blur of motion, then the engorged head began to spurt a stream of semen. Sinking down into the cushions, Terhune gasped. The girl knelt beside him. Neither spoke for several moments.

Looking at the shining dildo on the floor, then at the girl, Terhune said tiredly, "You liked it, didn't you?"

"Oh, yes!" she breathed. "It was wonderful!"

"The night's not over yet," he said, playing with her nipple.

She stripped completely, and they lay on the bed. Terhune drank and talked, absently feeling her breasts, the inside of her thigh, the lips of her vagina. His voice dropped off, words slurred, barely audible. Eyes closed, he asked sleepily, "What's your name?"

Turning her head on the pillow, she said, "Janice."

There was no way she could react in time to protect herself. Like a raging bull, Terhune leaped up and drove a fist into her face. She screamed and rolled off the bed.

With an agility that belied his age, Terhune scrambled down beside her and seized her hair. "Don't ever use that name around me, slut!" he raged, banging her head into the carpet. He smashed an open palm across her mouth. Blood ran from broken lips.

She tried to crawl away. Terhune dragged her back by the hair. Eyes glazed with madness, he rained blows on her face and head. The girl screamed but to no avail; Las Vegas hotels were soundproofed for maximum privacy.

The blows stopped, and Terhune's hands closed around her throat. Lying on her back with Terhune astride her hips, she read the terrible intent in his eyes. He intended to kill her.

Desperately, she looked around. A heavy lamp lay by her head; it had been knocked off the nightstand in the scuffle. Head swimming, vision out of focus, she reached for the lamp. Her fingers closed around the slender neck. With dwindling strength, she drew it closer. A moment of panic when the wall plug refused to release the cord. She tugged harder, and it came loose.

Preparing to swing the lamp, she knew she had only one chance. If she failed, she would die.

Terhune grunted with effort as he increased the pressure on her throat. Rolling the lamp behind her, the girl grasped it with both hands. Drawing her lips back over her teeth, she brought the lamp crashing into Terhune's face. He cried out and rolled off her body.

The girl knelt on the carpet, drawing deep breaths, the lamp still in her hands. Terhune faced her, hands flat on the floor, face dripping blood. Snarling like an animal, he launched himself at her, reaching out to grasp her body. She raised the lamp and smashed it down on his head. With a strength born of madness, he clawed at her belly, trying to topple her on her back. Again and again, she struck his head. Then it was over, Terhune's head lay in her lap, his hair a mass of blood.

With a scream of terror, she threw down the lamp and

pushed Terhune's lifeless body away. Backing against the wall, she stared unbelievingly at the bloody remains. Reality crashed down like a clap of thunder. She had killed a man. Not just any man. She had killed a United States Senator. She bit her knuckles and tried to think.

She thought of her lawyer; she kept him on retainer in case of arrest. No, he couldn't help her with this. Could anyone?

The senator's aide! She dashed to where her purse lay beside the couch. The contents spilled on the floor. Kneeling, she sorted through the scattered items. With a sharp intake of breath, she picked up the business card. She looked at the phone; it was on the nightstand beside the senator's body.

Approaching the bed from the opposite side, she crawled across and pulled the phone as far away as she could. Lying on her side, she gave the operator the room number.

Max Verdon answered on the second ring. "Are you alone?" she whispered.

"Yes," he said. "Who is this?"

"You left your card with me. Remember?" A sob escaped her throat.

"What is it?" Urgent now.

"Oh God," she moaned. "It's terrible!"

"Speak up!" he snapped. "What's happened?"

Her voice was a half-scream. "He's dead! He tried to kill me, and I killed him!"

The line hummed. "Are you there?" the girl asked.

"I'm here," Verdon said in a hollow voice. "Don't move. Don't do anything. I'll be there in thirty seconds. I've got a key. I'll let myself in."

Eyes glued to the door, the girl curled up in a fetal position, hugging the phone to her breast, the stench of death rising from the floor on the other side of the bed.

12

"Janice was his wife," Max Verdon said, sitting on the bed and staring down at Bob Terhune's body. He looked at the girl. "It was your misfortune to have the same name. He worshiped her when she was alive; I think even more so after she died." Verdon studied the girl's battered face. "Go clean up," he said gently. "Bring some extra towels. We'll talk then."

The shower started running as Verdon walked to the bar and picked up the ice bucket. Returning to the bed, he paused and looked at the body of the man he had served so long. Bob Terhune had already been finished in Washington; his excesses had ruined him for another term. He was just through a little earlier than planned.

The girl approached the bed carrying several towels. She made no attempt to hide her nudity. There were long scratches on her belly, droplets of blood seeping out and running down into her pubic hair. "Lie on your back," Verdon said. He laid a towel across her stomach to stanch the blood. With another towel, he made an ice pack. "Hold this against your face," he told the girl. She pressed it over an ugly bruise, never taking her eyes off Verdon's face.

Gazing around the room, Verdon considered the problem. Fifty years of age, he had weathered many political storms with a keen native shrewdness. He had been in binds before, but nothing like this.

He looked down at the girl; her large dark eyes stared back. "It's not easy to think right now," he began. He patted her arm. "I need your help. Most of it will be listening." A reassuring smile. "I do my best thinking out loud." Moving her torn lips, the girl tried to smile back. "Good!" Verdon said, pressing her arm. "We'll work something out."

Pulling on the lobe of his ear, he continued, "Next Tuesday's election day. Senator Terhune's backing was essential for Steadway to become D.A. Certain parties are interested in seeing Steadway make it. They've spent a lot of money. If necessary, they'll spend more." Verdon waved a hand toward the opposite side of the bed. "If this comes out, Steadway won't make dog catcher. Understand?"

"Yes," whispered the girl.

"I've got some ideas. Before I talk to those interested parties, I need to get your feelings. Okay?"

A quick nod.

Holding up his hand, Verdon pulled down a finger. "One, this has to look like an accident. We'll find a way.

"Two—and this is the part you're not going to like—you have to leave town."

No reaction. The dark eyes were staring at his hand now.

"Three, I think we can arrange some kind of payment for your silence. You're a smart girl. After you get over the shock, you may start thinking a smart lawyer can get you off. Maybe he can, but you'll get roughed up in the process. Follow me?"

Another quick nod.

Pursing his lips, Verdon studied his fingers. "That's it—for now, anyway." He touched the girl's hand. "You've got a tough two hours ahead of you. It's going to take at least that long for me to get things squared away. You've got to stay here alone; that's our only guarantee that no one will come in. Understand?"

"Yes," she said, voice stronger now. "I can handle it."

"Good!" Verdon said, smiling and squeezing her hand. "I knew I could count on you." His daughter and this girl were about the same age, but that's where the comparison ended. This one had guts, no doubt about that.

After Verdon left, the girl double-locked the door. Still in a daze, she gathered her belongings and carried them to the bed, averting her eyes from the sheet-draped body. Dressing, she went into the bathroom and tried to cover the facial damage with makeup. There was no way she could pass a close inspection.

She waited on the couch, flipping through a Las Vegas entertainment magazine. Little registered; her mind was in a whirl.

A soft knock. Edging up to the door, the girl called, "Who is it?"

"Verdon."

Stepping quickly inside, Verdon leaned against the door. "Take all your things and wait in the bathroom," he said. "Don't come out until I tell you."

As soon as the bathroom door closed, Verdon looked out into the hall and waved. Two men entered wheeling a large clothes hamper. Locking the door, Verdon hurried to help.

Terhune's body and the damaged lamp were loaded into the hamper. Verdon tossed the bottle and glasses into the grisly load. His eyes swept the room. Spotting the dildo at the base of the couch, he added it to the collection, then the towels, sheets and pillowcases from the bed.

Moving to the bathroom door, he knocked. "Just open the door enough to talk." The door cracked open, one huge eye peering at him questioningly. "Give me all the dirty towels and washcloths," he whispered. Moments later, she handed him a damp bundle, then closed the door.

Verdon threw the towels into the hamper. The two men topped off the load with a pile of dirty laundry and left. Locking the door, he knocked on the bathroom door. "You can come out now," he said.

The girl found Verdon emptying a large box on the couch, stacking sheets, pillowcases and towels on a chair. Looking at the girl as he removed a bucket and cleaning materials, he said, "Feel up to helping?"

"Of course," she said quietly. "What do you want me to do?"

"Clean up the bathroom and put fresh towels on the racks."

She was hanging up the towels when Verdon came in and

filled the bucket from the bathtub faucet. Going back out, he began to scrub the carpet by the bed. Her work done, the girl sat on the couch. "This is where it happened?" Verdon said, glancing up. "Right here?"

She nodded wordlessly.

Cleaning the bucket, Verdon returned the cleaning material to the box. "Okay," he said, "let's make the bed. That should do it."

They worked silently. Standing back, Verdon surveyed the room. "Looks good," he said. "We'll give it a once-over, just in case."

Moving to the girl, he lifted her chin and studied her face. "You'll have to lie low for a while," he said. "We don't want any questions about those marks." Taking her elbow, he led her to a chair. He sat down and ran a hand through his brown wavy hair. "Shit!" he exclaimed. "Was it just six hours ago when we were sitting here? Seems like a year."

Verdon closed his eyes for a moment, then looked around the room. "This room's in my name," he said. "I've got another one down the hall." A pause. "I've got to keep this room for a few days. We can't take a chance that we might have missed something, maybe left a spot or two that might raise questions. The best solution would be for you to stay here."

The girl's eyes widened. "Don't worry," Verdon continued, shaking his head. "I'm not going to put you through that. I'll take this room; you can have mine." He pointed at the box. "I've got to get rid of that. We'll stop by my room on the way. While I'm dumping it, make a list of things you'll need for the next three, four days. I don't want to go near your home, so give me sizes for clothing."

An hour later, Verdon had removed his things from his room and left with the girl's list. He returned the next morning with several packages. "I probably won't see you until tonight," he said. "Whatever you do, hide your face when a maid comes in or food's brought up. Wear those big sunglasses and that floppy hat. They'll help."

The girl tried to sleep. She woke around noon and turned

the radio on. The hourly news was filled with the story of Senator Bob Terhune's death. He had driven his car off an embankment and crashed into a deep canyon. Death was instantaneous from severe head injuries.

Verdon dropped by that night. "I'm being run ragged by every goddamn newsman in the country," he said tiredly. "It'll be several days before we can complete our business."

Four days later, the girl drove her Pontiac convertible out of Las Vegas and toward Arizona. With luck, she would reach Chicago by Sunday.

In the trunk was a zipper bag filled with $50,000 in used bills. That, added to the sizable sum she had saved, brought her within range of the financial goal she had set when she arrived in Las Vegas a little over a year ago.

She left behind a signed statement, detailing what happened last Thursday night. Steadway's backers had insisted on it; if she signed, they would pay. The girl knew that her life meant nothing to the kind of men who supported Steadway. With Verdon's help, she was being offered an attractive way out. She signed and was on her way within hours.

All across Arizona, she kept her radio tuned to a powerful Las Vegas radio station. As she neared the New Mexico border, she heard the satisfactory news that Steadway had lost badly in his bid to become Clark County D.A.

13

"Our Father Who Art in Heaven, Howard Is Thy Name."

It was said in the spring of 1967 that a fisherman out early one morning on Lake Meade happened to glance up just as Howard Hughes walked by.

Nevada governor Paul Laxalt happily announced that

Howard Hughes had put the "Good Housekeeping Seal of Approval" on Nevada gambling.

The *New York Daily News* reported that Howard Hughes had moved to Nevada to drive out organized crime.

"That son of a bitch is goin' to buy up everything in Nevada!" Tony Giuliano exploded, jabbing his cigar at Louis as they walked around the huge Fantasia Hotel casino.

"The more he buys, the better it is for us," Louis said. "Premium customers are leaving the DI and Sands in droves."

"Why not? That fuckin' Maheu is runnin' 'em like I.B.M. No more free booze, no compin' rooms and food, no broads. He's committin' suicide."

"Hughes came here with over four hundred million net from that TWA sale," Louis said. "That'll buy a lot."

"It's hard to turn down a man with that much cash," Tony Giuliano said. "Bill Harrah did. He turned down forty million."

"Money isn't everything to Bill," Louis said. "He likes to build things, probably gets more kicks out of watching things grow than checking his bank balance. Look at that automobile collection. And who would have imagined a five-hundred-seat showroom in downtown Reno?"

"Now Harrah is going to match our highrises."

"Twenty-four stories—just like the Sahara and the Dunes. Remember the big fuss when the Riviera built nine? Shit, that Sahara tower makes it look like a toy!"

"I hear Hughes is dickering to buy Harolds," Louis said.

"So have I. They'll probably sell now that Pappy's dead."

"I wonder if Hughes has approached Slaughter. His setup would be a nice plum."

Tony shook his head. "A waste of time. Slaughter's got the same idea as Harrah—go public."

Louis stopped and stared at his father. "Where did you get *that?*"

Tony Giuliano's eyes were hooded. "I've got people in the right places."

Louis didn't ask. His father's spy network was a closely

guarded secret; he had paid informants everywhere. Undoubtedly, someone was watching him.

"Going public is the number-one topic around here," Louis said.

"It's the only way out for Slaughter," Tony said. "The way he spends money, he could bankrupt the Bank of England."

"He's making money," Louis said cautiously. "I know several casinos that are thinking about going public, but they're small time compared to Slaughter. He's got ambitious plans."

"Like another Lear jet?" Tony sneered.

Louis shrugged. "It's a charge-off. He uses it to commute up and down the state. It's a classy way to bring high rollers in."

Tony stared at his son. "Remember what I said about Slaughter gettin' in too deep? I've got a gut feelin' this is it. If he goes public, he'll go nuts with all that dough and borrowin' power. He can go just as broke with a big bankroll as he can with a small one. Only difference, he'll come down a hell of a lot harder."

Louis considered his father's words. The old man was tightfisted. Was he also shortsighted? Had his hate for Meade Slaughter affected his reason?

Louis thought of his father still living in that old house in Reno. Tony wouldn't part with it; he had been born there. Louis had been shocked when he had dropped by last fall, his first visit to the house in years. The drapes were shabby, and there was a spot worn completely through the upholstery on the couch. When Louis voiced his disapproval, Tony argued that he was seldom there. When he was, the worn surroundings made him feel "comfortable."

While Tony Giuliano was content to move slowly, Howard Hughes was not. His Nevada empire grew until the man in the ninth floor penthouse of the Desert Inn owned six Las Vegas gambling properties—the Desert Inn, Sands, Frontier, Castaways, Silver Slipper and Landmark. He made one Northern Nevada purchase—Harolds Club in Reno.

Howard Hughes spent $300 million in Nevada buying hotels, a TV station, an airport, large pieces of land on the Strip, 30,000 acres of desert near Las Vegas and scores of mining claims.

If Hughes had had his way, he would have owned even more hotels. He tried to buy the Dunes, but negotiations fell apart. After five months of bargaining, Robert Maheu and Moe Dalitz shook hands on a deal that would see the Stardust, the biggest moneymaker in Nevada, go to Hughes for $31 million. Fearing that Hughes was forming a monopoly in the state, the U.S. Attorney General blocked the deal. It was a humiliating defeat for Hughes, a man whose ego was more alive than his wasted body.

For Moe Dalitz, it was a blessing in disguise. He sold the Stardust to Parvin-Dohrmann, owners of the Fremont, for $41 million. Thus, Moe Dalitz bowed out of active ownership on the Strip. His investments were varied, however, and his presence continued to be felt in Las Vegas.

On the night of November 25, 1970, Howard Hughes was spirited out of Las Vegas and flown to the Bahamas. Two days later, Robert Maheu was fired. The Hughes Nevada empire remained intact but with new leadership and an absentee owner who lay in a darkened room brooding on the millions he had lost in his gambling ventures.

Gambling clubs aren't run like General Motors. Fancy college degrees and government agency backgrounds mean nothing in a casino. In their blindness, Hughes's managers dismissed men who had learned their trade in Cleveland, Nashville, Detroit, Chicago, Miami and Minneapolis, not to mention the struggling clubs in Nevada's earlier days.

Summa replaced these gambling veterans with ex-IRS and ex-FBI men who frightened away the high rollers and failed to spot the cheaters who descended on their casinos like vultures to a feast. In time, certain naïve executives were replaced with hard-eyed men who gradually put the operations back in the black.

Many of the political and civic leaders who had welcomed Howard Hughes to Nevada in 1966, were now bitter that he

had left. They announced that he wasn't wanted back. Some
threatened to try to revoke his gaming licenses.

Forgotten was his purchase and completion of the Landmark Hotel, the thirty-one story concrete and reinforcing bar
skeleton that had blighted the skyline east of the Strip for
nearly seven years. Forgotten also was his purchase of the
Frontier Hotel, which as the New Frontier had closed in
1965 after years of failures and revolving ownership. Bankers
Life, the mortgage holder, had torn down the New Frontier
and was preparing to open the new 500-room Frontier in July
of 1967 when Hughes purchased the hotel.

Howard Hughes's motivation had been selfish, but Nevada
benefited. Property values skyrocketed, and for the first time
major U.S. corporations gave Nevada gaming serious consideration. Many considered this as miraculous as walking on
water.

14

It was silent in the office except for the turning of pages and
the scratching of Meade's pen. The light shone down on his
gray hair as he bent over the legal documents. Two well-
dressed men sat across the desk. A third stood beside Meade,
turning pages and pointing where he should sign.

Slouched on the couch, Smitty watched the proceedings.
From time to time, the men would glance his way, wondering
what part he had in the ceremonies. Smitty had slipped in
while they were explaining the papers to Meade. There had
been no introductions; Meade had acknowledged Smitty with
a quick glance and a nod.

The man standing beside Meade said, "That's it, Mr.
Slaughter." He glanced at his watch. "Your stock should be
trading now." Reaching into his slim briefcase, he took out

a check and laid it on the desk. "That concludes our business." He held out his hand.

Meade rose and shook hands with each of the men. As the door closed behind them, Meade said to Smitty, "What are you grinning about, you old goat?"

"Was I grinnin'?" said Smitty, a look of puzzlement on his face. He scratched his bald head. "Maybe I was. Suppose it had somethin' to do with that piece of paper on your desk?"

Meade waved the underwriter's check for $10,764,000 at Smitty. "Maybe I should use some of this to buy you a rich widow lady."

"A nice piece of land will do," Smitty said. "Beats a woman anytime. Lays there real quiet like and makes money."

That night, Meade raised his champagne glass and said, "To Nevada Investments. May the rich get richer!"

The candlelight flickered over their faces as they sipped from the long-stemmed glasses. Ann held her's up. "Are we supposed to throw these in the fireplace?" she asked.

"Don't you dare!" Gari cried. "They cost a fortune."

"With your loot, what do you care?" Smitty said. He raised his glass to Ann. "To the most beautiful millionaire in the world!"

Ann turned her big violet eyes on Meade. "Is it really true?" she breathed. "I'm a millionaire, or esse, or whatever?"

"If everything goes right," laughed Meade, "you'll be worth twice that in a few years."

"Wow!" bubbled Ann. "I can buy any man I want!"

Shaking her head, Gari said sorrowfully, "She's just set the women's movement back a hundred years."

Meade quietly observed his "family." The years had been good to Gari. At forty-six, she was still a dynamic, beautiful woman, turning men's heads wherever she went.

Ann was a blond version of her mother, with a cast to her features that reminded him somewhat of Shirley. Ann had inherited so much of Gari—the way she held her head, her tall slim figure, her quick lively mind. Meade smiled. Ann had done well in the mammary department, too, not as spectacular as her mother, but very impressive indeed. Next year, she would turn twenty-one. Meade didn't want to think about it.

Gari raised her glass. "I have a special toast," she said softly, eyes shining. "To Uncle Charlie, the man who made Ann a rich girl."

"Amen," Meade said. They drank their champagne silently.

Meade glanced at Smitty. He was 84. Had Charlie lived, he would be 85. The years had passed so quickly. Meade thought of his own age—68. So much had been accomplished, so much yet to do.

Certainly, Charlie had never dreamed that the $100,000 he left Ann would be worth a million before she was twenty-one.

Last year, on October 27, 1971, Bill Harrah had been the first to sell gaming stock on the New York Stock Exchange, offering 450,000 shares to the public at $16 a share.

Now, it was Meade's turn. Today, Nevada Investment's initial public offering of 650,000 shares came to market at $18. The underwriters had distributed a "Red Herring" prospectus three weeks ago, turning the stock into a hot issue nationwide. Long before closing this afternoon, the issue was over-subscribed and closed at an asking price of 22⅜ in the over-the-counter market.

After taxes, Meade would net about $8 million from the check he had received from the underwriters this morning. With it, he would make investments and launch some of the projects he had in mind.

More capital would be needed over the coming years. The prestige and power of a public corporation would help obtain long-term loans. Growth, stock splits and accompanying increases in value would allow Meade to sell additional stock and still retain control.

Control was everything. With the sale today, he still retained eighty percent of the corporation. When he had watched the sign go up on the Fremont Street club in 1938, he had vowed that the Plush Wheel would never be lost to him again.

Ground would be broken this spring for a fifteen-story hotel at Lake Tahoe. A highrise hotel was planned for Reno on Sierra Street, behind where the present club now stood. The old club would remain even after the new hotel opened.

In three to four years, Meade hoped to erect a thirty-story tower on the Strip. The plans were already drawn with a projected twin tower rising beside it. The new hotel would compete with the MGM Grand, which would open next year with 2,100 rooms.

Kirk Kerkorian had started the trend toward huge hotels when he opened the International on Paradise Road in 1969. He then sold it to the Hilton chain, along with the Flamingo, which he had purchased in 1967 as a training ground for the personnel who would take over the International. The Bonanza was presently serving in a similar capacity while Kerkorian's MGM Grand was being built next door.

Gari *pinged* her finger against a glass. "Ann has an important announcement to make," she said. "She wants you all to be the first to know."

Meade's jaw dropped. "You're not getting married!"

"No," Ann said sweetly.

"You're pregnant!" Smitty yelled. He ducked as a bread stick barely missed his head.

"Cut it out, you two!" Gari ordered. "This is serious."

Ann crinkled her nose at Meade. "It's about my career," she said. "I've decided to be a lawyer!"

Smitty gaped. "You're worth a million and you need a career?"

"Chauvinist," Gari muttered.

Meade got up and bent over Ann. "Congratulations, honey," he said, kissing her on the cheek.

"Better get a move on," Smitty said. "I ain't gettin' any younger. I want to be your first client."

They drank a toast to Ann. Meade's face dropped when she revealed that she would be attending the Stanford Law

School in Palo Alto. "It will only be for two years," Gari
said, patting Meade's hand. "She'll be coming back to work
in Vegas."

Lighting a cigar, Meade considered the challenges ahead.
At a time in life when most men lived in the past, he was
eagerly looking toward the future. As long as there were
goals, he would remain young. There would always be goals;
he would see to that.

BOOK FIVE

1977-1986

1

The miles flashed by as Reese Harrington drove toward Las
Vegas. It would be dark when he arrived, and the famous
Strip would be ablaze with light.

He settled deeper into the soft leather upholstery, the beat
of the powerful engine keeping time to the classical music
that swelled from the hidden speakers.

Reese smiled as he listened to the music. When the media
had learned about his secret indulgence, they had ballooned
it all out of proportion. Reese Harrington, one of the premier
quarterbacks in the National Football League—curled up
with Beethoven while his teammates toured the discos.

He had acquired a taste for classical music in college, when
he dated a girl who was a concert pianist. It wasn't a consuming passion; it just relaxed him when he was tired or driving.
Beyond that, he termed his choice of music, "selective Top
Forty."

The Aston Martin Volante convertible knifed through the
evening shadows. It had been a leisurely trip down from
Denver. Reese was in no hurry. No one was waiting; there
were no schedules to keep. After the hectic pace of pro football, it was a pleasant change.

Reese had never wanted to make football his life. When he

graduated with honors from Stanford University, his time-table called for no more than ten years in the game. Because of his scholastic achievements—and his popularity as an All-American first-team quarterback for two years running—he had received attractive offers from several major companies. Now, after a knee injury that had required major surgery, he was free to pursue his career in earnest.

He had received many sympathetic calls and telegrams when it was announced that he was definitely out of profes-sional ball. One of the callers had been his ex-wife, Catherine. She said that she and her new husband had been great fans of his, and she hoped that things would work out. Reese thanked her and hung up, wondering how a man could live with a woman for three years and end up feeling nothing when he heard her voice.

Two months ago, the cast on his leg had come off. After working with a therapist for six weeks, he was ready to leave. He had plenty of money saved; he could go anywhere.

He had known where he was going from the moment he decided to get out of professional football. For eleven years, he had been putting off a trip to Las Vegas. Football and marriage had stood in the way, most of all a gnawing reluc-tance. But he had made a promise, and the promise had to be kept.

A glow of lights in the distance brought a thrill of anticipa-tion. An hour later, Reese was driving along the Strip. Then Reese saw it. The Plush Wheel. The great hotel towered into the Nevada night, while across the front, blinking lights created a merry-go-round, ferris wheel and giant roller coaster.

"Welcome to the Plush Wheel," the doorman said, step-ping up to the car. His eyes roved over the classic lines of the Aston Martin. "Beautiful car, sir!"

"Thank you," Reese said, getting out and kneading the muscles in his back.

"Are you staying with us, sir?" the doorman asked.

"Yes," Reese said. "I have a reservation for a late check-in."

The doorman signaled to the bell captain who manned a booth by the door. As a bellboy unloaded Reese's luggage, the doorman said, "We'll keep your car by the door. A beautiful car like this deserves special treatment."

After debating how much special treatment was worth, Reese pressed a twenty into the man's hand. "Thank *you,* sir," the doorman said, getting in the Volante and parking it where they always displayed automobiles that reflected their special clientele's taste and wealth.

Reese was surprised at the relatively small size of the lobby. A few steps, and he would be in the casino, which he could see beyond the entrance. His practiced eye measured the size of the huge room. It would hold two football fields.

"Good evening, sir!" the desk clerk enthused, dollar signs in his eyes. Evidently, he had been made aware of the car. It was too damn conspicuous, but it was Reese's only luxury. He rationalized that it was cheaper than a wife.

Wanting to join the crowd unnoticed, he checked in as "R. S. Harrington."

In his room, Reese walked out on the terrace. Twenty-five stories below, the Strip was an awesome sight. To the east, the lights of the Hilton and Landmark beckoned from Paradise Road.

Changing, Reese went down to the casino. He understood cards, but craps was a mystery. After dropping a few dollars on roulette and breaking even on 21, he wandered into a lounge where a small band was playing. Tired and fighting to keep awake, he left after one drink and went to bed.

Waking early, Reese exited an elevator before eight, just in time to watch workers erect a large Christmas tree in the lobby. Stepping gingerly around a box of ornaments, he looked out through the large glass doors. A light rain was falling. So much for any ideas he had about exploring the Strip on foot.

An old man wearing a heavy sheepskin coat and a battered cowboy hat came in, stamping his wet booted feet on the carpet. As he neared Reese, he took off his hat, revealing a bald freckled head. Reese's imagination went to work. With the bald head, pale eyes and lean leathery neck rising out of the bulky coat, the man bore a distinct resemblance to a turtle.

Slapping his hat against his jeans, the old man glanced up. He froze in his tracks, a quizzical look on his face. Moving closer, he peered up into Reese's eyes. Reese smiled. What the hell, it was bound to happen.

"Don't I know you?" the old man asked.

"Don't think so," Reese replied.

"Not from these parts, huh?"

"First time here. Got in last night."

The old man shook his head. "Somethin' mighty familiar about you," he said, faded blue eyes squinting up at Reese. He stuck out a thin skeletal hand. "My name's Frank Smith. Everybody calls me Smitty."

Here it comes, Reese thought. "Reese Harrington," he said, shaking hands.

A pleasant surprise; the name meant nothing to the old man. "Had breakfast yet?" Smitty asked.

"No."

"Come on. I'm buyin'."

Smiling, Reese fell in beside Smitty. He'd enjoy the company, but he wasn't going to take advantage of the old man.

Reese was surprised when a security guard called out, "Morning, Smitty."

Smitty waved. A few steps further and a tuxedo-clad man beside a craps table lifted a hand. Smitty grinned and nodded. When they entered the restaurant, the hostess greeted Smitty by name and led them to a large booth in the rear, removing a "Reserved" sign as they sat down. Reese glanced at the red phone. Who *was* this old man?

"First time in Vegas, huh?" Smitty said.

"A wide-eyed innocent."

"Stick around me, boy," Smitty chuckled. "Maybe, some of my experience will rub off."

"You been here long?"

Lighting a cigarette, Smitty shook out the match. "Eighty-nine years," he said. "Long enough to know apples from oranges."

"No kidding?" Reese said. "I wouldn't have taken you for over sixty."

"We're goin' to get along just fine," Smitty grinned, eyes crinkling. "I know it's all bullshit. Some mornin's I look in the mirror and wonder how come I ain't dead."

Their breakfast arrived, and they were silent for a while. Spearing a sausage link with his fork, Smitty waved it at Reese. "We ain't too nosy out here; a man's got his right to privacy. I usually size a man up pretty quick. You got me kinda puzzled. You're wankerjawed, hard to fit."

"How so?" Reese asked in an amused voice.

"Certain types come to our fancy sandbox—conventioneers, salesmen passin' through, big-time gamblers, losers on the ropes, husbands hopin' their wives will stay on the slots long enough for them to grab a piece of ass, your typical everyday crowd.

"You don't fit. You're too big and healthy lookin' to be a mortician—that's the big convention goin' now. You're in too good shape to be a salesman; they spend most of their time in bars. You look too smart to be a gambler—or a loser. Too smart to be married, too. Right?"

Reese burst out laughing. "You're something else, Smitty," he said. "Right on every count!"

"Figured so," Smitty said, clacking his false teeth with satisfaction.

Smitty learned a good deal about Reese in the next half-hour. It was quite an achievement, requiring all of Smitty's skills as a seasoned interrogator. A very private person, Reese had been dubbed "The Hermit" by the press for his reluctance to talk about himself.

Reese held one thing back from Smitty. He told about graduating from Stanford but said nothing about football—there or in the pros. He made a passing reference to a job in the sports business. He was traveling while recovering from a knee injury.

Smitty said, "So, you're footloose and fancy free. Can't think of a better place to howl than Vegas."

"I'm not much of a howler," Reese said, running his hand over his thick black hair. "I tried gambling last night—fizzled out pretty quick. Maybe I was too tired," he added, shrugging.

"Maybe you're smart," Smitty grunted. "Only way to come out a winner in Vegas is to stay away from the tables."

"I thought you would want me to gamble," Reese said, a surprised look on his face. "It's what keeps your state going."

"True, but there's plenty of suckers. Let them do the losin'."

Smitty insisted on signing the check. "Doesn't cost me a thing," he said. "The house takes care of it."

Too late, Reese realized that had he done more listening and less talking, he might have found out what Smitty's connection was.

"Come on," Smitty said, picking up his heavy coat and dilapidated hat. "Got someone I want you to meet."

Reese's curiosity was aroused even more when they stepped out of the elevator on the second floor and approached a bronze sign reading "EXECUTIVE OFFICES."

Smitty opened a door marked "SPECIAL PROJECTS." A pretty receptionist looked up and said gaily, "Good morning, Smitty." Her eyes slid over Reese with more than a little interest.

"Hi, doll," he said. "Boss in?"

"Just arrived. Want me to buzz?"

Smitty held up a hand. "We'll surprise her."

Her? Reese lifted an eyebrow as he followed Smitty toward a beautifully carved door at the end of a short hall.

Putting a finger to his lips, Smitty said conspiratorially, "I'll take a look-see first."

Opening the door a crack, Smitty stuck his head in. "Smitty!" a woman's voice cried. "What brings you out so early?"

Smitty said, "Come on out from behind that desk, gal. Want you to meet someone."

Smitty opened the door wide, motioning for Reese to follow. Looking over Smitty's head, Reese saw a tall slender woman striding toward them. The combination of classic features, golden eyes and modishly-styled dark hair was stunning. She was smiling brightly.

Then she saw Reese. A hand flew to her mouth, and she gasped, eyes round and staring.

"Gari," Smitty said with a big grin, "meet Reese Harrington. Reese, this is Gari Slaughter." The name jolted Reese. Meade Slaughter owned the Plush Wheel!

Recovering her composure, Gari held out her hand. "How are you, Mr. Harrington?" she said in a low throaty voice. Her eyes twinkled. "Reese Harrington," she mused, cupping her chin and tapping a foot. "That name seems to ring a bell."

Reese grinned. "So does yours. Is that the same as Meade Slaughter?"

Gari laughed. "Like Reese Harrington is the same as the St. Louis Cardinals."

"What's goin' on?" Smitty said, looking irritably from one to the other.

"You mean you don't know?" Gari asked incredulously.

"Know what?" Smitty said, confused, sticking his jaw out belligerently.

Waving toward Reese, Gari repeated, "You don't know who he is?"

Smitty peered up at Reese. "I thought I did when we came in," he said.

"This is Reese Harrington," Gari announced. "The late great quarterback for the St. Louis Cardinals."

Smitty was still staring at Reese. "Son of a bitch," he muttered. "You're a closed-mouthed bastard, ain't you?" He turned toward Gari. "He said he was in the sports business."

"That's beautiful!" Gari cried, clapping her hands. "It's about time someone pulled the wool over your eyes."

"Just because you and Meade are such big football fans don't make you any smarter than me," Smitty grumbled.

"You don't like football?" Reese asked Smitty.

"Sure I do! But I don't get involved like Gari and Meade

do. They don't just watch—they fight! Always takin' opposite sides. There's been times I thought I was in the middle of a war!"

Gari ordered coffee, and they talked for a while. As Reese and Smitty prepared to leave, Gari said, "Please drop by and see me before you leave, Reese. I hope you're not leaving too soon."

"I'll be around for three, four days," Reese said.

"Just a minute," Gari said, going around behind her desk and flipping through a desk calendar. She looked up at Reese. "How about lunch Monday?"

"I'd like that," Reese said.

"Wonderful! Drop by around eleven-thirty?"

"I'll be here."

As they rode the elevator down to the main floor, Reese said, "That is one beautiful lady."

"Yep," Smitty agreed. "She used to be one of the most popular showgirls in Vegas."

Reese whistled softly. "She looks good enough to be on stage now."

"Be sure and tell her that," Smitty chuckled. "She'll appreciate the compliment, but she might change your mind about show business. It's a tough life. She got out when she was twenty-five." He shot a sidelong glance at Reese. "How old do you think she is now?"

Reese thought a moment. "Forty?"

Smitty laughed. "She'll be fifty-two next month."

Reese stared as the elevator doors opened. "Aw, come on, Smitty," he said unbelievingly.

"Truth," Smitty said, holding up his hand, leading Reese into the casino. "She keeps real active. Besides bein' Vice-President in Charge of Special Projects and handlin' important hostess duties, she plays tennis and rides horseback. 'Course, her big sport is sailboatin'. Guess she's a whiz. Don't know myself. I won't go near that leaky tub."

"Bet she's got a hell of a forehand," Reese said, recalling the strength he had seen in that tall sleek body.

"She can punch out most men. That keeps 'em off her back
—that and her bein' Meade's woman."

"Better not let a feminist hear you saying that," Reese
grinned. "They don't even like 'wife.' 'Woman' sends them
through the roof."

"Fuck 'em," Smitty said harshly, startling Reese. "They're
nothin' but a bunch of screechin' parrots." They entered a
nearly deserted lounge. "Let's set a spell," Smitty said, waving the cocktail waitress away.

Lighting a cigarette, Smitty looked at Reese. "I never said
that Gari is married to Meade, did I?"

Reese's jaw dropped. "She is, isn't she?"

Smitty was smiling now, enjoying himself. "It's no secret
about her and Meade. Gari's a Slaughter, all right. She's
Meade's daughter-in-law."

"But I got the impression—"

"Oh, they've been living together for twenty years. Kinda
confusin', ain't it?"

"You can say that again! What about Gari's husband,
Meade's son?"

"He died back in fifty-six," Smitty said brusquely.

Silence. Reese said, "You've known Meade for a long
time?"

"Since thirty-three. He was just a kid then."

While Reese was digesting that, Smitty's eyes lighted up.
"Meade and Gari raised her and David's daughter like she
was their own. You should see Ann. She looks like her
mother, except she's a blond."

"She must be beautiful."

"A knockout. Tall, with legs up to here," Smitty said,
holding the back of his hand under his chin. A mischievous
glance. "She looks like a showgirl—better than most. In high
heels, she's six, seven inches taller than me. Sometimes, she'll
dress up, and I'll waltz her around the casino. Everybody's
thinkin' I'm a dirty old man buyin' a sweet young thing for
the night. You should see the nasty looks them old biddies
give me!"

"She must have men standing in line," Reese said.

"That she does, but right now her career's more important."

"Career?"

"She graduated from law school a couple of years back. Come to think about it, it was Stanford. You were long gone by then. She's workin' for the Gaming Control Board."

"Beauty and brains," Reese said. "Quite a combination." A questioning look. "What's the Gaming Control Board?"

"I keep forgettin' you're new here," Smitty said. Lighting another cigarette, he launched into a lengthy description of Nevada's gaming agencies and their investigating, auditing and enforcement arms. The lounge was filling when he finished.

"I'll try to remember that," Reese said. "Some of it," he added weakly.

"Don't feel bad," Smitty chuckled. "I've been here since the beginnin', and I still get confused."

When they parted, the skies had cleared, so Reese decided to take a drive. He toured the Strip and Paradise Road, then Fremont Street. The downtown Casino Center matched Smitty's earlier description—a noisy circus that appealed to the shirt-sleeved, sawduster crowd.

Leaving Las Vegas, he drove north on Highway 95, opening the car up. The rain had left the air fresh and clean. To the west, Mt. Charleston rose majestically into the clear blue sky, a touch of snow around the peak. At Indian Springs, Reese made a U-turn and headed back.

He looked at his watch: 4:12. He hadn't been in town a day. Shaking his head, he stared out the windshield.

Things were happening too fast. What he should do is leave tonight and never see Las Vegas again. But he couldn't. He still had a promise to keep.

2

The following morning, Reese got up at four and packed a bag. Telling the desk clerk to hold his room, he gave him three $100 bills.

Daybreak found Reese in California. Traveling through a high pass, he looked at the scattered snow and wondered if it would be warm in Palm Springs. A long drive, but he had to get away.

Arriving back at the Plush Wheel Monday morning, he was handed several call slips. Three were from Smitty, two from Gari. She had called yesterday, again an hour ago.

"Reese!" she cried, relief in her voice. "We thought you had run away!"

Reese laughed. "Just a little trip. The lunch still on?"

"Of course. That's why I called. I needed to make sure you were coming. Meade is joining us." Her laughter rang over the phone. "He'd kill me if I pulled him off a busy schedule just to eat with me!"

Gripping the receiver hard, Reese stared at the white house phone.

"Reese?"

"Sure," Reese said in a low voice. "Meet you at your office?"

"Why not just come to the Gambler's Club? It's to the left of the casino. Any security guard will show you the way. Eleven-thirty?"

"Fine." Hanging up, Reese went to his room and changed, his mind in a turmoil.

The maitre d' of the intimate Gambler's Club restaurant led Reese to a booth in a far corner. As they approached,

Gari smiled and waved. The big white-haired man beside her rose to his feet.

"Meade Slaughter," he said in a deep rumbling voice. Gripping the extended hand, Reese looked into the piercing blue eyes, his feelings mixed, held by the power of this man he had waited so long to see.

How many times had he dreamed about what he would say at this first meeting—if there was a meeting? The well-prepared words fled, and all he could say was, "Glad to meet you, Mr. Slaughter."

A broad smile broke over Meade's face. "I've heard a good deal about you," he said. "Smitty's been wearing my ear out." Reese raised an eyebrow in surprise.

Drinks ordered, Meade said to Reese, "You gave me a lot of enjoyable Sundays. It's too damn bad about the leg."

"Maybe I was lucky," Reese said. "This might have been my year to slump."

"No way, Reese," Gari said. She shot a wicked glance at Meade. "This big jerk happens to be sold on the Rams. I won big on you."

Meade shot Gari a sour look. Turning to Reese, he explained, "We bet on all the games. If I don't pay my markers, Gari locks me out of the house."

"What happens if Gari doesn't pay?" Reese asked.

"I withhold my favors."

"Meade!" Gari cried, turning bright red and jabbing him in the ribs.

"*There* you are!" a female voice exclaimed. "I've been looking all *over* for you!"

Reese looked up to see a stunning blonde. She saw him just as she started to slide into the booth. "Oops!" she squeaked, long fingers flying to her mouth.

"This is my daughter, Ann," Gari said drily. "It seems that she's invited herself to lunch. Ann, this is Reese Harrington."

"*The* Reese Harrington?" Ann said breathlessly. "Stanford, class of sixty-nine?"

"The same," Reese smiled, sliding over to make room. "How did you know that?"

"Because I got my law degree at Stanford, class of seventy-five." An impish look. "Besides, when Mom said she had met you, I looked it up."

"Small world," Reese said lamely. He couldn't stop staring. Smitty's description hadn't done her justice. She was achingly beautiful.

Meade shook a big finger under Ann's nose. "We were just getting acquainted when you barged in. Butt in too much, I'll box you one."

"Oh, pooh," Ann said, sticking out her tongue.

Covering her eyes with her hand, Gari said, "Please forgive Ann. She's never learned to show respect."

"Mother!"

Reese laughed, glad that Ann had joined them. Things were going better than he had expected.

Over dessert, Meade lit a long slim cigar and looked at Reese. "Gari said you're leaving soon. In a hurry?"

"No. I only planned to stay a few days."

"I'm flying to Lake Tahoe tomorrow," Meade said. "Want to come along?"

Reese's heart leaped. Should he? *Could* he? He fumbled for an answer.

"Please, Reese," Gari urged. "I'm going, too."

The decision was made. "I accept," Reese said, strangely happy.

"Good," Gari said contentedly. "We'll get back in time for the opening of the Tropicana's new show." She smiled sweetly. "You're going with us, of course."

Meade grinned at Reese's bewildered look. "Smitty wants to show you the ranch."

"Christmas is coming!" Ann tossed in merrily, big violet eyes aglow.

"What's going on?" Reese stammered.

"Smitty would say you've been snookered," Meade said. "Give in, boy. You haven't got a chance." He crushed his cigar out in the tray. "Another thing, from now on, you're a guest of the Plush Wheel. If you spend one dime in this place, I'll be obliged to break that other leg."

Reese was too flabbergasted to speak.

"It won't hurt his pocketbook," Gari said. "He'll just write it off."

In a daze, Reese was chaperoned to the front desk by Gari and Ann, where Gari retrieved Reese's deposit and issued the new orders to an attentive desk clerk.

"There!" Gari said in a satisfied voice, turning to face Reese. She patted him on the cheek. "Be ready at eight in the morning. It's trying at times, but Meade insists on being prompt."

Mother and daughter walked off, leaving Reese standing dumbly in the center of the lobby. Turning, Ann waved gaily. Reese smiled and waved back.

A dry voice said, "I've been waitin' for you, boy."

Whirling, Reese stared down at Smitty. Tipping his hat back, Smitty said, "I think it's about time we talked about your dad." Looking into Reese's shocked face, he added in a quiet understanding voice, "Don't worry. I'm the only one who knows."

3

Except for a curt, "Come on," Smitty hadn't spoken since his stunning announcement. Numb and reeling from the startling events of the past hour, Reese followed the little man through the casino and into the elevator. On the second floor, Smitty unlocked an unmarked door and snapped on the light, revealing a paneled office, antique desk and black leather furniture. "My office," he explained, a look of amusement crossing his leathery face. "Yeah, I know, what the hell do I need an office for? Tell that to Meade. It's mine, anyway. A waste of money for all the use I get out of it." Tossing off his coat, he settled into a chair. "Have a seat."

Reese was quick to obey; his legs felt like jelly. He watched Smitty drop his hat on the floor and light a cigarette. "How did you get on to me?" Reese asked quietly.

"Nothin' to it," Smitty said. "That first sight of you 'bout put me six feet under. You're the spittin' image of Meade when he was your age."

"You . . . you really think so?"

"Hell, yes, I'm sure," Smitty snapped. "How many guys do you know with black hair and blue eyes? I've always suspected that Meade has some Cherokee in him. They throw off the damnedest combinations—dark hair and green eyes, brown eyes and red hair. 'Course, they ain't all big like you and Meade. You're not as heavy or thick through the shoulders, but, hell, you're young. If you two was the same age, you'd look like twins."

Smitty crushed out his cigarette. "When you told me about your mother, that shut the barn door. You're Meade's son, all right."

"You didn't bat an eye. Not once," Reese said in a low voice, visibly moved, hearing what he had known for eleven years.

"Tell me more about her, boy," Smitty said in a surprisingly gentle voice. "You said she died of cancer."

"It came on fast," Reese said, a dark sadness entering his eyes. "After the doctor told her, she lost all will to fight. She just wasted away. I don't think she weighed seventy pounds when she died."

"She was one of the most beautiful women I've ever known," Smitty said quietly. "It must have been hell seein' her go like that."

"They called me out of school one day," Reese said in a tortured half-whisper. "It was the eighteenth of January. I'll remember that day as long as I live.

"When I got to the hospital, the doctor told me straight. I was sixteen, a junior. He had treated me like the man of the house from the beginning. He told me that Mom could go anytime. She had insisted on talking to me; it didn't matter if it shortened her life by a few hours." Reese's voice took on

a dreamlike quality as he gazed over Smitty's head and recalled that winter day in 1967. . . .

The doctor opened the door and ushered the tall broad-
shouldered boy inside. Beckoning to the nurse as Reese approached the bed, they left him alone with his mother.

"Mom?" Reese whispered. "Mom, can you hear me?"

Cindy opened her eyes and tried to smile. "Reese," she
murmured. "I'm so glad you got here in time."

The chilling inference of her words made the boy shudder.
He drew up a chair and took her frail hand.

"I have something very important to tell you," she said,
struggling with each word. "I've put it off so long." A tear
ran down her cheek. "I can't wait anymore; there's so little
time."

"Mom!" Reese cried.

Feebly, Cindy shook her head. "Help me, Reese," she
pleaded. "I have to get it said."

Tears rolling down his face, Reese held his mother's hand
tenderly in both of his.

"It's about your father," Cindy whispered. "He was the
only man I loved."

How could this be? Reese wondered. His parents had divorced when he was two. His mother had kept no pictures,
seldom mentioned his name, never shown any sign of the love
she now professed.

Seeing Reese's perplexed look, Cindy said, "Jack Harrington *isn't* your father. He's a good man, and he married me
knowing I was carrying another man's child. I felt so dis-
honest knowing he loved me while I loved someone else. It
broke his heart when I left him, but I couldn't live with
myself any longer. He gave you his name, and I bless him for
it."

Cindy closed her eyes, and Reese thought she had drifted
away. He felt the press of her fingers. "Your father is a
famous man in Nevada," she continued, eyes half-closed.
"He owns several casinos."

Reese opened his mouth to speak.

"Please, dear," Cindy said. "Let me finish." A smile crossed her face. "You look like him, you know. You're big like him, too." Her voice faded, and she closed her eyes again. Reese bent over her anxiously.

"It's all right," Cindy whispered, looking up into his eyes. "I just get tired so fast." She paused for a moment. "Your father's name is Meade Slaughter. He owns the Plush Wheel Casino in Las Vegas. Promise you will go and see him. You don't even have to speak." Her eyes roved his face hungrily. "He would be proud of you. You won't forget his name? You will go and see him someday?"

A deep sob shook Reese's frame. "I promise, Mom," he said brokenly.

Cindy's eyes focused on distant memories. "When I learned I was pregnant, I hoped we would marry. I talked to him—about marriage. He never knew about me being pregnant with you. He wasn't ready to commit himself. While he was on a trip, I went away. He never knew. He never knew . . ."

Cindy closed her eyes and never spoke again. The doctor came in and led Reese away. Two hours later, he told the boy that his mother was dead. . . .

Blinking the dampness from his eyes, Reese said to Smitty, "I started going to libraries and reading the Las Vegas papers. Over the years, I kept seeing Meade Slaughter's name. There were often pictures of him in the papers. Sometimes, I hated him. I guess I did that most of the time. I used to daydream about walking up and introducing myself. Then I would punch him in the face and leave." A rueful look. "After meeting him, I don't think that would be so easy."

"You better believe it," Smitty said. "I've known a lot of tough men in my life, and Meade's got 'em all beat hollow." He shook a cigarette from the pack. "He was pretty broke up when your mother left him. He hired private detectives to find her. He moved heaven and earth to locate her. He loved Cindy, Reese. I'll stake my life on it."

"But why—"

Smitty raised a hand. "You'll have to ask him. I don't know any more than you do."

"I'm not about to do that," Reese said flatly. He pointed at his chest. "There's a lot of resentment built up in me."

"I understand," Smitty said sympathetically.

After a long silence, Reese rose and looked down at Smitty, a pensive expression on his face. "Do I really look that much like him?" he asked.

"Like two peas in a pod," Smitty said. "Did you see the look on Gari's face when you walked in her office? Thought she was goin' to faint. Lucky you were a big football player; that threw her off the scent." Smitty waggled a skinny finger. "Watch that woman, boy. She's smarter than a whip!"

Reese told Smitty about the trip to Lake Tahoe tomorrow and the way the family had "snookered" him.

"Hell, yes!" burst out Smitty. "Don't you know what's goin' on?"

Reese stopped pacing. "You tell me," he said. "I got lost somewhere during dessert."

"Meade's lookin' you over," Smitty chuckled. "He's thinkin' about puttin' you to work."

Reese was too stunned to reply.

Smitty grinned at the confused look on the big man's face. " 'Course, I might have egged him on a bit—been workin' on him since Friday."

Reese dropped into the chair. "Keep going," he said.

"You could do a hell of a lot worse, boy," Smitty said. "Meade's not gettin' any younger. I've been tellin' him for years that he needs a right-hand man. He's agreed, but the right one ain't come along."

Smitty leaned forward, hands clasped between his knees. "Meade puts faith in my instincts. I don't mind tellin' you that I'm a pretty wealthy man. I got there makin' the right moves and pickin' the right people. When I met Meade, I latched onto him fast. He was a comer, and I wanted to go along for the ride. We talked about that over the weekend. I told him you're another one. That'll help him make up his mind.

"Another thing that will help. You're his son. He don't know it, but blood ties are strong. He'll *feel* somethin'. He won't know what it is, but it'll be there."

Stretching his long legs, Reese rested his head against the cushion. "I don't know, Smitty," he said, staring at the ceiling. "I just don't know."

"You'll think about it?"

Reese looked sharply at Smitty. "Hell, yes, I'll think about it. That's probably *all* I'll do the next few days." He waved a hand. "Meade might not make the offer, anyway."

"He will," Smitty said confidently. "He ain't dumb; he knows a good man when he sees one." A sly grin. "Besides, I'll keep buggin' him."

Reese sat up straight, and a look came over his face that Smitty had been seeing for over forty years—the determined set of the jaw, the slight flare of the nostrils, the hardening of the steel-blue eyes. "If Meade makes an offer and I accept," Reese said, "it will be as Reese Harrington and not Meade Slaughter's son. That's my secret. No one has the right to tell him except me. Not even you."

Smitty nodded approvingly. "You got yourself a silent partner," he said, reaching out a bony hand. "And I mean silent."

New Years 1978 arrived. Two days later, Reese went to work for the Plush Wheel.

4

"The first time I saw this street," Meade said, "there were a few basement clubs on the north end of the block and that was it." He pointed at the First National Bank building on the corner of Virginia and Second Streets, its six Roman columns standing in colossal order. "That's the only building that hasn't changed; they called it the Reno National Bank then." A pause. "Eddie Questa gave Bill Harrah a big break when he loaned him money for a bingo club—back in thirty-nine or forty. The bank continued to back him until Harrah's operation got too big and went public."

Reese stood beside Meade in front of the Virginia Street Plush Wheel. This was his second trip to Reno since joining the company. The last time, they had flown in and out the same day. This trip, they were staying two days, so Meade could show Reese around.

"Fremont Street hasn't got anything on this, except it's bigger," Meade said, turning up the collar of his overcoat against the cold March wind. "The weather's better in Vegas, so it's busier year round." Meade stepped back as a taxi pulled up to the curb, splashing the walk with the slush from last night's snow.

Meade started walking toward Commercial Row, Reese keeping pace. For over two months, sometimes seven days a week and often into the night, Meade had been bombarding Reese with facts and figures, as if he had suddenly realized that he was seventy-four and had no designated successor.

Reese hadn't been hired with this understanding. Not directly, anyway. His official title was Assistant to the President. That had caused quite a stir in the corporate structure. A thinly-veiled resentment had been shown at certain top levels, particularly by Stanley Atwood, the Executive Vice President.

Extremely proud of his prodigy, and armed with the true knowledge of Reese's parentage, Smitty had sponsored Reese with unusual enthusiasm. Meade, who considered Smitty a sagebrush J.P. Morgan and valued his judgment accordingly, was puzzled by his old friend's enthusiasm, so much so that he put Reese's application through a more rigorous scrutiny than usual.

Knowing that should Reese reach a top position in the company, he would be investigated by the Gaming Board, Meade retained a private agency to search into Reese's background. He ended up making no connection between Beverly Harrington—once an active sponsor of a little theater group in upstate New York—and Cindy.

Reese came through with flying colors, some of the investigations not being completed until weeks after he had begun work. The most satisfactory report was of Reese's scholastic achievements at Stanford. Once again, Smitty's judgment had been more than justified.

Now, Meade had to see how Reese held up under daily pressure. Meade wasn't the easiest person to work for; he was demanding, a perfectionist, often short-tempered, and used to working alone. Reese knew that he would be dismissed if he didn't measure up. With regret—he and Meade had developed a good rapport—but dismissed nonetheless.

Turning on Sierra Street, Reese looked up at the sixteen-story Plush Wheel hotel. Completed the year before, it was part of the shift to the west of Virginia Street. Under the new Reno master plan, no new casinos could be built in the downtown area unless they included at least one hundred rooms.

"Gari calls this 'Meade's Folly,' " Meade said, following Reese's gaze. "She'll sing another tune in a few years. In the meantime, I'll have to sell some more stock to cover the temporary losses. I don't like doing it, but it's the only way out."

On the second floor, they entered the General Manager's office. Ross Gentry had started as a busboy at the Virginia Street club in 1949. He came out from behind his desk and shook hands. He looked up at the two big men. "Damnit, you guys," he said. "You're giving me an inferiority complex. Sit down before I start to cry."

"I've been telling Reese about your growth problems," Meade said as they joined Gentry around the desk.

"We're busting our seams," Gentry acknowledged. "There will be two hundred thousand people in the Reno-Sparks area before long. We've got water supply problems. With the drought over, maybe that will ease up. The air quality has to be cleaned up. Reno's sewage problems are enormous. We need new treatment plants, but that's being held up by environmental challenges. Everywhere you look, new houses and mobile homes are going up—along with building costs. Outside of that, we're doing great."

"You're a real joy, Ross," Meade said, lighting a cigar. "Say something to cheer Reese up."

"We ain't got no gangsters," Gentry said brightly.

"Ross, you ought to be in our showroom," Meade said as he rose and crushed out his cigar. "We're short on comedians." He nodded at Reese. "Let's get out of here before this guy ruins our day."

The following morning, the Lear jet lifted off the Cannon Field runway and streaked into the morning sky. Unlike the other two jets owned by the Plush Wheel which were designed for more seating, this one was like an airborne office. There were two large desk working areas and a smaller one for a secretary.

As they flew over Carson City, Meade pointed at the snow-capped peaks of the Sierra Nevadas. "In a couple of months, we'll do our annual spring cleaning at the cabin on the North Shore. Gari can introduce you to the _Lady Ann._" Seeing Reese's quizzical look, he explained, "Gari's first sailboat— a little four-meter job, about fourteen feet. She keeps it in a boathouse at the cabin.

"Now she wants to add a cruiser to that Tornado catamaran she's got at Lake Mead. Ann's as nuts about sailing as her mother—if that's possible."

"I know what you mean," Reese said. "One day on the lake with those two and I came home with my ego dragging. I thought I knew something about sailing. Beside them, I'm a rank amateur."

"Gari gets me out a few times a year," Meade said. "I'm sort of a coward in deep water, but it's worth going just to see the pleasure on her face. She loves to show off." The warmth in his voice was unmistakable.

Why didn't he love my mother like that? Reese wondered. Smitty said he did, but what did Smitty know about love?

It wasn't easy for Reese, being with Meade almost every day. Burdened with his secret and over a decade of resentment, Reese was battling a growing feeling of respect and a desire to know this man as a father.

Reese had loved his mother deeply. He missed her. They had been close, and he yearned to share memories with Meade. In such a quest, he had gone to Los Angeles eight years ago and met with Jack Harrington. It had been difficult; Cindy still held a dominant place in both their hearts. Reese had come away with a feeling of gratitude and mutual understanding. Harrington had kept in touch over the years, and Reese was pleased with his recent successes as a film director. Last year, Jack Harrington had won the Academy Award for Best Picture.

A few weeks ago, Reese had called Harrington and told him about his new job. They had talked for an hour, and Jack had been sympathetic. He, too, harbored bitterness toward Meade, but he understood Reese's need. He wished Reese well in his new job and promised to visit him in Vegas soon.

Fleetingly, Reese had resented the affection that was so apparent between Meade and Gari, as if Gari had stolen his mother's rightful place. It had left Reese feeling foolish, especially as his own affection for Gari grew.

She was like an older sister, a companion and confidante. Around her, he had to be extremely careful. His secret was in double jeopardy—from Gari's intuitive mind and his compelling desire to unburden himself.

"We'll take a long weekend and stay at the cabin in May," Meade said, breaking into Reese's reverie. "We'll bring Smitty along, too. He needs a few days with his nose out of that damn bankbook."

5

Smitty elected himself as Reese's gambling teacher. "I taught Meade; seems only right that I teach you," he said the first time he took Reese for an "owner's walk" through the Plush Wheel casino.

There had been many sessions since. Reese had learned about the management structure of a gaming hotel.

"I thought a hotel had one big boss who ran everything," Reese said.

"They got a president or general manager who's sorta top dog," Smitty said. "If he's smart, he keeps his nose out of the gaming end. That's the casino manager's territory. You don't put accountants in charge of a casino. It takes men with know-how, like Carl Cohen at the MGM and Ash Resnick at Caesars."

One night after Reese had spent several hours with Smitty on the catwalks above the casino observing the games through one-way mirrors, he was visited in his office by a blond whirlwind. "Reese Harrington," yelled Ann, "you were supposed to call me last night. We were going to have dinner. Remember?"

"Oh, God," moaned Reese, slapping his forehead. "I got tied up on a report and forgot."

Ann's lovely face was flushed with anger. "That's not the first time you've stood me up," she cried. "What's the matter with me? Do I have leprosy or something?"

"Ann—"

"You're a jerk, Reese Harrington. A real class jerk!" There was a swirl of blond hair and a brief glimpse of a rigid back. The door slammed, and a picture went slightly askew. Reese got up and straightened the picture, returned to the desk and sat down. He cursed softly and drummed his fingers on the chair arm.

How could he explain? He couldn't just say, "Gee, Ann, I would like to be with you a lot, maybe even fall in love. God knows, I'd like to bounce you around in the sack. But you see, there's this little problem. Through no fault of yours or mine, I happen to be your uncle."

A thought hit Reese, and he laughed aloud. If he married Ann, that would really complete the Slaughter zoo—Meade living with his daughter-in-law, and Ann married to her uncle!

As he pulled out of the Plush Wheel parking lot, Reese decided to have dinner at the Desert Inn. Entering the casino, he ran into a friend who invited him to a television movie wrap-up party in a penthouse suite. In the course of the evening, Reese met a lovely raven-haired model. They hit it off and left early to see the show at the MGM.

Nearing the front exit, with the girl clinging to his arm and chattering happily away, Reese looked up as Ann and two girls entered. His eyes met Ann's, and he could almost smell the odor of burning flesh.

Head held high, Ann swept by without a word. Reese was pleasantly surprised to learn that he and his lady friend hadn't disappeared in a cloud of smoke.

6

Tony and Louis Giuliano stood in front of the nearly completed house. The huge sprawling structure was built within a stand of ancient oaks. Behind the house, the ground began a gentle ascent toward Mt. Rose. To the northeast lay the city of Reno.

"Beautiful, isn't it?" Tony said, smiling broadly as he surveyed the house and grounds.

"You can say that again," Louis said, glancing at his father's face. The last year and a half had changed Tony from a tired penny-pinching recluse into a man who was boyishly eager to join the mainstream of life. And all because of a woman.

But what a woman! The day Tony introduced her to him, Louis' body responded like a finely tuned violin. He could almost hear the vibration. A happily married man with two grown daughters and a nineteen-year-old son, Louis had to give himself a mental slap.

At the time, Jan Lebeck was thirty-five, Tony sixty-seven. Tony had first mentioned her on a trip to Las Vegas. Noticing his father's new tailored suit and styled hair, Louis made it a point to travel to Reno and meet the woman who had inspired such unbelievable changes.

Jan Lebeck was a divorcée; she had been married to a wealthy Chicago industrialist. When their marriage ended several years ago, Jan had received a large sum of money, much of which she had invested in gaming stocks. Moving to Reno in 1973 and buying a home near the Hidden Valley Country Club, she had purchased several pieces of land and joined a syndicate that built a half-million square feet of warehouse space in Sparks. With a Freeport Law that exempted inventories from property tax if they were destined for out-of-state sale, Nevada had developed a highly profitable warehouse industry. Jan nearly doubled her wealth in four years.

An executive of the Del E. Webb Corporation, in which Jan had a substantial investment, introduced her to Tony Giuliano. Things moved rather fast from there.

Jan was an exquisite brunette only an inch shorter than Tony's five feet eight inches. The day Louis met her, he was amused to note that his father was wearing elevator shoes. He was not amused at the strong relationship that was developing between Tony and Jan.

His worst fears were realized when they were married in

the spring of 1977. Now, this house. Situated on one hundred acres, the package was costing Tony nearly a million dollars. "What the hell," Tony had said when he first showed Louis the architect's drawings. "It's about time I spent some money on myself."

Looking at his father's animated face, Louis shook his head in amazement. Jan had performed a miracle.

It had only been natural for Louis to be suspicious of his younger stepmother's intentions. Had she been poor, there would have been no question, but she had come to the marriage bed a wealthy woman.

Jan would come out of the marriage better off but with no part of the Giuliano empire; Tony hadn't taken leave of his senses. A marriage contract had been signed before the nuptials. Should the marriage be dissolved or Tony die, Jan would receive a handsome settlement but no ownership in the family interests.

Until Tony died, he would have absolute control of all his holdings. In his will, Louis would receive the gaming corporation and equally share the real estate and stocks with his younger brother, Mike. The construction company, one of the largest in Nevada, would go to Mike, who had been running it for nearly twenty years. Their sister, Carla, who had elected to go with her mother when the marriage dissolved, would receive a token settlement.

Turning away from the house, Tony said, "Let's go downtown." On his first visit to Reno in nearly six months, Louis had been brought directly from the airport to the new home. He would be having dinner with his father and Jan tonight at Jan's place. She and Tony had been living there since their marriage. When Tony had gone to live in Hidden Valley, he had sold the family residence near downtown Reno, another move that had shocked Louis. Looking ten years younger, Tony showed no reluctance in shedding his past.

Louis thought he was through being surprised until he stepped into his father's office at the Western Club. Years ago, the building had been renovated and a fourteen-story hotel tower added, but Tony's office had remained intact, looking exactly as it had when Carlo Giuliano purchased the club in 1915, right down to the original furniture.

"Jesus Christ!" Louis burst out, coming to an abrupt halt. One wall had been knocked out, more than doubling the office in size, a large draped window replacing the small one that had barely leaked light through a dusty venetian blind. Expensive paneling and wallpaper brightened the room. In front of the window, legs sinking into the deep pile carpet, was an eight-foot walnut desk that must have cost thousands. The high-backed executive chair was dark leather, as were the four chairs placed in front of the desk.

"Nice, huh?" Tony beamed. "Jan planned the whole thing, bought the plants herself."

Louis murmured his appreciation. This really brought home the measure of Jan's influence on the old man. The office had been Tony's inner sanctum, as it had been his father's before him. Not even Louis had been allowed its use.

Tony waved him toward one of the chairs. "Give me a second," he said, moving to a side wall. "Got something I want to show you."

Louis lit a cigarette while Tony moved a picture aside and twirled the dial on a safe. Taking out a soft leather case, he returned to the desk. "Nobody knows about this but me," he said, zipping it open. Sitting down, Tony removed a stack of documents. "I'll be making a move before long, so you should know what's goin' on." His voice hardened. "It's about Meade Slaughter."

Ah, thought Louis. *Something hasn't changed.*

Tony laid out several sheets of lined yellow paper; Louis recognized his father's handwriting. Running a thick finger down a column of figures, Tony stopped at the bottom. He looked up at Louis, his finger still in place. "In a couple of years," he said, "maybe more, maybe less, I'll have control of Nevada Investments."

Louis was stunned. Nothing had prepared him for this. He had thought that the years and Tony's infatuation with Jan had mellowed his father's attitude toward Meade Slaughter.

Tony had quietly been lining up the big guns while Louis
believed the war was over.

"How did you accomplish that?" Louis asked. One didn't
buy that heavily into a Nevada casino without being investigated by the Gaming Control Board.

"I hold fifty thousand shares under my name," Tony said.
"Everybody knows it, including the Gaming Commission."
A short laugh. "That must have shook Slaughter. Couldn't
have scared him much; that don't represent a half-percent of
the company."

"Then, how—"

Tony held up his hand. "I got friends, *good* friends. Some
individual stockholders, a couple of small union pension
funds. It's all here." He began to stuff the papers back in the
case. "The less you know, the better," he continued. "I
started layin' the groundwork for this fifteen years ago; it's
untraceable."

"Jesus!" Louis whispered.

"He's got nothin' to do with this," snapped Tony, the
veneer of his new image cracking under the strain. "I'm the
one who's done it, and I'm goin' to run that bastard out of
his own company!"

7

"Nevada owes Bill Harrah," Max Verdon said. "Maybe Las
Vegas didn't take much note of his passing, but he's going to
be missed up here."

"He never had much use for Vegas," Meade said.
"Thought it was full of phonies." A chuckle. "He considered
his place the standard, and no one measured up." They had
been reminiscing about Bill Harrah; the gaming pioneer had
died two weeks ago, June 30, 1978.

Verdon pointed at Smitty stretched out on a lounge chair, cowboy hat covering his face. "How do you like that?" Verdon said. "He asks me to come up and visit, then goes to sleep."

Meade yawned widely. "Don't blame him," he said. "Feel like it myself."

A gentle breeze stirred the colorful canvas awning of the beach cabana. It was a warm summer day at Lake Tahoe, the temperature in the upper seventies. Fifty yards away, the huge two-story cabin nestled in the pines.

Meade's eyes shifted from Smitty's sleeping form to the wide expanse of the lake, picking out a speck in the hazy distance. Gari and Reese had gone out on the *Lady Ann* after lunch for a "quick sail"; they had been gone for three hours.

Meade smiled to himself. Reese was part of the family now. It seemed like he'd been around for years, not just seven months.

Outside of Charlie and Smitty, Meade had avoided close friendships. He was generous but not with himself. For the middle part of his life, work had been his sole passion. Now, his interests were equally divided between his family and the Plush Wheels. The major challenges had been met, and his horizons were limited. At times, he felt more like a caretaker than anything else.

When Reese joined the company in January, Meade had been overly cautious. Influenced by Smitty's enthusiastic support and his own liking for Reese, he had fought to keep an objective position. With the passing of time and as Reese passed every test with flying colors, Meade began to drop his guard, noticing that Reese was doing the same. He had remarked to Gari once that Reese seemed to be uncomfortable in his presence, not as open as he was when they were all together. Gari had made light of it, saying half seriously that even ex-NFL quarterbacks could be intimidated by Meade's overpowering personality.

Meade glanced at Smitty. Age might have deprived him of his hair, but it hadn't affected his judgment. For forty-five years, Meade had been benefiting from Smitty's shrewd advice. Bringing Reese to his attention might turn out to be Smitty's crowning achievement.

Max Verdon's voice broke into his thoughts. "You've got to see Atlantic City, Meade," Verdon said. "It's unbelievable how people are lining up to lose their money."

"What's that?" Smitty said, lifting the hat off his face.

"Wouldn't you know it?" Verdon said. "Mention money and he's awake like a shot."

Smitty sat up blinking. "When you get to be my age, Max, that's the *only* thing that'll wake you up."

"Nobody gets your age," Verdon retorted. "Only God, and he's not much older."

Sixty-four years ago, Smitty had ridden through the snow to bring the doctor to Sam Verdon's cabin north of Reno, where Max was born the next morning. Smitty and Sam Verdon had gone to grade school together in Elko and had once been rivals for the hand of Betsy Olsen, who chose Sam and became Max's mother. Sam and Betsy were dead now, and Smitty was Max's link to the past. Max visited with Smitty at the ranch several times a year; Smitty rarely came north anymore.

After Bob Terhune's death, Max Verdon had left Washington and returned to Reno, where he utilized his experience and contacts gained from twenty-five years as Terhune's aide to establish a political consulting service. He had done well and often traveled the country on behalf of his clients. On one of those trips a month ago, he had visited Atlantic City.

"Imagine one casino with a market of thirty-five million within an eight-hour drive," Verdon said. "People standing in line outside! Slot players waiting two, three hours for a cash payoff. Crazy."

"Resorts has been open about two months now," Meade said. "If they keep this up, they'll post a record drop."

"The bottom line's the *win*," Smitty said. "Let's not get too excited until we see that."

Max Verdon looked toward the lake. "Our brave sailors returneth," he said.

The three men watched the *Lady Ann* skimming across the

water, heading toward the dock at what seemed an alarming speed. Gari nudged the tiny boat against the rubber bumpers. Leaping to the dock, Reese whipped a rope around a cleat.

"Make a pretty good team, those two," Verdon said.

"Gari's in heaven," Meade chuckled. "She's got someone to play with."

Just hours before flying to the lake, Ann had announced that she was bringing a guest, Don Blanden. Nothing unusual, except Meade happened to despise Blanden and Ann knew it. What puzzled Gari more was that Ann didn't like him much either. Ann had been taught to value honesty, both in herself and others; Blanden hardly fit that category.

He was the tennis pro at a local country club (a baby sitter for bored housewives, according to Meade). Tall, blond and trim from many hours on the court, Blanden had capitalized on his good looks to model for several TV commercials, usually in tennis shorts, smiling and swinging a racket, a gorgeous girl or girls in attendance. He had been chasing Ann for nearly a year.

Meade was highly suspicious of Blanden's motives. True, Ann was lovely, but there were hundreds of lovely women in Las Vegas. To Meade, Ann was the greatest catch in the world, but he was practical enough to admit that Blanden had a long list to choose from. So why this special interest in Ann?

Two million dollars, Meade concluded. Gari supported this belief. Blanden had completely failed in his attempts to charm Gari. Her rebuffs hadn't fazed him. He kept coming back for more, even dropping by her office from time to time.

As far as Gari knew, Ann hadn't seen Blanden for months, until she called from her apartment to say he was joining them for the trip to Lake Tahoe. At least she was smart enough to call first. If Blanden had shown up without warning, Meade might have lost his cool.

To make matters worse, Ann had acted outrageously, cooing around Blanden like he was God personified. Reese had accepted Blanden's presence with easy grace, trying to make him a part of the group. Ann's reaction had been to treat

Reese rudely and fawn even more over Blanden. Blanden was ecstatic, touching Ann and putting his arm around her at every opportunity, causing Meade to seethe with barely contained fury. It was going to be a long weekend.

8

"Well, the prodigal returns," Gari said drily, looking up from her book. "I thought you had forgotten where I live."

"Come on, Mom," Ann said, flopping down on the couch. "I was here a week ago."

"Two weeks," corrected Gari.

"Whatever," Ann said, combing her fingers through her long blonde hair.

Gari smiled. "I'm glad you're here. It gets lonely with Meade away."

"Where is he?"

"Reno. Flew up this morning."

"Alone?"

"Reese, too, of course. They're like Tweedledum and Tweedledee."

"Oh," Ann said. Chin on fist, she stared broodingly at the wall.

Gari asked softly, "What's the matter?"

Ann's head snapped around. "Who said anything's the matter?" she asked a little too quickly.

"You don't have to say. I'm your mother, remember?"

"It's nothing," Ann said, waving a hand. "Just a down day, I guess."

"You've had a lot of them lately," Gari said, not hiding the concern in her voice.

Blinking her eyes, Ann shook her head. Looking down, she

played with a loose thread on the cushion. "I can't talk about it," she said in a barely audible voice.

Alarmed, Gari moved over and sat beside Ann. "Let me help," she said, taking her daughter's hand. "Please."

Bursting into tears, Ann yanked her hand away and doubled it into a fist. Gari jumped as she smacked it into her palm. Ann's violet eyes blazed through the wetness. "I'd like to cold-cock that son of a bitch!" she cried.

"Who?" Gari was almost physically sick. There was only one per—

"Reese!" Ann shouted, stunning Gari.

"Reese?" croaked Gari.

"I'd like to wring his neck!" Ann yelled.

"Really, dear," Gari said, calming somewhat, unable to believe that Reese would harm Ann, "I think cold-cocking is enough."

"I'll do that first. *Then* I'll wring his neck!"

"What has Reese done?" Gari asked. "I can't imagine him hurting you."

Leaping to her feet, Ann cried, "I wish to hell he would!" She pointed a long finger at her crotch. "Right there!"

"Ann!" Gari exclaimed, staring up into the angry flushed face. "Have you been drinking?"

"No, but that's a good idea!" Ann snapped, marching to the bar and grabbing the gin bottle. Slamming ice cubes into a glass, she mixed a martini.

Gari sat down at the bar. "Fix one for me, too," she said. "For some strange reason, I'm suddenly in the mood."

Ann handed Gari a glass, then gulped down half of hers. "Reese is a class jerk," Ann said, tossing her head. "I've already told him so."

"When did you honor him with that?" Gari asked, arching an eyebrow.

"Months ago."

"I thought things were a bit strained."

"I've tried to be nice because of you and Meade," Ann said loftily.

"That's awfully nice of you," Gari said, "but Meade and

I are more concerned about your happiness than having our feelings ruffled." She shot a disapproving look at the top of her daughter's head as Ann bent to make herself another martini. "Have you had dinner?" she asked.

"No," Ann said, taking a long swallow. "Why?"

Gari pointed at the glass in Ann's hand. "Too many of those on an empty stomach and you're not going to have anything to worry about. You're going to be horizontal."

"Sounds heavenly," Ann said with a sigh.

Gari was becoming irritated. "All right, Ann," she ordered. "Spit it out. What's eating you?"

Ann banged the glass down on the bar, splashing the contents on her hand. "Reese Harrington treats me like I'm nobody!" she wailed.

"My God!" Gari gaped, sitting up straight. "You're in love!"

"Of course, I'm in love," Ann cried plaintively. "Do you think I hate him?"

"Well," Gari said mildly, "I got the distinct impression that you wanted to cold-cock him and wring his neck."

"Maybe after I get him in bed," Ann said wistfully.

"Ann Slaughter, that's terrible!"

"Is that what you think when you go to bed with Meade?"

Gari leaped to her feet. "Take that back!" she raged.

Ann's eyes filled with tears, and she reached blindly across the bar. "I'm sorry, Mom. I'm so mixed up I don't know what I'm saying."

Taking Ann's hands, Gari said, "I'm sorry, too. Make some fresh drinks, and let's sit on the couch."

Over three more martinis, Ann poured her heart out. "I'm so crazy about him I can't sleep," she concluded between sniffles. "He never asks me out. If I don't make up excuses to see him, we'd never even speak—except when we're all together."

"Maybe he needs time," Gari suggested.

"Time?" Ann shook her head, and the tears flew. "It's been almost a year. I hate to admit it," she said brokenly, "but he doesn't want anything to do with me."

Gari gazed down into her glass. She had been happy when
Reese didn't go weak-kneed and speechless in Ann's presence, as so many men did. She hadn't considered a match-up,
not until Reese had been with them for several months. The
possibilities were attractive, but she hadn't voiced her
thoughts, not even to Meade.

Gari took Ann's hand. "I've been so happy about what
Reese has done in taking the pressure off Meade that I've
been blind to everything else," she said.

Ann smiled through her tears. "Oh, Mom, it's so wonderful. I've never seen Meade so happy. He just comes alive
when Reese is around!"

Gari nodded. "It's a mutual admiration society. It's obvious that Reese feels the same way."

Ann burst into tears. "Why can't he feel that way about
me?"

Gari said, "Let's get you to bed. You're in no shape to
drive home. In the morning, we'll be able to think better."

Gari was wrong. Mother and daughter called in to work
sick. They spent most of the day in darkened rooms suffering
from grade-A hangovers.

9

Looking over the top of the newspaper, Meade's eyes met
Gari's. She was frowning and chewing on her lip. Recogniz-
ing the signs, he dropped the paper in his lap and took off his
glasses. "You were saying?" he prompted.

"Clever, Mr. Slaughter," she said, eyes narrowing. "Very
clever."

"So bright they put me under a tub at night," Meade said
cheerfully.

"Oh, boy," Gari groaned, looked prayerfully at the ceiling.

"I'm waiting," Meade said.

Gari sighed and looked at Meade. "It's Ann. She's got a problem."

The smile vanished from Meade's face. "Ann?" he said sharply.

"She's in sort of a one-sided affair."

"Blanden!" Meade exploded, throwing the newspaper aside. "I'll break—"

Gari laughed. "Oh, Meade, I'm sorry. It's nothing like that."

"All right, lady," Meade growled. "Explain yourself, and it better be good. You almost gave me a heart attack."

"It's a little complicated. Our lovely Ann has fallen head over heels in love with Reese."

"That's a problem?" Meade beamed.

"It is for Ann. Reese doesn't seem to know she's alive."

"No kidding?"

"Ann came over Wednesday. Between martinis and tears, the story dripped all over the couch. She stayed here in bed the next day with a terrible hangover. Her mother shared the same fate."

"I'll be damned."

"Something like that—what I can remember."

"You're sure about Reese?"

"Ann is. A girl knows about these things. It's killing her." A wicked gleam. "Serves her right. She's broken more hearts than Sarah Bernhardt."

"I'll be damned."

"Meade, if that's your only input, I might as well be talking to the wall."

"I hope you don't expect me to talk to Reese," Meade said, scowling darkly. "Ann's my responsibility; Reese isn't. I don't believe in monkeying around with people's lives."

"What about me?" Gari asked innocently.

"Is that what this is all about?"

"The thought occurred to me."

"I'll bet. You already had your mind made up, didn't you?"

"Well . . ."

Putting on his glasses, Meade picked up the paper. "Good luck, baby," he said, burying his face in the sports section. "Just don't come back all beat up and complaining."

The next morning, Gari rang Meade in his office. "Can you do without me tonight?" she asked. "I have a date."

"He'd better be short, fat and over a hundred," Meade said gruffly.

"How about tall, dark and twenty-nine?"

"That quick? You're talking to him tonight?"

"You know how I hate to procrastinate. Besides, I want to get Ann straightened out as soon as possible."

"Does she know?"

"Don't be silly. She'd kill me. I'd stay out of it if there was another way. Oh, yes, if Reese should ask, you've got piles of work to bring home tonight. You're too busy to have me around."

"A liar as well as a meddler. Never thought I'd see the day. You better be home by midnight or I'll get out the shotgun." Muttering something unintelligible, Meade hung up.

Reese had been suspicious from the moment Gari dropped by his office and invited him to have dinner with her in the Lake Room. Meade didn't have that much work to do, and nothing was more important than his evenings at home with Gari. The answer came over after-dinner drinks.

After a brief lull in the conversation, Gari blurted out, "It's tough being a mother."

"I wouldn't know," Reese said, smiling to cover his confusion.

"The problems don't stop when the child leaves home," Gari said, nervously playing with her glass.

"Oh?" Reese said weakly.

"Ann is having a tough time, Reese," she said. "I'm afraid you're involved."

Reese wished he could disappear.

Seeing Reese's discomfort, Gari touched his hand. "This isn't easy for either of us," she said, biting her lip. "Ann's fallen hard for you. Evidently, she's alone in her feelings. Is there some way you can let her down easy?"

Nothing else would make sense except the truth. "Can we talk in my office?" Reese said. Nodding mutely, Gari gathered up her things.

In the office, Reese pulled a chair up close to Gari's. "Meade can't know anything about this," he said, standing behind the chair while Gari kicked her shoes off.

Gari was taken aback. "You're sure?" she said, dreading the responsibility. She and Meade had never kept anything from each other.

"Positive. You have to give me your solemn word on this," Reese said, a tone of authority in his voice Gari had never heard before.

"All right, you have it," she said resignedly. "I hope you have good reason."

"The best," Reese said, sitting down. "When you first saw me, you acted like you'd seen a ghost. Remember?"

Frowning, Gari recalled their first meeting. "I thought I . . . I . . ."

"Recognized me?"

"Yes."

"Then you figured you had recognized me as Reese Harrington, quarterback."

"Right."

Leaning forward, Reese stared at Gari for several beats. "Think hard," he urged. "Who do I remind you of?"

Gari stared back, eyes growing bigger and bigger. Gripping the sides of the chair, she whispered, "No . . . *no!*"

Reese nodded. "Now you know why you were so shocked."

Pointing a shaking finger, Gari gasped, "You . . . Meade?"

Reese seized her hand. "Meade's my father. That's why I've avoided Ann."

"My God," Gari murmured. "I must have been blind. I thought the black hair and blue eyes were just an unbelievable coincidence. If Meade had been twenty years younger and his hair dark, nobody could have missed it. Meade doesn't know, of course."

"No," Reese said, "and it stays that way!"

"Why? It's not fair, to you *or* Meade."

"It's a long story, Gari."

"Well, you're not getting out of here until you tell me," she said, drawing her long legs up under her body.

Reese stared at the floor. Surely this wouldn't affect Gari's feelings toward Meade, an affair over thirty years ago! Gari was too sensible for that. He looked up. "My mother and Meade went together in the late forties."

"You were born in forty-nine," Gari said softly. "Meade teased you about that at your birthday party, said you should have played for San Francisco."

"Mom left him when she learned she was pregnant."

"Cindy." Gari's voice was barely audible.

A shocked look. "How did you know?"

"Meade told me, when Ann was just a little girl."

"Mom said he didn't know she was pregnant."

"He had absolutely no idea. He looked for her, even hired a detective agency. When he told me, the pain was still there. I remember saying how much he must have loved her."

Reese's heart leaped, relieved at last of a heavy burden. "What a waste," he said.

"How long have you known?" Gari asked.

"Since I was sixteen."

For the second time since arriving in Las Vegas, Reese told about Cindy's death. While Smitty had shown no outward emotion, Gari's face was streaked with tears. Moving closer, Reese took her in his arms, and they wept together. It was a cleansing time for Reese, washing away the last traces of resentment, preparing him to willingly accept Meade as his father.

They talked far into the night. Reese told Gari about his visit with Jack Harrington when he was a senior at Stanford. "Jack loved her, too," Reese concluded. "He said their marriage was the saddest, most wonderful time in his life, loving

Mom and knowing she loved someone else. It got too much for her, and she went back east."

"Why didn't she stay in Los Angeles?" Gari said. "All her contacts were there."

"Jack thinks she didn't trust her emotions, being so close to Meade. She had buried her past when she left Las Vegas, so it was easy to pick up and go."

"Meade didn't notice anything in your application."

"Mom never used the name Cindy again. All I ever heard was Beverly. Cindy was a studio name."

"How did she get into little theater work?"

"She was a good actress and had saved quite a bit of money. That combination was pretty hard to turn down. She owned half the company in Mt. Kisco when she died."

"She never married again?"

"No, her whole life was wrapped up in the theater and me. I couldn't have had a better mother. I grew up in a fairytale land, with a beautiful mother and theater people always around."

"It's surprising you didn't get into acting."

"Oh, Mom stuck me in a few shows when I was young. I didn't like it. She dropped the idea. She never pushed me; that was one of the great things about her."

"Do you have any pictures of her?"

"Dozens—hundreds. I dig them out once in a while."

"May I see them sometime?"

"Sure. I have one right here." Reese took out his wallet. "Jack took it right after I was born. He gave me a whole set." Reese handed the picture to Gari.

Gari's hand shook. She couldn't trust herself to look up. "Meade has to see this," she whispered.

"Not yet . . . maybe never," Reese said.

"You can't mean that!" Gari cried, waving the picture in Reese's face. "At least think of Meade! Do you think this is easy for me? Know something? Meade and I have never talked about love—not in twenty years! Oh, it's there; we both know it." She waved the picture. "How do you think I feel knowing he loved your mother more? It would be a

lot easier to forget the whole thing, but we can't. We
can't!"

Reese fumbled uncomfortably for a reply. "Give me time,"
he said. "I shouldn't have said never; I don't really feel that
way. I want to know Meade as a father, but I want him to
know me as a man first."

"Please don't take too long," Gari said. "Meade's seventy-
four. He's had so much sadness in his life."

"You're quite a woman," Reese said admiringly. "And
you shouldn't downplay the way Meade feels about you. You
two have something special."

"I know," Gari smiled. "We've been lucky." She gasped
and bolted upright. "Ann! I've forgotten all about her. She
has to know, Reese. It's the only way."

Reese started to protest.

"Do you think she'll talk?"

"She's awfully close to Meade," Reese cautioned.

"She's also an attorney."

"Touché," Reese said glumly.

"She won't understand, otherwise." Gari pressed.

"All right," Reese sighed.

Gari glanced at her wristwatch. "If I don't get home,
Meade's going to kill me. It's past one."

"Be careful," Reese said. "You're not used to keeping
secrets from Meade."

"Lordy, don't I know it. I'll be careful; don't worry."

Gari returned home in a fog. Dropping his book, Meade
looked up from the bed. "How did it go?" he asked.

"Okay," she said, smiling wanly. She sat down, yawning
while Meade unzipped her dress. "I'm so tired, I'm about
ready to pass out."

Meade watched appreciatively as Gari walked nude to the
closet and slipped a white nightgown over her head. "We'll
talk about it in the morning," he said, turning out the light
and molding his body to hers.

10

Anger, consternation, tears. Gari now knew the depth of her daughter's feelings for Reese. It was not the passing infatuation she had considered at first, then hoped for since last Thursday.

"What if neither of us had known?" Ann was saying. "Do you think some mysterious instinct would have kept us from getting together?"

"Be reasonable," Gari said. "You can't argue with the facts."

"This isn't a courtroom, Mother," Ann said, getting up and pacing the floor of her apartment. "What about how I feel inside? What am I supposed to do about that?"

Gari sighed and looked down at her hands. "You're the only one who can answer that," she said. "I wish I could help, but I can't."

"I wish I could help myself," Ann said, shoulders drooping. The anger returned. "Why did you have to tell Reese? I'll never be able to face him again!"

"That's not true. Reese is more than understanding. You can be good friends."

"We can be good friends," Ann repeated. A lopsided smile. "You don't know how many times I've said that when I was breaking things off. Steve—you remember him—looked so hurt when I said it. I laughed. Can you believe it, I *laughed!* Know something? It's not funny any more!"

Gari held out her arms, and Ann buried her face in her mother's lap. Filled with infinite sorrow, Gari stroked the long golden hair. There was nothing she could say.

Minutes passed. Ann rose and turned quickly away. "Let

me wash up," she said, leaving the room before Gari could reply.

When she returned, Gari was pouring two cups of coffee. They sat at the kitchen table. "I'm going out of town for a few days," Ann said. "I have vacation time coming. It will give me time to think."

The look in Ann's swollen defiant eyes frightened Gari. Seeing her mother's look, Ann said, "I'm not going off the deep end, Mom. I just need time to be alone. You said it earlier; I have to work this out by myself."

"Do you know where you're going?" Gari asked.

"I think so. I'll let you know when I get back."

Gari nodded. Ann was twenty-six. It was her life.

"I still can't believe it," Ann said, trying to smile. "How can you keep it from Meade?"

"One day at a time," Gari said. "I can't see them as anything else but father and son now. It's so obvious."

Gari left with Ann's promise that she would call as soon as she returned. Gari dreaded telling Meade. He wasn't going to understand Ann's leaving without a goodbye or explanation. She smiled ruefully. She would unburden herself on Reese. After all, he started the whole thing.

Ten days later, Ann returned with stunning news. She was going to work for the law firm of O'Connell and Matkins in Menlo Park, California. She had worked there as a clerk while attending Stanford. One of the partners had come to Las Vegas several months ago and asked her to join their corporate department. She had turned it down but considered it a gift from heaven after her mother's shocking revelation.

Meade took it hard, unaware of Ann's need to get away, while Reese was ridden with guilt, knowing his part in her sudden defection.

Reese and Ann met on several occasions before her departure, stilted, uncomfortable sessions, each trying to make light of their new status. Secretly, both were relieved when it came time for Ann to go.

Ann returned only once in the three months that remained

of 1978, for Christmas. She was doing well on her new job and seemed to be adjusting emotionally. Gari knew better. Ann was holding part of herself back. The old, open sharing was gone.

As the next summer approached, Gari became impatient with Reese. When was he going to tell Meade?

"Not yet," Reese said. "Maybe when the Gaming Board completes its investigation." Reese had applied for a license as a key employee at the Plush Wheel. If approved, he would be made Vice President of Marketing. Unofficially, he would continue in his role as Meade's personal assistant.

Gari leaned over Reese's desk. "What else have you got to prove?" she said angrily. "You've shot up faster in the organization than anyone's ever done. You were splashed all over the *Las Vegas Sun* as the 'Golden Boy of Gaming.' I think the whole thing is ridiculous!"

"Ridiculous or not, that's the way it stays," Reese shot back. "Will you please sit down? You make me nervous." He smiled as Gari's mouth flew open. "Come on, we're buddies, aren't we?"

"Don't bet on it," Gari said, plopping down in a chair. "You're as stubborn as Meade, if that's possible."

"Must be hard on you, being so easygoing and lovable," Reese said.

Gari shook her head. "You win this time, but don't think I'm giving up."

11

Looking out the big picture window, Louis Giuliano noted that most of the snow was gone from the Sierras. The summer sun would burn the rest off soon.

"This is the best time of the year," Jan said. "When everything's new and green."

Louis looked at his stepmother, cool and elegant in white slacks and blue lace blouse. Her rich black hair was piled on top of her head today, stray ringlets teasing ears and neck. Jan Giuliano was a woman of many faces, all of them beautiful.

Louis had acquired a deep respect for his father's much younger wife. She governed the household wisely, and her conduct at home and in public was above reproach.

Jan had been frank with Louis about her marriage. That had occurred last year, while they were walking the grounds of her new home. Stopping beside a marble fountain, Jan said abruptly, "You're wondering why I married Tony, aren't you?"

Startled, Louis said, "That's pretty direct."

"Why beat around the bush?" Jan said, moving on. "We're going to be seeing a lot of each other, and I think we can be friends. Things will go smoother if you understand."

"All right," Louis said.

"I've been competing in a man's world for several years," Jan began. "You don't know what it's like to show up at a meeting and have men resent your presence, treat you with contempt, then fall all over themselves trying to get you in bed. They can't imagine I succeeded any other way."

Jan's dark eyes challenged Louis. "Don't get me wrong. I'm not a man-hating feminist. I don't go in for sign waving and shouting slogans. Politics bores me. What I do, I do well, and that's making money."

Louis paused, tall and slender in a dark tailored suit, touches of gray at his temples. "Then why marry my father? You were doing well on your own, and he's got old-fashioned ideas about women. He didn't even like it that my wife graduated from college."

"Tony offered me protection, and he was willing to change his lifestyle to meet my needs. I can move about and make investments undisturbed; no one is going to bother the wife of Tony Giuliano. His attitude toward women? I'm not included. Tony respects money. It's something new for him, being able to discuss finances with a woman."

"You didn't say anything about feelings."

An amused look. "You want me to talk about love? Would you believe me if I did? We have a mutually benefiting union, Louis. Tony's enjoying life, something he's never done before. He likes to show me off. We're both happy with the arrangement. I admire him for what he's accomplished. We listen to each other; that's more than most couples do."

"You win," Louis said, smiling and holding out his hand. "Consider us friends."

That was a year ago. They were comfortable together now. With his father's approval, Louis often sought Jan's advice on business matters. He no longer wondered why Tony held Jan in such high regard. He didn't know any woman—and few men—who could match her keen analytical mind.

Jan rang the maid and ordered coffee. "Let's have it by the pool," she said to Louis.

They sipped their coffee under the large yellow umbrella. "This Meade Slaughter thing is coming to a head," Jan said, almost causing Louis to drop his cup.

"Where did you hear about that?" he asked.

"It didn't come all at once, a little here, a little there," Jan said. "I think I know the whole story now."

"Including what happened to my grandfather?"

A nod. "And what happened to Slaughter's fiancée."

Louis's eyes widened. "You know something I don't. My grandfather was killed when I was nine years old."

"I didn't get it all from Tony," Jan replied. "A private detective filled in the pieces."

"My God," Louis exclaimed. "Do you realize what a risk you've taken?"

"Yes," Jan said. "I also realize what this obsession is doing to Tony. Hate can destroy a man's reason; it can also destroy those around him. I had to know what was behind it."

"And?"

"It's not good. Slaughter had some justification."

Louis pushed his cup aside. "Go on," he said.

"Not long after we were married, Tony told me about his father's death. He said Slaughter killed him because Carlo was pushing Slaughter out of his club. That didn't make sense. What I know about Slaughter, he's not the kind of man who would kill because someone bested him in business. He'd fight back, but kill? I couldn't see it.

"I didn't do anything until I found out about the takeover Tony's planning. You know about that?"

Louis nodded.

"Tony's taking a terrible risk. He has to be breaking gaming laws. For revenge! If you ask me, both sides should leave well enough alone.

"The detective went back over old records and found that Slaughter was beaten and paralyzed and his fiancée killed by 'persons unknown.' Two years later, Carlo and his bodyguard were shot down—about the same time that Meade Slaughter returned to Nevada."

"That's all news to me," Louis said, struggling with this shocking revelation.

"You can read the reports," Jan said. "They're in my safe-deposit box downtown."

"Why?" Louis said. "Do you know what will happen if he finds out you've been snooping around with private detectives? He's been running a spy network most of his life. It's all right for him to do it, but nobody's going to do it to him."

"I'm not going to be destroyed by this," Jan said. "I've thought about giving Tony an ultimatum—either he drops it or I leave."

"Don't do it, Jan," Louis warned. "I've never known Papa to care for anyone like he cares for you, but he's been after Slaughter for over forty years. Think of the planning he's put into this—the millions he spent! Don't give him an ultimatum. Not unless you want to lose."

Jan looked at Louis, an odd smile on her face. "That might be winning," she said softly.

12

"Wake up, lazybones!"

Jeanette Thomas rolled over and squinted at the clock beside the bed. She closed her eyes and pressed the receiver of the phone to her ear. "What's with you, Nancy? It's only ten," she said.

"You've had almost eight hours sleep. Up and at 'em! It's a beautiful day outside."

Pulling the pillow back over her head, Jeanette mumbled, "Go away. I get tired just listening to you. Where do you get your ambition?"

"Need it with two kids. Hear them yelling? We're going to the lake, and you're going with us."

"Thanks, but make it another day," Jeanette yawned. "I haven't slept all the wrinkles out yet."

"Ready or not, we're coming to get you," Nancy said. "Al's packing the car. Be by in half an hour." The phone clicked in Jeanette's ear.

"Oh, gawd," Jeanette moaned, throwing the pillow aside and sitting up, the sheet slipping from her nude body. No use arguing with Nancy. Like talking to a stone wall.

Jeanette padded to the kitchen and plugged in the coffee pot. Bending her slender frame, she touched her toes. She patted her stomach. Better go to the bathroom before she did that again.

She was out of the shower in ten minutes. A cup of coffee was downed while she blow-dried her shoulder-length dark brown hair. She had just slipped into a black French-cut bikini when the doorbell rang. Small hands rattled the knob and beat on the door.

Opening the door, Jeanette was instantly attacked. "Let's go!" the girl cried, bright orange hair coming up to just above Jeanette's knee. Her older brother, just turned four, grabbed Jeanette's hand and pulled her toward the doorway.

"Slow down, guys," Jeanette said. "I have to get some clothes on. Besides, you're early."

"Three minutes early," Nancy said as she entered the room. "Let her go, kids." She opened the hall closet door and peered inside. "Where's that fancy umbrella?" she asked, pushing some coats aside. "Ours is busted."

"Under the bed," Jeanette said.

Nancy made a face. "Probably all dusty."

"You can clean it while I put something on."

"You've got something on," Nancy said, eyeing the skimpy suit. "Wish I could fit into that thing."

"Don't knock your bod. It makes you a living."

A sigh and a glance down at her heavy breasts. "These things more than the rest of me," Nancy said.

Jeanette laughed. "Tell you what, let's put yours and mine together, then split them up. That should make two normal-sized pairs."

"Let's go," the little girl urged, pushing on Nancy's leg.

Nancy looked down at her daughter. "Come on, Carrot-top, Petey. Let's crawl under Jeanette's bed." They dusted off the beach umbrella while Jeanette dressed in jeans, T-shirt and canvas sneakers.

They piled into the station wagon, Jeanette sitting in the back seat with the children. Al Martin, Nancy's husband, said woefully as he started the car, "To think I'm missing football for this."

"And I'm missing sleep," Jeanette said.

"Do you good, kids," Nancy said. She ruffled Al's red hair. "You can watch the game tomorrow night."

"Thanks a lot," Al said. "I'll have to leave for work about the time it gets good." He squeezed Nancy's hand. "Guess it's worth it, considering you're such a good-looking broad."

Nancy smiled at Jeanette. "Gee, ain't marriage grand?"

"For you," Jeanette said. "Not for me."

"Oops," Nancy said, looking at Al. "She's in one of those moods."

Al looked in the rear-view mirror at Jeanette. "Pay no attention. Nancy reads romance novels. Wants everybody to be in love. And married."

Arriving at Lake Mead, they set up the umbrella and laid out the picnic things. Al and the women stayed in the shade, Al because he burned easily and the women because their work didn't allow tans. Nancy was a showgirl and Jeanette the lead dancer at the Fantasia. Al, a stagehand, met Nancy there five years ago. Nancy called it a convenience marriage; they kept the same weird hours.

The beach was crowded, and boats moved in and out of the nearby marina. The warm September days were best, Jeanette thought as she sat watching the scene, arms around her long legs, chin on knees.

"Gotta go to the girl's room," Nancy said, jumping up, stunning in a white bikini, almost six feet tall with a head of ruffled blonde hair and sky-blue eyes. "How about you, Jay?" she asked, calling Jeanette by the nickname she had acquired when she began dancing in Las Vegas seven years ago.

"I'll pass," Jeanette said.

Nancy waved so long and walked off.

The children ran by, Becky screeching with Petey at her heels. Al raised his head. "Cool it, kids!" he yelled. They paid no attention.

Al said, "Guess I'll have to start beating them. They don't show me no respect."

The children snaked in front of a row of sunbathing girls, then Becky cut a sharp left. She saw two big hairy legs, then a strong arm swept her into the air.

"Hey, there," the big man grinned, blue eyes flashing in his darkly tanned face. "Where you headin'?"

Like her mother, Becky didn't have a bashful bone in her body. "That way!" she pointed. She looked down at her brother, then into the man's smiling face. "You're tall!" she said. "Taller than my daddy!"

"Where is your daddy?" the man asked.

"Over there." Becky pointed at the red-haired man standing beside a big white umbrella with red tassels, an anxious look on his face.

"Let's go see him," the big man said, perching Becky on his shoulder, an ice chest swinging from his other hand.

Al Martin lifted Becky down. "Thanks," he said. "These kids can be a danger at times." The children took off, yelling and screaming.

"No problem," the tall man said.

"Have a cold beer?" Al offered.

"Thanks, but I've had my quota for the day." The man looked at Jeanette who was kneeling on the blanket. "Cute kids you've got."

"Oh, yes!" she said. "I know I'm partial, but they really are darlings."

Al glanced at Jeanette. What was she up to?

"I'd better get going," the man said.

"Come out often?" Al asked.

"Mostly Sundays. I get in a little sailing. It's my escape."

"Know what you mean. By the way, my name's Al."

"Reese," the man said, shaking Al's hand. He looked at Jeanette.

"Jeanette," she said brightly.

"Well, see you." He walked off, white tank top and trunks contrasting sharply with his deep tan.

Nancy slipped under the umbrella. "Who was that?" she asked. She looked at Jeanette. "You let a hunk like that get away?"

"She lost his interest," Al said. "He didn't want to fool around with a married woman."

"*What?*"

"Would you believe this nut?" Al said. "Becky runs into this guy, so he carries her over. 'Cute kids you've got,' he says to Jay. 'Oh, yes!' she says, all pleased with herself. Off he goes, thinking she's married with two little brats."

"You didn't!" Nancy cried, catching Jeanette's smug look and breaking into laughter. "I can't believe it. Why did you do that?"

Jeanette shrugged. "It just sneaked out. And I *do* think the kids are cute."

"My aching back," Nancy said, digging into the ice chest. She handed out two cans of beer and popped one for herself.

13

Reese left the marina and walked along the beach. It was early October, and the crowds were thinning out.

She was helping her brother build a sandcastle, her orange-red hair flashing like a beacon. Reese squatted down on his heels. "Hi," he said to the little girl. "Remember me?"

She frowned, studying Reese over a mound of sand. The blond-haired boy said, "She's not very old. She forgets things a lot."

"I do not!" the girl cried indignantly. "I remember you. You picked me up."

Reese nodded. "What's your name?"

"Becky. My mom calls me Carrot-top."

"I wonder why," Reese said, looking at the dancing orange curls.

"Here comes Mom," Becky said, pointing a sandy finger at a tall blonde walking their way.

Reese rose, a puzzled look on his face.

"Hi!" Nancy said. "You must be the guy who saved my kid from getting her head knocked flat."

"I thought—" Reese grinned sheepishly.

"Yeah, I know. Jeanette can be a bundle of laughs at times. Come over and have a beer. We can talk while the kids dig to China."

Introductions over, they sat under the white umbrella, red tassels stirring in the gentle breeze. "Just you and the kids?" Reese said.

Nancy made a face. "Al put up such a howl I left him with the TV. He hates to miss the Forty-Niners."

"Most people are for the Rams here," Reese said.

"Not Al. He's from San Jose. Dyed-in-the-wool Niners' fan."

"You're not from there." It wasn't a question.

"Caught the accent, huh? Austin, Texas. My mother thinks I'm a ruined woman, here in Vegas and all."

"I take it you're not a secretary."

"Guess I don't look the type, huh?" Nancy grinned. "I'm in the show at the Fantasia. So is Jeanette. I have to stand around like a lump on a log while she dances up a storm. Ever seen her dance?"

"Don't think so. Not at the Fantasia, anyway. She danced anywhere else?"

"Oh, all over. She's really great. Except when she tries to steal my husband and kids. Al told me how she made like they were hers. She was grinning like a Cheshire cat when I got back right after you left."

"She's not married?"

"Nope. Never has been. Interested?"

Reese sipped his beer. "I've been in Vegas for almost two years, and I've never gone with a girl from the shows. Funny, isn't it?"

"Not really," Nancy said. She squinted at Reese. "You work at one of the hotels?"

A nod.

"Executive?"

Another nod.

"Well, there you are," she said, spreading her arms. "The girls don't mix much with the front office. Our social life revolves around the people we work with—performers, musicians, stagehands. That's how I met Al. He's a stagehand at the Fantasia."

"Makes it nice for the guys who work backstage," Reese grinned.

Nancy grinned back. "Must be a thousand of us sex-starved girls working in the shows. 'Course, a lot are old married ladies like me. Hey, you got me off the subject. Interested in Jeanette?"

Reese laughed. "I might be. She got anything to say about it?"

"I don't think she'd object. We have pretty much the same tastes. I'd go for you in a second if I weren't saddled with a husband and kids."

Reese laughed. He really liked this outspoken girl. "I'll give it a go," he said. "How do we do it?"

"We?"

"Come on, Nancy, you're not going to make me do this alone, are you?"

A wicked gleam. "Let's do it different. Okay?"

"How?"

"Let's think up something that will blow her mind," Nancy said, rubbing her hands together with delight. "I love surprises, don't you?"

14

"Bob, this is Reese Harrington. Can you get me in the late show tomorrow night?"

"How many?"

"Just me."

"Can do. Want me to come along?"

"Great! What time?"

"Meet me at the front entrance at eleven. We'll have a drink first."

Reese hung up and looked at his watch. Past noon and this call was all he'd accomplished today. Not surprising, considering he hadn't gotten to the office until a half-hour ago.

Last night, he had worked until past two putting the finishing touches on a new marketing program that would be presented to the board of directors next week.

This would be his first appearance before the board as Vice President of Marketing for the southern Nevada Plush Wheels. The Gaming Commission had approved his application for a key-employee license in August, and he had taken over his new duties on September first.

Reese entered the Fantasia shortly before eleven. With nineteen hundred rooms, the Fantasia was one of the largest hotels on the Strip. Its showroom stage rivaled the one in the MGM Grand's Ziegfeld Room.

The Fantasia was larger than the Plush Wheel but would not be for long. Next fall, ground would be broken for a second thirty-one story tower at the Plush Wheel, with completion set for eighteen months later in the spring of 1982. The Plush Wheel would then have twenty-seven hundred rooms, a new underground shopping arcade and 50,000 square feet of convention space.

Bob Lomax, the Fantasia's publicity director, led Reese into a lounge where a small showband was entertaining. They sat in a booth reserved for company executives. "Straighten your tie," Lomax said as a tall slim man entered the lounge. "The head honcho is coming our way."

Louis Giuliano held out his hand. "Good to see you, Reese."

They shook hands, and Louis sat down. Reese and Louis had met several times before at social functions and gaming meetings. At fifty, Louis had the reputation of being one of the most experienced hotel men in Nevada, as comfortable in the casino as he was behind a desk. Reese had liked him from the start.

Soon it was time for the show. Louis excused himself and walked toward the casino. Reese and Louis had arranged to meet for lunch.

Reese and Bob Lomax sat in a first tier, center booth, looking at the stage now filled with nearly a hundred performers. Reese had picked out Nancy right away, a towering beauty in a feathered costume that covered little and revealed almost everything. Reese counted Al Martin a lucky man.

Then Jeanette burst onto the stage, a lovely creature doing double and triple turns as she weaved in and out of the lines of lavishly costumed performers, silver heels flashing through intricate steps. Reese was enthralled.

"Like her?" Lomax said in Reese's ear, the crashing music drowning everything else out.

Reese nodded, then said quickly to throw Lomax off the scent, "She's kind of small upstairs."

"Flat, you mean? The Felicia Atkins-look is out, Reese. Slim is in—has been for five, six years. Besides, we all put in a few small pairs so the customers' wives and girlfriends can say theirs are just as big or bigger.

"With a dancer like Jeanette Thomas, who cares? She's short, too, just under five-six. But God, can she dance!"

Reese watched as Jeanette twirled from one boy dancer to another, beaded strands of her wispy costume flaring as she spun, teasing the audience with glimpses of spectacular legs and well-rounded buttocks. The number ended to a rousing ovation.

As the show progressed, Reese saw little else but Jeanette. She wore only a G-string for the adagio number, a romantic duet in which she was lifted and carried by her muscular male partner.

Reese didn't ask any more questions about Jeanette. He had satisfied his curiosity. Now to put his plan into effect.

15

Jeanette stared at the single red rose in the delicate vase. "That's French crystal," the brunette said who was looking over Jeanette's shoulder. "I've been collecting it for years. Who's it from?"

"Don't know," Jeanette said, fingering the card tied to the neck of the vase. "All it has is my name."

Nancy bent for a closer look. "It's a man's handwriting. Be glad, Jay. You're still attracting the right sex."

"Get your ass out of my face, Nancy," a short-haired blonde said. She stood on tiptoe. "One rose—that's all?" She walked off, naked buttocks bouncing. "You're slipping, Jay."

"Since when did you get even one rose, Jenny?" Nancy yelled.

The blonde kept walking. She flipped an Italian salute over her shoulder.

"Regency Florists," a girl said, bare breasts swaying as she read the card. "They're not cheap." She clutched the slender vase. "Think he meant this to be a phallic symbol? It must be ten, eleven inches."

"Beat it, you horny characters," Jeanette ordered. "Get some clothes on. You're vital parts are overreacting to exposure." She sat down as the girls drifted away. "I like it," she said, gazing at the vase. "If it's a phallic symbol, it's a nice one."

"It'll make a good club," the girl sitting next to her said. "In case the guy is waiting to pounce at the door."

"I'll keep that in mind," Jeanette said, not discarding the idea completely.

Shoulder bag swinging, holding the vase carefully in her right hand, Jeanette entered the parking lot. There had been no man with an expectant smile waiting at the door. She drove straight home and was asleep in an hour.

No single rose awaited her after the final show that night. "Three dozen!" a shapely girl announced, standing over the perfect buds, finishing her count with a long finger resting on a velvet-smooth petal.

"More French crystal, too," said the brunette who had identified the vase last night. "Big bucks."

"Same guy?" a voice asked.

A leggy girl looked on both sides of the card. "Looks like the same handwriting."

"Hey, those are my flowers!" Jeanette cried, fighting to keep from being relegated to the role of bystander.

"It's probably an Arab sheik," Nancy said. "He wants you in his harem."

"Thanks a bunch," Jeanette said. "I wonder who he is?"

"You sure rang his bell," Nancy said. "What do you think he's got planned next? A whole *bed* of roses?"

"Funny, funny," Jeanette said. She sniffed the flowers. "He's got class, I'll give him that."

Jeanette drove home, glancing from time to time at the roses that filled the passenger seat, wondering who the giver was. She hoped it wouldn't result in an embarrassing situation. This being Sunday, her mysterious suitor might be long gone by afternoon, a weekend visitor who got his kicks sending flowers to girls backstage.

That night, Jeanette didn't go directly to the dressing room after the final show; none of the performers did. This was the end of the work week. Payday and weigh-day.

As each performer stepped on the scales, with the others looking on, his or her weight was recorded to be forwarded to the producer. Woe betide the individual who was consistently off the assigned weight!

Jeanette's turn came. "One hundred eight," the weigher said to the woman holding Jeanette's card. Jeanette sighed with relief. She hadn't gained or lost a pound. She stood around with the others until the weighing was over and they could collect their paychecks. She spent additional minutes discussing some new routines with her adagio partner.

As Jeanette approached the dressing area, she heard squeals of surprise and delight. The room was filled with naked and half-naked girls, intent on some object in the corner. Jeanette hopped up and down, trying to see what was causing the commotion.

"Isn't it beautiful?" a breathless voice said.

"Why can't I get something like that?" someone said wistfully.

Pushing closer, Jeanette saw a bed of light yellow roses, about two feet square. An umbrella made of white roses with tiny red petals hanging like tassels was stuck in the center, a bottle of champagne lying underneath. It looked like a miniature float in the Rose Parade.

A girl read from the card that dangled from the umbrella, "I liked you married, but I like you better single." She looked up, confused. "What the hell does that mean? And who's Reese?"

Jeanette froze. "Let me through!" she cried, pressing forward. She read the card. An envelope leaned against the umbrella pole. She opened it. "Call you backstage Tuesday night." She took a business card out of the envelope. The gold Plush Wheel emblem was embossed in the upper left-hand corner, "Reese Harrington, Vice President Marketing," in the lower right.

Nancy was peering over Jeanette's shoulder. "The same Reese who was at the beach?"

"Who else?" Jeanette said, lifting the card that hung from the umbrella. "Likes me better single! How did he find out?"

"Got me." Nancy screwed up her face in concentration. "Reese Harrington. Where have I heard that name?"

"Did you say Reese Harrington?" a towering showgirl asked.

Jeanette and Nancy nodded in unison.

"Oh, wow!" the showgirl enthused. "Jay, you lucky girl!"

"I know him," a blonde with straight hair and bangs said, hugging her naked breasts. "Not like a friend, but I know who he is. He's a big man at the Plush Wheel. Used to be the quarterback for the St. Louis Cardinals. My hometown."

"Yea, team!" whooped a girl with breasts that would make three of Jeanette's. "He can tackle me anytime."

"Quarterbacks don't tackle, dummy," Nancy said.

"Bet he would if I asked him," the girl shot back.

Nancy looked down at Jeanette. "You're going to talk to him, aren't you? He seems like a nice guy."

Jeanette smiled and picked up the bottle of Dom Perignon. "He has good taste, too. Sure, I'll talk to him. If nothing else, I want to find out how he learned about me."

Nancy rolled her eyes. "Oh, I'm sure you will."

A parade of girls escorted Jeanette to her car, several helping her carry the rose-covered beach scene. It was an odd-looking procession, some wearing stage makeup, others with faces scrubbed clean, clad in jeans and an assortment of tops, mostly T-shirts. One girl was wearing hiking boots.

Jeanette drove off to a chorus of cheers.

16

Reese lounged on the deck of the catamaran and looked at Jeanette. This was her first time on a sailboat, and she was enjoying every minute. Dressed in white Levis and top, she lay on her back, hands behind her head, gazing up at the billowing sail. It was in the mid-eighties, a late October day on Lake Mead.

This was their third date. The first had been ten days ago, a few nights after Reese called. They had met at the Alpine Village Inn for an early dinner. It was an informal atmosphere, and they drank a bottle of Liebfraumilch with the German food.

Reese learned quickly that Jeanette was an inquisitive, direct individual. In her teens, she had been one of the flower-children in San Francisco's Haight-Ashbury district, and she had retained that group's contempt for pretense. Reese was intrigued and sometimes taken aback. Jeanette Thomas was definitely not your ordinary run-of-the-mill girl.

Their second meeting had been in a lounge at the Fantasia between shows. Jeanette was in full makeup, a marked contrast from their earlier meeting when Jeanette had worn no makeup and just a touch of lipstick.

The time had been too short for both, and they arranged to go sailing on Monday. When Reese called yesterday to verify the time, Jeanette suggested bringing the Dom Perignon. It was chilling in her ice chest, waiting for the right moment to be opened.

Jeanette proved a real help on the boat, nimbly jumping about and helping Reese rig the sail. She was full of questions and wouldn't accept incomplete answers. After Reese explained that the twenty-foot Tornado catamaran had been Ann's since Gari bought the thirty-two foot cruiser last year, he had to give a detailed description of the Slaughter family. By the time they were sailing in the wide expanse of Boulder Basin, Jeanette had absorbed a considerable amount of information.

From her prone position, she looked up at Reese. "You really like them, don't you?"

Reese nodded. "They're good people," he said, going on to tell about his work with Meade and his close friendship with Gari. He said little about Ann.

Jeanette thought that over for a moment, then glanced at the ice chest. "Ready for the champagne?" she said.

Locking the tiller, Reese moved forward and poured the wine. Touching his glass to Jeanette's, he said, "To Nancy's kids. They're cute, but I'm glad they're not yours."

The laughter came easy. Jeanette had learned all about Nancy's intrigue. She was forgiven; things were working out well.

Side by side, Reese and Jeanette ate shrimp cocktails and sipped champagne, the boat bobbing gently on the water.

Reese learned that Jeanette started taking dance lessons at the age of three, becoming active in an Orange County, California, ballet company while in grade school, appearing as a featured performer at dance festivals throughout the state during her high school years.

"Then something snapped," Jeanette said, holding out her glass while Reese added more champagne. "I wanted to be free. For one thing, I found boys a lot more interesting than working out on a horizontal bar with a bunch of sweaty girls. I was barely out of high school when I took off for San Francisco with my boyfriend to join the hippie movement. Things went okay for about a year, then he left me. I thought

I would die. I had turned my back on my family to go with a boyfriend, and I was too proud to go back. I was alone, really alone."

Reese glanced at Jeanette. She was gripping her champagne glass tightly, staring at nothing. "I worked as a part-time clerk in a store and enrolled in dance classes at the University of San Francisco," she went on. "It took two years for me to get over that breakup. It probably sounds silly to you—taking a teenage romance so seriously."

"Did it seem silly to you?"

"No."

"Then it doesn't seem silly to me."

She touched his arm, then drew her hand back quickly.

Thrilling from that simple gesture, Reese said, "How did you end up in Vegas?"

"Most of my dance training in San Francisco was jazz," Jeanette said. "Combining that with all those years of ballet and tap, I figured I was ready for the big time. I moved to Vegas, thinking I could pick up a job in a month or so." A short laugh. "It took over a year.

"I attended several dance schools and went to every audition that came up. If nothing else, I got over being scared. The first few auditions were frightening—those huge show-rooms and everybody so sure of themselves. I worked as a teller in a bank to keep alive."

"And?" Reese prompted.

"One day I was hired. I must have looked funny with my mouth hanging open after they had eliminated the last person, and I was still there. Can you imagine how I felt? I had been turned down dozens of times! I kept my contract by the bed, so I could read it whenever I woke up. I didn't sleep much that first night."

"How long ago was that?" Reese asked.

"Seven years last July. I've done five separate productions since then. I'm beginning to feel old."

"I was going to say something about that," Reese grinned. "All those grey hairs and wrinkles."

Jeanette punched him lightly. They traded birth dates and

made suitable comments about their age differences, Jeanette being 28, Reese 30.

The combination of the idyllic setting and champagne brought them closer together and loosened their tongues. Reese talked about his marriage to Catherine when he was twenty-two, the conflicts that arose and the divorce six years ago.

"I almost got married a couple of times," Jeanette said when Reese was finished. "The first time was six months after I arrived here. I was so discouraged about finding work as a dancer, and one of the bank officers was so nice to me. We got along fine, but I couldn't see myself settling down with a banker husband. It didn't seem workable then; it's impossible now." Lying on her back, she looked up at Reese, who was lounging against a cushion. "I can't relate to such an unimaginative kind of life."

She continued, "The second close call was with a musician. Most of the girls date musicians and stagehands . . . and boy dancers. It's sad about the boys. Some are out-and-out gays. Others are trying to find out what they are, and girls are really hurt when their boyfriends suddenly decide they are gay. You can compete with another woman but not with that."

Jeanette's slender fingers caressed the empty champagne glass. "I met a musician named Tom. We went together for two years and came close to getting married several times. It's easy in Las Vegas. Make up your mind anytime day or night and *boom,* one hour later you're married. Eventually, we drifted apart. That was a year ago. He's playing at the Hilton."

"Anyone since?" Reese asked, sliding down so he was lying beside Jeanette.

"Dates. Nothing serious. Working six nights a week, I keep pretty busy. You?"

"About the same. Football took up most of my time for years. Since arriving here, about all I've done is work." A smile. "Except sailing. If I hadn't been out that Sunday, I wouldn't have met you."

"Glad you did?"

Reese closed his hand over Jeanette's. "Gladder by the minute."

She looked into Reese's eyes with childlike frankness. "I would be lying if I said I didn't enjoy being with you."

"That's good enough for me," Reese said. "Seal it with a kiss?"

Lying side by side with only their hands and lips touching, they shared their first intimate moment. Reese rolled on his side and drew Jeanette close. Between kisses, they murmured short, broken sentences, touching, feeling, paying no attention to the passing of time, aware only of each other.

17

Meade was in a pensive mood. Probably just the Christmas season, he told himself as he stood gazing out over the Strip from his office on the top floor of the Plush Wheel tower. This was his "Eagle's Nest," a place where he could be alone or have meetings away from the busy corporate headquarters on the second floor.

Meade looked down at the cleared area where the twin tower would be started next fall, a fifty-four-million-dollar expansion. Twenty-seven hundred rooms total! There weren't that many rooms in all of Nevada when he opened the first Plush Wheel on the Strip in 1943. He had been so proud of that little casino nestled in its horseshoe ring of one hundred twenty cottages. Meade shook himself. Living in the past! A sure sign of old age.

Hearing the door open behind him, Meade turned, annoyed; he had told his secretary he was not to be disturbed. The scowl was replaced with a big smile. "Ann!" he shouted, crossing the room and taking the girl in his arms. "You weren't supposed to be here until next week."

"Couldn't wait," Ann murmured. She raised her face. "I've missed you so much," she said, kissing him on the cheek.

"Not half as much as I've missed you," Meade said. "Come, sit down." He led her to a chair.

"You first," Ann said, pressing a long finger against his chest. Throwing her coat and purse aside, she sat on Meade's lap, laying her head on his shoulder.

"Does your mother know you're here?" Meade asked.

"She picked me up at the airport," Ann said. She lifted her head and smiled. "We fooled you, huh?"

Meade nodded, filled with love for this girl who reminded him so much of David—the blonde hair, the wide-spaced eyes that David had inherited from Shirley, a look of innocence that the years would never erase.

Meade held her tightly. "When are you coming back for good, honey?" he said. "We need you at the PW."

Ann sat up straight and took Meade's face in her hands, fingers playing with his thick white hair, big eyes serious now. "I've thought about that a lot the last year," she said. "I want to, but I'm not ready yet."

"Why not now?" Meade asked. His arms encircled her waist. "Is it Reese?"

A hiss of indrawn breath. Ann yanked her hands back as if stung. "How did you know? Did Mother—"

Meade shook his head. "It was as plain as the nose on Smitty's face. Gari's said very little. The rest I've guessed. She talked to me once, a few weeks before you left. She was worried and asked my advice. I wasn't much help. After that, she acted like she was guarding a state secret." He smiled. "I didn't have to be a Sherlock Holmes to figure out why you suddenly decided to leave. I know what it's like to be hurt. I went through it once myself."

Ann's eyes widened. "You?" she said incredulously.

"Me," Meade said, taking her hands. "A long time ago. I was about your age, maybe, a little older." A faded memory of a young man kneeling in the surf, sobbing his heart out over his wife's infidelity.

Ann gripped his hands. "You're not just saying that to make me feel better?"

"No, honey. Just to let you know I understand."

"Know what my problem is?" Ann said. "I measure every man by you. Reese is the first one that came close." She paused. She already had said too much. What was the matter with Reese? Wasn't he ever going to tell Meade?

"And I thought you were smart," Meade said, pulling her head back on his shoulder. A moment of silence. "I wanted to be mad at Reese," Meade went on. "I considered him a fool, but who am I to say who should fall in love with who? He's got a girlfriend now."

Ann nodded into his neck. "I know," she said. "Mom told me. I've grown up a lot since I left, Meade. Have you met her?"

"A couple of times. Reese brought her over for dinner once."

"What's she like?"

"I like her. She's pretty down-to-earth, not harebrained like a lot of the women in this town." A chuckle. "Your mother was prepared not to like her."

Ann sat up again. "Why?"

"You won't believe it, but she didn't like the idea of her being a dancer. Know what I did? I threatened to take some old eight-by-ten glossies I have of Gari at the El Rancho and hang them in my office."

"Good for you!" Ann cried. "How come you've never shown them to me?"

"Because I didn't know about them until a few months ago. They were in one of our old filing cabinets. Publicity was throwing out a bunch of stuff and found a box of photos from the Strip hotels in the forties and early fifties." A wicked gleam. "They're hidden where Gari can't find them. I'll dig them out while you're here."

"Does Mom like her now?" Ann asked.

"Who? Oh, Jeanette. They get along okay. Gari acts like

a mother checking out a possible daughter-in-law. Not that her opinion will mean that much to Reese."

"Is it that serious?"

"Got me. They're together quite a bit. Check it out for yourself. I'm sure Reese will have her over. Her show's shut down for the Christmas season; most of the big ones are." Meade cocked his head to one side. "You got me off the subject back there. When are you coming to work for the PW?"

"I need another year, maybe more. It's not Reese. I can handle that now. I need more corporate practice. I'm learning so much, Meade!" She yanked at Meade's black string tie. "With that and my experience in gaming law, you'll have to pay me a bundle."

Meade grinned. "What's a big salary to you? You're rich. You can live off your dividends." The smile faded. "Seriously, I like the idea of having family in the corporation. I'm beginning to wonder who I can trust. Stan Atwood's been bent out of shape ever since I brought Reese in. There's some dissension among the ranks. If I could definitely pin it on Atwood, I'd give him his walking papers. He's had aspirations of being top dog for a long time. Originally, I encouraged it. Reese is pegged for that spot now. He's doing a great job, honey. More than one hotel would like to grab him."

"You don't have to sell me," Ann said, bending over to kiss Meade on the forehead. She jumped off his lap. "Speaking of your prodigy, he's having lunch with us. In fifteen minutes. Mom's waiting."

Before they left the office, Ann brushed some lint off Meade's black western-style suitcoat. She placed her hands on his shoulders. "You'll always be my hero," she whispered, nuzzling his cheek with hers.

18

Reese awoke around eleven. A thin ray of sunshine was visible along the edge of the heavy drapes that covered the sliding glass door. It would be warm outside, summer being less than two months away.

There was a stir to his left as Jeanette burrowed deeper under the covers. A bare arm appeared and adjusted the pillow tighter over her head.

Reese smiled at the memory of their first night together. That had been six months ago. He had invited Jeanette to his apartment after the final show, persuading her to stay after they had consumed a bucket of fried chicken and a bottle of chenin blanc.

He had awakened at eight, with Jeanette's naked body pressed spoon-fashion into his. She was sound asleep, one hand clutching the edge of a pillow that covered her head, only the tip of her nose showing.

Unlike Jeanette, Reese wasn't used to sleeping until noon. He got up and showered, then read the paper, peeking into the bedroom every half-hour or so, greeted each time by a shapeless lump with no head. Jeanette explained over a late breakfast.

"I got into the habit when I started working nights," she said. "The daylight and noise would wake me up after only a few hours of sleep. The pillow was a perfect solution—once I learned how to breathe."

Reese stared at the dark ceiling. They had been seeing each other on a steady basis since last October, neither expressing a need for commitments. Reese had been burned once, and was still leery. Jeanette's emotions ran deep, and she guarded them carefully, too honest to make frivolous statements, afraid of being hurt as only an introvert can be.

Reese had been concerned with a much bigger problem. He knew he couldn't put off telling Meade much longer. It would have uncomplicated many things if he had done so a year ago.

At first, he hadn't known just how he felt about Meade, ten years of resentment clouding his judgment. That had been wiped out overnight when Gari revealed Meade's true feelings about Cindy. Respect for Meade and a secret pride in their relationship had taken a dominant place in Reese's heart by that time, anyway.

The longer Reese waited, the harder it got. He invented a hundred scenarios, agonizing over the outcome of each. What if Meade rejected him? Would he be angry, thinking he had been made a fool of? Was it emotionally possible for him to accept Reese as his son? How would they react to each other afterwards?

Reese had a special reason for regretting his procrastination. Last month, Jack Harrington had come to Las Vegas. It had put him in the position of lying to Jeanette. He could have told her the truth; he realized now that he should have.

Jeanette was in Reese's apartment when Harrington called. Jack had been in meetings all day and was returning to Los Angeles on the nine o'clock plane. He could stop by Reese's place and go directly to the airport from there. Telling him to come right over, Reese hung up. Jeanette was sitting across the living room, a plate with a half-eaten hamburger in her lap. "Who's Jack?" she asked.

Reese didn't think. The words just slipped out. "My father," he said.

Jeanette almost dropped her Seven-Up. "I thought you didn't even know him," she said. Reese had told her that his parents were divorced when he was two.

"We see each other now and then," Reese said. He dropped the next bomb. "You've probably heard of him— Jack Harrington, the movie director?"

Jeanette's mouth made a big O. "He directed *The Gilded*

Rose, the movie that won all those Academy Awards. I saw it three times." She was suddenly angry. "Why didn't you tell me? Is it privileged information?" Placing the glass on her plate, she stood up. "I'd better get going."

"Oh, no, you don't," Reese said, jumping up and blocking her exit. "Sit down, silly," he ordered, taking the plate and putting it on the coffee table. "You're my girl. Jack will want to meet you."

Jeanette sat down and picked up the hamburger. "I still think you should have told me," she said quietly.

"I should have," Reese said as he returned to his chair. "I didn't even know Jack was in the country. He's been in Europe the last four, five months."

Jeanette wiped her mouth with a napkin, then took a sip from the glass. She didn't grab her purse and touch up her face, which was devoid of makeup; a scattering of freckles and the slightly upturned nose gave her an elfin look. Nor was she bothered that her hair was tousled and jeans too short, revealing bare ankles and rough-out leather sandals. Famous director or not, Jack Harrington would have to accept her as is.

Reese avoided introducing him as his father; however, Jeanette brought it up. Reese knew that Jack's surprise was no less than Jeanette's, but he covered it well. Jeanette and Jack hit it off, and that pleased Reese. Jeanette declined the offer to go with the men to the airport. On the way, Jack warned Reese that he was treading on dangerous waters. Reese glumly agreed.

Sixty-nine years of age, rust-colored hair turning gray, Jack Harrington was so thin that he looked taller than his six feet. The years had etched craggy lines in his face, and when he smiled, it was like catching a glimpse of an animated Mt. Rushmore.

Brought back to the present, Reese edged away from Jeanette's warm body.

Jeanette's hand left the pillow and reached under the covers to touch Reese's leg, fingers playfully walking toward his stomach, stopping to explore between his legs. Reese smiled and moved closer. Working his head under the pillow, he kissed her long neck. "You know that turns me on," Jeanette's muffled voice said as she bent her head forward.

Reese pushed her dark hair aside and touched his lips lightly to the soft white skin, making little round-trips from her shoulders to the base of her skull. He cupped one small breast and kneaded it gently.

Reese was fully erect now, and Jeanette was massaging him into almost painful hardness. Drawing her long legs up into a fetal position, she guided him into her warm moistness. With one long smooth thrust, Reese drove himself deep into her body. Moaning softly, Jeanette ground her bottom into his crotch. Reese continued kissing her arching neck and kneading her swollen breast, the hardened nipple rasping against his palm.

Their movements increased, efforts becoming more vocal. Suddenly, Jeanette went rigid, gripping the bottom sheet, pushing so Reese could penetrate deeper. With a cry that would have been a piercing scream had her face not been buried under the pillow, Jeanette reached a jolting climax, drawing Reese helplessly along so he exploded moments afterwards.

Still joined, they lay quietly for several minutes. They might not be sure of their feelings, but physically they couldn't have been more perfectly matched.

19

Meade looked up from his desk as Smitty walked in and tossed his hat on the floor. "Can't you at least knock?" Meade growled as the little man sat down. Smitty snorted and pulled out a crushed pack of cigarettes.

"Good idea," Meade said, taking a cigar out of the humidor. "Coffee?" He reached out to buzz his secretary.

"Not so fast," Smitty said, holding up a hand. "You might want somethin' stronger after I'm through." Meade's hand froze as he caught the expression on Smitty's face.

"Not this early in the morning," Meade groaned.

Smitty lit a cigarette, peering over his cupped hands at Meade. "I didn't want to say anything until I had proof," he said. "I've got it now." The light reflected off his bald head as he leaned forward. "There's goin' to be a run on Nevada Investments. The way it stands now, you're goin' to be the loser."

Meade was stunned into momentary silence. He took the unlighted cigar out of his mouth and laid it in an ashtray. "All right, Smitty," he said. "Tell me."

"I'm sure you know who's makin' the run," Smitty began.

"Giuliano," Meade said, voice heavy with resignation.

Smitty's faded blue eyes merely flickered. Taking a piece of paper out of his shirt pocket, he smoothed it out on the desk. "Here's what I've got," he said, ticking off each item with a stubby pencil. "Giuliano has eleven percent. He's got some friends with five. You've got thirty-one percent; Ann, two and a half; me, one. Frazer has nineteen. That leaves thirty and a half percent owned by around twenty-six thousand shareholders." Smitty looked up. "Sound about right?"

Meade was writing on a yellow pad. He nodded curtly, waving for Smitty to go on.

Smitty referred to the piece of paper. "NI stock has ranged between nine and a quarter to twelve-fifty over the last two years, closed yesterday at eleven and an eighth." The pencil made another check mark. Smitty waited until Meade stopped writing. "Giuliano's goin' to make a tender offer of fourteen dollars a share."

"What if he buys every one of those twenty-six thousand shareholders out?" Meade said. "That will only give him an additional thirty and a half percent. And there's no way he's going to buy all of them out. He's—"

"He don't need that much," Smitty cut in. "He only needs sixteen percent."

Meade glanced at the yellow pad, then back up to Smitty. "Frazer?" he asked in a disbelieving voice. Clyde Frazer was a wealthy Texas rancher who had started buying Nevada Investment stock years ago.

"Giuliano's given him a million dollar letter of credit to bind the deal. Fourteen and a quarter a share."

"You're sure?" Meade said—a drowning man clutching at straws.

"Hell, yes, I'm sure," Smitty snapped. "Do you think I'd say it if I wasn't?"

"No," Meade said heavily. "That's the problem; you're always too damn accurate. I wish to hell you'd be wrong for once."

Mollified, Smitty said, "I wish so, too, but it ain't so."

"It will have to be approved by the Gaming Commission," Meade said.

"They won't turn Giuliano down," Smitty said decisively. "He's got one of the oldest licenses in the state. You can bet he's pulled some fast ones, but the Board won't find 'em. He's covered his tracks so good, he probably don't even know everything himself."

"Sixteen percent," Meade mused. "Think he can get it?"

"My sources say he's got verbal commitments for a million shares already."

Meade suddenly looked all of his seventy-six years. "If that's true, then he'll win," he said in a barely audible voice.

There was no way to soften the blow. "Looks like it," Smitty said. "Giuliano wouldn't be makin' this move unless he was a hundred percent sure."

Meade did some quick figuring. "That's almost a hundred twenty million."

"A heap of hate," Smitty said, "but even with that extra thirteen or so million he'll be payin' out, he'll eventually come out. It's a good investment."

Meade got up and paced the floor. Bunching his big fists, he stared down at Smitty. "This isn't my kind of fight," he said. "I feel so damn helpless! What am I supposed to do—stand still and let him kill me?"

"It's not like the end of the world," Smitty said mildly. "Your share's worth ninety million or so. You can sell and live the life of an A-rab sheik."

"That would be the same as dying," Meade replied.

Smitty looked up at his friend, hearing his words but feeling no empathy. Smitty didn't believe in attachments, personal or physical. He had no investments he couldn't rid himself of overnight. Profits were all that mattered. "You fought back once before," he suggested.

"I was younger then," Meade said. He towered over Smitty, eyes suddenly cold. "The Plush Wheel is mine! I won't give it up without a fight."

"Frazer's your only chance," Smitty said. "Mighty slim, but no deal's complete until the papers are signed and the money's in the bank."

"Do you suppose Giuliano's paying cash?" Meade said.

Smitty shrugged. "Don't know. If he has to, he can come up with it."

Meade sat down and ran some figures through his calculator. "Almost sixty-five million to buy Frazer out. I can borrow some, but not that much."

Smitty shifted his narrow body around in the chair. "You bring Frazer around, we'll find the money."

Meade studied the little man. "Sure?" he said.

"Goddamnit," Smitty bristled. "Will you quit askin' me if I'm sure? I'm old enough to know my own mind."

Meade grinned. "Just checking." He picked up the phone. "I want Gari and Reese in on this."

An hour later, Meade had completed an overview of the situation. He didn't have to communicate his feelings to Gari and Reese; they understood and shared his anguish.

Because Reese knew nothing about the long-standing feud between him and Tony Giuliano and Gari very little, Meade outlined his troubles with the Giulianos, beginning with Carlo's attempt to destroy the Reno Plush Wheel in 1934. There was no reason to hide the killing of the two hired thugs; it was a matter of public record. As to Carlo's death, Meade only said that Tony believed him responsible and had nursed a grudge ever since. After Bob Terhune's intervention in the quarrel, Tony had apparently backed off. Today's revelation proved that he had merely taken another, more legitimate road toward revenge.

The meeting broke up with only one firm decision being made. Meade would take immediate steps to contact Clive Frazer. There was no doubt of the outcome if Frazer's stock was unavailable. Tony Giuliano would be in control of Nevada Investments.

20

The *Las Vegas Sun* broke the story two days later, the *Wall Street Journal* on Friday. By that time, Meade had received the bad news from Clive Frazer. Frazer could do nothing unless Giuliano failed to complete the transaction by July 1st, less than six weeks away.

"You could blow it wide open if we could prove a previous connection between Giuliano and Frazer," Smitty said. They were seated in the living room, papers scattered about. The picture window provided a spectacular view of the Plush Wheel golf course, but no one noticed.

"Small chance of that," Ann said. "The Control Board updated their information on Tony Giuliano while I was there, when he bought that casino in Tonopah. And he was investigated when he started buying heavily in Nevada Investments. No connection was found. All they have to do now is check out the last two years."

It was Saturday, four days after Smitty walked into Meade's office with the news. Ann had flown down from San Francisco this morning. Gari met her at the airport, and they had arrived at the house an hour ago, where Meade, Reese and Smitty were waiting.

"Tony Giuliano's dad was a sneaky son of a bitch," Smitty said. "He had his hand in everything—like a goddamned octopus. I'm not against payin' for information, but compared to the Giulianos I'm an amateur. Tony inherited Carlo's spy system, and he's been buildin' it for fifty years. He's paid out a fortune, but he's made it back a hundred times. He enjoys gettin' into other people's business."

Meade said, "Smitty thinks some of our people are on Giuliano's payroll."

"Anybody in particular?" Reese asked.

"Just guessin' so far," Smitty said. "Got any suspicions?"

Reese stared at Smitty. "Atwood?"

"Maybe."

Meade said: "If Giuliano reached him, it's probably only been in the last year or so. Guess I'm getting soft, but I still find it hard to believe. If Giuliano got to him, he's done it with a promise of a top job in the new organization. The word is out that Giuliano has the support of some of our key management people. That will help if he has to depend on votes to seize control."

"Atwood's got a pretty good reputation," Reese said. "Any way to check it out?"

"I'm going to take a page out of Giuliano's book," Meade said. "A Los Angeles detective firm is sending ten men up on Monday. They'll put a twenty-four-hour watch on Atwood, Rosen and Hackett and do some general snooping on the street."

"I'm for it," Reese said. He looked at Meade. "Rosen and Hackett, too?"

"They're in tight with Atwood. Best to check it out. Only those three will be watched day and night."

"Do you think Louis Giuliano is in on this?" Reese asked. "He seems like a pretty straight guy to me."

Smitty said, "Louis may run the Fantasia, but he don't own one light bulb. What Tony decides to do, he'll do with

or without Louis' approval. The gumshoe boys will check
Louis out with the rest."

"Should I stay away from Louis?" Reese asked.

Meade shook his head. "Keep on like nothing's happened.
You might learn something."

The following afternoon, Reese and Jeanette had a long
talk at his apartment. The story was still making the front
pages of both Las Vegas papers.

"What will you do if Giuliano takes over?" Jeanette asked.

"I won't be at the Plush Wheel, that's for sure," Reese
said. He was slumped down in the couch beside Jeanette, bare
feet on the coffee table. "Actually, I haven't given it much
thought."

"You could go to another hotel," Jeanette suggested.

Reese stared at his bare toes. "Wouldn't be the same. I
belong at the Plush Wheel." He looked up at Jeanette. "I'm
not sure I can feel the same anywhere else."

Jeanette frowned. "You've got to do *something.*"

"Hey, we haven't lost yet."

"According to the newspapers you have."

"Don't believe everything you read," Reese chided. He
tugged at one of her fingers. "Maybe I'll live off of you."

Jeanette cocked her head to one side. "You'll have to sell
your car," she said. "The upkeep is half my salary."

"Gee, I don't know," Reese said. "Can you work days,
too?"

"Well, I did get another job offer."

Reese looked up sharply. "Serious?"

Jeanette nodded. "It's a good one. I would be lead dancer
and help with the choreography. Ron and I would do adagio
numbers, too."

"Which hotel?"

"Not here. It's a road show, opening in Detroit."

Reese's feet came off the table. He sat up and faced Jeanette. "How long?"

"It's a year contract."

"Are you going to do it?"

"I haven't decided yet. I'll have to make up my mind in

the next few weeks. My contract at the Fantasia comes up for renewal in July."

"You'd go, just like that? Leave me alone?"

"It only came up the other day. I may not take it."

"You were talking about opening a dance studio."

"That's in the future, dummy. I've got a few good years of dancing left."

"I think the dance studio's a good idea."

Jeanette smiled. "I'm glad."

Reese took her hand. "My opinion means something?"

"Of course. It means a lot."

"Then don't leave Vegas."

"I didn't say it meant *that* much."

Taking Jeanette by the shoulders, Reese looked into her large brown eyes. "I'm getting used to having you around," he said quietly.

Jeanette smiled crookedly. "Same here."

Reese wanted to say more, but it wasn't the time. "You'll keep that in mind while you're deciding?"

"Sure." She leaned forward and gave him a quick kiss. "Looks like June will be a big decision month for us both," she said.

Reese kissed the tiny freckles on her nose, then drew her close. He was surprised at the sudden surge of feeling for this lithe girl in his arms.

21

On the morning of Wednesday, June 11, 1980, Tony Giuliano was less than three weeks away from final victory.

"Forty-two years!" he shouted, waving a copy of the *Nevada State Journal* in the air. "Forty-two years I've been after the bastard. Now I've got him!"

Louis watched his father walk excitedly around the office, a maniacal gleam in his eyes. He had been like this since yesterday afternoon when the Nevada State Control Board had unanimously approved his application to buy Clive Frazer's stock. All Tony needed now was final approval by the Gaming Commission, and he could close the deal. The Commission would meet in Carson City on the twenty-sixth. With the Board's unanimous decision and Tony Giuliano's previous track record, the outcome was a foregone conclusion.

Tony waved the newspaper, the Control Board's action a banner headline. "This will give me forty-eight percent," he said. "That bastard Benton in Chicago is holdin' me up for fifteen a share; he knows he's got me by the balls. Same with that family trust in Phoenix. I'll have those in a week, grab a few others that have been flirtin' around, and I'll have it. Fifty-one percent, maybe fifty-two."

"When will you complete things with Frazer?"

"The twenty-eighth."

"Then what?"

"I want you to carry the ball in Vegas. I'll call a special board meeting of Nevada Investments for about July tenth. We'll vote Slaughter out and start cleanin' house. You'll be president. That will keep the shareholders happy. No need for a panic durin' the transition."

"Does everybody go? What about Atwood?"

"We'll go slow—see how he works out. I don't like a man who'll turn on his boss."

"My thoughts, too," Louis said. "You hear a lot about gaming executives having no security and getting the shaft, but it's a two-way street. The way some of them move around, it's like a game of musical chairs. Atwood worries me. If he'll knife Slaughter in the back, who says he won't do it to us?"

Tony sat down behind his desk. "Watch him," he said. "One wrong move, kick his ass out."

"What about Harrington?"

"He goes. He's Slaughter's right-hand man."

Louis nodded. He had expected that. "Guess that's it, then," he said. "No chance of Frazer backing out, is there?"

Tony's laugh was a short bark. "No chance at all." His eyes were hooded, thoughtful, as he measured Louis. "No harm tellin' you. I've had Frazer in my pocket for almost twenty years."

Louis shouldn't have been surprised; he was well aware of his father's devious ways. But it still came as a shock. "How?" he asked.

"You know about Embarcadero Ventures."

"Rozini's company."

"Old Sam started it back in the late Twenties. At first, it was nothin' but a room in his house. He lent out money, mostly to dockworkers; that's how come the name. Him and Papa were real close. They did a lot of business together, even after Papa left San Francisco for Reno. They trusted each other but nobody else. Machiavelli would have been proud of the way they put things together.

"Sam built Embarcadero up durin' the Depression. By the mid-Forties, the company was spread all over the country, makin' venture capital loans. When Sam died, his son Sal took over. He and I work together as good as Sam and Papa did—maybe better. We've paid a fortune to lawyers to keep things buried. It would take fifty years to uncover everything."

Tony unwrapped a cigar. He was enjoying himself. "Back in sixty-two, Frazer was a two-bit farmer with some hot ideas. Embarcadero checked him out and figured he was worth backing. He was long on ideas but short on how to handle money. Embarcadero became a silent partner, and Frazer was watched every step of the way. Wasn't long before Rozini had enough on Frazer to put him away for twenty years. Rozini's owned him ever since."

Louis was getting the picture. "You and Rozini . . ."

"We're partners. I own half of Embarcadero."

Louis just stared.

"Thought that would get you," laughed Tony. "What the hell, it's about time you learned what's goin' on."

The picture was complete now. "So it never was Frazer buying into Nevada Investments."

"It was my money, funneled through Embarcadero. By the time Slaughter went public, I had Frazer's nuts in a vice. He can't complain. He's done okay. But when I say jump, he jumps."

"So when you buy his stock, you'll just be paying yourself."

"Mostly," Tony said. "Frazer owns some."

"Does Jan know about this?" Louis asked.

Tony shook his head. "This is family business. Sal and I have talked it over. He wants you to take my place in Embarcadero when I'm gone. I agree. Mike's not got the head for this. Rudi will take Sal's place. He's been workin' with his father for fifteen years now, so he knows his way around. As soon as we get Nevada Investments straightened out, you'll spend time with Rudi. He'll lay it all out."

The enormity of what he had learned weighed heavily on Louis as he flew back to Las Vegas that night. He had never asked for this. He was satisfied running the Fantasia. That, along with overseeing the Fremont Street club, kept him fully occupied. He had no heart or desire to enter into the maze of intrigue and shadowy business dealings his father and grandfather had woven over two lifetimes. It wasn't his way of doing things.

Louis knew his father was aware of this, but Tony had no choice. Mike was totally unsuited for such a complicated undertaking. Like it or not, Louis reluctantly would have to follow his father's orders.

As president of the Fantasia Hotel, Louis made a six-figure income. He had invested carefully and was far from a pauper, but Tony held the purse strings to his future.

Louis was deeply disturbed by his father's takeover of Nevada Investments. When Jan had told him about the murder of Meade Slaughter's fiancée, he, like her, had seen the law of the jungle justification for Carlo's death. It should have all stopped there.

Louis was a sensitive man, something his father was not.

He had never known his grandfather; he couldn't share Tony's hate. Louis loved his work and thrived on the challenges of running a successful gaming hotel, but he had little heart for what lay ahead.

22

As Reese rode the elevator to the thirty-first floor, he didn't hear the chatter of the hotel guests. Squeezed into a corner, he watched as each ascending number lit up, paying little attention as the doors opened and closed, the passengers filtering out until he was alone.

Three days ago, the Control Board had approved Tony Giuliano's application, tolling a death knell for Meade's reign as head of the Plush Wheel. The atmosphere had changed dramatically around the hotel, starting with Meade. He had become withdrawn, defeat showing in the haggard lines on his face and the slump of his shoulders.

Gari had taken Reese aside this morning. "Ann will be down tomorrow," she said. "Maybe she can get through to him." There were angry tears in her eyes. "I'm about to punch him in the face! He won't listen to me, not even to Smitty. I never thought I'd see the day that Meade Slaughter would feel sorry for himself. He's been holed up on the top floor for two days. He came home late last night and hardly said a word. I'm so mad I could spit!"

"It won't last," Reese said. "Look at what he's accomplished! He's got nothing to be ashamed of."

"I've tried to tell him that. It's like talking to a stone wall." Gari turned Reese around and pushed him toward her office door. "You go up and tell him that. I've done my duty."

Reese looked up at the blinking numbers. Jeanette had said June would be a big decision month. She wasn't kidding.

Jeanette. What was he going to do about her? They had seen little of each other the past two weeks. He had been putting in sixteen-hour days fighting the inevitable.

The doors opened on the thirty-first floor. Like a man going to his execution, Reese walked toward the door of Meade's office. They had talked only briefly during the last two days.

Joan Babbit, Meade's secretary for fifteen years, looked up helplessly at Reese. "He said he doesn't want to be disturbed," she said in a funereal whisper.

"Even me?"

Joan glanced at the closed door, then back at Reese. "He said no one was to be let in. That's all."

Anger seized Reese. He picked up Joan's purse off the desk and thrust it into her hands. "Take a break," he said. "Shut off the phones and lock the outside door. I'll page you when it's time to come back."

"But—"

"No buts, just go." Reese forced a smile. "Don't worry; it's my decision." He made a shooing motion. "Out."

Throwing the door of Meade's office an apprehensive look, Joan slipped out into the hall. Reese smiled and made a turning motion with his hand. The door closed, and he heard the click of the lock. For a moment, Reese's resolve wavered. Shaking himself, he knocked sharply on Meade's door, counted to three and walked in.

Meade was standing by the corner windows that gave him a sweeping view of the Strip and the downtown skyline. He was coatless, face pale, dark circles under his eyes. The paleness was replaced with a dark flush. "I want to be alone, Reese," he snapped. "Didn't Joan tell you?"

"She did, and I sent her packing," Reese said.

"You did *what?*" Meade shouted.

"I told her to shut off the phones and lock the outside door. She'll come back when she's paged."

Reese had never seen such anger in a man. Meade's white shirt almost stretched to the tearing point as he swelled with rage. "You've got no fucking right to do that, mister!" he roared.

"As much right as you've got hiding out in this fucking office!" Reese shouted back.

Meade was struck dumb. No man had ever talked back to him like this. "I'll tell you what you can do," Meade said, biting off each word. "You can get out of this fucking office and stay out until I invite you back!"

They stood twenty feet apart, the air snapping with tension. "I'm sorry," Reese said in the same clipped tone. "I'm not going until you cut this shit out."

"What shit?" Meade's voice thundered. Reese was glad he had sent Joan away. He hoped the soundproofed walls lived up to their name.

Reese spread his arms. "*This* shit! Staying up here and acting like the world's come to an end." He pointed at the floor. "There are people down there who need you. Gari for one. Think of somebody besides yourself for a change!"

That did it. Meade moved so his face was inches from Reese's. "You goddamn punk," he whispered. "What the fuck do you know about life? Where were you when I was building all this?" Meade held up a huge fist. "I fought every inch of the way. My blood's in this place. When you've gone through that, come back and tell me how I feel."

Reese started to speak. Meade cut him off with a slashing motion. "Get out," he said, voice rumbling deep in his chest. "Get out before this goes too far."

"Like you'll fire me?" Reese shot back.

"Don't push me," Meade warned. "You'll certainly be out in a few weeks, anyway. I can make it sooner if you want."

Reese was angry almost beyond words. "Don't bother," he said, stepping back a few paces. "I thought I'd found a real man when I came here. My mistake." He turned toward the door. "I'll clean things up and be out in an hour."

Meade was hurt to the quick, too proud to back down. "Go ahead," he said. "I don't need you anymore."

Reese whirled, lashing out blindly, "Like you didn't need my mother?"

Silence dropped over them like a cloak. They stared at each other, one appalled at what he had said, the other bewildered at the sudden turn of events. Meade's mouth worked soundlessly. He moved closer. "Your mother? What's she got to do with this?"

"Oh, shit," Reese said, looking around for some unseen guidance.

Meade's anger had vanished into a pool of confusion. He gripped Reese's arm. "What about your mother?" he asked.

Reese responded in an anguished voice, "I didn't want you to find out this way."

Meade gave Reese a little shake. "I knew her?"

Reese nodded. "Years ago. In the Forties."

Meade jerked back as if stung. "When in the Forties?"

"Forty-seven, forty-eight."

Both men stared at each other. Meade spoke first. A hoarse whisper. "Cindy?"

Reese nodded, unable to speak.

"How did you know about us?"

"She told me just before she died."

"Cindy went away," Meade said in a dazed voice. "I tried to find her. Why, why did she disappear like that?"

"She didn't want you to know."

"Know what?"

Reese's voice was barely audible. "About me."

Meade's fingers dug painfully into Reese's arm. "You?"

Reese looked defiantly into Meade's eyes. "She was pregnant when she left."

"My God," Meade moaned. He was holding both of Reese's arms now. "Your name's Harrington. How—?"

"Mom went to Jack Harrington for help," Reese said. "They had been friends for years. Jack offered to marry her and give me a name."

Tears came into Meade's eyes. "You're my—" His voice choked.

Rease nodded, his own vision blurred. Meade's big shoulders began to shake, and he reached out. They threw their arms around each other. Tears filled both men's eyes.

Time passed. Neither man spoke. Meade moved back and said the words Reese had imagined hearing so many times. "My son." Meade's voice was charged with emotion, tears streaming down his face.

Reese smiled, blurting out the first thing that came to his mind, "Sure you want me?"

"*Want* you?" It was a shout that rang off the walls. "Hell, yes, I want you!" Meade gripped Reese's shoulders and looked hard into his face. "I have to know everything. Your mother—"

Reese shook his head. "She died thirteen years ago, when I was sixteen."

If Reese needed proof that Meade had loved his mother, he had it now; it was written all over his face. "Yes, of course," Meade said. "I knew that. I just didn't connect—" He turned away. Seconds ticked by. Staring at the far wall, Meade said, "How long have you known?"

"She told me in the hospital the day she died."

"Why? Why then?"

"She said you were the only man she ever loved. She made me promise to come and see you someday. I didn't have to talk, just see you. That's why I came to Vegas. If it hadn't been for Smitty, we wouldn't have met."

Meade was still absorbing the picture of Cindy dying, still loving him, wanting their son to know his father. He turned slowly. "Does Smitty know?"

They sat down, and Reese told the story from the beginning. An hour passed, then another. Reese's greatest fears were laid to rest when Meade accepted the reasons why he had kept silent, why Gari and Ann had been told and sworn to secrecy.

Meade smiled and recalled the night Gari said she was going to talk to Reese about Ann. "I told her she might be biting off more than she could chew," he said. "Serves her right that she's had to keep it quiet all this time. I can't think of a better punishment."

Reese smiled. "This will get her off my back. She's been

driving me nuts wanting to know when I was going to tell you."

Reese was talking about Cindy's theater work in New York when Meade's private line phone rang. He glanced at the wall clock, surprised to find it was past three. He picked up the receiver.

"Meade?" It was Gari.

"Hi, baby," Meade said, winking at Reese.

Gari tore the receiver away from her ear, staring at it with disbelief. Meade sounded *happy*. "Are you all right?" she asked tentatively.

"Sure, I'm all right. Are you?"

"I am if you are. Meade, have you forgotten about poor Joan? She's had a two-hour lunch and has been moping around my office ever since."

"Oh, God, tell her to come back."

"Is Reese there or have you buried him somewhere?"

"Sitting right beside me. Looks too healthy to bury."

"Meade, what's going on?"

"I can't believe it, you three joining Reese in this conspiracy."

Gari's shriek was clearly audible to Reese. "Meade, oh, Meade, did Reese, did he—?"

"Sure did. Broke down and confessed. Said you drove him to it."

"I'm sending Joan home," Gari cried. "I'll be up with a bottle of champagne in ten minutes." The phone went dead.

Three bottles of champagne were consumed before the evening was over, along with a lavish dinner sent up from the Lake Room. Nevada Investments stock would have shot up two points if the public could have seen the group.

Meade was alive again, filled with good food and wine, talking optimistically about the future, a future without the Plush Wheels but with a son. "We'll start again," he said, lifting his glass toward Gari and Reese. "We'll have the money and borrowing power to set the state on its ear."

The young couple that entered the elevator on the twentieth floor looked askance at the three tall people who were

howling with laughter and slapping each other on the back.
The girl later suggested to her husband that maybe there was
a Tip-Topper's convention in town. If so, they must be a fun
bunch.

If they had asked what was so funny, the woman would
have said she had just remembered that this was Friday the
thirteenth.

23

On Monday morning, Reese drove out to the ranch to see
Smitty. The old man was sitting on the porch of his converted
bunkhouse, a cigarette dangling from his lips. "See you survived the weekend," he said.

"Barely," Reese said as he sat down. It had been a busy
two days, Ann arriving on Saturday, the many things the
family had to discuss, the big Sunday afternoon dinner that
Smitty had attended.

"Well, you got things out in the open with Meade now.
That should make the week look better."

"It's a hell of a relief. I feel like I've gotten rid of a baby
I've been carrying around for half my life."

"That's one way of puttin' it," Smitty said, looking at
Reese's jeans and short-sleeved shirt. "Where's your suit?"

"I'm playing hooky. Thought I'd spend the day with you,
part of it, anyway."

"Shall I tell Gladys to plan on you for lunch?" Gladys and
Steve Austin lived as caretakers in the big ranch house.
Smitty usually ate lunch and dinner with them.

"I'll have to leave after that," Reese said. "This is Jeanette's day off. We haven't seen much of each other lately."

"Things gettin' on okay?"

"She's thinking about going on the road for a year. I don't like the idea."

"Tell her so?"

"In a way. I haven't got a lot to say about it. We're not that serious."

"We? She ain't either?"

Reese thought a moment. "She's never said anything along that line. Her work's pretty important. We get along great. I wouldn't want to be with anyone else. I think she feels the same way."

"When I was your age," Smitty said, "most women didn't think beyond a house and kids. I remember the ruckus on the Strip when Meade made Gari a vice president. That was before they started livin' together. Her bein' independent and all, that was one of the big things that attracted Meade. Maybe you're like your dad; you like your women with a mind of their own."

Reese recalled his ex-wife, Catherine. She had been jealous of his every move, a clinging-vine type. It had helped destroy their marriage. Perhaps Smitty had a point.

"Hey, Mose!" Smitty yelled, startling Reese. The big shaggy brown dog loped down from the direction of the ranch house and laid his head on Smitty's lap, sorrowful eyes rolled upwards in supplication. "Hang on a minute," Smitty said to Reese, scratching the dog behind the ears. Taking a notebook and pencil out of his shirt pocket, Smitty printed a few words in block type. "Can't write longhand worth a damn," he muttered as he tore out the page and stuffed it under the dog's collar. Giving the dog another scratch, he pointed toward the house. "Go see Gladys." The dog trotted off.

"What was that about?" Reese asked.

"Saves me havin' to use the phone," Smitty said. "I let Gladys know you'll be here for lunch."

Reese laughed. "I'll be damned." He watched the dog disappear into the grove of trees that surrounded the house. "I've never been able to figure out who that dog belongs to."

"Gladys and Steve brought Mose here as a puppy five years

ago. Me and him get along pretty good, so he splits his time between them and me. They're goin' to leave him with me when they move back to Florida this winter. They'll be livin' in a condominium. No big dogs allowed. Besides, Mose would go nuts closed up like that."

They went inside, and Smitty made a pot of coffee. Sitting at the round oak table, Reese revealed the real reason for his visit. "I know it sounds hopeless," he said, "but I thought I could talk with Louis Giuliano. Maybe he can get me through to see his father."

"Forget it," Smitty said brusquely. "A chicken sleepin' with a coyote's got a better chance."

"It's worth a try, isn't it? I can't believe a man can hate that much over something that happened so long ago. And then it's just conjecture at that!"

Smitty didn't answer right away. He got up and refilled their cups, sat down and lit a cigarette. "I'm goin' to stick my neck out, boy," he began, puffing out a cloud of smoke. "Your dad and me's been friends for a long time, but I'm not about to test that friendship by lettin' him find out what I'm goin' to say. You swear you'll never repeat this?"

Reese nodded, held by the intensity of Smitty's gaze.

"You've got the same toughness as Meade," Smitty said. "It's goin' to be tested in the comin' years, but let's hope not in the way your dad's was. David was a good kid, but he was no help to Meade when the chips were down. Maybe things would have been different if David had taken after his dad instead of his mom."

So Reese learned the truth about Carlo Giuliano's death and Tony's cruel retaliation through David fifteen years later, ending with Mario Gatori's murder and Tony's humiliation.

"Now you see why it ain't worth seein' Louis Giuliano," Smitty said when he had finished.

Reese could only shake his head. How naïve he had been!

Smitty abruptly dropped the subject, and the rest of the time before lunch was spent discussing the investigations conducted by the detective firm, the collusion that had been uncovered between Tony Giuliano and Stan Atwood and the three other employees that were also a part of the conspiracy. Nothing would be done. The matter would be out of Meade's hands in a few short weeks. No connection between Clive Frazer and Giuliano had been found.

Reese left a little after one, and Smitty sat on the porch, the dog Mose at his feet. Smitty looked off toward Las Vegas and wondered if Meade had the strength and stamina to start over again. He hoped it wouldn't take too long. He wanted to be around to see it underway.

24

Max Verdon called Smitty Thursday night. "I'm flying down from Reno tomorrow morning. I have something important to discuss with you," Verdon said. "You going to be around?"

"Alive and kickin', I hope."

"I'll be there around ten."

Smitty was standing on the porch when Verdon drove up. "Coffee's on," Smitty said, going inside.

Verdon entered, carrying a briefcase. "We goin' to do business?" Smitty asked.

"Maybe," Verdon said, sitting down at the table. He took a sip of coffee and made a face. "What is this stuff—some kind of secret weapon?"

Smitty grinned. "Good, huh? I never wash my pot. That's what gives it texture."

"Texture! It's more like liquid sandpaper." Verdon took another sip. "I think I will need this, considering what we have to talk about."

Smitty glanced at the briefcase. "Shoot."

Max Verdon said, "I've been sitting on this for some time,

never thought of using it until lately. Being in politics all my life, I've been involved in some underhanded things in my time. Here is a dusty skeleton in the closet that could help Slaughter." Verdon opened the briefcase and took out a folder. "Meade's your friend. Mine, too. This might be a way out."

Smitty's pale eyes narrowed. "Shouldn't Meade be in on this?"

"This is dirty business, Smitty. It's not his style."

"But you think it's mine," Smitty said drily.

"I've never known you to let scruples stand in the way of winning."

"Right you are. Let's hear it."

"I told you how Bob Terhune really died."

"Killed by a whore. So?"

"So that whore is married to Tony Giuliano."

"Jesus jumpin' Christ!" Smitty burst out, biting his cigarette in half.

Verdon's lean face broke into a wolfish grin. "Got you that time, didn't I?"

Smitty saw the possibilities in an instant. "Proof?"

"*I* don't need proof. You don't forget a face and body like that, and the way she carries herself. That lady's got class.

"I saw her at a shareholders' meeting in Reno. She wasn't married to Giuliano then. I didn't let on I recognized her, and when she looked at me there wasn't even a flicker. She had guts coming back to Nevada, but she's a gutsy gal. I did some checking, and she's the one.

"She never got on the police books in Vegas, nowhere for that matter. She's smart; I think one of the smartest women I've known. I'm not proud of what I'm doing. Frankly, I admire her. It's a raw deal, but Meade's getting a worse one, so I'm going with Meade.

"She married a rich guy in Chicago named Lebeck. They got divorced five years later, and she came out with a bundle. The rest you know."

"I can't do anything without solid proof," Smitty said.

"I've got a signed confession. She traded that for fifty

grand and safe passage out of town. I'll leave the confession with you. The rest of the papers I'll keep. If your bluff is called—and that's pretty much what it is—I'll deny any knowledge. Her word won't mean a damn against mine in Nevada. There aren't any names on that paper, just hers and Bob's. It's up to you if you want to give it a try."

"Blackmail, pure and simple," Smitty said.

"Bother you?"

"Shit, no." Smitty sat back and eyed the folder. "The Gaming Commission's meeting next Thursday. If I'm goin' to do anything, I've got to do it quick." He rocked his chair back and forth. "The problem's gettin' to Giuliano. He knows I'm Meade's friend; he wouldn't let me within ten miles of his place."

"What about Louis? He's right here in Vegas."

"Let me see what you've got," Smitty said, holding out his hand. "Best to take this one step at a time." Smitty read the confession and went through the notes while Max Verdon took a walk outside.

Smitty finished going through the papers and joined Verdon by the pasture fence. "What I need is a typed resumé of the facts," Smitty said. "Somethin' I can stick in an envelope along with a Xerox of the confession and give it to the son. This ain't the kind of thing you take to a typin' service."

Verdon hooked a thumb toward the car. "Funny thing, I just happened to bring a typewriter along."

Smitty squinted up at Verdon. "You willin' to buy in that much? Typefaces can be traced, you know."

"Not this typewriter, not to me, anyway. When I go, it stays. You'll know how to get rid of it."

Smitty chuckled. "I should have known better than to teach you how to suck eggs. Let's get at it."

That night, Smitty and Verdon had dinner with Meade. On the way to the Plush Wheel, they had stopped at a copy shop. Max Verdon kept the papers in his briefcase and at his side throughout the evening.

Verdon stayed with Smitty that night and left early the next morning. Shortly after nine, Smitty called the Fantasia.

He was put through to Louis Giuliano and made an appointment for two-thirty.

Smitty left the ranch with two sets of copies sealed in large manila envelopes. He dropped one set off at a safe-deposit box. The other was clutched in his gnarled hand when he entered Louis Giuliano's office.

Louis greeted him cordially. Knowing of Smitty and Meade's close association, Louis expected this had something to do with the takeover bid. He wasn't disappointed.

Smitty came right to the point. Handing the envelope to Louis, he said brusquely, "Get this up to Reno. It's got to do with the negotiations on Nevada Investments."

"Why me?" Louis asked. "My father's in charge of that. Send it to him."

Smitty's eyes were cold under the brim of his cowboy hat. "I didn't say it was for him. It's for his wife."

"Jan? She's got nothing to do with this."

"Just see that she gets it," Smitty said. "You can read it if you want, but I wouldn't advise it. She'll know what to do. Tell her to make sure that Tony hears about it or I'll see he gets a copy direct."

Louis knew Smitty's reputation and that he had many powerful friends; otherwise, he would not have seen him. "Is this Meade Slaughter's doing?" he demanded angrily.

"Nope. It's all mine." Smitty's voice turned harsh. "I've got a copy locked up. Tell Tony—in case he gets funny ideas."

Louis laughed disbelievingly. "That's crazy talk."

"You wouldn't say that if you'd been around as long as I have," Smitty snapped. "Just get it there."

Louis tossed the envelope on his desk. "And if I don't?"

"You're goin' to be responsible for one helluva mess."

Louis sighed and looked at the sealed envelope. He returned his gaze to Smitty. "What's the bottom line?"

"Tony backs off and lets Meade Slaughter buy Frazer's stock."

"That's all?" Louis laughed. "Why not ask for the moon?"

"Get it to Tony's wife," Smitty said, pointing at the enve-

lope. He turned to go. "If I don't hear from you by Tuesday
noon, I'm goin' to spread that information all over Nevada.
Ask Tony; he knows I'll do it."

"I don't like threats," Louis said, standing rigidly beside
his desk.

. "Neither do I," Smitty said. "I just believe in keepin'
promises." He was gone before Louis could answer.

25

The hawk flew in great swooping circles, screeching its defiance at the world below. A few minutes ago, Jan Giuliano
had been lying by the pool, shading her eyes against the sun's
glare, reveling in the beauty of the sight. The bird screeched
again, but Jan didn't hear. She was sitting up, the receiver
pressed to her ear, shivering as a breeze stirred the water at
her feet. "He didn't give you any idea?" she asked.

"No," Louis said. "Do you want me to look?"

Jan glanced up just as the hawk dropped like a rock, a dark
bullet diving for the kill. She flinched as if the cruel talons
had dug into her heart. "I'd better see it first, Louis," she
said. "Do you want me to fly down?"

"I think it would be better if I come up there. Jan, I have
an uneasy feeling about this. Let's keep Papa out of this at
first, anyway."

A sigh of relief. "We can't meet here, then. Tony will be
around all weekend. Would Monday be better?"

"That's cutting it too close. I'm tied up with the family on
Saturday, but I can make it on Sunday."

"I'll come up with some excuse for going out," Jan said.
"Tony's so involved with this takeover, he probably won't
miss me, anyway."

"I'll get there on the eleven o'clock flight and take a taxi

out to that shopping center on Plumb Lane near Virginia. I'll
wait inside the entrance. Park on the lot and stay in the car;
I'll find you. Let's make it twelve noon. We'll go somewhere
and talk."

"I'll be there," Jan said, adding a short goodbye. She hung
up and stared at the pool. She had planned on a swim—a
lifetime ago. Starting for the house, she stopped and gazed
back at the pool. Shaking her head with disgust, she marched
back, the white one-piece swimsuit clinging to every curve.
Dropping the towel and kicking off her cotton sandals, Jan
dove into the water, heading for the far end with long clean
strokes, repeating the process, back and forth, back and
forth, for twenty minutes. When she emerged, she was once
more in control.

Louis arrived at the shopping center a half-hour early. To
kill time, he walked slowly through the inside mall, window
shopping aimlessly. Jan drove past the entrance shortly before twelve. They were heading east of town a few minutes
later, the envelope lying between them like some malevolent
thing.

Jan stopped at a small neighborhood park. "Let's sit at a
table," she said. "I feel closed up in here." Without waiting
for an answer, she picked up the envelope and both left the
car.

Louis lit a cigarette while Jan slit the envelope with a nail
file. Turning away, he watched two little girls playing on a
slide. Several minutes passed. Louis looked at Jan. She was
staring off into space, several papers in her hands. "Bad?" he
asked, already knowing the answer.

"It could be better," Jan said, the color completely gone
from her face. "This Frank Smith, I've heard about him. Is
he as tough as they say?"

"I'm afraid so. He's about the only one left of the old
Tonopah-Goldfield crowd. They don't come any tougher."

Jan tapped the papers. "Then you think he'll do what he
says."

"He may be running a bluff."

Jan brushed a strand of raven hair away from her cheek.

"Do you believe that?" she asked, regarding Louis with quiet speculation.

Louis shrugged. "I really don't know, Jan. What's it about?"

Jan looked away for a moment. Her dark eyes returned to search his. "Are we friends, Louis?" she asked. "It seems I need one now."

Louis' smile was genuine. "We're friends," he said.

"This may sound strange," Jan said, "but you're the only real friend I've got. I've always gone it alone, proud that I didn't need anybody." A crooked smile. "There was one time, however. Now it's come back to haunt me." She raised the papers. "That's what this is about."

"I'll do what I can," Louis said.

Jan held out the papers. "Read these. We'll talk when you're through."

It was Jan's turn to watch the children play. The papers rustled. Silence. "Jan?"

She turned slowly, not knowing what to expect. "Still friends," Louis said, shaking his head with amazement. "You've been carrying this around inside all these years? According to this document, he tried to kill you. I need a better picture; this is pretty sketchy."

Jan talked, the children's cries providing a bizarre background to the grisly tale. When she was finished, Louis said, "Max Verdon is part of the old boy network in Reno. Do you think he's behind this?"

"I'd like not to think so," Jan said. "He was good to me at the time. I think he protected me from those people. I've seen him a few times, always at a distance. It's possible he recognized me; I took that chance when I came back. What about Frank Smith? He could have been working with Terhune and that group that was backing Steadway. If so, he might have held the evidence."

"It's possible," Louis said. "Smitty's no political animal, but you can bet a lot of politicians have danced to his tune. Wherever there's money, he won't be far behind."

Jan looked directly at Louis. "You haven't said anything about my former 'profession.' "

Louis laughed. "Jan, this is *Nevada!* As a kid, I used to play down by the stockade on Front Street, got to know the girls by name. I can name ten, eleven women who got out and are happily married."

"Tony doesn't know."

"You're sure? You better believe he checked you out."

"I don't have a police record."

"Did you tell him you used to live in Vegas?"

"No, my past is my business. I didn't think anything would come up to affect us."

Louis let out a long breath. "To every problem, there's a solution—so they say. What happens now?"

"Tony has to know," Jan said. "I'll tell him when I get back."

"Just like that—walk in and tell him everything?"

"Know a better way?"

Louis watched the children for a few moments. "I guess not," he said, eyes still on the playground.

He heard the rustle of papers. Jan said, "I'd better get back."

Louis turned toward Jan, a quiet smile on his face. "*We'd* better get back. I'm not going to let you do this alone, Jan. We're friends, remember?"

Jan was touched. "No, Louis, thanks anyway," she said, a determined look coming over her face. "This is my fight."

"Your fight, my father. I'm involved. We do it together." Louis took the papers from Jan and stuffed them in the envelope. "No arguments. Let's go."

Jan wasn't used to taking orders from a man. She started to speak, then saw the look on Louis' face. She rose and joined Louis in the walk to the car. He held the door open while she slid behind the wheel. She watched Louis move around to the passenger side, feeling his strength. It comforted her.

26

It went wrong from the start. Tony Giuliano didn't like to be surprised. "What the hell are you doin' here?" he demanded as Louis appeared in the doorway of his study, Jan close behind.

"Something important came up," Louis said. "I thought it best to see you in person."

Tony looked past Louis at Jan. "You know about this?"

"I met him in town. It was about something that affects us all."

"You said you were goin' shopping," Tony said, barely containing his anger.

"Louis and I had to talk first," Jan said calmly. "I had hoped it wouldn't involve you."

Tony's fist smashed down on the desk. "Everything that happens around here is my business!" he shouted. He pointed a thick finger at Jan. "Including you."

Jan's head lifted, and a steely tone entered her voice. "You don't own me, Tony. We went over that before our marriage. Let's not get into that now; we have more important matters to discuss."

"More important than this?" Tony rapped out, waving an arm at the papers on his desk.

"That's what it's about," Louis said.

"Nevada Investments?" Tony said, anger flaring. "You've been talkin' about this behind my back?"

"Oh, cut it out, Tony," Jan said, tired of the foolish by-play. She moved into the room and sat down. Louis joined her.

Tony was seething. He looked from Jan to Louis, back to Jan. "Talk," he snapped.

Drawing the papers from the envelope, Jan tossed the typed resume on the desk. She held the confession back. Louis lit cigarettes for Jan and himself while Tony scanned the material.

A roar left Tony's mouth before he had completed the first page. "A goddamn whore!" he cried disbelievingly. He read the next few lines. "You fucked Terhune, then killed him?" he shouted, pinning Jan to the chair with savage eyes. He glanced at the second page, then swept it aside. Leaning forward, he looked at Louis. "Out! This is between me and this bitch. I'll deal with you later."

Louis' only move was to re-cross his legs. "You had better hear the rest," he said. "I told you this involves Nevada Investments."

Except for the whiteness of her face and the tight lines around her lips, Jan showed no reaction to Tony's outburst. This, along with Louis's dispassionate attitude, infuriated Tony further. "You've got two minutes," he told Louis. "Then get your ass out."

Louis told him. Tony's face turned darker and darker until it was black with rage. His English failed him. "This don't mean no fuckin' thing to me!" he yelled. "You think I'm goin' to lose what I work for all my life for this cunt? Let her hang!"

Rising, Jan turned to Louis. "Thank you," she said quietly. "I'm sorry you had to be in on this." She looked down at Tony with contempt. "Lisa will help me pack. I suggest we do this as quietly as possible."

Tony was standing now, Louis too. Anything was possible when Tony went into one of his blind rages.

Tony's hands were rigid at his sides, fingers opening and closing. "Cunt!" he spat out. "You're trash. Fuckin' trash!" The last words were said to Jan's departing back.

Tony swung on Louis. "Now it's your turn," he barked. "Sit down. Pay me some respect. What's been goin' on between you two? You been playin' around behind my back?"

Louis had been easing down into the chair. He stopped his descent and stood up. "That's enough," he said in a tight voice. "There's nothing between Jan and me. We're friends; that's all. She's your wife. I was only trying to help." His eyes locked with his father's. "You're going to throw her to the wolves?"

"You think I'm givin' up Nevada Investments for that whore? If you do, you've got another thought comin'."

Louis looked at his father for a long time. He saw the hate and absolute refusal to back down. Nothing would stand in the way of this final victory over his lifelong enemy. Louis moved toward the door. "I'll be back in a few minutes."

"You stay until I'm through," Tony said.

Louis stopped. He shook his head. "No," he said quietly, "No, I think not." He went out and shut the door.

Jan was in her bedroom, piling clothes across the maid's outstretched arms. Louis made a little shake of the head. Jan said to the girl, "Take those out to the car." She put a folded sheet and the keys on top of the clothes. "Spread the sheet in the trunk. We'll fill that first." The girl left, an apprehensive look on her face.

Louis said, "Don't leave without me, Jan. I'm going to settle this matter. When I'm through, I may be no more welcome than you."

"Leave it," Jan said. "Smith may be bluffing. Don't get in any deeper than you are."

Louis' face remained impassive. "You'll wait?"

Jan sighed. "All right."

Tony was pacing the floor of his study. "Been talkin' to the whore?" he asked.

Louis' patience snapped. He walked behind the desk. The typed resume was on the blotter. Jan had kept the confession. Louis folded the resume and put it in his inside coat pocket.

"Put that back!" exploded Tony, advancing across the room as Louis moved away from the desk.

Folding his arms, Louis rested his back against the wall. "You're going to order Frazer to sell his shares to Slaughter," he said. "I want Slaughter notified by Tuesday night. If he isn't, I'll be up before the Commission on Thursday. I'll tell them all about your connection with Frazer."

Had Tony Giuliano not been in excellent health for his seventy-four years, he might have dropped dead from a heart attack, so enormous was his rage. His whole body shook as if seized by a virulent fever. He took one tottering step, then another. A fist was raised. "Two-faced cocksucker!" he lashed out, spraying spittle on his shirt.

At that moment, Tony was a madman, and he reacted like one. He rushed behind the desk and reached for a drawer. Reading his intent, Louis moved swiftly, gripping Tony's wrist.

They fought silently, Tony tearing at Louis' face, producing long bloody scratches. When Louis wrestled that hand away, Tony tried to bite his arm, gnawing at the cloth of Louis' coat, growling like a jungle animal.

Tony's legs were at work, too, kicking and kneeing Louis, seeking the groin. He needed only a few seconds of freedom to reach the gun in the desk drawer.

Increasing his efforts, Tony drove a leg between Louis', throwing them both to the floor. Back and forth they rolled, but Tony's strength was ebbing, age and Louis' wiry muscles taking their toll. Louis pushed Tony's face into the carpet and held it there until Tony ceased struggling. Releasing his father, Louis remained on his knees, breathing deeply.

Louis got slowly to his feet. He stared down at the ruin of his coat, buttons gone, a ragged tear where Tony's teeth had found their mark. There was blood on his tie. He wiped his cheek. His fingers came away streaked with red.

Tony was quiet, too weak to move. Louis lifted the phone and dialed Jan's room. She answered on the third ring. "When will you be ready?" Louis asked.

"Five, ten minutes," Jan said. "Louis, what's the matter? You sound terrible."

"Never mind. Can you send Lisa home before we go?"

"Already done. She's frightened to death. Tony was heard all over the house."

"All right. When you're ready, knock on the study door.

Don't come in—not under any circumstances. Go straight to the car and start the engine. I'll be right behind you."

"Louis, what is it? What's happened?"

"No time. Move as fast as you can." Louis hung up.

Tony was scrabbling about on the floor. "You and the whore," he whispered, struggling to his feet. "I give her to you. That's *all* you get. You'll be out of my will tomorrow."

Louis was too numb to care. He opened the drawer and put the gun in his pocket. "I'll leave this for you in Vegas," he said. He knelt on one knee, keeping well out of reach. "Make sure you make the arrangements with Frazer. Slaughter's to get the word by Tuesday night. If not, I'll be at the Commission meeting on Wednesday." Louis hesitated, recalling how he had laughed at Smitty. Only two days ago? "I'm going to put everything in writing—Frazer, Embarcadero, everything I know," Louis added wearily. "Should anything happen to your wife or me, everything will be turned over to the proper authorities."

Tony's hate reached out like a living thing. "Be out of the Fantasia by tomorrow night or I'll have you thrown out," he said hoarsely, struggling to a sitting position.

Louis rose. He had never felt love for this man. Respect, yes, but that had been tested and found wanting. He knew instinctively they would never speak again.

There was a knock on the door, then silence. "Goodbye, Papa," Louis said. Tony spat on the floor and looked away.

27

Smitty's phone rang a few minutes after nine on Monday morning. A man's voice, vaguely familiar. "Mr. Smith?"

"Yep."

"This is Louis Giuliano. We have to talk."

"Shoot."

"Not on the phone. It's best we meet."

"Want me to come to your office?"

"No. What about your place?"

"It's 'way to hell and gone, fifteen miles out of town."

"That's even better. Are you alone?"

"An old couple in the big house. A few cowhands. They don't know nothin'."

"Tell me how to get there. I'll come right out."

When Louis arrived, there was no shaking of hands. The temperature was already in the eighties, so they went inside.

"I'm not going to pretend I like you, Mr. Smith," Louis said as he sat down across from Smitty. "I wouldn't be seeing you like this, but this matter has gone beyond anything I imagined. Your action has cost Jan a husband and me a father. I've been dismissed from the Fantasia and cut out of my father's will. I hope you're satisfied."

Smitty's only reaction was to blink and pause in the midst of lighting a cigarette. "There wasn't anything personal in this," he said. "I had to make the try. It was the only possible way to keep Tony from doin' more dirt to Meade Slaughter."

"What's this 'more dirt,' Mr. Smith? My father's hated Meade Slaughter for most of his life, but this is the first time he's made any direct move against him. Unless you mean the stock he's bought over the last ten years."

Smitty studied Louis for several moments. He nodded, as if reaching a satisfactory conclusion. "I expect you're tellin' the truth, Mr. Giuliano," he said. "We never thought you had any part in it."

"Any part of what?"

"You know how David Slaughter died?"

Louis' eyes narrowed. "I heard he died of a drug overdose."

"That's right. And it was your father that got him hooked."

"That's ridiculous! My father's never had anything to do with drugs. I'll stake my life on that."

"Maybe not as a business," Smitty said, "but he sure as hell got David addicted. Meade spent ten grand havin' it investigated. He's still got the report tucked away."

Suddenly, anything seemed possible. Louis asked Smitty to give him the details, and Smitty did.

"I want to read that report," Louis said.

"It's around, I'll see you get it," Smitty said.

"I'd better finish what I came for," Louis said. "I told my father I would release certain information to the Gaming Commission if he doesn't back off from his deal with Frazer. Frazer is supposed to offer his stock to Slaughter by tomorrow night."

Smitty leaned forward. "What did you do that for, boy?"

"It's really none of your business," Louis said shortly. "I wasn't going to see Jan ruined over an apparently senseless feud, for one thing."

Smitty clacked his false teeth, then smiled. "There's more to you than I thought," he said. "I don't usually make mistakes."

Had Louis been in a more receptive mood, he might have realized what an admission this was, coming from a man who rarely apologized or offered a compliment. He chose not to comment.

"Tomorrow, huh?" Smitty said. "What happens if Frazer don't come through?"

"I go to the Commission. I'm a man of my word, Mr. Smith. I don't think it will come to that."

"I'll pass the word to Meade."

"Tell me, did Meade Slaughter orchestrate all this?"

"He knows nothin'," Smitty said flatly. "This was my show all the way. Meade will be shocked out of his boots."

"How much will you tell him?"

"Only what's necessary. Tell Tony's wife her secret is safe. When Frazer's stock is in Meade's possession, I'll destroy my copies."

Louis stood up. He took out a business card and wrote on the back. "This is my home number. Call me Wednesday morning if you don't hear from Frazer."

Smitty got up and took the card. "What you goin' to do now that you're unemployed?" he asked.

"I'm not worried. There are always good jobs open for a man with experience. I won't make any moves until this thing is settled." A wry smile. "The news of my dismissal is most likely already on the street. Las Vegas is still a small town in that respect."

Smitty nodded. He reached out. "I'd like to shake your hand."

Louis looked at Smitty's outstretched arm. He should hate this man. He thought of Meade Slaughter's fiancée, David's addiction, what hate had done to his father. He took Smitty's bony hand in his.

They parted at the door. The dog, Mose, watched curiously as Louis walked to his car, a tall slim figure in an elegantly tailored suit.

Smitty went inside and called Meade.

28

"We're going home early," Meade said over the phone to Gari. "Reese, too."

"Should I ask why?"

"Ask, but I can't tell you. Smitty just called and said he's coming in. He wants us to meet at the house; it's more private."

"He does love his mysteries, doesn't he?"

"He thrives on intrigue. If it were edible, he'd live to be a thousand."

Smitty had an attentive audience. They sat on the edge of their chairs, mystified at the grin that was spreading over his face. "Meade, how would you like to keep the Plush Wheels?" he said.

Meade was stunned. He hadn't expected anything like this. "That's a stupid question," he said. "You already know the answer to that."

"I'd say you've got a fair to better chance," Smitty said. "We'll know by tomorrow night."

"Keep going."

"Don't get your nuggets in an uproar," Smitty said, "but I'm only goin' to give you the highlights. All right?"

Meade nodded impatiently.

"Louis Giuliano came to see me this mornin'. Clive Frazer is supposed to contact you by tomorrow night and offer you his stock."

Meade grunted as if struck. "All of it?"

"Every share, a little over four and a half million of 'em, the way I calculate."

"How did this all come about?"

"There was a big blowup yesterday. Tony kicked his wife out and fired Louis. Tony's probably drawin' up a new will right now."

"They were playing around?" Meade said. "What's that got to do with me?"

"It's nothin' like that," Smitty said. "I ain't goin' to elaborate. But you owe those two, Meade. Louis told Tony he'll go before the Gaming Commission and release some damagin' information if Tony don't persuade Frazer to sell his stock to you. That's all I'm goin' to tell."

Gari was as bewildered as Meade and Reese. "Louis Giuliano standing up for us?"

"You'll have to take my word," Smitty said. "I believe him. If Frazer don't come through by tomorrow night, I'm to let Louis know."

Reese said, "Why did Giuliano kick his wife out?"

Smitty shook his head. "Sorry, boy. Story ends here."

The news was beginning to sink in. "We might not lose it," Meade said, looking at Gari and Reese. "Did you hear that, guys? We might not lose it after all!"

"Let's not celebrate yet," Gari said cautiously. She couldn't bear to see Meade knocked down again.

"How about celebrating a little?" Meade said, grinning like a boy trying to con his mother. "Haven't we got a bottle of champagne in the fridge?"

Gari smiled and jumped up.

"None of that lizard piss for me," Smitty said. "You know what I drink."

Smitty left early, but the rest talked late into the night, too excited to sleep.

Meade got the call at 11:15 the next morning. With little explanation, Clive Frazer offered Meade his shares in Nevada Investments. The exact terms would be decided in the next ten days.

Hanging up, Meade called Gari and Reese. While they were on the way up to his office, he called the Gaming Commission in Carson City. They confirmed that Tony Giuliano had withdrawn his application.

As soon as Gari and Reese arrived, they put through a call to Ann. She was practically sitting on the phone, having been given the news last night. She would be down tomorrow for a celebration and business meeting.

It had been an unbelievable two weeks. Meade had gained a son and regained the Plush Wheels. He was happy almost beyond words.

There were some not so happy. Stan Atwood, Phil Hackett and two other top executives were let go. Because he was caught up in the euphoria of the moment, Meade allowed them to resign. They would say nothing about the true reason for their dismissal, Meade having shown them the reports.

Between the five hotels and clubs, eleven other employees were fired, the investigative net having caught them while in the search for bigger fish.

For Reese, his happiness ended during the early Sunday morning hours. Jeanette had called on Saturday to say she would come straight from work to his apartment. There had been a strange tone in her voice. Reese feared the worst, thinking she had accepted the road-show job.

Jeanette didn't ease into the subject; it wasn't her way. Pushing past Reese, she leaned against the closed door. "Is it true?" she asked in an accusing voice. "Is Meade Slaughter your father?"

Reese spread his arms helplessly. "I was going to tell you," he said. "Things have been so crazy lately I haven't had the chance. How did you hear?"

"Never mind. You had a chance, Reese Harrington— months ago. Why did you lie to me when Jack came by?"

"Everything happened so quick. I was stuck. Meade didn't even know then."

Jeanette's eyes sparkled angrily. "You couldn't trust me," she said in a low cutting voice. "What am I, just another piece of ass to you? Am I a passing ship in the night, no trust between us?"

Reese wished she would yell; her bottled-up anger frightened him. "No, it wasn't that," he said, wilting under her unrelenting gaze. "I . . . I, oh, hell, I don't know."

"You lied to me, Reese; it's as simple as that," Jeanette said. "If you had trusted me, you wouldn't have lied. I trusted you. I never lied to you. Relationships are built on trust. Without that, we haven't anything. I told you all about my hippie life in San Francisco—everything. I held nothing back. I was beginning to hope—really hope!"

"Sweetheart—"

"I'm taking that job, Reese." Her voice broke. "I wasn't going to."

Reese stepped forward. Jeanette's voice was a sharp cry of pain. "No! It's over, Reese. My contract ends in two weeks and I'm leaving. Don't contact me. You'll show me *that* much respect, won't you?"

"Can't we talk it over?" Reese asked beseechingly.

"Promise you will leave me alone. That's all I ask."

"I promise," he said, teetering on the edge of his emotions, afraid to say more.

"Thank you," Jeanette whispered. A moment later, she was gone.

Jeanette never called, and Reese kept his promise. On one

occasion, he yielded to a masochistic urge and went to the
Fantasia to see her dance. He hadn't promised not to watch
her.

29

It was mid-August, seven weeks since Clive Frazer had
agreed to sell his shares in Nevada Investments. The final
transfer had taken place the week before, three days after the
Nevada State Gaming Commission had approved the purchase.

It had cost Meade sixty-five million to buy Frazer's stock,
almost eleven million over the current market price. To
Meade, it had been worth every penny. He now owned
11,920,000 shares of Nevada Investments, representing fifty
percent ownership. Ann had two and a half percent, Smitty,
one percent. Together, they controlled the corporation. During the next year, Meade would buy another one or two
percent.

Frazer's stock had been purchased with loans from three
different banks and High Sierra Federal Savings in Northern
California. With Smitty's backing, the financial package had
been put together in record time.

Tony Giuliano was slowly unloading his Nevada Investment shares. He had purchased an additional seventeen percent during his takeover attempt, giving him a total of
twenty-nine percent. Should he sell all his recent purchases
at the prevailing price, he would lose over six million dollars.

"He's goin' nuts," Smitty said in the Plush Wheel coffee
shop. "Tony never knew how much he depended on Louis
until he got rid of him. He's hirin' and firin' right and left.
If he keeps this up, he'll lose his best men. Some have already
left—like rats from a sinkin' ship."

"Reese pointed Tony's wife out to me the other day," Meade said. "She's quite a looker."

"*Ex*-wife," Smitty said. "The divorce was final two weeks after she left him."

"She still go by the name of Giuliano?"

"No way. She went back to Lebeck, her name before she married Tony. She didn't want his name or his money. 'Course, she's got money comin' out of her ears. Oh, yeah, she wants to see you."

"Me? What for? Gari's not the jealous type, but if she sees me with that woman, she might lop my head off for good luck."

"Let Gari sit in," Smitty said. "It's business."

"What kind of business?"

"Got me. I'm just passin' a message from Louis. Guess he sees her now and then since she moved to Tahoe."

"Tahoe?" Meade asked, raising an eyebrow.

"She signed a long-term lease at the Tahoe Country Club and Estates. That's a plum. You got to have contacts to get in there."

"How come you know so much about her?" Meade said. "Seeing her on the side?"

"Not that one," Smitty said vehemently. "Not if I was fifty years younger. I hear tell that she's got a ball-bearin' brain that runs like an IBM machine. Highfalutin, too. Tahoe Country Club! She ain't the only good-lookin' gal with a tight-assed walk."

Catching the eye of the waitress, Meade signaled for more coffee. He turned back to Smitty. "Do you know why Louis wanted those papers?" Last month, he had given Smitty a copy of Branch Thorton's report detailing Tony Giuliano's part in David's drug addiction.

"Jan ran a little investigation of her own," Smitty said. "Two, three years ago. It uncovered what happened to you and Sandra—all news to Louis. Puttin' that together with what I had told him about David, Louis figured he'd better take some protective measures. But he wanted to see that report first. If he had any doubts, that settled it. He typed up a summary of all the dirt he has on Tony and mailed him a copy, told him if anything happens to Jan or him, it would be made public. Whatever he's got on his father, it must be dynamite."

"It's hard to imagine even Tony Giuliano harming his son," Meade said. "His ex-wife's another matter; I wouldn't put it past him to dump her down a mine shaft."

"Louis has got him locked up now," Smitty said. "A smart move, far as I'm concerned."

30

"So we went to old prospector Colonel Fink's funeral," Benny Binion was saying. "There was me, Hank Greenspun, Vail Pittman, Judge Nores from Pioche and a shill from the Fremont. Just us five. I leaned over to Hank and said, 'Hank, I tell you one thing I noticed in this town. A man dies here and he ain't got no money, he don't draw worth a damn.' "

The men at the table laughed. Gari had left them an hour ago, mumbling something about the "old boys' club." She was smiling when she said it. This was Meade's birthday party, and it was only right that he should spend time with friends who had been a part of his life in Nevada.

Over five hundred guests had crowded into the big room that served as the Plush Wheel's convention facility. It was October 8, 1980, and Meade was seventy-six. The party had started at six and it was now past ten. Meade had grumbled about all the attention he was getting, but Gari knew he was enjoying every minute.

It was after two in the morning when Meade, Gari, Ann and Reese arrived back at the big house on the golf course. Meade's many presents would be brought over from the Plush Wheel later that day.

Ann sat on the arm of Meade's chair. "I've been saving my big present to give to you now," she said, ruffling Meade's hair.

"Where is it hid?" Meade said, looking at the low-cut gown that concealed little.

Ann placed a slender hand over her left breast. "It's in here," she said. She put an arm around Meade's shoulders and pressed her cheek to his. "I'm giving you *me!*"

"How's that?" Meade said, reaching up to touch her face.

"You're going to have me around all the time—starting the first."

"You're coming home?"

Ann nodded happily. "Better get my office ready."

"How do you like that, guys?" Meade said, looking around Ann at Gari and Reese. "Now, that's what I call a *present!*"

"Thought you'd like it," Gari said.

Hugging Ann, Meade looked at his family. "I'm a lucky man," he said softly.

31

The Lear jet swept over Mt. Rose. There had been a light snow the weekend before, and patches of white dotted the mountains that ringed Lake Tahoe.

Reese thrilled everytime he saw this mammoth alpine lake. As the jet reached the North Shore, the Hyatt Tahoe appearing off the left wing and the Cal-Neva Lodge off the right, Reese saw the family cabin almost immediately below. It disappeared as the jet started its long downward glide toward the airport at the south end of the lake.

Reese would be spending a week at the cabin next month while he worked with Frank Di Santo, the new general manager of the Tahoe Plush Wheel.

Nevada Investments had pulled off a major coup when they hired Di Santo away from Caesars Palace on the Strip. He had taken up his new post on November first.

It was difficult for Meade, but he tried to leave his top men alone, giving them the authority to make day-to-day decisions. Frank Di Santo had been on the job for two weeks, and Meade was chafing at the bit to get a first-hand progress report. This was their second stop on this trip, having spent yesterday and last night in Reno.

Meade pointed to the left. "That bomb blast at Harvey's last August made all of us sit up and take notice," he said. "The possibility's always there that some loser might take his frustrations out on a casino. It's cost the Wagon Wheel ten, twelve million to clean the mess up.

"They've got another big job on their hands, getting that second highrise built. They've been fighting the environmentalists tooth and nail over that for years. Harvey's will eventually win; they got approval from the Tahoe Regional Planning Agency in seventy-three. But that's going to be the last tower at the lake.

"I saw it coming back in the sixties. That's one of the big reasons why I went public. The plans for our highrise had already been approved, but I knew if we didn't get going, we'd be in a court fight like the Wagon Wheel's in now."

Meade waved a hand as the jet approached the runway. "We're already in, so I guess I can afford to be charitable toward the environmentalists. It's a beautiful lake. If they hadn't stepped in, the whole area would have ended up looking like the South Shore—a hodgepodge mess."

A hotel limousine was waiting. A half-hour later, they were seated in the restaurant at the top of the fifteen-story Plush Wheel tower.

Frank Di Santo didn't waste time getting to the point. He was fifty-three and had been in the gaming business for over thirty years. A squat intensive man with black hair and eyes, he talked in short explosive sentences. "Meade," he said, "this recession is going to hurt; Nevada won't be lucky like during the past when things got tough. Combine that with the push from Atlantic City, and we've got troubles. We've got to make changes, forget everything but the bottom line."

"I'm listening," Meade said.

"We've got to bring in more slots, especially video slots. I'm not saying we should turn our backs on the premium customer. They're important, but in the long run, slots will be the biggest revenue makers."

Meade held up a hand. "Draw up what you see for Tahoe, Frank. If everything jibes, we'll give it a go here first."

"You can have the analysis today," Di Santo said. "I had it typed up last week."

Startled, Meade said, "You've done all that since the first?"

Di Santo shook his head. "I started on the outline as soon as we signed our contract. I've been gathering data since seventy-six."

Meade sighed. "Like you say, Frank, it's the bottom line that counts."

Di Santo took a sip from his Coke. "You'll find it easy to take when you see the projected profits, Meade. Relax, you don't have to carry all the worries now that you've got Reese to take up the reins."

A pleased look flashed between Meade and Reese. It was common knowledge now that they were father and son. In early July, the Plush Wheel's publicity department had released the information, leaving certain details to the imagination. Such an announcement might have raised eyebrows twenty years ago, but not in 1980.

Reese was especially happy with the way Meade had accepted Jack Harrington. With Cindy as the initial focal point of their interest, they were well on their way to becoming good friends. Jack was spending nearly half his time in Las Vegas of late, making preparations to shoot a movie near Tonopah.

Later that afternoon, Meade and Reese visited the other stateline hotels and clubs. They ended up at Harrah's, a few steps from the California border.

Entering Harrah's, they were greeted by row upon row of

slot and video machines. The noise lessened as they entered
the hotel lobby area. Meade paused in front of the jewelry
counter. Getting this concession in a gaming hotel required
"juice." It took connections; one had to be a relative or have
the right friends.

"That was a pretty slick move Jan Lebeck made," Meade
said. "She had done her homework by the time she saw me.
I knew the Wilsons wanted to retire but not when. It will cost
her at least a half-million to take over their jewelry concession. I was glad to okay the deal. She'll add class to our Tahoe
arcade."

"Considering what she did for us, it wasn't really asking
that much," Reese said. "I'd sure like to get to the bottom
of that someday."

"Louis never said anything?"

"Not a word. It must have been something else, whatever
it was. I'm glad he got on with the Sahara. He's overqualified
for the job, but it's a good organization. He'll head up another hotel someday."

Meade switched the subject. It was still strange to talk in
friendly terms about a Giuliano.

32

Jeanette had been gone for five months—one hundred forty-
five days to be exact. With relentless efficiency, Reese's mental calendar added to the count each day. Even now, he
couldn't get her out of his mind.

Through Nancy, Reese had obtained the itinerary of *Las
Vegas Burlesque Follies*, the show Jeanette had signed on
with. It was currently in Manassas, Virginia and would move
on to Miami on January first. After much debate, Reese had

sent her a Christmas card. No message, just her name and, "Love, Reese."

Reese arrived at Smitty's ranch a little after eight. The Austins had retired to Florida last month, and Reese had moved into the big ranch house. It suited his new lifestyle. Now that he was second in command of Nevada Investments, he often worked seven days a week. When a hectic day ended, he looked forward to the relaxing quietness of the ranch. His social life had narrowed dramatically since Jeanette left. When he did entertain a woman, it was at the apartment he maintained in town. The ranch house was his private castle, off limits to all but the family and Smitty. And Mose.

Reese hadn't adopted the big shaggy dog; if anything, it was the other way around. After Smitty retired for the night, Mose would move up to the huge covered porch that enclosed the ranch house, flopping down on his rug beside the front door and waiting for Reese's return and a goodnight scratch accompanied by a bowl of goodies.

So, Reese, Smitty and Mose settled into comfortable coexistence. Reese and Smitty had breakfast together and dinner when Reese came home early. Smitty did most of the cooking, and the dinners were heavy with meat and potatoes, as were the breakfasts with stacks of pancakes. Reese could almost hear the *thud* as the food hit the bottom of his stomach. To preserve his waistline, he tried to limit his at-home dinners to twice a week.

33

As summer approached, Meade had some decisions to make. "Let's go out on the patio," he said to Gari. It had turned dark a half-hour ago, but it was still warm. They sat in padded lounge chairs, Meade lighting a cigar, Gari toying with a glass of iced tea.

"I've got to do something about my will," Meade said. "Problem is, I don't know what to do."

Gari squinted at Meade, three feet away. "Meade Slaughter not knowing his mind? Never thought I'd see the day."

Meade grinned in the soft light of the patio lanterns. "You're seeing it. Not the first, either. I've come to depend on you a lot the last twenty-five years, baby," he said, reaching out to take her hand.

"Twenty-five years? It's been that long?"

"Will be next year."

Gari squeezed his hand. "Almost a quarter of a century," she said. "How do you like holding hands with an old woman?"

"If you're old, I'm ancient," Meade said, squeezing back. "I like holding hands with you, but there are some things I like even better."

"Ditto," Gari smiled. Their sex life was undiminished, a private joy.

"Back to the business at hand," Meade said, releasing Gari's hand. "Any thoughts?"

Gari said, "I've been concerned that you haven't changed your will since you found out about Reese. It's been almost a year."

"There's Ann, Reese and you," Meade said. "As it stands, you're my heir with Ann next in line."

"Ann and I have already talked this over," Gari said. "Reese is your son; he should come first."

"Not if you were my wife."

"Well, I'm not."

"It would be a great way to start off the next twenty-five years," Meade said.

Gari's head snapped around. "I thought we were talking about a will."

"Among other things. What do you say, kid—are we too old to marry?"

Gari was too stunned to answer. She just stared.

"Cat got your tongue?" Meade asked, teeth flashing whitely in the subdued light.

Gari shook her head, mouth half-open. "Meade, you come up with the damnedest off-the-wall ideas."

"Hardly off-the-wall," Meade said. "I've been giving it careful attention for months."

Gari sat up straight, feet falling to the ground. "Are you serious?"

"Never been more serious in my life."

Gari dropped back on the cushion and stared up at the night sky. "We haven't discussed this once, not since the first week together. Why now?"

Meade jabbed his cigar into an ashtray. "It first came to mind last year, when it seemed like Giuliano was going to take over. It looked like we would be having a lot of time on our hands . . . we could travel, do things together. Marriage seemed like icing on the cake, if you know what I mean."

Gari frowned.

Meade sat up and took her hand in both of his. "Then I found out about Reese, and the Giuliano threat blew over. Something started bugging me, but things were so hectic the next few months I didn't have time to figure out what it was. It didn't really start to hit me until after the first of the year."

Meade continued, "I felt so good about having found a son and hearing about Cindy after all these years. It made me realize how much I had loved her." Gari's hand tensed.

Meade smiled and stroked her long fingers. "Alone and with Reese—and with Jack Harrington—I dredged up a lot of old memories. Old feelings, too. Know something? None of those feelings were better than the ones I have for you. Before long, I wasn't thinking about Cindy; I was thinking about *you.* One morning I was standing by the bed watching you sleep, and I realized what was bugging me. Damnit, I *loved* you! I loved you so much I couldn't imagine ever living without you. That was when I knew we should get married. I don't want you just as my best friend and lover. I want you as my *wife!*"

"Oh, Meade," Gari whispered, eyes filling. "Oh, Meade." She reached up and smoothed a lock of white hair off his forehead. "Don't you know how much I love you? I've wanted to tell you for so long, but I was afraid you wouldn't want to hear it."

Meade bent and kissed her, tasting the salt of her tears. They clung to each other for a long time. Meade drew his head back, noses touching. "Okay?" he said.

"Okay what?"

"Don't be a smart-ass."

"Is it necessary? I know how you feel; that's what matters to me."

"It's not necessary," Meade said, "but it's what I want."

"You usually get your way, don't you?"

"I try."

"When?"

"Wedding chapels are open twenty-four hours a day in Vegas."

Gari laughed and sat up. She placed her hands on Meade's shoulders. "I'm game if you are," she said, "but I'll pass on the wedding chapel bit."

They were married in the living room of their home. A justice of the peace performed the ceremony, and only Smitty attended, with Reese acting as best man and Ann as brides-maid.

34

The will wasn't forgotten during the twelve days that led up to the wedding. Papers were drawn up, including a marriage contract, that would leave Nevada Investments equally divided between Gari, Ann and Reese, taking into consideration that Ann already owned two and one-half percent of the company. No shares could be sold to the public or transferred to spouses as the result of death or separation until they were first offered to the original principals, allowing six months for purchase.

Gari had expected Meade to leave more to Reese. "He's going to be pretty well off as it is," Meade said. "I'm supposed to keep this quiet, but you should know. Smitty set up a fairly large trust for me and a smaller one for Ann and you years ago, after he had that bout with pneumonia. Last March, he started transferring the bulk of the rest of his estate into a trust for Reese."

"That must be millions!" Gari exclaimed. "Does Reese know?"

Meade shook his head. "Just me and the lawyer. Now you. If there's anything Smitty hates, it's government controls. Without any heirs and no will or trusts, the government would get his money. With the trusts, he's insuring the government will get the minimum in taxes. Sort of a last laugh, if you know what I mean."

Gari sat back in the booth. They were waiting for Ann and Reese to join them for lunch in the Gambler's Club. "This week is full of surprises," she said.

Meade grinned. "Smitty's damn possessive about Reese. He considers himself the sole reason we met."

"I hate to stroke the old goat's ego," Gari said, "but isn't it pretty close to the truth?"

"Sure, but I'm not going to advertise it."

"I wonder about Reese stuck out on that ranch with just Smitty for company," Gari said. "Is that good?"

"Don't see any harm," Meade said. "It's what Reese wants. I thought he'd be over that girl by now."

Gari shot Meade a reproachful look. "Who do you think he got his bleeding heart from? How long did it take you to get over Cindy?"

Meade hid a sheepish look behind his hands while he lit a cigar.

A male voice began to sing, "Hello, young lovers . . ." They looked up into two smiling faces. "Hope we're not intruding," Reese said as he and Ann slid into the booth.

"Glad you stopped by," Meade said. "This woman's been giving me a bad time."

"That's not good strategy, Mom," Ann said. "You're supposed to wait until you're married a while."

"Ann's got some news," Reese said. "Tell them," he ordered, nudging her in the ribs.

Ann's face flushed with excitement. "Know that movie Jack's going to shoot here in August? He got me a bit part. I'm going to be a showgirl!"

"Oh, no!" Gari cried.

"Hey, great!" Meade said. "Jack mentioned something about that being in the works. I told him I was all for having our chief counsel's image brightened up."

"You didn't!" Ann exclaimed.

"Well, not quite, but I think another showgirl in the family is terrific."

"Looks like we've got several things to celebrate," Gari said quickly. "Why don't we order champagne?" Meade signaled the waiter.

"*Several* things?" Reese said.

Meade held up a hand. "We're taking a drive after lunch," he said mysteriously, turning to the waiter and shutting off further questions.

Two hours later, Meade parked at the construction site. They stepped out of the Cadillac into the shadow of the new thirty-one story tower. Crews had started installing the plate glass the week before. By September, the exterior would be completed.

"We build; they rebuild," Meade said, looking south in the direction of the MGM Grand, where a disastrous fire had claimed eighty-four lives and caused nearly fifty-million in damage the previous November.

The new Plush Wheel tower, unlike the MGM which was constructed under old building codes, would be fitted with sprinklers, smoke detectors and closed-circuit TV systems in every room. With the passing of a new fire law by the Nevada legislature two months ago, all Nevada hotels had to be retrofitted with sprinkler and warning systems by June 15, 1984. As soon as the new Plush Wheel tower was opened in May, the retrofitting would begin on the older section.

Meade lifted a hand in greeting as Jim Bailey approached from the construction trailer. "Looking good, Jim," Meade said.

"I always feel better when the outside starts closing up," Bailey said, nodding toward a rooftop crane that was lifting a sheet of glass toward the waiting glaziers.

Meade said, "When your dad came to Vegas, building a two-bedroom house was a big thing."

"I was only four, so I don't remember much about that era," Jim Bailey said. He smiled at Meade with the ease of longtime friendship. "Dad built a hell of a lot over the years, but I think he was proudest of that half-assed exercise rig he built for you in San Francisco. He used to talk about it all the time—helping you to walk again."

"I'll never forget what he did for me," Meade said. "We came a long way together." His wave encompassed the twin towers and the main casino. "Neither of us imagined anything like this."

Leaving Jim Bailey, they borrowed hard hats and went inside, picking their way over electrical cords and around equipment. The 50,000-square-foot convention facility was just a shell, and their voices echoed in the gigantic room. "Race you to the other end," Reese said to Gari.

"Real funny," she said. "I'm so full of lunch and champagne, it's a wonder I got this far."

Passing through the site of the future race and sports book, they descended to the underground arcade. Temporary lights were strung along the ceiling, and the shops were beginning to take shape.

Gari looked at Meade. "Don't you think we should show the children their surprise?"

"Yeah, Meade," Ann said. "I've been looking around every corner. Where is it?"

"Not here," Meade said. "Sorry about the diversion, but I wanted to see how things were going." He headed toward the stairs, the others trailing behind.

Meade drove along the golf course, passing one magnificent home after another. He parked beside a large vacant area. Gari took an envelope out of the car pocket. "Lots one fifty-eight and -nine," she said, handing the envelope to Ann in the back seat. "That's the deed. The land and the house are on us. You can build whatever and whenever you want." A warning look. "Within reason, of course."

Ann's mouth opened and closed. The envelope dropped in her lap. Meade grinned. "Say something, counselor."

"I'm flabbergasted," Ann said. "I would have never guessed. I didn't know there were any lots left out here!"

"Meade hung onto a few," Gari said. "Glad?"

"Oh, yes—yes! I've dreamed about having a home here. I can have one built right away?"

"Get busy, and it will be ready for Christmas," Meade said.

"I love you!" Ann cried, leaning forward and kissing Meade and Gari.

Gari untangled herself from her daughter's arms. She handed an envelope to Reese as Meade started the car. "You get lots three fifty-one and -two," she said. "That's across the lake from us. We'll pick up the tab for the house, but there's a catch; you have to feed my ducks when I'm out of town."

"I don't get it," Reese said as the car approached the Plush Wheel. "You guys get married and you're giving gifts. It's supposed to be the other way around."

"Right!" chimed in Ann.

"Don't forget that on Saturday," Meade said. "We'll be expecting something appropriate to our maturity and exquisite taste."

Gari twisted around to face the rear-seat passengers. "Meade and I have been updating personal matters the last week, and we decided to give you the lots now. We had planned it for Christmas." She looked at Ann. "We thought you'd like to get out of that apartment by then. If your house is finished by Christmas, we'll have dinner at your place."

"I'll start on the menu tonight."

Gari threw a disapproving look at Reese. "I suppose you're not in a rush to get away from the ranch."

Reese grinned. A thought had been burning in his mind for the last fifteen minutes. "I might surprise you," he said. "Maybe, we'll have Christmas at my place *next* year."

35

Jeanette threw another crumpled sheet of hotel stationary into the waste basket. This was her first letter to Reese, and she couldn't even get the opening sentence right.

When he had sent her a Christmas card six months ago, she had sent one in return, following his example and penning nothing but "Love" and her name.

A humorous Valentine card arrived in February. Again, no message. Jeanette visited four shops before she found a card that was just right. She wondered if Reese's search had been as difficult. His card had made her laugh, and it had reminded her of the good times they had together. He couldn't have found such a perfect card quickly. At least, she didn't want to think so.

The Easter card was also carefully selected, beautifully designed, with two short lines of thoughtful printed verse, followed by, "Love, Reese," at the bottom. Finding one of similar quality wasn't going to be easy. The show was moving to Detroit and Jeanette had to make a mad dash from the hotel just hours before flight time. She prepared the card in the air and mailed it when they landed.

Jeanette's birthday was a few weeks later. Reese enclosed a three-page letter with the card. It was worded cautiously, asking how she was, wondering if she would be continuing in the show, passing on tidbits of Vegas news he knew she would be interested in. A slight deviation at the bottom. "Love you," instead of just, "Love."

So here she was, two weeks later, trying to answer his letter. She had considered not answering it at all. Her friend, Brenda, who had danced with her three years ago at the Las Vegas Hilton and was her roommate on the road, had lectured unsparingly. "Don't be a fool, Jay," Brenda had said. "You know that isn't what you want. I'd give up my silicone to have that guy. And I'm not the only one. You two had something really good. If you think you can have it again with somebody else, then don't answer his letter."

Jeanette was effectively silenced by that last argument. No other relationship had approached the one she had had with Reese. Not even the teenage one she had thought could never be duplicated. There had been two affairs during the past year, but they had left her feeling empty and burdened with a strange sense of guilt.

Jeanette struggled with the letter. She finally got through the first page, a bunch of nonsense about the weather and some changes in the show.

"I've signed a contract for six more months," Jeanette wrote. "They wanted a year, but I have an opportunity to teach dancing under Phil Black in New York City, starting in January. As I still have dreams of having my own dance studio someday, I can't pass up this chance. Besides, I'm getting too old for all this traveling (ha)."

Warming to her task, Jeanette found to her horror that she was well into the sixth page. What would Reese think if her letter was *twice* as long as his? She glanced over the pages and couldn't see anything she wanted to take out.

She thought about her decision to leave the show. She had been joking about being too old—she could dance professionally for years yet if she wanted—but her enthusiasm had been waning lately, much of it due to the increasing desire to open her own dance studio.

It wasn't out of the realm of possibility. She had discovered a natural talent for teaching five years ago when she volunteered to help put together a community show. Since then, she had taught part-time in several Las Vegas dance studios. Working under Phil Black in New York City would be a definite leg up toward reaching her goal. After that, all she had to do was rob a bank. Her insecure lifestyle had left her finances sadly lacking.

Chewing on her pen, Jeanette debated how to sign the letter. Reese's, "Love you," was pretty strong, and she shouldn't be a copycat, anyway. Frowning, she scribbled several sample lines on a notepad. Settling on one, she wrote, "With love." She signed the letter with a flourish and sealed the envelope.

Zipping up her robe, she hurried out to the hall mail drop. Best to get it on the way before she changed her mind.

36

"It was rough, wasn't it?" Jan Lebeck said. They were standing just inside the entrance to her apartment.

"Worse than I expected," Louis Giuliano replied, face gray and drawn from the ordeal of the last two days.

"Let's sit down," Jan said, leading the way into the living room. "Coffee?"

"No thanks," Louis said. He sat in a chair and rested his head against the back cushion, closing his eyes for a moment.

Jan sat on the edge of the couch, hands clasped in her lap. "Maybe it would be better if you came back after you've rested," she said, concern in her eyes.

Louis shook his head and straightened up. "No, I'll sleep better after I've talked it out. It's like closing one of the biggest chapters in my life—*our* lives."

Jan nodded, understanding better than anyone else what Louis was going through. "Was it a big funeral?"

"Medium. Papa had a pretty strong standing in the community, so all the big-wigs were there. My mother and sister came up from San Francisco. Mike, of course, although you wouldn't have known we were brothers the way he acted. I swear he came within an inch of slugging me."

Jan's face twisted with dislike. "Mike's always had a heavy hand. He inherited all of Tony's worst traits and added some of his own. Tony told me once that he beats his wife."

"She was there—and their three kids. I don't have much use for the boys, but their daughter is nice."

"Rita," Jan said. "She must be eighteen or nineteen. I gather Tony must have told Mike what happened."

"I guess so, some of it, anyway." Louis pulled a legal

605

document from his inside coat pocket. "Papa got a good poke at me from the grave," he said, handing the document to Jan. "Read the middle paragraph, page two."

Jan's dark eyes ran down the page. "What a vindictive hateful thing to say," she murmured, her lovely face sparking with anger. She looked up, stabbing the paper with a long slender finger. "He couldn't be satisfied with just cutting you out of the will," she said hotly. "He had to say all these lies —calling you a thief, cheating with me behind his back, trying to steal his casinos. I'm sorry, Louis, but your father was a bastard!"

"Hey!" Louis said, moving over to the couch and putting his arm around Jan. "You're the lady who never loses her cool, remember?"

Leaning her head against his shoulder, Jan stared down at the papers. "I know," she said, "but it's so *unfair.* No son ever worked harder for his father." The papers slid off her lap as she clinched and unclinched her hands. "What really makes me angry is that I'm the cause of this."

Louis smoothed her silky black hair. "We promised not to talk about that," he said quietly.

Jan sat up and grasped Louis' hand. "Fight them," she hissed. "*Fight* them, Louis. You can't let Tony beat you even after he's dead."

"I can and I will," he said, face setting into the stubborn lines she had come to know so well. "Mike has enough money to drown me before I get to first base. Rozini looked like he could kill me at the funeral. He'll put Embarcadero behind Mike in a fight, and those boys can play rough."

Louis cupped Jan's face in his hands. "You would be dragged into the mess. They would find out everything about you. Besides," he added, running his fingers over her small ears and through her hair, "we're not totally innocent anymore. We never cheated behind Tony's back, but we're doing it behind my wife's now."

Jan moved her head to one side and kissed the palm of Louis' hand. She pressed the hand against her cheek. "I'm selfish," she said. "I've found a man I respect and care for, and I won't let him go."

"Just try," Louis said, drawing her into his arms.

"Are you too tired to make love?" Jan asked, clutching him with that fierce energy that always set him on fire.

Louis rose quickly, pulling her with him. "On your way," he said, turning her toward the bedroom, slapping her gently on the rump.

Wordlessly, they undressed and met in the middle of the big bed, kissing and rubbing each other with their bodies and hands, taming the first burst of passion so they could explore each other in a more leisurely manner.

Louis kissed a high firm breast, running his tongue around the dark areola, nipping the jutting nipple. "I'll never get tired of this," he murmured, "not in two lifetimes."

Jan arched her back, pressing the nipple into his mouth. Her arms were straight along her sides, fingers of one hand playing with the soft head of his swollen member. She smiled down at his wavy gray-streaked hair. "That's easy to say after only six months; you'll be tired of me by the end of the year."

"Ha!" Louis exclaimed, sliding down so his face rested in the fine hair at the base of her smooth belly. Jan opened her thighs so he could bury himself in her moistness. His tongue flicked over the little pearl of flesh that nestled between pink velvet lips. Jan began to rotate her hips, and Louis inserted two fingers into the opening just below his mouth. As Jan's climax neared, his fingers worked faster. She came with a sudden thrust of her whole body, grasping Louis' head with urgent hands.

Louis moved up and rolled on his back. Jan snuggled close, throwing a slender leg over his hips, warm breath stirring the thick hair on his chest. She sighed deeply and ran a hand over his ribs.

It was a game they played well, having practiced and refined it from the day they became lovers, a year after the break with Tony.

Whenever Louis brought Jan orally to climax and didn't want her to reciprocate, he would hold her, waiting for her

strength to return. Then he would enter her in a variety of
positions, until they were driven to unbelievable heights of
passion, followed by an exhausted contentment neither had
ever thought possible.

37

"Dearest Jeanette:

"It's Sunday, and I'm holed up at the ranch with the phone
unplugged. I've warned everyone, even Smitty, that I will
shoot to kill if I'm bothered before I'm through.

"Through with what? you ask. Through with this letter,
through with talking about you, me, our future together if
there's going to be one. You may shudder at the thought, but
I almost flew back to New York. I didn't because the emotional part of me is afraid, and the logical part wants you to
make up your mind without outside interference—me!

"I've had a crazy week, and it's driven me to write this
letter . . ."

Her letters had grown steadily warmer over the past year,
but she had no plans to return in the near future to Las Vegas.
Only in the last few letters had Reese begun to hint about
getting together again. She had referred lightly to his suggestions but had made no positive statements.

Reese returned to the letter: "I love you, and I think you
love me. I was wrong to lie to you about Meade, but it was
an honest lie, if there is such a thing. I'm not going to make
excuses, but I hope you will understand and forgive me.
Meade and I are very close now, and I'm glad it's out in the
open. Someday, I hope I will have the chance to tell you the
whole story."

He filled two more pages, talking about the good times

they had had together and his futile quest to find someone to
take her place:

"I love you, and I know what I want—*who* I want. People
run from love and making commitments because they don't
want to get hurt. Well, I'm going to take that chance. I love
you, and I want you to be my wife. If saying this gets me hurt,
then so be it.

"I'm not asking you to make up your mind right now, but
I would like for you to come back to Vegas and give us a
chance.

"You want to open a dance studio, and I want to help you
do it. A straight business deal, sweetheart, with no obliga-
tions. I'll back a loan. It will be in your name, and you will
make the payments. If things don't work out with us, you
won't have to feel you owe me anything. Consider it a friend
helping a friend."

Reese drew a deep breath. Now for the biggie. "I've told
you about Ann's new home—it's the talk of the country club.
Well, I've got one, too. Construction started in January, and
it's finished now . . . sort of. It's got five thousand square feet,
and it's a beauty. I'm enclosing a couple of pictures.

"It's sitting on a bare patch of land and the interior is
sheet-rocked and taped. That's all. I haven't even had the
fireplace or the exterior rocked. If necessary, it's going to stay
that way for six months. If you send me a 'Dear John' in
answer to this, I'll have everything completed right away.
Otherwise, I'll wait.

"There's not much more to say except that I love you and
think about you all the time. I'm ready to settle down, and
there is only one girl I want to do it with. Give us a chance.
That's all I ask.

All my love,
Reese."

Jeanette received the letter on Wednesday. She skimmed
over it as she rode the elevator up to her Manhattan apartment, her spirits soaring higher with each new page.

As soon as she got in her apartment, she sat down and

finished the letter, then re-read it again, laughing out loud at
the sudden joy that filled her heart, knowing at last that
everything was going to be all right.

She had known for months that Reese was building up to
something like this. She had known, also, what her answer
would be. The part about the house touched her. How could
a girl deny a love like that?

Three days later, a long happy letter was on its way, asking
Reese to fly out for a weekend as soon as possible. She was
ready to return to Vegas, but she thought they should discuss
it in person first.

Besides, she couldn't wait to be in his arms again.

38

"You're cuttin' it pretty fine," Smitty said, skirting a stack
of boxes that partially blocked the twenty-fifth floor corridor.
The May 28th opening of the new Plush Wheel tower was
less than eight weeks away.

"We'll make it," Meade said. "Some of the sub-contractors
will be working twenty-four hours a day, but that's their
problem."

Smitty peered into a guest room where two men had just
finished painting. A third man was preparing to wallpaper
the west wall. "When will they start puttin' in the carpet?"
Smitty asked.

"Three weeks or so," Meade said. "All the rooms are
painted through the tenth floor; they may start sooner."

Reese was walking ahead, looking up at the open corridor
ceiling. Two men were assembling the air-conditioning duct-
ing. One sneezed. "Damn insulation!" he burst out. Reese
grinned and turned back toward Meade and Smitty.

Three stories below in a corner suite, a welder stood on a

ladder, connecting a support for the sprinkler system. The foreman was pushing the crew hard; the system was scheduled for its final testing the middle of next week.

The black welding mask severely limited the man's vision, so he didn't see the spark ignite a wadded paper bag —all that remained of the doughnuts that had served as his breakfast.

The burning bag fell from the ceiling frame onto a pile of trash—sacks and cups from other meals, flattened cardboard boxes, empty paint cans. The acetylene and oxygen tanks had been wheeled into the three-foot-high heap.

The fire might have been contained, if the case of paint thinner hadn't been pushed into the rubbish in a careless attempt to make room for men and equipment. The scene was repeated in the corridor and dozens of rooms. Construction workers aren't noted for their housekeeping skills.

The trash caught fire quickly, spurred on by the residue in the empty paint cans. By the time the frightened welder had shut off his torch and torn away his mask, the flames were licking at the base of his ladder, burning around the tanks and nearing the corridor.

The man jumped to the right, landing clumsily on one foot, wrenching his ankle. Hobbling toward the tanks, he reached out to pull them away from the fire.

With an explosion that reminded the welder briefly of Vietnam before he died, the cans of thinner went up. That rolling thunder had barely subsided when the tanks burst, shattering the windows and sending out a shock wave that stopped traffic on the Strip.

The fire raced down the corridor, cases of paint, wallpaper glue and thinner exploding in its wake. A painting crew ran out of a room into a wall of flame that engulfed their bodies and sucked the air from their lungs.

Halfway down the corridor, a man wearing a leather carpenter's pouch frantically stabbed the elevator buttons; there were six elevators in all, three on each side of the corridor. One set of doors opened just as the fire hit the man. Shirt and hair burning, he staggered inside and punched the lobby button. Shouting and beating at his hair, he fell on the floor and rolled around.

The elevator dropped five floors, then stopped. A young woman started to step inside. Screaming, she dropped an armload of papers. "What is it, Fran?" a bearded man said, dashing up to hold the doors open. His eyes widened at the sight of the man on the floor.

"Fire!" the man gasped through his pain. "Twenty-first floor."

The bearded man shouted at a man watching from the end of the corridor, "Fire—get everybody out!" Drawing the girl inside the elevator, the bearded man hit the down button. While he smothered the carpenter's smoldering shirt, the moaning man described the holocaust he had escaped.

When they arrived at the ground floor, the bearded man and the girl helped the carpenter out of the elevator. As the burn victim sank to a sitting position against the wall, the bearded man ran for the phone. "Fire—clear the building!" he shouted to the half-dozen workers in view.

"Where?" one shouted back.

"Twenty-first floor!" the bearded man answered as he grabbed the receiver. "Get moving; the whole floor's gone!"

Nine-eleven answered. The bearded man was told that fire and rescue equipment was on the way. The flames were visible from hotels all along the Strip, and scores of calls had come in. He was instructed to wait by the entrance so he could submit a first-hand account.

The muffled explosion jolted the three men on the twenty-fifth floor. "What the hell?" Smitty exclaimed, whirling, looking in all directions.

"Somewhere below," Meade said, moving quickly toward the elevators. The panels showed that all six were on their way down, four from the floors below, two from above. Workers gathered around, heads turned upward as they watched the lighted numbers blink on and off.

One set of doors opened, and five men crammed into the already packed elevator. "Can't take anymore!" a burly man cried, pushing the others back as the doors closed.

"Goddamn!" cried a man in white overalls, pointing. "That one is holding two floors up."

"Probably be full when it gets here," muttered another.

Reese said, "I'm going to try for the service elevator. Whoever gets one, hang onto it." He headed toward the Strip side of the long corridor, Meade and Smitty falling in beside him.

They had barely reached the service elevator when a cry came from down the corridor. The men were fighting their way into an elevator. Reese took off like a linebacker, but he was seconds too late. The doors closed inches from his outstretched hand. All were gone except for Meade, Smitty and Reese.

Reese punched the down buttons. All six elevators were on the lower floors. He called to Meade and Smitty who were watching the panel above their heads, "Anything?"

"It got up to the sixteenth floor, then went back down again," Meade said.

Suddenly, the lights above Reese went out. He whipped around. Out there, too. He punched the buttons. Nothing. Reese looked down the hall. Meade and Smitty were still staring upward. "Lights went out here," Reese called.

"Come on down," Meade replied. "They're probably gone."

"I'll check the stairwell first," Reese shouted, running to the opposite end of the corridor. When he opened the door, he was met by a dense cloud of smoke. He ran back toward the two men.

Meade checked the stairwell next to the service elevator. It, too, was filled with smoke. "Shitty way to start the day," Smitty said as Reese arrived beside them.

Reese walked over to the floor-length glass pane that looked out over the Strip. "Whatever it is, it must be pretty big," he said, gazing down. "Take a look." He took up a stance in front of the elevator, waving them toward the window.

"Son of a bitch," Meade murmured, looking down at the congested street—fire engines, police cars and ambulances pressing toward the Plush Wheel, people running from all directions, staring up and pointing at the new tower.

"We lost these lights, too," Reese said from behind them.

"I'm not surprised," Meade said, turning and looking up at the blank panel.

39

Gari's office phone rang. "Do you know where Mr. Slaughter is?" Paris Lynch, the security chief, said. "There's a fire in the new tower."

"How bad?" Gari asked, clutching the receiver.

"There was an explosion on the twenty-first floor. Several floors are burning."

"Oh God," Gari said, recalling Meade's words an hour ago. "Meade's in the tower. He went up about nine. Reese is with him. Are you sure they're not down?"

"Not as of two minutes ago. I've got a man keeping a line open at the elevators. I'm going there as soon as we hang up."

"Get going," Gari said. "I'll see you there."

Gari dialed Ann's office. "She's in a meeting at the Resort Association, Mrs. Slaughter," Ann's secretary said. Gari told her to get Ann back to the Plush Wheel as soon as possible.

The new section was a mass of confusion, and Gari had to show her identification twice before she could reach the lobby area where Paris Lynch was waiting.

Meade was nowhere in sight. "One of the painters saw them on the twenty-fifth floor," Lynch said. "Sounds like Smitty's with them."

"Why didn't they come down?"

Lynch shrugged. "Guess there wasn't room. The man said there were ten or so left when he came down."

"Any since?"

"One bunch." Looking uncomfortable, Lynch added, "The elevators can't make it up there now."

Gari thought her knees would collapse. "Why not?"

"At least six floors are burning out of control," Lynch said. "The elevator shafts act like chimneys. The fire chief says they'll have to stop the elevators on the lower floors pretty soon. They can blow anytime."

"The stairs?"

"The firemen are using the lower ones; their ladders can only reach the ninth floor. The stairs will be impossible above the fire. Those left up there will have to go for the roof. Helicopters are on the way from Nellis Air Force Base."

Memories of rooftop rescues from the MGM flashed through Gari's mind. Those people had been fleeing smoke, not flames. Not just the elevator shafts, but the entire Plush Wheel tower would become a giant chimney.

A sweating fireman reported to the chief, standing a few feet from Gari, "Three jumpers outside, all dead," he said. "Windows are popping all over the place."

The first bodies were brought down—two looking like they were asleep, three charred beyond recognition, a grisly parade that would haunt Gari the rest of her life. As the bodies came down the stairwells, additional fire hoses were dragged up. They were trying to stop the fire's downward plunge at the twelfth floor. The elevators were no longer in use.

Nearly three hundred feet above, the three men had retreated into one of the suites on the northeast corner of the tower. The side facing the older tower was threatening to ignite any moment.

Reese went out on the balcony and looked down. Flames were leaping from at least eight lower floors. A hundred feet to his left on their level a window exploded and red-streaked smoke poured out. Reese glanced up toward the roof, then dashed back inside.

"We've got to go up," Reese said. "The fire's moving in all around us."

"We ain't monkeys," Smitty said. "Least I ain't."

"How far up?" Meade asked.

"Two, three floors," Reese said. "Until the helicopters get here."

"Let's do it."

"You might as well ask me to walk up the side of the buildin' barefooted," Smitty said. "You guys go ahead. I'll take my chances here."

"Like hell you will," Meade said, towering over the little man. Ignoring Smitty's protests, Meade asked Reese, "How do we do it? You're the athlete in the family."

"I go first," Reese said. "When I get on the next balcony, I'll pull you up."

"See," Meade said to Smitty, "nothing to it." Inwardly, Meade was cringing. He had never liked heights. Dangling hundreds of feet above the ground would be a nightmare come true. His courage would have suffered an even further setback had he known that Reese felt the same way.

They went out on the balcony, Meade practically dragging Smitty. Reese took off his coat, removing his wallet and sticking it in a back pocket. He tossed the coat over the balcony; they watched the swirling fall that seemed to last forever. Yanking off his tie, Reese sent it sailing after.

Meade's coat and tie followed. It was a warm April day, and Smitty wasn't wearing a jacket.

Reese climbed onto the rail and reached up for the balcony above. "You're going first, Smitty."

It looked easy the way Reese did it. Fifteen seconds and he was ready. Smitty flicked his cigarette over the rail. "Now what?"

"I'll lean down and grab your belt," Reese said. "Meade, help him up."

Meade lifted Smitty to the top rail. The little man couldn't have weighed more than one hundred twenty. Meade looked up at Smitty, holding him by the waist. "Hang onto my shoulders," Meade said.

Reese's legs were locked around the iron rails, the top one and a smaller vertical one. Smitty's belt was just out of reach. "Give him a boost," Reese said.

Meade heaved, and Reese had the belt. With one powerful

motion, he lifted Smitty so he was hanging half over the top rail. Kicking, Smitty threw himself onto the balcony.

Meade adjusted his position so he was sitting facing the balcony, arms wrapped around the vertical rails. "Just a second until I catch my breath," he said to Meade who was looking up questioningly.

After a few moments, Reese said, "I'm going to hang like a trapeze artist," adding a wisecrack to cover his fear, "Maybe I can get a job at Circus Circus after this. Climb up so we can catch each other's wrists. I'll pull you up so you can grab a rail. Then I'll boost you the rest of the way. Okay?"

Meade nodded, not trusting himself to speak. Seizing Reese's hand, he climbed on the rail. Fumbling, Meade swaying on the narrow rail, they locked their hands together. Meade outweighed Smitty by almost double, and Reese's shoulder muscles popped as he drew his father slowly up, concentrating his eyes on Meade's head—anything to avoid looking at that appalling drop.

Meade grasped the rail with one hand, then the other. Grabbing Meade's belt, Reese lifted him until he tumbled over the top rail. Meade had just enough strength left to help Reese up. They lay side by side, grinning foolishly at each other, then laughing weakly at the sight of Smitty hunched down on his heels, dragging on a cigarette.

"That's one," Smitty said, tugging at his battered hat brim. "I take back what I said earlier, Reese. You'd make a damn good monkey."

40

Gari was standing in the vast pool and garden area between the twin towers. She had been of no use inside; the stairwells were being used only for firefighting now. Most of the lower floors were cleared of workers, and the remaining few were being taken down by ladder rigs positioned on each side of the tower. A new battle line had been formed on the eighth floor, the flames having driven the firefighters down from the twelfth.

Gari heard her name called and looked around to see Ann pushing her way out of the crowd. "Paris Lynch said Meade and Reese are up there!" Ann cried, anguished eyes searching Gari's face in hopes of denial.

Gari put an arm around her daughter, giving as well as receiving comfort. "Smitty, too," she said. "They were in the top section when it started, so they should be on the roof by now."

Ann looked up as a police helicopter circled the building, appearing and disappearing through the billowing smoke. "Have they taken anyone off the roof yet?" she asked.

"A few," Gari said. "Civilian helicopters are doing what they can. The big helicopters should be here from Nellis soon."

A collective scream issued from the throats of the hundreds of watchers on the ground and balconies of the older tower. Ann gripped Gari's arm. A man was dashing about on a balcony a few floors from the top, clothes on fire. He tried to climb to the next balcony, and the flames engulfed his face. Twisting and turning, he fell toward the ground, his cries drowned out by those of the crowd. He crashed into a stone bench, folding over it, a boneless smoking shape.

In the next ten minutes, three others followed, flaming cartwheels welcoming eternal release from unbearable pain.

"I can't. I can't . . ." Ann said under her breath, holding her mother and looking away.

Shattered glass rained down through smoke-filtered sunlight on the firefighters as they dragged hoses up ladder rigs and maneuvered hosewagons. At a nearby emergency station, doctors treated firemen who had been caught on the eighth floor. The attempt to halt the fire there had failed, and new lines had been formed on the sixth.

Paris Lynch hurried up to the two women. "Meade—the others, they're climbing the balconies on the other side," he said, brushing a mixture of soot and sweat from his forehead. "Come on. I'll get you through." He started walking toward the Strip end of the tower.

Gari was numb with fear. "All three—you're sure?" she asked, wanting to know before they rounded the building.

"So I was told," Lynch said, waving an arm in frustration. "One of my men reported it." He stopped suddenly and pointed upwards. "There they are!"

Gari's hand flew to her mouth. Reese was on the balcony above, pulling Smitty up, Meade guiding the slight body until it was out of reach. The watchers cheered as Smitty crawled over the rail and dropped safely.

Gari and Ann held each other tightly, wanting to close their eyes but unable to. "Meade . . . Meade," Gari whispered, hearing the activity of a television crew behind them as they recorded the frightening climb.

The crowd gasped as Reese's hands locked with Meade's. Television cameras whirred, catching the moment when Meade's legs swung free of the rail, and he dangled in space for several heart-stopping seconds.

Ann's fingernails dug into Gari's back as they clung to each other, too terrified to speak.

Upward, slowly upward. Time seemed to stand still, but it was actually less than a minute. Meade reached the top rail,

Reese pushing on his legs, heaving him onto the balcony. The crowd shouted and cheered. Gari and Ann didn't move until Reese safely disappeared over the balcony rail.

A television reporter approached. "Mrs. Slaughter—"

"Not now!" Gari snapped, shielding Ann from the cameras. "Haven't you people any decency? Look at those flames! They're not safe yet."

Waving the camera away, the reporter prudently retreated.

"Here they come!" a man shouted, pointing to the north. A cheer went up as three huge CH-3 helicopters came flying in close formation from the direction of Nellis Air Force Base.

Ann screamed, and Gari's gaze whipped from the helicopters to the balcony. Flames were shooting out of the room directly below where the three men sat.

41

Reese leaped to his feet, reaching for Smitty. They hadn't expected the fire to move so quickly.

Smitty's face had turned a dull gray, the paleness of his skin accentuating the freckles on his bald head. He put his hat back on and peered weakly from under the brim. "You guys take it from here," he said. "I'm 'bout done in."

Reese looked at Meade. "I'm going up," he said, nodding toward Smitty. "Be ready."

Reese's ascent was swift. As he leaned from the balcony, the beat of a CH-3 thundered overhead, and a boatswain's chair began to winch down.

Meade passed Smitty up, and Reese seized the little man under the arms. Smitty's head rolled listlessly as Reese lifted him to the top rail. Muscles straining, Reese balanced Smitty there while he drew himself up. Climbing over the rail, he gently laid Smitty down.

When Reese leaned back over the rail, it was like looking down into hell. Flames bordered the balcony, and Meade was moving from one foot to the other, seeking relief from the heat that was penetrating the soles of his boots.

Father and son looked at each other, sharing a moment of unspoken love, regretting the years they had missed being together. They understood the almost impossible task that lay before them. There would be no time for Meade to balance on the rail and lock hands with Reese. The flames would be all around them, igniting Meade's clothes the moment he got near the edge.

"Only one way!" Reese shouted. "Cinch your belt around your wrist. I'll hang down and grab the end of the belt." Reese sat on the rail and dropped over backwards, securing his feet behind the vertical rails, boots protecting his ankles.

Meade had taken his belt off, but he was shaking his head. "It won't work," he said, knowing the terrible risk Reese was taking. "I'm going to pack it in."

"No, goddamnit!" Reese rapped out, looking upside down at Meade. "If you won't think of me, think of Gari! Are you going to leave her a widow without a fight?"

Meade swore and tightened the belt around his waist. The flames were leaping three feet high all around the balcony, and they singed their arms as Meade passed the belt end to Reese. Wrapping the belt several times around his hand, Reese said, "On the count of three—you jump, I'll pull!"

Meade nodded and gripped the belt with both hands.

"One, two, three!" Meade leaped for the rail, and Reese swung him out into space. The belt couldn't be seen from the ground, and it looked like Meade had missed Reese's hands. The watchers screamed.

The two men dangled there, Meade's pants smoking, a tongue of flame licking at the cuff of one leg. Reese drew Meade so their faces were two feet apart. "See if you can grab my belt," Reese whispered through gritted teeth. Closing his eyes, he pulled Meade higher.

Meade's questing fingers found the belt, caught hold. Reese released the belt that was wrapped around Meade's other wrist, grabbing Meade's legs at the same time. Meade's pants had started to burn, but Reese's grip snuffed the flames out. Neither noticed the pain as Reese lifted Meade up.

Meade grasped the top rail with one hand, then both. With superhuman strength, Reese pushed Meade up over the rail. Meade fell in a heap, breath coming in ragged gasps.

Reese hung from the rail, the people and machines twenty-eight stories below tiny blurred objects. He knew he had to move now or he would never make it up. He tried once, twice, clutching a rail the third time. Then Meade appeared, reaching down and gripping his arm. While Meade pulled, Reese grabbed a rail with his free hand. Moments later, they were kneeling on the balcony, arms hanging limply at their sides.

The boatswain's chair appeared beside them, swinging gently back and forth. Reese staggered to his feet and held the chair against the rail.

"Shit!" Meade burst out behind him.

Reese swung around. Meade was kneeling beside Smitty, ear pressed to the little man's chest. Reese's voice was hushed, "Meade?"

Meade looked up, and his eyes said it all. "I think he's dead."

Reese shook away his own sorrow. "Let's get him up," Reese said. They strapped Smitty into the chair and watched the body winch up toward the helicopter.

Minutes later, Reese was helping Meade into the chair. Reese said, "I'm going to climb the last two balconies." He pointed up at the men who were lined along the roof, looking down. "Tell the guys in the helicopter that I'm going to see if those men can drop me a rope. I can help on the roof. Got it?"

"You've done enough!" Meade shouted as the chair began to rise.

"Later!" Reese shouted back, leaping on the rail with renewed strength. He waved at Meade, then climbed to the next balcony. "Got a rope?" he called to the watching men.

"Yeah!" a man in a hard hat yelled. "Back in a sec." His head disappeared, and the others shouted encouragement as Reese drew himself up toward the last balcony.

42

Gari watched the descent of the "Jolly Green Giant" CH-3 helicopter; her eyes had followed its every movement after Meade and Smitty had been drawn up into its belly.

She had almost vomited following the success of the final climb. While Meade had swung, linked to Reese by the unseen belt, Ann had kept repeating, "Hold me, Mom, hold me," over and over again, stopping only when both men were safely on the balcony.

While that was happening, a man behind them kept telling his companion that Meade and Reese wouldn't make it. When the climbers were safe, Gari whirled and hissed, "Don't ever underestimate *real* men!"

The helicopter landed, and the two women ran toward it. They stopped suddenly as Meade appeared in the doorway, Smitty in his arms, an Air Force crewman moving ahead down the steps, holding Meade's elbow to steady him. Meade had refused to put Smitty on a stretcher. He would carry his friend to the ambulance. A medic on the helicopter had confirmed that Smitty was dead.

"Oh, Meade," Gari said softly. The two women flanked Meade on the short walk to the ambulance, TV crews recording the scene.

"He didn't know what hit him," Meade said to Gari and Ann. "He was dead when we got him onto the balcony."

As soon as Smitty was released to the ambulance attendants, Meade seized the women in an iron embrace. "Reese?" Ann asked in a choked voice.

"Helping on the roof," Meade said. "He wouldn't listen when I told him to come down."

Gari leaned wearily on Meade's broad chest. "You'd better talk to the media people; they won't leave you alone until you do." Meade swore softly. After a few minutes, he walked toward the waiting reporters, arms around the two women.

As the first question was being asked, Reese was waving the helicopters toward the Strip side of the tower. Flames were appearing on the roof at the opposite end. Only seven remained to be lifted off, but it was going to be close. The roof could collapse at any moment.

The men grouped around Reese. A helicopter hovered overhead, and then there were six.

Flames raced toward them at frightening speed, driven by a light wind and fueled by the oil-impregnated roofing composition. Another man was lifted up . . . another. Four to go, then three.

But there was no more time. Flames six feet high were only seconds away. "Up there!" Reese yelled, running toward the Plush Wheel sign, a twin of the one on the opposite tower. Feet smarting from the melting tar, the men climbed the steel maintenance ladder, not stopping until they reached the top of the fifty-foot-high letters.

They sat on the letter E, the Plush Wheel emblem rising ten feet above their heads. The electricity had long since been cut off, so the wheel wasn't turning.

A helicopter arrived above; its great blades whacking the air, providing fresh air and blowing smoke away from the men. As the fire roared directly below, a man began the slow winch up.

The steel girders were becoming too hot to touch. Reese stood and ripped off his shirt, wrapping it around one hand so he could hold on without getting burned.

The remaining man followed suit. He stood beside Reese, looking up at the descending boatswain's chair. "Come on! Come on!" he urged. Below them, the plastic letters began to melt.

The chair arrived. "Yours," Reese said, grabbing the chair and holding it for the man.

The man looked at Reese apologetically as he got in. Seconds later, the chair was on the way up.

The heat was almost unbearable, melting the letters on each side of Reese. Then with a rending crash, part of the roof fell in, the sign going with it, the heat-weakened steel bending so the sign hung at a forty-five-degree angle.

Reese had barely hung on, suffering severe burns on his unprotected hand as he grabbed the fiery steel for support. All around him, girders were bending, welds snapping.

The boatswain's chair was almost within Reese's grasp. As he reached out, a beam broke loose, driving a half-inch reinforcing bar into the right side of his back, cracking ribs and piercing his chest, leaving two inches of ridged iron rod protruding from under his nipple, blood seeping out and down over his stomach.

The bar had separated from the frame, but as Reese slid down, it wedged between two plates, pinning Reese to the structure. He had become part of the Plush Wheel sign.

43

It was nearly one, an hour and a half since Reese had undergone emergency surgery at Valley Hospital.

Few on the ground had witnessed Reese's horrifying injury and rescue from the Plush Wheel sign, but it had been filmed by Channel 13 from a civilian helicopter. The family had watched the replay in the hospital waiting room.

Steve Schorr was reporting: ". . . and by eleven, fifty-five minutes after the fire broke out, only one man was left on the roof—Reese Harrington, President of Nevada Investments, parent company of the Plush Wheel hotels and casinos.

"Harrington, son of Plush Wheel founder Meade Slaughter and the quarterback who nearly led the St. Louis Cardinals to the Super Bowl in seventy-seven, had climbed to the roof after the daring rescue of his father and Frank Smith, a Nevada pioneer who died of an apparent heart attack during the balcony-by-balcony climb toward the roof. We'll be showing film of that climb later."

The television camera zoomed in on the Plush Wheel sign, the picture blurred by rolling clouds of smoke. Reese was looking up as the boatswain's chair dropped down. The entire roof was ablaze. The tower had indeed become a giant chimney.

"At this point," Steve Schorr continued, "the sign fell backwards, and a steel reinforcing rod broke loose, pinning Harrington to the sign and piercing his chest."

The boatswain's chair was coming down again, in it a man wearing Air Force garb. "One of the heroes of the day," Schorr said, "was Technical Sergeant Jim Kain, who risked his life to free Harrington and lift him to safety. Less than five minutes later, the roof and the sign collapsed into the floors below." A vivid six-second shot of this flashed on the screen.

From the ground, another camera crew picked up the lowering of the boatswain's chair with the sergeant holding Reese's unconscious body. For the purpose of speed, they hadn't been winched aboard. The chair swayed thirty feet below the helicopter all the way down.

Steve Schorr was saying, "From there, the Flight for Life helicopter rushed Harrington to the Valley Hospital rooftop two and a half air miles away.

"Usually," Schorr said, wrapping up the story, "Flight for Life patients are taken down to the ground floor for surgery; however, in extremely critical cases like Harrington's, the patient is resuscitated in the helicopter resuscitation room on the fifth floor, just fifty feet from the landing pad.

"Reese Harrington is there now, as surgeons work to remove the length of reinforcing bar from his chest. We will keep you informed of this and other related stories as we continue our on-the-spot coverage of the disastrous Plush Wheel fire."

Meade sat staring at the television, an arm around Ann, whose head was resting on his shoulder. Gari had his other hand in her lap, fingers intertwined with his. There were bandages on Meade's arms, others on one leg. The burns weren't serious, and they would quickly heal.

The waiting room was crowded. Ambulances and the Flight for Life helicopter had been bringing in fire victims all morning. The other hospitals—Desert Springs, Sunrise and Southern Nevada Memorial—were working at peak capacity to save lives and repair burned and broken bodies, with the most critically burned going to Southern Nevada.

The latest toll was twenty-three dead and eighty-four injured. The construction work had been winding down, or the casualties would have been much higher.

The fire had been stopped at the sixth floor, and crews would stand by until the upper floors had been knocked down. Helicopters were dropping chemicals and releasing water bags into the gutted shell.

A doctor with a surgical mask hanging around his neck came off the elevator and approached the family. Meade rose, drawing Gari and Ann with him.

"Mr. Slaughter?" the doctor said.

"Yes." The women drew closer to Meade.

"We've removed the bar," the surgeon said. "Fortunately, it only nicked a lung, but it tore up a lot of blood vessels and broke some ribs. The bar was rusty, so sepsis is a danger.

"He has third degree burns on his back, arms and one hand. That's complicating things."

"How does it look?" Meade said.

"It will be touch and go for the next forty-eight hours," the surgeon said. "The patient is in the recovery room. We'll let you see him in an hour, then you should go home and get some rest."

After the doctor had gone, Meade said, "I want to stay, but I'd better make a quick run to the hotel."

"Same here," Gari said. She had a very important job to do and not much time left.

Ann shifted the strap of her purse and looked around. "I'll stay," she said. "Okay?"

"Sure, honey," Meade said, squeezing her arm. "We'll be back in an hour."

Ann kissed them, then sat down, clasped hands in her lap, eyes drawn in morbid fascination to the television screen.

Gari went straight to Reese's office. Jeanette had to know before she got the story second-hand. The week before, Reese had told Gari over lunch about his letter to Jeanette asking her to return to Las Vegas. Gari had thought about this at the hospital. If Jeanette loved Reese, she should be at his side.

When Gari entered Reese's office, the first thing she did was look at the morning's mail that lay on his desk. Near the top was a letter from Jeanette. Gari would have given anything to know what was in it before she called, but there was no way she would violate the couple's privacy.

Quickly, Gari flipped the cards in the Rolodex. It was just after four in New York. She wanted to catch Jeanette at work before she learned about the fire; it would be featured on all the networks.

She found it. Below Jeanette's name was an address, the same as on the envelope. No phone number. Gari's heart leaped. At the bottom of the card was printed, "Phil Black Dance Studio." No number, but she could get that. Minutes later, she reached the dance studio. "Is Jeanette Thomas there?" Gari asked, wondering what she would do if she wasn't.

"Sure." A girl's voice with a New York accent. The receiver clattered on something hard, making Gari jump.

"Hello?" Gari recognized the soft voice, seeing in her mind the dark hair and wide-spaced brown eyes.

"Jeanette, this is Gari Slaughter. I'm calling from Las Vegas."

A hiss of indrawn breath. "From the Plush Wheel?"

"Yes. Jeanette, we've had a fire here—a bad one. Reese has been injured."

"*Reese?*"

"Jeanette," Gari snapped, trying to get through to the suddenly distraught girl, "Reese told me last week that he asked you to come back. I have to know—did you say yes? There's an unopened letter from you on his desk."

"Yes!" cried Jeanette. "Yes! I love him. I—oh, God . . ."

"That's what I wanted to hear," Gari said, taking charge. "Reese is in critical condition; they finished operating an hour ago. Can you come out? If you love him, you should be here. Knowing how you feel will help him pull through."

"I'll leave right away! I'll have to call the airport—"

"All taken care of," Gari said. "One of our jets is on the way up from Atlantic City; it will be waiting at the Marine Air Terminal at La Guardia. Go right from there—grab a taxi fast!"

"Oh, Gari, I love Reese—I've always loved him. I've been such a fool!"

"We've all been at one time or another," Gari said quietly, knowing now that she had done the right thing.

"When he wakes up," Jeanette cried, "tell him I love him! *Please.*"

"Sure, dear. We have a telephone on the plane, so we'll keep you aware of any changes. Try and rest during the flight. You probably won't get much the next few days."

44

Jeanette would never forget that flight, racing toward the setting sun and the man she loved who might be dying. The flight attendant, a tall brunette who knew the Slaughter family well and was deeply distressed herself, left Jeanette alone in the luxurious cabin for most of the four and a half hours it took to reach Las Vegas.

Jeanette had snatched a copy of the *New York Post* from
a newsstand as she ran from the dance studio to hail a cab.
The fire was featured on the front page but it was just a short
item, few details being available at press time.

Jeanette picked at a lavish meal the attendant, Gloria, had
insisted she eat. This was one of the three Plush Wheel VIP
jets, with all the accoutrements premium customers would
expect.

The fading sun colored the sky, and Jeanette looked down
on an endless sea of pink fluffy clouds. *Why hadn't she sent
the letter one day sooner?* If she had, Reese would have that
to think about. She had written from the heart, telling him
what he wanted to know—what she had known but wouldn't
admit to herself all during these years of separation.

She was afraid, afraid for Reese, afraid for herself if she
should lose him. She knew that her life would never be complete without Reese. He had said it in his last letter: "We
belong together, honey. We're a matched pair; nature
planned it that way." Jeanette had laughed and cried when
she read it. She was only crying now.

From today's perspective, Reese's not being completely
honest about his parentage and his past seemed so insignifi-
cant. She should have tried to understand instead of putting
such importance on her noble values. It was childish for her
to be such a prima donna.

Jeanette straightened up and viciously speared a piece of
steak. Reese was going to live, damnit, and that was that!
Poking the meat in her mouth, she chewed thoughtfully.

Both Gari and Meade were waiting when the plane landed.
Meade hugged Jeanette as if she were already part of the
family. "How is he?" Jeanette asked, kissing Gari.

"Nothing new," Gari said. "We're going to the hospital
now."

It was a weary group, Meade looking the worst of all. He
had gone through a day that would have immobilized a man
half his age. He was running on sheer willpower, and Gari
wanted to get him to bed. "Anything?" she asked Ann.

Ann shook her head. "No change. They're not going to let us see him. I talked to the doctor ten minutes ago."

Meade sighed. "Then let's go, hon," he said to Gari. "You, too, Ann. Getting yourself sick isn't going to help."

Jeanette lay awake a long time in the bedroom Gari had said was once Ann's. Twelve hours ago, Jeanette was teaching jazz steps to one of the most promising students at the school in Manhattan, thinking as she worked of the joyful possibility that Reese might fly in this weekend. They were only a few miles apart now, and she hadn't even seen him.

While the family slept, alarms brought a medical team rushing to Reese's side. All his vital signs had ceased, and he was clinically dead. The team worked swiftly, and their efforts were rewarded when his heart began to beat again.

At the Plush Wheel, traces of smoke were still rising from the ruined shaft that yawned from the sixth floor upward, a stripped skeleton except for dangling bits of steel and broken masonry. Like empty eyes, blackened windows stared impassively down on the bright lights of the Strip.

The sign still clung together, hanging precariously to a few supports from the roof, the huge Plush Wheel now an unrecognizable circle of twisted steel.

45

It was eight in the morning, and everyone was wandering about in robes. Meade had been on the phone for two hours, checking with the hospital and directing salvage operations at the site of the fire.

At nine, Jeanette and the family were in the waiting room being briefed by the doctor. "The next twenty-four hours will tell," the doctor said.

After the doctor left, they stood around in stunned silence. Yesterday had left them physically and emotionally drained, unable to cope with much more. This news was like a crushing blow.

Meade looked helplessly at Gari. "We really should go to the PW for a while."

"I know," she said heavily, looking at the two girls. "All right if we leave you alone?"

They nodded in unison. "We'll be okay," Ann said. It was a reluctant parting; they had been drawing off each other for strength.

Jeanette and Ann sat on a couch. Ann had been reading the *Las Vegas Sun,* and a two-page spread of fire pictures lay between them. There was a picture of Reese and Meade dangling from the twenty-eighth-floor balcony, another showing the Air Force helicopter lowering the sergeant with Reese's body in his arms.

Jeanette whispered, "How could you stand watching it?"

"Mom and I propped each other up," Ann said. "Actually, Mom was doing most of the propping. I guess I was in shock most of the time. Everything was dreamy and floating. They say that's what shock does to you—sort of a protection from reality."

The two girls continued talking in low voices, darting nervous glances toward the entrance to the intensive care unit.

In the car, Meade was saying to Gari, "I have to make arrangements for Smitty." He gripped the steering wheel. "I still can't believe he's gone. We were together almost fifty years!"

Gari rested a comforting hand on Meade's leg, the only solace she could give.

"He wanted to be buried in Reno," Meade continued. "He was always a northerner at heart. We'll have a memorial service here and in Reno. Smitty wouldn't have wanted it, but there are a lot of people in Nevada who will want to pay their last respects. It's sad that Reese won't be able to attend. If Smitty ever came close to loving someone, I think it was

Reese. He was as proud of Reese as if he were his own son."

"Don't forget yourself," Gari said. "Smitty loved you, too."

"And I him," Meade said. "Damn! Charlie and Smitty—two big chunks out of my life."

At the Plush Wheel, Meade had his hands full. The toll was now twenty-eight dead and seventy-nine injured, twelve critically.

The insurance investigators were at work—and lawyers were descending on the scene like locusts. There would be millions in claims for the victims and more millions needed to rebuild the tower. Structurally, it was intact, but everything would have to be replaced from the sixth floor up.

"There's smoke and water damage all the way down," Jim Bailey said from across Meade's desk.

Meade said: "Next April twenty-third is the fifty-third anniversary of the opening of the first Plush Wheel. Think you can have everything in order by then?"

Jim Bailey leaned back and closed his eyes. "The MGM reopened ten months after their fire, but that was mostly smoke and glass damage. They had to rebuild the casino and arcade. We don't. They had to retrofit the fire safety system; we'll have to do most of ours over, but that will be new construction. This is April fourteenth. If we work double, triple shifts, I think we can make it. We won't be able to do heavy construction work at night because of the noise. That will have to be taken into consideration."

"Let's shoot for it then," Meade said. "I don't feel like celebrating right now, but I hope I will next year. Anything else?"

"A million things, but they can wait. I'll try to get some preliminary cost figures together within a week. We'll start rigging for cleanup as soon as the Fire Department and the insurance investigators let us."

The afternoon went badly. Meade and Gari were called out of an executive meeting a little past three; Reese's temperature had reached 105. They rushed to the hospital and formed ranks with the distraught girls, huddling on a couch until late into the night. Reese's fever broke at ten, and they went home an hour later, assured by the doctor that this crisis was over.

Thursday evening, they were briefly allowed to see Reese. He was heavily sedated and knew nothing of their visit. It had been a frightening experience for the family, especially for Jeanette who hadn't seen Reese for years and had to see him like this—attached to machines by tubes running from his nose and body.

It was a quiet group that returned home that night. They were staying together as much as possible. Ann hadn't returned home after that first sleepless night alone.

Friday passed, and Reese slowly began to improve. The crisis had passed. On Saturday morning, the smiling doctor announced, "He's awake. Hopefully, you can see him this afternoon. I think it's safe to say he's going to be all right."

Meade pressed the doctor's hand, then enfolded the women in his arms. Tears flowed, and Jeanette sobbed against Meade's chest. Looking through blurred eyes at Jeanette, Meade thought, *The family still numbers five.*

They sat down, all talking at once. The hours dragged, but the reports continued to be favorable. At two, the doctor came to take them to Reese.

Jeanette hung back, twisting a tissue between her hands. "May I go in alone—after you're through?" she asked. "Please don't tell him I'm here."

"Of course, dear," Gari said, understanding Jeanette's need. "We won't say anything."

Reese's eyes brightened when they entered the room. Gari and Ann moved to each side of the bed. Reese's hands and arms were bandaged, so all the women could do was stand there and look. Meade squeezed in beside Gari. "Hi, gang," Reese said in a weak voice.

The women kissed him, and Meade awkwardly touched Reese's leg under the sheet. "You had us worried," Meade said, barely in control of his voice.

A slow smile came over Reese's face. "Your damn sign almost killed me."

"Oh, Reese, you nut," Gari cried, wiping her eyes. The tension eased, and they passed along just enough news to let Reese know everything was working out. After five minutes, the doctor came and took them away.

Meade had told the doctor earlier about the situation between Reese and Jeanette. "I think we'd better give the man an hour or so to rest up before she goes in," the doctor said as they approached the waiting room. "It's going to be a pretty traumatic experience."

Jeanette agreed; it would give her a chance to calm down. She had been sitting in a chair, knees tight together to keep them from knocking.

Shortly before four, Reese felt the touch of a hand on his shoulder. "Jeanette?" His voice was hoarse, disbelieving.

"Yes, darling, it's me." Her hair caressed his face as she bent to kiss him. She drew back, and they stared at each other.

"It's not a dream?" Reese said.

"No dream," Jeanette said, smoothing his hair back from his forehead.

"How long have you been here?"

"Since Tuesday night. I'm staying with Gari and Meade."

"You got my letter?"

"Yes, and mine missed you by a day. I'm here to stay, darling. I love you."

Reese smiled. "Half as much as I love you."

"Impossible," Jeanette said, shaking her head, dark hair flying.

"Enough to marry me?"

"More than enough."

"Have you seen the house?"

"Only at a distance. I want us to see it together."

"Got a better idea. I'm going to be here a while. Why don't you start fixing it up? Surprise me. Gari will help you with the details."

"Sure?"

"Positive."

"It's a beautiful house."

"You're a beautiful girl."

"No, you're beautiful."

"Men aren't beautiful."

Jeanette started to move away. "I've already overstayed my time," she said. "The doctor doesn't want you to get too excited."

"Too late for that," Reese grinned. "If I could only get you in this bed . . ."

Jeanette smiled, trailing her fingers over his cheek. "When it happens, it will be in *our* bed in *our* home."

"Better start looking for furniture."

Jeanette was at the foot of the bed, backing slowly toward the door. "Monday, I promise."

"It's going to be a good marriage," Reese said.

"I know, darling, I know."

Jeanette's words hung in the air for a long time after she had gone.

Epilogue

The sun had set, and the Strip was ablaze with light. It was a warm September night, and the gentle breeze was a welcome relief.

Over a hundred people were gathered on the roof of the new Plush Wheel tower—the Slaughter family, company employees, friends and Air Force Technical Sergeant Jim Kain and his wife.

Sergeant Kain had received a special reward from Meade and an all-expense-paid vacation for him and his family to Hawaii, flying both ways in the private luxury of a company jet. Meade considered it the least he could do for the man who had risked his life to save Reese.

The dark Plush Wheel sign reached high into the night sky, dwarfing the people below. The last letters had been hoisted into place two weeks ago, the final electrical connections made yesterday.

Meade and Reese stood together, their wives at their sides, Ann next to Gari. Everyone had a champagne glass. Ten cases of Dom Perignon had been consumed while they had waited for the sun to go down.

"Ready?" Jim Bailey said, holding up a switch box connected to a long cord.

"Ready," Meade said, and a cheer went up.

Bailey handed the switch box to Reese. Jeanette looked up at her husband. "I'll take your glass, darling."

Reese released it reluctantly. "I still think you should do it," he said.

Smiling, Jeanette kissed his cheek. "No way. Get to it, mister."

Everyone looked up. Reese pressed a button, and the giant letters PLUSH WHEEL lit up, bathing the upturned faces in an eerie assortment of colors. Shouts and whistles filled the air, and glasses were raised.

"More!" a voice called. It became a chant, "More, more, MORE!"

Reese grinned and pressed the second button. Outlined in gold, letters in white, the great Plush Wheel emblem burst into life. Seventy feet in diameter, it was an exact replica of the Wheels of Fortune that stood in the entrances to all five Plush Wheel casinos.

This time, the shouts and cheers were deafening, carrying to the ground three hundred fifty feet below. Meade was silent, gazing up at the glowing emblem, thinking back to the day in 1933 when he had stood on the Virginia Street sidewalk in Reno and proudly watched the painter put the finishing touches on that first symbol, a simple gold wheel on a weathered pane of glass.

Hands slapped Meade on the back, but he didn't react. Seeing the look on his face, his little family instinctively closed in, a tightly-knit group in the midst of the waving, cheering crowd.

Meade held his glass out. Reese took his from Jeanette, and they formed a circle. "To my family," Meade said. "I love you all." They drank, and the women kissed him.

Reese's arm went around Meade's shoulders. "Quiet, everyone!" he shouted. "Quiet!" Reese had learned how to make his voice carry on the football field, and his words brought instant results.

Reese raised the switch above his head. "I think my father should push the last button. Everyone agree?"

The crowd roared its approval.

In the silence that followed, Reese handed the switch to Meade.

The last button was pressed, and the giant wheel began to turn. It stopped at a number, moved on, stopped at another number, moved on again. The rooftop erupted with cheers and the popping of corks, making heads turn upward from the Strip.

An hour later, only the family remained. Meade and Reese were standing below the sign, looking out over the Strip. They had been talking quietly for several minutes.

Gari looked at Ann and Jeanette. "Why don't we leave them alone for a while?" she said, nodding toward the men. "I sense something special going on."

Jeanette did a little dance step. "I have to go to the bathroom. All this champagne!"

"Ditto," Ann said.

Gari called out, "We're going to the ladies' room. Take your time. We'll be in the Gambler's Club."

The men waved, then turned back to the four-foot wall that enclosed the roof. Meade had been talking about the past, but the mood had left him. He lit a cigar. "Remember what Di Santo said at Tahoe a couple of years ago?" Meade said. "He was right. Things are changing. The damn recession and Atlantic City have taken a real bite out of Nevada. We've got to be more flexible, spread our wings."

Reese smiled, knowing what was coming.

Meade flicked an ash from his cigar. "Let's take a hard look at that projection. We paid big bucks to that company to work it up for us. There are a lot of new horizons out there. Think of it—a Plush Wheel in Australia! Right now, the most realistic projection is Atlantic City. Ready to jump?"

Reese looked down. "Not from here," he grinned, "but I'm all for giving Atlantic City a go."

"We can be there in three, four years," Meade said. "Smitty made sure of that."

Reese nodded, watching the cars move along the Strip. He

hadn't been told until he had left the hospital to convalesce in the room Jeanette had prepared at their new home.

Smitty's fortune—cash, stocks and real estate—had been left to the family, nearly a million each after taxes to Gari and Ann, ten million to Meade, and almost twenty-five million to Reese. After taxes! It was mind-boggling. Smitty had handed them all a ticket to a limitless future.

"We're going to need top people," Reese said. "It will take one of the best to run our place in Atlantic City."

"Any ideas?"

"Yes, but you won't like it."

"Try me."

"Louis Giuliano."

Meade stuck his hands in his pockets and peered at Reese. "Giuliano?"

Reese braced himself, waiting for the storm. Some of their disagreements took on heroic proportions.

Meade's eyes crinkled with humor. "You've been building up to this for some time, haven't you?"

"A year or so."

"A Giuliano working for the Plush Wheel," Meade mused. "Now that's *really* what I call flexible. Think he'll come over?"

"It's suited to him—an opportunity of a lifetime. He's fifty-two, a lot of good years ahead of him yet. We've talked, but never about this. He'll take it."

"Stock options and such?"

"The only way to keep a good man."

Meade smiled. "Set up a meeting. We'll talk."

"That was pretty easy," Reese said.

"Not really. Matter of fact, been thinking about it myself."

"You're pretty cagey."

"Watch out, it's catching."

Reese laughed and looked down on the Strip. "Louis can help set up our hotel in Laughlin. That way, he can start right away. It'll be good experience, and he'll be in on the ground floor with Atlantic City."

"Think I'll live long enough to see us in Miami Beach?" Meade asked.

Reese elbowed Meade in the ribs. "Hell, yes. You can sit out front of our Miami Beach Plush Wheel and watch your grandkids play in the sand."

"I want great-grandkids, too," Meade said. "If Ann doesn't get busy, I'm going to find a guy for her myself."

"It'll happen," Reese said. "Be patient."

"Patient? She's thirty!"

"So's Jeanette. Women get married at an older age these days."

They leaned on the wall, contemplating the future. Above them, the great Plush Wheel stopped at a number, turned, stopped . . . turned. Thirty-one stories below, thousands moved up and down the Strip—searching, dreaming, hoping also to be winners.

CLINT MCCULLOUGH graduated from a Bible school, and has been a missionary with the Navajo Indians and an itinerant preacher. He later worked as a ranchhand and then became the Secretary Manager of Kern County, California, Farm Bureau. For a time he ran his own advertising agency (which won several art direction awards), designed and built houses, and worked as a rafting guide. *Nevada* is his first novel.

GRIPPING DRAMA—AS URGENT AS TODAY'S HEADLINES

RAMPAGE by William P. Wood

A scorching novel of a passionate district attorney and a brutal, amoral killer whose defense—not guilty by reason of insanity—is a slap in the face of justice. "A taut courtroom drama...Hard to put down."
> —William J. Caunitz, author of *One Police Plaza*

_____ 90306-5 $3.95 U.S. _____ 90307-3 $4.95 Can.

LAUGHING WHITEFISH by Robert Traver

A searing courtroom drama about an Indian woman who fights a powerful and corrupt mining company for her land. By the author of *Anatomy of a Murder*. "A constant delight that should not be missed."—Ed McBain

_____ 90217-4 $3.95 U.S. _____ 90216-6 $4.95 Can.

1988 by Governor Richard Lamm and Arnold Grossman

A taut novel of an international conspiracy to capture the presidency—a media genius, a puppet politician, a seductive beauty, a revered black congresswoman, and a sinister Middle-Eastern cabal all caught up in a drama of blackmail, double-dealing, terrorism and expedient murder...

_____ 90287-5 $3.95 U.S. _____ 90288-3 $4.95 Can.

Sex...Glamour...Money...

PRETENSIONS by Sally Rinard
Set in the glittery world of high fashion and high society, where money is a weapon and sex the means of exchange, this dazzling tale combines the erotic, exotic, and the cutthroat world of business.
"A glitzy contemporary novel that's a delight to read."
—Publishers Weekly
_____ 90301-4 $4.50 U.S.   _____ 90302-2 $5.50 Can.

LISA LOGAN by Marie Joseph
Ambition and pride take Lisa Logan from poverty to the heights of success in haute couture. Money, power, fame, she finally has it all—except the man she wanted most.
_____ 90218-2 $3.95 U.S.

DECISIONS by Freda Bright
Dasha Croy rockets to the top in a brilliant law career, but will her marriage be the price? Can love and security compete with the seduction of power?
_____ 90169-0 $3.95 U.S.   _____ 90171-2 $4.50 Can.

HER ONLY SIN by Benjamin Stein
Susan-Marie had the beauty, brains, and sexuality to achieve her dream of heading the biggest studio in Hollywood, but her ambitions could cost her her love and even her life. "A power-packed, star-studded page turner."
—Los Angeles Herald-Examiner
_____ 90636-6 $4.50 U.S.   _____ 90637-4 $5.50 Can.

IMAGES by Cara Saylor Polk
"A hip, inside, behind-the-scenes page turner about a woman's climb to prime-time in big-time television news."
—Dan Rather
_____ 90456-8 $4.50 U.S.   _____ 90458-4 $5.50 Can.

ST. MARTIN'S PRESS—MAIL SALES
175 Fifth Avenue, New York, NY 10010

Please send me the book(s) I have checked above. I am enclosing a check or money order (not cash) for $_____ plus 75¢ per order to cover postage and handling (New York residents add applicable sales tax).

Name _____

Address _____

City _____ State_____ Zip Code_____
Allow at least 4 to 6 weeks for delivery